THE DARK TUNNEL

By

PATRICK HENDERSON

A Tale of childhood, passion, and war

ISBN 978-1-957956-87-9 (Paperback)
ISBN 978-1-957956-88-6 (Ebook)

Inquiries and Book Orders should be addressed to:

Leavitt Peak Press
17901 Pioneer Blvd Ste L #298, Artesia, California 90701
Phone #: 2092191548

To my beloved wife,
Rita,
without whom this book
would not have been published.

Also, my thanks to Annelies Clarke
who designed and painted
the cover.

The author was born in Brighton, and, after 3 years at a small private school, attended the Brighton, Hove and Sussex Grammar School. He is married to Rita, to whom the book is dedicated, and has 3 children. He has lived and worked in Brighton all his life.

He has a connection with Somerset and especially the area in the vicinity of Clevedon Court - the large fictional estate in Somerset is based on this house. His interest with both World Wars, the Hitler Youth Organisations and a visit to the small town of Grave in Holland, where the climax of this story takes place, has been a valuable asset in the creation of this novel.

SYNOPSIS.

The Dark Tunnel.

This is a story of a family, young love and betrayal, and the tragedy of war. The story revolves round 3 cousins; an English boy, a German boy and a Dutch girl, and their upbringing between the wars. The boys' affection for each other is intense, but, as they mature, their natural desire for the love of a girl enters their lives.

During the summer of 1932, when the 3 cousins are on holiday at their grandparent's country house near the small town of Grave in Brabant, an incident occurs that will have tragic repercussions on their lives during the Second World War, when each are serving their country.

Historical Characters

BALDWIN. Stanley. Conservative Prime Minister 1923; 1924-29 and 1935-37.

EVART. Sir Spencer. Adjutant-General at the time of the Curragh mutiny in 1914.

FRENCH. Field-Marshal Sir John. Chief of the Imperial General Staff 1912 to March 1914. Later Commander-in-Chief of the British Expeditionary Force in France.

GOEBBELS. Paul Joseph. Reich minister for propaganda.

GOUGH. Hubert. Brigadier-General commanding Third Cavalry Brigade 1914.

HAIG. General Sir Douglas. Aide-de-Camp General 1914. Later Field-Marshal. Succeeded French as Commander-in-Chief BEF in France.

HEYDRICH. Reinhard, SS General. One time head of the Gestapo. Head of the Gestapo. Head of the Sicherheitsdienst (SS Security Service). Appointed as Reich Protector of Bohemia and Moravia in 1941. Assassinated 1942.

HIMMLER. Heinrich, Chief of the German police and the Gestapo. Reichführer SS.

HINDENBURG. Field-Marshal Paul von. President of the German Republic 1925-1934.

HITLER. Adolf. Became chancellor of Germany in 1933. On the death of Hindenburg be became President as well, remaining Führer (leader) of the Reich until his death in 1945.

KHALIFA. Sudanese religious leader who, with his father, the Mahdi, led a revolt against Egyptian rule and held the Sudan from 1885 until defeated in 1898 by a combined British and Egyptian farce under Sir Herbert Kitchener.

LEY. Doctor Robert. A chemist by profession. An early member of the Nazis Party and supporter of Hitler. Gauleiter of Cologne and leader of the German Labour Front. Hanged himself in 1946 before standing trial at Nurenberg.

MACDERMOTT. 19th Century music hall singer, sometimes known as the Great Macdermott, whose war song introduced the word jingoism into the English language in 1878,

MUSSEET. Antoon, Dutch engineer with an outstanding record in civil service. Founded NSB (Dutch. Nazi Organisation) in 1931. Executed 1946.

PAGET. General Sir Arthur, General Officer Commanding in Ireland 1914,

PAPEN. Franz von, German politician. Chancellor in 1932.

SCHIRACH. Baldur von. Youth leader of Germany. Became Gauleiter of Vienna during the second world war.

SEELY. Colonel. Secretary of State for War at the time of the Curragh mutiny in 1914.

WOLSELEY. Field-Marshal Sir Garnet. Later Vicount. Commander-in-chief British Army. 1885-1900.

GLOSSARY

A.T.S. Auxiliary Territorial Service. (Women)

A.W.O.L Absent without leave.

BANNFüHRER. Hitler Youth rank. Leader of a group of about 3000 boys, although this number varied from time to time.

CO. Commanding Officer.

DEUTSCHES JUNGVOLK. German youth organisation absorbed into the Hitler Youth and catered for age groups up to 14.

DOG TAGS. Identification Discs. (American)

GAULEITER. Highest ranking party official in a territorial division of the Nazi Party.

GEBIET. Organisational district of the Hitler Youth. The boys wore their Gebiet number on their uniform.

HAUPTMANN. German army rank - captain.

HAUPTSTURMFüHRER. SS rank - captain,

JUNGBANNFüHRER, Group leader in Deutsches Jungvolk.

KAMERADSCHAFT. Section of about 15 Hitler youths

KAMERADSCHAFTSFüRER. Hitler Youth section leader.

LEUTNANT. German army rank – (2nd. Lieutenant).

MAASDIJK. Road on top of the dike.

MAASPOORT. Ancient town gate on north side of Ravenstein.

MC. Military Cross.

NSB. Dutch Nazi Organisation.

OBERSTURMBANNFüHRER. SS rank – (lieutenant-colonel).

OTC. Officer Training Corps. Grammar schools and public schools usually had a company of cadets. Forerunner of the Combined Cadet Force,

SCHAR. Troop of about 50 Hitler youths.

SCHARFüHRER. Hitler Youth Troop leader.

SCHUTZSTAFFELN. (SS). Originally formed as Hitler's bodyguard. Gradually developed into a large organisation with a number of departments, and included many fighting units which fought as part of the German army. SICHERHEITSDIENST. (SD). SS security service.

STURMABTEILUNG. (SA) . Nazi Party troops.

STURMSCHARFüHRER. SS rank – (warrant officer).

UNTERSTURMFüHRER. SS rank – (2nd. Lieutenant).

PART 1

CHAPTER 1

There was an ear-splitting crack as the road erupted, sending up a shower of dust and debris. The staff car shuddered to a stop and stalled as the driver slammed on the brakes and ducked down behind the dashboard. The Brigadier General in the rear jerked forward, and then fell back heavily in his seat, wincing with pain from an old wound.

"Damn it!" he whispered. It had been two years since the Somme, when the shrapnel had torn into him, but although the wound had healed, the doctor had been unable to remove all the splinters, and on occasions this caused him discomfort. He could put up with this, but had not come to terms with the fact that he would never ride again.

"Stray Whizzbang, sir!" said the driver, appearing from below the dashboard and putting his cap straight.

"I am aware of that, Perks."

"Thought we'd copped it that time, sir,"

"More likely to cop it from your damned driving than from anything the Hun artillery can throw at us," the passenger drawled absently, his attention now turning to a small detachment of infantry picking themselves up from the side of the road.

The young officer in charge, seeing the red-banded service cap worn by the figure hunched in the open back car, saluted, and the general, his trench coat buttoned to the neck and the collar turned up to afford same protection against the chill of the overcast November morning, lazily raised his hand to his cap in acknowledgement,

Must be new out, he thought, glancing at the boyish faces as the soldiers moved away. His thoughts drifted back to his own first time under fire twenty years before. How young and inexperienced he had been then. Twenty years, so long ago. Yet it only seemed yesterday when he had left Sandhurst – he would have been twenty at the time - for the regimental depot at Winchester. He had grown a moustache to cover his boyish features and to give himself confidence. He hoped it would impress his new colleagues in the regiment, but on arrival at the depot he found no colleagues to impress, for his battalion was in the Sudan with Kitchener. Taking a ship to Egypt he had eventually joined them near the town of Omdurman, only to find himself ignored by busy officers, who were preparing for a large scale action expected on the following day. His first action. Not in the scale of things he had experienced in France in the last four years, but nevertheless, a bullet could kill whether it be Dervish or German. He remembered vividly the sickening fear as the mass of the Khalifa's army came thundering straight at the British line, and later the sense of elation when the general advance was ordered and victory assured.

Then it was off to South Africa. The Boers had taught him a thing or two. How pleased father had been to hear of his V.C. at Ladysmith. He smiled to himself as he remembered the adjutant's monocle falling from his eye, and his exclamation 'Good God! Young Johnnie Rutherford's got a V.C.', when the officer had read the news of the award in the mess at Pretoria. What a reckless young idiot he had been at the time, but he wasn't ignored anymore, and he needed no moustache to impress after that. Past memories faded as the car jerked forward again, avoiding the shell crater and splashing through puddles left by earlier rain on the uneven road surface. It passed the smouldering remains of a small brick building, once a French frontier post, and began to climb towards higher ground, reaching the top of the rise without further mishap and then travelling along the side of a low ridge through a more varied landscape. .

At times it was possible to see some distance across the rolling countryside with its isolated farms, and villages nestling in small hollows. The war had moved swiftly across this area, leaving it generally unscathed. About a than a mile away from the road the fields gradually climbed up to form another ridge, and a short distance beyond this was the British front line. The road was now straight, lined on either side by trees, and the car began to pick up speed, causing a cool breeze to play on the unprotected passenger huddled in the rear seat. John, who had been feeling cold for some time, decided it was time to stop and stretch his legs and get some warmth into his body. "Pull in a minute, Perks," he said. The driver stopped the car, and John heaved himself stiffly from his seat and got out. With his hands thrust deeply into his pockets he walked a short distance back along the road and turned into the entrance of a track. About a hundred yards down the track he could see a large white farmhouse with a red tiled roof. There were a number of horses in the yard being groomed by khaki clad figures, and in a field on the other side of the buildings stood a line of six field guns, guarded by a solitary soldier. A motor ambulance came slowly along the track from the opposite direction, turned into the field in front of the farm and bumped its way across to the far corner, where a few tents had been set up as a field dressing-station. He walked into the field, thumping his arms across his chest as he went in an attempt to get warm. In the distance some way down the line could be heard the dull thunder of the guns. Except for the arrival of the ambulance; there appeared to be little activity at the dressing station. This didn't surprise him, for the casualty rate had dropped dramatically during the past few days. How different it had been not so long ago during the great offensives of the war, when the field dressing stations and field hospitals had been swamped by the constant stream of wounded returning from the front.

He wondered at the greenness of the countryside, the unshattered trees, the undamaged farm, and remembered the desolation, the destruction and the mud where the trenches had run like a festering wound across the land. Since the German retreat the scarred land had been left far behind. It was difficult to believe how the fortune of war had changed so rapidly during the past few months. He remembered that early morning in March, when the German barrage had opened up on the British front line along the forty mile sector between the rivers Oise and Sensée. He'd gone up the line to assess the situation and found a third of the brigade wiped out. Then the German infantry had crashed into the remains of the British front positions, and he had been forced to pull back his surviving men. It had been the same story everywhere. He had been lucky to escape with his life. In certain areas the British had retreated forty miles. But they eventually stood firm, and the great offensive ran out of steam and slowly ground to a halt. The German army had exhausted itself,

In July the Allied armies had counter attacked, and by 8th August the advance to the Rhine had begun. The advance had been so swift during the last few weeks; it was sometimes difficult to know the exact position of the front line. He knew the Guards had just taken Maubeuge, and, by the sound of the guns in the distance, it was obvious to him that the Canadians were still fighting their way into Mons.

As he walked towards the dressing station, keeping close to the hedge at the side of the field, a stretcher was taken from the ambulance and placed on the ground in front of one of the tents. A white coated doctor emerged, and having taken a brief look at the casualty, went back inside the tent. Two orderlies then removed the stretcher and placed it a short distance away near the hedge. They saw the brigadier general approaching and stiffened to attention, and the corporal saluted. John returned the salute and the two men moved away and disappeared into one of the other tents. He paused for a moment to light a cigarette, and was just about to walk on, when there was a groan from the patient on the stretcher. Turning, he saw a fair haired boy - he could be no more than eighteen - trying to sit up to attention in order to show the proper respect due to a. senior officer, "For God's sake, there's no need for that!" John said, quickly kneeling down and putting his arm round the youth's back to support him. He took his cigarette and put it in the boy's mouth, and this seemed to bring some relief from the pain.

"Thank you, sir," whispered the boy when the cigarette was removed. John tried to gently lay him back on to the stretcher, but the boy grasped his hand tightly and pleaded, "Don't leave me! Please!" He had gained comfort from having this strong arm round him, and he looked with gratitude at the officer as he felt the arm tighten to support him once more.

"Alright now, calm yourself," John said quietly. What could he say to comfort the boy? A man of few words, his own youth now in the distant past, he found it difficult to talk naturally with the young.

It seemed as if he had lost touch with them, especially since his army career had advanced and the barrier of rank had set him apart from his subordinates, yet he felt an affinity with this boy. Perhaps because he also had known fear, loneliness and pain, and had suffered as a front line soldier. He removed his hand for a moment from the boy's grip, and taking a handkerchief from his pocket gently wiped the cold sweat from the young brow.

A spasm of pain seized the youth. He cried out in agony and buried his face in the officer's chest. John held the boy's head until the pain had eased, and then wiped away the tears from the ashen face. He noticed the dark red stain appearing on the blanket and knew the end was not far off.

"I'll be all right, sir, won't I?" the boy asked weakly; the anguished look still on his face.

"Of course you will, lad!"

"The doctor said I was done for. I don't want to die!" said the boy, his large eyes searching the general's face for reassurance. For some reason he knew he could trust this very tall, strong man. There was a warmth and concern about him, and he felt secure in his arms as he used to feel as a child when Dad had held him close. It was strange that he should be in the arms of a general. He'd rarely seen one before, let alone spoken to one. They were men of another world; stern men with serious faces who didn't even notice private soldiers. At first he'd thought this one looked stern, but now he was close to him it was different. How proud Dad and Mum will be when they hear that he's been looked after by an officer. The pain seemed to be getting easier, and he felt a pleasant drowsiness creeping over him. He knew the general would be right, he was beginning to feel better already. "I feel a bit better, sir. The pain's going," he said.

John felt the boy relax, and noticed the strained look on the young face gradually disappear. But he knew this was not improvement, but the numbness of death spreading over the body, and that the life he was holding in his arms was slowly slipping away. The boy smiled at him and then closed his eyes. He saw the boy's lips move and bent his head lower in an effort to catch the words.

"Dad?" The boy's voice was now almost inaudible as the darkness closed in on his mind. He slowly raised his hands groping towards John's face. "Kiss me," he whispered.

John was not a demonstrative man and had never kissed another male in his life, except his own father. But what else could he do he asked himself? He knew that he would regret it for the rest of his life if he neglected to comfort this boy right to the end. His face was already almost touching the boy's. He placed his lips lightly on the pale brow, and then, as he drew back, he saw a look of contentment spread over the young face.

Somewhere down the line, he heard the sharp crackle of a German machine gun spitting out its murderous venom in a last gesture of defiance. In the distance the ceaseless rumble of the guns. Without warning a nearby field erupted as a stray shell exploded, tearing open the surface of the ground and sending debris flying high into the air. Then, quite suddenly, the sound of the guns ceased, and there was silence; an uncanny silence all the way down the line. It was as if the world had at last become conscious of the carnage, and, for a moment, had stood in silent horror of its folly before the fallen millions. The boy in his arms gave a deep sigh and his body went limp. The young life had finally drifted away.

A shiver went down John's spine, and for a fleeting second he imagined himself deaf, because the sounds that had become so familiar were no longer there, and an alien quietness had descended over the land. He listened intently, but could hear only the wind softly whispering in the tops of the trees and gently singing through the telegraph wires. Carefully lying the dead youth back on to the stretcher, he fumbled inside his coat for his watch - it was exactly 11 a.m.

The war was over. He looked down on the boy and pulled the blanket up over the peaceful face. He'd felt the same sorrow a thousand times, but there were no tears left in him to shed; they had vanished years ago. Once again he strained his ears to listen, for now another sound was being carried on the breeze. The sound of church, bells. It was at this moment his mind began to take in that the guns really had ceased the destruction of his generation. Were the bells ringing for the living or the dead, he wondered? Perhaps they tolled for the boy who had found his peace, or did they ring out for himself and those like him who had survived the slaughter? Which ever way it was, he had no prayer to offer - the bells must speak for him.

A deep sense of weariness came over him. Why was he so bothered about one boy, he wondered, when thousands had died alone in the mud, or screamed out their last moments forsaken on the wire? He asked himself why the doctor had made no effort to comfort the boy? Perhaps the man was also tired, or maybe he had become so used to the sight of death that his compassion had died,

John returned to the waiting car; his driver held open the rear door for him. "I'll sit in the front. I'm still damned cold."

"Right you are, sir!" said the driver, quickly opening the front door. "You're dead tired, sir, that's your trouble. It's time you 'ad a long rest."

"You're probably right, Perks, you usually are,"

"Would you like the 'ood up, sir?"

"No, don't bother. It'll make no difference."

Perks returned to his seat, started the engine and drove on. "So it's over at last, sir. Oo'd 'ave thought when we came out in fourteen it would 'ave took this long?"

"Who'd have thought it?" said John inattentively, his mind wandering back over the years, remembering friends long dead. He closed his eyes but, tired as he was, sleep evaded him. Pictures of the past refused to leave his mind. He saw himself as a boy riding free over the green hills of his beloved Somerset. And then at school, always with his dearest friends, Robert and Reggie. But these sunlit days had gone forever, and cold reality intervened once more to sicken his heart. He thought of Robert, who had died in the mud of Passchendaele just a year ago - his body had never been found. Then he couldn't rid his mind of the face of the boy on the stretcher. There was a look on that boy's face as he died that would haunt him for the rest of his life. He couldn't fathom what it was; he couldn't even describe it to himself. He asked himself why he had survived when so many had died, but found no answer. Although he had survived in body, part of him had died in the trenches and would always remain there, and he knew his life would never be quite the same again. The experience had cut too deep for the scars to heal completely.

The car entered a village, where small groups of people had gathered in the main street. Some of them raised a cheer as it passed, but most were too intent on talking to a squadron of dismounted cavalry to notice. It was still difficult to believe it was all over, and to pass the time he pulled from his pocket an army form C212 and read the first few lines once again just to reassure himself:

> *Hostilities will cease at 1100 today Novr 11ᵗʰ*
> *Troops will stand fast on the line reached at that*
> *hour -*

He didn't bother to read the whole order but carefully folded the paper and put it back into his pocket. He would keep it as a memento.

It was late afternoon, and. the light was fading, when the Sunbeam drove through the gates of brigade headquarters, a chateau some miles behind the line near the fortress town of Mauberge.

"General's car just come in, sir," the guard sergeant rapped down the telephone. The brigade major at the other end of the line grunted acknowledgement, replaced the receiver, and hurriedly left his office to meet his chief. By the time he had reached the entrance hall, his general was already out of the car and mounting the stone steps leading up to the massive front door. Two sentries presented arms, and John returned the salute as he walked briskly into the house,

"Good afternoon, Shaw," he said to the young major.

"Good afternoon, sir. If you will come this way, I will show you to your quarters," replied the officer respectfully leading the way down a long corridor,

"Any messages?" John enquired.

"Yes sir. Division called and wish you to contact them."

"What the devil do they want?"

"They didn't say, sir. It was the G.O.C. himself who wished to speak with you."

"Was it, by Jove! I wonder what he wants?"

The major opened one of the many doors and John moved past him into an elegant room, tastefully furnished, which was obviously one of the chateau's drawing-rooms. He flung his trench coat on to a large sofa, walked across to the enormous hearth, and gave the glowing logs in the fireplace a hefty kick, rekindling the blaze.

"I trust this room will be suitable, sir?" the young man enquired anxiously, hoping to have pleased his general, for whom he had a great respect.

"Excellent, thank you. Makes a change to have a bit of luxury. Doubt if it'll be for long, though. They're bound to move us on again before long." said John as he stood with his back to the now blazing fire, enjoying the warmth seeping into his chilled body. "I wonder what Division want?" he pondered, "the show's over. Couple of days rest wouldn't go amiss."

"Not much chance of that, sir," replied the major, who was just about to make further comment, when the inner door at the far end of the room burst open, revealing a slim, shortish man with bright sparkling eyes and a thin cheeky face.

"All the fun of the fair, old boy!" said the newcomer exuberantly to John. He bounded into the room, giving a hearty laugh.

"What are you playing at now, Reggie?" said John, indicating a piece of string, which his friend was holding in his hand and which extended back through the open door into the adjoining room.

Reggie began to wind the string as if he was reeling in a fish. "Ha Ha! Wait for it, old boy!" Then, with a shout of triumph, "Here she comes!" and a final pull, a bottle of whisky came sliding across the floor, and was immediately hoisted up by its captor and placed on the table.

"You are a bloody fool, Reggie, " said John, smiling.

"Celebration chaps!" Reggie exclaimed. Then turning to the major he said, "Glasses, Nigel!"

The young officer gave a despairing look, although he was used to the antics of Colonel Sanders.

"Before we start celebrating, Reggie, I must phone Division," said John.

"Wish 'em all the fun of the fair from me, old boy."

John sat down at his desk, lifted the receiver of the field telephone, which had been specially set up for him, and wound the handle. The operator, somewhere in the chateau, answered immediately and connected him with divisional headquarters. There was a long pause, during which time the major placed the glasses on the table and Reggie opened the bottle.

Minutes passed. Then a voice was heard at the other end of the line. "That you, Rutherford?"

"Rutherford here, sir,"

"Congratulations, old chap!"

What the devil's he talking about, John asked himself, wondering whether he had heard correctly? The line was poor, and both officers were having to raise their voices to be heard. "I'm sorry, can you repeat that. This line is very bad."

"I said congratulations. Can you hear me?" The major general raised his voice again and spoke slowly.

"Yes, that's better,' John replied, but still not understanding why he should be congratulated. It was too early for any further promotion and it was unlikely that he was being sent, home. But the voice at the other end was speaking again.

"I've received a message via the British Embassy in Holland." There was a pause while the divisional commander searched through the papers on his desk, "Ah, here it is," he continued. "I'll read it to you. It says, please inform Brigadier General John Rutherford that at eleven ack emma this morning his wife gave birth to a son. Both mother and child are in excellent health."

John sat quite still, for a moment not comprehending the news, and lost for words. He had had little time to think of his personal affairs during the past weeks, with his mind concentrated on the fast moving offensive as the war came to an end. He felt a sense of guilt that he had momentarily forgotten his child was due to be born, even though it was a week early. But as he began to grasp the message, and his thoughts settled on his beloved wife and new son, a warm glow of joy crept over him. His tiredness and its consequent depression seemed to leave him.

He had never been an emotional man, always the strong, calm, straightforward soldier, but a flood of feeling swept over him now with which he found it difficult to contend. He fumbled for his handkerchief and held it to his forehead, hoping the others would not see the flush on his face.

The voice at the end of the phone interrupted his thoughts. "You still there, Rutherford?"

"Yes. Yes, I'm still here, sir," he stumbled, collecting himself.

"I thought you'd lost your tongue, man. Anyway, I'll arrange leave for you as soon as I can, so you can go and see the young fellow. When the Hun gets out of Belgium you'll be able to take a train into Holland. Must go now. Regards to Elizabeth."

"Thank you. Goodbye." John replaced the receiver, and Reggie placed a glass of whisky in front of him.

"You look a bit tense, old boy. Not bad news, I hope?"

"Elizabeth had a son this morning."

"Well I'm blessed! And you sit there like a damp squib. If it had been me, I'd have gone up like a whiz-bang. Congratulations, my dear chap! I give you a toast." Reggie raised his glass. "Your new son."

On that Armistice Day evening, the chateau was ablaze with light as preparations went on for a celebration dinner which John was giving for his battalion commanders and some of their officers. Although the news of his son, and a hot bath had revived his spirits somewhat, he would have preferred to have eaten his dinner in the quietness of his own room, but felt duty bound to entertain his officers on this particular evening.

He arrived early in the dining room to ensure that the table was set to his satisfaction, for he demanded efficiency from all his staff, and could not abide a lowering of standards even though some considered that difficult circumstances permitted it. He believed that etiquette and good manners were an essential part of life, especially when entertaining guests.

Standing with his back to the blaming log fire, his uniform immaculate and his dark straight hair neatly parted in the centre and brushed down on either side, he surveyed the room with certain contentment. The long oak table with all the places neatly set, and the candelabras standing at intervals along the centre. The flickering light from the candles playing on the faces of the portraits on the walls gave them an unearthly appearance.

Reggie, who was temporarily working with the brigade staff and consequently billeted in the chateau, was the first to arrive, much to John's pleasure, for with Reggie present the conversation was sure to flow smoothly. The other guests presented themselves promptly, none wishing to be late with the brigadier present, and everyone took their place at the table exactly on time.

John, at the head of the table with Reggie on his right, glanced at the faces before him and thought how young they looked, some no more than boys. Even his battalion commanders, except for Reggie, could be no more than twenty five. He had watched the faces change over the years of war as the casualty rate mounted and the old regular army was wiped out. The old faces were replaced by young eager boys who, when they arrived at the front, had no conception of the hell into which they were entering. He tried to recall some words Robert once quoted about hell, but he found it difficult to remember quotations or poetry, for the arts had never been his strong subject.

"Penny for your thoughts, old boy!" said Reggie, who had just been relating an amusing tale to the young officer next to him, and was once again attacking his meal with relish. It always amazed John how Reggie usually managed to clear his plate before anyone else and yet never appeared to cease in conversation.

"I was trying to bring to mind some words that Rob once quoted about the war and hell. Something about a covenant with death."

"Don't ask me, old boy; Rob could quote from so many things."

The young officer beside Reggie looked uncertainly at John as if about to enter into the conversation, but not wishing to appear presumptuous, remained silent. John, perceiving his hesitation, invited a solution, from him.

"I think you may be referring to a verse from Isaiah, sir. 'We have made a covenant with death hend with hell are we at agreement'." The young man flushed with embarrassment as he spoke, feeling foolish to have aired, what, he considered his very limited knowledge in front of his brigadier. Although John did not realise it, indeed, the subject never crossed his mind, most of his subordinates and young people in general stood in awe of him. They had great respect for him but, lacking the knowledge of the kindness and generosity which lay below the surface, sometimes felt uncomfortable in his presence. The few friends of his young days, who had been close to him and knew the real man, were all gone; lost, one by one, in the years of war. Only Reggie survived.

"I'm obliged to you," said John, hesitating and trying to remember if this young subaltern had been introduced to him. "I don't believe I know your name."

"Irving, sir. Matthew Irving."

John eyed the intelligent young face. Rather thin and pale, he thought, but the eyes were alert and penetrating. "Ah yes, thank you, Irving," he added.

"Irving tells me that he is going to read law at Oxford when his army service is finished. In any case, he's too intelligent to be a regular soldier," said Reggie with a twinkle in his eye.

John smiled and wondered whether there was any truth in Reggie's last remark, but was not drawn to argue the point. He said, "I wish you well in your chosen career, Irving. But don't let your time in the army be wasted. It's all good experience in life, and you'll need plenty of that if you're going to be a successful lawyer."

The young officer smiled modestly. "Thank you, sir. I'll remember that."

After the loyal toast, Reggie banged the table calling for silence, and then Matthew Irving rose from his chair. "Gentlemen," he said rather uncertainly. "Although this is an informal occasion and speeches are not the order of the day, I, as the youngest guest, have been asked, or more correctly, instructed" - a soft ripple of laughter went round the table - "to make a short speech." He went on to thank John for his hospitality, and still referring to John he continued, "Your leadership, daring, and consideration for your men is legendary in the brigade, and I would have given much to have served under you during the years of fighting. As it is, I've missed all the action, and I much regret it." He was now speaking with more confidence. "However, I am proud to be serving in this great British army and especially in this famous brigade." A hum of approval came from the other officers. "I am proud of my country, and I believe in the just cause for which we have been fighting."

Picking up his glass, he turned and faced John and ended by saying, "Before finishing I would just like to congratulate you, sir, on the birth of your son this morning, and I know that everyone will join me in wishing you and your family well for the future." He paused and raised his glass. "Gentlemen. Our host."

After the toast as the young man sat down, Reggie said to him, "Well done, old chap. That's what I like, something short and to the point. You'll make a splendid advocate one of these days. You've certainly got the gift of the gab."

"That makes two of you," John interjected, and then added, "I suppose you put him up to this, Reggie, just to get me on my feet."

"Well, I thought we ought to have a little something from you tonight, old boy. End of show, and all that. Some of these young chaps have never heard you speak."

"Doubt if that will retard their military careers," John retorted dryly.

As John stood up to reply the new officers, who had recently joined the brigade, looked with envy at the crimson ribbon on his left breast. He had realised that he would probably have to say a few words during the evening, but he had not bothered to make any preparation.

He said, "Gentlemen, I thank you for your kind wishes, and am touched by the loyalty you have shown me during these difficult times. Irving has spoken as I would have expected any young man of spirit to speak, and many years ago I would have said the same. But as one grows older our thoughts are tempered by experience, and I would like to submit to you a few thoughts of an older man. I welcome the new officers here tonight, 'but unlike Irving I am glad you have missed, the action in this murderous war, because we are going to need you for the future, not lying out there rotting on the wire. You are the fortunate ones, although you probably won't believe it. Very few of you will remember how we came out in fourteen, with bands playing and flags flying, to fight for some great cause like knights in shining armour. But the cause, whatever it was, got lost in the mud and died in the slaughter." He paused, seemingly to gather his thoughts. He picked up his glass and stared down into the clear wine. He could feel again the heat of the sun on that July day as he left the trench with his battalion spread out either side of him, and remembered asking himself, after having advanced only a few yards, why his men were kneeling in prayer instead of going forward with him. Then the sudden realisation that they were not kneeling but slowly collapsing to the ground as the German machine guns cut them down. "What a waste," he said quietly, more to himself than to his audience. Then clearing his throat he continued, "Millions have died, and unless we take the right path now and ensure that it doesn't happen again the dead will have died in vain, for nothing." A puzzled look had clouded some of the faces before him, and he wondered whether they understood what he was trying to say. "The point I am trying to make, gentlemen, is this. We have won this war at a terrible cost, and I pray, for the sake of you young men and my new son, that our politicians are wise enough not to sow the seeds of another, by acts of revenge." He raised his glass. "Gentlemen, I drink to you - The survivors. Long may you be allowed to live in peace."

After the guests had gone, John and Reggie sat in front of the dying fire in two large armchairs. Each had a glass of brandy in one hand and a cigar in the other.

"Did you really mean, what you said about the dead dying in vain?" Reggie enquired.

"I most certainly did. Think about it. The French are already crying for revenge, and mark my words; revenge will lead to another war. You will not be able to keep Germany down for ever, and unless she is treated wisely now, God help the next generation."

"Don't you think that Lloyd George will be able to stop the French from going too far?"

"No, I don't. There's too much of an outcry against Germany at the moment, and as a politician he will bend with the wind. In any case it is France which has been devastated, not Britain, and Clemanceu will ensure that he has the greater say in what conditions are to be imposed. What with the French crying for revenge and the

Americans trying to force on them a democracy they don't want, the Germans are in for a difficult time in the next few years."

Reggie held his glass under his nose, inhaling the fumes, his eyes half closed and an expression of contentment on his face. He could be serious when the occasion demanded, and never tired of his discussions with John, whom, he thought, had a perception into the subject of politics far greater than his own. "Surely, you don't think they should get away Scot free?" he asked.

"All I'm saying is that there should be reconciliation, not revenge. The German army fought to defend their Fatherland. They fought honourably too so far as one can fight honourably in war. And their fighting men have suffered hell just as we have. I just think that there should be an honourable peace. I am worried that the next generation will have to suffer as we have." John looked earnestly at his friend, who was now-blowing cigar smoke up into the air. Reggie was about to reply, but before he could speak John continued, "Talking of the next generation, Reggie, we, that is Elizabeth and I, would be very happy if you would consent to be the new baby's Godfather. We also decided that, if the child was a boy, we would call him Robert Reginald."

Reggie's face lit up and he felt a glow of pride inside himself. He had been married for sixteen years and had not been blessed with any children. What a joy, he thought, to be able to take a special interest in this boy. He saw his friend looking at him, but, for once, was at a loss for words. He coughed to clear his throat and then said huskily, "Most honoured, John. I'd be glad to."

Then, more to himself than to his friend, he added quietly, "My name too for the child. Most gratifying."

"I hope you don't mind, Reggie, your name in second place, I mean. I just thought that Robert..."

"That's all right, old boy," Reggie interrupted. "It's just how it should be. It sounds right that way."

As Reggie finished speaking the clock on the mantelpiece started the long chime to midnight, and the day, which had seen peace return to the world, and the birth of a new child for John, drew to its close.

Chapter 2

The train shuddered before jerking to a stop, and this was followed by a loud discharge of steam from the locomotive. The newspaper covering John's face slipped down onto his lap. He had not managed to sleep and was finding the journey tedious. There had been delays at Namur and Liege, and now there was obviously going to be another at the Dutch frontier. He would get out at Einhoven and stay there overnight if the damned thing ever got that far before nightfall, he thought. He had no intention of spending the whole night being shunted about Holland trying to catch a few moments of fitful sleep. Vivid memories came back to him of past journeys when returning from leave, sitting bolt upright in a crowded carriage through the interminable hours of the night, his head falling forward in sleep only to be jerked back to consciousness after what seemed to be only a few minutes. Then, getting out on to a cold and draughty platform in the early hours of the morning, he was in a state of fatigue and depression. Never again. At least now he had a reserved compartment, but he did not relish the idea of spending a night in it - it was too cold. The thought of it made him turn up his collar and pull his civilian overcoat more tightly round him.

The wearing of his civilian clothes that day had given him a pleasant feeling of freedom. For the first time in years he felt completely relaxed. The Armistice had released him from the constant subconscious fear of death and the burden of leading his men into action.

To pass the time he felt in his overcoat pocket and took out a small black box which contained a solid gold medallion about the size of a florin. Studying it closely he saw that one side had been decoratively engraved with the interweaving initials *RRR*. The other side bore the heads of Disraeli and Bismarck encircled by laurel leaves, and the inscription *Peace with Honour - Berlin 1878*.

1878 had been the year of John's birth. It was also a time of crisis in Europe. His father had commanded the battalion at that time, and he could remember Mother telling him, when quite young, how worried she had been on the day he was born because of the war fever which had swept the country. She had expected the regiment to be drafted overseas and war with Russia to break out at any moment.

The Russians had attacked the Turks during the previous year, and compelled them to accept the Treaty of San Stefano. The conditions imposed on the Turks were considered unsatisfactory by Britain and Austria, and a crisis developed. A congress of powers was convened at Berlin, with Bismarck presiding, and a full scale war prevented by negotiation. Disraeli, on his return from the congress, claimed he had brought back *Peace with Honour*.

It was the time during which *Jingoism* was born, when Macdermott was singing his song in the music halls:

> *We don't want to fight, but by jingo, if we do,*
> *We've got the ships; we've got the men, and got the*
> *money too!*

John smiled as he remembered how, when a boy, he was sometimes called Johnny Jingo by his family if they wished to tease him.

Earlier that day, as he had walked down the steps in front of the chateau to the waiting car prior to leaving for the station, Reggie had handed him the black box and explained that the medallion had been given to an uncle of his by Disraeli in recognition of the excellent work he had done behind the scenes at the Congress of Berlin. The uncle had been a member of the diplomatic corps at the time, and his initials had been *RRR*. The medallion was to be a present for the new baby.

Returning the box to his pocket, he glanced out of the window into the cold, dull December afternoon. He saw some Dutch frontier guards getting on to the train, and shortly afterwards the door of his compartment opened and a dumpy, unsmiling officer with piggy

eyes stood glaring down at him. John thought he looked rather ridiculous in his ill-fitting uniform. The man said something in a deep
guttural accent and stretched out his hand, by which John presumed
he was being asked for his passport and papers. The officer glanced
briefly at the passport but carefully read the papers, which had been
prepared by the British Embassy explaining the purpose of the visit.
His attitude began to mellow as he discovered that he was in the presence of an English general on his way to visit his wife and new born
son. Eventually the round face beamed and began speaking slowly,
if somewhat loudly, emphasising each word to ensure the foreigner
would, understand. "Engelsche Generaal. Goed, goed...Zoon. Goed,
goed. Ja, ja."

John, who could speak no language but his own, was amused
to be receiving this lesson in Dutch. Then the thought struck him
that perhaps it was double Dutch. Stupid as it was, the more he tried
to push the thought out of his mind the more it tickled him, and
he found it difficult to keep a straight face. Feeling he should say
something out of politeness, he copied the man and said, "Ja, ja." It
was the limit of his vocabulary, but the other seemed pleased by his
linguistic effort and, handing him back his papers, shook his hand
vigorously, saluted, and then made to leave the compartment still
beaming and nodding his head. With a last, "Zoon, Goed, goed," the
moon face disappeared and the door closed.

When the man had gone John found that he could control himself no longer, and laughed until the tears came to his eyes. Every
time he tried to stop, the thought of the officer and his double Dutch
set him off again. It was a few minutes before he was able to constrain
his laughter, and when he eventually did, he wondered what he had
found so funny. He tried to remember the last time he had laughed
like that, but found he couldn't. It must have been so long ago, he
thought. Perhaps he had needed to laugh just to relieve the tensions
of the past years and to prove to himself that he was still capable of
doing so. In any case it had raised his spirits and relieved the boredom of the journey,

He must have sat there for about twenty minutes listening to
the gentle, rhythmic hiss of steam issuing from the locomotive, when

there was a jerk and the sound of clanking all the way down the train as the couplings took up the strain. He was on the move again. Looking out of the window, he saw that at last he was crossing into Holland. He had been there only once before, and that was in the year when his life had been altered so dramatically – 1914.

*

In March 1914 John had returned to England with his battalion after spending some years in India, to be greeted with the news that he had been gazetted lieutenant colonel to command the 1st. Battalion. His promotion was to take effect on Monday 29th June. He had recently celebrated his 36th birthday. Ever since he was eighteen his life had been dedicated to the army, and as an efficient and conscientious officer he had risen slowly up the promotion ladder. His courage and leadership in action and his administrative ability were well known to all who served with him. And in India a political shrewdness had been noticed by his superiors; when he had managed to settle peacefully a dangerous and delicate situation involving one of the independent princely states. Although it was not likely to affect his career, it was considered unfortunate that he had never married. He had spent his life in a male environment, firstly at school, then with the regiment, and had never sought the company of women. As a result his contact with them had been restricted, and he had remained a bachelor.

A cold, damp Monday morning in early spring found him strolling through Trafalgar Square. He was staying at his London club prior to returning home to Somerset, having left the regimental depot at Winchester a few days previously to take nearly four months leave. Leaving the War Office, after attending an interview regarding his forthcoming promotion, he decided to return to the club on foot and enjoy the sights of the busy London streets which he had not seen for some time. He was in good spirits and looking forward to the evening when his two great friends, Robert and Reggie, would join him for dinner.

A mass of traffic was moving slowly through the Square. Carriages of the rich; motor cabs - there were few hansoms left on the streets of London now; drays, with the iron rims of their wheels polished bright by constant contact with the cobbled streets; cart's; red motor omnibuses with solid rubber tyres; and gleaming black motorcars. The drumming of horses' hooves and the roar of the ever increasing number of motor vehicles on the roads gave him a feeling of excitement, and so provoked his interest that he stood for a moment watching the scene. He noticed, with a twinge of regret, that there was not a horse drawn bus to be seen - the London General Omnibus Company having withdrawn its last one in 1911. A great brewer's dray beautifully painted in glossy chocolate brown thundered past drawn by two magnificent Clydesdales, their trappings jingling above the noise of the traffic. John - an expert on horses and an excellent rider - never tired of seeing these giant animals. A new, bright red motor bus, with its varnished wooden slats fixed under the high bodywork between the wheels to prevent pedestrians from falling underneath, crawled at snail's pace in front of him. Slowed by the sheer volume of traffic, the overheated engine was giving off clouds of steam which was blowing back into the driver's face. The bus gradually moved past him and was then forced to stop. The conductor came down the open stairs from the top deck, "Quicker to walk, Guv!" he grinned at John, who acknowledged the man with a smile, and then noticed a brightly coloured advertisement poster affixed to the back of the stairway. The poster showed a smiling, fresh faced Dutch girl in traditional costume, and a large tulip field in the background,

"Bit of alright, Mister, ain't she!" A newspaper boy with a cheeky face was just setting up his pitch and had noticed John's interest in the poster. "Paper, Mister?" said, the boy holding out The Times.

"Thank you," said John, placing a penny into the grubby hand and turning to continue his walk.

"All Sir Garnet, sir!" said the boy, guessing he was talking to a soldier. He had noticed the gentleman's military style moustache, the bowler hat and black overcoat, and the rolled umbrella being carried resting on the right shoulder.

John stopped and looked down into the bright eyes peering up at him from under the peak of a scruffy cap,

Memories of the Sudan and South Africa came flooding back into his mind. He hadn't heard that expression for years.

"Bet you're a soldier, Mister. Me dad, 'e was a soldier of the old Queen."

"What regiment?" John asked,,

"Royal Fusiliers, Mister. I'm joining when I'm old enough."

"In that case, as one soldier to another, here's your first King's shilling," said John, taking a shilling from his pocket and pushing it into the eager hand.

The boy stared at the coin in disbelief. "Cor blimey, a real bleedin' bob! Just wait, till me dad 'ears abart this. Thanks, Mister! You're a toff, and no mistake." He gave a smart salute, as taught him by his father; John smiled at him and, raising his hat, walked away.

As he went down Haymarket, his mind kept returning to the picture of the Dutch girl. Trying to turn his thoughts on to some other subject, he recollected the paperboy. It was strange how just an expression, which was barely remembered now, could conjure up in his mind such vivid pictures of the army just before the turn of the century, when the saying had been in common use with the troops. But try as he would to think of something else, the Dutch girl's smiling face seemed to insist on all his attention. He wondered why the Dutch grew so many tulips, but before coming to any conclusion he imagined the girl saying to him," Why don't you come and find out?"

That evening John sat at a table in the dining-room of his club. An elderly, white haired steward approached followed by another man.

"Captain Nicholson, sir," said the steward, who then quietly withdrew.

"Robert, my dear chap. So glad you could come," said John rising and shaking his friend by the hand.

The dining room was not full, but there was a low buzz of conversation coming from the tables where other officers were seated. The steward returned and took their orders and, shortly afterwards, served them soup.

"By the way, Reggie has been in Paris for a fortnight and I've had a wire to say he'll be late," said John.

"I'm glad he's coming, it will be just like old times. I suppose he's still making pots of money?"

"I've never known it otherwise," John chuckled.

"What do you think about him joining the Territorials?" Robert asked. "Can't imagine old Reggie as an army man."

"Oh, I don't know. He might be unconventional, but men will follow him, and that's the secret of success for a good officer. "

"Well, John, and what are you going to do with all this leave?" Robert enquired.

John, who had finished his soup, sat stroking his chin for a moment. "I've been thinking about that," he drawled. "I've a notion to take a holiday. Perhaps on the continent." He paused, and then said quickly as if he had just remembered something, "Holland." He couldn't understand what made him say it, for he'd had no intention of going to Holland. It just seemed to slip out.

"Holland!" exclaimed Robert in a tone of voice which indicated that it was the last place on earth where one should take a holiday. "Why the devil do you want to go to Holland? All tulips and wind-mills." Then he added quickly, "Not that I've been there." He had rarely known his friend show any inclination to spend his leave any-where other than at his father's estate in Somerset, where he could indulge his passion for riding. "Not your cup of tea I should have thought," he added.

"There was this poster," said John, trying to sound nonchalant.

"What poster?" interjected Robert whilst his friend paused to think how best to explain.

"Oh, just a poster on the back of a bus showing a Dutch girl advertising something or other. I can't get the thing out of my mind."

Robert's dreamy eyes lit up and he began to laugh. He always enjoyed teasing his friend. "I never thought I'd see the day when a staid old bachelor like you would fall in love with a Dutch girl on the back of a bus."

"Don't talk such damned nonsense!" said John, rising to the bait. "All I want is a couple of weeks' holiday somewhere other than

Somerset, just for a change." Why he should be defending himself he didn't know. "I've never been to Holland before," he added quickly. And he'd no intention of going now, he thought, or he hadn't before this conversation started. He had the feeling that he was being drawn into something against his will. "I thought it may be quite interesting."

"You must go, old chap, fate has decreed it. You'll probably find the girl of your dreams and come back married." Robert let out another peel of laughter.

The steward unobtrusively approached the table and began to remove the empty soup plates. Robert, trying to suppress his laughter, said to him, "I say, Merton, what do you know about Holland?"

The elderly man raised one of his bushy eyebrows, but otherwise his face remained impassive. He continued with his duties and then, after a pause, said in a grave, flat tone, "I have never been to that country, sir. However, I am led to believe that it is flat, and that the inhabitants wear clogs and ride bicycles."

"Thank you, Merton, for that most interesting piece of information," said Robert, hardly managing to control himself.

"Thank you, sir," replied the steward, bowing slightly before moving slowly away with the plates. Robert pulled out his handkerchief and began to weep with laughter into it.

"I don't see what's so damned funny," said John dryly, trying hard to keep a straight face, but finding it increasingly difficult not to be affected by his friend's humour.

"I was just picturing you," Robert began disjointedly between further sobs of laughter, still holding the handkerchief to his eyes. For a moment he was unable to go on, and then trying again, he said, "I can see you riding a bicycle along the top of a dyke, wearing-clogs, chasing a Dutch girl on the back of a bus." He just managed to finish the sentence before his next convulsion. "That man Merton is a real gem," he managed to add.

"He's a bloody fool, like you! Bicycles and clogs. Tulips and windmills," said John, trying to sound disdainful. "Neither of you know a damned thing about the place. In any case I'm perfectly capable of riding a cycle."

"'And chasing a Dutch girl," Robert quickly added.

"Shut up about that blasted girl!"

"You brought her up in the first place," Robert replied, wiping the tears from his eyes.

"I wish I hadn't mentioned her. I was only trying to explain what had made me think of Holland."

A mischievous gleam came into Robert's eyes. He said, "I'll tell you what, John. I'll wager you a guinea you won't tour Holland on a bicycle."

"Done!" John exclaimed without thinking, instantly regretting it.

"And if you bring back a Dutch girl I'll chuck in an extra ten bob," Robert added with confidence.

At that moment Reggie entered the far side of the room, carrying a bottle of champagne under each arm. "All the fun of the fair, you chaps," he called as he approached his friends, causing at least one elderly officer to give him a hard look.

"For God's sake, Reggie, don't make so much row!" John called out in a loud whisper when his friend was near enough to hear. "What with this idiot, and you with your fun of the fair, we'll all be drummed out. You're not at Maxim' s now, you know."

"Sorry, old boy," Reggie whispered, holding a finger up to his mouth, and tip-toeing the rest of the way to his chair.

Laughing at his antics, John and Robert greeted their friend with obvious delight.

"Let's open the bubbly," said Reggie, seizing the napkin from the steward's arm. Wrapping it round one of the bottles, he unfastened the cork. Merton, who had just returned to serve the main course, looked on unmoved, although the expert way which Reggie carried out the operation was not lost on him. While Reggie was pouring the wine, Robert mischievously drew the steward into the conversation again. "Do you know, Merton, Major Rutherford is going to tour Holland on a bicycle."

Merton, whose grave expression remained unaltered, looked at John and replied calmly, "My sympathy, sir. A most disagreeable form of transport, if I might say so, sir. Nasty things, bicycles. Cold and wet."

Perhaps that Merton wasn't such a bloody fool after all, John thought. He was still secretly regretting that his friend had manoeuvred him into accepting the bet. Only Robert could have done it. The two had always enjoyed each others company, and their good humoured banter was the product of a deep friendship. In their early years they were rarely apart, but since Robert's marriage and the birth of his two daughters their time together, when not on regimental duty, had naturally been reduced. John had a great regard for his friend's wife, Helen, and was pleased that he had found such happiness. He was also fond of the girls, although he could not abide all the fuss that was made of them when they were babies. He didn't like babies.

Reggie, who had poured an extra glass, handed one to the steward. "Have a quick swig of this, Merton. Do you good. All the best to the wife and kids!"

"Although highly irregular, sir, I am most obliged to you, and will carry out your instructions at the earliest, opportunity." The man's face almost lost its sombre expression as he took the glass and moved away, wondering to which kids the gentleman could be referring.

"Now you chaps, what's all this about Holland?" said Reggie.

Robert began to laugh again, but before he could speak, John said, "I'm just going to Holland, for a holiday, that's all."

"On a bicycle," Robert interjected.

"Great Scott!" said Reggie, looking genuinely surprised. "A bicycle! I thought horses were more in your line, old boy."

"They are," said John, "But I'm reliably informed that in Holland one rides a bicycle." John then related to Reggie the conversation which had taken place before his arrival. However, he was unable to prevent Robert butting in to ensure that Reggie heard about the Dutch girl on the back of the bus.

"Well I'm blessed!" Reggie exclaimed, after hearing the full story. "A bicycle!" That's taking things a bit far. Now, why not try a motor bike. Noisy things, but great sport. Got one at home you can have. Triumph, belt driven. You have to give her a hefty shove to start, but once she does she goes like the wind. Can't use the old girl any more because Daisy doesn't like it, at least she doesn't now, since she dropped off."

"Dropped off? John queried,

"Good Lord yes! Ha! Ha!" Reggie gave one of his loud laughs. "Absolute scream! Though Daisy didn't think so. There we were just out for an afternoon spin. Got to that steep bend just out of Poynings - you know the one, John."

John nodded, remembering the village nestling under the Sussex Downs.

"Thought we'd go up the Devil's Dyke for tea. Anyway, to cut a long story short, I opened up the old throttle and we shot round the bend and up the hill. At least I did," Reggie chuckled. "I thought the old bike was going well, but imagine my surprise, chaps, when I got up the Dyke and found Daisy wasn't there. She'd dropped off. Ha ha." Reggie paused for a drink and then continued. "I went all the way down again, and there she was sitting at the side of the road, swearing like a trooper, and still clutching her handbag. Couldn't help laughing until she hit me with the wretched thing. Swears she'll never ride again."

"Don't blame her!" John commented, grinning at the thought of the language that slipped out of Daisy on occasions, revealing her upbringing in the dockland slums.

Robert was once again in stitches. "I can just see Daisy sitting there with that enormous handbag of hers," he said. "I don't think I've ever laughed so much in all my life. I feel quite weak with it all."

"By the way, how is Daisy?" asked John.

"Full of the joys of spring, old boy. Started to give dancing lessons, don't you know. Doesn't have to, of course, but she enjoys it. Never quite got over her days at the Gaiety, I suppose." Reggie grinned, and then added with, a twinkle in his eye, "Can't say I mind what with the constant stream of young lovelies in and out the house. Keeps the old eyes boggling."

At a table on the other side of the room, a florid faced officer in his early sixties with a large white moustache, which hung down over the sides of his mouth, was eyeing the three friends. His attention had been attracted by Robert's laughter which, although not excessively loud, was noticeable in the quiet of the dining room. "Who's that fellow over there?" he enquired of his companion, and indicated Robert with a nod of his head.

"I've no idea, but the dark one with him is Rutherford."

"Not old Georgie Rutherford's boy?"

"Yes, that's the one. Did rather well with us in South Africa, you may remember."

"Of course, I remember," the older man retorted rather testily. "V.C. at Ladysmith. Not that I'd have known him. Only met once, and he was a slip of a boy at the time. Pity he's not one of us; Georgie was just the same, would go into the damned foot. Splendid rider too. Could have had any horse regiment he wanted. "

"Wasn't there another son?" asked the younger man.

"Oh, yes. Civil servant. Something in the Home Office, I believe. Unfit for the army, don't you know. Poor specimen. Disappointment to old Georgie. Still this one's made up for it." After a pause to sip his port he went on. "And what about the other fellow. Who's he?"

"Ah, now he's something in the City. Very rich, but no regiment,"

"No regiment! Good God! What the devil's he doing in here then?"

"I believe he's in the Territorials."

"Might just as well be in old Baden Powell's Boy Scouts for all the good that'll do him. Territorials!" the florid faced man muttered with a disparaging note in his voice, and then turning his attention back to his port poured himself another glass.

John had noticed the two older officers looking his way. "Old Johnny French is looking at you, Rob, wondering what you find so amusing, I'll be bound," he said.

"I bet he's got more than me on his mind at the moment. This mutiny at the Curragh must be a headache for him. Do you think he'll resign?"

"Difficult to say. I did hear that he saw the King on Saturday and was given some strong advice on how to handle the situation," John replied.

"What's all this about a mutiny?" asked Reggie, who had been out of touch with the news during his visit to Paris. "Ireland again, of course. All our troubles come from there. It beats me why we don't get out of it,"

"That's exactly what we're trying to do," John replied. The Home Rule Bill should be passed later on this year, but there's Edward Carson and his Ulster Volunteers who are pledged to resist it because it's a threat to Orange rights and privileges". If Asquith doesn't handle the matter properly there could be civil war in Ireland."

"But what's this about a mutiny?"' Reggie persisted.

John related how, the week before, Arthur Paget, General Officer Commanding in Ireland, was called to London, and seen by the Cabinet Committee on Ireland and by others, including Sir John French. He was given certain instructions and then returned to Dublin, where he presented an ultimatum to his officers that they must either agree to take part in active operations in Ulster, or resign and forfeit their pensions. General Gough, commanding the third Cavalry Brigade, returned to the Curragh barracks, outside Dublin, and informed his officers that he had decided, to resign rather than fight against Ulster. Over fifty of his officers decided to follow his example.

"Good heavens, old boy!" Reggie exclaimed, "The balloon really has gone up."

"Well, the Government have been quick off the mark," John continued; explaining that a statement had been issued saying that the ultimatum was the result of a misunderstanding, and that troops would not be used against Ulster, except to guard the ammunition depots. Certainly not to crush political opposition to the Home Rule Bill. "Gough has been instructed" to resume his command, and things appear to have returned to normal. But it was a nasty business, and the King is most upset, I'm told."

"Who's to blame?"

"Nobody seems to know, because Paget's instructions were verbal and not in writing. Of course, Paget is not the most tactful of men and never chooses his words with care. He could have been misunderstood, but on the other hand he might have been given those instructions. Anyway, the matter seems to have been resolved for the moment, but what the consequences will be is anyone's guess."

The steward came quietly to the table and gave a gentle cough. "Yes, Merton?" said John.

"General French sends his complements, sir, and asks if you could join him for a few minutes."

"Thank you, Merton. Excuse me, you fellows, I'll be back shortly," said John, rising from the table. He went to the other side of the room where the two senior officers were sitting. "Good, evening, Sir John," he said.

"Ah, Rutherford. Sorry to interrupt your party. Just wanted to congratulate you on your promotion. You know Haig, don't you." The General indicated his companion and John gave a slight bow to the other General. "I remember you as a boy," he went on. "Once stayed at your father's place in Somerset. How is old George?"

"He hasn't been too well, sir;"

"Sorry to hear that. Georgie was one of the best. Should have been a cavalry man, you know. So should you."

"I'm pleased to see a Clifton man doing well." The other General spoke to John in a courteous and restrained manner. "I was also at Clifton, but before your time of course," he added.

"Yes I knew that, sir. My two friends were also there. It was where we first met," John replied.

"I suppose you consider that's something in their favour, Haig?" Sir John interposed. "We won't keep you from your friends, Rutherford. Give my regards to your father."

"I will indeed, Sir John."

The two older men nodded at John and he returned to his table. "What did they want?" asked Robert before John had even sat down.

"Just wanted to know the name of the clown making all the noise, so that they could transfer him to the cavalry to be with all the other thick heads," John replied.

"There's no answer to that, Rob," said Reggie, giving one of his hearty laughs. "You've been bowled out for a duck, old boy,"

"All right, but you must admit this Holland business is a real side-splitter," Robert replied, starting to laugh again.

"For God's sake change the subject before he starts again," said John.

The meal over, the three friends withdrew to the smoking-room where they sat talking, content in one another's company, remembering schooldays and the happy times they had spent together in past years. "Do you chaps realise it's past midnight?" said Reggie during a pause in the conversation. The others made no comment, nor did they make any move to bring the party to an end.

Robert's carefree frame of mind of the early evening had given way to a pensive mood. "It's been a wonderful evening," he sighed. "If only we could stop the clock and hold, on to these precious moments."

"All good things must come to an end, old boy," said Reggie.

"Yes, that's just what's happening," Robert reflected.

"What's that, Rob?" Reggie asked,

"Good things coming to an end. Do you ever feel that, Reggie?"

"No, can't say I do. I'm sure there'll be good times to come. You can't hang on to the past, Rob." Reggie replied kindly.

"Not even when the past is all you've got left?"

Reggie looked at John, but they both remained silent.

Robert was sitting forward on the edge of his armchair with his elbows on his knees and his hands clasped under his chin. He sat watching the dying embers in the fireplace, and then said, "I should like to believe that, Reggie, but sometimes I feel life is just slipping away from me, and the wonderful times we enjoy together will be no more. What was it that Rupert Brooke wrote?" He thought for a moment and then said softly,

> *"And we that knew the best*
> *Down wonderful hours grew happier yet.*
> *I sang at heart, and talked, and ate.*
> *And lived from laugh to laugh, I too,*
> *When you were there, and you, and you."*

Robert noticeably shivered, "Someone walked over my grave," he said. He stood up and smiled at the others. "Time for bed, I think. Goodnight you two."

His friends watched him disappear through the door.

The following morning the three breakfasted together, all having stayed overnight at the club and then John saw the others off on their separate ways.

Before leaving, Robert reminded him of their bet, and John, feeling there was no way out, spent the next few days arranging the tour.

John had decided that he would travel light whilst actually cycling, and would have his trunk sent on ahead to certain hotels along the route so that on alternate days he would have reserved accommodation and a change of clothes. On the other days he would stay at smaller inns wherever he happened to be.

At the end of the week, having made all his arrangements, he wired his father giving his time of arrival and then took the Bristol train from Paddington.

That afternoon, after changing at Bristol, he arrived at Clevedon. At the sight of the familiar platform memories of boyhood came back to him. He remembered the excitement of travelling home from Clifton at the end of term with the long holidays ahead. The anticipation, of riding, fishing, helping on the estate, and all the activities of a happy home. He could still feel this joy of homecoming, although, since his mother's death, a light had gone out in his life and things would never be quite the same. But he was very close to his father, and they gained mutual comfort in each others company.

At last he was back in Somerset, the magic word which meant home, its mysterious history stretching back beyond Arthur and his knights into the mists of time had always fascinated him.

And there was father waiting for him. Still tall, but not so upright, as he was. His hair, now completely grey. He had aged considerably in the last four years, John thought. Father and son embraced, and John kissed him lightly on the cheek.

"Welcome home, my dear boy," said the old man, making no attempt to hide his feelings. His pride and affection for his younger son was plain for all to see.

''Father, how good to see you." John took his father's arm as they walked to the waiting pony and trap.

Driving out of the station, Sir George turned along the main road in the direction of Bristol. "It's so good to have you home again after all this time." he said with obvious pleasure. "Maud is home, you know. Looking forward to seeing you,"

"That's wonderful! I thought she was still in the States."

They passed the great oak tree, with the seat encircling the base of the trunk, standing where the road branched to Portishead, and shortly after turned into the drive leading to the old, grey stoned manor house.

Maud was standing at the front door waiting for them. She waved as they came into view, and thought how alike they were. John was tall like his father, whereas she and their brother George took after their mother and were much shorter.

John leapt out of the trap and brother and sister flung their arms round each other. "My little brother," she said warmly, looking up at him. "I do declare you look taller and stronger than ever."

"And you haven't changed at all, Maud."

The stable boy led the pony away, and after John had been greeted by the servants, Sir George and his two children mounted the steps to the front door. John remembered how he had always counted *one, two, three, four,* as he went up the steps when he was a child. The sound of the front door latch and the smell of log fires as he entered the hallway brought more memories flooding back into his mind. He was indeed home at last.

It had been a pleasant evening, with just the three of them enjoying a good meal and talking of days gone by. They had all sat at one end of the long table in the oak panelled dining room, father at the head and his children either side of him. The log fire had been lit to take the evening chill from the room.

"How's business. Maud?" asked John.

"I've found publishing in the States most profitable." Maud replied. "And what about you? What are your plans?"

"I intend to stay here for a few days and then spend a fortnight in Holland. After that I'll be back here again," John replied.

"Holland! Why Holland?" his father enquired with a note of surprise in his voice.

"Just a change, that's all." John had no intention of explaining the real reason for his forthcoming trip and inviting further amusement at his expense. He hoped, for a change of subject.

"I believe it's a very interesting country. I'll lend you a book on it," said Maud. "By the way, I must congratulate you on your promotion. You deserve it." She had always taken an interest in John, who was 10 years her junior, and in their younger days had acted more like a little mother to him than a sister.

"Thank you."

"And now I'm going to retire. It's getting late. I shall leave you two men to talk about whatever men do talk about." Maud rose, kissed them both, and left the room.

"She's a good girl, you know. Makes sure I'm well looked after," said Sir George as he pushed the port decanter towards his son. He also held out a box of cigars, "Come on, light up. Must celebrate your homecoming,"

"Thank you. Father,"

The old man leant back in his chair, and after a pause to collect his thoughts he said, "I'm pleased to have this opportunity to speak to you alone. I've been wanting to say a few things to you for some time." Sir George was not to be hurried with what he had to say and paused frequently to savour his cigar. "I'm seventy one now, and life moves on so quickly. Who knows how long I shall last? It was a great blow to me when your mother went, and one never quite gets over these things." He sighed as he remembered his beloved wife, and thought how empty life had been since she died. "It's no good beating about the bush," he continued. "As you may have guessed, *you* are my favourite son. I'm not saying I don't love George. He's a good enough fellow, a little pompous perhaps. This civil service job of his makes him a bit of a stick in the mud, in my opinion. Typical office wallah. But he seems to like it, and his heart's in the right place."

"You must admit, Father, he has done well."

"True enough, but he's not the man you are. I always wished you were the elder son so that you could inherit all this." He gestured with his hand indicating the room. "But there it is, m'boy, the place and the title have to go to George. Unfortunately, he's not interested in the estate – doesn't understand farming or the country way of life. Never made any attempt to do so. He hasn't got the feel of the land as you have and what' s more, he rides like a damned costermonger. I know you wanted to be a farmer. Had to put a stop to that. But there were good reasons."

"I realise you had my interest at heart, Father."

"I must admit that one reason was selfish. I wanted a son in the regiment. And, by God, you've done me proud." He took his handkerchief out of his pocket and blew his nose loudly, and then said softly, as if to himself. "Proud of you." Looking intently at his son he said, "Hope you didn't mind too much?"

"I've been happy in the army, but at the time I was sad to leave home. I came to realise that I could never farm this estate. After all, it wouldn't be mine, and I'd have to leave it one day."

"That was my other reason for putting you in the army. So you'd have a career of your own and not have to rely on George and this estate."

"I understand now, but I didn't at the time," said John, remembering himself as a sixteen year old, angrily objecting when told, he could not take up farming.

"Which brings me to what I want to say," said Sir George, sending a large cloud of cigar smoke into the air. He watched it rise up towards the high ceiling, and then, looking directly at John, said, "I've decided to let you children have your inheritance now. No point in waiting 'til I'm dead. With any luck, doing it this way, you might escape heavy death duties. I've also decided that you will have what I call my private fortune. This is money that doesn't come from the estate; it comes from a number of successful investments I have made over the years,"

To say John was surprised at this unexpected announcement would be an understatement, for, being the second son, he had never contemplated that he would receive any special consideration in the matter of his father's will, and that all would go to George. "I don't know what to say, Father. You have always been most generous with my allowance all these years, but I never expected this. What about George and Maud?"

"I have provided for Maud, and I know you'll always look after her. In any case her business is doing very nicely. As for George, he'll have the money which comes from the estate. If he runs things in a business like fashion the estate will give him a good income. If he doesn't, he'll have only himself to blame. But as a safeguard I have entailed the estate, with you and Maud as trustees."

"I don't think Henrietta will like it," said. John

"Damn Henrietta! It's got nothing to do with her; I'll leave my money to who I wish. What the devil George married her for I'll never know. Never did like her." If there was one thing calculated to agitate Sir George it was the mention of his daughter-in-law. From their first meeting he felt that her character lacked sincerity, and he could not bring himself to trust her. He put up with her for George's sake, but was under no illusion, and considered her reasons for marrying his son were the prospects of being the wife of a Baronet and a good inheritance. "You just make sure she doesn't get her hands on the money I leave you. I don't want it thrown away on her extravagant desires. She and George will have quite enough of their own."

As with his father, John also could not bring himself to like his brother's wife. He had seen her for the first time when he returned from the Boer War in 1902. She had met George at a civil service ball a few months earlier, and shortly after, the couple had become engaged. He considered her a snob and counted himself fortunate that their paths seldom crossed,

Sir George got up and went across the room to a small table where he picked up a file of papers. "I believe you have the right temperament to be entrusted with a large amount of money. That is why I am leaving it to you. Money could ruin the life of a lesser man," he said as he came back and handed the file to his son. "These are the legal documents transferring my investments and capital to you," he added.

"Are you sure about this, Father?"

"Of course I'm sure, boy. I know what I'm doing. You needn't worry. I've kept enough for my needs, which are not very great now-a-days. Although this house will belong to George, I have made provision that I shall live here 'til I die.'"

John casually glanced at the papers on his lap, but his surprise at his father's announcement to leave him a large sum of money could not compare with the astonishment he experienced when he began to realise the extent of the fortune. When young, as with most boys, he had taken little interest in his father's affairs. He had been strictly brought up, and although he had never wanted for the essentials in life, his father had not allowed him what he considered unnecessary luxuries. The effect of this simple, almost austere, upbringing had remained with him throughout his life, and he was noted in the mess as an officer who lived well within his means. But now he was to be rich.

"This is a considerable fortune, Father!" he exclaimed.

"I am well aware of my financial situation," Sir George replied, and then went on to explain that even before he left the army he had discovered a good business head an his shoulders and an aptitude for successful investment. Over the years he had gradually built up his fortune. He had also run the estate profitably.

"I had no idea, Father."

"Nor had anybody else. It was my secret."

John sat silent, unable to put his feelings into words.

"There's one condition," said Sir George. The money is yours. You have thanked me. It's my wish that you never mention the matter again either to me or to anyone else. The subject is closed."

The two sat in silence for a time, content in each other's company, the father looking with satisfaction at the handsome face and strong figure of his son. He remembered the years of John's boyhood. His son had always been a strong, healthy boy, who loved to run wild on the estate, and who was completely at home with animals and a fearless rider. He would have made a good farmer, but he had made a good soldier instead. It is probably for the best, he thought.

It was Sir George who broke the silence. "I see that French has resigned," he said.

"Yes. Father, it was in The Times. He's obviously done the honourable thing, but I doubt whether it was necessary. After all the Curragh incident wasn't his fault."

"Perhaps not. But he was the Chief of the Imperial General Staff and a certain responsibility lay with him. Seely and Ewart have also resigned so he had little option."

"By the way, I met French at the club last week. Sends his regards."

"Well I'm blessed!. Haven't seen him for years. I'll bet he said you should be in the cavalry."

"He did as a matter of fact. Said he'd met me when I was a boy. I can't remember that,"

"That's right, he did. It was in eighty eight, if my memory serves me right. The year that damn fool of a Kaiser came to the throne. I was taking you to lunch in Town, special treat I think, and we happened to bump into Johnnie French, so I invited him to join us. You were ten at the time." Sir George thought for a moment and then said, "And now you're thirty six. It only seems yesterday when you were born, and we were having all that trouble with those Russkies. How the time goes," he sighed, remembering his children as little ones and regretting the passing of the years.

"You still have a good memory, Father,"

"I can remember the past well enough. It's the present that's difficult. That's what age does to you." Sir George smiled, and then, as if he had been waiting for a suitable time and did not wish the moment to pass, quickly said, "Pity you're not married. A man needs a good woman to look after him. I find it difficult to understand how a good looking, strapping chap like you has managed to remain a bachelor. And there's George, who's no oil painting, been married for years."

"Perhaps that's the reason, Father. I see him under the thumb and I'm glad I've avoided it."

"But have you never fancied a girl?"

John smiled and said, "Well, there was Sheila Butcher."

Sir George laughed. "Oh, yes. You were fifteen at the time and she was a village girl from down the road."

"She was a very nice girl too," John replied. He brought to mind the long fair hair, the happy face and the smiling lips he had once kissed, and wondered where she was now.

"Yes, that's why I gently put a stop to it. I'd heard rumours," Sir George said with a twinkle in his eye. "You can't keep things quiet in a village, you know,"

"So it was you who ruined my first true love," said John dryly. "Now you know why I never married."

The two laughed and Sir George let the subject drop.

The old man rose stiffly from his chair using the table for support until he was upright. "I get a touch of arthritis," he said. "I'm getting old, John. I must to my bed." John got up and took his father's arm and the two left the room together.

John lay awake for some time revelling in the perfect stillness of the night. Not a sound came through the open window except the occasional hoot of an owl in the high wood on the side of the hill behind the house. How he loved this old house, and especially this room. It had been his bedroom since earliest childhood. He tried not to think of the future when he would no longer be welcome here, but was unable to keep it from his mind. It will not be the same when Father goes, and it would probably be better if he kept away from the estate altogether when that happened. Perhaps he would buy a small cottage somewhere. After all, he had only himself to consider. On the other hand, a property with good stables would be more interesting. He began to think about his forthcoming holiday in Holland, and the more he thought about it the more he disliked the idea. He cheered himself up with the thought that it would only be for two weeks, and then he would come back to Somerset and really enjoy himself, One day he would get his own back on Robert, meantime he would win that guinea from him. With these thoughts swirling in his head he gradually drifted into sleep.

He was awakened by the sound of milk churns being placed on the wooden stand at the end of the lane, which ran down the side of the garden. He had always gone straight to the window after getting out of bed, and although he had been away for a number of years, he found that the habit was still with him. His bedroom overlooked the front lawn, and he saw that the lush green grass was wet with an early morning mist coming off the moors and hanging low over the countryside. There was promise of a warm day ahead when the sun gained enough strength to dry the moisture laden air. He heard the deep, monotonous drone of fog horns sounding far out in the Bristol Channel as ships made their way slowly through the treacherous waters to and from Avonmouth. It was a sound that had fascinated him as long as he could remember. He tried to imagine what part of the Empire those unseen ships would visit.

Having washed and shaved and put on his riding-clothes, he went to the stable yard behind the house where he found Maud waiting for him, "I thought you'd soon be here," she said, "You're never one to miss your early morning ride. I trust you don't mind me joining you?"

The horses ready, John and Maud mounted and rode out of the yard, turning up the track which gently climbed the side of the hill. They rode in single file with John in the lead, and on reaching the top they stopped and gazed out over the countryside. In the distance, far to the south, the dark form of the Mendips stood out on the horizon like a mysterious island. John took a deep breath, intoxicating himself with the pure morning air. "Wonderful!" he exclaimed. "Just look at that view, Maud."

"It's beautiful," she replied, pleased to see her brother so happy.

John stared at the distant hills and said, "Do you know, when I was a small boy I used to feel frightened when I saw the Mendips in the distance. They always sent a shiver down my spine. They appeared so dark and foreboding. I used to imagine them as an enchanted land where witches did all sorts of magic things."

"That's because old granny Collins used to fill your head full of stories about witches and heaven knows what."

John smiled, remembering the old woman who once lived down the road near the mill.

Maud let her animal trot on. She gave rein and began an easy canter, calling back to her brother, "Come on, I'll race you to Cadbury!" John followed, and brother and sister rode along the crest of the hill with the easy confidence years of experience had given them. The bright morning sun and the freshness of the wet countryside exhilarated them, and it was only when they had covered about two miles and reached the ancient camp site did they rein in. Dismounting, they walked their mounts to the edge of the hill where they could see the village church below, and the moor beyond.

"This is the most beautiful part of England," said John.

"That's only because it's home and you spent all those happy years here when you were young," replied Maud.

"You're right. I was only thinking last night how I shall miss coming here when Father goes."

"But you can still visit. I'm sure George will be pleased to see you."

"Maybe. But it's Henrietta. "Oh, she won't mind the visit, but only to show me she's the mistress of the house."

"You're always welcome to make your home with me, John. Providing you don't mind being looked after by a poor old spinster." She spoke with genuine affection, for he had always been her favourite brother.

"You may be a spinster, Maud, but you're not old. It surprises me that you've never married. I can remember a number of fellows who'd have married you like a shot if you given them half a chance." John had heard it said that her one true love had been killed in India. He had been too young to know about it at the time, and it was a subject that was never mentioned within the family.

"You're just as bad," retorted Maud laughing. "What a couple of stick-in-the-muds we are." They laughed easily together as they remounted and rode back the way they had come,

Brother and sister found that their father had almost finished his breakfast when they arrived in the breakfast room. Maud kissed him and said, "We've just been for the most lovely ride, Father."

"I thought that's where you were." I wish I could have joined you, but I'm not up to it nowadays." He held his daughter's hand for a moment and squeezed it affectionately. "By the way, George and that wife of his are coming for the week-end. I hope having that woman here won't drive you two away. I want you to stay as long as possible,"

"She's not that bad," said Maud kindly. "She's just . . ."

"A ruddy pain in the neck," interjected John before Maud could finish.

"John, you must try and be nice to her," said Maud, who had never been known to say an unkind word about anyone.

"I'm always trying to be nice to her, but she gets my back up with all her airs and graces. And her background's nothing special."

"Now who's being snobby?" Maud smiled and wagged her finger at her brother.

"I'm not a snob. I don't mind what background a person comes from providing they don't try to pretend they're something else. She acts as if she's a duchess or something, and dresses like one as well. And all that jewellery; she looks like a damn chandelier. I really don't know where old George finds the money to pay for it all."

"Nor do I," said Sir George.

Maud cut the conversation short and announced that they would all take the train and spend the day in Bath. "For some culture," as she put it.

George and Henrietta arrived late on the Friday afternoon. John was looking out of the alcove window in the great hall when the carriage drove in through the gate. He saw Jamie, the fourteen year old stable boy, sitting very straight and driving competently, obviously trying hard to carry out his duty well. George was slumped in his seat with his top hat set too far back on his head, giving him an untidy appearance. Henrietta was beside him, sitting bolt upright and looking straight ahead, with both hands resting on the top of the handle of her parasol.

"Good God!" John exclaimed as the carriage approached the front door. "You'd think it was Queen Mary herself in the state coach."

"Now John, stop it!" urged Maud. She had been quietly playing the piano but now stopped and joined her brother at the window.

But John was not to be put off from his critical study of his sister-in-law. "Just look at that hat," he continued. "It's like a bowl of fruit stuck on her head."

Maud said nothing but couldn't help agreeing with her brother's description and the incredulous look on his face made her want to laugh.

"And why the devil does George always look so damned scruffy even when he's got his best togs on?" John added. "He needs a couple of weeks with the battalion. That'd smarten him up."

"John! Stop being so critical!" scolded Maud

The vehicle stopped outside the front door, and seeing that Jamie made no attempt to get down from his seat and open the carriage door - he had been instructed that a footman would carry out this duty - Henrietta poked him in the back with her parasol and said sharply, "Get down here and open this door you idle wretch!"

"Allow me, my dear," said George meekly.

"You stay where you are! Let the idle brat earn his keep. I expect he's overpaid as it is."

Jamie leapt down and opened the door, taking off his hat and remembering the whipping he had been promised by the head groom if he gave any cause for complaint when the visitors arrived. George got down first and assisted his wife. He was the shorter of the two and at thirty nine had become overweight through lack of exercise and rather more food and drink than were good for him. He held a good position at the Home Office, which was in some measure due to the domineering character of his wife, who had ensured that his considerable administrative talents did not go unnoticed by the right people.

The butler had opened the front door and waited to welcome the guests, but Henrietta swept past him without a word, followed by her husband who did at least manage to exchange a greeting with the man. John and Maud came into the entrance hall. "Henrietta dear, welcome," said Maud with genuine warmth.

"Good afternoon, Maud," Henrietta replied as her sister-in-law took her arm and led her towards the drawing room. "Why does this place always smell so musty?" She raised her nose and sniffed, and eyed the house critically. "How I hate these old places."

John's natural good manners prevented him from springing to the defence of his beloved home and telling his sister-in-law that the smell was that of a good old country house. He had resolved to greet Henrietta in a friendly fashion, but was finding it difficult to keep his good intentions.

"You're not in Wimbledon now, my dear," said George with a weak laugh, trying to make light of his wife's unnecessary remark.

"More's the pity," retorted Henrietta sharply. "I can't abide the country as you well know."

"Good afternoon, Henrietta," cut in John, trying to be affable but finding it difficult. Although he was a soldier and known to be cool and calm in the most difficult situations, he hadn't got Maud's placid nature, and there was nothing more likely to make him bristle than a rude and domineering woman.

"So you're home again," said Henrietta, pretending to notice John for the first time. Although outwardly her attitude towards him was one of aloof tolerance, inwardly she never felt at ease in his presence. She found his piercing eyes disconcerting, and felt that he could always discern her innermost thoughts. She was, in fact, a little afraid of him. She looked at him standing there towering over his brother, and could not help comparing his dark, handsome features with the round, puffy face of her husband. If only he had been, the eldest son she would have married him. But perhaps that would not have been so easy as her conquest of George, she decided. At least George would have the title and the estate, and for that she could put up with his lack of physical attraction. Although she hated the old house, it gave her satisfaction to know that one day, in what she hoped would be the not too distant future, she would be mistress here.

The gentlemen followed the ladies into what had always been known as the great hall, but what was now a comfortable drawing-room, where afternoon tea awaited them. "Father will be down soon," said Maud.

"Who's talking about me?" The old man stood in the doorway smiling at his family. Henrietta hurried over to him with her arms outstretched, forcing on one of her rare smiles.

"Father dear, how lovely to see you," she said with an affectation which usually became apparent when she was playing a part not in keeping with her nature.

Sir George said, "I'm sorry I wasn't here to greet you, but I always rest in the afternoons nowadays." His daughter-in-law took his arm and led him to his chair. He wondered to himself if she would have been so attentive had she known how he had settled his financial affairs in his will.

Henrietta noticed John looking at her, and she was unable to maintain the smile on her face. He had always felt there was no warmth in that smile - she didn't smile with her eyes. She wasn't a bad looking woman, he decided, but her mouth was too large and gave a sullen expression to the face.

"I thought you would have brought my grandsons with you, George."

"Henrietta thought it better they stayed at home, Father," George replied. He knew that he should have insisted when they had argued the matter two days before. He had wanted to bring the boys, but always found it so difficult to go against his wife's wishes.

"I find they get so dirty here running wild with that common stable boy," Henrietta replied.

"A bit of good Somerset dirt might do them a world of good," said John, "I spent my young life getting dirty on the farms round here."

"Yes, I can imagine that," Henrietta replied sarcastically. John ignored her remark and said, "And as for Jamie, he's a perfectly good boy. He could teach your lads a thing or two."

"Rubbish! He can't even speak the King's English," retorted Henrietta. She was not used to being contradicted and was becoming irritated with John.

In her ignorance Henrietta did not realise that the boy was not speaking badly, but speaking a different language. The Somerset dialect, which he spoke and which his forefathers had spoken for centuries, was of Anglo-Saxon origin and one of the foundations of modern English. As a boy, John had been happy in the company of humble folk. He understood their dialect and knew their ways, and it pained him to hear them belittled by ignorance. He overcame his inclination to make a cutting remark and said evenly. "I can assure you, Henrietta, he speaks English in its purest form. It's the remains of the language spoken at the court of King Alfred."

"I can do without the history lesson," she replied sharply, but before she could launch into another attack, Maud quickly changed the subject.

"And how are things with you, George? Anything interesting happening at the Home Office?" Maud asked.

"The usual round of problems," he replied with a touch of pomposity, glad that he had been asked. Underneath his thin skin he felt that others considered him a dull fellow with an uninteresting job, and he found it difficult to compete with the romance and excitement which all seemed attached to his brother's military career. He never blamed John for this, for his brother rarely mentioned his army life, but it made him feel inferior; a state which he unconsciously countered with a self important attitude. "There's the constant trouble from these confounded suffragettes," he continued.

"You sound as if you don't think we women should have the vote," said Maud.

George was sorry he had mentioned the subject, because that was exactly what he did think; only he could not say so for fear that it would bring forth an outburst from Henrietta, who was forever complaining that women were trodden down by men. George could never understand how she came to this conclusion, bearing in mind their own married relationship. Before he could make any reply his father interrupted.

"Lock 'em up! Damn trouble makers!" grunted Sir George.

"But Father, don't you think we should have a say in the running of our country?" Maud asked gently. "There's got to be change you know,"

"I've seen too many changes in my life time to be bothered with any more. When I was born only one man in six could vote, and that was enough to run this country properly. Now every Tom, Dick and Harry has the vote, and things are no better than they were - worse probably. And now you women want it. God knows what for, but I suppose you'll get your way in the end. You usually do."

Maud smiled at her father, but made no attempt to contradict his views. He was hardly likely to change them at his time of life, she decided.

Henrietta looked at John belligerently and said, "I suppose you think that women should never have the vote."

John smiled and replied firmly, "I'm sorry to disappoint you, Henrietta, but I believe you should have it, and you will have it in the end. What I don't agree with is the way some women are breaking the law to obtain their ends."

Glaring at John, Henrietta let the subject drop. Happy that he had not been pressed further for his opinion on suffragettes, George quickly thought of a different subject. "How's your friend Reggie?" he asked John."

"Very well. I had dinner with him the other evening; he's the same old Reggie."

"Isn't that the man with that odious wife?" Henrietta enquired, knowing full well it was. "We met them here once at a party. So dreadfully common. I find it impossible to understand how a man of his quality could marry such a person."

"At least she doesn't pretend to be something she isn't," John replied hotly. "And might I remind you Henrietta that Daisy is a fine person and there's nothing odious about her."

You seem to spend your time defending the lower classes," Henrietta retorted. "It's quite plain to all that your friend married beneath him."

"Maybe, but she's got a heart of gold."

Maud noticed a nerve twitching under John's right eye, a sure sign that her brother's anger was rising. "I think we'd better change the subject," she said evenly, smiling at her brother.

Sir George was enjoying his afternoon tea, and was amused by the abrasive banter between his younger son and Henrietta. He glanced with satisfaction at his three children, pleased in the knowledge that they were a happy and united family. They had of course, never wanted for anything - he had made sure of that. But he had never indulged them when they were young, except perhaps Maud just a little. All fathers should spoil their daughters on occasions, he considered. It had been his wish to give his children more than just material well being, and he had tried to demonstrate his love by the interest he had shown in them, and by giving them as much of his time as his busy life had allowed. He believed that he had been successful in this.

After breakfast on the following day Sir George called his sons to his study. His father's announcement that he was to receive the house and estate immediately took George by surprise in the same way as John had been surprised a few days earlier when he learnt of his good fortune. The old man mentioned nothing about his financial settlement on his younger son, but he did explain to George the conditions he had made as a safeguard to the disposal of the property. George, however, appeared little interested in these conditions, his mind being focussed only on the difficulties of running the estate. "I don't really want the estate, Father," he said.

"It's got nothing to do with whether you want it or not," Sir George replied, sharply. "You are the eldest son and will inherit the title, and it's your duty to take over the estate as well."

"What about money?" George enquired. He would have much preferred to be left a substantial sum of money rather than this wretched estate, which would only bring him extra work and responsibility. "I can't run the place without money."

"The estate pays for itself and should give you a good profit if you run it properly," Sir George replied,

"That's all very well in the good years, but what if there's a depression? I'm no farmer."

"That's your fault. You should have taken more interest when you had the chance. In any case, you've got a good administrative brain. You will have to rely on your estate manager and the tenant farmers to handle the practical side." Sir George was inclined to be impatient with those who did not share his love of the land,

"But do I get any money?" George persisted.

"Fifty thousand pounds goes with estate, and there will be a little more when I die. You have a good salary and your house in Wimbledon, so you should be well satisfied." Sir George had never lost his military manner, and spoke with the confident authority as when, in days gone by, he had briefed his battalion officers. "And by the way," he added, "I'm not dead yet, so I shall still have m' quarters in this house."

Although he knew nothing of his father's fortune, George had expected to inherit a larger sum. It was not that he wasn't satisfied. He was; but he doubted if Henrietta would be. The one thing he had made up his mind about was that he would still live in Wimbledon, and only visit the estate when necessary. As he pondered on these things, he saw his father looking at him as if expecting a reply. "Thank you, Father. I'm most grateful," he said, but with little conviction.

John had sat silent during the conversation and considered his presence unnecessary, but his father had insisted he be there. Later, when alone with his brother, George had expressed his fears for the future. It seemed to John, although it was not mentioned, that Henrietta's extravagance was at the root of George's worries. To have been left the estate with the option of being able to sell it would have suited George nicely. But without this option he felt it was like having a mill stone round his neck.

"I'm stuck with the blasted place and I don't want it. Would to God it had gone to you," George complained. "Life is so damned stupid. I've got it and don't want it. You want it and can't have it. Ridiculous isn't it?"

"Don't worry, old chap, I'm sure all will be well," John replied, trying to allay his brother's fears.

It was a bad day for George. He managed to avoid being alone with his wife to delay the inevitable interrogation about his discussion with his father, but he knew that it would be the first thing she would enquire about when they retired to bed. And he was right.

"And what were you discussing with your father and that brother of yours this morning?" Henrietta asked directly the bedroom door closed. "I noticed the ladies were not invited to take part,"

"Father was giving us some idea as to how he had left his estate," George replied. He spoke with his civil servant's tactful discretion which always irritated Henrietta.

"Come to the point!" she rasped. "How much has the old skin-flint left us?"

"I do wish you wouldn't speak about him like that, my dear. He's been very generous to us over the years."

Henrietta ignored her husband's remarks and went on. "Why has he suddenly brought all this up? Is he expecting to die?" She sat at her dressing table removing her jewellery, wondering how long the old man would last.

"Of course not, but he's getting on now, and he wants to get a few things settled. He is handing over the house and estate to us immediately."

"Is he now." Henrietta pondered, stroking her chin. "Then we'll sell it,"

"We can't."

"Why not?" Henrietta retorted angrily, glaring at her husband.

"I haven't been given the full details yet, but Father has made provision as to what happens to the estate." Before George could continue, Henrietta shouted at him, "You idiot! Trust you not to get the important points."

"Steady on, my dear. I was going to say that after me the estate must go to young George. It can't be sold outside the family without permission of the trustees."

"And who are they might I ask?"

"John and Maud, and the solicitors."

"I might have known it," Henrietta spat out venomously, her eyes blazing with anger. She crashed her hair brush onto the dressing table smashing a glass container and scattering beads over the floor. "And I suppose you said nothing, you spineless fool. It's our estate and we should be able to do what we like with it."

"He's given us fifty thousand pounds as well," George added, hoping to calm his wife's rage.

"Fifty thousand pounds," Henrietta repeated slowly. "The mean old swine! He's worth a fortune and all he can give us is fifty thousand pounds."

"But that is a fortune," George replied weakly. "He can't be worth much more than that."

"I happen to know that he's worth well over a million, perhaps nearly two."

"That's impossible. How do you know that anyway?"

"It doesn't matter how I know, but amongst other things I once heard him talking to his bank manager." Henrietta replied with an air of triumph in her voice. "I wonder what he's doing with it all?" she pondered.

Having got into bed, George had settled down ready for sleep. "Father did say there will be more to come when he dies," he said, hoping that the matter would now be dropped. But Henrietta was not satisfied,

"What are the others getting?" she went on.

"I've no idea, Father didn't mention them," George mumbled, pulling the sheet up over the back of his head.

"But the favourite son was with you. What did he get?"

"What do you mean, favourite son?" George asked.

"You're so naive. Don't you see that brother John is the favourite?" Henrietta was now pacing up and down the room tapping a hair brush in the palm of her hand, still pondering the matter.

"Father has always treated us equally."

"Then what's happened to all that money? The old man discussed your inheritance in front of him, so why wasn't his inheritance discussed in front of you?"

"I really haven't thought about it," George replied wearily.

"Then it's time you did, or we'll end up with nothing, and dear John will get the lot, if he hasn't already done so," Henrietta's exasperation was complete when she received no answer and heard the heavy breathing of her now sleeping husband.

*

George and Henrietta left on the Sunday afternoon, and the atmosphere in the house noticeably lightened.

John and Maud left for London together the next day. They parted at Paddington and John crossed to Liverpool Street where he caught the Harwich train. He had a reserved sleeping berth on the night ferry to the Hook of Holland. It was a good crossing and the ship berthed on time the following morning.

The first hotel had been arranged for him at Dordrecht, and it was here he would collect his cycle. Dordrecht was only a distance of some 26 miles, so he broke the short journey at Rotterdam and spent some of the day exploring the old city. This small city which, since the opening in 1884 of the Nieuwe Waterweg - a wide and deep canal for sea going ships, leading to the North Sea - had become one of the greatest ports in the world. However, it did not hold his interest as had some other places he had visited, so he left for Dordrecht in the early afternoon.

With military precision he had made sure his agents had supplied him with a map of each town he was to visit, and the exact location of his hotels. As his luggage had been sent on ahead, he decided to walk the short distance to the hotel and view the beautiful old town at the same time. He strolled along the cobbled streets fascinated by the design of the houses, many of them high and narrow, each differing from its neighbour. All so different from an English town. He was struck by the lack of stonework on the houses, and even the Grote Kerk, whose clock was striking four as he gazed up at the high tower, was made of brick. A short walk from the church across two small canal bridges found him in front of his small hotel; a fine old house facing the canal basin across a cobbled street.

He stood for a moment at the edge of the quay admiring the house and noticing the lack of activity in the vicinity. One barge was moored alongside the quay but appeared deserted, and, except for the lapping of the water against its hull, there was no sound to disturb the peace of the afternoon. The hotel door was shut, but on trying the handle the door opened and he entered. The small homely entrance hall was as deserted and silent as the street outside, but seeing a hand bell on a small table he picked it up and rang it. Somewhere in the distance he heard a door shut, and then the sound of light footsteps approaching along the adjoining corridor. Eventually, a. girl of about fourteen appeared and gave a little curtsey.

"Do you speak English?" John enquired.

"Ja. A little," the girl replied shyly.

"My name Is Rutherford. I have a room reserved for tonight." John spoke slowly, hoping the girl would understand.

"Wait please." The girl ran off and disappeared along the corridor, and for a time there was silence once more.

He had not long to wait before the silence was broken, this time by the sound of many footsteps. In fact it seemed to John that the whole household had sprung to life. Not only did the girl reappear, but two other girls, one being a little older and the other a little younger than the first; obviously her sisters. The girls were followed by their parents, the proprietor and his wife, and a number of the hotel staff, all wishing to see the English major. It was clear he was expected.

"I give you welcome, Major Rooterford." The proprietor had come forward to shake John's hand. He spoke with a pronounced accent and a quaint turn of phrase, but his English was good. He introduced his family one by one, each of whom curtsied, and then ushered John into a cosy lounge. A comfortable chair had been placed near a low table on which had been set out all the items the Dutchman considered necessary for an Englishman to take his traditional tea.

"English tea, Ja!" the proprietor exclaimed proudly as the tea pot and hot water jug were placed on the table by the eldest daughter.

"Most kind of you," John replied. It was clear that his host wished to continue in conversation, and John managed to gain much information about the country in general and the route he was to travel during his tour.

"I give you much praise, Major," the Dutchman said. "It is good that you use the bicycle here. You see much of the country."

"I hope you're right," John replied, glad of the encouragement, but not convinced he was doing the right thing. He was slightly apprehensive about his lack of cycling skill. He had never owned a cycle as a boy - his interest had always been in horses. He was seven in 1885 when the modern cycle, with two wheels of equal size, fitted to a frame, and driven by pedals and chain, was evolved, However, in 1890 George had been given, one of the newly invented diamond frame models, It was fitted with the new pneumatic tyres. George had allowed John to ride his precious machine, provided he mended all punctures. John, who was three years younger than his brother, had thought this a satisfactory arrangement at first, but the state of the roads was so poor at that time, and punctures so frequent, that he soon got tired of it and went back to his horses.

The Dutch family had taken great pains to ensure their special guest enjoyed a true English tea, and John was genuinely pleased with the effort made on his behalf. He tried to look suitably impressed. However, he was mistaken if he believed he was to be left to enjoy it on his own. His hosts seemed intent on sharing his pleasure and remained with him until he had finished.

It was the same at dinner. There were three other guests at their tables in the dining room - John thought they must be travelling business men - but it was John who once more found himself the centre of attention. The proprietor's daughters all wished to serve him, so, to prevent a quarrel, they had been allowed to share the task. With blushes and a few giggles the girls fussed in and out of the room bringing him far more than he could manage to eat. If all his holiday was to be like this it will be most agreeable, he thought.

After a good night's sleep, he found himself a little more optimistic about the day ahead and his cycling ability. He enjoyed his breakfast and then, dressed in knickerbockers and tweed jacket, made his way to the front door. He considered his clothes correct for cycling even if his riding lacked skill.

John found his host already waiting outside holding the cycle ready. He was surprised and a little embarrassed to find the man surrounded by his family and three of the hotel staff, all eager to see him off. In addition, two of the other guests were also present, and he noticed a number of people on the barges moored at the quay were taking an interest in the little group outside the hotel.

He cursed Robert for tricking him into this wretched tour, but, putting on a brave face, smiled at his audience.

He had put on his cap and an old army raincoat, which he had cut short to make it suitable for cycling. It would no longer keep all the rain out, but he had a waterproof cape in his knapsack - at least he hoped it was waterproof; the shop assistant in Oxford Street had said it was.

John tried to look confident as he took the cycle from the Dutchman, but he was thinking what a disaster it would be if he fell off in front of all these onlookers. He was sure he felt more nervous than he had done when he faced the Boer guns at Ladysmith. At least there he hadn't been alone.

As he put his leg over the cross bar everyone seemed to be talking at once and trying to shake his hand. At last the happy crowd drew back and the time had come. He stood on the pedal making the machine shoot forward faster than he had anticipated. This made him sit back heavily on the saddle, and caused his other foot to miss its pedal as it came up. For a, moment both pedals revolved freely while his feet tried to find them, and the cycle wobbled forward bumping him over the cobbles. The little crowd cheered. Eventually, he got his feet on the pedals and began to gain control. He heard the Dutchman shout, "Ride on the right." Lifting his hand from the handlebars just long enough to wave an acknowledgement, he moved across to the other side of the street.

The cobbled surface was not easy to ride on, and he had to hold the handlebars very tightly to keep a straight course. In fact the machine shook so violently that he had visions of it disintegrating under him.

As this was his first day he decided that 20 miles would be far enough. He travelled south and stayed at Breda that night. The next day, now quite confident on his cycle and not as stiff as he had anticipated, he set out for 's-Hertogenbosch, a distance of some 30 miles to the east. His plan was to spend a few days in the southern part of the country, an area where tourists did not usually penetrate, before going on to the more picturesque northern parts.

He woke on the third day after a sound sleep, but did not immediately get out of bed. He pulled himself up so that his head was resting on the headboard, and just lay there for a time. He had lost all sense of time. It must be Friday the tenth, he thought. So many thoughts seemed to fill his mind as he lay there. He asked himself if he was really enjoying the holiday. Here he was, alone in a foreign land, when he could have been riding over his beloved green hills in Somerset. Although the people had been, most friendly, he had begun to feel an acute sense of loneliness. He remembered, with certain envy, the Dutchman at Dordrecht so happy with his little family about him. Why had he this feeling of apprehension today? It was unlike him to feel depressed just because he was alone.

John pushed back the covers and swung his legs over the side of the bed. He sat there for a moment with his head resting in his hands. Should he give up and go home, he asked himself? It was very unusual for him to be indecisive. On the one hand he wished to go home, and yet he had this feeling that something would not be right if he did. Perhaps it was the bet with Robert he wished to win, or maybe it was just to gain a sense of achievement in that he had completed the tour. They were not very satisfactory explanations, but whatever it was, something seemed to drive him on.

Later that morning he rode through many villages as he made his way towards the river Maas. By midday he had arrived at the small fortified town of Ravenstein. He dismounted as he entered the south end of the town, and pushed his machine through the cobbled main street. At the other end of the street he passed through the town gate and found himself on a road, which ran on top of the dyke with the great river flowing alongside it. On his left the river was spanned by a railway bridge which, according to his little guide book, was called the Edith Bridge, opened in 1881. He turned away from the bridge, and after walking a short distance along the dyke, sat down on the grass near the ferry house to eat his picnic lunch.

The day had been completely overcast, but now the clouds were breaking and the sun was beginning to force its way through. There was a cool north easterly wind blowing directly across the river so he did not remain long over his meal, because he began to feel chilly.

The road to the east had been made along the top of the dyke; consequently he was travelling along a high embankment, enabling him to have a good view of the surrounding countryside. The river's course took it away from the dyke for a few miles as a result there were flat fields on either side of the raised road. It struck him how empty they seemed - no large herds of cows, just a few grazing horses - and he passed few people. To the south the flat land stretched away as far as the eye could see, and to the north he could make out the river, which was now over a mile away.

Looking with a soldier's eye he pondered whether, in a future war between France and Germany, either side might be tempted to send their armies across these flat lands. It was a possible route into Prussia for a French army. Right across the north German plain to Berlin. It had been used before, but the great rivers were always a barrier. It was unlikely that the Germans would need to swing as wide as this in order to encircle Paris now that they held Alsace and Lorraine. God forbid that there should be a war, he thought, but the future is always uncertain. The French had never forgiven the Prussians for their defeat in 1870, and yearned for the return of the two lost provinces. It wouldn't take much to set Europe alight.

After about three miles he stopped to take another look at the view before the road ahead left the dyke and gently descended to the flat land below. At this point the dyke swept back towards the river, and the road went straight on. Occasionally the sun broke through lighting up a tall, thin needle like tower of a church far to the south. But he was unable to work up any enthusiasm for the countryside. It was far too flat for his liking. Some distance ahead he could see the fortifications of the old town of Grave.

He had intended to stay the night at Grave, but the depression he had experienced that morning had returned, and he decided that he would go into the town, take the ferry across the river, and go on to Nijmegen. He would stay there overnight instead, and then go home. Robert could laugh as much as he liked, but he'd had enough of this damned cycling. A glint in the distance caught his eye, as if the sun was reflecting off a window. It was coming from between a clump of trees in the direction of Grave. He thought it was probably another farmhouse near the river.

He rode on, and at the bottom of the slope the road became absolutely straight until it wound its way through the village of Velp. Now cycling fast, intent on reaching the ferry, he took little notice of the few village houses and was quickly past. A short distance ahead he thought the road divided, but, if he had been concentrating properly, he would have seen that the left fork was merely a track and that the road went to the right. Without thinking, he took the left fork, immediately realising his mistake as the surface became uneven and the cycle began to shake and rattle under him. "Blast!" he exclaimed. "What the hell am I doing?" He put on the brakes gently, not wishing to slide on the loose surface. The track had curved sharply to the left but he managed to turn with it, coming to a stop just before hitting the opposite verge.

There were tall hedges an either side, and ahead a high brick wall where the track turned sharply to the right and went out of sight behind the hedge. John stopped and dismounted with the intention of pushing his cycle back to the road. But then, he had a sudden impulse to see what was round this corner. Perhaps it was the place he had seen glinting in the sun. What he had expected to find he did not know, but he felt a pang of disappointment when he reached the corner. The track continued for about 100 yards and then came to dead end in front of the doors of an old barn. The hedge on his right did not continue round the corner, and he could now see that it had been concealing a small orchard. He was just about to turn away when he noticed that the height of the wall diminished a short distance along the track, and beyond this point he would be able to see over it.

Why he bothered to walk along he never knew. But he did. When he could see over the low wall, what met his eyes was like a picture painted by one of the great masters. He could have almost been back in England, for the scene was far more English than Dutch. There in front of him, set back behind perfectly tended lawns and surrounded by beds of shrubs and a mass of spring flowers in bloom, was a large and beautiful, old red bricked house. It had a unique charm, and it was plain to see that here was a place of affluence. The sky was now clear giving the scene a backcloth of blue with the sun's rays enhancing the redness of the brickwork. John had always shown an interest in old buildings, and this one had immediately taken his eye. He considered the main centre section to be the oldest part of the building. Two dormer windows set above the first floor gave it a symmetrical appearance, and were a pleasing variation to the otherwise large expanse of steep tiled roof. He noticed that one of these windows was open. It was probably the one he had seen glinting in the sun. At each end of the old part of the house were gabled wings of much later construction. He decided that at one time there may have been five ground floor windows in the main section of the house, but that the centre one had been removed to make space for the present front door. The old door had probably been covered when the wings were built on, about a hundred years ago, he estimated. He was quite pleased with his assessment of the house, but found difficulty in deciding the age of the original section. Being sheltered from the wind, which he had found very trying earlier in the day, the afternoon sun had warmed him, and the whole scene was pleasantly restful. He had not seen a garden like this since leaving England. It was impossible to see how far it extended behind the house because of the shrubberies, but he guessed that it went back for about a hundred yards and that its boundary was the dyke itself.

Mounting his cycle, he sat with one foot resting on the grass verge and the other on the pedal ready to move off. But, reluctant to leave the peaceful setting, he remained a few minutes longer. He noticed that there was someone sitting at an open ground floor window, and he heard the faint sound of a piano being played. A young man came out of the front door and began to walk towards the garden gate. It was time to go. His English reserve made him reluctant to become involved in conversation with a stranger, and in any case he still had some distance to travel if he was to reach Nijmegen that day.

He pushed off from the grass verge, but as he did so the front wheel ran into a rut on the uneven surface and was twisted sharply to the right throwing him off balance. He fell heavily to the ground with the cycle landing on top of him. "Damn!" he exclaimed as he lay there on his back. Sitting up, he impatiently pushed the cycle from him, cursing himself for his incompetence. He tried to get up, but as he did so, found that he must have fallen awkwardly, because a sharp pain shot through his left ankle.

"Sind Sie verletzt, mein Herr?"

The voice came from behind him. John turned and saw the man whom he had seen come from the front door of the house. "I say, do you happen to speak English?" he asked.

"Ah, so you are English," the stranger said pleasantly. He took the cycle and stood it against the wall. "Doctor Karl Heinemann, at your service." The young man clicked his heels and gave a slight bow before kneeling down beside John. "Are you hurt?"

"I think I have twisted my ankle."

"Just be still. I will get you into the house."

The doctor stood up and called loudly towards the open window of the house, "Natascha! Hilfst du mir bitte, Liebling!"

"That doesn't sound like Dutch," John remarked.

"No, I am a German, you understand. My wife is Dutch."

John, realising he had not formally introduced himself, fumbled in his pocket and eventually produced his card. "My card, Doctor," he said.

As the doctor took the card from him John heard the click of the garden gate, and casually glancing round saw a young woman emerge. It was not often he looked twice at a woman, but on this occasion he instantly had to look again. She was of medium height and had short fair hair, but without doubt she was the most beautiful young woman he had ever set eyes upon.

"May I present my wife, sir," the doctor said, and then after a quick glance at John's card he continued, "Natascha, this is Major John Rutherford of the British Army."

John held up his hand and apologised for not rising. He looked into her large bright eyes, which seemed to radiate a confident and vivacious personality, and took an immediate liking to her.

"I am delighted to meet you, Major Rutherford," she smiled.

Although Karl spoke good English, it was with a German accent. But with Natascha, her English was so perfect that John could hardly believe she was Dutch.

"My wife is also a doctor, Major Rutherford. So you are in good hands, as you English say."

With Karl supporting one side and Natascha the other. John slowly got to his feet. He tried to put his left foot on the ground, but found it too painful to take his full weight.

"Just lean on me," said Karl.

Karl was quite tall and John thought he looked typically German. Perhaps it was his hair which gave this impression. Cut short across the top as well as on the sides, it gave a square look to the head, which John had always associated with Germans.

"I'm sorry to put you to all this trouble."

"Not at all," Natascha replied cheerfully, "I'd have been most disappointed if you'd had your accident anywhere but here. I've always wanted to nurse a wounded British soldier."

John felt better for her infectious humour. He even found his depression, had vanished.

Progress was slow as they moved towards the front door. "What a beautiful house you have here," he said.

"Oh, it's not ours," said Natascha. "It belongs to my parents. We actually live in Cologne. We're only here for a few days."

An older woman appeared at the front door. She was taller than Natascha and had a well made figure.

"Mama, this is Major Rutherford of the British Army. He's unfortunately hurt his ankle," said Natascha.

"My dear man, do come in," said the older woman. She took John's arm from her daughter, and assisted him into the entrance hall. There was a homely presence about the well made figure of Flora van der Leyden, and John warmed to her at once. It was obvious from where Natascha got her cheerful disposition,

The day seemed full of the unexpected for John. Here he was deep in the province North Brabant with this charming lady speaking to him in an accent which was unmistakably Scottish. "You are very kind, madam. I feel I am being such a nuisance," he replied, wondering what further surprises this house might hold for him.

The high ceiling with protruding beams gave the house a spacious look. A large brick fireplace caught his eye in the hallway. Above the fireplace a decorative coat of arms had been painted on the chimney breast. A large staircase with beautifully carved banisters made its way to the upper floors to the right of the fireplace. At each end of the hall, passages led to the rooms in the two wings. Although large, the tasteful elegance of its furnishings had retained for the house the feeling of warmth and homeliness of a much smaller place. John was led towards the room where the piano was being played. He was no expert on music, but he knew enough to appreciate that whoever was playing had the exquisite touch of a real artist. It was a large room he entered, with the open window in the front where Natascha had been sitting. The grand piano at the far end of the room was placed so that the young woman who was playing had her back to him. The rays of the afternoon sun were falling on her, giving sheen to her lovely fair hair - hair that was somehow familiar to him. Why he should notice this he did not know. It was most unlike him to take in such feminine matters. And to find himself on such easy terms with these strangers was another surprise for this reserved Englishman. If John thought his surprises were over he was mistaken. The music stopped and the young woman rose from her stool and turned to face him. He tried to suppress the astonishment which he was sure must be showing on his face, for here in front of him was Natascha Heinemann, which was impossible because she was standing behind him. But she was exactly the same height and the beautiful features were absolutely identical; the high cheek bones, the perfectly formed nose and the large brown eyes. And, of course, the lovely fair hair. Yet there was a difference, he thought, but he was unable to fathom it.

Flora van der Leyden was used to the surprise which people showed when first meeting her twin daughters, but it came to her mind that, on this occasion, the stranger's face registered something more than just astonishment. "You will no doubt have guessed, Major Rutherford, that this is also my daughter. May I present Elizabeth," she said to John. The young woman came forward with a natural grace, her hand extended towards him. "This is Major Rutherford, my dear. He's had an unfortunate accident," said her mother.

"Major Rutherford, I'm so sorry. I do hope it's not serious," Elizabeth said, looking up at him with concern.

Now that he was close to her it occurred to him where the difference lay between the sisters. Natascha's eyes were sparkling and full of life, but here was a deep tender beauty which, for an instant, held him as if under a spell. He felt he'd seen her somewhere before. But that was ridiculous, he thought. "Nothing serious, Miss van der Leyden," he heard himself say, as he took her delicate hand. The feel of the smooth tender skin sent a flush of excitement through him, and he held on to it for just a fraction longer than was usual for a formal introduction. This momentary hesitation did not escape the notice of the girl's perceptive mother, who was still holding his arm even though Karl was the main support on the other side.

Elizabeth's outward composure covered an inner turmoil. She had heard her family entering the room, but was unaware of the stranger's presence until she had turned round. Her legs had nearly given way at the sight of this exceptionally tall, powerfully built, handsome man, with his dark piercing eyes seemingly looking right into her. From that moment her thoughts, her feelings, in fact her life, were never to be the same again. She could remember Natascha teasing her by saying that she never gave a man a second look. Her retort had been that one look would be enough to know the right man. And now she knew that she had been right - one look had been enough.

It was diagnosed that John's injury was not serious, and that with a few days rest his ankle would be back to normal. The family insisted that he remain as their guest for as long as he wished, and certainly until he was fit to continue his journey. He was informed that a servant would be sent to Nijmegen the following day to retrieve his trunk from the hotel he was due to visit. He had tried to excuse himself from dinner that evening on the grounds that his dinner suit was in the trunk, but, according to the family, it was out of the question that he should not be present. "Mama, we must all dress informally this evening so that Major Rutherford does not feel out of place," suggested Natascha. And so it was decided.

John had been given a walking stick, and later that evening had managed, with some difficulty, to make his own way from his bedroom to the dining room. It was here he was introduced to the owner of the house and head of the family, Jan van der Leyden, a man, John judged, to be in his mid fifties.

The van der Leydens were an old, wealthy merchant family, with their trading company flourishing in many parts of the world. Jan controlled the company, but his son Hugo managed the business from the head office in Rotterdam. Jan's pride in the company in no way compared with the intensity of that which he had for his children. John formed the impression as they spoke, alone together for a few minutes before dinner, that the older man would have been happier if Natascha had married within the circle of wealthy merchant families as Hugo had done, rather than to a German doctor whom she had met when both were students at Edinburgh University.

At dinner John sat on Flora's right, next to Natascha, with Elizabeth opposite him, and Karl opposite his wife.

"Tell us something of yourself and your family, Major Rutherford," said Jan in the rather proud manner of an aristocrat used to authority.

"Now Papa, you're not interviewing somebody for one of your merchant houses," said Natascha. Then, turning to John, she went on, "Papa is a terrible snob, Major Rutherford. He always interrogates our guests to find, out whether they are suitable to sit at the van der Leyden table." Natascha spoke with a wicked smile on her face, and she patted her father's hand affectionately.

Jan laughed indulgently, and said, "You see, Major Rutherford, what a father has to put up with. My beloved Natascha is always so direct."

John realised, however, that Jan was not to be put off from gaining his information. "I come from a Somerset family, sir," he said. "My father is General Sir George Rutherford, of Warren Court, near Clevedon." He had the feeling that Jan's attitude towards him mellowed when his host heard of his father's title.

"I believe Somerset is what you call the West Country, is it not, Major Rutherford?" Karl enquired.

"That's right, Doctor. It is the most beautiful county in England."

"It seems you are passionately in love with your county," Elizabeth remarked quietly, looking directly at him, but lowering her gaze as their eyes met.

He was glad of the excuse to openly look at her, instead of having to restrict himself to furtive glances which her previous silence had forced on him. "Indeed I am, Miss van der Leyden. I never tire of its green hills and silent moors," he replied, and then added, "I'm sorry, but I mustn't bore you."

"Not at all. It sounds fascinating, "Elizabeth said.

"Tell me, Major Rutherford. Does your father's title make him a member of your Parliament?" Jan asked.

"No sir," John replied. "Father is a Baronet, which is the lowest hereditary English title. One of my ancestors bought the title from King James the First, for £1000 in 1611, but it doesn't make him a member of the peerage, so he has no seat in the House of Lords."

"And have you served in the army for many years?" asked Jan, now even more interested in his guest.

"It seems a lifetime, sir. I actually joined my regiment in ninety eight."

"And did you fight in South Africa?" interjected Karl with a note of coolness in his voice.

"Yes I did."

"How exciting!" exclaimed Natascha enthusiastically.

"I doubt if the Boers would share your excitement. It was their country which was taken from them," Karl retorted with a look of disapproval at his wife. As a patriotic German boy during this war, Karl had followed the lead of his Kaiser in supporting the Boer cause.

"I realise that we British were not popular in Europe at that time, especially with His Imperial Majesty the Kaiser," John began. He went out of his way to show due respect to the Kaiser so as not to give offence to Karl. "I hope that the years have healed any rift between countries," he added diplomatically.

"Come on, Major Rutherford, tell us about the war," urged Natascha. "Who cares what the stuffy old Kaiser thought about it. He's only jealous because his empire isn't as big as yours."

It was obvious that Karl was most put out by his wife's unpatriotic remarks, but he managed to control his anger and said stiffly, "Natascha, just remember that you are a German citizen and that His Imperial Majesty is your Kaiser."

"Now you're being stuffy, Karl," Natascha retorted, enjoying the fun of teasing her husband, She knew he was a kind and generous man, but he lacked her sense of humour, and was always very serious on any issue connected with his beloved Fatherland.

"You should not talk as if that war was fun, Natascha. How would you like your country invaded by the British army?" said Karl, in a self righteous tone.

"If they were all like the Major, I wouldn't mind at all," Natascha replied brightly, with a cheeky look at her husband. Natascha's light-hearted attitude towards a serious subject only made Karl more determined to stress his argument against the British. He ignored his wife's last remark and came back at John with another point. "And what have you to say about the thousands of women and children you British killed in your concentration camps?"

John admired the directness of the German's look, considering him to be a strong character, but he could see that Karl was one of those people whose knowledge of the war was narrow, and who had missed the wider truth of the matter. He caught Elizabeth looking at him intently, and as their eyes met he lost his train of thought and forgot all about Karl's question.

Jan was not pleased that his guest should be questioned in this way, and gave his son-in-law a disapproving glance. It was one thing to enquire about him and his family, but quite another to question the integrity of the army in which he served.

"What a pity the human race cannot live without war," said Elizabeth. She spoke softly in her retiring manner and smiled at John.

Why was it, he asked himself, whenever she spoke it gave him such pleasure, and made him feel quite young again? It wasn't so much what she said, but the way she said it; the movement of her mouth, the gentle voice, and the fact that she was speaking to him. "Ah, yes, Miss van der Leyden. The perfect world."

"Who wants a perfect world!" Natascha exclaimed. "It would be so boring. I much prefer being wicked."

They all laughed, except Karl, who was just about to speak again only to be forestalled by Flora.

"I am sure Major Rutherford, doesn't wish to spend, his whole evening answering questions about the rights and wrongs of war," she said firmly, looking at her son-in-law.

"I am sorry, Mama," said Karl, and then turning to John added, "I meant no offence, Major Rutherford."

"None taken, Doctor," John replied smiling at the young German. "Perhaps I might be permitted to ask a question?" he added.

"Of course," said Flora,

"You are obviously a Scot, Mrs van der Leyden, but how is it your daughters speak such perfect English? I cannot hear a trace of an accent. They could easily pass for English girls."

"From the very first I have always spoken to them in English, and in their early years they had an English governess. And then they were educated in England," Flora replied.

"My girls have a gift for languages," Jan added proudly. "They also speak German and French fluently."

"Would that I could do the same, but like most Englishmen I speak only English," John admitted.

In addition to discovering the family's British connection, John also had his thoughts on the van der Leyden's home confirmed by Jan. The centre section was indeed an old house. Jan's grandfather had bought and renovated it, having the new wings built on at the same time. The grandfather had used it as a country residence for the holidays. However, Jan had made it his permanent home, because now that Hugo, his son, was helping to run the family business Jan found he could spend more time away from Rotterdam.

Jan was never happier than when telling the story of his house, and was pleased that John had shown such interest. He explained to his guest that the Spanish, under the Duke of Parma, had laid siege to

Grave in 1586, and it was said that they had erected the first building on the site during the 3 months they surrounded the town.

"When I was a child my grandfather used to tell me tales of how the Spaniards had tried to tunnel their way into the town," Jan related. "The story goes that the original building was the starting point for their tunnelling. It is said that their first tunnel got out of alignment and surfaced outside the walls on the side of the dyke. They tried again but the siege ended, before the second tunnel was finished."

Flora remarked, "Of course it is true that the Spanish did lay siege to the town, but the rest are only Grandfather's tales. It was a farm when he bought it, and it was probably built as a farm centuries ago."

"They would have had to tunnel about four hundred yards," John commented. "Seems a long way. Strange, though, how these old tales were often based on fact. Are there any cellars under the house?" he enquired.

"Oh, yes," said Jan. "As a child I was forbidden to go down there."

"And Papa has never allowed any of us to go down," Natascha interrupted. "Do you know, Major Rutherford, there is still a vicious looking strap hanging outside the cellar door, Papa put it there years ago as a warning to keep out. Hugo was a real mischief, but even he didn't venture inside the door for fear of that strap."

Jan said, "I rarely go down myself, except to inspect the wine stock. I've never seen a tunnel." He laughed.

"But Papa, what about the French officer?" Elizabeth asked. "You see, Major Rutherford, the French were at the gates of the town in seventeen ninety four, and they occupied the house for a time. A French officer was said to have reported that he had found the farmer and his family hiding in a tunnel under the house."

"I expect he meant the cellar," said Jan, adding, "If there was such a man."

The conversation turned away from the house to John's cycling tour. The family heard how he had entered into a wager to tour

Holland on a bicycle. "And now I have a good excuse not to continue," he grinned.

"But you can't give up now!" Natascha exclaimed. "What fun to win the bet. After all, your ankle will be better in a few days, and we can soon rearrange your hotels."

"Be careful or my daughter will have you cycling round half of Europe. Natascha is the organiser of the family. She keeps us all on the go," said Flora.

John laughed and then said to Natascha, "No, Frau Heinemann, when I'm better I shall go home. I've found that cycles do not agree with me. But I'll claim that I've won the bet. After all, I have toured Holland on a cycle. Or at least some of it."

"It all sounds stupid to me," said Karl. "But then, of course, the English are eccentric."

"And that's another thing," Natascha interjected, changing the subject with a speed which sometimes bewildered her listeners. "May we call you by your Christian name? We can't go on calling you Major Rutherford. You must call me Natascha, and then there's Karl and Elizabeth."

John smiled and nodded his approval, surprising himself that he had consented to such informality among people he hardly knew. And yet, somehow he felt at home in this house, and his reserve, which was always most apparent in the company of the opposite sex, had been overcome by the warmth of his reception. When he retired to bed that night he lay awake thinking of the day's events, and wondered what strange fate had brought him to this house. But wherever his thoughts wandered they continually returned to Elizabeth. She was certainly a lovely creature, but why should she keep forcing her way into his mind? He had seen beautiful women before, but once they were out of sight he had not given them a second thought. Was it the way she looked at him, he asked himself, or was it what she said? Normally he found women a damned nuisance and took little notice of them, but somehow she was different. In the end he drifted into sleep wondering what the morrow would bring.

It had sometimes entered John's mind that he was growing old before his time. He had no children to keep him young and had little social contact with other young people, so it was with some surprise that he found himself completely at ease in the company of the van der Leyden girls, whom, he considered, must be at least ten years his junior. They seemed to readily accept him, and he found that their good humour and high spirits had removed the difference in years between them, and they were soon treating him as almost one of the family.

When Natascha and Karl left for home, John was sorry to see them go, and knew he would miss Natascha's sparking personality and sense of fun. In a way he would also miss Karl, even though the German missed no opportunity in luring him into political discussions usually designed to prove that Imperial Germany was of equal importance in the world as the British Empire. John never argued the matter, for he knew it pleased Karl, as it did his Kaiser, to ensure that others knew of his country's greatness. Natascha would usually manage to rescue John by some witty remark, which, on occasions, would even make her serious minded husband laugh. Karl liked to believe he was the masterful husband, and in some ways he was, but Natascha knew exactly how to handle him. She once remarked when Karl was not listening, "He makes me do exactly as I want."

With Natascha present it had been like staring into the sun and being blinded by the dazzling rays. But when she had gone John found he could see her sister more clearly. In the days following he was to spend his time with Elizabeth. She was fun, but in a different way from her sister, and possessed a gentle and serene nature. He had been attracted to her from the first moment he had seen her at the piano, but it was only during these days when they were alone together that he realised this was more than just a passing fancy. As day followed day feelings within him were being awakened which previously he would have believed impossible, and the short periods out of her presence made him impatient to see her again. At first, the effect Elizabeth had upon him lay deep within and was not noticeable on the surface. But as time went on his dormant feelings began to emerge in many small ways.

He was enjoying himself so much that he began to regret his ankle was healing so quickly, and that the day would soon come when he would have to leave. There came a time when he knew that he could do without the walking-stick, but did not dispense with it for fear that his hosts might see how well he was walking.

His enforced rest made him subject to pastimes which previously he would not have entertained. Elizabeth would play to him, or read him poetry and short stories she had written, and, to his surprise, he was quite content to listen; happy just to be in her presence. Each day she would accompany him into the garden when he would exercise his ankle with a slow walk.

He was shown over the house, and in one passage, which led from the entrance hall, he noticed an old door with a leather strap hanging beside it.

Elizabeth gained much knowledge of the world during the long talks they had together. It was here that their age gap was most prominent, for his experience was so wide that she could not hope to be on equal terms. He had a modest and interesting way of imparting information, never speaking down to her. It was always discussion, never a lecture. The one difficulty she had was to get him to talk about himself, and it was only by clever manipulation of the conversation that she was able to delve into his character and learn about incidents in his own life. The one failure they had was when she tried to teach him Dutch. He appeared to have no aptitude for the language, and she laughed so much at his facial expressions when he attempted to pronounce the simplest of words, that he swore he would never utter another word of the confounded language.

"Why do you stare at me like that?" she asked one morning as she sat drawing his portrait. "You are supposed to be looking at that wall so I can see your profile."

"You can't expect me to look at a wall all the time, when there is so much beauty in the room." As he turned his head away he saw her blush.

"That's better," she said, trying to sound calm and to give the impression that his words had not affected her. "I would not have supposed you to be the type of man to flatter women," she added casually.

"Your supposition is entirely correct. I have never flattered a woman in my life." He glanced at her out of the corner of his eye and saw the flicker of an uncertain smile on her face. "Since I have been here you have surrounded me with beauty. Music; painting; poetry." He paused and then added quietly, "And you."

"For a man who has no time for women, you seem remarkably experienced in the way you pay complements."

"I've never said I have no time for women, just that there have been no women in my life. Except, of course, my mother and sister. Oh, yes, and Sheila Butcher," he added, laughing.

"Whoever was Sheila Butcher?"

"Never you mind," he replied.

"A secret love," she said. "Now I'm finding out the truth about my mysterious guest." They both laughed as she pencilled in the last few lines and completed her work. "There! It's finished!" She held it up for him to see.

"So that's how you see me," he said thoughtfully.

"Don't you like it?" she asked.

"Oh, yes, I do. It's just strange to see yourself as others see you." He looked hard at the drawing and tried to detect if she had any deep feeling for him. But like her it was an enigma, which he knew would soon have to be solved.

The following day the pony and trap had been made ready so that John might take her for a drive. As Elizabeth had made to get up into the trap, he had offered his hand to assist her. He had not touched her since their introduction, but as he once again felt the soft skin of her delicate hand his heart began to thump. For a moment he stood watching her as she settled herself into the seat, and it was then that he knew he couldn't contemplate life without her. The state he had thought he'd never have to face had overtaken him without him realising. He was in love. As he looked at her lovely face, he remembered the picture of the Dutch girl on the bus in London and realised why he'd thought he'd seen her before. Perhaps this was why he had come to Holland. Maybe he was meant to come all along.

"Come along, John, stop staring at me as if you'd seen a ghost, and take me for a drive."

"I'm sorry. I was far away."

He flung his stick into the trap and, forgetting his ankle, quickly got in himself.

"Your ankle seems much improved," Elizabeth said, as he sat down beside her and took the reins. She gave him a furtive glance with a wisp of a smile on her face.

"It's been better for days," he admitted nonchalantly.

"You fraud!" she exclaimed with false indignation. "And I've been waiting on you hand and foot, and all the time you've been perfectly fit. Why ever didn't you tell me?"

He smiled at her but didn't answer. They drove down the track and into the road where, three weeks before, John had cycled depressed and set on going home. He was silent for some time. She did not disturb his thoughts but sat quietly and waited for him to speak again. After a mile or so the trap climbed the gentle slope where the road met the dyke, and there he stopped. "I didn't tell you because I cannot leave yet. There's something I must do first," he said, at last answering the question which she thought he had forgotten. He took one her hands in his and again thrilled at the touch. She made no attempt to draw away.

No man had affected her like this before, and she felt her heart flutter. "You don't need an excuse to stay on," she said trying to control the emotion in her voice. "You can stay as long as you like."

"Then I may have to stay forever," he replied. He was not looking at her, but gazing into the distance.

She gave a little laugh and said, "Surely it won't take that long?"

"I hope not."

"If you'd stop being so mysterious and tell me what, it is, perhaps I could help."

"Indeed you could."

"Then what can I do?"

He turned and looked straight into her eyes. "Marry me," he said tenderly.

All her life she had imagined such a moment as this. When, the tall, dark man of her dreams would say these words to her. She had always believed that she would remain completely calm and give a firm answer, but now it had happened, her good intentions melted away in the heat of her emotions. His words had completely taken her by surprise and she didn't know what to say. After a pause she heard herself stammer. "But you hardly know me."

He lifted her hand to his lips and gently kissed it. "In my heart I have known you all my life. I just didn't know where to find you. But now that I have, I can never let you go." He put his hands on her shoulders and gently pulled her towards him so that their faces were quite close. "I love you, Elisabeth, and I want you for my wife."

"I don't know what to say. You quite take a girl's breath away."

"I'm sorry if I have shocked you, but I'm not very good at this sort of thing."

"I wouldn't say that," she said, regaining her composure. "I must have time to think."

"But do you love me?" he asked.

"You know I do."

"Then marry me."

"Is that an order, Major Rutherford?" she asked, teasing him.

"Yes," he replied, screwing up his eyes into that irresistible smile which seemed to light the whole of his face.

"Then what can a poor girl do?" she said demurely. His dark eyes seemed to look into the depth of her soul and she knew, as she had done from the beginning, that here was the love she had waited for. Her eyes filled with tears of joy. It was futile to resist any longer. "I have loved you from the first moment I saw you," she whispered. "I am yours forever, my darling." She put her arms round his neck and drew him towards her until their lips blended with a fervent rapture which, until that moment, they had not imagined possible.

That evening after dinner Elisabeth left John alone with her parents. "I see you've given up using a stick," said Jan.

"Indeed sir, I'm almost recovered," John replied.

Jan was sitting in his high backed chair smoking a traditional long stemmed Dutch pipe, while Flora and John sat facing him at each end of a sofa, Flora was never idle and was busy knitting.

Jan looked at his wife with pride and said, "You see, Major Rutherford, how my wife is always busy looking after us, and yet, as I tell her, there is no need for her to work so hard. It could all be done for her."

"Aye, and as I tell you, my dear, you are my family and I shall look after you. No servant is going to take that from me. They never have done, and they never will." Flora looked directly at John and added, "You remember that. Rich or not, always look after your own family. Never let others do it for you, or you'll regret it in the end."

"But the man's not married so he's hardly likely to need your advice, my dear," said Jan, chuckling at his wife.

"But he will be", and sooner than you think," Flora replied.

John sat forward on the edge of the chair and clasped his hands in front of him. Surely she doesn't know, he thought. "Which rather brings me to a subject I should like to speak to you about," he said, feeling his throat go dry.

"Shall I leave you two alone?" asked Flora.

"Whatever for?" said Jan.

"Because he wishes to speak to you."

"What about?"

"Marriage, I should think."

"Marriage! What marriage?" Jan spluttered, inadvertently blowing smoke at his wife.

Flora flapped her hand up and down in front of her face to clear the air and then said, "If you'll listen I am sure John will explain."

"I would be obliged if you would stay, Mrs van der Leyden," John said, sensing an ally in the canny Scot, and at the same time asking himself how the devil she knew what he was going to talk about. He had not allowed for a mother's instinct in these matters.

"In that case, my dear man, you can hold this wool," she said with a knowing look. She placed some wool over John's hands and pushed them apart to make it taut, and then began winding it into a ball. "It'll give you something to do while you tell us all about it."

John sat, for a moment collecting his thoughts and wondering how to begin. "I wish to request permission to marry your daughter," he said at last rather formally.

Jan, who had just put his pipe back into his mouth, snatched it out again. "What's that!" he exclaimed, wondering If he'd heard correctly.

"What he means is that he's going to marry Elizabeth," said Flora.

"Marry Elizabeth!" Jan retorted more bewildered than ever. "Who says he is?"

"He did. Only he's too much of a gentleman to say it so bluntly."

"You knew about this, didn't you?"

"Of course I did!" Flora retorted. "It was obvious from the first. You men are so blind"

"In any case they hardly know each other. Three weeks. It's ridiculous!" He did not object to John, but believed that such a short acquaintance between the young people was not a good basis for a lasting marriage. However, Jan might be the most successful merchant in Holland, but he was no match for his wife when it came to affairs such as this.

"Aye, but it didn't take you three minutes to decide I was the one for you, when you purposely bumped into me in that restaurant in Princes Street." She spoke with that charming Scottish lilt in her voice. John asked himself why it was that the Scots never lost their accent no matter how long they had been away from the land of their birth. He was looking from one to the other as the conversation went back and forth, and had the feeling that his presence was completely unnecessary.

"What do you mean, purposely? It was an accident," Jan retorted.

"Poof! You'd been eyeing me for half an hour, just waiting for me to get up." Flora was enjoying herself as she remembered her first meeting with her husband. "I'll admit I walked very slowly to the door to let you catch up," she chuckled.

"I don't believe it!"

"Of course you don't. You men know nothing about the ways of women." Flora, who had finished winding her wool, got up and went to open the door of the room. "You might as well come in, Elizabeth, and support your man instead of listening at the door." The girl was led in by her mother and made to sit next to John. Her cheeks were slightly flushed with embarrassment, but John thought it made her more attractive than ever. He felt a small hand slip into his, and his heart leapt for joy.

"Now we can settle the matter properly," Flora added.

"It appears to be settled already" sighed Jan. "You know, Major Rutherford, I have had three women to contend with in this family. They always get their own way, and I'm supposed to be the master here."

"You must stop calling him major, Papa. Please call him John," said Elisabeth. "In any case he will be a colonel in June," she added proudly.

Flora knew when to keep quiet and let her husband take over the conversation. In a more serious vein Jan asked some searching questions of the young people, and it seemed to them some time before he had satisfied himself as to the suitability of the match. But Flora could see that her husband was pleased with Elizabeth's choice of this fine aristocratic Englishman, and his seeming delay in granting his blessing was just a cover to give himself time to think. It was obvious that he deeply loved his daughter, and his only desire was for her to have the right man. But in his heart he knew she had chosen well. "I have tried to find reasons why this marriage should not be the perfect match, but it seems that I have failed. Why both my daughters have chosen foreigners I shall never know."

"Perhaps they are copying you," Flora gently reminded him.

Jan smiled and stood up. He held out his hands to his daughter. "I pray you will always be happy, my little one," he said as Elizabeth got up and flung her arms around him. Still holding her with one arm, he held out his hand to John and said, "So be it, John."

The wedding day was set for the first Saturday in June even though Jan considered the date too early. But, as John explained, he had to return to duty on 29th. June, and after that it would be some months before he could properly take leave long enough for a reasonable honeymoon. Natascha's wedding had been a large affair with plenty of scope for Jan to invite his rich merchant friends, and many others besides. But Elizabeth wanted a quiet wedding with only the immediate family present at the actual wedding breakfast. There would be the usual celebrations in the week leading up to the actual day. Jan was a little disappointed but Flora was relieved, for time was too short to organise a large reception.

John wrote to his colonel formally requesting permission to marry, and asking that the matter be kept secret. He wished to surprise his friends in the regiment, and. get his own back on Robert for having tricked him into the dreadful cycle tour. Lieutenant-Colonel Arthur Stanhope had been John's commanding officer for many years and was now about to retire. It was his place that John would take on promotion. Both the colonel and his wife Lady Victoria Stanhope - she derived her title by being the daughter of an Earl - had known John since he joined the regiment as a young subaltern, and had watched his career with interest. They had seen the exceptional talent in the young officer and realised that one day he too might command the battalion. And now that time had almost arrived.

The colonel replied by return of post giving his permission, but also enclosing a private letter of congratulation.

Peninsula Barracks
Winchester,
Hampshire.
10th. May 1914,

My Dear Rutherford,

> *It was with great pleasure that I read your news, and both my wife and I extend to you our heartiest congratulations. It has made us very happy to know that you have found someone to help and support you in the years ahead.*
>
> *With Elizabeth at your side I know that the burden of your future responsibilities as commanding officer will be so much lighter.*
>
> *I have noted your request for secrecy and will try my best to oblige. But as you know, the War*

Office has to be informed and there is the possibility that the news might reach your friends from that quarter. We shall see. I must say that I look forward to seeing the faces of Nicholson and, your other colleagues when they see your new bride.

I have enclosed an invitation for your attendance at my farewell ball, which will take place on Saturday 27th June, so I wish you well until we meet on that occasion.

Warmest wishes,
Arthur Stanhope.

John smiled to himself as he read the letter, thinking of the surprise he would give Robert and Reggie when he took Elizabeth to the ball. Reggie would sure to be there, because, although not a regular officer, he was a personal friend of the Stanhopes.

As the cool spring days warmed in anticipation of summer, and the sleeping countryside awoke with new life, John and Elizabeth were rarely out of each others company. On occasions they walked on to the dyke at the end of the garden and watched the barges plying up and down the river not more than two hundred yards away. They rode into the surrounding countryside to visit friends so Elizabeth could show off her Englishman to the ones who had believed she would never marry. Sometimes they were seen strolling in the town, but their greatest pleasure, when the day was warm enough, was to sit in the garden under the shade of a tree and while away the hours, just happy to be together.

Flora noticed radiance in Elizabeth which she had not seen before. It was as if this dark stranger, who had suddenly appeared in their lives, had drawn something new out of her daughter, making her a more complete and confident young woman. Each day the lovers would discover some new delight in the other's character.

Replies to the few wedding invitations were gradually received. Sir George, to his great regret, could not attend. Since John had been away, his father had suffered a chill and his doctor had forbidden him to travel. He had been overjoyed to hear of his son's forthcoming marriage. "Damn it, Maud!" he had exclaimed to his daughter on hearing the news, "Always knew some girl would catch him in the end. The young blighter's certainly caught us on the hop, though. Why all the hurry, I should like to know?" Sir George stroked his chin and considered the matter and then said, "You don't think . . .?" but before he could continue, Maud interrupted.

"John did explain in his letter."

"I only thought that he might have been making up for lost time," Sir George replied with a twinkle in his eye, enjoying the shocked look on his daughter's face.

"Really, father, what will you be thinking next!"

Maud would be attending the wedding. John had given her details of the dress uniform he would require, and she had promised to take it with her.

George and Henrietta received an invitation and a letter requesting George to act as best man. George was thrilled but, as usual, Henrietta dampened his enthusiasm. "If you think for one moment I am going to traipse halfway across Europe to see that brother of yours marry some foreign creature, and you make a fool of yourself as best man, then you're mistaken. You can go if you like, but I shall stay here," she said. But to her surprise and annoyance, George, in a rare moment of initiative, accepted her suggestion that he should go alone.

As is the Dutch custom, the week which led up to the wedding day was crammed with parties given by the van der Leyden family and their friends to celebrate the coming event. On the day before the church wedding John and Elizabeth and all their guests were driven to the town hall in Grave, where the quite lengthy and important civil ceremony took place. The marriage was now recognised in Dutch law. It appeared to John that the Dutch considered this event of almost equal importance to the church wedding service, but until the church service had taken place both he and Elizabeth acted out their single status.

As often happens and this wedding day was no exception, so much took place in the space of a few hours that Elizabeth felt she was being carried along on a wave of joy and excitement, which seemed to move so rapidly that she hardly had time to savour the moment. It was only when she awoke the following morning that her mind could begin to take in the happenings of the most wonderful day of her life.

So it was not a dream, she thought, as she looked at the contented features of the still sleeping man beside her. She lived again the moment when she and her father had arrived by carriage at the church and the town band had struck up. It seemed that the whole town had turned out to welcome them. She had felt like a princess in her beautiful wedding gown. Although nervous, she felt secure in the presence of her father, and in the knowledge that she was to be given by one strong man to another. On entering, she had seen that the church was full, but she only had eyes for one man, and he towered over all others. How fine he had looked, standing there waiting for her in his dark green uniform, sword at his side, and his shiny black cross strap and silver accoutrements glinting in the sun. He had given her confidence, for he had not stood meekly with his back towards her as she approached, but, with the self assurance of maturity, had turned to face her as she approached up the aisle.

The wedding breakfast had been fun. How she loved having her family about her. Her brother Hugo and his wife Kate were there with their small daughter Isabel. Also Natascha and Karl, and a number of aunts, uncles and cousins. Even Grandmama van der Leyden was there, making one of her increasingly rare excursions from Rotterdam. "You've picked yourself a real man," the old woman had told her as she and John had moved among the guests. Grandmama had tapped John on the chest with the bone handle of her walking stick and added, "I like tall, dark men!"

Elizabeth had been sorry that her father-in-law was not able to come, but had been pleased to meet George and Maud. George seemed unusually relaxed.

*

Experienced travellers will say that Paris is a charming place. But Paris in the springtime seen through the eyes of lovers becomes the most beautiful city in the world. Although love makes all things beautiful, perhaps Paris has a claim to this accolade. The straight, wide, tree-lined boulevards, and in contrast the varied sizes and shapes of the streets in the old town fitting together like pieces of a jig-saw puzzle. The Seine curving its way through the city, and crossed by the 32 bridges. Painting, sculpture, architecture, all have a home here, and for John and Elizabeth, who had fallen under the spell of this city of light, the days passed in a whirl of enjoyment, which they had never dreamed possible.

One warm afternoon they strolled in the Parc du Champ-de-Mars, marvelling at the construction of the great steel girdered tower before them. "Did you know that it is nine hundred and eighty four feet high, and that there are two million five hundred thousand rivets holding it together?" John asked casually, looking at his new wife with a smug expression on his face.

"John, how clever you are to know all these things," Elizabeth replied. She saw him grinning, and then noticed him slipping the guide book into his pocket.

"You tease! You've just looked it up." She laughed and looked up at him; this man who had given her such happiness.

"And you, my love, are so beautiful," he whispered as he bent down and kissed her lightly on the forehead. "They say that Gustav Eiffel had his own room at the top, but I'm too much of a coward to go up and find out."

"Nonsense," she said remembering the row of medals she had seen on his chest on their wedding day. "A coward! And you with all those medals," she grinned.

"Just campaign medals, dearest. Everyone gets one."

It occurred to her that, although he had told her much of the places he had seen in the world, he had never-spoken about himself as a soldier. "I'm not stupid, John, I saw the bronze cross.

"Oh, they give those to the young and foolish, or those too old to care," he laughed, but would not be drawn on the subject.

There was so much to see and do. Each day they wandered at will with no set plan, or just sat - drinking coffee on the cafe terraces, watching the constant stream of people pass by. They danced the evenings away under the great chandelier in the hotel ballroom to the waltzes of Strauss and Lehar. And later, after the unimaginable ecstasy of their new found love, they would fall asleep in each other's arms.

As spring moved into summer they were oblivious of the storm clouds gathering over them. The world they knew would soon vanish forever, becoming just a sunlit dream of a bygone age, never to return.

Towards the end of June they journeyed home. As the ferry approached the English shore, Elizabeth saw the passionate love her husband had for his native land. They had remained on deck, him with his arm around her, so as not to miss, even for a moment, the sight of the afternoon sun shining on the white cliffs ahead.

They stayed in London overnight and took the train to the west the following day. They sat close to each other in the corner seats of the compartment, both silent and lost in thought. Elizabeth felt her hand gently squeezed and glanced at John out of the corner of her eye. If life ended at this moment, she thought, she would be content, for she had known love - love which would last for eternity.

"My dear girl." Sir George embraced his new daughter-in-law and kissed her on the cheek. He had been waiting impatiently for the arrival of the young couple, and had hurried to the front door when he had seen the carriage enter the drive. Elizabeth only just had time to alight before he enclosed her in his arms. Then holding her away from himself, still with his hands on her shoulders, he said, "Now let me look at you. Maud said you were lovely, and she was right. How did that boy have the good fortune to find you? It's incredible."

She blushed, but it was unnecessary to reply for her eyes spelt out her happiness and her immediate affection for the old man. Sir George put his arm round her shoulders, and together they walked into the house.

"I say, don't I get a welcome anymore?" John called out after his father. He was happy to see his father's enthusiasm for his new found daughter.

Sir George didn't stop but called back over his shoulder in the dry manner which his son had inherited, "I'd almost forgotten you, m'boy. But if you will bring back such a beautiful bride, what *can* you expect?"

But when all three were in the drawing-room and father and son embraced, Elizabeth saw the bond between them and knew she belonged to a united family.

Sir George was disappointed that the visit, on this occasion, was to be a short one. The young people would leave for Winchester the following day to attend the ball, and to take up their new quarters. On the Monday John would assume command of the battalion.

The officer's mess was ablaze with light that-evening. Arthur Stanhope had spared no effort to ensure the success of his farewell celebration. A well connected man, mainly through his wife, a number of important people had been invited including members of the peerage, and the guest of honour was to be the Colonel-in-Chief of the regiment himself. It was with much satisfaction that he stood with Lady Victoria in the entrance hall receiving his guests. The sound of the regimental dance orchestra could be heard coming from one of the inner rooms where already some of the younger officers had started to dance.

Robert and Helen were among the early arrivals.

Reggie and Daisy had driven down from Brighton in Reggie's brand new Rolls Royce Alpine Eagle. They arrived wearing long raincoats over their evening dress, and both wore leather flying helmets and goggles. "Keep your goggles on, old girl," said Reggie as he parked the car. "Give old Stanhope the fright of his life!"

Reggie entered the building with Daisy dragging behind hanging on to his belt. "Not so fast!" she called in a loud whisper. "My bloody goggles 'ave steamed, up. I can't see a bleedin' thing." Daisy had not lost her London accent, but she tried hard not to drop too many aitches at functions such as this - not that Reggie minded one way or the other. However, in moments of difficulty, she automatically reverted to her natural manner of speech, often inserting a few extra adjectives much to the amusement of her friends.

"I say, old boy, is this the way to the T.T. races?" Reggie spoke to the sergeant at the door, who was announcing the guests, and was amused to see the shocked look on the man's face.

"Sorry sir. This is a private function. Entry by invitation only," the sergeant replied formally, trying to cover his surprise.

The colonel had also been taken aback by the appearance of the heavily disguised couple, but, although his monocle fell from his eye, he then realised who it was and called over to the newcomers. "Come on Sanders, stop playing the fool."

Reggie gave one of his loud laughs. He slapped the bewildered sergeant lightly on the back. "All the Fun of the Fair, Sergeant. How're the wife and kids?"

Daisy winked at the man and drew a smile from him when she said, "It's all right, luv, he's always like this, even before he's 'ad a tipple."

Once inside, Reggie searched out Robert and Helen, who were standing at the far end of the reception room. "John not here yet, Rob?" he enquired.

"No, I thought he might be with you."

"Not with us, old boy. Haven't seen or heard from him since we left the club that morning."

"I had two postcards." said Robert. "The lazy blighter had just written three words an each. The post mark on the first one was a place called something or other bosch."

"Hertogenbosch," Helen corrected.

"That's the name," Robert continued. "Anyway, all he said was 'tulips and windmills'. And on the second one 'bicycles and clogs'. Didn't even sign the things."

"Having you on, old boy. Just getting his own back for sending him on that wild goose chase," Reggie replied with a laugh.

"I didn't do anything of the sort!" said Robert with mock indignation. "I wonder why he's taken so long to get in touch. He should have been home weeks ago. I must say I can't wait to hear how he got on."

"Well luv, you ain't going to 'ave long to wait. He's here," said Daisy. She had caught sight of John shaking hands with the colonel just outside the door. The room was now crowded with guests taking wine before moving into the other rooms, and the others had not noticed the arrival of their friend.

"I say, who's the lovely creature talking to Lady Victoria?" Robert said as he craned his neck round some of the other guests for a better view.

"No Idea, old boy," Reggie peered across the room. "By jingo, she's a stunner! I've seen some beauties in my time, but she takes the ticket."

Daisy gave her husband a dig in the ribs. "'ere you watch that roving eye of yours, Reggie Sanders."

"Ha ha, sorry, old girl. Must admit though she's a cracker. And just look at that, dress." Still staring towards the door Reggie added, "Surely she's not with John?"

"Don't be ridiculous! You know he doesn't bother with women, and he certainly wouldn't bring one to a mess function," Robert replied.

Daisy began to take an interest in the new arrivals. She was quite a tall woman, and standing on tip-toes she managed to see what was going on. "She's not only with him, she's in love with him," she said knowingly.

"Don't talk rot, old girl!" Reggie retorted.

"You mark my words," Daisy replied.

"Good God!" Robert exclaimed. "She's taken his arm."

Daisy waved and caught John's attention, and he made his way towards them. A way seemed to open up in front of him as astonished officers and their ladies moved aside to let him pass with this lovely girl on his arm. For a moment silence fell on the room as the murmur of conversation lapsed, and all that could be heard was the rustle of Elizabeth's elegant gown and the delicate sound of a waltz coming from one of the other rooms. All eyes seemed to be looking at her, and Elizabeth felt her legs go weak with nervousness. She modestly looked down to cover her embarrassment and gripped the strong arm beside her more firmly. She felt John put his hand on hers, and her confidence returned. As they reached their friends the conversation in the room gradually returned to normal.

"I say, grand to see you again, old boy. Can't wait to be introduced to your lovely friend." Reggie took Elizabeth's hand and then said, "I'm Reggie, my dear."

"Now Reggie, behave yourself, you'll embarrass the girl," Daisy said. "Don't mind him, dear." She looked at the girl's large eyes and then said seriously, "But he's right, you really are lovely."

"I should like to present Elizabeth," said John. He purposely paused in order to watch their faces and then added, "My wife."

There was a stunned silence. Robert's mouth dropped open but no words came forth. He just looked helplessly at Helen as if waiting for her to explain. Reggie's face went blank. It was only Daisy who reacted true to form by blurting out, "Luv a duck, John, you're a dark ' orse, and no mistake!"

"Isn't anyone going to congratulate us?" John asked with a note of triumph in his voice.

Daisy was the first to react and hugged and kissed Elizabeth. "You've got a good un "ere, John', I can tell," she said with tears of joy trickling down her heavily made up cheeks. She took Elizabeth's hands and said, "Don't mind me, dear. I always 'ave a good blub when I'm 'appy. It's me upbringing you see. I wasn't taught all the graces like this lot, but they pretend not to notice. They're all toffs here," she went on with her usual mixture of speech. "But they treat me right, even though I aint really one of 'em."

"She's got a heart of gold, Beth, and everyone loves her," said John, taking one of Daisy's hands and kissing it.

Reggie kissed Elizabeth on the cheek. "I'm speechless," he sighed.

"Well, that makes a change," said John dryly.

Elizabeth was introduced to Helen, and then John said to his wife, "And last but not least, this is Robert. He may try to claim some of the credit for bringing us together, when he comes out of his trance." Elizabeth looked at the sensitive face and extended her hand, which Robert took and kissed.

"I must be dreaming," he said.

"I'll explain it all later, but if you could drag out the thirty one bob you owe me, it may help you to realise you're wide awake," drawled John.

"It was a guinea," Robert protested.

"It was a guinea for the confounded cycle ride," John retorted. "An extra ten bob for bringing back a Dutch girl," he added.

That's true, old boy," Reggie interjected.

"You're not telling me Elizabeth is Dutch?" said Robert in a voice which seemed resigned to the fact that nothing was impossible anymore.

"That's exactly what I'm telling you."

"I don't believe it," Robert protested.

"I'm afraid it's true," said Elizabeth gently, smiling at him.

"He always gets the better of me in the end," said Robert with a sigh as he counted out the coins into John's hand. "It was just the same at school."

"Are you sure you didn't marry me for the extra ten shillings?" Elisabeth asked, giving John a mischievous look. Before he could defend himself, a group of young officers had gathered round to be introduced to their future colonel's new wife. In fact John found conversation with his friends almost impossible as guest after guest came to offer congratulations and to be introduced to Elizabeth. It was obvious that his young wife had won the hearts of all by her poise and graceful charm. One young officer pleaded for a dance, and not having the heart to refuse him, Elizabeth was whisked away onto the floor in the adjoining room. On returning, she found John in conversation with Arthur Stanhope and the colonel-in-chief, an elderly and distinguished looking officer with a bald head and a large curled moustache. On his dark green uniform, below a long row of medals, he wore the Garter Star.

"Your Royal Highness, may I have the honour to present my wife?" As John spoke he looked at Elizabeth hoping she would realise that this was the man he had mentioned earlier in the day. He need not have worried. Elizabeth sank into a deep, graceful curtsey. The colonel-in-chief stepped forward, and, taking her hand, raised her up.

"My dear young lady, the honour is mine," he said, kissing her hand. "We are most pleased to have you with us. You are now as much part of the regiment as your husband." Turning to John he continued, "You are indeed a fortunate man, Rutherford. I believe it's important that our colonels should have the support of a wife. A great asset for the regiment, don't you know. . . Now Stanhope, we must not stop the young people enjoying themselves."

"Thank you, sir," John replied, bowing slightly as the two older officers moved away.

During the evening a constant stream of guests tried to book dances with Elizabeth. But to prevent himself from being completely excluded, John had written his own name against most of the numbers in her little white dance diary. And so they danced their honeymoon to an end.

The night was pleasantly warm as they walked arm in arm along the deserted street after the ball, talking quietly about the wonderful evening. They were looking forward to being alone in their first home; a terraced house overlooking the barracks in a small road on the other side of the deep railway cutting. John had rented the premises because of its convenient position. They stood for a moment outside the house reluctant to leave the magic of the night and unable to take their eyes from the bejewelled sky.

"Is it possible to tell the future by the stars?" Elizabeth asked.

"Only if you're in love," John replied, pretending to read a message in the sky. "They tell me that as long as they are in the sky I shall love you." He put his arm round her and pulled her close.

"I never thought you would be such a romantic," she said.

"What did you think I would be?"

"When I first saw you I thought you very stern. You looked at me as if you were inspecting your soldiers."

"Which shows you just can't judge by looks."

"That's true. For instance, I would never have guessed Robert was a soldier. He has such a sensitive face, and such sad eyes."

"You know, he once told me he would die before he was forty. He couldn't explain it, except by saying there was no picture in his mind of himself in old age."

"How strange. Such a nice man. I always knew you would have good friends, John." Even as they talked the sky in the east began to lighten, heralding the new day,

"Look you can see the dawn coming up," John reflected for a moment and then added, "Sunday the twenty eighth of June, the last day of my leave.

Rising late that morning, Elizabeth prepared a light lunch which was taken in the tiny garden. She had placed a rug on the grass in a position that was partially shaded from the hot noon-day sun by a small apple tree. And there they sat content with each other and oblivious to all else. They drank in the peace of it all like some priceless wine, and tried to grasp the precious moment by willing it to last forever. But already the European telegraph wires had begun to hum, and the old world – their world – had nearly run its course.

That afternoon Agnes arrived. She lived down near the cathedral, and had been sent by an agency with a view to being taken on as a maid. Both John and Elisabeth were much impressed by the girl, so she moved in that day and started her duties immediately.

They attended evening service at the cathedral, and afterwards strolled by the river. The past weeks came into John's mind, and he wandered how he had lived without this girl beside him. What strange chance had taken him to that solitary house in a foreign land? Was it chance? He had asked himself this question so many times, but, whether it was or not, he had found the girl of his dreams, and with her beside him he could face anything.

John returned to duty the following morning and attended his first parade as colonel. After parade he briefed his officers as to his general policies, and then went to the mess for morning refreshment.

"I say have you seen this, Colonel?" It was the adjutant who spoke. He was sitting in an armchair casually turning the pages of The Times. John, who was standing nearby talking to some junior officers glanced at the speaker and said, "What's the news, Stuart?"

"Listen to this," the adjutant said, and then read out, "The Tragedy of Sarajevo. With the deepest and most profound regret we record today the tragic news of the assassination of the Archduke

Franz Ferdinand, Heir Presumptive to the Austro-Hungarian Throne, and of his wife, the Duchess of Hohenberg."

"May I look?" said John, taking the paper.

"It's a long article," said the adjutant. "They were evidently shot by a high school student."

"Who's been shot?" asked Robert, who had just caught some of the conversation.

"The Archduke Franz Ferdinand," John replied.

"Who the devil's he?"

"The heir to the Austro-Hungarian Throne."

"I suppose this'll mean yet another war in the Balkans," said the adjutant.

"That's a certainty if Serbia had a hand in it, and they probably did," John replied. They've been trying to cause trouble with Austria for years. Trouble is, it could set the whole of Europe alight."

"Surely not," the adjutant said. "I can't believe the big powers would get involved in a silly little quarrel like this."

"Much will depend on Russia," said John. He had made a study of European history and had kept abreast of the political situation for a number of years, even while he was away in India.

"What's it got to do with Russia, Colonel?" asked one of the younger officers.

"Russia considers herself the traditional protector of the Slavs. If Austria declares war on Serbia and Russia goes to Serbia's assistance, Germany could honour her alliance with Austria and come in on her side. Russia has an alliance with France, "and if she is attacked France would no doubt assist her. France has been spoiling for a fight with Germany ever since, eighteen seventy, when she lost Alsace and Lorraine."

"And what about us, Colonel?"

"Who knows? I can't see us being dragged in. What do you think, Rob?"

"I pray you're right. But I think that 'Summer's lease hath all too short a date'," Robert replied absently.

John's fears that there would be a general European war subsided during the following three weeks. It had been expected that there would be sharp reaction from Austria, but as the days passed and nothing happened people pushed the matter from their minds. Many thought it was just another incident in a far off land which had nothing to do with Britain anyway. It was the Irish question which was occupying the public mind. But on 23rd July events began to move fast, when Austria at last sent an ultimatum to Serbia, demanding full acceptance of the conditions within 48 hours. It was the last ultimatum to be drafted in diplomatic French. The statesmen had begun to lose control of events.

On the evening of the 24th the British Cabinet, after having sat for hours trying to find a solution as to what should be the geographical limits of Ulster, were startled when Sir Edward Grey, the Foreign Minister, read them the text of the Austrian ultimatum. It was only then that they realised the serious state of affairs that was developing and the possibility of a general European war. It was asked how could a country possibly accept such terms?

At 2 minutes past 6 on the evening of the 25th, Serbia handed her answer to the Austrian Ambassador. She had accepted nearly all the demands, and, offered to submit to arbitration those few points she had been unable to accept. But although there were diplomatic moves to calm the situation, Austria declared war on Serbia on the 28th.

There were desperate attempts by some of the Rulers during the last hours of peace to prevent a war which none of them wanted. In the past, to mobilise was the last and most effective diplomatic move to bring pressure to bear without war. But the European statesmen of 1914 had failed to realise that this was no longer the case with the now massive conscript armies. No longer could they be put in a state of readiness and then, at the stroke of a pen, sent back home. General mobilisation meant war. Events had taken control.

The Tzar had ordered general mobilisation on the 30th. At midnight the following day Germany sent an ultimatum to Russia demanding the immediate suspension of her mobilisation, but the following afternoon, without waiting for an answer, Germany declared war on Russia. On that day France mobilised.

Monday 3rd August was a Bank Holiday, but John had spent the whole day at the depot. With the, worsening situation he was determined that his battalion should be in a proper state of readiness. He was still at work during the evening when the news came through that Germany had declared war on France.

The next day it was learnt, that German troops had crossed into Belgium. John returned home that evening to find Elisabeth and Agnes waiting for him in the hall eager for the news. "We've sent an ultimatum to Germany demanding they withdraw from Belgium. They must answer by midnight - that's eleven our time," he informed them.

"What if they don't answer, sir?" Agnes asked.

"Then there will be war," he replied.

It was just before midnight as they were preparing to go up to bed. There was a bang on the front door. When John opened it, a young soldier from the depot stood there. He saluted and handed John a message from the orderly officer. John knew what it would say before he read it and so did Elizabeth, who was waiting for him at the foot of the stairs. "It's happened," he said as he took her hand and led her up the stairs.

A few days later the regiment left for France. With the band in the lead, they marched the short distance from the depot to the station to the cheers of people lining the pavements. At the station, Elizabeth and many other wives were there to see their loved ones go. She tried not to cry as he held her in a last embrace. The colonel's lady would be expected to be strong and set a good example to the other wives. But her heart was in shreds, and she could only manage a weak smile as he put her from him and got into the carriage as the whistle blew. The door shut, and as the train began to move, he put his hand out through the open window and for a moment their finger tips just touched.

She had meant to say so much before they parted, but when the moment came she could find no words. And then he was gone and it was too late. She watched the train go down the long straight until it disappeared from sight, and then made her lonely way home.

John settled down into his seat as the train passed through the deep cutting below his home. Robert and the adjutant were also in the compartment, but none spoke. He felt exhausted after the past few days of feverish activity preparing the battalion for embarkation. He sat for a moment and saw Robert smile at him from the opposite seat, and then his eyes became heavy with sleep.

*

"Nijmegen! Nijmegen!" Somehow the words seemed to force their way through the haze of sleep. The train juddered to a stop, and then in his semi-conscious state John heard the sound of steam being released from the locomotive. "Are we there, Rob?" he mumbled, opening his eyes. But the compartment was empty. "God, I must have been dreaming!" he whispered to himself as his mind began to clear. "It was all so long ago." He shook; his head, trying to bring himself back to reality. He was cold, and a feeling of hopelessness gripped him as he glanced round the empty carriage. There was no Rob anymore. Everything had changed.

The door of the carriage opened and a porter entered to take his case. How long had he slept, he asked himself? It was dark and late, far too late to go on to Grave. He would have to find a hotel near the station.

The following morning he took a cab to the ferry, and then, after crossing the Maas to Grave, hired a carriage to take him to the van der Leyden house. He had not seen Elizabeth since February that year and now it was nearly Christmas. This would be the first Christmas he had spent with his little family.

Elizabeth had remained in their small Winchester house throughout the war, even though John was willing to buy a much larger place, she had been happy there in her little nest, as she called it, for it was there she had known the joy of their first golden weeks together. Their first child, Joanna, had been born there in 1915. Agnes had stayed with her, and had become very much part of the family.

Elizabeth spent a few weeks with her parents in Holland each year. During her current visit, when she had made to leave for home, she had felt faint and had been advised to have her baby before making the journey. And so it was that Robert was born in Holland.

As the carriage turned into the rough track leading to the house, John remembered the time he had cycled that way. He had often thought about the day when he rode up the track by mistake. It was a lifetime ago. Turning the corner at the end of the track, he saw the mounting block which his head had nearly struck when he fell from that wretched cycle. The carriage stopped at the garden gate and, after paying the driver, John stood for a moment trying to adjust his mind to enter once again a life of peace among normal people. He was so lost in thought that he had not noticed the small girl come through the garden gate, Feeling a tug at his coat and a voice saying, "Daddy, Daddy!" he looked down and saw a pair of large brown eyes peering up at him. His mood changed as he picked up the child and held her close, smothering her with kisses. The sight of his first born brought life back into him. She was so like him, and he loved her with such intensity that he knew he would have to be careful not to spoil her as she grew up.

Elizabeth came down the path to greet him and flung her arms round his neck, standing on tip-toes to kiss him. They walked up the path arm in arm with John carrying Joanna. He could find few words. None were necessary. His loved ones were with him and that was all that mattered.

Jan and Flora were waiting at the front door. They had not seen him since the day he left on his honeymoon. He was still the fine, upright, handsome man that Flora remembered, but the years had taken their toll and his dark hair was now showing flecks of grey

Inside, Natascha was there to greet him. She came forward and kissed him on the cheek. "You don't mind being kissed by the enemy?" she asked, giving him the same provocative smile he remembered so well. "At least there's an armistice between us," she laughed.

"You, Natascha, the enemy. Never!" he exclaimed. "How's Karl?"

"Still with the medical corps, but very disillusioned. Perhaps even a little bitter."

"Aren't we all?" John, had been looking hard at her. She was still lovely, and still the same vivacious Natascha. But he could tell that she too had seen the horrors of war during her service in a German military hospital near the front. There was an affinity between them, which could not be grasped by those who had lived outside this experience.

Natascha had become pregnant earlier in the year, and Karl had insisted that she return to Holland to have the baby. Karl Heinz had been born on 3rd October, and as the British blockade was causing serious food shortages in Germany it was felt that both mother and child would be better cared for if they remained in Holland until conditions in Germany improved.

"Would you like to see your son?" Elizabeth asked.

"Of course," he replied with a smile, hoping to disguise the fact that he had forgotten all about the boy. He put Joanna down and then squatted down and held her hands. "Will you take Daddy to see your baby brother?" he asked gently.

The child's eyes lit up, and looking at her mother for a nod of approval, she proudly led her father up the stairs to the nursery, followed by the rest of the family. John followed his daughter's lead by tip-toeing into the room with much exaggeration and with a finger to his mouth. Two cots stood side by side.

"It's all right, you needn't be that quiet, they'll be waking soon," said Elizabeth, amused at their antics.

"Which is which?" John asked, looking first at one boy then the other.

"This is Robert," said Joanna triumphantly, pointing into one of the cots. "And that's Karl Heinz," she added.

"All babies look alike to me," said John

"They most certainly don't, you naughty man!" scolded Flora.

"Oh, come along, Mama, admit it, these two do," he replied. "They look exactly alike to me."

"Aye, well, I must say these two do look alike," Flora conceded. "But not all babies look alike," she added quickly,

John stood for a moment looking at his son. He took the medallion, which Reggie had given him, and rested it lightly on the child's hand before replacing it in the black box and handing it to his wife for her to examine. "A present from Reggie," he explained.

John continued to look into the cot. He had lived with death for so long that he'd almost forgotten the miracle of life.

"It's strange to think that these two boys have been born enemies," Natascha observed.

"But the war's over?" said Elizabeth.

"The war isn't over," John remarked. "There's an armistice, but we're still at war until a peace treaty is signed. At the moment we are in a state of armed truce."

"Don't say it's going to start all over again?" Elizabeth tried to keep her voice steady and suppress a feeling of panic.

"It could, but it won't," John replied. "The German army is no longer capable of resisting. They're exhausted."

"Thank God!" Elizabeth exclaimed with relief. She glanced at the cots. "The future lies with these children. I hope to God they find a way without war," she added, taking John's hand and leading him from the room.

PART 2

Chapter 3

The boy had lost all sense of time as he stood fascinated at the rail unable to take his dreamy eyes from the massive moving hills of water which slowly raised the ship on to the high, smooth summit of the next roller only to lower it once more into a sunken valley, removing from his view all but the sky. There was no wind, but the warm Atlantic air, stirred by the movement of the ship, ruffled his fair hair. In the far distance he caught sight of the sunlit coast of Spain, only to lose it again as the deck sank into the next trough. Perhaps the ship would go down and down, he imagined, gripping the rail a little tighter, and never come up again, and he would live forever in a watery kingdom beneath the sea.

The ship was making way under a brilliant blue sky four hours out from Gibraltar on the last leg home to England.

He couldn't remember home, for he had never lived there, but he did remember visiting Grandpa just once before he died. That was such a long time ago, and he must have been very young. Home was where the king lived. He knew that because Daddy had told him. How he had loved sitting on Daddy's knees on their veranda in the cool of the evening listening to exciting tales of kings and knights in armour and old battles. If only Daddy was always like that. Agnes said it was always raining at home, but he didn't believe that. Oh yes, and a man called Mr Baldwin lived there, as well. He'd heard lots of grown-ups talking about him. He felt sorry for Mr Baldwin because it seemed that the unions – whoever they might be – were always trying to strike him, at least what the grown-ups said. When he'd asked his governess why this was, she had caned him for stupidity. The silly old cow had always been pleased to find an excuse to cane him. He wondered whether it was the cane he hated most, or having to take his trousers down in front of the two girls who shared his lessons - they were never beaten and it wasn't fair. Besides, girls were sissy. He was always ashamed of himself for crying and had hoped Daddy would never find out what a coward he was.

The boy leaned hard against the rail as the ship lurched into another trough, but he fancied that the great rollers were becoming smaller. Not that he minded one way or the other, for it was good fun hanging on and watching the water rush along the side of the ship never quite reaching the deck. How Karl Heinz would have loved it, he thought. They'd had such good fun when they'd lived together at Grootvaders house in Holland (he always referred to his Dutch grandfather as Grootvader even when speaking English).

He felt as if he had been on board for months - it must have been all of sixteen days since leaving Bombay. He knew that it was six thousand two hundred and sixty miles from Bombay to London, because it said so in his atlas, and that beastly governess had made him learn the distance by heart. The voyage seemed never ending, and, although he had been absorbed by the sights he'd seen, he was now looking forward to the arrival in London.

He had never been completely happy in India, perhaps because he'd missed Karl Heinz, and was often lonely, the few friendships he had made failing to make up for the separation from his cousin. He had taken to music as a comfort, and it was his greatest joy just to be left alone with piano or violin. Music had become part of his life and unknowingly he had developed a love for the art which went far beyond the normal. His mother had been his teacher, and, being herself a first class musician, had recognised the talent which had taken root in her son.

"Well, young man, you look deep in thought. What's your name?"

"Robert, sir," the boy replied as he turned and saw a ship's officer looking down at him. He thought the man must be important because he had three gold rings on each sleeve. "I don't think we've met, Robert."

The officer extended his hand and smiled at the good looking lad before him. "When did you come aboard, Robert?" he asked as they shook hands.

"Bombay, sir."

"Are you interested in ships?"

"Yes, sir."

"Would you like to come up on the bridge?"

"Oh, yes please, sir!"

Robert found the bridge even more exciting than he had imagined. He was shown the compass, and the helmsman allowed him to hold the wheel. He couldn't wait to tell Daddy about this adventure.

"There's Cape Trafalgar," the chief officer pointed out. "Do you know what happened there, Robert?"

"That's where Lord Nelson beat the French," Robert replied proudly. He liked history, and it gave him pleasure to be able to answer correctly. It helped to make up for the other times when he was asked things he didn't know.

"Good boy!"

"Captain coming up, sir," a young apprentice called out to the chief officer.

A few moments later an elderly officer, with a red weather beaten face and a white beard, blew into the wheel house like a violent squall. The seaman on the wheel visibly stiffened, and the younger officers affected a flurry of activity. Robert noticed that the only one who seemed unconcerned by the arrival of the captain was his friend.

"Who's this shrimp on my bridge, Chief?" bawled the captain as if he was trying to be heard above a gale.

Robert considered the captain very stormy, and he did wonder whether the man in the crow's nest might have heard his question.

"A young man returning from India, Captain. He's interested in ships and thought he'd like to inspect the bridge just to make sure everything's ship-shape and Bristol fashion. A faint smile went across the chief officer's face.

"You sure he's not an Arab?" the captain roared, eyeing Robert's brown body, which so contrasted with the white shorts he was wearing that he looked the picture of health and boyish vitality. "First class, I hope! I want none of your Tom, Dick or Harry on my bridge."

The captain glared at Robert, who began to wonder whether his excursion to the bridge had been such a good idea after all.

"What's your name, boy? Come on, speak up or I'll clap you in irons."

By this time Robert was standing stiffly to attention, mainly because he found this position prevented his knees from knocking. "Robert Rutherford, sir," he managed to stammer.

"Not Major General Rutherford's boy?"

"Yes, sir," Robert replied with a little more confidence. The sound of his father's name always gave him courage – except when he was naughty and then it had the opposite effect - and he had noticed that it often made other people's attitude towards him become more agreeable.

"Well, that's one thing in your favour, boy," said the captain. And then turning to the chief officer he added, "Rutherford and that lovely wife of his are the only ones on this damn voyage who talk any sense. I don't mind them at m'table, but as for the rest." He paused for a moment to glare at the helmsman. Hold your course, man!" he called before turning his attention back to the chief officer. "That reminds me, Chief. Who the devil put that damned woman on my table last night? The Honourable somebody or other. What a bore! Blasted bird watcher - looks like a cockatoo. Make sure she's not put there again."

"Aye, aye, sir,"

"You're dismissed, boy," The captain walked away, having turned his attention on to one of the young deck apprentices, who was either doing something or not doing something - Robert couldn't decide which - but which ever way it was the storm had gathered over the unfortunate youth.

The chief officer put his hand on Robert's shoulder, and led him back down to the upper deck.

"Phew!" Robert exclaimed, relieved to have escaped being clapped in irons, although he was not quite sure what it meant.

"The captain's not as fierce as he sounds," said the chief as the two parted.

The great swell had died down as the ship had moved away from the coast into deeper water, and Robert no longer needed to hold on to the rail as he sauntered away along the deck. He had not got very far when he heard Agnes's voice. "So there you are, you naughty boy! Where have you been? We've been looking for you everywhere."

"You couldn't have looked everywhere or you'd have found me," Robert replied defiantly, wondering what all the fuss was about.

"You won't be so cheeky when your father gets hold of you."

She took hold of his ear and led him off along the deck, his head on one side forcing him to walk on tip-toe to relieve the pressure.

"Ouch! You're hurting me!" he whined. "What have I done now?"

"You've been missing for an hour. We've been frantic that something might have happened. And what's more important, we're late for lunch."

John and Elizabeth returned to their cabin after searching for their son, and John was just about to ring for the steward to have a further search carried out, when Joanna bounced in and said, "It's all right, Agnes has found him. They're along the other end."

"When I get hold of that brat I'll. . .!"

"Now, now, John," Elizabeth interrupted softly, knowing that her husband's irritation had been brought on by concern for the boy. "Let me talk to him."

"The boy needs discipline, Beth. You're too soft with him."

"If it'd been Joanna you'd have reacted quite differently, yet it's Robert who's the sensitive one," Elizabeth replied.

"Sensitive or effeminate? I don't want any of that sort of thing in a son of mine."

"Oh, John, don't be ridiculous! There's nothing effeminate about him. You only have to look at him to see he's a normal, healthy boy."

He grinned at her, pleased with her reassurance and admitting to himself that the boy was certainly tall for his age and had a strong, healthy body. "How is it you always get your way?"

"I don't know what you mean," she laughed. Robert was bundled into the cabin, and by the look on his father's face he thought his doom was sealed. What he didn't see was the underlying relief. "Hurry up and get yourself ready for luncheon. We're already late," snapped John. "You can explain yourself at the table."

"Yes sir."

Robert ran to his cabin next door and put on a white shirt. Why did grown ups always make him dress up at meal times? He much preferred just being in shorts and sandals when it was so hot. He ran his fingers through his hair in a quick effort to make it look tidy, and then as an afterthought remembered to wash his hands - at least he wouldn't get told off about that.

The ship was no longer pitching and rolling as it had. been earlier that morning, and was now making way in fairly calm conditions, so it was without difficulty that the little family walked along the deck to the dining saloon. The quartet was playing as they were ushered to their table.

Once seated, Robert kept very quiet, hoping to be forgotten. However, he was not forgotten, but to his surprise it was his mother who spoke to him.

"Robert, do you realise you were missing for an hour, and we were very worried about you?"

"I was on the bridge, Mummy, and I couldn't leave because. . ." he paused, wandering how to continue his excuse, and then, added quickly, "Because the captain said he would put me in irons."

"That sounds a very remarkable story," said John. His annoyance had subsided, and he had to restrain a smile.

"It sounds like a fib to me," Joanna interrupted. "He's always fibbing, Mummy."

"No I'm not," Robert snapped back, going red in the face, because he knew that he did sometimes.

"That will do, Joanna. We all know that Robert has a vivid imagination, but it doesn't mean that he's a fibber."

Elizabeth spoke firmly, but Robert could tell by her face that he would not be punished.

"Now Robert, you must promise not to wander off an your own. Supposing you'd fallen overboard?"

"I promise, Mummy," Robert replied, feeling relieved.

"Next time it will be the stick for you, my lad," said John,

"You can't, Daddy. The canes are in the sea chest. I saw Agnes putting them in before we left."

Robert thought that for once he had got the better of his father but his triumph was short lived.

"I'm sure the captain would lend me a cat-o'-nine-tails," John countered, in such a way that Robert couldn't make out whether or not he was joking.

"What's that, Daddy?"

"It's a whip with nine tails. Used on sailors in the old days."

Robert considered this information for a moment and then said, "That's not fair. It means I'd get nine whacks for every stroke."

"I'd never thought of that," John replied, stroking his chin and looking thoughtful. "I think I'll ask the captain to let me have one. It would save me no end of effort."

"Oh, no, Daddy. I think I'd prefer the cane," said Robert seriously, and then seeing his father grinning at him, added, "Daddy! Stop teasing." How he loved these moments when his father had fun with him, and how he hated the other times when that look came over his father's face, Robert called it his war look, because Mummy said he was like that when he remembered the war, and he was best left alone until the sadness passed.

John saw his son's look of relief. They both burst out laughing. He put out his hand and touched the boy affectionately on the cheek.

Robert amused the family when he related the tale of his adventure on the bridge, especially his vivid description of the captain and his objection to the bird watcher at his table. On learning that a cockatoo was a kind of parrot, Robert drew their attention to a lady sitting on the far side of the saloon. "That must be her," he whispered loudly, and they all chuckled as they furtively glanced in that direction.

"And now I have some news for you all," said John, trying to sound mysterious. Both children began to chatter, impatient to hear what their father had to tell them. Two elderly ladies at a nearby table," smiled at each other on hearing the raised voices and seeing the excited look on the faces of the eager children.

"Hush children, let Daddy get a word in or you'll never know what he has to tell you," said their mother.

"Be quiet, Robert!" said Joanna.

"Be quiet yourself! You're making as much row as I am."

John was silent until the two of them were quiet, and then said, "I've bought a house. It's going to be our new home."

"Oh, Daddy, that's wonderful! Where is it? Is it big? Can we see it?" Joanna was so excited that she did not know what to ask next. She was eleven years old and had never lived in a house that really belonged to them.

"One question at a time, young lady," John replied. "It is a big house, and it's near a place called Brighton."

"Where's Brighton?" asked the excited girl.

"It's a seaside town in Sussex. Do you know where Sussex is?" John asked.

Robert, looked blank, but Joanna replied, "It's that long county at the bottom of England?"

"Good girl! That's the one,"

"I know," said Robert, "Sussex by the sea. That's what the band played when we left Lucknow."

"By Jove! So it did," said John, surprised at his son's remark.

Robert thought for a moment and then asked, "Daddy, how can you have bought a house in England, when you haven't been there for a long time?"

"That's a sensible question, Robert. Well, your Uncle Reggie has arranged everything for me. I suppose you don't remember him?"

"Is he the one who sends me a birthday present every year?" Robert asked.

"I remember him," Joanna laughed. "He came and saw us off when we left for India. He was very jolly. He said, 'All the fun of the fair, old girl, have a stick of Brighton rock'. Can we see him again, Daddy?"

"Yes you can. He's meeting us when we dock."

John felt a sense of pleasure at the prospect of meeting his dear old friend again in a few days.

"Hurray!" both children cheered loudly.

"Hush children, people are looking," Elizabeth whispered.

"Sorry, Mummy. But Uncle Reggie sounds a jolly good sport," said Robert.

John explained that the house stood in large grounds next to Reggie's home. He had admired the place some years previous when staying with Reggie. They would be staying with Reggie until they had furnished the place, so the children would have plenty of time to get to know him and their Aunty Daisy.

John's next posting was to be the War Office, and this was one of the reasons he had chosen this particular area in which to settle. The house was within easy reach of a Southern Railway station and the excellent London to Brighton line. He intended to travel daily, and would only stay in London on those occasions when duty prevented him from returning home.

A young ship's officer approached the table and apologised for interrupting their meal. He introduced himself as the entertainments officer and explained that he had been given the task of finding children who would be willing to entertain the passengers during afternoon tea.

"My brother plays the piano and the violin," Joanna quickly cut in before the man could say more.

Robert felt his face flush and he looked down at the table, wishing his sister would shut up. Although he enjoyed playing, he knew he would not be able to play in front of all these people. In any case, he thought, he wasn't good enough.

"Well, that's just what we want. How about it, young man?" the officer asked. "With your parents' permission, of course," he added, making a slight bow towards John and Elizabeth.

Robert looked up at his mother and whispered the first excuse that came into his head.

"I haven't got anything to play."

"Yes you have, dear. You have the Elgar piece we've been practising."

"But Mummy, I make so many mistakes, people will laugh."

He had only played in front of family friends. He just couldn't play in front of all these people, he told himself again. He must get out of it somehow.

"Stop making excuses," said John abruptly. "You spend all this time on your music, and when it comes to showing people this talent you're supposed to have you don't want to do it. Music isn't just for you; it's to give other people pleasure."

Robert was looking down again. He found it difficult to meet his father's eyes when being lectured. "Look at me when I'm talking, boy." Robert looked up and was happy to see that his father was not wearing that black scowl which always terrified him. Nevertheless, he was wearing his military look - as Robert called it - and it was not the time to argue.

"You will play," said John.

"But..." The excuse faded on his lips as he looked at his father. Yes, sir."

He tried not to sound too reluctant for fear of another lecture, but his reply was accompanied by a pained expression on his face.

"Now stand up and thank the gentleman for his kind request and tell him you accept."

Robert got up and stood to attention, and falteringly said his piece.

"Directly after lunch you will go to your cabin and practice for an hour," said John.

"Yes, sir."

"And you are excused your other lessons this afternoon."

"Yes, sir. Thank you, sir."

Robert beamed at the thought of no lessons, and for a few moments forgot his concern about playing. But his anxiety soon returned.

The young officer was much impressed by the way the matter had been dealt with, and by the boy's obedience. In the course of his duties he had to deal with so many spoilt brats that it was refreshing to find such a lack of argument. Mind you, he thought as he walked away, the boy's father was not the sort for anyone to argue with, certainly not a boy.

"You make it all sound like military manoeuvres, John dear," Elizabeth grinned. She was quite used to her husband's military ways, but the way he organised the family on occasions still amused her. However, she did realise that it was going to take a great deal of courage on Robert's part for him to be able to perform, but considered it would without doubt do him good, and it was time he overcame his reluctance to demonstrate his talent. "Well you know I can't stand all this humbug; can't do this, can't do that. He knows damn well that he can do it, and he jolly well will."

John saw Elizabeth looking at him with an amused expression on her lovely face, and he couldn't prevent himself grinning back at her. She loved to see his face light up into that attractive smile which had always been ready to appear in those few carefree weeks they had spent together in 1914. So often since the war she had noticed that strained look, when he quietly brooded on the experiences he could never speak about.

When Robert returned to his cabin he rejoiced that there were to be no lessons that afternoon. How he hated lessons, and yet they hadn't been quite so bad since his mother had taken them.

During the voyage, Elizabeth had given the children their lessons. She had surprised them, not only with her strictness in insisting that they work two hours in the morning and one in the afternoon, but also because she was found to have a talent for teaching. She was a very cultivated woman, and especially managed to impart her gift for languages to her children. Robert was especially talented in this sphere, no doubt because it came easily to him, but with other subjects he was lazy and they suffered as a consequence. Joanna, on the other hands had a good grasp of most subjects. She was a bright girl and had shown good results since attending La Martiniere School, Lucknow.

Having found freedom from the governess and the frequent thrashings, Robert had not at first taken his mother's lessons seriously. But after finding himself standing in the corner for an hour after lessons had finished on the first morning, he decided that perhaps it would be best to cooperate. To his surprise he found that he began to make some progress, but it would be going too far to say he actually enjoyed the work – he would never have admitted to it even if it had been true. Sometimes he was stubborn and exasperating, but afterwards would feel sorry and apologise.

Robert took his violin from its case and, after tuning it, played a few bars of the piece he was to perform. But he felt too restless and nervous to settle down to any serious practice, and soon put the instrument down. It was a nice violin, he thought. Not full size, of course, but it had a good tone. It was kind of Daddy to have bought it for him, especially as he didn't seem to like musicians very much. He knew this because he'd, once heard him telling Mummy that he hoped no son of his would become a musician. Then Daddy had mentioned pansies, but he couldn't understand what flowers had got to do with it.

To pass the time and to take his mind off the coming ordeal, he took out some of his lead soldiers and placed them on the floor. He had a good collection of these toys, and had been allowed to bring a few with him on the voyage to keep him amused. His vivid imagination always enabled him to play happily on his own. In his eyes the patterns on the carpet were roads for his troops to march down, forts to be attacked, and places of ambush. But even at this young age he sensed it was strange that he should like playing with soldiers, because he didn't feel a very warlike sort of person, and he was almost sure he wouldn't like to be a soldier. At least he wouldn't like to have a sword stuck in him or be shot, but then he supposed that soldiers didn't like that either. Then why did they become soldiers, he wondered? His thoughts were interrupted by the sound of his parents entering their cabin next door, and he quickly took up his instrument and played a few more bars. He had not got very far, when Agnes came in to take him to the saloon, because the pianist, who was to accompany him, wished to run through the music.

The pianist seemed a nice man, and Robert gained some confidence on being told how well he played. Mummy sometimes told him that, but he thought she only said it to be kind because he knew that he was really not very good at all. Although, when he had played at the Residency last Christmas, the Governor had praised him, but then grown ups don't always say what they mean. Perhaps he wasn't the only one who fibbed sometimes.

After the practice he sat near the door, watching the saloon fill with those passengers about to take tea. He put his hand on his tummy and pressed hard in an effort to get rid of the butterflies inside. Why was he always so nervous, he wondered? Perhaps he was a coward. Other people always seemed so calm, especially the boy who had played at teatime yesterday – he was a proper swank, and a rotten player as well. If only he could be calm and brave like Daddy. Mummy had told him that Daddy was very brave in the war. But why would he never speak about it?

"Come along, dreamer." The voice of his father interrupted his thoughts, and a hand gently gripped his shoulder. He picked up his violin and joined his family as they made their way to the table. The saloon was almost full, and the orchestra had already started to play as they took their seats. When they were served, Joanna started to tuck in immediately.

"I'm starving," she said.

Robert glared at her. It was her fault that he had to go through this ordeal, he thought, and there she was stuffing herself, with not a care in the world. Elizabeth offered him some bread and butter.

"I'm not hungry," he pouted.

"That's no way to answer," snapped John.

"Sorry."

"Perhaps you'll feel like something after you've played," Elizabeth soothed.

A girl was the first of the children to perform. She played the piano reasonably well, not that anybody appeared to be listening, for the general chatter and the clink of cups and saucers contin-ued throughout the rather long piece. But she did get a reasonable applause when she finished.

A boy was next. He sat at a nearby table and, when his time came, marched confidently to the stage. Robert saw it was the swank who had played the violin the day before. He wore glasses, and his dark hair was unnaturally plastered down. He was obviously dressed for the occasion, wearing a white silk blouse and black velvet short trousers, with long white socks neatly pulled up to just below the knees. Robert noticed he had on black patent leather shoes fastened by a strap and a large silver buckle. "What a sissy," he whispered to Joanna, who started to giggle. Robert didn't like the boy because he had heard him being rude to his parents, and his father had done nothing about it. He thought the father looked as soppy as the son, and was glad Daddy wasn't soppy like that, even though it sometimes meant a swishing. But he wished he had the boy's confidence.

When the boy began to play it was obvious to those who did happen to be listening that his confidence exceeded his talent.

"What a blessing the chatter hasn't stopped or we might be able to hear him," John remarked dryly.

The two children stifled their laughter so as not to be heard by the boy's parents. But the parents were far to engrossed in their son's performance to notice.

"He's trying his best," said Elizabeth.

"Trying his best to break my eardrums," John put in, playing up to his children, who were by now shaking with laughter and holding their hands over their mouths.

"John!" Elizabeth exclaimed with false severity, trying hard not to laugh.

"He sounds like a pelican in pain," John went on, trying quite successfully, to help Robert forget his apprehensions.

"Daddy, you've never heard a pelican in pain," Joanna retorted.

"I know, but I'm sure it must sound like that."

"You are all very naughty," Elizabeth rebuked.

The music stopped and there was some polite applause. The boy bowed stiffly and went back to his seat looking as confident as ever.

"It's your turn now," said Joanna gleefully.

She was very fond of her brother - except when he was in one of his beastly moods - and was generally kind to him, but she was the elder and considered it her right to order him about when she felt like it.

"I can't stand up," Robert whispered urgently. "My legs are shaking. What am I going to do?" he whimpered.

John pushed his chair back and turned it so that he was sitting alongside the table. He took Robert by the hands and gently encouraged him to stand. The boy stood facing his father and John held him at the hips. He could feel the boy quivering,

"Now stop snivelling and listen to me, Robert." John said firmly. "I know exactly how you feel, because we've all had butterflies in the tummy at some time or another."

Robert stared at the massive figure of his father and could not believe that he had ever felt afraid.

But John's fear had been real enough when the German machine guns had opened up from behind the unbroken wire. If only he could tell the boy. But he couldn't. Nothing could pass his lips about the war. But he must say something to help, he thought. "You can't be brave without first feeling afraid," he said, and then wondered whether the boy understood what he was talking about.

Robert was not sure whether he understood or not, but the fact that his father was trying to help him, and giving him all his attention, had gradually loosened the grip of fear and replaced it by an eagerness to please.

"Now Robert, you will go up there and play. Just remember we are all proud of you."

"Yes Daddy."

Robert was released from his father's grip. He picked up the violin and walked slowly towards the small stage.

"Oh dear, he does look a little untidy," Elizabeth remarked.

Robert made his way between the tables, feeling an acute sense of loneliness and wishing to run back into his father's arms. He felt that all eyes were upon him, whereas, in fact, few people had even noticed him.

There was one small, dapper man, however, who had noticed. His sharp features and dark piercing eyes seemed to indicate a fiery temperament. A neat goatee beard and receding brown hair, already turning grey, ensured his distinguished looks once seen would not be forgotten. It was after the ship had put in at Naples that he and his companion had appeared at the table next to the Rutherford family. Since then he had taken his seat at each meal, but had made it perfectly clear that he had no intention of acknowledging the presence of the other passengers, not even to exchange the time of day. He was accompanied by a rather effeminate young man with an American accent, who appeared to be some sort of companion assistant by the offhand way he was treated. The two had just taken their seats for tea when the older man spotted Robert mounting the rostrum. "Do my eyes deceive me, or are we, yet again, to have our musical sensibilities racked by these juvenile torturers?" The goatee beard spoke with cutting severity, and loud enough to be heard at the nearby tables. John and Elizabeth looked at each other as the man rose abruptly from his chair.

"Cecil, order tea in my cabin. I can't stand another of these performances."

"Yes, Maestro," the young man replied, leaping up and signalling the head waiter.

On the rostrum the entertainments officer had welcomed Robert and shaken his quivering hand. As Robert prepared to play, the officer made his announcement. "Ladies and gentlemen, we now have another young man to entertain us. His name is Robert and he tells me he is seven and a half years old." The officer paused and then read from a piece of paper, "He is going to play an arrangement for piano and violin of the Larghetto from Elgar's Serenade in E for strings."

Meanwhile the head waiter, seeing the man with the beard angrily rise from his seat, hurried across and. enquired with much servility, "Is anything wrong, Maestro?"

"Is anything wrong, you ask? I come here for tea, and for the last two afternoons I have had my eardrums torn in shreds, and you ask if anything is wrong."

"I'm sorry, Maestro," the head waiter replied, ringing his hands. But the goatee beard had turned away from him as If he didn't exist, and had slowly sat down again lost in thought.

"The Maestro will take tea in his cabin," the young companion said loudly.

"Quiet, you fool! I'm listening"," snapped the older man. The sound of the violin had come to his ears, and something about the playing had taken his attention. He had expected another rasping, discordant performance, but instead had found his interest held by the boy's delicate touch and mature interpretation of the music. He sat on the edge of his chair with one elbow resting on the table, stroking his beard.

The chatter in the saloon gradually subsided as one by one people became captivated by the appealing melody, which this boy was playing with such feeling. Many passengers, especially those who had not seen their country for some years, could feel an underlying sadness in the picture of England the music conjured in their minds.

By now Robert's fears had almost vanished, and he had stopped shaking. There had been some little technical mistakes at the beginning, which he had tried to cover and hoped had gone unnoticed. But now he had begun to feel the music and knew that everything would be all right. A joy entered his heart and he wished he could go an playing for ever. But the piece was not long and was soon over. For a moment there was silence, and then, a second later there was such a crack of applause that it made him jump. He stood there feeling embarrassed, and then made to leave the stage, but remembering, stopped and gave a low bow, after which he walked quickly back towards his table. On his way he heard voices saying, "Well done," and, "Good boy," but he kept his eyes down. His father's praise would be sufficient for him.

John's musical knowledge was not deep enough to assess the technical merit of his son's performance. The boy had played nicely, and in tune, but what was more important, he had overcome his fear of playing in front of all these people. John lacked the understanding that Robert's desire to please him was greater than his fear of failure in front of an audience.

Robert was about to resume his place at the table when he felt someone grip his arm. Turning, he saw the man with the goatee beard peering at him. He had previously noticed this man at the next table, and had considered that he looked rather a disagreeable person. He had been fascinated by the his large bow tie, and had spent lunch time trying to work out why it had five red spots on one side and six on the other. He had come to the conclusion that fierce face couldn't tie a bow properly,

"I suppose you think you've been sent by the gods to enchant us with your musical prowess?" The man spoke sharply, clipping his words to the bare minimum as if he feared wasting even one syllable.

Robert did not understand what the man was talking about, so he said nothing. He felt uncomfortable and glanced nervously across at his mother, who gave him a reassuring smile. John had his back to the stranger's table and had not seen that his son had been accosted.

"Well boy, have you lost your tongue?"

"N. . .No sir," Robert stammered, wishing the man would release him.

"I fear even poor Sir Edward cannot escape the fate of having his music placed in the clumsy hands of a boy."

Robert, still not sure how to reply, just blurted out, "I'm sorry sir. I know I'm not very good."

"I'm not asking for your opinion. The quality of your performance will be decided by those who understand the art, not by you or these idiotic tea takers, who have obviously been carried away more by the undoubted attraction of your face rather than by any musical ability you may possess."

Robert was hoping the man had now finished with him, but the grip on his arm did not lessen, and after a short pause the fierce face continued. "However." he said, peering even closer into Robert's face. "I have detected something about your playing worth noting." Again he paused as if he was considering carefully the words to use. "A certain deep sensitivity, unusual for one so young. That is a rare gift for which all the technical perfection in the world cannot compensate."

Elizabeth listened intently to what the stranger was saying, and John had turned in his chair to see what was going on behind him. Robert's arm was released and he moved the two steps to his father's side and felt secure.

The man also turned in his chair. He eyed John and Elizabeth, and then said "Be careful with this child. I find within him a certain quality, imperceptible to all but those who have a highly trained musical sensibility. He will experience the frustration of one who cannot find himself until he can express in music what lies deep within him. Mere technical perfection will never satisfy him. But perhaps, if he tastes the passion of love and his heart is broken, then he may find what he searches for, and even achieve fame. On the other hand, this inward quality may escape from his grasp, or, in the turmoil of life, the fragile brilliance may be shattered like glass, and he will then suffer the emptiness of the unfulfilled."

The stranger spoke with the dispassionate assurance of one who brooked no argument or discussion. Having made his statement he turned in his chair, and the family were left only with a view of his back. He had given them the benefit of his knowledge, and there was an end of the matter. Shortly afterwards he got up and left the saloon followed by his young companion.

"What a strange man," Elizabeth said when he had gone.

John was not impressed. "Conceited ass, more like. Talking all that bilge. Hadn't even the courtesy to introduce himself. Damn, cheek!"

"I must admit he was not the most likeable of men, but he did seem to know what he was talking about," Elizabeth replied.

"Nonsense! Robert's playing is good for someone of his age, I grant you. But it's nothing special. I've heard a number of children who can play just as well, if not better."

John found it difficult to praise his son's musical talent. He had no real objection to the boy playing an Instrument, providing it remained just a hobby and went no further than that. But he would have preferred him to follow, what he considered, more manly pursuits such as riding. It had pleased him that Joanna had ridden since she was four, but it had been a great disappointment to him that when he had sat Robert on a horse for the first time the boy had cried until he was lifted down, and had never been persuaded to get near a horse again.

Elizabeth could not let the matter rest, because she felt that one day Robert might wish to dedicate his life to music. She sensed it as that strange man had done.

"I think you missed the point, John. He didn't praise Robert for his playing, which I think was a little unkind, because he did play nicely. He said that Robert has a special gift, which could lead to great things."

"Great things, be damned! I want no son of mine becoming a long haired fiddler. Who was th' fellow, anyway?"

"I have no idea."

Elizabeth said no more, but it did cross her mind that sometime in the future John could have to face the fact that Robert may wish to tread a path of which he did not approve.

Five days later the family sat at breakfast as the ship moved slowly up the Thames towards the London docks. The previous evening Robert had seen the Kent coast come into sight, and had marvelled at the greenness of the countryside, a sight that had been erased from his young mind by three scorching summers on the Indian subcontinent.

John was deep in thought as he sipped his coffee, turning over in his mind the news he had heard from the chief officer that morning.

"Stop kicking me!" Joanna exclaimed, glaring at her brother, who was swinging his legs to and fro under the table. Robert had finished his breakfast and was impatiently waiting to get down from the table so that he could go on deck and see the sights of the river.

"I'm not kicking."

"You are, you rotten little fibber!"

John looked at his son and Robert immediately sat up and stopped fidgeting.

"Please may I leave the table?" Robert asked.

"No, you sit still for five minutes," John ordered. Then, turning to Elizabeth, he said, "I was told this morning that the TUC has called for a general strike. Some papers say that nearly five million stopped work yesterday, but I can't believe it was that many."

"Will it affect our docking?" Elizabeth asked.

"I don't think so, because the navy have been brought in," John replied. "It's such a shame when ordinary decent working men get led into this sort of thing. They suffer hardship and eventually return to work, and haven't gained a thing."

"What's a strike, Daddy?" Joanna asked.

Robert was pleased that his sister had asked, remembering what had happened when he had asked his governess a similar question. After hearing his father's explanation, he was even more pleased he had remained silent. He didn't want Daddy to think he was stupid.

Anyway, why don't people say what they mean? How was he to know it meant stopping work? He wished he could go on strike instead of doing horrible arithmetic and tables.

"What's it all about, John?" Elizabeth enquired.

"It's the miners," John explained. "The industry's in a bad way at the moment. They've been told to take a cut in wages and to work longer hours. They've refused, and have been locked out by the owners. Now the TUC had called out everyone else in support."

"Is five minutes up yet, Daddy?" Robert asked, eager to get away from boring talk about strikes.

"Come on," said John. "We'll all go on deck and watch the docking. See if you can recognise your Uncle Reggie and Aunty Daisy."

When on deck John pointed out a submarine to the children, and explained it was there to generate electricity because of the strike.

"Look Daddy, is that Uncle Reggie over there?" Joanna cried out in excitement.

"You're right."

"I saw him first! I won," Joanna shouted triumphantly.

"It's not fair. I can't remember him, so it doesn't count," Robert shouted back, pouting at his sister. "Why does Uncle Reggie wear his cap round the wrong way?" he asked.

"It's so the peak doesn't get in the way of his goggles when he's driving," John answered. "Hope he hasn't brought that open sports car of his. Noisy, draughty thing!"

"Look! There's your Aunty Daisy, "said Elizabeth, pointing, and then waving as she caught Daisy's eye.

Joanna burst out laughing and said, "What a big hat, and just look at that enormous handbag."

"I thought it was a suitcase," Robert laughed.

John chuckled at his son's humour, and Elizabeth, trying to keep a straight face said, "Now children it's rude to make personal remarks about other people. Your Aunty just happens to like large hats and large handbags."

"Golly! I should think she does," Joanna added.

The ship inched its way towards the quay. The heaving lines went over and the mooring ropes were pulled across and fastened to the massive iron bollards. Eventually the large rope fenders were crushed against the quayside as the ship came to rest. The long voyage home was over.

The starboard deck was crowded with passengers waiting to disembark, and the dockside was equally crowded with people waiting to greet, them. John led his family through the crush and down the gangway, and then struggled towards Reggie, who was waving his cap round and round in the air.

"All the fun of the fair, you chaps!" Reggie called out. He came forward and violently shook John by the hand, kissed Elizabeth and Joanna, and then lifted Robert completely off his feet and hugged him. Then, putting Robert down, he greeted them all over again.

Daisy was in tears as she kissed everyone. She had found it necessary to push her large hat to the back of her head to ensure that the brim didn't hit the faces of those she kissed. Joanna asked why she was crying.

"I can't 'elp it dear. I always cry when I'm 'appy."

Daisy took out her powder compact and dabbed her cheeks to cover the streaks the tears had made.

"You do speak funnily, Aunty," Joanna said innocently

"Joanna!" Elizabeth exclaimed, looking embarrassed.

"I know, dear. I didn't get taught proper when I was a nipper. My Reggie says you can't 'elp the way you speak, dear."

"You're awfully nice, Aunty. I don't mind a bit," Joanna replied.

"Thank you, dear. That's made my day."

Daisy then affected a high class accent and made the children laugh. "Hi can speak proper posh when hi wish, and never drop mai haiches." She gave a loud screeching laugh, which was so infectious that even the adults had to join in.

"Come an old girl, stop your play acting and let's get moving," said Reggie.

Followed by Agnes, and two of the ships stewards carrying the hand luggage, the party moved off towards the customs shed. Robert, who was usually shy and reserved with strangers, endeared himself to his godfather by spontaneously taking his hand as they walked along.

Formalities completed and the luggage loaded, they all clambered into Reggie's brand new, gleaming black Rolls Royce. John sat in the front with Robert on his knee. All the women sat in luxury in the back.

Picketing the dock gates were a number of tough looking dockers, who exchanged a few good humoured gibes with Reggie as he drove slowly past. Driving a few yards down the street, Reggie stopped outside a drab looking public house. He got out of the car and disappeared inside.

"Now what's he up to?" Daisy asked.

A few minutes later, Reggie emerged carrying a large tray on which were six pint glasses of beer, two loaves and some cheese. A number of people had come to the door of the bar to see what this man with the cheeky face was up to, only to see him walk back down the road to the dockers, and serve each man with a pint.

Robert, who was by this time leaning out of the window watching the proceedings, called back to the others, "Uncle's made them all laugh."

"He makes everybody laugh, dear. I always tell ' im he should have been on the 'alls," Daisy replied.

John thought how true that was, and remembered Reggie in the war. Even in the most depressing and dangerous circumstances Reggie's carefree spirit had never been suppressed - he was a truly happy soul.

Reggie got back in, and waving his cap out of the window to the bewildered group at the pub door, and receiving a cheer from the dockers up the road, he drove on.

It was a depressing dockland area of back streets through which they had to drive before reaching Commercial Road, but Reggie seemed to know the way. In any case if he didn't, Daisy certainly did. As they swung into one street they were suddenly confronted by a large crowd, which had spread right across the roadway, and Reggie had to brake heavily to avoid running into them. Before he could back up, the car was surrounded and angry faces began to appear staring in at the windows. Robert felt his father's arms tense and hold him tighter.

Although most of the crowd looked as if they were ordinary working men, it could be seen that there was a hostile element among them. On the pavement in front of the crowd, were two men holding poles, between which was stretched a red banner. At each end of the banner was a hammer and sickle, and scrawled across the centre in white were the words *Workers Unite.* Standing on an upturned box under the banner a youngish, unshaven, pasty faced man with longhair was waving a clenched fist in the air, and haranguing the crowd. Round him were a number of other men of similar appearance, seemingly of some political group, because they were certainly not working men.

At the doorways of almost all the houses in the street women had appeared to watch the proceedings.

The speaker appeared to be having some success, judging by the cheers and shouts of agreement coining from the crowd. But a number of women, standing sullenly together outside one of the houses behind the speaker, did not seem impressed.

"I say you fellows has the revolution started?" Reggie called out.

One man of the political group, incensed by Reggie's light hearted attitude, rush over and pulled open the driver's door. He screamed at the crowd, "Brothers! Look what we have here! Capitalist scum grown fat on your labours."

John was sitting calmly assessing the scene. He decided to do nothing unless the situation turned violent with a likelihood of danger to the women and children. His exceptional strength had saved his life many times in the war during the ghastly hand to Hand fighting, the memory of which he desperately tried to forget. But this was not war. However, war or not, no one was going to lay a finger on his family while he was there to prevent it. It would be difficult to handle an angry mob all on his own, and if he did severely injure or perhaps even kill one of these men it would only make matters worse. Would he get any support in a court of law, he asked himself? In any case he didn't wish to hurt them; after all, they were only ordinary people, however misled. But if they attacked the women and children he would have to do something. As these thoughts passed, through his mind, the back door opened and Daisy leapt out.

"Push off you little bleeder," she shouted at the trouble maker.

Daisy gave the man a hefty push in the chest, which sent him reeling back into the crowd with a look of astonishment on his face. The last thing he had expected was for a woman with a strong dock-land accent, and no lady at that, to emerge from a car of this sort.

"Comrades!" screamed the man on the soap box pointing at the car. "These are the bloated, capitalists who keep you trodden down, thieving all the good things for themselves while you go hungry."

By this time Daisy had pushed herself to the front of the crowd, and was standing in front of the speaker, "Don't you talk to me about bleedin' 'unger, you poxy faced little runt," she yelled.

With a wild swing of her handbag she crashed it into his tes-ticles. He doubled up in pain, missed his footing, and fell from the box. Seeing his leader falling, one of the men holding the banner let go of his pole in an effort to prevent this from happening. But he only made matters worse, because the banner sank, and the speaker fell on to it as he toppled to the pavement, pulling the other pole down as well. Speaker and banner ended up in an entwined heap in the gutter with the two poles resting on top. A roar of laughter went up from the crowd followed by a cheer when they saw Daisy clamber on to the box and stand there defiantly with her hands on her hips.

"The sparks are going to fly now," said Reggie.

"Do you think we ought to give Daisy a hand?" John asked,

"No old boy, best we stay here. Leave it to her." Some of the ex-speaker's henchmen rushed to his assistance, and started to shout at Daisy, but she shouted at the audience over their heads.

"'ere you lot!" Daisy shouted at the crowd. "You want your bleedin' brains tested listening to these stupid bastards. Look at 'em!" she shrieked, pointing at the group in front of her, some of whom had by now helped their leader to his feet. "They've still got the nappy rash on their bums."

More laughter came from the' crowd as they warmed to this woman, who spoke their language.

Reggie wound up the window now that Daisy was getting into her stride, in an effort to prevent her speech being heard inside the car. He knew that in the excitement of the moment her language would not be suitable for the children. But children have sharp ears.

By this time, Daisy had the crowd well on her side. "I was born 'ere, and proud of it. And I don't want any bleedin' pimply faced little twerp telling me what it's like to be poor and 'ungry."

The ex-speaker tried to reassert his control over the crowd. He shouted up at Daisy. "Get down you bloody cow." He turned to the crowd, "Don't listen to her, brothers," he screamed, but at that moment he crashed to the ground again, only this time his nose was streaming with blood.

"Don't you talk to 'er like that, you bastard." A big man in the front of the crowd had planted his fist squarely in the agitator's face.

None of the other agitators put up any resistance, sensing the crowd had turned against them.

"I remember you, duck," the big man shouted to Daisy. "Daisy Day ain't yer. Use to be on the 'alls."

"That's right, luv."

"You done all right for yourself, girl. Good luck to yer."

He helped Daisy down from the box. "Come on lads mind yer backs, let the lady through," he called.

The agitators had been jostled back up against the houses, and the crowd made way for Daisy as she walked back to the car.

When she was in, and the crowd had cleared to the side of the street, Reggie slowly drove on.

"You showed 'em, old girl," Reggie said, while Daisy sat in the back straightening her hat.

"I wish we'd had you on the Somme, Daisy. The Bosch wouldn't have lasted five minutes," John drawled.

"Aunty, why did you call that man a bleeder?" asked Joanna. "He wasn't bleeding was he?"

"No dear, but he would 'ave been if he 'adn't got out the way." Daisy gave one of her high pitched laughs.

"What's a bastard, Aunty?" Robert asked, not to be outdone.

"Never you mind, dear."

Elizabeth wondered what question might come next, and thought it best to intervene. "That's enough questions, children. Let's talk about something else."

As they passed through central London, there were many signs of the unusual conditions. They saw that the buses were manned by people who were obviously not the usual crews - some of them looked like students. The police were in evidence everywhere, and in one place a detachment, of eight mounted specials rode past, all in civilian clothing, with riding boots and breeches, and each man wearing a sola-topi and carrying a stout stick over his right shoulder. On their left arms they wore the blue and white armlet of the police to show they were officially on duty.

"Looks like a polo club," Reggie remarked.

A convoy of food lorries went by guarded by armed soldiers wearing steel helmets.

Reggie gave the children a running commentary on all the sights of the town, Robert was listening intently, and thought that home seemed a very exciting place. Then the car stopped for a traffic policeman's signal, and Robert noticed a man being pushed in a wheel chair waiting to cross the road. The man had no legs and only one arm. A dreadful scar ran diagonally across his face from his forehead to his chin, and there was no nose. His head was lolling to one side, and a vacant look covered that part of the face still capable of showing expression. The sight horrified the boy, but he was unable to take his eyes from it, and from a quiet comment made by his uncle he understood that the injuries would have been caused in the war.

Until that moment Robert's tender mind had not taken in the reality of war. As with most boys, he had imagined it as a glorious adventure with soldiers like his father and uncle returning as heroes. Could this have happened to *his* father, he asked himself?

As the car drew away, he turned and watched the man until out of sight. His imagination ran wild, and he tortured himself with thoughts of his own arms and legs being blown off and his face cut in half. He squeezed his eyes tight shut in an effort to rid his mind of the picture. It was a mistake, because travelling with his eyes shut made him feel sick.

Robert had rarely ridden in a car, and when he had the journeys had only been short. This was the first long ride he had experienced, and he had enjoyed it up until this moment. But now this nasty queasy feeling would not go away. If only he hadn't shut his eyes. He'd been all right before that. And he'd been all right on the boat when everyone else had felt ill. For some time he managed not to say anything but just sat quietly on his father's knee hoping he wouldn't suddenly get sick all over the car. Eventually, just after they had passed under the railway bridge at Coulsdon, he whispered to .John, "I feel sick, Daddy."

Reggie stopped the car immediately. "Sit tight everyone," he said, getting out and going round to the passenger door. "I'll see to him."

"Reggie's like a dog with two tails now he's got Robert to fuss over," Daisy remarked.

Robert was taken on to the grass verge and bent over, Reggie holding the boy's forehead while he vomited. After a short time he felt better, and the two walked a little way along the grass to give Robert some exercise in the fresh air.

"What's this round your neck, old boy?" Reggie asked. He had seen part of a gold chain protruding from under Robert's shirt and it appeared familiar.

"It's what you gave me, Uncle, when I was born." Robert pulled out the gold medallion," and proudly showed it to Reggie.

"I hope you like it, old son."

"Oh, I do. And I know all about it." It was on his fifth birthday that he had been first shown the medallion, and he remembered his father explaining its history to him. "I wasn't allowed to have it for a long time, but now I'm older and more re. . . responsible, Daddy says I can wear it sometimes if I really take care of it. But I shan't be allowed to wear it to school."

Reggie smiled to himself at the old fashioned way the boy talked. It pleased him that his godson's reserve had thawed, and as they walked back to the car hand in hand with Robert now chatting quite freely, it occurred to Reggie how much he had missed by not having a son.

"Are you looking forward to going to school?"

"I don't know. I've never been to school. I always did lessons at home." In his heart Robert was not looking forward to the coming experience at all. He had seen the masters at La Martiniere Boys College, and had thought they looked rather fierce in their black gowns and their funny looking mortar-board caps. In his mind he had built up a picture of what school was going to be like, and it was not something he liked to dwell upon.

The rest of the journey was uneventful, but they did stop on Handcross Hill to let Robert have another short walk. It was there that he caught a glimpse of the top of some hills standing out boldly in the distance.

"South Downs," Reggie remarked, seeing the boy's interest. "That's where you're going to live."

Robert stared at the softly rolling contours along the skyline. These hills would be his friends, and they would allow him to enter their enchanted land without harm, he imagined. Others would have to beware, but not him, for they were his hills and he would live there protected by their magic. All his enemies - especially that governess - would just disappear the moment they set foot there. The road eventually became enveloped by the Downs as it climbed the hill to Pyecombe, and for the rest of the way the hills sloped gently up on either side. After the village of Patcham they wound their way into an attractive valley much covered in trees, and it was here that a number of large Victorian houses stood, set well back from the road in their own spacious grounds. Reggie explained that a small stream ran along the bottom of the valley under the road and went down to the sea at Brighton. This stream had been enclosed over a hundred and thirty years before and the road built over it, but in times of exceptionally heavy rainfall the water would still bubble up and flood the road.

"Here we are!" said Reggie as he turned the car into an entrance on the left hand side of the road.

They passed a small lodge house, and then drove on up the curving driveway past, trees and shrubs purposely planted to hide the house from the road.

"Golly! Is that all ours?" Joanna cried when the house came into view.

Elizabeth found the building pleasing to her artistic eye. It was a very large red brick house, typically Victorian, and perhaps a little fussy in its design. But nevertheless, a homely looking place, and it did have character. A place to bring up her children where they would be happy. "It's lovely," she said.

Behind, the house and beyond the large main lawn, the grounds very gradually sloped up the hill. They were a children's paradise, with extensive lawns for games, and many paths through the shrubs and trees for hide and seek.

John felt satisfied now that he knew his family were happy with his choice. When he had first seen the place all those years ago, he had imagined himself living there with loved ones about him, and his pleasurable daydream had now come to reality. He noticed that the garden was reasonably tidy, thanks to Reggie, who had arranged for the gardening staff to remain on after the previous owner had left. In fact Reggie had done a first class job in arranging everything. All that remained to do was to furnish the place and employ some household staff. That would be done while they stayed with Reggie during the next few weeks.

Before they drove on to Reggie's home next door, the children were allowed to explore the garden for a few minutes. Reggie took them along one particular path in the shrubbery. "This is the secret way," he said in a tone of mystery. He had the knack of turning everything into an adventure for the children, and they followed him wide eyed with excitement as he led them behind some bushes to an old door in the wall. Ivy covered the wall, and the doorway was partially overgrown. It was clear that the door had not been used for years. "Now listen, you chaps." Reggie spoke softly as if he was about to relate some dark secret. "This is the secret door, and only you and I know about it."

"Where does it lead to, Uncle?" Joanna whispered.

"Into my garden."

With a little effort Reggie pushed the door just far enough open for one person to squeeze through. The children took it in turns to look through the gap, where they saw another path leading through more bushes on the other side.

"Now, whenever you children want to come and visit your old Uncle Reggie, you just come through here."

When they returned to the car, Robert said, "We know a secret."

"What's that?" John asked.

"Oh, Daddy, you know we can't tell you or it won't be a secret anymore," Joanna replied in a tone indicating that grown-ups were sometimes rather stupid. Then she snapped at Robert, "What did you want to say that for?"

Robert wished he had said nothing and thought it best not to argue.

Reggie drove the short distance along the road and turned into his own drive. The grounds were about the same acreage as John's, the house also being large and Victorian, but of a very different design.

From the first, Robert felt at home in his uncle's house. He sensed that there were no restrictions here, and he didn't have to be on his best behaviour all the time as in some other houses he had visited. He knew it was going to be a happy time. Then there was the visit to Holland, to look forward to in June when he would see Karl Heinz again. The only cloud on his horizon was school, but that was too far off to worry about at the moment. Her children's schooling had been on Elizabeth's mind for some time. The subject had caused her a great deal of heart searching, and the conclusions she had reached had made her realise that she would now have to speak to John about the matter at the earliest opportunity.

In John's mind there were no such difficulties. The matter was quite clear. Robert would go to Clifton as he himself had done, and Joanna would attend Elizabeth's old school at Roedean. John had never considered the matter in doubt, the children's names having been put down at these schools some years before. It was, therefore, with some surprise that he heard Elizabeth broach the subject that evening when they had retired to their room.

Elizabeth was sitting at her dressing table combing her hair in. front of the mirror. "John," she said, trying to sound unconcerned.

"What is it, Beth?"

"About the children's schooling,"

"Don't worry, darling, it's all arranged."

"That's just it." She could see his reflection in the mirror, and noticed a puzzled look come over his face.

John had just got into bed and was sitting there with a book in his hand. He had intended to read for a short time before settling down, but his wife's last remark made him put the book down and give her all his attention. "What do you mean, that's just it?"

Elizabeth hesitated and then came straight to the point. "John, dear, I don't wish the children to go to boarding schools," she said. Then seeing John was about to say something, she quickly continued. "Please hear me out. We were forced apart during the war, and I never wish to go through that experience again, either with you or the children. Now that we have two lovely children I will not be constantly parted from them at the end of every school holiday. Nor will I let anyone else have a share in their upbringing. They are our children, and we must bring them up." As all her pent up thoughts came out the apprehension she had felt about mentioning the subject disappeared, and she spoke with a passionate sincerity.

"I never knew you felt like this."

"I know I should have mentioned it earlier. I realise that it will be a great disappointment for you, but I must ask this of you, John. If you never agree to anything else, I must ask you to agree to this."

John, was silent for a moment. He had to admit to himself that some of his reasons for wishing Robert to attend a public school were selfish. It gave him great pleasure to think that his son would follow him at his old school, and then, of course, into the army. The boy was certainly physically strong enough to cope with these tough institutions, but sometimes he had wondered whether he was the right material for the army. But, then again, that was a stupid thought, for the boy was too young as yet for anyone to judge. He remembered that his great friend Robert had a sensitive nature, but he had made a splendid soldier. As for Joanna, his feelings about her schooling were not so strong, but this was only because she was a girl, not because he loved her any the less. As long as she got a good education he would be satisfied. He had to admit to himself that he did enjoy having the children about the house, even though they were sometimes a damn nuisance. His one regret was that he couldn't give them more of his time. Perhaps Beth was right. She usually was about this sort of thing. In any case, how could he refuse her anything, for no sacrifice on his part could repay her for the undreamed of happiness she had given him.

"You do realise, darling, that the best education a boy can get is at a public school? It gives him such a good start in life."

"I'm sure you're right, John. But the best upbringing a child can get is with its parents as a member of a loving family. I can never forget how I used to feel at the end of the holidays, when I had to tear myself away from a happy home and return to school. I don't want my children to suffer that." Elizabeth had hated those moments, and had often wondered how she would have coped if Natascha hadn't been with her.

"It's different for a girl, I'll admit."

"Boys have feelings as well, you know."

"Maybe, but Robert has got to learn to stand on his own feet. It'll do him good to be a boarder."

"I think it would be more likely to do him harm. He's the sort of boy who needs a home environment. I know you don't agree, but I ask you to do this for me."

"You know full well I can never refuse you anything. Tell me what you want for the children and I'll see to it. Arrangements will have to be made quickly." He sighed, and then smiled at her.

She came across the room and sat on the bed beside him, taking his hand. How she loved this giant of a man, so strong, and yet with an unfathomable streak of tenderness running through him.

"Robert can go to the local grammar school in Brighton, and there's a new municipal girls school, it's only up the hill from our garden."

"How do you know all this?"

"I asked Reggie. He says they are both excellent schools."

"And what sort of girls will Joanna mix with at a municipal school? Surely we can do better than that. There must be other places."

"Joanna has a strong character and she'll cope. Let's just go and look before we decide."

"And what if these schools can't take them?"

"Oh, but they can. You see I wrote to Reggie some time ago and asked him to put their names down just in case we changed our minds about where to send them."

Elizabeth squeezed his hand and smiled at him, amused at his incredulous expression.

"Did you, by God!"

"In any case, Reggie is a governor at the grammar school."

"Well, I'm blest! You had it all worked out. I remember your father once saying, that he sometimes wondered who was the head of his family. Now I understand what he meant." John slipped down under the sheets, hoping all would turn out for the best. Only time would tell, he thought.

And so their new life in England began.

CHAPTER 4

Agnes entered the darkened room without making any special effort to keep quiet. She pulled back the heavy drape curtains, and the bright, early morning, spring sunlight burst into the room. Robert pulled the bedclothes up over his head. "Oh, no! Not that time already," he groaned.

"So you're awake, are you? Well I must say that makes a change," said Agnes. He was usually sound asleep when she entered.

"I've hardly slept a wink." Robert turned over on to his back, and pulled himself up a little so that his head rested on the head-board, then he lowered the sheet so that his eyes were just showing. But finding the glare of the sun too much, he tugged it over his face again. It was going to be a rotten day, he thought.

"Oh dear, we do sound grumpy this morning," said Agnes as she fussed about the room.

"Do I have to get up? Couldn't I be ill or something? " he whined.

"Come along, get up, your bath is ready. . . ill indeed! Whatever next?"

Robert was lucky because, unlike the rest of the family, his room had its own adjoining bathroom. It was a spacious room in the wing which extended out at the back of the house, A large bay window overlooked the back lawn, and a smaller side window faced south, from which could be seen the back of the house and the rest of the garden. Reggie's house could also be seen through the trees. Two single beds side by side and pushed close together stood near the side window. Robert always slept in the one nearest the window, the other one being used when any of his friends came to stay. Karl Heinz always slept there on his visits.

Against the wall opposite the bottom of the beds stood a book-case with lines of brightly covered boys' manuals and some beauti-fully bound novels along its shelves. Next to it was his desk on top of which was the small black box containing his treasured medallion. He loved his room, it was his little world to do with as he wished, and nobody entered without his permission - except Agnes, of course, but then she kept it tidy for him.

Usually he was happy to get up early at this time of the year. But not this morning. He didn't even feel like gazing out of the win-dow across the dew soaked lawn to the trees beyond; something he always did when he first got up. He pushed back the covers and slowly swung his legs over the side of the bed, and for a moment sat there holding his head in his hands. If only it was tomorrow, he said to himself. He took off his pyjamas top, and went to the end of the bed, where he pulled the cord of his trousers and let them fall to the floor. He didn't mind Agnes seeing him with nothing on — she was different somehow – but lately he had experienced a little embarrass-ment when his mother had entered the bathroom and seen him in this state. It had all stemmed from a night about three weeks before, when he had been lying in bed just before settling down to sleep. He had been experiencing this pleasurable feeling for some weeks, and as usual he had put his hand through the slit in the front of his pyjamas trousers to hold himself in a place where he knew he shouldn't. With his hand there he could make the feeling even better. It was then he had discovered that the skin in the surrounding area was no longer completely smooth. Thinking he must have caught some disease, panic had struck him, and he had leapt out of bed to examine him-self in the mirror. He had discovered a faint growth of hair. Why was hair growing there, he had asked himself? For one terrible moment he wondered whether his whole body was going to be covered, and had looked hard at other places and felt himself all over, but to his relief he had found no further growth. God must be punishing him for doing dirty things to himself, and for thinking dirty thoughts, Getting back into bed, he had prayed hard, promising to be good in the hope that he would be cured by the morning. But he wasn't, and he went to school that day a worried boy. However, later in the showers a sense of relief had come over him when he had noticed that some of the other boys had a faint growth in the same place as himself. Perhaps it wasn't a punishment after all, because surely the others couldn't have dirty thoughts like he did.

"Now you just pick up those pyjamas. I've got better things to do than tidy up after you, my lad," Agnes ordered. Much to the amazement of the other servants, she exercised a firm control over the two children. Master Robert, of course, was easier to deal with than the high spirited Miss Joanna, but even Robert could be a perfect pest at times.

She watched him pick them up and place them on the bed. She was so proud of him, and never ceased to talk about him to the other servants. He was her boy, and so good looking, and tall for his age as well, she would tell them. She enjoyed seeing him naked, not just because of his nicely proportioned body and lightly tanned skin, and certainly not for any improper reason, but because his innocent love for her allowed it, giving her a privileged position in his life. She had noticed the signs of puberty on him, also the damp patch on the front of his pyjamas trousers, which she had invariably found in the mornings over the past few weeks. She wondered whether it was worry over this that had made him seem a little depressed that morning. Boys did worry over these things, especially when they didn't know what was happening to them. She remembered her own brothers.

Robert was usually reasonably bright when he woke up, often hurling a pillow at her when her back was turned.

"Cheer up," she said, giving him a gentle slap across the bottom as he walked past her to the bathroom. "I've laid out your clean underwear on the chair."

Stopping at the bathroom door, he turned and looked at her sheepishly. "Agnes." He tried to sound casual, but she knew him too well to be taken in. "Could I have two pairs of pants this morning?"

"Certainly not! I've never heard of such a thing! Just you get into that bath before I put a slipper across your bottom."

Robert didn't wait to argue. He had only been in the bath a short time when Agnes came in and looked hard at him. It had just struck her that there was something else worrying him other than what she had previously thought, and now she had guessed what it was.

" What are you staring at?" he asked.

"I know what's the matter with you, young man. You're in trouble. What have you been up to?"

"Nothing," he said, innocently. But his eyes could not meet hers as he spoke.

"None of your fibs now! You're expecting a whacking, aren't you?"

It was no use trying to keep things from Agnes, and gradually it all spilled out. He and his best friend at school had been caught smoking and were due to see the headmaster that morning.

He sat in the bath holding his tummy as Agnes applied the soap to his back. As was usual, when the truth came out he poured out his heart as well. He was so nervous, he told her, that he felt like running away and hiding. How was he going to get through it?

"Oh, Agnes, I feel sick. Why am I such a coward?"

"Don't talk such nonsense!"

"But I am. Daddy thinks so. I know he does."

"He thinks nothing of the sort! Where do you get these ideas?"

"It's true! Because I won't ride he thinks I'm soft. I can't help it, I hate horses."

"Now you're being silly. Lots of people don't like riding."

"Please Agnes, let me have two pairs of pants?" he pleaded again.

"No," she replied firmly. "You've been a very naughty boy, and you'll take your punishment like a man."

"It's not fair," he grumbled. The beastly things made me feel sick anyway. And now I'm going to be punished again."

Robert remembered choking and coughing as he had inhaled the smoke, and then the feeling of nausea as it had settled into his stomach. Also the smoke had got into his eyes making them water so much that he'd had to use his handkerchief to dry the tears. It was when he removed the handkerchief that the master was seen standing there watching, and his smoking adventure had ended as quickly as it had begun.

"It serves you right! Ruining your health with those filthy things...Now hurry up or you'll be late for breakfast."

But he didn't feel like breakfast.

Robert got out of the bath and with Agnes's help was quickly dried. Back in the bedroom he tried to sneak another pair of pants out of the drawer, but Agnes was too sharp for him and slapped his hand, making him put them back. He dressed in his grey flannels and grey shirt, and put on his red and green school tie.

"You'd better look smart this morning for the headmaster," she said, straightening his tie.

"A fat lot of good that'll do. He'll only see the seat of my pants," Robert replied sulkily.

He put on his green blazer and went down to breakfast.

The breakfast room was not large; its bay window looking out to the front of the house. The furnishings Elizabeth had chosen, which included a round breakfast table, had succeeded, in giving it a cosy atmosphere. She had always insisted that breakfast be completely relaxed and informal, so that John could read his newspaper and the children their school books if necessary. She rarely read at the table herself, remaining available for conversation or content just to sit and watch the faces of her loved ones.

Maud was at breakfast with them - she had arrived the previous day to stay the week-end. John sat opening his morning post.

It was the King's birthday, and he was to drive to Epsom for the Oaks and a celebration luncheon. As ADC General, John was to have attended the Royal party, but he had not been well for the past few days, and the King had commanded that, he stay at home and rest until he felt better. He had awoken that morning feeling almost back to normal, and was looking forward to a nice relaxing weekend at home.

"You're looking very much better today, schat," Elizabeth remarked. *Schat* (meaning darling) was the only Dutch word that John and Elizabeth used to each other. Elizabeth had tried to teach him the correct Dutch intonation, but John found it impossible, and ended up by pronouncing it in true English fashion as 'scat'.

"Yes, I do feel better. I'm sorry to have missed the Oaks. The Aga Khan's filly, Udaipur, is running."

Gloomily, Robert entered the room. He went to the sideboard to examine the choice which had been laid out for breakfast, but lifting one of the silver platter covers and finding kippers underneath his stomach turned over and he quickly replaced the lid."

"Aren't we to be greeted this morning?" You might at least say good morning to your Aunty Maud," said Elizabeth.

"Sorry. Good morning. Aunty."

"Good morning, Robert."

At that moment Joanna burst into the room.

"Morning everyone!" she called, going to the sideboard and quickly inspecting each dish in turn. "And what's for breakers this morning?"

God! Robert exclaimed to himself, why does she have to be so jolly breezy? Then he remembered he shouldn't be using God's name like that, because he was trying to keep in with him today in the hope of some help when he saw the headmaster.

Joanna filled a plate so full of porridge and milk that she had to walk carefully to her place for fear of spilling it.

"This will do for starters," she said with relish.

Robert, by this time, had put one piece of toast on a plate. This he moodily dumped on the table where he proceeded to scrape some butter onto it.

"Is that all your having, dear?" Elizabeth enquired,

"I'm not hungry," Robert snapped.

John glared at his son. "Don't talk to your mother like that!"

"What a grump you are this morning. Not your usual piggy self today," Joanna teased, knowing that her brother's appetite normally matched her own.

"I'm not such a pig as you," Robert retorted. "Just look at your plate."

"Robbie's in a bait this morning." Joanna laughed; she knew exactly how to annoy her brother.

In his early years Robert had always been called Robbie, but at the age of ten he had informed the family that he was now grown up, and that he wished to be called by his proper name, Robert. Everyone had complied with his wishes, except Joanna when she was in the mood for teasing him.

"Mummy, tell her not to call me that. She knows I don't like it."

"Now you two, that's enough. What will your Aunty think?" said Elizabeth.

"I bet he's in trouble again," Joanna provoked.

"Shut up, you!" Robert could feel his eyes filling with tears of frustration. He tried to fight them back, hoping that Joanna hadn't noticed or she'd call him a cry baby. Sometimes he felt he could kill that sister of his, especially when she kept baiting him. How did she always manage to guess when he was in trouble?

Elizabeth had noticed the expression on John's face change as he read one of his letters. The nerve under his right eye twitched slightly, which it invariably did when he was upset. "Something wrong?" she asked him.

"Perhaps you'd better read this," said John sharply, handing the letter to Robert.

A quick glance and Robert saw the school address at the top of the page, and his headmaster's thick, heavy signature at the bottom. "Oh, no," he whispered as his heart sank. He felt positively sick as he slowly read of his wickedness and the fate that awaited him. When he had finished he handed it back with shaking hand, unable to meet his father's gaze.

The letter was actually quite mild in content, written out of courtesy to John in order to enlist his help in preventing a reoccurrence of his son's foolish act. It merely informed him that Robert had been caught smoking, and that the matter would be dealt with under school rules. But to Robert's young mind it couldn't have been worse if it had been an indictment for murder.

"Well, what have you got to say for yourself?" John snapped, his thoughts of a pleasant week-end disintegrating. He could feel his temper rising, but knew he must keep it under control especially with Maud present. Why was it, he asked himself, that he could deal with all the problems of life in a calm manner, but when it came to Robert's misdemeanours he felt like boiling over?

Robert began to feel hot, and he knew his face had gone red with embarrassment. "Nothing, sir," he whispered.

"There! I knew it! He is in trouble!" Joanna exclaimed, triumphantly. "What's he done, Daddy? I bet he's in for a good swishing."

"Oh, shut up, you silly sod!" Robert cried.

There was a stunned silence.

Maud nearly choked on a piece of toast she had just put into her mouth. It was with great difficulty that she kept a straight face, for the looks of surprise on the other faces had made her want to burst out laughing. But she was sorry for her nephew, for his face was a picture of shock, bewilderment and apprehension.

Elizabeth didn't know where to look. "Robert!" she blurted out. She saw the boy's lower lip quiver, and noticed the nerve twitch under his right eye in the same manner as his father's. How alike her two men were in so many ways and mannerisms, and yet so different.

Joanna's mouth dropped open in surprise, but on this occasion no words came out. She gave an embarrassed giggle, and felt a little sorry for her brother.

Robert looked in alarm at his father, and wished the floor would open up and swallow him. The word had come out without thinking. He had never used a word like that at home before. "I. . .I'm," he stammered, trying to apologize. But he was cut short.

"How dare you use that disgusting language in my house," John blazed. "And in front of the ladies too," he added. "Leave the table. I'll deal with you later."

Robert got up and almost ran from the room, hoping to reach the door before the tears overflowed down his cheeks.

"That was your fault, Joanna," said Elizabeth, when Robert had gone. "You shouldn't tease him like that."

"That's not fair, Mummy. I didn't make him say that word."

John said. "I'll slaughter that boy! He wants a damned good thrashing, and that's what he'll get. I've heard enough bad language in my time, but I'll not tolerate it in my own home. And as for his other escapade." At that point John ran out of words, and handed the letter to Elizabeth.

"Whatever made him do it?" was all Elizabeth could think to say after reading the letter."

Maud was also allowed to read the letter, and Joanna made sure she knew its contents before leaving the table.

John impatiently picked up his newspapers and shook it open, glancing quickly at some of the article headings:

Charterhouse draw with Winchester; Dulwlch by-election, Conservative majority 17005. He then closed it again and looked over at his sister, "Sorry about that, Maud," he said. "I apologize for my son's behaviour."

"My dear John, there's no need to apologize to me; I am part of the family you know. He wouldn't be a proper boy if he didn't get into trouble sometimes. I find Robert a very attractive and charming boy. You're very lucky to have such a son."

John just grunted and disappeared behind his paper once more, but although he tried to read, thoughts began to revolve in his mind. Trust Maud to say something like that. These damn women always take the boy's side. But still, there was probably something in what she said. How was he going to deal with the boy? The son of the chairman of the governors caught smoking - that would be a good article for the school mag. Was he so angry because of what people might say? No, damn it! Of course he wasn't. Then why was he so angry? After all it was only a boyish prank, and Beth thought he was too hard on the boy sometimes. Perhaps he was, he concluded.

When Robert had first been sent to the school John had wondered whether he was doing the right thing in complying with Elizabeth's wishes. But time had proved Elizabeth right. The headmaster and staff were excellent and the education was good, and John had realised that having the children living at home was what he had really wanted all along.

As the years went on, he had found himself taking an increasing interest in the school activities, and had eventually been asked to serve on the board of governors. Now he was the chairman. His frequent contact with the headmaster made it inevitable that he should know a great deal more about his son's school activities, including his misdeeds, than would have otherwise been the case. Although John tried to make sure that the boy didn't suffer as a result of this knowledge, Robert sometimes felt at a disadvantage.

Agnes found Robert lying on his bed gently weeping, with his face buried in his pillow. She went to the bathroom and fetched his flannel and towel, and then sat down, beside him. "Come along now," she said. "Let's wipe those tears away, or you'll be late for school." She took him by the shoulder and raised him so that he was sitting beside her, and then put her arm round him as he rubbed the flannel over his face.

"Oh, Agnes, I'm so miserable. I've just been terribly rude, and they're all angry with me."

She straightened his tie and ran her fingers through his hair. Then rising, she took his hands pulled him to his feet, and holding him at arms length looked him up and down. "That's better," she said with a nod of approval.

They left the bedroom, and as they reached the landing Joanna came bounding up the stairs. She gave her brother an affectionate slap on the back and said, "Good luck, old bean! Sorry about your troubles."

When they reached the hall Robert took his cap and satchel from the hallstand, but Agnes immediately made him put them down again.

"Now Robert, go and apologize to your parents," she said firmly.

"Please Agnes, I can't. Please don't make me. You know I'm a coward."

"If I ever hear you call yourself that name again I'll put my hair brush across your bare backside," she flared. "You've got a bad habit of calling yourself a coward, and if you don't watch out you'll start to believe it. It's not true, and you're to stop saying it! Do you hear?" She caught him by the ear and pulled him up on to his toes, with his head on one side. Agnes had a habit of doing this when he annoyed her.

Robert screwed up his face. "Yes, mam. "Ouch! I'm sorry, I'm sorry:"

When Agnes was satisfied that her pinch had served its purpose, she released him, and then entered the breakfast room alone, leaving Robert outside rubbing his ear. John was still hidden behind his newspaper, so she gave a little bob to Elizabeth.

"Good morning, Agnes," said Elizabeth, pleasantly, "Good morning, m'lady. Good morning Miss Rutherford."

With much rustling and folding John emerged from behind the collapsing paper. He was very fond of Agnes. He had never forgotten what a great help and comfort she had been to Elizabeth in the war years. He knew the children loved her by the way they frequently spoke about her, often quoting the sensible advice she gave them. According to them, what Agnes said had to be done. "Good morning, Agnes, what can we do for you?"

"Good morning, Sir John. I'm sorry to disturb you, but I've brought Robert to apologize. He asked me to come in first, to see if it's safe." She raised her eyes with a knowing look on her face.

John smiled at her and said, "Oh, so you're the advance guard, Agnes. Well, I suppose he should get full marks for putting out scouts and testing the enemy's position. Send him in."

Robert hesitantly came in, obviously much embarrassed, and stood beside the table. He held his arms at his side, his hands fidgeting with the bottom of his blazer betraying his nervousness.

"And what can we do for you, sir?" John asked abruptly.

"I've come to say sorry, sir."

"Have you, indeed." John fixed the boy with a stern look. "Let's hear you then," he said.

"I'm very sorry for being rude. Please forgive me," Robert said, remembering exactly what Agnes had told him to say.

Elizabeth held out heir hand and, taking him by the arm, pulled him gently towards her. As usual her heart had melted and she couldn't be angry with him for long. He kissed her and then went round the table and kissed his aunty, Maud, who had taken sixpence from her handbag, pushed it into his hand and whispered something to him.

Robert stood at his father's side wondering whether he dare kiss him as well. He would have given anything to have had the courage to throw his arms round his father's neck and kiss him to show him how much he loved him. But he feared to be rebuffed,

Maud's right, John said to himself, looking at the dejected face beside him, he is an attractive boy. He felt a sudden urge to pull Robert into his arms and hug him. Instead, he said firmly, "I shall speak to you later, but don't make any plans for tomorrow" - tomorrow was Saturday – "because after school you will go straight to your room, and that's where you'll stay for the rest of the day. Now off with you."

"Yes, sir." Robert hesitated for a moment, and then, on impulse, quickly kissed his father on the cheek and ran from the room.

John fidgeted on his chair and went back to his paper. Elizabeth excused herself and left the table to be at the front door when the children left for school. Brother and sister were left alone at the table.

"You spoil that boy, Maud. I saw you tip him. He's supposed to be in disgrace. Instead he gets paid for his rudeness."

"I hope you're not going to be too hard on him this evening," Maud countered.

"Am I ever too hard on him?" John mumbled inattentively. He put the paper down on the table with finality. It was no use trying to read a damn thing this morning, he grumbled to himself. He'd wanted a quiet breakfast, and had been looking forward to a pleasant week-end, and now that brat had caused all this upset. He would have to let Maud have her say, or he'd get no peace. Blasted women are all the same, chatter, chatter, chatter. "He only gets what he deserves," he added.

"Just remember he's only a boy," Maud went on. She glanced at her brother with a whimsical look on her face. "I remember another boy once who was caught smoking in the stables on a certain estate in Somerset, and that same boy said a very rude word to his elder sister when she teased him about it."

It amused her to see her brother's blank look. "What the devil are you talking about, Maud?"

"What a short memory you have, my dear," as his sister related the forgotten incident in his own boyhood it all came back to him. The shock of being caught, and the apprehension about what was to happen to him. His father had made him smoke until he was sick, and then reminded him of what would have happened to his beloved horses if he had set the stable on fire. The sobering thought of a stable fire had made such an impression on him that he had not smoked again until the South African war. As for his rudeness, he remembered being stood in front of the family and invited to repeat the offending word. But, in his embarrassment, he couldn't, and he had never used the word again.

"Confound you, Maud, "John drawled with a faint flicker of a smile. "I don't know why I invite you here. How the devil can I act the stern father when you bring up things like this?"

"I only have one other thing to say, my dear, and then I'll let you read your paper." She gave him that charming smile which had always endeared her to him. "When you do consider Robert's punishment this evening, just bear in mind that he worships the very ground you walk on."

John watched her get up and leave the room. "Damn the woman. In fact damn all women," he quietly grunted. She had completely unsettled him, and now he didn't want to read. How was it that women always seemed to get their own way in the end, he asked himself? Still, he wouldn't be without them. But it was Maud's last remark that kept returning to his mind - could it really be true?

He got up and went to the window, and watched the children leaving for school. Joanna turned and gave him a frantic wave, and blew him a kiss. What a whirlwind that girl is, he thought, waving back. Robert, who was following behind his sister, had his head bowed and his hands thrust into his blazer pockets. He didn't turn round.

Each morning Robert would meet his friend at the end of the drive, and then, on fine days, they would walk down through the village and up the hill to school. In bad weather John's chauffeur would take them by car.

Ian came in from the country by bus and got off near the drive entrance. The boys had not immediately taken to each other when they had first met at the school - just the opposite. After two years their dislike for each other had ended in a fight, when Ian had received a black eye and Robert a bloody nose. This incident had been, the cause of their first introduction to the cane at the school, and it was this shared discomfort which had since bound them together in friendship.

After a short discussion on the trials of having fathers, the boys were silent for the rest of the way, thinking more about what was going to happen rather than what had.

Robert tried to think of happy things such as the coming summer holidays when he would once again visit Grave. Karl Heinz would, be there, and this gave him the greatest pleasure. Robert's years away in India had made no difference to his close relationship with his German cousin. When they had met again, this relationship had continued just where it had left off, in fact, as the years passed, they had become still closer, even corresponding with each other, each writing in the other's language.

In assembly that morning, when the whole school gathered in the hall, the headmaster announced that two boys had been caught smoking. Robert's stomach turned over. He felt that everyone was looking at him as indeed many boys were. He tried not to listen, looking at the massive oil paintings round the walls of the hall. These had always impressed him, especially the one showing Henry lll and Simon De Montford after the battle of Lewes. He pondered on what King Henry felt like after his defeat by De Montford. Surely the king couldn't have felt as bad as he did now, he concluded. After a short lecture on the subject, at which time Robert slumped down as far as he could on his chair without falling off in an effort not to be noticed, the headmaster ended by saying that Shaw and Rutherford were to report to his study immediately after assembly.

When the two boys reached the study, there was a small queue waiting outside, so they joined the end. Eventually Shaw went in leaving Robert to wait on his own.

For what seemed an age, there was only silence behind the large, black door. Robert tried again to think of other things. He looked up and down the long corridor, which ran alongside the assembly hall, and remembered his first day at the school. He had been taken into the empty hall with the other new boys, there to wait until the rest of the school assembled. When the rest of the school had begun to pour in he had wondered when they were going to stop coming. When the hall had filled with the 400 boys, the headmaster had entered and mounted the stage. Along with the other new boys, Robert had had to answer his name, and he could remember being quite pleased with himself for speaking up. That was 6 years ago. He no longer sat at the front, for as a boy moved up the school each year so the class position moved towards the back of the hall.

Much to his surprise, he had been happy at the school, at least as happy as was possible considering it was a place of work. Discipline was strict, but fair - he was use to that at home - and punishment was not excessive. The most he'd had were a few detentions and the cane on two occasions. It was this thought that brought his mind back to the closed door in front of him.

The prolonged silence in the study had raised his hopes that perhaps he may not be caned after all. But his optimism was shattered by the sound of a heavy *thwack*. "Oh, no," he said to himself.

He tried desperately to think of something that was even worse than the cane, but all that came to mind was his Aunt Henrietta and that horrible cousin Jason. Robert had first met this side of the family a few months after returning from India, and had taken an immediate dislike to his aunt. He had held out his hand when introduced to her, but she hadn't taken it, merely turning to his father and saying, "So this is your other brat." And another thing, she was rude to Agnes, calling her 'that servant woman'. And as for cousin Jason, he thought, he was an absolute rotter.

Try as he would, his fleeting thoughts could not blot from his mind the sound coming from the other side of the door. He counted four and thought it was finished. But it hadn't, and there were two more loud *thwacks* before the silence. It was to be the full six. He was trembling and could do nothing about it. "Suddenly the door opened, and his friend came out, red faced and watery eyed, and holding his buttocks. He said nothing, but quickly made off down the corridor.

Robert entered the study and shut the door. His headmaster was standing in front of his desk waiting for him. The tall figure with the steely grey hair looked stern, and what was worse he was holding that beastly cane.

"Well, Rutherford?" the head growled.

Robert often mimicked the way the headmaster said the word well, but today it didn't sound so funny.

"You sent for me, sir," he choked.

After a short lecture, Robert, felt that his shame could not have been worse if he had burnt the school down, but he did wish the head would get on with it, instead of making him stand there waiting for the execution.

"I must say, I'm surprised at you, Rutherford. Have you anything to say for yourself?"

"No, sir," he whispered. In his nervousness he could hardy get the words out.

"Well, you've broken school rules. Is there any reason why you shouldn't be punished?"

Robert thought that if he tried hard he would be able to think of a hundred reasons, but all that came out was, "No sir."

"Bend over."

Robert complied and touched his toes. At least in this position the butterflies in his tummy were squeezed tight, and the muscles in his legs were taut, so that it could not be seen that he was shaking. He could feel his trousers tight round his bottom, offering little protection from what was to come. His blazer was tucked up and the stick laid lightly across him, but, just as he steeled himself to receive the first stroke, the door opened and the headmaster's secretary walked in. He could see the lower part, of her between his open legs. Why did the silly fool have to come in now, he asked himself? Everything was against him today, and God was no help. In fact, he seemed to be making things worse. Agnes said that God didn't like bad people,

Eventually, the headmaster took up the cane once more, and this time the agony of waiting was over. He heard the swish and then a loud crack as the cane cut into him. For a second he felt nothing, and then he gasped and gripped his ankles hard as the stinging pain stabbed his buttocks. The second stroke brought the tears to his eyes. The cuts were almost unbearable. He bit his lip in an effort to stop himself crying out. He forced himself to count the strokes - three — four. "Ow!" he cried, unable to constrain himself any longer. The fourth stroke must have cut across another, because now it felt as if his backside was on fire. The last two strokes were the worst of all, for they fell on skin already cut and bruised. Five, "Oh, no!" Six, "Ow!" But then it was over. He stood up, his face contorted with pain and the tears running down his cheeks. Dismissed, he fled the study gripping his burning buttocks as hard as he could in a futile effort, to squeeze the pain out.

In the corridor he ran blindly into Carter, the head boy and captain of cricket.

"Just the man I want," said Carter. But Robert was gone. He didn't want Carter to see his tears. Carter was his hero, and wouldn't want anything to do with him if he knew what a cry baby he was. He was always ashamed of his tears.

Robert rushed into the back of the hall, and hid in the narrow passage behind the stage. There he waited, quietly sobbing, feeling weak at the knees as the tension broke. He didn't know what to do with himself to stop the agony, but after a few minutes the pain eased, and the stinging was replaced by a hot, aching throb. Eventually, he gained control of himself, and ambled slowly back to his classroom.

He steeled himself to enter the classroom, thankful it was a French lesson. Being fluent in French, thanks to his mother, Robert found these lessons easy. He got on well with the French master, who always treated him kindly and, on occasions, even asked Robert's advice on matters of pronunciation. Robert thought that Mr Wills spoke French with a terribly English accent, and he once even had the nerve to tell him so. But the master didn't seem a bit put out, and took the criticism in good part.

Robert entered the room and felt all eyes were on him. He was still gripping himself hard, hoping the throbbing would soon stop. But it didn't.

"Ah, the wanderer has returned!" the master exclaimed, beaming at Robert.

"I'm sorry I'm late, sir. I had to see the head."

"So it would appear, Rutherford. I assume that your face is not the only red part of your anatomy at the moment."

Robert blushed and his classmates laughed.

"I would ask you to sit down, but having a certain sympathy for you, I have decided that you may stand out in front of the class and read us this story." Mr Wills handed Robert his own book. "For the benefit of the duffers, you will translate as you go along."

Robert was glad of the chance to take his mind from his discomfort, and was soon engrossed in the work. He loved reading and was secretly proud of his perfect French accent. He thought that Mr Wills had purposely chosen this particular story, because it related to a French boy who was caught smoking, and he had to suffer some barracking from his friends when he read certain passages which closely resembled his own escapade.

The master listened with pleasure, wishing all his pupils were as good. A nice boy, he had decided when Robert had first come up into his class; always polite and well mannered, although often mischievous. Sometimes a little bit of a dreamer in the class, but that didn't matter, because he was so good at the language he could afford the odd lapse of attention. He had heard the boy spoke German and Dutch as well, but he had never enquired further.

Robert had just finished reading when the head boy entered the room.

"I'm sorry to trouble you, sir. But could I see Rutherford for a moment?" Carter asked.

"In the mire again, Rutherford?" one of his friends called.

Robert pulled a face at the boy, at the same time racking his brains to think what else he had done wrong.

Outside the classroom Robert quickly apologised to Carter. "I'm terribly sorry, Carter, I didn't stop when you called me earlier."

"That's all right, young Robert. Don't worry, I understand."

Robert's heart leaped. Fancy being called by his Christian name by the captain of cricket. He never thought that Carter had even noticed him, let alone knew his name.

"Now listen," Carter continued. I don't have to tell you tomorrow is the most important match of the season. We've got to win or we'll lose the championship. Wilson has sprained his wrist, so I want you to play in his place."

Robert's head was spinning. He could hardly believe his ears. Here he was, a young third former, who played for the second eleven, being asked to play in the school first eleven amongst the greats of the fifth and sixth forms.

"Some say you're not old enough, but you're fairly big for your age. Anyway, I've chosen you."

Robert nearly jumped for joy, and then Carter saw his face change as all the youngster's hopes fell apart as quickly as they had been built up.

"I'm sorry, Carter, I can't play," Robert stammered.

"What are you talking about? You must play. You can't let the school down."

"It's not that I don't want to. It's my father. I've got to stay in tomorrow afternoon as a punishment."

"I was relying on you." Carter was obviously disappointed. "You need a good boot up the backside, young Robert."

"Yes, Carter," Robert replied, hoping that the head boy wouldn't take him up on his agreement, for his bottom had taken enough punishment for one day."

"But your old man is a good card. He'd let you off if you asked a favour for the school."

"I daren't ask. He's in such bait."

When Carter went, Robert stood for a moment cursing himself for being so stupid. Whatever made him try those horrible fags? Agnes was right; they were filthy things. But he'd been punished for that. If only Joanna hadn't teased him, he wouldn't have been rude, and then he wouldn't have had to stay in tomorrow. Anyway, she is a silly sod. And a fat lot of use it had been praying to God - he hadn't been, any help at all.

The bell rang for lesson change, and Mr Wills came out of the classroom and disappeared along the corridor. Robert re-entered the classroom, and had to suffer a great deal of good humoured banter from his friends about his recent flogging. His punishment had not disgraced him in their eyes, rather the reverse. He was seen as a modest boy, rather on the quiet side, although, when the occasion demanded, he could be as wild and noisy as the rest. Nobody seemed to mind his quiet reserve, whereas, with some less popular boys it tended to ensure that they were picked on and teased from time to time. Robert was strong enough to ensure that others of his own age did not take advantage of him physically, but he was never aggressive himself.

"What did Carter want?" enquired a fair haired boy called Edwards, who sat in the desk in front of Robert.

Robert's explanation was punctuated by gasps of surprise from his listeners when they learnt of his selection for the school first eleven. And there was disappointment when, he explained that he couldn't play.

"Your old man sounds a bit of a tartar," said Edwards.

"He is sometimes. But he's all right really," Robert replied.

"Don't worry, Ruth old boy, you'll get another chance to play in the first," said another boy.

"Tick!" called the boy keeping watch at the door. For some reason the word *Tick* was used by the boys to herald the approach of a master.

The conversation finished abruptly, and the boys quickly returned to their desks. The next lesson was algebra. Oh lor, what a bore, Robert moaned inwardly. Why did old Cavey always come in with his book open in his hand as if he hadn't a moment to spare? Why can't he be like everyone else and waste a few minutes getting books out and finding the place? He was so disgustingly keen. It was such a soppy subject. How could *a* equal anything except *a*. *A* for apple made sense. That was the first thing he'd learnt from his governess. *B* for boat. *C* for cat. The piece of chalk struck him on the forehead.

"Do you think we might have your annual answer, Rutherford?" Mr Cavey, who spoke with a mild north country accent, was looking at him over the top of his spectacles.

Robert sat up with a start. "Sorry sir! What was the question?"

"I fear it will make little difference what it was, Rutherford. No doubt the answer, or, more correctly, lack of answer, will be the same."

"Yes, sir."

"Yes, sir," sighed the master, mimicking his pupil. "Perhaps another time, Rutherford. Meanwhile try and remain awake, just in case we require your expert advice."

Robert coloured up, and gave an embarrassed smile. He also got a dig in the back from the boy behind. "Wake up, Rutherford," he teased in a whisper.

Mr Cavey, as was his habit when he wished to wake up the class, began to throw out a few lightening questions. "Edwards, if *abc* equals twenty eight, and *a* equals seven. What is *bc*?"

"Brighton Corporation!" Robert whispered to his friend in front, having seen the initials on the deck chairs on the seafront.

Edwards sniggered and lost track of the question.

"What was that remark, Rutherford?" Mr Cavey glared at Robert.

"Nothing, sir."

"Stand up, boy!" The master was becoming irritated. "Now repeat what you said so that we can all enjoy the joke."

Robert stood up, looking sheepish. "Brighton Corporation, sir," he stammered, feeling foolish and wishing he had kept his mouth shut.

The rest of the class burst into laughter, which only helped to further provoke Mr Cavey's anger. "Come out," he said.

Robert dragged himself out from his desk and slowly walked to the front of the room. He received a sharp slap round the head from the waiting master, who then took; him firmly by the collar and stood him facing the wall.

"And you can take a detention," was Mr Cavey's final sentence.

"Oh, no sir! Please! It was only a joke," Robert pleaded. But Mr Cavey did not appreciate jokes which wasted his time, and Robert's pleas fell on deaf ears. He remained facing the wall for the rest of the lesson in fear that the headmaster might walk in and find him in trouble again, in which case he had visions of receiving another dose of the stick. Luckily for Robert his fear did not materialise. However, he was pleased at being able to stand, for the constant throbbing of the weals on his buttocks as he sat on the hard wooded seat at his desk.

Even the dinner hour dragged for Robert that day. Normally it flew by in a whirl of activity, but the mishaps of the morning had gradually lowered his spirits, and by the time the end of morning bell rang he was feeling quite dismal.

He moped down into the lower playground, and stood leaning against one of the cycle shed supports watching some of the others playing stinks. Why the game was called stinks he never really knew, but that was what it had always been called. It had to be played in the lower playground, because it required a high wall with an abutting sloping roof, and it was here that the scout shed supplied a suitable roof, and the back of the armoury, which was actually in the top playground, the wall. A tennis ball was thrown on to the roof to hit the back wall and rebound, and a boy's name called by the thrower. This boy had to catch the ball before it hit the ground. If he didn't, he had to bend down in front of the shed and have the ball thrown at his bottom by the other players.

"Want a game, Rutherford?"

"Not likely!" Robert replied. He was good with a ball, but was not taking any chances. It would be just his luck to drop the wretched thing, and he'd no intention of having anything else hurled at his bottom. He managed to get through the rest of the day without further mishap, and arriving home late that afternoon he found the house quiet on entering the hallway. The only sound was the loud tick of the grandfather clock. He looked in the drawing room, but seeing no one he made his way to the kitchen. Mrs Hicks, the cook, was making cakes when he walked in.

"Where is everybody, Mrs Hicks?"

"Your father's resting, and your mother and aunty are in the garden. And get those dirty fingers out of that bowl," the cook added sharply, as Robert sampled one of her cake mixtures.

Robert usually had a little tea with his mother directly he arrived home from school, but today he had decided to make himself scarce, because he still had the feeling he was in disgrace. He went to his room and got on with his homework, feeling that at least no one could grumble at him on that account. Also, if Daddy didn't see him he might forget to deal with him. Deal was a rotten word. It could mean anything, but with Daddy it usually meant a caning with his pants down. Surely Daddy wouldn't be so jolly rotten as to beat him again today. He wasn't too sure about that. Daddy could be pretty fierce when he was angry.

In his room he could see his mother and aunty having tea at the far end of the lawn. How he wished he could be out there with them on the lovely June afternoon. The weather looked set fine for the match tomorrow. Oh, he wished, if only he could have played.

He had finished his homework when the dinner gong sounded, but he made no attempt to go down. He felt safe in his room. He lay on his bed thinking that here there was no one to beat him, or slap his head, or give him rotten work to do, or detentions. And, no stupid sister to get him into trouble. It was only when Agnes came in and told him he was expected at the table that he made his way downstairs to the dining room. When he entered all the family were seated.

"You're late, young man," said John.

"Sorry, sir. I thought I'd better wait to be invited."

"Well, I suppose that's a reasonable excuse, considering every-thing," John replied, suppressing a smile. "You may sit down."

"How did you get on at school today, Joanna?" Elizabeth enquired.

Joanna was a great success at her school. She loved every moment of it, and that, combined with her strong, vivacious character, made her present position as head girl inevitable. Elizabeth had often seen Natascha in her; they had this same love of life. John's early worries about the class of girl his daughter might have to mix with had been quickly dispelled. Joanna was happy to mix with anybody, but she was the leader, not the led, so it was her influence that was exerted on others, not theirs on her, and of this John approved.

"OK thanks, Mummy." Joanna's reply was short, because she was more interested in how her brother had got on. She always took a cheerful interest in his thrashings, which irritated him no end, especially as she never received any herself.

"And what about you, Robert?" Elizabeth asked with a knowing look.

"Rotten!" Robert replied, looking down, because he felt that everyone would be looking at him, and expecting a full account of his interview with the headmaster.

"Come on, Rob, tell us all about it," Joanna encouraged with relish. "Did you get a really good thrashing?"

"You know jolly well I did."

"Did it hurt?"

"Of course it did, stupid!"

"How many did you get?"

"Six."

"Tuppence to see your stripes," Joanna laughed. Robert felt his face flush, but just managed to stop himself saying something he would regret. "Oh, please tell her to leave me alone." John glanced at his daughter and shook his head. "Sorry, I only asked." Joanna, as usual, wanted the last word, but thought it wiser to drop the subject.

Robert was allowed to eat the rest of his meal in peace, and was pleased to be excluded from any further conversation.

There was one interruption during the meal, when the butler came in and informed John that the headmaster wished to speak to him on the telephone. Although this was not unusual, John being the chairman of governors, Robert was still feeling guilty and wondered what else he could have done wrong. He kept his head bowed, trying not to invite further comment from Joanna.

After a short interval, John returned.

At the end of the meal, Robert asked if he might leave the table,

"Yes, you may," said John. "And you can go and wait in my study."

When Robert had left the room, John said, "It's all right, Maud, I know what you're thinking. I'm not going to be hard on him."

Maud smiled approvingly.

"I have one thing in common with my son," John concluded.

"What's that, my dear?" Maud asked.

"We both have sisters who keep reminding us of things we wish to forget." John slowly got up, and smiling at Maud, left the room.

He found Robert waiting apprehensively in the study. John sat down in his favourite armchair, and leant back looking up at his son.

God! He looks like Elizabeth, he thought to himself. The same lovely eyes. He wondered what the boy really thought of him. Could it be true what Maud said? Why do fathers have this disagreeable job of punishing their sons? But it was wrong to be sloppy with a boy, they didn't respect that. Boys expect their fathers to be strong, otherwise what have they got to hold on to?

"Well, what am I going to do with you?"

"I don't know, sir."

"I presume you agree that you were very rude at my table this morning,"

"Yes, sir," Robert replied. He was going to say that it was Joanna's fault, but then decided it would be unmanly.

"If you were in my place, would you hand out a beating for this? If so you'd better get yourself ready."

Robert hesitated. He was caught in a trap of his own making. He was sure that Daddy already thought he was a coward, so what would he think of him if he said no? The thoughts rushed round and round in his head, and he could not let go this condemnation of himself. Perhaps, if he said yes, Daddy might be pleased with him.

John could see the turmoil in his son's mind written on the young face. He noticed the little nerve move under the boy's right eye. Uncertainly, Robert went across the room and picked up the dreaded punishment chair, placing it in the centre of the room as he had done many times before. He took off his blazer and stood in front of the chair. Undoing his belt he let his trousers fall to the ground, and then took his pant's down and bent over.

John saw the angry weals across his son buttocks. The boy has got guts, he thought. "You can stand up, "he said, "And put the chair back."

Robert stood up and looked at his father in surprise. "Am I not going to be caned?" he asked.

"No, you're not," John replied. "Sometimes a father must remember to temper justice with mercy, and this is one of those times."

Robert dressed himself and, replacing the chair, came back and stood in front of John.

"Don't mistake this for weakness, Robert."

"Of course not."

"Is there anything else you would like to tell me? Anything that happened at school today that I could help you with." John searched his son's face and thought he was about to say something, but the words seemed to fade on the boy's lips.

"No, sir," Robert replied. He could not bring himself to mention the cricket match, now that he had been spared a whipping.

John reminded him that he was to remain in his room on the following day after school, and then Robert left the room.

Robert decided to spend a few minutes getting cheered up, so he ran into the garden and through the secret way into his Uncle Reggie's place. He entered a side door of the house, which was always open for him – he never rang or knocked – but finding no one in, went out again into the garden and spotted Reggie and Daisy lounging on deck chairs at the far end of the lawn. Reggie had a panama hat tipped over his eyes and was lying almost flat; a picture of contentment, while Daisy sat more upright, under her parasol, keeping up the flow of conversation.

Daisy saw Robert approaching, "Cooee. Hallo luv," she called loudly, shaking her parasol violently.

Reggie's snatched his hat from his eyes, and sat up. Robert was the son he had always yearned for, and as John had once remarked, if Robert asked, Reggie would give him all he had.

"All the fun of the fair old lad!"

"Same to you, Uncle." Robert could always be sure of a rousing welcome from these two wonderful people. He was very often the centre of attention at home and at school although he didn't realise it. But here, with Reggie and Daisy, when Robert appeared, their whole world revolved round him.

"You look a bit down in the dumps, Robert," said Daisy.

"You need a good stiff whisky, old boy. Take a swig of this." Reggie held out a glass to him, and Robert carefully put it to his lips and dipped his tongue in.

"Eerr," Robert shuddered, making a grimace.

"Stop encouraging the boy. What would John say?" Daisy scolded.

"Well, he ain't here, old girl," Reggie gave Robert a wink.

Robert cautiously sat down on the grass, and related the events of the day. He had always found it easy to talk to them, and tell them his troubles. His humorous description of Mr Cavey and the Maths lesson kept Daisy in stitches, and when, he came to his remark about Brighton Corporation, he thought she was going into hysterics.

"You're a caution, dear, and no mistake!" Daisy shrieked, wiping the tears from her eyes.

"It wasn't so funny when he slapped my head, " Robert replied wistfully, now wondering whether it was funny at all, especially as he had got a detention as well. "Oh, God!" he exclaimed, quickly sitting up. He'd forgotten the detention.

"What's the matter, old boy?" Reggie enquired,

"I'd forgotten that beastly detention. That means I've got to stay in at school tomorrow afternoon."

"I say, that's hard luck!"

"Yes. The trouble is, Daddy's making me stay in at home tomorrow afternoon. Now what am I going to do?"

"Oh lor!" said Reggie. "You are in a pickle, young fellow m'lad. You'll just have to own up."

Dejectedly Robert got up. "What do you think he'll say, Uncle?"

"I'm sure I don't know, Robert. But take my word on it, it'll be all right."

"I'd better go." Robert thrust his hands into his pockets and sauntered off across the lawn.

"Goodbye, dear," Daisy called after him.

"Keep your pecker up, old boy," said Reggie.

Robert arrived back in the house to find the rest of the family taking coffee in the drawing room.

"So there you are, Robert!" said his mother.

He flung himself on to the sofa beside his aunt, wishing, too late, that he had been more careful with his sore bottom.

"Coffee, Robert?"

"No thanks, Mummy."

He was glad that Joanna had gone to do her homework, for although they generally got on well together, he felt he'd had enough of her for one day. The idea did strike him, though, that he might sell her a view of his stripes for a bob. He was a bit short of cash. What a stingy devil she is, he thought, only offering tuppence.

Maud tried to engage her nephew in conversation, but she could see he was obviously not in the mood. She found him a bright and intelligent boy, who normally chatted to her in quite an old fashioned manner. However, this evening he seemed pensive, just looking at the floor, with his hands gripped tightly together.

At that moment the door burst open and Joanna almost fell into the room, followed by the butler. "Daddy, Daddy! It's Buck House on the telephone," she cried.

"For goodness sake, Joanna, calm down." John nodded to the butler and added, "Thank you, Maitland, I'll take it here." He picked up the telephone beside him, and Joanna quickly snuggled on to his lap and pushed her ear as close as possible to his. Everyone was quiet while they waited, and then there was a click and a crackle, and a gruff voice spoke at the other end.

"It's the King, it's the King!" Joanna whispered loudly, not knowing how to contain her excitement.

Elizabeth put her finger to her mouth and whispered, "Hush, Joanna."

"Your Majesty is most kind." John was heard to say. "Much better thank you, sir." Then after listening further he said, "And may I wish you, sir, 'many happy returns of the day',"

The voice at the other end continued for a moment, and then John said, "I have one of them on my knee, sir." He put the ear piece against Joanna's ear, and held the mouth piece in front of her,

"Joanna, Your Majesty," she said. . . "I will, Your Majesty"... "Thank you very much."

There was a click at the other end, and the voice was gone. John replaced the receiver.

"Yes, Your Majesty. No, Your Majesty. Joanna, Your Majesty," Robert mimicked, trying to get his own back on his sister.

"And you can shut up!" Joanna retorted. "You're only jealous because he didn't speak to you."

"He wouldn't have spoken to you either if he'd known what you're like."

"Stop it, you two," Elizabeth interrupted. "What did His Majesty want, schat?" she enquired.

"Just to ask if I was feeling better. Damn thoughtful of him, don't you think! He's sixty seven today, you know."

"He sounded jolly kind," Joanna said.

"He is," John replied. "And yet his own children are afraid of him, all except his daughter-in-law, the Duchess of York. He seems to dote on her."

"I'm not afraid of you, Daddy," Joanna laughed, flinging her arms round John's neck and kissing him on the cheek. "I expect, Robert is though, because he's such a naughty beast."

"No I'm not!" snapped her brother.

"I bet you are when Daddy's just about to give you a good whipping."

"That's different. So would you be."

"You two are the absolute limit today with all this arguing. I really don't know what your Aunty will think of you," Elizabeth chided.

Joanna gave her father another resounding kiss and then bounced out of the room, announcing that she was off to finish her homework.

"That girl leaves me breathless," John joked.

It's a pity she doesn't leave herself breathless, and then she wouldn't have so much to say, Robert reflected. He looked at his father, who was just helping himself to another cup of coffee, wondering whether it was the right time to mention his wretched detention. Robert considered he looked happy enough. The telephone call had pleased him, and Joanna's antics always seemed to put him in a good mood. That soppy girl was some use even though she was so annoying. Robert came to the conclusion that he would have to pluck up courage and say something now,

"Daddy, I forgot to tell you something."

John looked doubtfully at his son, and did not fail to notice that the boy was uneasy. "What's that, Robert?" he asked.

"Well, you see, I. . . "There was a pause while Robert decided how best to go on. "That is, I. . . I got a detention today, and that means I have to go back to school tomorrow afternoon." Robert gabbled through the last few words in an effort to get, the matter over with quickly.

"I see," John said, wondering what else the boy could have got up to. "First it's smoking, then rudeness, and now a detention." John spoke very deliberately, emphasising each offence in such a way that Robert winced inwardly at the sound of them. "And how are you going to be in two places at once? We had agreed, that you would stay in your room tomorrow afternoon."

"I know, Daddy. But I shall get into terrible trouble if I don't turn up for the detention."

"And you'll be in terrible trouble if you're not in your room," John retorted. "So, now what are you going to do?"

"I could stay in my room on Sunday afternoon instead?" Robert suggested.

"Perhaps you would like to tell us why you were given a detention?" Elizabeth said.

Robert felt he wouldn't like to do anything of the sort, but he thought he'd better try to explain.

"Whatever made you say that, dear?" Elizabeth enquired, trying to suppress a smile.

"It just slipped out. Anyway, old Cavey's always picking on me. He's always saying, 'Eh, Rutherford, your maths is abysmal," Robert mimicked.

"I'm not surprised, if that's the sort of answer you give," John replied.

Maud began to laugh, and John was forced to smile. "All right, Robert," he agreed. "You can stay in your room on Sunday, instead."

" Oh, thanks, Daddy!"

"And now, Robert, I think we've all had enough of you and your misdemeanours for one day. You'd better go to bed," John said, not unkindly.

Robert got up, but hesitated, wandering whether his disgrace precluded him from kissing them all goodnight. However, he was immediately left in no doubt that he wasn't considered that wicked, and he kissed them each in turn.

"I believe you may find that tomorrow will be a far more pleasant day, Robert," John remarked.

Robert agreed with his father, if only because tomorrow couldn't be worse than today, but he didn't consider that much of a recommendation, and he wasn't looking forward to the afternoon in detention. He got up and left the room, but a moment later his head appeared again round the door. "Sorry for being naughty," he said, and then closed the door quietly behind him.

"Such a nice boy. You should be very proud, John."

"So you keep telling me, Maud," John replied, "But he can be a terror at times, and you know it. Besides, you don't have to deal with him."

"Well, you always wanted a real boy and not a sissy, so how can you complain when he acts like one?"

John knew better than to get involved in an argument with his sister, or any other woman for that matter. They always seemed to have the last word, nevertheless, he thought he'd fire one last shot. "That wonderful boy, as you call him, is going to get something he's not expecting tomorrow," he said, ominously.

"Oh, John, you're not going to punish him again!" Elizabeth exclaimed, looking worried.

"That would be unfair, John," Maud added. But John just sat sipping his coffee, and no matter how hard they tried, neither could induce him to make further comment. It was that infuriating silence after a purposely obscure remark which Maud remembered from their early days was the way her brother would cleverly withdraw from an argument. It was his weapon against a woman's last word.

The following morning when Agnes woke him, Robert slowly pushed his head out from under the sheets and, through the haze of drowsiness, thought he saw his cricket clothes lying on the spare bed beside him. He turned over and shut his eyes again, expecting Agnes to order him out of bed as she usually did if he tried to catch a few extra moments under the covers. But nothing happened. He could hear her humming as she pottered about the room, but she seemed to be in no hurry to get him up. Eventually, his curiosity got the better of him and he sat up rubbing his eyes. That's strange, they are my cricket togs, he thought to himself.

"What's the time, Agnes?" he yawned.

"Nearly eight o'clock."

For a moment it didn't sink in. Then it struck him like a thunderbolt. "Oh, crumbs!" he cried. "I'll be late!" He flung the bed covers off and leapt out of bed almost tearing off his pyjamas, and. pulling the cord right out of his pyjamas trousers in his panic. "Why didn't you wake me? What shall I do?"

Agnes caught hold of him as he rushed across the room to get his underwear. "For a start you can calm down," she said firmly.

"But I'll be late!"

Agnes had taken hold of both his arms and held him in front of her. "Now listen," she ordered. "Your father has given these instructions." Agnes then copied the military style in which John had given her his orders. "Number one, you will take your bath. Number two, you will dress for cricket. Number three, you will go down to breakfast when you're ready. Number four," Agnes hesitated for a moment, having forgotten what number four was, "Oh, yes. Number four, you will be taken to school by your father at ten twenty, something Emma, whoever she might be."

"Ack emma, silly. That's what they say in the army." But having corrected Agnes, it began to dawn on him what all the instructions meant. "Agnes, I must be going to play after all!" he yelled, flinging his arms round her and frantically kissing her.

At that moment the bedroom door, which was already ajar, was pushed open and Joanna's face appeared. "Cor! what a smashing free view of your stripes, baby brother," she laughed.

Robert let go of Agnes and quickly picking up a shoe flung it at his sister's face, which promptly disappeared. "Get out you bloody pig!" he shouted in frustration, rushing to the door. But before he could get there Joanna was laughing along the end of the passage.

"I'll tell all my friends what a lovely striped bottom my little brother has," she called back.

Robert was about to shout back that he was taller than she was, but before he could a hair brush struck him hard on the appropriate place and he was hauled into the bathroom.

"Ouch! That hurt!"

"It was meant to. I've never heard such language!" Agnes exclaimed. "Where do you pick it up from? You're lucky they didn't hear you downstairs."

"Well she shouldn't look when I've got nothing on. I always get it in the neck because of her. It's not fair."

But Robert knew that Agnes was right, and that it was lucky he had not been heard by his father!

When he entered, the breakfast room, Robert was greeted with surprised looks on the faces of the womenfolk.

"I didn't realise it was cricket today, Robert," Elizabeth said, seeing her son in his gleaming whites and green blazer. When she had realised the boy was late for breakfast, she had been about to go and hurry him, but John had informed her that the matter was in hand.

Robert was not quite sure how to reply.

John, who was, as usual, reading his paper, peered round the open pages and said with exaggerated surprise, "Oh, I see we're all dressed for cricket. I didn't know we had to wear cricket togs for detentions. Is this new rule?"

Robert looked bewildered and could feel himself going red in the face, wondering whether Agnes had got it all wrong. His father disappeared behind the paper again, so he took the opportunity of taking his breakfast from the sideboard and quickly sitting down at the table.

It began to dawn on Elizabeth that her husband wasn't so surprised as he made out, and then she remembered his remark of the previous evening. "John, you're up to something. Come out from behind that paper and stop teasing the boy."

Robert saw the paper collapse and his father appear again, only this time there was a self satisfied grin faintly showing on his face. With relief Robert said shyly, "Oh, Daddy."

"Do you realise, Elizabeth, that our son has been selected to play for the school first eleven today?"

"Robert, that's marvellous!" She stretched out and took his hand, squeezing it and holding it for a moment. She could feel his excitement, but it was not only this that gave her pleasure, it was the fact that Robert had found some way of pleasing his father.

"Well done, old bean!" Joanna exclaimed.

"Well done, indeed!" Maud added.

"Why didn't you say something yesterday, Robert?" John asked.

"I didn't like to, Daddy, because of all the trouble I'm in. I didn't think you'd let me play."

They all learnt from John that, if it had not been for the headmaster telephoning him the previous evening, he would not have known that Robert had been asked to play. After hearing from Robert that he couldn't play, the cricket captain had not let the matter drop, but had approached the headmaster to seek his help.

John found it difficult to understand why his son had not confided in him, although he did feel a grudging admiration for the boy for being prepared to accept his punishment and not use cricket as a way out. He did not understand that there were occasions when his son was afraid of him. He had never spared the rod. Although he had tried always to be scrupulously fair, believing that a father should be a father, and not just another friendly playmate. A boy should see his father as a rock - a rock to hold on to in time of trouble, and to founder on when he does wrong.

The match was due to start at 11 a.m. members of the team were excused lessons that morning, but had to be at the cricket pavilion on the school field twenty minutes before play. John had decided that he would accompany Robert to school and watch the match from the beginning, and had ordered the chauffeur to be waiting at the front door at 10.20 a.m. precisely.

Robert was pleased to hear that his mother and aunty would come and watch during the afternoon and stay for tea with the teams, but he was not quite so sure about having Joanna there. Girls were so soppy, and Joanna could be jolly embarrassing with some of the things she said about him. "And don't call me baby brother in front of the other chaps," he instructed.

"I might," Joanna laughed.

"Mummy, please tell her not to."

"Don't worry, dear. You know she's only teasing." Elizabeth assured him.

Father and son got into the car exactly on time. It was only a short journey to the school, but it was long enough for Robert to realise that his father was in an exceptionally good frame of mind and unusually talkative.

"Do you wish to go in the front entrance, Daddy?"

"No. I'll come in with you," John replied. Only the staff and visitors entered the school through the front door, the boys having to use the playground entrances at the rear. The school was an attractive red brick building which had been completed in 1913 and which had been used as a military hospital during the war. It was built in the V of a cross roads, with the front block facing the junction and the two wings extending back, each fronting on to one of the roads. At the rear there was an upper and a lower playground, which were separated by a gymnasium and an armoury. At the far end of the upper playground was the boarding house and the headmasters house, and beyond these across a narrow path - known by the boys as the cinder track - was the very extensive playing field.

The chauffeur dropped them at the upper playground entrance, and they walked in past of the boarding house. It was break time and the playground was packed with boys. On seeing Robert arrive, a number of his friends came running over, obviously proud to show that they were associated with a member of the first eleven.

John had not realised that his son was so popular with his fellows, always imagining him to be far too retiring and quiet a boy to be so well liked.

Robert introduced some of the small crowd that had collected, and they came one by one and shook John's hand.

"I say, sir, it's jolly decent of you to let old Ruth - I mean, Robert, play. I told him it would be all right, but he was in such a funk about asking."

If Robert hadn't interrupted the speaker would have gone on, possibly forever, he thought. "Shut up, Edwards, we don't want to hear all that again,"

Eventually the two managed move on and cross the playing field to the pavilion where the home team was already assembling ready to welcome their guests. Carter came forward to greet them, feeling especially pleased that the chairman of the governors himself had seen fit to turn out to watch. John already knew the team captain, and considered him a suitable boy for Robert to look up to. But having been greeted, John withdrew to a deck-chair in order not to hinder Robert's new relationship with the older boys in the team. He knew it was sometimes difficult for a younger boy to be accepted before he had proved his worth, and did not wish anyone to think that his son had been chosen because he had influence. He noticed that as the team collected Robert was standing slightly apart from the older and mainly taller boys, and it reminded him of the way he was ignored by his colleagues when he first joined the regiment at Omdurman. The boy will be all right, when he starts playing he decided.

John settled himself comfortably in his chair, content with the thought of a full day's cricket ahead. What a bit of luck to have been excused accompanying the King at the Trooping today, he thought.

The visitors won the toss and decided to bat. They had a strong team with some powerful looking boys among them. In the first over Carter had placed Robert at Mid on, and had then proceeded to put up some fast balls to the opening batsman. The fourth ball was exceptionally fast and well placed; the batsman making an uncertain stroke. The ball shot towards Robert and struck him hard in the palm of his outstretched hand, making him wince with the sting. In his anxiety to do well he fumbled and lost his grips and the ball dropped to the ground. "Oh, God, what have I done!" he whispered to himself. He felt his face flush and experienced that prickly feeling in the back of his neck which he always got when embarrassed. He knew all eyes were watching him. What a terrible start, he thought. Carter will never ask him to play again. He could see some of the team glaring at him. Whatever must they be thinking?

When he threw the ball back to Carter, the captain just smiled at him and said, "Don't get so tense, Robert. Just relax and enjoy yourself."

In the first hour the opening batsmen went on to score 49 runs, and with every run scored Robert felt himself responsible.

By lunch time the score stood at 63 for 5.

The day had turned out very warm, and the tables for lunch had been set out on the grass. John sat with the headmaster and other members of the staff from both schools, and also the team captains.

Robert was not involved in much conversation during the meal, the other boys on his table being six formers, who talked among themselves rather than to a young third former and one who had fumbled a catch as well. But he didn't mind, being happy within himself just to be there. How different from yesterday, even the headmaster looked human again. He was still sore, but he didn't mind that either, because he was here playing for the school, and Daddy was here, and Mummy was coming, and the sun was shining, and everything was wonderful. If only today would go on for ever.

How often had he lain in bed before going to sleep at night imagining just such a day as this. Only, in his imagination, he was the hero of the hour, not one who dropped an easy catch. But it was nice to dream. At least in dreams he could make as many runs as he liked, and hold all the most difficult catches. He would usually bowl out all the other team as well with his tricky spin. But today Carter hadn't even asked him to bowl. But Carter had spoken to him. 'Don't get so tense, Robert. Just relax and enjoy yourself', he recalled the great man saying. And Carter had called him 'Robert' even after he'd dropped that catch, so everything really was wonderful.

After lunch 4 more wickets fell in quick succession, only adding 13 runs to the score. Then the last man came in and joined one of the opening batsmen, who was still batting strongly. The score quickly shot up to 103, and it seemed that this partnership was set to last.

By this time many more spectators had arrived and were lining the boundary, and Robert was pleased to see some of his own form there. Then he saw his mother and Aunty Maud arrive. Oh, lor, Joanna's come too. If only she'd keep her mouth shut and not say anything to embarrass him in front of his friends. And there's cousin Lisa, what's she doing here? Girls are so soppy, although come to think of it, cousin Lisa was the only girl he had ever met who wasn't soppy. He had to admit to himself that she was a bit of a Tom boy, who could run and throw a ball almost as well as he could. But she was a blinking nuisance, always staring at him with those dark flashing-eyes of hers, and following him and Karl Heinz about when they wanted to play boys' games or swim in the nude in the river Maas. There! She was looking at him now, all dressed up in her posh school uniform. Aunty Natascha said that one day he would change his ideas about girls, and then he'd be the one to follow Lisa about; though what he'd want to follow her about for, he couldn't think. What a silly thing to say.

Like her aunts and her sister, Isabel, before her, Lisa van der Leyden had been sent to Roedean School. As with all girls attending that school from abroad, she had to have a guardian, resident in the country, and the obvious choice had fallen on John and Elizabeth, living so close to the school as they did. On certain week-ends during the term girls at Roedean were allowed to be taken out of the school by their parents or guardians so on these occasions Lisa would come to stay with her relatives in Brighton.

With all the excitement of the match, Robert had forgotten that it was the week-end that Lisa was due to stay. He usually tried to keep out of the way when she was about; he had better things to do than play with a girl.

At, the end of the over Robert began to walk across to the out field near the boundary on the pavilion side of the pitch. Carter had sent him there, telling him to be ready for some catches, so he would have to be very alert. He'd better not drop any this time. He could see out of the corner of his eye that his mother had been given a deck-chair, with Aunty Maud on one side of her and his maths master, Mr Cavey, on the other. Lisa was sitting on the grass in front of Elizabeth, and Joanna was standing behind hoping to be noticed by the boys, Robert thought. Both his mother and Mr Cavey appeared to be enjoying a joke, and Robert couldn't help feeling it was at his expense.

Before he reached his new position, Robert heard the sound of a hunting-horn. It could only be one person, he thought, and turning, he found that he was right, for there, walking across the field inside the boundary line was Uncle Reggie. He was dressed in one of his loud blazers and a boater. The boys lining the boundary were in fits as Reggie gave them another blast on the horn. "Tally ho! Up the school! All the fun of the fair, you chaps. Ha ha," he called out as he walked by. Reggie was not unknown to the boys, for he would frequently turn out to support the second eleven when Robert was playing.

"Give 'em the old one two," Reggie called over to Robert as he passed.

"Hurry up, Uncle, you're holding up the game," Robert quietly called out, feeling self conscious.

"Sorry, old boy." Reggie hurried off the field to where John and the other spectators were sitting.

Daisy had also arrived; with the inevitable large hat and parasol, but, unlike her husband, she had not walked within the boundary area. "What can you do with 'im, John?" she said as John, rose to greet her.

"Absolutely nothing, Daisy, the Germans never managed to stop his antics, so I'm sure we never shall," John replied.

Reggie had carried his hunting-horn all through the war, much to the amusement of his men. He would move up and down the trench keeping their spirits up just before the terrible moment of the attack, and then lead them over the top, blowing away as if there was nothing more to worry about than the cunning of a fox.

There was a dull thud as the batsman struck the ball square in the centre of his bat. Robert, saw the ball lift high into the air. It was coming in his direction and there was no one else who could possibly reach it. For a moment he stood rooted to the ground not knowing whether to run forward or step back. Again he could feel that all eyes were on him. He would never be able to face anyone again if he dropped it this time. As the ball shot up, he lost sight of it in the glare of the afternoon sun. For a split second he had to turn his head away to relieve the strain on his eyes. He moved to where he thought it would come down, and tried to shade his eyes with his hand. "God!" he groaned, "Where is it?" It was coming down straight at him. He strained every nerve to keep his now watering eyes firmly fixed on the rapidly descending black spot. He cupped his hands close to him, and a second later he felt the ball strike him on the chest. For one agonizing moment he felt it slipping between his hands and his chest. He fell on his knees and grasped it hard to his stomach, and then gripping it firmly, he lifted it high above his head for all to see, as if he was praying to the sun. There was an explosion of excitement from the boys lining the boundary, some of them waving their caps in the air and shouting his name. For a short time he remained on his knees holding the ball tightly to his chest, almost afraid to let go of it." He was shaking with excitement, and then realised that he was being applauded.

Robert sneaked a look at Lisa and saw her looking at him, but he quickly looked away. For some reason it gave him pleasure to impress her, in fact sometimes he felt himself showing off when she was present. He soon forgot Lisa when Carter came over and put his arm round him. "Well held, Robert," he said. He even got a slap on the back from some of the others in the team.

The visiting team were all out for 105.

Robert would be tenth in the batting order, and so had plenty of time to lounge about the pavilion area. He thought he'd better go and pay his respects to his mother and the rest of his guests, but he didn't particularly want to get too near the headmaster; he had been too near him for comfort yesterday.

"Well done, Robert," said Elizabeth.

"Yes, well done," said Mr Cavey. "It's a pity your maths isn't as good as your cricket, Rutherford," he added.

"Yes, sir," Robert replied, and then thought, and it's a pity you don't let me off that rotten detention.

Robert looked at Lisa, who was still sitting on the grass in front of Elizabeth. Although he would never admit it to himself, he secretly admired his cousin's swarthy skin. It gave her a healthy look, he thought, not like some sissy girls who always looked so pale. He made to walk away back to the pavilion.

"Aren't you going to say hallo to Lisa?" Elizabeth remarked.

He wasn't, but he thought he'd better since his mother had mentioned it. "What cher," he said.

"Robert!" Elizabeth glared at him. "Speak properly!"

"Hallo, then," he said, reluctantly.

His cousin looked, up at him with an indifferent expression on her face. "Hallo," she said, and then looked away, giving Robert the impression that it was of little importance whether he acknowledged her or not. For some reason, this irritated him. Who does she think she is, anyway?

As he walked back to the pavilion three of the sixth formers in the team surrounded him. "I say, Rutherford, who's that lovely thing with your old man over there?" one asked, indicating Joanna, who was standing talking to John and Reggie.

"What lovely thing?" Robert asked, looking somewhat bewildered.

"That girl, stupid."

"Oh, her. That's my sister, worse luck," Robert apologized, pleased that the older boys should have spoken to him, but wishing they had chosen a better subject to talk about.

"How about introducing us?"

"Whatever for?" Robert asked.

"Never you mind. Just introduce us, that's all."

Robert took them across to Joanna, and having introduced them, found that his services were no longer needed. He shrugged and walked away, thinking that some people ask for trouble.

Reggie joined him in front of the pavilion and, having been an Oxford Blue, was soon surrounded by a number of boys firing questions at him.

The opening bat for the home side was out for a duck, and then Carter went in and started to make a stand against the fierce bowling. One bowler in particular was exceptionally fast, and Robert began to feel a little apprehensive, for he had not experienced a pace as fast as this before.

"Don't worry, Robert. You'll be all right. You've got a quick eye and you can use his pace to your advantage," Reggie encouraged.

Four more wickets went, and then another. The home side's score reached. 87 and another wicket fell. By now Robert had got his pads on and was sitting waiting on the pavilion steps. He had his eyes shut and was holding his head in his hands. He felt just as he did when he had been waiting to play the violin in front of all those people in the dining saloon on the ship coming home from India. The waiting had been terrible, but once he had started to play everything had been all right. A shout, "Howzat!" made him look up, and he saw the boy, who had just walked out to bat, corning back again. This is it, Robert my lad, he said to himself. He stood up holding his bat - the marvellous new bat his parents had given him for Christmas - and. began the long trek to the wicket. He kept his head bowed as he walked out so as not to see the faces staring at him.

Carter came to meet him, "We're in trouble, Robert. We need nineteen to win," he said.

Robert quietly took his position at the wicket, making no show of studying the pitch or the position of the fielders like some swanks did. He didn't like that sort of thing, and besides, if he was out for a duck, he would feel so stupid having made all that show. He didn't like the look of the bowler either. He was a large well made boy with a flabby face, and Robert, felt he was leering at him. The bowler began his walk back, and Robert wondered when he was going to stop. The thought came to him that the flabby face was going to walk right off the field and back to the changing rooms. The thought tickled him and helped release some of the tension.

The bowler had stopped and turned to face him. Thoughts started to rush through his mind. He saw the boy begin his run, and imagined him as a mass column of French cavalry charging the British squares at Waterloo, "Steady, Rutherford, hold your fire," he whispered.

The ball came hurling down the pitch at him. He just nicked it with the edge of his bat and it went shooting away between the wicket keeper and the slips before being fielded for one run. That was a bit of luck, he thought, but at least he had broken his duck, and had put Carter to face the bowler again. All he had to do was play safe and let Carter do the batting was the advice he had been given.

Carter, with a little help from Robert, who, much to his surprise, had scored 3, took the score to 101, and with this score on the board play stopped for tea.

At tea Robert thought that the attitude towards him by some of the team had altered since lunch time, when they hardly spoke to him. It was almost as if some of them wanted to sit next to him. What he couldn't understand was why they wanted to keep talking about Joanna instead of cricket. It was such a waste of time talking about girls, especially that one. He noticed that when Joanna sat down for tea, the chairs next to her were quickly taken by the boys he had earlier introduced. He made sure that he sat as far away as possible from the family and staff, because he didn't want anyone to accuse him of being a swank or a show off, taking advantage of his father's privileged position.

With the first ball after tea disaster struck and Carter was clean bowled. Robert knew that the last boy in was not a good bat, he also knew that between them they had to score 5 to win. The boy struck out wildly at the first ball but missed it altogether. Luckily, it missed his wicket, it was also missed by the wicket keeper so Robert shouted out to run and they just managed to take a single.

Robert now faced the bowler, and now it dawned on him that as Carter had gone, the responsibility for winning or losing the match was his. What was he going to do, he groaned to himself? Everyone was watching him. He would never be able to score the 4 runs needed to win. He had convinced himself that the 3 he had scored had been due to luck; and his luck could not hold much longer.

The tension among the spectators was electric. Even the noisy junior boys were quiet as they waited for the next ball, giving loud signs of relief each time Robert's wicket remained intact.

During the next over the other boy hit out at one ball and scored 2, but only just managed to survive by blocking every other ball. Then it was Robert's turn again, and to his consternation he found that he had to face the very fast flabby faced bowler once again. Robert miss hit the first ball, catching it on the side of his bat, but luckily deflecting it from his wicket. The next ball was delivered short, and Robert found it rising straight towards his face. He had the presence of mind to turn his face to the side and bring up his hand. The ball glanced off his hand and slapped into his cheek. For a moment the sting was excruciating and the tears came to his eyes. He dropped his bat and fell to his knees holding his face, with his head touching the ground. A loud moan went up from the spectators as the vision of victory for the home team faded. The umpire and some of the fielders crowded round him, and Carter ran out to the wicket. He knelt down and put his arm round the younger boy's shoulders, very gently encouraging him to sit up. But Robert still kept his hands over his face for fear they would see him crying.

Carter said nothing but got Robert to his feet and, giving him a handkerchief, led him towards the pavilion. As the two boys approached the pavilion, John got up and went inside with them. Robert sat down holding the handkerchief over his face.

"Let's have a look at you," said John, removing the handkerchief.

Robert knew that now his father was with him there would be no fuss, just straightforward instructions to be obeyed tears or no tears. John felt the cheek. "No bones broken, Robert, just a nasty sting," he said. "Fill that basin with cold water and wash your face. Give yourself a couple of minutes rest and then you'll be fine." John smiled at his son as he went to the door. "Then I expect to see you come out and win the match for us," he added. Robert nodded and gave his father a weak smile. When John had gone Carter said, "Your old man's alright, Robert. He knows what's what."

When Robert emerged from the pavilion he got a cheer from the waiting boys and applause from the adult spectators. He glanced at his father and was pleased to get a nod of approval, which helped lift his confidence.

Just two for a win, he thought as he walked back to the wicket. If only he could do it.

When play recommenced, it was the bowler who appeared to have been put off by the interruption, whereas Robert felt himself encouraged by the applause he had just received. He played the next two balls safely back along the pitch to the bowler. The large boy was tiring, for the pace had slackened, but Robert was purposely waiting for the right ball before hitting out for the two runs needed to win.

There were only two balls left in this over, so he would have to do something soon. The next ball was fielded quickly, and there was no chance of a run. It was now, or maybe never, he thought. One for a draw, two for a win.

He bent over his bat, and could feel the sun of the glorious June evening warming his back. It had been a wonderful day, perhaps even the best in his life. Whatever happened now could not alter that. He had tried his best, even though he had only scored 3, but it would be nice to carry his bat for 5 and win the match as well. The bowler had turned to face him again. They're going to charge again, Rutherford. He smiled at his own fantasy. His dreams had often kept him calm in times of stress; Agnes said he ought to be a writer, for he seemed to be able to make a story out o f anything. Sometimes, though, she didn't appreciate his stories, but those were the ones when he was fibbing to try and avoid one of her tannings. Their banners are flying, but this time it was the banners, not of the French cavalry, but of the Old Guard themselves. Many times Daddy had told him the story of Waterloo, and although he did not like the idea of war, he had to admit that the story fascinated him. Well, even the Old Guard were defeated in the end, so there was still hope. Steady, Rutherford, they're coming. As the bowler thundered nearer and nearer, he imagined the sound of the run up to be the drumming of the *pas de charge.*

In one last desperate effort the flabby face hurled himself into his delivery. Robert's clear, young eyes saw the ball was off centre. He stepped out, and with a beautiful action, cracked it with all his strength, sending it scudding across the grass passed Square leg.

"Yes!" he yelled, and began to run,

His partner reacted immediately to his call. They both raced up the pitch. A fielder near the boundary ran and picked up the ball. "And again." Robert screamed as he thrust the end of his bat on to the crease of the other wicket and turned for the second run. He could see the ball hovering high in the air like a bird of prey about to fall an its victim, and there was the wicket keeper poised at the stumps in front of him, waiting for the kill. Both batsmen scorched back down the pitch." If they made it, they would have won. The ball was falling almost on top of the stumps, and if the wicket keeper had let it fall, it would probably have taken the bails off itself. But in his haste the boy caught it, high, and by the time he had struck off the bails, Robert had flung himself flat on the pitch with his bat stretched out and over the crease.

"Howzat?"

The umpire shook his head.

For a moment he lay there on the grass unable to believe that he had done it. They had won. Robert would never forget that moment as he walked back to the pavilion to the cheers of the boys and the applause of the other spectators, who were now all standing as they clapped. He had never seen his father look so pleased in all the years he could remember. Perhaps it would in some way make up for the disappointment he had been to Daddy, he thought.

After dinner that evening, the family sat in the drawing room. John sat reading while Elizabeth and Maud chatted. Robert was playing cards with Joanna, and Lisa, but he was beginning to get fed up because Lisa kept winning. He could always tell what sort of hand Joanna had, because her face gave her away, or she would say something so that he knew what she was up to. But it was not so with Lisa. She didn't say much, and he never knew what she was thinking.

"You're out again, Robert," said Lisa, calmly placing one of her cards on top of Robert's pile.

"Damn and blast!" Robert protested.

"Robert! Your language! You really are a naughty boy," Elizabeth scolded.

"Daddy says damn."

John hid his face behind his book.

"That's no reason why you should," Elizabeth retorted.

"Well I've got to say something when I'm annoyed. Couldn't I say damn sometimes?"

"What shall we do with you, Robert?" Elizabeth sighed. "You shouldn't swear in front of the girls.

"But they're just the ones I want to swear in front of, because they're so damned annoying - sorry, I mean blasted annoying."

Maud didn't know how to keep a straight face.

Elizabeth was at a loss for words, and was relieved to see the butler enter the room. "Yes, Maitland?" she said.

"It's Lady Henrietta on the telephone, m'lady," he said, taking the telephone from the small table and handing it to Elizabeth.

The conversation appeared to be very one sided, with Elizabeth having to restrict herself to single words. Eventually she said, "We'll look forward to that. Goodbye, Henrietta."

"What did that old cow want?" Robert asked, realising too late that he had said the wrong thing again. "I'm sorry, I'm sorry, I didn't mean it," he quickly added, knowing very well that he did mean it.

"John, will you come out from behind that book and speak to your son," Elizabeth urged.

John lowered his book, pretending not to have heard properly. He hoped that he hadn't got double standards regarding Robert's language, but felt that there was a world of difference between the word the boy had used at table yesterday and what he had just come out with. He had to admit to himself that his son's description of Henrietta rather matched his own, and in any case he wished to avoid having to rebuke the boy and spoil such a wonderful day. "What's that, dear? What did Henrietta want?" he said, changing the subject.

"Henrietta and George will be coming for luncheon tomorrow."

"Groan," said Robert.

"Oh, no!" Joanna exclaimed.

"Don't be unkind, children," Elizabeth said, "and all the boys will be coming too."

"What the devil do they want!" John exclaimed.

"John, your language!" Robert blurted out, mimicking his mother. He put his hand over his mouth, realising that he might have gone too far.

The girls collapsed with laughter, and Maud and Elizabeth did the same.

"You cheeky young devil," said John, leaping from his seat. Robert ran for the door, but as he tried to open it John caught him round the waist and then lifted him high in the air. Robert found himself being held by his ankles, dangling upside down. "What shall we do with him, girls?"

"Tickle him to death, Uncle," said Lisa, rushing over to join the fun and running her fingers under her cousin's armpits.

"Mercy!" Robert screamed.

John slowly lowered the wriggling boy on to the floor, and then returned to his chair. Both girls tried to hold Robert down, but he was too strong for them and was soon up and taking refuge beside his Aunty Maud. He had really enjoyed that bundle, especially as Daddy had been such a sport.

"I can still, handle you, my lad, as big as you are," said John. But the boy was growing, and he had felt the strength in the young body. He wouldn't be able to lift his son like that for much longer. "Well, how are we going to amuse ourselves?" he asked.

"Let's have the wireless on, Daddy," said Robert.

"No, I don't think so. We've had it on once this evening, and that's quite enough."

"What about a sing-song round the piano," Joanna suggested.

"That's a good idea," said her brother.

"How nice to hear you two agree on something," laughed John.

After half an hour of singing some of the old songs from the shows, among which Robert gave his cockney rendering of 'My Old Man Said Follow the Van', and had them all laughing again, Maud said, "You once sang me my favourite song, Robert. Would you sing it for me again?"

"I remember, Aunty, it's *Danny Boy*." Robert had remembered this song from his first day at school. He had gone with his new class into the assembly hall for their first music lesson, and it was this song he had been singing when he had been slightly sick over his brand new song book. Nobody had noticed, but afterwards he had thrown the book away, and pretended that he'd lost it.

"I'll try, but my voice is breaking, and sometimes I can't get the high notes anymore," Robert replied. He had recently given up as head boy in the church choir because of this.

And so with Elizabeth playing the gentle accompaniment, the strains of the beautiful, pure voice of the boy floated out of the open French doors into the twilight of that warm June evening.

Oh, Danny Boy, the pipes, the pipes are calling
From glen to glen, and down the mountain side,
The summer's gone and all the roses falling,
It's you, it's you must go and I must bide.
But come ye back when summer's in the meadow,
Or when the valley's hushed and white with snow,
It's I'll be here in sunshine or in shadow,
Oh, Danny Boy, I love you so, love you so.

Robert's voice had not faltered, and he had managed the top note comfortably. He could see his aunty dabbing her eyes with her handkerchief, and remembered how the sad words had affected her before. Lisa was looking at him. What was she thinking? She was such a puzzle.

But when ye come, and all the flowers are dying,
If I am dead as dead I well may be,
Ye'll come and find the place where I am lying,
And kneel and say an 'Ave' there for me;
And I shall hear, though soft ye tread above me,
And all my grave will warmer, sweeter be,
For you will bend and tell me that you love me,
And I shall sleep in peace until you come to me! (see P625)

It was the last time Robert, was able to sing perfectly with his boy's voice.

"That was beautiful, my dear," said Maud.

"Why does it make you so sad, Aunty," Joanna asked.

"It reminds me of someone I knew long, long ago."

"Why does my voice have to break?" Robert asked.

"You're growing up, my son," John replied. "Nothing in life stays the same for long, not even the beautiful things."

"I wish this day could go on for forever," said Robert.

"Unfortunately it can't," John smiled. "Now off to bed with you."

CHAPTER 5

It was unusual for the household at Wimbledon to stir before noon on a Sunday. Even when the four boys were home the only sign of life in the morning would be a maid going silently about her duties. There had to be no noise for fear of disturbing her ladyship. However, on this particular Sunday, as the whole family had been instructed by Henrietta to be ready by ten thirty for the journey to Brighton, a number of glum looking faces had appeared at the breakfast table. Henrietta herself never graced the breakfast table, always taking her breakfast in bed, and young George - so called to distinguish him from his father - was also missing, having arrived home in the early hours of the morning after attending two parties in Town, and having consumed more drink than was good for him.

"I say, Pater, do we have to drag ourselves down to that dreadful Brighton? Relatives can be so boring," said Percy, his tall, spare frame draped across his chair, which he had turned alongside the table so that he could rest his elbow on it while he pecked at his breakfast. It was far too early to eat, he considered.

George looked at his second son and sighed. What had he done to deserve Percy? Twenty six years old and wasting his time trying to be an actor, although what else he was fit for he couldn't imagine. "Your Mother wishes the whole family to go, and in any case I fail to see why you should object. You've nothing else to do."

"I detect a note of censure, Pater old thing. I can't help it if I'm resting at the moment."

"You're always resting," sneered Jason.

"You shut up you little brute! What do you know about the stage?" retorted his brother.

"About as much as you do. Two parts, that's all you've had. And you didn't have to say a word," Jason snapped back. He disliked Percy, considering him to be an effeminate idiot. "You could play the fairy queen in panto, that's just about your mark," he added with a snigger.

"The opinion of a nasty, ignorant, little wretch like you, Jason, is not worth tuppence," Percy retorted, putting on a dignified air, more through being at a loss to know how else to deal with his precocious brother, than for any natural feelings of self control. He could have quite easily throttled the horrid brat.

"I'm l-look-ing forward t-to seeing Uncle John again," Henry stuttered, trying to change the subject. "He's always b-b-been very k-kind to me," he added.

"That's because you crawl round, him," said Percy. "As far as I'm concerned he's just an ignorant oaf like most soldiers. I don't like the way he looks at me."

"That's because he thinks you're a pansy. And he's not the only one," Jason cut in.

"And *you've* got a dirty mind. One of these days you'll get what you deserve," snapped Percy, raising his long, straight nose and looking with distaste at his youngest brother. "We all know what you get up to at school," he added, pleased to see by the surprised look on the boy's face that he had touched on a tender spot.

"For heavens sake let's have some peace at the table!" George interrupted. How he longed for peace and quiet. What with Henrietta always demanding something, usually money, and young George drinking too much, and these two always at each other's throats, life for George had not been easy. He realised that many of his troubles sprang from his own weakness; he had never stood up to Henrietta, and had rarely disciplined his boys when they were young. Now, at the age of fifty seven, he was very much overweight, and frequently complained of feeling tired, a condition for which he received little sympathy from his wife.

Jason snatched some more toast from the centre of the table and plastered it with a thick layer of butter before spooning on a large lump of marmalade. He was a strong sixteen year old, and was finishing his last term at Clifton before joining the Merchant Service.

He would normally have been at school this weekend, but had been allowed home in order to attend an interview in London on the Monday morning with a shipping company. "Well, I'm glad we're going to Brighton even if you're not," he said to Percy, trying to goad his brother into a fresh argument.

"Of course you are, dearie. You just can't wait to get your nasty little hands on that good looking cousin of ours, and make his life a misery for an hour or two. Just you watch out that dear Uncle doesn't catch you. He's very handy with the cane you know," Percy replied, renewing the attack and pleased for the opportunity to get the better of his brother. He could see the fury in Jason's eyes, but before the battle could continue Henrietta entered, the room and all argument ceased.

"It is now exactly a quarter past ten. I expect everyone to be ready to leave in ten minutes," she instructed.

Jason hurriedly left the room with his mouth still full of toast, followed by Percy. George went to the sideboard and poured himself a whisky.

"How you can drink that muck at this time in the morning I shall never know," Henrietta chided. "No wonder you're fat. And do try not to forget our purpose in visiting Brighton today."

"How can I, my dear? You have already reminded me six times."

"Indeed I have, and with good reason. Now you just tell that brother of yours that we want to be rid of the estate, and that it's up to him as a trustee to find a way through all the legal nonsense. And we want a good price for it."

Henrietta then turned on Henry. "And what are you sitting there gaping at? And just remember I don't want you stuttering away to that uncle of yours and taking his attention when your father should be talking business with him. I shall never understand why, of all people, he should take so much interest in you. Just keep out of the way."

Henry tried to reply, but his mother had left the room before he could force out the words.

The family congregated in the hall, waiting for the car to be brought to the front door. That is, all except young George, who eventually made his way unsteadily down the stairs holding on to the banisters with one hand and his head with the other, looking decidedly pale and blear-eyed. "Do hurry up, George!" ordered his mother.

"I say, what an advertisement for the British army," guffawed Percy. "Captain Rutherford springing into action on a Sunday morning. You really should attend the disarmament conference, Georgie. One glance at you and everyone would want to disarm for fear of being shot by their own side. I can't imagine anyone in their right mind giving you one of those beastly pop-gun things to play with."

Percy's remarks were not uppermost in his brother's mind, and he made no attempt to reply, for it was taking all young George's concentration to get himself safely down the stairs. However, Percy was not to be put off, and his amusement increased when young George reached the bottom of the stairs and had to stand for a moment to regain a proper balance.

"If only the army could see you now, they wouldn't even give you a pea-shooter," Percy continued. "What a bit of luck they're sending you to India. There's so much more space out there, so it won't matter if you miss whatever it is you're supposed to shoot at, and nobody'll mind if you happen to pop off a native or two by mistake."

"For God's sake shut up, Percy! Keep your play acting for those weird friends of yours," his brother replied as he lurched his way across the hall ignoring the rest of the family. Going into the dining room, he went to the sideboard and took the stopper from a very expensive cut glass decanter which, according to Percy 'Mother dear had looted from the house in Somerset', and half filled a tumbler with whisky. Drinking it down, he then filled his hip flash just in case he was unable to get at his uncle's decanter in Brighton. What the hell he had to be dragged down to Brighton for, he couldn't think. When Mother gets these damn silly ideas nothing can shift her. God! He felt rotten. If only he was back in bed.

"It's going to be absolutely foul travelling in this heat all boxed up like a tin of sardines. It really is too bad of you, Mother dear, forcing us into this dreadful journey," Percy complained as he opened the rear door of the Daimler for his mother. His gaudy blazer was flung over his shoulder, and he fanned himself vigorously with his boater. "If only that fool George hadn't cracked up the old tourer, we could have used two cars. Now we all have to squeeze ourselves into this wretched box and risk our lives with that idiot Henry at the wheel."

"Henry happens to be a very good driver," replied his father.

"It must be the only thing he is any good at," Henrietta declared. She rarely had a good word to say for her third son. His limp - he had been born with one leg slightly shorter than the other - irritated her, and his stutter infuriated her. "Nevertheless," she added, "There is no room for the chauffeur today, so we'll have to put up with Henry."

Jason and his father got in the front of the car with Henry and Percy remained holding the rear door until his brother George had settled himself next to his mother.

"I never realised you were so considerate, Percy," young George slurred.

"Don't deceive yourself, dearie. I wish to sit next to the open window to prevent myself being rendered unconscious by the obnoxious fumes which will no doubt be issuing from your besotted body." Percy got in and settled into the corner seat as far from his brother as possible, quickly winding down the window and making great play of breathing in the fresh air. But young George had already closed his eyes and paid no further attention to his brother.

"Drive on, Henry!" Henrietta commanded.

*

Sunday, for the family at Brighton, had always consisted of church in the morning and home for the rest of the day. The only variation to this pattern of events would be, perhaps, a walk on the Downs or a picnic in the country on a summer's afternoon. For Robert, whilst he was in the choir, a second visit to church was required in the evening, but as that was no longer necessary, he was normally free for the rest of the day after the morning-service.

As usual on a fine, warm day, the family walked the short distance to the church. The girls in their light summer frocks walked ahead, followed by Robert and Agnes, with Elizabeth and Maud bringing up the rear. Robert, much to his annoyance, had been made to wear his smart grey suit. It was a blooming nuisance having to dress up in a suit on a day like this. Why, couldn't he go in just shorts and sandals, he asked himself? He couldn't wait to get back to his room and fling off everything and get his shorts on. He pulled at his shirt collar, feeling it tight and sticking to his neck in the heat.

"Do stop pulling at your collar, Robert," said Elizabeth.

"Can't I take my tie off, my beastly collar's too tight?"

"Certainly not! Whatever would the vicar think?"

In the cause of comfort, Robert was prepared to risk what the vicar might think. "Don't you care if your dear son is strangled?" He turned, and gave his mother a facetious look. "I shall probably choke to death in the sermon."

"I'm sure it's not that bad, dear," Elizabeth smiled.

"The only way he'd choke to death would be by stuffing too many gob-stoppers," Joanna giggled to Lisa.

Robert chose to ignore his sister's remark. It then occurred to him that Daddy might make him keep his suit on all day as part of his punishment. And another equally disagreeable thought came to him, that Mummy had set him some work to do that afternoon. Oh, hell! It was all that stupid Joanna's fault. If it hadn't been for her he would never have used that word at the table. Look at her bouncing along with that other pest, Lisa. They never got into trouble. If only he could get his own back on Joanna. But he'd heard the vicar say that you shouldn't try to get your own back, because God didn't like it. Perhaps sisters didn't count. On the other hand Daddy wouldn't like it, and he seemed so much more powerful than God. God would sometimes bonk around with thunderstorms and that sort of thing, but that didn't hurt like Daddy's cane. Daddy says he should treat his sister like a young lady. Some lady!

John had not accompanied his family to church that morning, but was waiting for them at the front door when they returned. "The family should be here soon," he reminded them. "Robert, you will remain with us until we've greeted them, and then go to your room."

"I don't like them. Can't I go to my room now?"

"You like Henry and your uncle George," Elizabeth put in.

"Yes, they're all right, but I don't like the rest."

"It's got nothing to do with whether or not you like them. You're my son and I wish you to be present to help me greet our guests," John instructed.

"Yes, sir."

Ten minutes later the Daimler drove sedately into the drive and stopped at the bottom of the steps leading up to the front door. John led his family out to greet their relatives. George heaved himself from the front seat followed by Jason, who leapt out after him. "Good to see you, George," said John with genuine affection, shaking his brother's hand. Robert, making an effort, to show that he was polite like his father, opened the rear door, and out came Percy. "Thank God that's over!" he exclaimed. Then, looking closely at Robert, he said, "My, my, you've grown, and better looking than ever. You'll have to be careful, little cousin." Robert did not like being called little, because he wasn't little. In any case, why should, he have to be careful, he asked himself? Percy always said such silly things.

Cousin George stumbled out after Percy and stood unsteadily as Robert shook his hand. How untidy he looks, Robert thought. Daddy would never allow him to be untidy like that when calling on people. He felt pleased that Daddy wanted his help to greet their relatives, and was glad to be wearing his smart suit after all. It made him feel quite grown up.

John shook hands with his brother's eldest son, but looked with distaste at his appearance. However, young George's condition had not altogether surprised him, for he had received information from certain military sources regarding his nephew's deteriorating behaviour. Evidently young George's drunken conduct in the mess was now the talk of the battalion, and his gambling had come to the ears of his colonel, who would soon be forced to take action if matters didn't improve, John had decided, to take his own action.

Robert held out his hand to assist his aunty Henrietta from the car, and was quite surprised when she took it. He was less surprised when she otherwise ignored him. Henrietta imperiously swept up the steps, briefly pausing to reassure Elizabeth, to whom she referred to at home as that foreign woman, and Maud that she had noticed them.

The sisters-in-law knowingly smiled at each other and followed her ladyship into the house, the rest of the family following suit, except for John and Robert. They waited to greet Henry, who, as usual, had been forgotten.

"Hallo, Henry," said Robert. He felt sorry for his cousin, who seemed pleased that someone had taken the trouble to welcome him.

"Come along, Henry," said John, putting his arm round his nephew's shoulder and leading him up the steps into the house. I didn't know you could drive."

"Oh y-yes, Uncle. I ler-ler." Henry stopped and then, after a pause to collect himself, tried again. "I l-learnt on th-the estate. J-J-Jamie taught me."

"Well I'm blessed! He must be in his thirties by now. Nice boy."

"He's b-been very k-k-kind to me, Uncle."

"I wish I could drive like you, Henry," said Robert, giving Henry the satisfaction of knowing that at least his young cousin admired him for something.

At this point Robert disappeared to his room. He flung off his suit, in fact he felt so hot that he flung off everything, even his shoes and socks, and just put on a pair of shorts. He leaped on to the bed and lay flat on his back, staring at the ceiling with his hands clasped behind his head. He would have a think. It was nice to have a think sometimes. What was he going to do for the rest of the day? It was a rotten swiz that he should have to stay in on a day like this. Still, it was better than another whacking — he was still sore from Friday's lot. Perhaps he could sneak out for a bit. No, that wouldn't be right because Daddy had put him on his honour. He had never been locked in his room; the lock had no key anyway. It was time he stopped saying daddy, after all he would be fourteen in four months, no, just over five months, actually. Anyway, he would say father from now on – it sounded more grown up. And he'd better say mother, as well. He wondered what they were doing downstairs, drinking probably, grown ups always drank when they had nothing better to do.

Robert was right. The new arrivals had been served with an aperitif, although young George had refused John's best Madeira and helped himself to the whisky decanter. Then all eleven members of the family sat down to luncheon.

"Where's my young nephew?" asked George.

John briefly explained Robert's absence, and then led the conversation on to the previous day's cricket match and Robert's good performance.

"Why you men get so carried away with cricket I can't imagine," said Henrietta. "Such a stupid game, hitting a ball about with a piece of wood. In fact, when one considers the matter, all games are rather pointless."

"That's the whole point, Aunty," said Joanna, not really knowing quite what she was trying to say. "If there was any point it wouldn't be a game, if you see what I mean."

Henrietta didn't, and her glare at Joanna finished the subject.

"And how are you getting on, Henry?" John enquired.

A look of surprise came over the young man s face. He was not used to being spoken to at the table, except by way of criticism or when being laughed at by his brothers, and there was a pause before he could bring himself to answer. "Oh, Henry's in charge of the pig swill on the estate," said Percy with a malicious grin.

Jason sniggered,

"Henry does not get on, he merely labours," Henrietta replied in answer to John's question to her son.

John wished that she would be quiet and let Henry answer for himself. "Do you like the work, Henry?" he persisted.

"Y-Yes, v-very much th-thank you, Uncle. I-I. I-l-like working with an-animals."

"That's because he doesn't have to talk to them," Jason grinned. "They don't make him stutter."

"Have you heard that young George has been posted to India?" asked George, changing the subject.

"He's frightfully peeved about it, "Percy cut in.

"Can't think why," said John.

"He'll miss all the high jinks in Town, Uncle," said Percy.

"It's a God forsaken hole," young George snarled.

"It's a splendid place for a young officer," John rejoined. "You may get some action on the frontier."

"Heavens! That's the last thing he wants. He might get pinged by one of those nasty bullet things, or blown up or something. And then what would all the girls do?" Percy baited.

"Be quiet, Percy!" Henrietta ordered. She was tired of the subject, so for the rest of the meal monopolised the conversation with talk about fashion, a subject on which she was an expert.

As Robert lay thinking on his bed, the bedroom door opened and Agnes entered with a tray of food. She never forgot his needs even when he was confined to his room. While he hungrily cleared the plates, she scolded him for having left his suit lying on the bed where he had thrown it in his hurry to get it off. After Agnes had gone he lounged on the sill of the open window, putting off the moment when he would have to start doing the work which he had been set by his mother. He watched the family come out into the garden after luncheon. The older members seating themselves at the far end of the lawn near the summer house; the young ones, except for cousin George, who flung himself on the grass for a rest, and Henry, who was left out anyway, setting up the croquet-hoops for a game. Lisa saw him at the window and gave him a smile. For some reason this pleased him, and he shyly waved an acknowledgement. When he was fourteen he would be as old as she was, he thought. But he was always that six months behind, and that sometimes irritated him, especially when to tease him she referred to him as her young cousin.

Jason followed Lisa into the summer house to collect the mallets and balls for the game. "You're not a bad looker," he said, catching her round the waist and pulling her close to himself.

"What's it got to do with you," she snapped, struggling to get, him away.

"Came on, how about a kiss?"

"Let me go, Jason!" She pushed him hard and he stumbled back, tripping over the mallets and sitting down. "Who do you think you are?"

"You stuck up little miss."

Jason snatched up the mallets and angrily walked back out on to the lawn.

After coffee John and George walked together round the garden. "I've been wanting to talk to you about Somerset, John."

John said nothing but waited for his brother to continue.

"I want to be rid of the estate,"

"That's not possible, George, and you know it."

"But I need the money. The estate is not paying its way, you know."

"Then it should be," John replied curtly. Sometimes George tried his patience. "Perhaps you need a new manager."

"I don't see why. The man does his best."

"Then it's not good enough," John retorted. "Why don't you let Henry have a try?" he suggested.

"Henry?" George laughed. "My dear John, I've come to you for serious advice, not witty remarks." George felt a little irritated that his brother should take such a light hearted view of his difficulties. As much as he loved Henry, he had no illusions about the boy's ability - or rather lack of it. In any case, Henrietta would ridicule the idea.

"I'm serious, George. Just because, he stutters you think he's a fool. But he's not a fool, and he knows a great deal more about farming than you give him credit for. That, of course, is an understatement, because you give him credit for almost nothing."

"You're not seriously suggesting that I make Henry the manager?"

"Why not give him a chance. After all, he is twenty two, and I think he has a feeling for the land, as father used to say. Given the right encouragement he could do well."

"You need more than a feeling for the land, nowadays. You need a good business head."

"Then why don't you send him to one of those agricultural colleges to learn the modern methods and the business side of things?"

"I can't afford it. In any case, Henrietta would never agree. She wants to sell, and that's that."

"Well, she can't. Father made provision to stop this from happening."

"You're a trustee; surely you can get round all that legal nonsense. There are always ways and means."

"Maybe, but I've no intention of going against Father's wishes."

George realised that it was useless continuing the conversation. In his heart he had known that John would never consent to the estate being sold, but Henrietta had insisted that he raise the matter.

The two brothers walked back towards the lawn in silence until George, nodding towards his eldest son, who was still resting under the tree, remarked, "And there's another problem. I'm not sure I can go on much longer paying that boy's allowance."

"This is ridiculous!" John exclaimed. "What the devil do you do with all your money?"

George shrugged.

"If you're that short, I'm willing to help, but it beats me how you've got yourself into this mess," said John. "If it'll help, I'll settle young George's allowance for a time. I'll settle his gambling debts as well."

"Gambling debts! What gambling debts?"

"He owes three hundred pounds."

"Three hundred pounds!" George repeated, astonished. "How do you know this, John?"

"I make it my business to know what goes on in the regiment. Why the devil do you think he's been sent to India?"

"I've no idea."

"He's been sent to another battalion to give him a new start. If he doesn't pull himself together, I'll see to it personally that he resigns his commission."

George sighed and mopped his brow. "I wish you'd talk to him, John."

"At twenty eight, he shouldn't need talking to. You talk to him, and you can tell him from me that if he doesn't pull his socks up he'll be out of a job," John replied. However, he decided that he would take this opportunity to admonish his nephew.

Robert had been trying to finish the work he had been set, but sounds from the garden of the young people playing croquet had constantly distracted him and he had returned to the window a number of times wishing he could be playing with them. He noticed the game had finished and that all except Jason had gone back to the summer house. Once more he returned to his desk to make another effort, but he had no sooner started when the door to his room opened and in walked Jason.

"You should knock before you come in here," said Robert, looking daggers at his unwelcome guest.

"I don't knock for a grammar school worm. If you were at my school I'd beat you for your cheek," Jason snarled. He went to the window and checked that the rest of the family were still at the other end of the garden. He wanted no interruptions whilst dealing with his cousin.

"Well, I'm not at your school and this is my room, so go away."

"You need a lesson in manners." Jason caught Robert by the arm, knocking the pen from his hand and spotting his work with ink.

"You bloody fool, Jason, look what you've done!"

Jason dragged his cousin from his chair. "I'll teach you to call me names," he sneered, twisting Robert's arm up behind his back. "Go on, say your sorry!" he demanded.

"Ouch! Stop it, Jason! You're hurting!" Strong as he was, Robert was still unable to match the strength of the older boy, and found that he was helpless with his arm locked behind him. "I'm sorry!"

"That's better," Jason smirked as he forced Robert to bend over.

Jason was enjoying himself. He enjoyed the power he had over the younger boys at school, and now cousin Robert would be taught a few lessons.

Robert felt his shorts unfastened and drop to the floor. "Well, well, our grammar school tick has been beaten," Jason leered, pressing hard on Robert's weals and making him wince. "What do you say to a bit of fun?"

"What sort of fun?" Robert asked innocently. But his innocence soon disappeared as his cousin expertly turned his curiosity into desire, then into pleasure, and finally into shame. Robert quickly tired of his cousin's attentions, but it was some time before, seeing his chance to escape, he slipped out of Jason's grasp and ran for the door. Jason was quickly after him, but as Robert flung the bedroom door open, Jason ran into it and struck his nose, and Robert ran into the passageway straight into the arms of Agnes.

"What's going on?" she demanded. "And you, Robert, with nothing on!"

Robert said nothing, but just watched as Jason ran off down the passage holding his nose, which was now bleeding.

Agnes pushed Robert back into the bedroom. "What have you two been up to?" she demanded again.

"Nothing, Agnes, honestly. We were just messing about, that's all."

Agnes gave him a quizzical look, but let the matter drop.

As Jason came running across the lawn holding his bleeding nose, the rest of the family were taking tea.

"I never thought I'd see the day when brother George actually accepted a cup of tea," Percy was saying as young George was handed his cup by Elizabeth. "I thought the old hard stuff was more in your line. Taking the cure, are we?"

"It's a pity you don't take the cure for your inane chatter," young George growled. Still smarting from his recent, and unpleasant, conversation with his uncle, but determined not to be done out of all his pleasures, he furtively took out his hip flask and added whisky to his tea. For a moment he thought Percy had seen him, but his brother's attention had now focussed on Jason.

"Walked into a tree, Jason?" Percy laughed.

Jason ignored his brother and went straight to his mother. The front of his white shirt was now spotted with blood. "Look what Robert's done," he moaned, at the same time holding his nose in an effort to stop the bleeding.

"Sit down and hold your head back," said John. "Joanna, run and get a cloth and some cold water from the kitchen."

"This is a disgrace!" exclaimed Henrietta.

Maud thought her sister-in-law sounded like the Queen of Hearts about to order Alice's execution. Off with her head, she thought to herself.

With the cold cloth on Jason's nose the bleeding stopped. "What's this all about, Jason?" John enquired.

"It was Robert!

"What, did he hit you?"

"He was being rotten. He didn't want me in his room."

"Why was that?" John inquired.

"It doesn't matter why!" Henrietta interrupted. "That boy needs a good thrashing."

"It matters very much, why," John quietly replied.

"Are you going to do nothing?"

"I'm sure John will deal with the matter, my dear," said George.

"You keep out of this!" Henrietta ordered.

"Can't see what all the fuss is about," Percy interjected. "I've been wanting to give the little blighter a nose bleed for years. I say give the boy a bar of chocolate."

"Be quiet, Percy! How dare you make light of this matter." Henrietta was furious.

"Did he hit you, Jason?" John persisted. "He flung the door open and it hit me, Uncle," Jason pouted. "He did it purposely."

"A likely story, I don't think," Percy drawled. "I'll wager I know what you were up to."

"Mind your own business!" snapped Jason, glaring at his brother,

"Are you sure it was on purpose?" John repeated.

"That's what he said," snapped Henrietta.

"And is that what Robert will tell me?" John asked.

"I trust, you are not insinuating that my son is a liar?" said Henrietta haughtily. "You've heard the facts of the matter. Now do something about it and give that boy the whipping he deserves."

"You'll just have to leave the matter in my hands, Henrietta," John replied evenly.

"I don't mind what I have to do, providing that boy is punished," said Henrietta making her final pronouncement on the subject.

"Well I must say," said Percy, "The day's been far more of a whiz that I thought it would be. What with old Georgie being almost sober, and that brute Jason getting his just deserts, who knows, perhaps Henry will stop stuttering before we leave."

"Do stop talking such drivel, Percy, and come and have another game of croquet," said Joanna. "All of you," she added pulling young George and Henry to their feet. "And you, Jason."

"I can't play. My nose hurts," whined Jason. He was sitting on the grass beside his mother. Henrietta patted him on the head.

"That's right, darling, you just sit here quietly."

"Oh, don't be such a baby, Jason." Joanna got hold of her reluctant cousin and pulled him to his feet. She thrust a mallet into his hand and pushed him across the lawn. "A fine sailor you'll be if you can't stand a little bonk on the nose."

The astonished look on Henrietta's face as her son was marched away gave Maud further cause for amusement.

"Sensible girl, your Joanna," said George to his brother, pleased that the matter of Jason's nose had been temporarily forgotten. He sank back in his deck chair sipping his tea and listening contentedly to the laughter coming from the croquet lawn. Even young George was laughing, he noticed, which made a change. It was good that young people should laugh together. There should be more laughter in his own house, but he hadn't the sense of humour to encourage it, and Henrietta had no sense of humour at all. Perhaps, that was her trouble. It was these rare moments of peace which made life bearable for him. The sound of the violin coming from a bedroom window made him close his eyes and drink in the pure notes. He had always loved music and, in a hidden romantic streak in his soul, had imagined himself a great virtuoso. But he couldn't even play an instrument let alone play one well. In fact, there wasn't very much he could do well, he thought. Even when he tried to be kind it was mistaken for weakness. He knew some people thought him pompous, but he couldn't think why, because he never meant to be.

"Do stop rattling that cup and saucer, George." Henrietta interrupted a non-stop narrative she was giving to the other ladies about Jason's excellent progress at school and his forthcoming entry into the merchant navy, to put a stop to her husband's latest irritating habit.

"Sorry, my dear,"

"How long has your hand been shaking like that, George?" John asked, noticing that his brother's action was involuntary.

George seemed furtive about the matter and whispered his answer as if he didn't wish Henrietta to hear. But she was too involved with her own conversation to be listening to him. "Six months or so. Doctor says he can't do anything." He abruptly changed the subject. "Robert appears to be making good progress with the violin from what I hear."

"It's a pity he doesn't make such good progress with his school work," John replied.

George felt he had chosen the wrong subject so he tried again. "What do you think of the situation in Germany, John?"

"I saw in The Times on Friday that Papen has got his Cabinet virtually complete, with Freiherr von Neurath as Foreign Minister. It said that Hindenburg obviously wishes to pursue a constitutional course."

"But what about this man Hitler?" George asked.

"I would think an unknown quantity at the moment, but he strikes me as a little unstable for high office. Besides he's not a Gentleman, and Hindenburg would never make him Chancellor unless he had no other option."

"If you've finished all your business, George, we'll take our leave and go," Henrietta interrupted.

The sound of voices coming across the lawn took Robert to his window. He saw the whole family, except Lisa, who had already been driven back to school, strolling back towards the house. They're going at last, he said to himself. Jason looked up at him with a face as black as thunder, but he pretended not to notice. He knew he'd had naughty thoughts, but he wondered what God would think of him now that Jason had taught him worse things.

Later that evening, after his relations had left, Robert was lying on his bed reading, when the knock came on his door. "Come in," he called. "Oh, it's you, Daddy, I mean Father."

Robert stood up as John entered the room.

"I just thought I'd pop in and see you for a moment," John said. He often felt the need to be alone with his son, but somehow his busy life so often frustrated his good intentions.

"It's awfully decent of you, Father. Do you mind if I call you father? It's more grown up, isn't it?"

"Oh, yes, indeed. I don't mind a bit." John smiled to himself.

They sat down side by side on the bed.

"I wish you would come and see me more often," Robert said.

The words struck at John's heart. He had forgotten what it was like to be young and how his son needed his attention. It was only when he tried hard and focussed his mind on himself as a boy that he remembered his own joy in the presence of his father. "Yes. I must try." He saw Robert looking up at him with those large eyes of his. "I'm sorry you had to be confined to your room today, but fathers have to punish their sons when necessary. It's not always easy being a father, you understand."

"I think I do, Father. Anyway, thanks for not swishing me."

"Are you still sore?"

"A little," Robert smiled shyly.

"I wanted to say," John began, clearing his throat. He hesitated and wondered why it should be so difficult to say what was in his heart. He was never at a loss for words when the boy had to be told off. "I wanted you to know how. . ." He paused for a moment, glancing at the young face beside him. "How proud I was of you yesterday. I think you put up a first class show. And thank you for helping me welcome our guests today. I thought you acted most correctly. It is right that a father should have his son's support on these occasions."

"Oh, thank you, Father. It's jolly good of you to say so, especially after . . . well, you know." Robert felt his heart swell with pride. He took his father's hand. He thought he would so that Father would feel at ease in his room, and then he might come back more often.

John then said, "I hear you had an unwelcome visit from Jason." He felt Robert try to withdraw his hand, but John gripped it more firmly and wouldn't let it go.

Robert felt his face flush. "Yes."

"Do you wish to tell me about it?"

"I'd rather not," Robert replied, keeping his eyes on the floor and wondering what his cousin had said.

"As you wish. But just tell me one thing. Did you hit Jason?"

"No, Father. He ran into the door. . ."

John smiled. "Then the matter is closed."

The two sat in silence for a short time.

"Father, what was it really like in the war?

The question appeared to John to bear no relation to what they had been talking about, and he found it difficult to understand why his son should have suddenly asked it. But it was a question that had been on Robert's mind for a long time, and having his father alone with him was too good an opportunity to miss.

John saw out of the corner of his eye the earnest face staring up at him. It reminded him of that other young face which had once looked up at him those many years ago. The boy on the stretcher had wanted to live, and yet his life had slipped away like water through a sieve, and there had been nothing that John could do to prevent it. He had felt helpless then, and he had the same feeling now. His own son wanted a simple explanation, and here he was, General Sir John Rutherford, friend of the king, a man with the doors of all the great houses open to him, and he had no answer. How could he explain something completely outside the experience of the boy's young mind? It would be like trying to paint a picture without a canvas to paint on. It was the unanswerable question.

Robert had noticed John's hesitation and that strained look coming over his father's face. Perhaps he should not have asked that question, he thought. He tried again and said, "The vicar says war is wrong".

"It is," John replied, pleased that he had evaded the first question.

"Then why are you a soldier?" Robert came back.

"I had no choice; I was sent into the army by my father."

"Will you send me into the army?"

"Do you want to go?"

"I don't know. I like reading about battles and things, but I don't think I want to kill anyone, and I should hate to be wounded. It must hurt dreadfully."

"You must try not to think about that sort of thing. Are you looking forward to joining the OTC next term?"

"I'm not sure."

"You'll look smart in your uniform. And you want to learn to shoot, don't you?"

"I think I prefer playing the violin."

John was a little disappointed at his son's lack of enthusiasm for military training, but he tried not to show it. "Well, we shall see, old chap. I'm sure you'll do splendidly."

The following day Robert went to school quite happily, even though it was a Monday. Mondays were not usually the best of days in his way of thinking, the weekend being over and having to get through another five and a half days until the next one. But remembering how he had felt last Friday it didn't seem so bad. The situation was different in assembly that morning. On Friday he had felt like a criminal and had slunk down in his seat when the head had mentioned his name, but today his name was read out with pride, not only as a member of the victorious cricket team, but as the one who had hit the winning run. He basked in his moment of glory, fully aware that he was not a permanent member of the first eleven and would be unlikely to play with them again that season.

He was due to play with the second eleven on the coming Saturday, but had to inform his captain that he was not available. "I got a detention from that rotter, Cavey," Robert replied in explanation.

"You really are a bloody fool, Rutherford. We were relying on you. You'll have to go to the Head and ask for the swish instead."

It was normal procedure at the school that a boy with a Saturday afternoon detention could ask the headmaster to cane him instead.

"I can't."

"Why not? You're not afraid are you?"

"Of course not," Robert lied. "But I had a swishing last Friday."

"Think about the honour of the team," said the captain. But Robert was thinking more about his backside, and nothing could persuade him to change his mind. He knew he would regret what he thought of as his cowardice when Saturday afternoon arrived and he had to sit in school when he could be playing cricket, but he just couldn't pluck up the courage to go to the headmaster again.

He didn't play, and he did regret it, but during the detention kept reminding himself that at least he could sit down without too much discomfort.

The rest of the summer term of 1932 passed without incident. Towards the end of term, as did every boy in the school, Robert spent a few minutes with the headmaster having his report read, and signed. Each class was sent down in batches to wait outside the study, and each boy went in individually when called. On these occasions the headmaster would have the boy standing beside him as he sat at his desk. "Well, Rutherford, not a very good effort this term," said the headmaster.

"No, Sir."

"You've done well as usual in Latin, French and English, but the rest is a sorry story." The headmaster went down the list on the report, reading out some of the comments and grunting his disapproval at the boy's lack of effort. He gave Robert a couple of firm pats on the bottom and pulled him closer to his chair, putting his arm round Robert's thighs as he often did on these occasions when trying to emphasize a point to a nervous boy. "You are going to have to do better than this."

"Yes, sir."

"What is your father going to say?"

Robert was more worried about what he might do. "I don't know, sir."

"Well, I want better results next term, Rutherford. Off you go now."

"Yes, sir. Thank you, sir."

Robert went from the room thinking he ought to work harder next term, but next term was ages away and not worth worrying about at the moment. It was the summer holidays that were uppermost in his thoughts, and the forthcoming trip to the Grootvaders house at Grave.

There was only one more obstacle to overcome before Robert could feel completely relaxed. After that the long summer holidays would stretch out before him like an endless dream. On the last day of term every boy was handed a long, brown envelope on which he had to put his father's name and address. This was the report. The dreaded report as Robert thought of it. It had to be taken home and handed to his father. He was determined to get the matter over with quickly so, when his father returned home from London that evening, he handed him the envelope in the drawing-room while they waited for the dinner gong.

"Don't sneak away, young man," said John as Robert made to leave the room. Robert came and stood at his father's side while John tore open the envelope and took out the form.

"Listen to this, schat," John said. He then read out certain items to Elizabeth. "Maths, very weak. Tries sometimes when he feels like it. History, disappointing. I thought you liked history."

"I do, sir. But they asked me all the things I didn't know," Robert replied indignantly, thinking exams were stupid anyway.

"So it would appear," John commented, and then continued the sorry list. "Geography, answers too slight."

"I could have written about India and the places I saw on the way home, but they wanted to know about rivers and coal mines and that sort of thing. I don't know where the wretched coal mines are. I could have told them about the general strike though, and how Aunty Daisy socked that nasty bastard, or whatever he was called, with her handbag."

Elizabeth and John looked at each other.

"That's not a nice word to use, Robert," Elizabeth remarked gently.

"What word?"

"Never mind that now," John rejoined. "It's time you knew where the coal mines are. And what about physics and chemistry? It says very weak and no improvement made."

"I just don't understand what he's talking about."

"Do you ask when you don't understand?" Elizabeth enquired.

"I don't know what to ask. Besides, he always snaps my head off if I say anything. He's Welsh dand he's got a rotten temper."

"I fail to see what being Welsh has got to do with it," John remarked, wondering what his son would come out with next. "And this is your form master's comment," John went on. "Has ability and could do well if he made an effort. He is inclined to be a dreamer in class."

"He doesn't like me, because he said something about India once, and I told him he was wrong. He was wrong too. Anyway, we call him The Goon."

John decided he was getting nowhere. "Now you listen to me, Robert, I'm not interested in what strange names you call your form master, but if there's not an improvement by the end of next term I shall stop your music."

"Oh, don't do that, Father, please!"

"It's up to you. And you will have to do some work during the holidays instead of spending so much time playing the violin."

The matter seemed to be closed and Robert breathed a sign of relief. The idea of work in the holidays was not nice, but, with any luck they may forget it, he decided. But he really would try harder next term, for, although his constant struggle for perfection in his playing was becoming increasingly frustrating, life without his music would be terrible.

The last week of July was spent with mounting excitement and preparation for the forthcoming holiday in Holland. Each morning Robert woke, his first thoughts were to remind himself it was one day closer to the great day. And then the great day arrived. He could hardly believe it. Cases and trunks appeared in the hall, and Agues was bustling about checking and re-checking that nothing had been forgotten. And then in the afternoon the chauffeur brought the car to the front door, and all the luggage was loaded. Elizabeth and the children - John was in London and not going on this occasion - after saying their goodbyes to the servants, made themselves comfortable in the back of the car, and Agnes got in the front. All was ready for the short drive to the station. The engine started and the car began to move down the drive. The dream had begun, and Robert was happy.

CHAPTER 6

"There's the bridge!" cried Robert. It had been a long journey, but at last they were nearly there. He couldn't contain his excitement as the great nine span bridge came into view. In a moment he might just be able to see the red roof of Grootvaders house nestling in the trees on the other side of the river.

The family had come across on the night ferry from Harwich, as was their usual practice, and had landed at the Hook of Holland early that morning. One of Jan's cars had picked them up at Nijmegen station to bring them the last few miles to their destination. And now as the car moved on to the bridge, between the massive steel girders, and the glittering river Maas passed beneath them, the familiar sight of the old fortress town of Grave could be seen standing boldly on the far bank.

In 1926 when they had returned from India the construction of the new bridge had already been, in progress for two years. It was to be another three years before it was completed, and the use, of the ferry rendered unnecessary. Robert had watched the construction with great interest and on each visit had noted carefully in his mind how it had grown since the time before. A number of the great concrete blocks, on which the bridge stood, had been placed in the fields between, the dyke and the river where Robert and Karl Heinz frequently roamed. For the most part the bridge took the road across these low lying fields, and only three spans actually stood over the water. Over the years the boys became well known to the construction gangs, and were sometimes even allowed, a close look at the work going on. But it was after completion that they became really familiar with the bridge, or at least the underneath of it. They had been forbidden to play on it on pain of a severe thrashing, but that only added, to the excitement and adventure. It had become their bridge and nothing was going to keep them from it. A track on top of the dyke ran under the end of the first span, giving them easy access to the girders, which supported the road from underneath. It was only a matter of walking along the dike from Grootvaders garden until they were under the bridge, then up the grass bank beside the first concrete support, and with arms outstretched they could swing themselves up on to the girders. From here, when the maintenance men were not about, they would often clamber along above the fields until they were almost over the water. On one occasion they actually crossed the river and went the whole length of the bridge. They had never been caught.

This friendly monster with the nine humps had frequently forced its way into Robert's mind as he sat dreaming and chewing the end of his pencil during maths lessons, trying, usually without much success, to keep his mind on what old Cavey was saying. To pass across the bridge was to escape to the land of his birth where he could dream his dreams in peace, and the wicked world of work and masters and maths and nasty cousins and next term were all shut out on the other side.

The girders of the final span flashed by, and they were over. At last, the summer holiday had really started, Robert said to himself.

Most of the old fortress on the west side of Grave had been demolished to make way for the new approach road to the bridge. Grave was no longer isolated as it had been for centuries, and the road from Nijmegen in the north now led, uninterrupted by the river barrier, to Uden and Eindhoven in the south.

Karl Heinz had arrived the day before and was waiting impatiently at the end of the rough track for his cousin to arrive. As the car slowly turned from the road on to the uneven surface he jumped on the running board and pushed his head and shoulders through the open window, "Hallo everybody!" he laughed excitedly.

"Karl Heinz!" Robert cried, grabbing his cousin's hand and tugging it.

"Careful, Robert, or you'll pull him right in," said Elizabeth.

Joanna said, "They've started already. They can't even wait 'til we arrive before they start a bundle".

The whole family were waiting for them in the front garden. Jan, his hair now completely white, and not quite so upright as he used to be but still carrying his seventy two years well, with Flora beside him looking a young sixty eight.

Robert and Joanna rushed from the car into the arms of their grandmother and were immediately smothered in kisses. Jan was next for Joanna's attention, but Robert, now that he considered himself almost grown up, was not quite sure whether to kiss his Grootvader, so he just offered his hand. The old man smiled at his grandson's hesitation. "It is not unmanly to kiss, my Robert," he said, pulling the boy to him and kissing him on both cheeks.

"Have you a kiss for me, my handsome Prince?" said Natascha. "You and Karl Heinz become more and more alike."

Robert was happy to kiss his aunty, but he didn't particularly want to kiss his uncle Karl, so he greeted him in true German style by clicking his heels and bowing his head as he shook hands. This seemed to please Karl, whom Robert considered a rather formal person. It was unusual for Karl to accompany his family to Grave, but on this occasion Natascha had managed to drag him away from his now lucrative practice for a short holiday.

Hugo and Kate were also present, and Isabel, who was now twenty one. And there's Lisa, Robert said to himself, quickly looking away as his cousin fixed her dark eyes on him. He was certainly not going to kiss *her*, but he had to admit to himself that he would have been disappointed if she hadn't been there. He tried not to think about her, but, as the family exchanged greetings, found himself sneaking a look every now and then to see what she was doing. He didn't know why, but he often found himself thinking about her now. It was ever since that cricket match. Somehow he had enjoyed her being there to see him doing something well, even if she didn't understand the game. Girls don't understand much, anyway, he decided.

The greetings over, the whole party, except Robert and Karl Heinz, who had run off into the back garden, moved into the house where refreshments awaited the new arrivals.

"I'm sorry John couldn't come," said Natascha. "I do like to hear him and Karl arguing about politics. Karl gets so worked up, and John always remains so calm."

"The English are so complacent about politics," Karl replied. He did not hate the English as he did the French, but he had not forgiven them for their support of France in the war. It was quite beyond him why the English had gone to war just because the German army had marched through Belgium. The British army was continually marching into other countries throughout the world, so what was the difference, he often asked himself? No doubt the English would find some excuse for their own conduct, but then they were a strange people. The thought of the war still embittered his national pride, especially when he considered, as he often did, how badly his beloved Fatherland had been treated by the victorious allies. Still a fervent royalist, he considered that Germany would have been far more politically stable if the Kaiser had remained on the throne. Germany, he would tell anyone willing to listen, was not ready to be a republic. It was the one point on which he and John agreed.

His relationship with John had never been comfortable. He admired John for his high rank in the army, but in Karl's mind John was the typical Englishman, and the English were not to be trusted. He had once said to John that the English owned half the world, and expected the other half to comply with their wishes. When John had replied, dryly that he considered this a most agreeable arrangement; Karl had not appreciated the other's humour.

Life had been difficult for Karl, but he had worked hard, and after leaving the army had returned to Cologne and set up his own practice. The terrible economic situation in Germany in the twenties had meant years of struggle and a low standard of living. Although Jan had been willing to help his son-in-law, Karl was a proud man and insisted in making his own way in the world. The only concession he had made on this account was to allow Natascha and Karl Heinz to remain at Grave for the first few difficult years after the war, when he was still serving in the army.

There was nothing that Flora enjoyed more than having her whole family round her. She was sorry that John was not with them at dinner that evening, for, of her three children's marriage partners, he was her favourite. She admired his strength of character, and considered him the true English gentleman as well as a loving husband and father. It had given her much comfort to know that her daughter had married such a man. Most people thought Robert like his mother, but Flora could see John in the boy. "And how are you getting on at school, Robert?" she asked.

Robert, remembering the lecture he had recently received regarding his bad report, looked at his mother and smiled sheepishly. "I'm not quite sure, Grandma." (The children always spoke English to Flora and Dutch to Jan.) "Cricket's all right, but I don't like work very much."

"He's terribly naughty, Grandma. He's always getting the cane, Joanna interjected.

"Shut up, you!" Robert snapped, glaring at his' sister, feeling himself colour up.

"Och, I can't believe that," Flora laughed.

"He's certainly going to have to work harder, Mama, but he's not quite as bad as Joanna makes out," Elizabeth smiled.

"He's really good at music," said Karl Heinz enthusiastically.

Flora said, "And what about you, Karl Heinz?"

"I was top of my class, Grandma," Karl Heinz replied as if his success was of little importance and not unexpected. He then went on with obvious pleasure, "But I've got some special news to tell you."

"I'm sure being top of your class was special, and I'm very proud of you," said Flora.

"Come on, Karl Heinz, what's the special news?" Joanna as usual was unable to contain her curiosity.

"I've joined the Hitler Youth," Karl Heinz pronounced, looking round the table with satisfaction.

"Whatever's that?" Joanna inquired.

Karl Heinz looked a little taken aback at Joanna's ignorance, and made no effort to explain. He was also a little disappointed at the lack of response from the rest of the family.

"To be precise," said Karl, and Karl was always precise, "Karl Heinz has joined the Deutsches Jungvolk." He went on to explain that this had been a separate youth organisation which had amalgamated with the Hitler Youth and was considered ideal for boys up to the age of fourteen. "When he is fourteen he will be sworn in and enter the senior section."

"Then I'm given a dagger," Karl Heinz added eagerly.

"What for? Are you going to kill someone?" Joanna asked innocently, with a wicked twinkle in her eye.

"Of course not, stupid!" Karl Heinz was not amused at his cousin's frivolous remark. He expected these things to be taken seriously. But his father had always said that the English had a strange sense of humour.

"What's the Hitler Youth?" asked Robert.

Karl Heinz had not been called upon to explain this before and seemed unsure of himself. But he remembered what his *Jungbannführer* had told him when he joined, and recited, "We are the young people of the National Socialist German Workers Party who are sworn to serve Adolf Hitler and Germany."

Robert looked bewildered by his cousin's rather formal explanation - he had never heard of the national something or other, and knew nothing about Adolf Hitler for that matter - but before he could ask anything else Joanna butted in.

"Isn't that the man with the funny moustache who shouts a lot? I've seen him on the, news at the pictures."

Flora could see that both Karl Heinz and his father were not pleased by Joanna's light hearted comments. "We are very pleased, for you, my dear," she said to Karl Heinz.

"Why did he choose the Hitler Youth, when there are so many other youth organisations in Germany?" Jan asked; directing his question at Natascha.

"It's just that Karl has a patient who is an important Party member; he's a friend, of Herr Hitler, I believe. He suggested it," Natascha replied.

Karl put in proudly, "Germany has more youth organisations than any other country in Europe, and in my opinion, this is the best one. There is no class distinction and it is good that Karl Heinz will mix with all types of boy."

"It sounds a little too political for my liking," Hugo commented.

"Couldn't he have joined the boy scouts?" asked Flora.

"He could have done, Mama, but he didn't," Karl rejoined testily. "It appears that none of you realise what is going on in Germany. The election last week was an overwhelming victory for the national Socialists and they are now the strongest party in the Reichstag. Sooner or later President Hindenburg will have to invite Herr Hitler to be Chancellor, and then we shall have a new and strong Germany. It is the duty of our young people to be part of this, and to have joined the Hitler Youth will be Karl Heinz's contribution."

"Are you a National Socialist, Karl?" asked Hugo.

"I'm not a party member, but I believe in some of the things they stand for. Germany must regain its place in the world, and I think Herr Hitler is the man to make sure we do."

Karl Heinz looked at his father with pride. He didn't understand about, elections and politics, but father knew everything and it was good to hear him telling the others about his wonderful country. Like most of the boys he had met in the movement he hadn't joined for political reasons, but to be with other boys of his own age and to take part in exciting activities such as camping, hiking and sport. He also liked the parades, especially now that he was being taught to play the drum.

"*So* you support Hitler, Karl," said Jan.

"I do, because Germany needs strong government. Since we are not allowed to have a Kaiser, I believe that Adolph Hitler is the only man who can save us from the communists. I'll support anyone who can stop this foul disease creeping across Europe."

"Is he not against the Jews, as well?" Hugo was not convinced by his brother-in-law's reasoning, and had the feeling that some of the policies of the National Socialists made their leader an unsuitable candidate for the Chancellorship of Germany.

"If he is, then he is not alone in History. I'm sure nothing will happen to the Jews, but even if they are inconvenienced, in some way they will survive. They always have done." Karl's mind brushed aside that minor Issue for the more important task of driving back the filthy communists, as he frequently referred to them.

"I think it's time to stop talking politics before Karl gets carried away," Natascha interrupted.

Robert had not been listening he was more interested removing the last scraps of pudding from his plate. Karl Heinz's attention had also wandered and he was amusing himself by stretching his leg out under the table and trying to touch Lisa's knee with his foot. The table was fairly wide and he began to sink in his chair. "Sit up properly, Karl Heinz!" Karl rapped. The boy sat up smartly.

Flora, seeing that the children were getting bored called upon Jan to let them leave the table. This being allowed, the two boys quickly left the dining room for the garden where they remained until called in for bed.

In Grootvaders house the boys had always slept together In the same bedroom in which their cots had once stood when they were babies. When they were old enough the cots had been replaced by a double bed, which was a change from their single beds at home and added to the novelty of their holiday in the old house. It was always fun to try and push each other out of bed or wrestle beneath the bedclothes before falling asleep. Each enjoyed the closeness of the other, and sometimes they would find themselves wrapped in each other's arms when they woke in the morning. In their hearts they were brothers; perhaps even closer than brothers.

They both knelt together and said their prayers as they had always done since their very earliest days, Karl Heinz prayed for Mother and Father, and for Herr Hitler. He thanked God for bringing him to Grave to be with Robert, whom he loved very much and he hoped God did too, because then he would keep him safe. Robert asked God to forgive him for thinking dirty thoughts, and doing naughty things to himself. It was these feelings he kept getting, he explained. He couldn't help it and hoped God would understand. He prayed for Father and Mother, Joanna and Karl Heinz, and, of course, for Agnes and the rest of the family, but he wouldn't pray for Jason even though God would be angry about that, because the vicar says God expects people to pray for their enemies.

Robert finished first and got to his feet. After undressing he sat on the edge of the bed in his pyjama trousers - he didn't wear a top in the summer. As he sat there and watched his cousin undress, sensations came over him with such intensity that he felt himself becoming aroused. He felt a little ashamed and tried to suppress his feelings, but he couldn't get certain thoughts out of his mind. Why did he feel so naughty? What was happening to him, he asked himself? He had seen Karl Heinz naked before, but he'd never felt like this.

As Karl Heinz tried to pull on his trousers, Robert couldn't resist the temptation to push him on to the bed. Karl Heinz fell flat on his face, and Robert leapt on his back.

"That's not fair. I wasn't ready," laughed Karl Heinz as his cousin held him down. Physically the boys were evenly matched, but Karl Heinz usually won more of their wrestling bouts than Robert, because his will to win was the greater of the two. To Robert it was just a game and it didn't matter whether he won or lost. Sometimes he would laugh so much that it was impossible for him to put up any resistance. Although Karl Heinz took all games seriously, he never resented losing to his cousin, and when he was defeated he respected Robert the more, and always praised him for his good performance. This time Robert had won, assisted by the surprise of the attack and the fact that Karl Heinz's pyjamas had become wrapped round his ankles so that the movement of his legs was restricted.

"You're my prisoner and you've got to do what I say," said Robert, expecting his cousin to fling him off and start wrestling again. But to his surprise Karl Heinz did nothing.

Karl Heinz said quietly, "I surrender. You can do what you like with me."

Robert got off, his cousin's back and knelt on the bed beside him. He felt himself quiver with excitement at the sight of the naked boy lying in front of him, but for a moment hesitated to use the power he had been given. He knew what he wanted to do but wondered whether he dare. He plucked up courage and made Karl Heinz turn over. It pleased him to see that his cousin was in the same state as himself, and that he was not the only one to get like this. During the next few minutes as he gratified his wriggling victim, such was

Robert's excitement that he was unable to control himself, and his own feelings overflowed. After it was over a mixture of shame and embarrassment made them unable to meet each other's eyes, but the moment was short lived, and, switching out the light and leaving their pyjama trousers on the floor, they happily got between the sheets and lay back contented.

"I've always wanted a brother," Karl Heinz whispered.

"So've I."

"It's not sissy to love a brother, is it?" I don't mean like girls, with their stupid kissing and all that sort of thing."

"Course it isn't," Robert replied.

"Let's make ourselves blood brothers like the Red Indians do."

"But they cut themselves with knives," "Robert faltered, feeling he would be too scared to do a thing like that.

"They have to mix their blood." Karl Heinz could tell his cousin was unsure. "It won't hurt, Robert. It's only a little cut."

Robert desperately wanted to do it but doubted his courage to cut his own arm. However, he finally agreed, and it was decided that they would do it on the river bank the next time they went swimming.

They lay talking until past midnight before their minds became drowsy and sleep eventually took over.

The next day the weather was not suitable for swimming in the river, and the boys had to amuse themselves in other ways. A secret expedition along the underneath of the bridge filled in the first morning. They went only as far as the water's edge, because the maintenance men were working on the other side of the river. It was the first time that Lisa had accompanied them to the bridge. Before they would let her go with them she had to be sworn to secrecy, and she was firmly informed that if she was afraid of falling off or getting hurt she shouldn't go in the first place. To their surprise, Lisa swung herself up on to the girders and clambered along with as much skill as they did.

The following day offered more promise for a swim, and after breakfast, realising it was going to be hot, the boys decided to go to the river. "I've got my penknife for the blood ceremony," said Karl Heinz.

"Are you sure it'll be all right?" Robert asked, shuddering at the thought of it. "I mean, we won't get gangrene or something will we?"

"Of course we won't. Don't worry, Robert. We'll make a little fire so we can burn the germs off the blade. I've read that's what you have to do."

Robert wasn't entirely convinced, but knew he would have to go through with it. He helped his cousin find some paper and pieces of dry wood. And Karl Heinz took some matches from the kitchen. They left the house by a rear door, relieved to see that Lisa wasn't following, and, crossing the lawn, took the path through the shrubbery. But to their annoyance, when they climbed up on to the top of the dyke, there was Lisa sitting waiting for them. "I know you two are up to something," she said.

"No we're not!" Robert exclaimed.

"We're going swimming, and you can't come," said Karl Heinz.

"Why not?"

"You know jolly well why," said Robert.

"It's your fault if you don't wear anything. I shall come anyway, and you can't stop me." Lisa tossed her head as was her habit when putting the boys in their place.

Karl Heinz shrugged. He knew it was no use arguing with Lisa once she had made up her mind. "'Come on, Robert," he said, running down the other side of the dyke into the field. The others followed suit.

"We can't swim if she's here," Robert whispered urgently.

"Oh yes we can!" Karl Heinz retorted. "She's not stopping me. If she doesn't like it she shouldn't come."

Robert didn't feel as confident as Karl Heinz. He didn't want to undress in front of Lisa, and he knew she wouldn't go away. She could be such a rotten nuisance sometimes. Why couldn't she let them have a swim in peace? And another thing, he didn't want her to see him cut his arm. Supposing he funked it? Then she'd know he was a coward. Both she and Karl Heinz were so jolly stubborn, and he felt caught between the two of them. Oh, hell, what was he going to do now?

The boys wore no shoes and the damp grass felt like a soft carpet under their bare feet as they crossed the fields towards the river. The sun was now high enough to have dispersed the wisps of mist hovering near the river, but the dew still lay heavily on the grass covering their feet with its cooling balm.

Karl Heinz strode out in front with Lisa next following defiantly. Robert had dropped behind as he tried to think what to do. It was no good saying anything as neither of them would give way, and in any case he didn't want to appear a sissy or a spoil sport."

They crossed the fields to the riverbank then walked down stream for same distance so that they were well away from the bridge. There was one particular secluded place which they always used for swimming. Here was a small shallow inlet where the bank shelved very gradually, giving easy access to the water.

Having arrived and chosen a suitable spot near the water, Karl Heinz wasted no time, but immediately laid out the paper and pieces of wood ready for lighting. He took out his penknife and the matches, and neatly laid them down nearby. "That's all ready for when we come out," he said, with satisfaction.

"What's all that for?" questioned Lisa, who had sat down to watch.

"You'll see," Karl Heinz replied, starting to unfasten his shorts.

Robert also sat down but made no attempt to remove his shorts. He could see his cousin had that determined look on his face. Oh, lor, he thought, he really is doing it.

Lisa made no attempt to look away, in fact just the opposite. When Karl Heinz had stripped himself, he gave Lisa a challenging look and then walked slowly into the water. "Hurry up, Robert," he called.

The sun was well up now, and Robert could feel the heat beating on his bare back. He longed to be in the cool water, but he knew that Lisa was sitting there looking at him just to make him feel awkward. She's jolly well enjoying it, he thought,

"Couldn't you just shut your eyes for a minute?" Robert pleaded.

"Why should I? It's not my fault if you're so bashful," she provoked, giving one of her haughty looks.

He wondered why he was being so stupid. What did it matter anyway if she did see him, he asked himself? But somehow it did. But he would have to do it, or Karl Heinz would think there was something wrong with him. He was fiddling with the medallion round his neck. He had meant to take it off after breakfast, because he was not supposed to wear it when he went to play during the day and especially when he went swimming. He removed it and carefully wrapped it in his handkerchief, and then put it in the pocket of his shorts. He got up and, keeping his back to Lisa, quickly threw off his shorts and rushed into the water.

Once the water had closed round him, caressing his skin and protecting him from Lisa's stares, he felt secure and wondered why he should have made such a fuss. He swam back towards the bank and noticed that Lisa was starting to undo her dress. He couldn't take his eyes from her as she stood up and kicked off her shoes.

"Now who's staring, she called, grinning mischievously as their eyes met. He felt embarrassed and pretended to look away, but saw her dress slip to the ground only to reveal her bathing costume underneath. With a laugh she ran into the water. She never ceased to surprise them, and in a moment she was swimming as fast and as strongly as they were. Any doubts in the minds of the boys about having her with them had vanished, she was almost another boy, and they were happy, the three of them together. At last she had made her mark, and was never again to be excluded from their company.

When they all came out of the water, Karl Heinz lit the fire. Robert noticed that his cousin made no attempt to dress, but just sat naked on the grass, so he did likewise, although he did try to hide himself as much as possible from Lisa's gaze.

While Robert watched apprehensively, Karl Heinz held his penknife over the small flame until he was satisfied it was properly sterilized. When the blade had cooled, he carefully wiped it on his clean handkerchief.

Lisa looked on with interest but said nothing,

"Okay Robert, we're ready," said Karl Heinz. "I'll cut my right arm and you cut your left. That will make it easier for you, because you can use your right hand to do it."

Robert wished, he'd never agreed to do it. Why was Karl Heinz so much braver than he was? But he couldn't get out of it now, because Lisa was watching, and he didn't want her to know he was a coward. If only she'd go away. He watched Karl Heinz take the knife and place the blade on his forearm, gradually drawing it across the skin until blood was issuing from a small cut. "There!" he said, "Now it's your turn, Robert."

Robert had looked away as his cousin had made his cut, but now he could see the blood dribbling down the arm he felt quite weak. He took the knife from Karl Heinz, trying to disguise the fact that his hand was shaking, and sat for a moment to get control of himself. He could see Lisa looking at him, and knew there was no drawing back. Putting the blade on his arm in the same manner as Karl Heinz had done, he held his head down and hunched his shoulders, and then shut his eyes. He felt his cousin put an arm round his shoulders, and it gave him courage to feel Karl Heinz's body so close.

"It'll be all right, Robert, you'll see," Karl Heinz comforted.

With hand still shaking, Robert pressed the blade down and began to draw it across his skin. "Ow," he gasped as the pain seared, into him, and the tears welled up in his eyes. "I can't," he wailed.

"That's enough, Robert, you've done it," said Karl Heinz.

Robert opened his eyes and to his surprise saw blood oozing from his wound. It hadn't been as bad as he had imagined, it was just the thought of it that had made him feel squeamish. The boys put their arms together, and Karl Heinz bound them firmly with a handkerchief. Karl Heinz said, "Now we must swear an oath." He shut his eyes and thought for a moment. "What shall we say?"

Robert remained silent waiting for his cousin to think of something.

"I know," Karl Heinz continued. "I swear that my blood is your blood, and your blood is my blood, and we are brothers forever. Now you say it, Robert." After Robert had repeated the words, Karl Heinz said, "Good, that's done. Now we really are brothers."

Lisa sat fascinated by what the two boys had done. "I could do that," she said.

"It's not for girls," Robert replied, feeling proud of himself now that the ordeal was over.

"I suppose you think you're brave," said Lisa.

"Braver than you," Robert retorted.

"Prove it."

"Why should I?"

"There! You're scared!"

"No I'm not."

"Do something really brave, then," Lisa teased.

"Such as?!"

Lisa hesitated. She was at a loss to know what to say now that it had come to suggesting something. But she had no intention of letting cousin Robert get the better of her. "Go down the cellar," she blurted out.

"That's easy," Robert boasted.

"Do it then."

"All right, I will."

"When?"

"This afternoon."

"No, Robert, you mustn't," said Karl Heinz. "There will be terrible trouble if you are found out."

"There! You see! Trying to get out of it already," Lisa taunted.

"I'm not," Robert replied, beginning to feel dubious about the matter, and realising that Lisa had trapped him.

Karl Heinz tried to change the subject. He unwound the handkerchief, and their arms parted to reveal a sticky mess of congealed blood. "Come on, let's all go in again and wash off this mess," he said.

It was so good being in the water that it was with reluctance they eventually dragged themselves out to dry in the hot sun. As they lay sunning themselves Lisa said, "You'll need a torch, Robert."

"What for," Karl Heinz questioned.

"The cellar, of course. He can't go down without a torch."

"He's not going down," said Karl Heinz firmly.

"If he doesn't, he's a coward."

"He'll get a terrible strapping if he's caught," Karl Heinz replied, adopting a protective role towards Robert. He felt his cousin should be firmer in his dealings with Lisa.

"Well, it wouldn't be brave if there wasn't a risk." Lisa was not to be put off, and Karl Heinz realised he was losing the battle.

"It's no good, Karl Heinz, I'll have to do it, or we'll never hear the last of it," Robert concluded.

They arrived back at the house just in time for a light lunch in the garden with the rest of the family.

"Did you children have a good morning?" asked Jan.

"Yes thanks, Grootvader, " said Robert. "It was smashing in the water."

"What's happened to your arm, Karl Heinz?" asked Natascha.

"We cut ourselves. Now we're blood brothers."

"Good heavens! Whatever will you boys think of next!" exclaimed Elizabeth.

"You'll have a scar if I don't put a stitch in it," said Karl.

"We want a scar," Karl Heinz replied, feeling a little impatient with his father for suggesting such a thing. After going to all that trouble to get a scar, he wants to sew it up, he thought to himself. "We want everybody to know we're brothers forever."

Having eaten, the boys were not allowed to rest. "Come on, you two," urged Lisa. She had no intention of letting Robert forget his promise.

The boys reluctantly got up from the lawn, where they had been lying and enjoying the sun on their backs, and followed their cousin into the house. For a moment Robert tried to play the innocent, but Lisa soon put a stop to that. "Are you going to do it or not?" she asked impatiently.

"Yes, all right," Robert replied.

As he had been unable to stop the expedition, to the cellar Karl Heinz decided that he would take command of the organisation. He couldn't have a girl doing that. He sent Robert to put on a shirt, for, as he explained, it might be cold down below. "And put your sandals on," he added.

Lisa produced a torch. "Hurry up!" she said when Robert returned. "We must get started before the others come in."

"It's all right for you, giving orders. I couldn't find my shirt." Robert swore to himself that he would never boast again. Especially to a girl.

Karl Heinz explained the plan as the three sat in the hall at the bottom of the main, staircase. He was to stand guard at the end of the passage while Lisa went with Robert to the cellar door.' When he gave the signal that the coast was clear, Lisa was to pull back the curtain, and Robert would quickly enter and shut the door behind him. Lisa would then close the curtain and return to the end of the passage. "Go down for five minutes, Robert. When you come up again, wait behind the door until we give you three knocks. Then come out quickly. Don't come out before we knock, because someone might be around," Karl Heinz concluded.

"What if someone is around?" Robert asked.

"Then you'll just have to wait until they've gone."

They sat for a moment longer to ensure that the house was quiet.

"Ready then?" Lisa asked,

Robert felt that he would never be ready, but that he ought to get it over with. "Yes," he replied, trying to appear nonchalant. After all, he decided, there was nothing to be nervous about. He'd come straight up again, and then it would be over.

Robert and Lisa walked quickly down the passage, which was no more than a narrow recess about twenty five feet in length on the opposite side of the great fireplace to the main stairs. The cellar door was on the right nearly at the far end, and covered by a curtain. Robert felt his stomach turn over at the sight of the leather strap hanging on the wall, but it was too late to think about that now. Karl Heinz had signalled, Lisa pulled back the curtain, and he opened the door and went in. When the door closed behind him, he shone his torch and found a light switch. With the light on he could see the stone steps descending steeply in front of him. The actual passage down which the steps went was wide, but there was no handrail and the steps themselves were very uneven in height. Some were not more than six inches deep, but others were as much as a foot. One, about halfway down, looked as if it was even deeper than a foot. It was as if they had purposely been made like this as a trap for the unwary intruder.

Robert thrust his torch into his pocket in order to have both hands free for the descent. Down he went, carefully, one step at a time, with one hand touching the wall to steady himself. Halfway and here was the deepest step. Fancy making steps like these, he thought. No wonder they were not allowed to play down here. He was beginning to enjoy the adventure, it wasn't so bad after all and at least Lisa wouldn't be able to call him a coward.

Safely over the steep step, he found the rest much easier and eventually arrived at the bottom. He hadn't counted the steps, but it seemed a long way down. Luckily the stair passage was well lit. It must have been quite dangerous before Grootvader had electric light put in. So far he had only managed to light the stair passage, and now that he had arrived at the bottom he found that the cellar itself was only a dim outline and difficult to see clearly. But then he noticed two more switches on the wall, and, pushing them down, the whole cellar lit up, albeit not too brightly.

He was standing in a vault measuring about thirty five feet square, the walls, like the upper part of the house, being made of brick. It was how he imagined a torture chamber to be in the olden days, and he shuddered at the thought of his being a prisoner locked down here in the darkness and then put to the torment. Fancy being branded with a red hot iron, he thought. They must have been really rotten in those days. He would have done anything they wanted rather than put up with all that pain.

The stair passage wall continued along on his right hand side to the opposite wall of the cellar. It acted as a dividing wall between the chamber in which he was standing and that part of the cellar where the wine was stored, which was entered through an archway halfway along this wall. Robert moved forward and peered in at the rows of wine bottles placed neatly in their racks, but this did not hold his interest so he made no attempt to venture in. Turning his back on the archway so that the steps were now on his left, he looked down the length of the chamber. There was a very large wooden table standing against the wall on the left, and a few old barrels clustered around the far corner on the right. Other than that there was nothing. No boxes of treasure; no secret passages. Nothing. How jolly disappointing, he thought. The only other thing he noticed was an old iron stove standing on the hearth of a very large fireplace, which was set into the far wall straight in front of him. This looked boring as well. All the same, he might as well have a look. The stove was very old and very dirty, but he was able to lean over it and peer up the enormous chimney. Not that he could see much, just a couple of flat iron pieces about a foot apart, one higher than the other, protruding out about six inches from the wall above the stove. Perhaps that's how they climbed up the chimney to clean it. He remembered reading about sweep boys being sent up chimneys. What a rotten job that must have been, he considered. Perhaps school wasn't so bad after all.

It was time to go up again, five minutes must be up.

He returned to the foot of the steps and was about to start climbing back up, when he felt his heart miss a beat and his whole body seemed to turn to jelly. Someone was rattling the handle on the cellar door, and, what was worse, the door was slowly being pushed open. Then he heard voices. "Where are you going, Grootvader?" It was Lisa.

"I want some special wine for dinner tonight," Robert heard Grootvader reply.

Lisa spoke again, but Robert did not hear what she said. Oh God! What should he do? Grootvader was going to come down. He dragged the torch out of his pocket, his handkerchief, coming out as well, fell noiselessly to the floor, but in his panic he didn't notice. He fled to the fireplace. The only chance he had of hiding was to stand on the old stove and hope that Grootvader wouldn't see him. He clambered up as quietly as he could, the dirt covering his hands and legs as he did so. His body must be out of Grootvader's view, but his legs could still be seen below the top of the fireplace. Shining his torch up the chimney he saw that there were more iron steps above him. Gripping on to these, he managed to put his feet on the lower ones and climb so that no part of him remained visible to anyone in the cellar below.

"Someone's left the light on," he heard Grootvader say. But he couldn't hear Lisa's reply. He heard, the cellar door shut, and the sound of Grootvader making his way down the steps.

The chimney had narrowed as he had climbed, and he managed to hold himself steady by leaning back against the wall behind him. His feet must have been about six feet above the hearth. It seemed an age he was balanced in that chimney listening to the clink of bottles as Grootvader pottered in the wine cellar. Then he heard the sound of feet, on the stone steps, and the cellar door opening. The lights went out, the door slammed shut, and all was dark and quiet.

Up above in the hall Lisa and Karl Heinz were sitting at the foot of the stairs - the stairs had been a favourite position for the children to sit and talk since they were quite young. Sometimes, when they wished to keep out of the way, they would sit behind the carved banisters on the balcony which ran from the top of the stairs, overlooking that half of the hall. This had always been a vantage point where they could observe the activities of the grown-ups passing beneath them.

When Jan emerged from the cellar they expected him to be dragging Robert with him, but when there was no sign of their cousin they just looked at each other in surprise.

"Can't you two find a more comfortable place to sit? We have plenty of chairs you know," said Jan.

"We like it here, Grootvader," said Lisa. She fancied Grootvader's tone was a little cool, and asked herself whether his suspicions could possibly have been aroused. What had happened to Robert she wondered.

"Where's Robert?" asked Jan.

Lisa caught her breath and had to swallow hard. "Oh, he's gone for a walk," she replied hastily. "May we help you with those bottles, Grootvader?" she offered, hoping to change the subject.

Jan's expression softened a little, and he gave them each a bottle to carry into the dining-room. He kept them talking for some time and then, just before leaving them, said, "When Robert returns from his er. . . walk, he emphasized the word walk. "Tell him I wish to see him."

"Yes, Grootvader," said Karl Heinz.

The two watched impatiently for Jan to disappear, then hurried back to the cellar door. Karl Heinz gave three knocks, but nothing happened. "Perhaps he's come out already," he said.

"We'll try again in a few minutes, and if he doesn't come out we'll see if he's around the house somewhere," Lisa decided.

Meanwhile, Robert had decided it was time to climb down. He put his hand out into the recess in the chimney wall, which was directly in, front of him, in order to steady himself as he stepped down on to the lower iron foot plates. It was a jolly deep recess, he thought, he couldn't even see the wall at the back of it. He switched on his torch and pointed it straight ahead just to see how deep it really was. What he saw was just a hole in the chimney wall where some bricks had fallen out, but the strange thing was there didn't appear to be anything behind the wall. Perhaps a prisoner had been bricked up in a secret cell. They used to do nasty things like that in the olden days. Or maybe the hole was where the chimney once went? He shone the torch upwards. No, that didn't make sense, because the chimney went straight up in the normal way. So why was there nothing behind the wall?

He climbed a little higher and leant right in to the blackness, shining the torch to see what he could discover. It was obviously not part of the chimney. It was some sort of a room, although rather narrow and not very high. There seemed to be a floor about four feet below the opening. It looked as if at one time there had been a large gap in the chimney wall, which had been bricked up. Only the top bricks had fallen out, making a hole just big enough to look through. As he leant in he could feel the bricks beneath his chest were loose, so he climbed above the hole and, after pushing out a few more bricks with his feet, made it just large enough for him to get through. Somehow he managed to gradually lower himself into the darkness until his feet touched the floor on the other side of the wall. He found that he could stand upright. Perhaps it was a secret cell after all, although it seemed to go back a long way. Thankfully, there was no skeleton lying on the floor.

He noticed that the floor was just hard earth, but the walls were of brick like the cellar. These curved over his head like a tunnel. And then the thought struck him; was it possible that Grootvader's stories could be true after all, and that, there was a tunnel? He must go back quickly and tell everyone what he had found. But then he stopped himself abruptly. He couldn't do that without admitting that he had been disobedient. And supposing it wasn't a tunnel, he would look stupid and get a strapping as well. No, he would have to find out first if it was a tunnel. But was he brave enough to walk into the darkness. He hated darkness. But he mustn't be a funk in everything. He must try. After all, he had got a torch, and there wasn't really anything to be afraid of, he hoped. Still undecided, he looked at the hole through which he had come, and it occurred to him that, although it had been relatively easy to lower himself in, it was going to be almost impossible to get out again unless he could remove some more bricks. But the rest of the wall felt firm. He was in and he couldn't get out. His decision was made for him - there was no turning back.

Robert took a deep breath and then cautiously moved towards the darkness where the torchlight had not yet penetrated. After a few paces he realised it must be a tunnel for there was no wall blocking his way. The first part the way was straight, for which he was thankful, because had it been otherwise he knew that he would have been constantly asking himself what horror might be found round the next corner. As it was, his fertile imagination was already playing tricks on him and sending cold shivers down his spine. Was there someone following him? He knew there wasn't, but had to keep checking. Then the sound of his own feet made him think he could hear footsteps behind him.

His curiosity began to overcome his fear. He must find out where it led. The tunnel wasn't very wide; if he stretched out his arms he could touch the sides with his finger tips. At first the walls were dry, but then he noticed that they had become damp, and in places water was actually dribbling down and forming puddles on the floor. The walls had been lined with brick for a short distance only, and after this the earth was held back by planks of wood shored in position by wooden poles, which Robert had constantly to avoid. There were small sections of wall which had been lined with blocks of stone but these were few. Every now and then he had to dodge round a shoring pole set in the middle of the tunnel to support the roof. In places where rot had set in and the planks had broken away, he had to climb over small mounds of earth which had fallen in. For all this, the tunnel was in surprisingly good condition.

Try as he would his imagination refused to be suppressed. At one time he thought he heard the roar of water in the distance. Perhaps it will get nearer and nearer, and then flood the tunnel and sweep him to his death. He stopped and held his hands over his face, trying to control himself and telling himself not to be so silly. If the tunnel flooded it would all go down the chimney into Grootvader's cellar, so it was stupid thinking like that.

He had lost track of time and had no idea how far he had walked, when, without warning, his foot caught on a fallen plank. He stumbled and was unable to prevent himself from falling flat on his face. As he struck the ground the torch flew out of his hand and clattered away from him. The light went out and he found himself in darkness. He must have fallen into one of the numerous puddles, for he could feel the dampness seeping into his shirt and shorts. For a moment he just lay there with his eyes squeezed shut, hoping it was all, a nasty dream, but when he opened them he found it made no difference, the blackness was total. He had never imagined such fearful darkness. He could see absolutely nothing. He pushed himself up on to his knees. "Help me!" he yelled at the top of his voice, if for no other reason, to release his tension and irritation with himself at having fallen and lost his torch. Supposing he couldn't get out at the other end, would he be trapped in this dark tunnel for ever? Perhaps this blackness was what death was like. Since his mind had first been able to accept the thought that one day he would die, he had seen death as being enshrouded in an everlasting grey cloud from which he couldn't escape. Now he imagined it as complete blackness. Where God and heaven fitted in to this he had no idea. After all, heaven was suppose to be a nice place, but then it was only for good people, and he had a feeling that that didn't include him,

Robert .could feel the cold creeping into him, and his damp shirt was not helping matters. He was beginning to shiver. In his frustration and fear he felt a tear run down his cheek. "Stop it, you fool, don't start blubbing!" He struck himself on the cheek. The thought of Lisa calling him a cry baby made him stop. Perhaps he should go back the way he had come and try to get back down the chimney. He could guide himself in the darkness by touching the wall. Then he fancied he could see old Cavey glaring at him. Don't just sit there doing nothing, Rutherford, the problem won't answer itself. Do something, boy!

No! He jolly well wouldn't go back. Robert moved forward on his hands and knees, feeling the floor as he went in an effort to find the torch. His hand touched something cold and slimy in front of him, and he quickly started back. But then he realised it was only the wall, and this part must be of stone. He stretched out his hands into the darkness and could feel the wall barring his path. It must be a dead end, so now he'd have to go back, and if he couldn't get out at the chimney he really was trapped. As he turned his foot kicked something and he heard the clatter of the torch. Frantically, he put his hand to where he thought it would be. "Got it," he cried, and to his relief it still worked.

With light from the torch once more his spirits rose, and he could see that he had not come to a dead end after all. The wall was not blocking his path; the tunnel had just turned sharply to the left and continued on into the blackness. He would go on. He wasn't going to give up now. If the others could be stubborn, so could he. A few paces further on he found that the tunnel divided. Should he take the right way or the left, he wondered? The vicar says always take the right road, so he did, but he hadn't gone far when he found it came to a dead end – the vicar wasn't always right. Retracing his steps he came back to the fork and tried the other way.

"When is the right road not the right road? When it's the wrong one. Don't be stupid, Robert, anyone could guess that riddle," he said, trying to keep his spirits up.

How much further should he go? It must come to somewhere soon. Or perhaps it went on for ever, and he would never find his way out. He began to wonder how much longer his torch would last; it was already getting dim. What was that rumbling noise? Perhaps there was something terrifying ahead. There it was again. It really was something this time. It wasn't just imagination. Well, there was nothing he could do now except go on and face whatever it was. He could feel his heart beating faster, and then stumbling he fell forward on to his knees, landing, it seemed, on a pile of loose earth.

The torch had almost faded, and he could now see very little. With what light there was left he discovered that both the ceiling and walls had fallen in, and that there was no way forward. Something violent had caused the fall in, because some of the wooden wall planks had been broken and were lying on the ground with the shoring poles. This really was the end. At that moment the torch finally gave up and went out. He shook it violently in an effort to make it light, but no matter what he did the wretched thing would not show even a glimmer. He hurled it from him in a burst of anger, and heard it clatter away down the tunnel. He really did feel like crying. He flung himself down on to the soft earth in front of him and banged it with his clenched fists in sheer frustration. "Sod it! Sod it! Sod it! Damn and bloody blast!" he shouted, wishing the entire world could hear him. And he hoped God could hear too, because He should have stopped him getting into this mess. He had come all this way to find only a dead end, and now the bloody torch had gone out, and he'd have to feel his way back to that blasted chimney. And yet how was it he could dimly see the movement of his hands? It was not completely dark. There must be light coning from somewhere. "Wake up, Rutherford," he scolded. "Why don't you look, instead of swearing and making such a fuss?" He felt a little ashamed of himself. Perhaps God was looking after him, after all. The faint glow seemed to be coming from his left hand side. He put out his hand and felt only loose earth where the planks had fallen away. Quickly scooping some of the earth away, it took only a moment before the bright daylight flooded into his dark prison.

Robert almost danced for joy. Now he could see that although earth was blocking the way ahead, the left wall of the tunnel had almost come to the surface and was only covered by a thin layer of earth. It didn't take him long to make a hole large enough to wriggle through, and pushing his head and shoulders out into the daylight he lay for a moment drinking in the pure air. But his troubles were not over, for he appeared to be at the bottom of a deep V shaped gully, not that this was any difficulty for he could soon scramble up the bank. But above his head and cutting him off from the top of the bank was a thick canopy of brambles. However was he going to get through those, he groaned? He would be scratched to pieces.

He could hear the sound of traffic above him. That must have been the rumbling sound he had heard in the tunnel, he decided. He must have come out underneath the road embankment. And the steep bank right in front of him was the dyke. He could only be a few yards from the bridge. The fall in must have been caused when the new road was built, he concluded.

It took Robert at least half an hour to manoeuvre his way through the undergrowth of thorns. It was impossible to avoid being pricked and scratched, and his white shirt, which was now more the colour of khaki, had been badly torn down the back. Putting his hand on his bottom he could feel the bare skin, and he realised that the seat of his shorts had almost been ripped off. When he did eventually reach the top he found that he had came out on the dyke path with the bridge just a few yards away. For a time he lay exhausted on the grass with the sweat pouring off of him.

After a few minutes rest he sat up and examined himself. "Oh God, what a mess," he groaned. His arms and legs were caked in dirt, and he knew his face must be the same, because he had been wiping the sweat away with his muddy hands. Luckily, he was not badly scratched, but his shirt and shorts were ruined. What would he tell mother and Agnes? Thank goodness Father wasn't here. With a bit of luck he would get away with just a touch of Agnes's hair brush. How long had he been away? The afternoon seemed well on, but it was still very sultry. He stood up to make his way back to the house, and it was then that he felt the first drops of rain. He could see the large black thunder cloud and the heavy rain sweeping across the river towards him. He would never get home in time to avoid being drenched even if he ran all the way. What did it matter, anyway, he was in such a mess that a shower of rain wouldn't make any difference.

Karl Heinz and Lisa had knocked on the cellar door a number of times during the first half hour of Robert's absence, but, getting no response, had then searched the house. They had seen Jan return to the cellar on one occasion, but had made themselves scarce in case he should ask more questions as to Robert's whereabouts. "He must have come up while we were talking to Grootvader. He's probably gone down to the river," Lisa remarked. But their search in that direction also proved unsuccessful. When they returned late that afternoon they found the rest of the family gathered in the hall, having just come in from the garden as the rain came on.

"I presume you've been looking for Robert," Jan said.

"Yes, Grootvader," Karl Heinz replied.

"And you obviously haven't found him."

"No, Grootvader."

Flora asked, "Is Robert missing?"

"Don't worry, he'll turn up," Jan replied with confidence.

"Where did he say he was going?" asked Elizabeth.

"Just for a walk," Lisa replied.

"I thought you were all together as usual," Elizabeth said. She had not realised that Robert had been missing for so long and was trying her best to keep calm, but her voice betrayed her worry. "There might have been an accident. Papa, we must do something," she urged.

"Talk of the devil, look what the tide's washed up," laughed Joanna as her bedraggled brother appeared from the passage, which led to the back of the house.

Robert had entered through the back door, hoping to be able to creep up to his bedroom unnoticed, but not thinking that the family would be in the hall he had blundered in without first checking that the coast was clear.

"Great heavens!" Flora shrieked, her face, beaming at the sight of her grandson standing there dripping-water. Robert's hair, which was normally slightly wavy and brushed to one side, had been completely flattened by the rain, the locks in the front, having fallen, forward, were plastered over his forehead. The rest of him can only be described as streaked mud and torn clothes. The whole family turned and looked with astonishment at the sight before them.

Elizabeth didn't know whether to laugh or cry. She felt perhaps she should be angry with him. "Robert! Where have you been? What have you been doing?" was all that she could say.

"I er. . . I, I went. . ." Robert hesitated. They were all looking at him waiting for his answer. He could see Lisa standing at the back mouthing a word to him. "I went for a walk, and on the way back I fell down a bank into some brambles," he added quickly.

"But you know you shouldn't go off on your own without telling us. You really are very naughty," Elizabeth scolded. "Supposing something had happened."

"Sorry, Mother." The matter seemed closed.

"There's just one other thing, young man," said Jan, looking sternly at Robert. "Do you know where I found this?" Jan produced a handkerchief which he laid on one hand and carefully unfolded with the other revealing, as he did so, the gold medallion. Robert's hand automatically slid into what was left of his pocket. "No it's not in your pocket. It's here," said Jan.

"I put it in my pocket when I went swimming this morning, Grootvader. It must have fallen out by the river," Robert explained.

"No, Robert, it did not fall out by the river. I found it in the cellar this afternoon." There was a long pause while Jan's words began to register with everyone present.

"Here we go again!" said Joanna.

"I'm waiting for an answer, Robert," said Jan. But Robert couldn't find an answer, and just kept looking at the floor.

Elizabeth was near to tears. "Have you been down in that cellar, Robert?" she asked.

Robert looked up at her shamefaced. He just couldn't bear to tell her a lie. In any case, what was the use, Grootvader had found the medallion. "Yes, Mother," he replied quietly.

"Oh, Robert, how could you? You are a naughty, disobedient boy! I'm so ashamed, of you. How could you do such a thing in your Grootvader's house when he has forbidden it? For all the years that children have been forbidden to go into the cellar not one has disobeyed, except you." Elizabeth was so proud of her children; it had upset her that it should be her son who had disgraced himself in front of the family. For a moment she felt lost without John to take charge of the matter. Well, John wasn't here, she thought, so she, must be strong and do her duty.

Robert stood with his head bowed and his hands behind his back as he received his reprimand. He was trying to hold the seat of his torn shorts together so as not to expose too much of himself.

"I'm sorry, Mother," he said penitently. Then he exclaimed brightly as if to put the whole matter right, "But I found a tunnel!"

Joanna and Lisa giggled. Flora smiled and wondered what excuse her grandson would think of next, but Elisabeth did not find the remark amusing. "That's enough, Robert! This is a serious matter and I don't want any of your stories," she said. "I know exactly what your father would do if he were here." Elizabeth tried hard to keep her voice firm. She dispatched Agnes to fetch the strap hanging at the cellar door, and then ordered her to take Robert upstairs and ensure he had a good bath. Robert was then to wait for her in his bedroom. "And throw away those filthy clothes, Agnes," she added. "Yes, m'lady."

"Oh, Mother, not the strap, please," Robert pleaded, trying hard to melt Elizabeth's heart. He very nearly succeeded, but she steeled herself and pointed firmly to the stairs.

"Upstairs immediately!" she ordered.

"Don't bother to take your pants down for the whipping, Robbie, we can see your bum already," Joanna called after him as he was led away up the stairs.

"Shut up, you!" Robert retorted angrily, trying desperately, but without much success, to hold his torn shorts together.

"Joanna, don't be so vulgar!" Elizabeth rounded on her daughter.

Joanna sniggered, but quickly disappeared into the draw-ing-room. Karl Heinz was not amused, and Lisa felt guilty for having suggested the escapade in the first place.

Having watched Robert solemnly marched upstairs, the rest of the family followed into the drawing-room, except for Karl Heinz and Lisa, who decided to keep out of the way for a time in case they were questioned about their involvement in the cellar expedition.

"Elizabeth, my dear, I didn't mean to have the boy punished," Jan said kindly. "I only wished to stop him from doing it again. The stairs are dangerous, you know."

"I'm sorry. Papa, but on this occasion I must be firm. Robert has been disobedient and must take the consequences. Elizabeth would have liked to back down but felt it her duty to John to deal with the matter in this way.

"I can hear John talking there," Flora smiled.

"I think Elizabeth is right," said Karl. "One must be firm."

"Now Karl, it's nothing to do with you," said Natascha.

"I'm not so sure," said Karl. He then went to the door and called loudly for Karl Heinz. Eventually Karl Heinz and Lisa appeared, and whole story of the cellar affair came out.

"Did either of you go down the cellar?" Karl asked.

"No, Father. And I didn't want Robert to go."

"No, Uncle. And Robert wouldn't have gone if I hadn't teased him," Lisa added.

"You shouldn't have done that, Lisa. It was unkind," Kate scolded.

"And who's going to give that poor boy his punishment?" Flora inquired. "I can't imagine you giving him the strap, Elizabeth."

This was a point that Elizabeth had failed to consider. Mama was right. She certainly couldn't bring herself to do it. But, she hes-itated only for a moment and then said, "Perhaps you would help me, Karl?"

Upstairs, Agnes had left Robert in his bedroom to take off his ruined clothes while she had gone to run his bath. When she returned to the bedroom she found him sitting on the edge of the bed examin-ing the strap. He didn't like the look of it at all. It had a hard, round handle out of which came two nasty, flat and firm leather thongs, each about an inch wide and eighteen inches long.

"Come along, Robert, get those rags off," she snapped. "You'll get the feel of that strap soon enough."

Robert threw the strap on the bed and began to peel off what was left of his clothes.

"Heaven preserve us! What a mess you're in. And you've got a nasty scratch on your back." Agues produced a small metal cylinder from her apron pocket and began to unscrew the top.

"Oh no, Agnes, not iodine, please. It stings." The sight of the metal cylinder and the glass file inside was familiar to Robert. Whenever Agnes spotted a cut on him, out would come the iodine and a few drops of the stinging antiseptic would be applied. His pleas usually failed, and today was no exception. Agnes made him bend over and then quickly ran the end of the file along the scratch. "Ow-ow-ow!" Robert leapt up, and danced round the room until the sting wore off. He was then marched off to the bathroom where he suffered more discomfort as Agnes applied the scrubbing brush to his legs.

"What will you get up to next?" Agnes exclaimed. It was one of her favourite expressions, but Robert had other thoughts on his mind.

"Who's going to strap me. Agnes?"

"I'm sure I don't know."

"If it's you, promise you won't make it too hard."

Agnes smiled to herself. It was hard to be cross with him, she thought. He was such an attractive lad. "I'll do no such thing," she retorted.

"Oh, Agnes, please," he pleaded.

"You've proper upset your mother, and her such a sweet, kind person. You're very naughty," she went on.

Robert knew this was true. His disobedience had not worried him too much, but he hated to upset his mother. "I did find a tunnel, you know, Agnes."

"Now don't start that again." Agnes had heard some of his romantic tales before and was not to be taken in this time.

"Nobody believes me," he grumbled.

Robert and Agnes had only just got back into the bedroom when the door opened and Elizabeth and Karl came in. If Robert had imagined that he was to get away with a light strapping from either Elizabeth or Agnes he was mistaken. His mouth dropped open when Elizabeth announced that Uncle Karl was to be the executioner, and he had to obey his uncle when ordered to remove the towel from around his waist. Before bending across a chair he looked pleadingly at his mother, hoping she would relent, but she just looked away and he knew there was no escape. He wished she was not present because he knew she would be upset. As much as she hated the idea, Elizabeth had felt it her duty to be present on this occasion. But when the punishment started the tears began to role down her cheeks, for she couldn't bear the sight of Robert in pain.

Karl Heinz and Lisa sat at the bottom of the stairs listening to the loud slap of the strap and the cries of their cousin. Uncle Karl was obviously taking things slowly and laying it on hard, and Lisa counted fourteen strokes before there was silence.

When, it was over and the others had left the room, Robert flung himself on the bed holding his bare bottom, and quietly weeping. Karl Heinz crept in for a few minutes to change for dinner. They didn't speak, but Robert got an affectionate pat on the back before his cousin went out again.

After some time the pain subsided and Robert found he was feeling desperately hungry. It didn't seem that he was to be invited down for dinner that evening which wasn't fair because he'd had his punishment and even convicts got fed. Besides, the punishment for going down the cellar was a strapping, not starvation. As he carefully pulled his pants over his sore bottom he decided what he'd do. He would get some dinner one way or the other. He felt a little defiant that evening, probably because Father wasn't here to give him one of his frightening looks. Father could be very frightening sometimes, but he did love him all the same.

The family had taken their seats at the dining table, "I hope you weren't too hard on Robert, Karl," Natascha said.

"He got what he deserved, no, more, no less," Karl replied.

Elizabeth had found the experience of watching her son strapped very distressing, but at least she had done her duty, she thought. Karl had applied the strap a little too harshly for her liking, but having carried out the punishment at her request, she had not interfered.

"Are you not going to call Robert for dinner, Elizabeth?" Flora asked.

"No, Mama. He's to stay in his room."

"Well, I shan't interfere, my child. But isn't that a little harsh. If I'd had my way the boy would just have been scolded."

"Yes, Mama, but you're a grandmother, and grandmothers are notorious for being indulgent to their grandchildren," Hugo interjected. "You were not so lenient with me, I remember, when I was a boy."

"Thank you, dear brother," Elizabeth smiled.

"Och, away with you both!" Flora laughed. "Nevertheless," she continued, "I want this to be a house of happiness for my grandchildren, not a place of punishment. I think we've been too hard on the boy."

"So do I," Jan agreed.

"I don't agree," said Karl. "If Karl Heinz had been disobedient like that, I would have given him double what Robert got."

"Hush. What's that?" exclaimed Joanna. The sound of some chords being quietly played on the piano came from the drawing-room on the other side of the hall. Everyone listened.

The firm, steady, sombre chords of the Funeral March from Chopin's Second Sonata could now be clearly heard, increasing in volume. Then Robert's voice was heard, singing in time with the music.

> *"I WANT some din-ner, I WANT some din-ner now,*
> *I WANT some din-ner, I WANT some din-ner now,*
> *Plea-ease may I have some,*
> *Plea-ease may I have some,*
> *I WANT some din-ner, I WANT some din-ner now."*

"The boy's still got a sense of humour," Hugo chuckled.

"Listen! He's off again," said Joanna as Robert changed key and started to sing again.

"I've had a strap-ping, because I'm real-ly bad,
I've got a sore-or bot-tom, and now I'm ver-ry sad.
Plea-ease don't starve me,
Plea-ease don't starve me,
I promise I'll be good now, a ver-ry go-od lad."

By now the whole family was laughing except for Karl. The more contact he had with the English the more difficult he found it to understand them. The boy had been soundly thrashed and now he was making light of the matter. Karl regretted that he had not done his job of applying the strap thoroughly enough, but he appeased himself by remembering that it was really nothing to do with him, and that he had merely been assisting Elizabeth.

"Are you going to fetch him or shall I?" Flora asked Elizabeth.

Elizabeth was happy to relent. "I'll go, Mama," she replied, leaving the table. When she reached the drawing room, Robert had ceased to sing and was playing the second part of the movement seriously. The crystal clear notes of the delicate theme brought a lump to her throat. She stood listening for a moment and then went up behind him and put her hands on his shoulders. He stopped playing and wistfully looked up at her. "That was beautiful; my dear," she said, and he knew that he had been forgiven.

Robert leapt up and threw his arms around her. "I'm terribly sorry for making you unhappy," he said. Elizabeth kissed him on the forehead, ran her fingers through his hair, and led him to the dining room. He went to his usual seat next to his grandmother and, much, to her amusement, before sitting down he placed a soft cushion on the chair.

"Sensible boy," Flora laughed.

Robert was happy once more. He would try and forget that rotten cellar. As for that horrible tunnel, supposing he had been trapped down there or there had been a fall-in and he had been buried alive. It made him shudder to think of it. Sitting there eating his hot food with the family cheerfully chatting around him, he could hardly believe it had all happened.

"And what is my grandson thinking so deeply about?" Flora smiled.

"Nothing, Grandma," Robert replied. He saw Lisa looking at him. It was that look which always brought on the feeling that he would do anything she asked. He could feel his sore bottom glowing with heat, and wondered whether she cared that he had suffered because of her. He would never have risked getting into trouble if it hadn't been for her. Why did she have this effect on him now, he asked himself? He had never taken much notice of her before. It seemed to have started on the week-end of the cricket match. He couldn't understand it so gave up trying.

After dinner the three children went to the boys' room where they lounged on the bed talking. The subject of the cellar expedition was only briefly mentioned. It had served them all in a different way. Robert felt he had not let himself down in front of a girl. Lisa experienced a certain satisfaction that a boy should do this to impress her. And Karl Heinz was pleased to have been proved right when he had warned Robert not to do it. They had no real interest in the cellar itself. It had served its purpose as a challenge and was now of no more use to them.

Robert could not bring himself to speak of the tunnel. Somehow his fear of the total darkness he had experienced made him feel ashamed. Or was it for some other reason, he asked himself?

"Let's go for a cycle ride tomorrow," Lisa suggested. But Robert didn't agree.

"It'll be at least two days before I can sit on a saddle," he argued. "So let's go swimming instead." And so it was decided.

It was a week before they brought out their cycles, but the delay was not wholly because of the state of Robert's backside. There had been so many other things to do. They had not only swum, but hiked along the river. Uncle Hugo, who they all agreed was a great sport, played games with them and took them on a number of exciting trips in his car. Sometimes they would walk into Grave to buy chocolate with the money which grandparents, aunties and uncles would frequently slip into their hands.

In an idle moment one afternoon Robert demonstrated how he made water bombs by cleverly folding pieces of exercise paper into the shape of a ball, leaving a small hole at the top where the water was poured in. When full, the bomb was then hurled at someone with the object of giving them a good dousing,

"What a good idea!" Karl Heinz exclaimed. "How do you think of these things, Robert?"

"I've got an idea!" said Robert. The others were immediately all attention. "The first thing is to make two water bombs each," he went on. This having been done, they went into the garden and placed them on the old wooden table ready to be filled from the watering can. "When Uncle Hugo comes into the garden we all throw our bombs at him, and then run like blazes," Robert laughed.

"But he's in the drawing-room reading a book. He won't come out here?" Lisa declared.

But Robert had other plans. "Wait here," he said, and then disappeared into the house to find Agnes. As luck would have it she was in the hall. "Agnes, if you see Uncle Hugo tell him there's someone to see him in the garden," he said, trying not to sound too innocent or she'd become suspicious. "If you could look in the drawing-room, I'll look upstairs." Agnes obliged and when she had disappeared into the drawing-room, Robert ran back to the garden.

"Standby! He'll be out in a minute," Robert called. They quickly filled their bombs from the watering can and then took cover behind some shrubs near the house.

"I hope he's quick, mine's leaking," said Lisa.

"Here he comes!" whispered Karl Heinz as Hugo wandered into the garden looking about him for his visitor.

"Open fire!" Robert cried. And with that they all burst out of their hiding place, hurling their bombs at the unsuspecting victim.

Four of the missiles struck the target, one hitting Hugo in the face. He was saturated, but before he could do anything his assailants fled across the garden, not stopping until they reached the dyke.

"You young devils!" Hugo shouted after them, shaking his fist. But all he got in return were shrieks of laughter.

"Whatever happened, Mr Hugo? You're drenched!" Agnes exclaimed when Hugo returned to the house.

"It was a trap, Agnes," Hugo laughed. "I've been water bombed."

"And I know who's behind that," Agnes replied knowingly.

"I'll have my revenge, Agnes, don't you worry."

Meanwhile, the children had crept back into the garden. "I've got an even better idea," Robert chuckled.

The others couldn't wait to hear, so they all sat down on the lawn, keeping a wary eye for Uncle Hugo, ready for Robert to disclose his next piece of mischief.

"I made a giant bomb once," Robert began as the others gazed at him in anticipation of some more fun. He had the knack of telling a good story. "I got this great big sheet of brown paper and covered, it in cooking fat to make it really waterproof. I filled it in the bathroom, and then. . ." Robert paused and began to laugh.

"Go on," said Lisa impatient to hear what happened next.

"Well, old Perks - you know him, he's our chauffeur - usually comes to the side door for a cup of tea at three thirty. You know the window right over that door." Robert's audience nodded. "Well, I waited there with the bomb all ready. It was as big as a football. And sure enough old Perks came along on time. When he was right underneath I dropped it on his head."

Karl Heinz collapsed helpless with laughter. He laughed so much that he had to draw up his knees and hold his stomach, the tears pouring down his cheeks. It was some minutes before he was able to control himself, and then every time he tried to speak he just burst out laughing again.

"Do you want me to go on?" Robert asked.

"Go on, Robert," said Lisa. "Tell us the rest."

Still clutching his stomach and rolling on the grass, Karl Heinz could only nod in agreement.

"As I was saying," Robert continued, trying to pick up the thread of his story. "The bomb hit old Perks fair and square right on the head. The bottom of the paper burst open and the rest, of it went right over his head like a hood. He looked like the man in the iron mask dancing about down there. He was drowned, and he couldn't see a thing."

Karl Heinz doubled up again.

"Go on," Lisa urged. "What happened then?"

"Well, old Perks guessed it was me."

"I wonder how?" Lisa laughed.

"Later on I saw him talking to Father and thought I was really for it. But nothing happened until I went to the garage a few days later, and that rotter Perks turned the hose on me. I'm sure Father put him up to it."

"Oh, what fun you are, Robert!" exclaimed Karl Heinz. "If only we lived together all the time."

"Are we going to make a giant bomb to drop on Papa?" Lisa asked.

"No, he's had his lot," Robert replied. "I have a better idea. Let's go on to the bridge, and when a barge goes underneath we'll drop it on anyone on the deck."

"That's a terrific idea!" Karl Heinz exclaimed, holding his sides. "I'll split myself in a minute."

So a large sheet of thick paper was found and covered with grease. Then the three set out for the bridge, Robert carrying the bomb and Karl Heinz the watering can. On reaching the span under which the barges usually passed, they stood innocently leaning over the rail watching the river traffic underneath. What they didn't know was that they were being observed from the dyke. Hugo had seen them leave the garden with the watering can and knew they were up to something, so he had taken his binoculars to the end of the garden and lay on the side of the dyke watching them.

Karl Heinz decided that the bombing operation was a technical matter so he had brought two small stones with him. "We must see how long it takes for a stone to hit the water," he said. He dropped one stone over and counted, "One, two, three." Then he repeated the experiment. "So we've got to remember it takes the count of three for the bomb to get down," he added.

Robert was most impressed with his cousin's preparations. "You're a genius, Karl Heinz," he said.

"Who's going to drop it?" Lisa asked.

"I will!" said Karl Heinz.

"Okay," Robert agreed.

They had to wait for some time before a suitable target presented itself. But then Lisa noticed that there was a barge coming up stream with a man standing in the bows holding a rope in his hands. "Look!" she cried. "It's one of ours. It's flying the van der Leyden flag. Must be up from Rotterdam."

"Get the man on the bows, Karl Heinz," said Robert.

"I'll go to the other side and you signal when the bows have passed under," Karl Heinz instructed. He quickly loaded the bomb, crossed to the other side of the bridge, and got himself in a position below which he believed the barge would emerge. There, he waited for Robert's call.

"Get ready," Robert cautioned. "It's under," he shouted, and then he and Lisa dashed across the road and stood one either side of their cousin. Luckily there was little road traffic that afternoon, and they almost had the bridge to themselves.

"Now!" Karl Heinz let go.

If the crewman below had remained standing upright the bomb would have fallen at his feet, but at the wrong moment - at least it was wrong from his point of view - he bent forward to settle the rope and caught the full impact on the back of his neck. The paper exploded, the water soaking his head and shoulders. For a moment he didn't realise what had happened, but when he did react he saw the children dodge back from the rail. He shook his fist at them, and it was only when the barge had moved some way up stream that his oaths ceased to reach their ears.

"I think he's putting in at the town. Come on, let's get away from here," Robert urged. They picked up the watering can and ran to the end of the bridge. It was not until they got back on to the dyke path that they flung themselves down to rest.

"I got him!" Karl Heinz panted, rubbing his hands with glee at the thought of his success.

"You're a terrific shot, Karl Heinz. Well done!" said Robert. But a moment later he leapt to his feet. "Look out!" he cried. "Uncle Hugo's coming."

Although Hugo had seen the children on the bridge, he had not seen exactly what they were up to, because the bombing had taken place on the far side. He had seen one of his own barges coming up from Rotterdam and had decided to walk along to Grave for a chat with the skipper. When the children spotted him, they fled into the fields below.

Hugo shook his fist at them and laughed. He already had certain ideas for revenge, but within a short time these were to be radically revised.

It was a small party for tea in the garden that afternoon, consisting only of the three children and their grandparents. The rest of the family had gone shopping in Nijmegen. Hugo had remained behind, for, as he put it, shopping is for ladies.

"Where's your Uncle Hugo?" Flora asked.

"He's gone for a walk, Grandma," Carl Heinz replied.

While tea was in progress, Agnes brought out an envelope which she handed to Jan. After reading its contents, he handed it to Flora, who also read it. Robert thought it was something amusing, for although his grandparents did not laugh, he fancied they were finding it difficult to keep straight faces. But Robert soon forgot the letter, because a few minutes later Agnes returned to the garden followed by the local policeman.

"Good afternoon, Mr. Visser. What can we do for you?" said Jan, winking at the man.

The policeman's explanation was rather long and formal, but as he went on, so the children's faces began to change. The bombing incident was related in detail, but what was worse they had been positively identified as the culprits. "Anything to say?" the policeman ended by asking, at the same time looking hard at the children. All three kept their heads bowed but said nothing. "In that case, I must take you to the police station for questioning," he said.

"You'd better handcuff these boys in case they escape," said Jan.

"Oh no, Grootvader, we won't. I promise," said Karl Heinz.

But before leading his prisoners away, Mr Visser fastened the two boys together by their wrists.

Jan suggested that they go by the dyke path as the quickest way back to Grave. "Grootvader, what will they do to us?" Robert called as he was marched away,

"Lock you in a dungeon, I expect," Jan replied. Three worried but silent children were led along the dyke path. However, when they reached the town it was not the police station they were taken to but the quay where the barge was moored. And there on deck waiting for them was the skipper and the crewman. Once on board the handcuffs were taken off, and they were lined up in front of the two bargemen.

"These are the ones," said the crewman.

"Do you admit it?" asked the policeman.

"It was my fault, I suggested it," Robert admitted.

"They're all guilty," said the skipper.

"Right," said the policeman, "You can either come with me to the police station or take any punishment the skipper decides on. What's it to be?"

The skipper's punishment was the unanimous choice so with that the policeman left. The three were taken to the side of the barge and made to stand stiffly at attention with their backs to the water. The skipper and the crewman stood in front of them. The skipper then said, "You are sentenced to a ducking." And before they knew what was happening, the three youngsters were pushed backwards over the side, each hitting the water flat on their backs, making a resounding splash. When the children surfaced, spluttering after their ducking, the roars of laughter that greeted them came not only from the bargees but also from Hugo, who had emerged from the cabin, where he had been furtively watching the proceedings. There was more laughter when the three dripping youngsters clambered back on deck.

"You beast, Papa!" Lisa cried, bursting into laughter.

"What a rotten trick, Uncle. I thought I was going to prison," Robert spluttered, much relieved that he wasn't,

"So did I," said Karl Heinz.

"Serves you right," Hugo laughed. "That's my revenge, and you got the wettest."

But Uncle Hugo's surprises were not over, for when the youngsters had stripped off their wet things and dried themselves in the cabins below, they were given dry clothes to put on. It didn't matter that the clothes they were given were far too big for them, and caused further laughter from the crew, for when they were changed and returned to the main cabin they found that an enormous meal had been prepared for them by the skipper's wife. And there they spent a happy evening, eating, drinking, singing and listening to the tales of the crew.

It was a happy group that returned along the dyke path that evening, singing and shouting at the tops of their voices. When they burst into the house it was immediately apparent to the rest of the family, who were sitting quietly in the drawing-room, that their peace was about to be shattered. The two boys raced into the room wrestling with each other to be first in to tell the tale of their adventure.

"Good Lord preserve us! What have we got here?" Flora cried.

Both boys were dressed in baggy trousers the bottoms of which had been turned up to enable them to walk. The pullovers they wore almost reached their knees, and Robert, pretending to be an ape, had unrolled his sleeves until they almost touched the floor. Lisa made a more dignified entrance but her appearance caused as much laughter as that of the boys. Even Karl was seen to laugh.

It was some time before the boys completed their story, each vying with the other to relate that part which had amused him most. Robert told, with an incredulous look on his face and with obvious admiration for his uncle, how Hugo had used his friend the policeman to bring a note to Grootvader. The family had already heard the story from Jan, but they listened again patiently, watching with pleasure the joy written on the young faces.

Hugo, who had settled himself into an armchair, said, "And no more dropping water bombs on my barges, because next time it really will be the police station for you."

"We promise," Robert replied. "We'll drop the next big one on your head instead."

The delayed cycle ride took place the following day, Robert having decided that his sore backside was now fit enough to sit on a saddle. The three youngsters set off in the direction of Ravenstein, the small fortified town about five miles down the road In the opposite direction to Grave, where John had passed through eighteen years before intent on giving up his cycle tour. It was a favourite ride of theirs, and after passing the few houses at Velp they came to that section of road which, for obvious reasons, they called the long straight. It was here that the two boys raced ahead, each trying to manoeuvre the other into the ditch in an effort to keep in front. Lisa rode sedately behind with an expression of disdain on her face, as one who did not wish to be associated with her unruly companions. At the far end of the long straight the boys swept up the slope and stopped on top of the dyke to wait for Lisa, who was steadily pedalling along some distance behind. "Come on!" Karl Heinz called as she approached.

"What's the hurry," she replied. "We've got all day. If Grootvader saw you swerving and pushing about like that, he'd take your cycles away."

"Well, he didn't see," Robert replied. Girls are such goody goodies sometimes, he thought. Nevertheless, the boys heeded their reprimand and rode properly from there on. It was a clear day and they amused themselves as they rode along the Maasdijk by naming as many distant villages as they could. A light breeze blew in their faces and they had to pedal steadily to keep up a reasonable speed. "It'll be a smashing ride back with the wind behind us," Robert remarked.

For a time the Maasdijk ran some distance away from the river, but near the village of Overlangel it swept back again so that as the children approached Ravenstein they were riding alongside the river.

"There's the old ferry house!" cried Karl Heinz.

"Let's call in and see old mother Meijer," said Robert.

Elsa Meijer was neither old nor was she a mother, but her forty years, greying hair and unkempt appearance had been enough to earn her the first of these titles from those with young eyes. And as for being a mother, this had been her life long yearning which had never materialised, but which made itself obvious in the way she showered her love on any child with whom she came in contact.

A little eccentric in her ways, Elsa was sometimes laughed at by the children behind her back. They didn't mean to be unkind, because they had a genuine liking for her and enjoyed the welcome she gave them on their frequent visits to her home. They would never pass without calling in.

Elsa's preoccupations in life were firstly, the welfare of her numerous cats - Robert once counted ten - and secondly, looking after her brother, Dignus, who ran the ferry at this point on the river.

As the youngsters arrived and leant their cycles against the wall, Elsa appeared from a large wooden shed which stood beside the house. "Hallo, children," she called. In her arms she carried four black kittens.

"Oh, how sweet!" Lisa exclaimed, taking one of the animals.

The boys also took a kitten each as they were led into the house. The front door opened directly into a large room with an old table standing in the centre and wooden chairs scattered around it. Other pieces of furniture stood against the walls, and these included a large dresser in the far corner.

"Here are the children, Dignus," said Elsa to the large, sullen man sitting at the table smoking his long pipe. But it was as if her words had fallen on deaf ears, for there was no reaction from her brother. He didn't even, turn his head. However, the children were used to his silence and were inclined to ignore him. In fact, Robert could not remember one occasion when the man had done anymore than grunt in reply to a greeting. If he happened to be present during the children's visits, which he usually wasn't, Dignus would some-times talk about them to his sister but never to them.

They moved into the room, Lisa and Karl Heinz sitting down at the table, playing with the kittens. But Robert's kitten jumped out of his arms, and he had to chase it as it ran along the table and leapt across on to the dresser where it landed in a box containing old kitchen utensils.

Robert had seen this box before, and there was one thing in it that always fascinated him but, at the same time, made him shudder. It was a vicious looking carving knife with a bone handle and a very long, sharp, pointed blade. As he grabbed the kitten he saw that the knife was still there. He thought it looked terribly dangerous and had often wondered why it was left there.

Holding the kitten, in one hand, Robert picked up the knife. "Look at this, Karl Heinz!" he exclaimed.

"Just right for the Chinese torture, death by a thousand cuts," laughed his cousin.

Robert quickly returned the knife to its box. "What a horrible way to die," he said. "One cut with your penknife was bad enough, just fancy having a thousand." Robert noticed Dignus eyeing him through the haze of smoke, and thought to himself that he could just imagine Dignus giving him the cuts.

Elsa always insisted on giving her guests food and drink, and she bustled in and out of the kitchen carrying plates of bread and cheese and anything else she could find. She also brought in a bottle of her home made brew, which was a sweet drink that the children loved but had no idea what it was. When all was set, she came and sat beside them at the table. It gave her such pleasure to have the young ones in her home, and to be able to sit and watch their eager young faces enjoying their feast.

The plates were chipped and the glasses were not particularly clean, and from time to time a cat would jump on to the table and snatch a piece of cheese or a slice of meat. But the children didn't mind. It was all part of the adventure. There was no necessity to make conversation for Elsa did that for them. They only had to answer the questions she asked them.

"And what have you been doing with yourselves? I expect you've all done well at school," Elsa remarked.

Robert thought it would be as well to steer the conversation away from the subject of school so he quickly replied, "Karl Heinz has joined the Hitler Youth."

Robert was to remember his chance remark and what followed for many years to come. Sometimes he imagined that if he had been a wizard he could not have cast a better spell, for it seemed to him that the figure of Dignus, sitting morosely smoking his pipe and with his head sunk on to his chest had suddenly been, given a new lease of life.

At the sound of Robert's words a change came over the ferryman. His eyes seemed to light up. He put down his pipe and. stood up facing Karl Heinz."

"Heil Hitler!" He almost shouted the words, and as he did so he raised his right arm in salute.

Karl Heinz was as taken aback as Robert and Lisa, but the reaction of constant training was swift and he leapt to his feet. "Heil Hitler!" he replied. Karl Heinz couldn't help feeling a little self-conscious when he saw the faces of his two cousins staring up at him in astonishment. He quickly sat down and went on with his meal.

Dignus also sat down, but if he had been silent before it was now impossible to stop him talking. Even his sister was forced into silence. He looked intently at Karl Heinz. "So you are in the Hitler Youth," he said. This news had obviously impressed him. "Then we are comrades in the fight for a new world and the destruction of communism. I am proud to have a member of the Party under my roof," he went on. "For years Europe has been ruled by weak fools, but now things are changing. Adolph Hitler has already given us a lead in this country, and I look forward to the day when he will be the leader of all the countries in Europe. Soon he'll have power in Germany and then great things will happen."

Karl Heinz looked bewildered, "I'm not actually in the Party," he said. "I'm just in the junior section of the Hitler Youth."

"No matter," Dignus replied. "One day you'll be a Party member."

If the children appeared interested in the lecture, it was not because of what Dignus was saying - they didn't understand what he was talking about - but because they had never seen him like this before. Interested or not, they did not cease to eat and drink, and at the same time gave one another sly looks, trying not to laugh. I wish he'd shut up, Robert said to himself.

But Dignus had not finished. "I have watched him rise. What a man! If I was a German I'd be in the Party," he continued.

"What's he talking about?" Robert whispered in Lisa's ear.

"Hitler, of course."

Dignus went on, oblivious to the two whispering youngsters. "I'm a member of the Dutch National Socialist Party." He proudly pointed to a badge on his jacket. "We too have a man of vision. Antoon Mussert. When he founded the Dutch Party last December, I joined immediately."

"I think we'll have to be going," Robert remarked.

"You're the English boy, aren't you?" said Dignus.

"Yes, sir."

"Even though you English are politically stupid, your Sir Mosley and his British Fascists will lead you to better government if you'll let him."

Robert had never liked Dignus even in the days of his quietness, but now he appeared to have found his tongue he liked him even less. And who was this Sir Mosley, anyway? He'd, never heard of him.

It was another five minutes before relief came and Dignus was called away to take the ferry across the river.

"Phew! Thank goodness he's gone," Robert whispered to Lisa.

For the sake of Elsa, who was so kind to them, they stayed another half an hour before setting out again. "Come again, my dears," said Elsa. "And don't take any notice of Dignus. He's really quite harmless." But Robert wasn't convinced about that.

As they cycled away, they could see the figure of the ferryman on the boat returning from the other side of the river. Lisa said, "That Dignus is a real twerp, but I wouldn't trust him an inch."

"He's barmy, if you ask me," said Robert.

But Dignus was soon forgotten as they turned off the *Maasdijk* into the town under the archway of the old town gate, and rattled down the cobbled *Markt Straat,* Robert thought it better to lift his bottom off the saddle while bouncing over the cobbled street, but they were soon through the town and out into the flat country once more. Their route took them away from the river through, the villages of Herpen, Schaijk and Reek, and it was tired, hungry children who returned home late that afternoon to tell of the day's events and especially of Dignus's strange behaviour.

*

According to Robert there was one great disadvantage of having holidays; they all too soon came to an end. It seemed such a short time ago that he had been driven over the bridge in joyful anticipation of the wonderful weeks ahead, and now the bridge had disappeared from sight as the car made its way towards Nijmegen on the journey home.

"Don't look so sad, dear. Think of all the good things there are at home," Elizabeth comforted.

But Robert was not to be comforted. His mind went back over the six glorious weeks, recalling the fun as well as the mischief he had got up to. He brought to mind the cellar incident, and was much relieved that the matter of his disobedience was not to be mentioned to his father. Even Joanna had promised not to say anything. But now it was just a memory, and somehow it seemed to him as if it had never happened. He could hardly believe he had walked through that dark tunnel. Was he the only person in the world to know it was there, he asked himself? And yet, perhaps it was all a dream and it wasn't there at all.

Robert yawned, and he knew why he was so tired. It was always a sad time just before leaving for home, and so as not to waste even a minute of their precious time together, he and Karl Heinz had lain awake for hours after they had gone to bed the previous evening. Sometimes he felt ashamed at the things they did together, but now that they had started they couldn't stop. One boy at school had said it was bad for you, he remembered, and another had said it made you go blind, but he didn't feel rotten and he could still see perfectly well. Anyway, what did they know about it? But it was a comfort to know that Karl Heinz had the same feelings as he had. He asked himself what Father and Mother would think of him if they knew the things he did in secret?

Karl Heinz and Natascha were also returning home that day, but Karl had left some three weeks previous. Robert had felt quite pleased when his uncle had gone home. It was not that he disliked him, but since being strapped by him, Robert was not completely at ease in his presence. In some way he resented the fact that Uncle Karl had carried out the punishment, even though he knew it wasn't his uncle's fault. He could have accepted it from Grootvader or Uncle Hugo, but then they wouldn't have laid it on so hard, he decided.

The return journey was long and tedious, and there was nothing at the end of it to look forward to except school and all that rotten work he would have to do. But when he did reach home, Robert was happy to see his own room again and all his treasures, and soon fell into the usual daily routine as the holiday receded and became just a sunlit memory. At least he could dream of the happy times and think of next year.

CHAPTER 7

What Karl had predicted took place in Berlin just before noon on Monday 30th January, 1933. At that hour Adolph Hitler became Chancellor of Germany. The aged President of the Republic, Field Marshal Paul von Hindenburgh, had at last been persuaded to name as Chancellor the despised 'Bohemian Corporal' - he was actually Austrian by birth - who, in the next twelve years, was to lead a great people to the dizzy heights of power, and finally to destruction. To a great number of ordinary, decent German families there was the hope that they had found a man who would lead them to a better future. They did not get what they deserved, but that was the inevitable consequence of German history.

Karl was a good, middle class German, whose support for the new Chancellor was deeply grounded in his heritage, and he was not alone in his belief that Germany needed strong government. It was only sixty two years since the new nation in the form of the Second Reich had been forged by Bismarck's strong leadership and the power of the Prussian Army. The unification of the German States had created the strongest nation, in Europe, held together under the Emperor, who was also the Prussian King, and the magnificent German army.

However gratifying it might have been at the time for the victors of the First World War to insist that there should no longer be an emperor, and that the German Army should be rendered impotent, it was a mistake which, in time, was to open the door to dictatorship. In the minds of men like Karl, the golden thread, in the form of the Emperor and his army, which had held the Empire together, had been cut, and they searched desperately for something to take its place. The Weimar Republic had not caught their imagination, but in Adolph Hitler they believed they had found their saviour. His demand for absolute obedience was not a new experience for the German nation, and it was to be given freely and legally. He was to achieve more power than any prince or emperor had ever dreamed of.

The willing acceptance of autocracy and a deep sense of nationalism had made the German people into a great nation. But their anger and frustration at the way their country had been treated after the war and the humiliation of seeing their army reduced, to a mere shadow of its former glory, had driven many, and Karl was one of them, into the arms of Hitler. Karl had gone to war in 1914 to defend the frontiers of the Fatherland. He had not wanted war, nor had he wished, to take territory from any other country, and he found it difficult to understand the harsh terms of the Treaty of Versailles. He longed for the strong Germany he had known in the days of his youth. Someone had, once more, to bind the nation together. Adolph Hitler said he could do it, so Karl and millions like him were willing to give him the chance. They were not the only ones to be deceived.

On the evening of the day their Führer had been called to power the Nazi storm troopers (SA) and Hitler Youth, formations marched in their thousands through the main cities of Germany to celebrate the victory.

Karl Heinz had been allowed to stay up late to watch the massive torchlight processions. His home stood in the centre of the old city of Cologne. Leaning out of the open window on the first floor, he saw that the whole scene below was a mass of lighted torches, and the great Cathedral of St. Peter at the end of the street stood out in the glow like a two horned monster reaching up into the night sky. He could feel the atmosphere of excitement as the jackboots pounded the street below, and the bands played the traditional German military marches, and, of course, the new Horst Wessel song, which had become the official song of the Nazi party. The son of a Protestant chaplain, Horst Vessel had given up his family to live with a former prostitute and to devote his life to the Nazi party. He had been killed by the Communists in 1930, and would have been forgotten as were the hundreds of others who had been casualties of the political street brawls, had it not been for the song he had written. Doctor Goebbels was to ensure that in this youth the Nazi party had it greatest martyr.

Karl stood behind his son at the open window with his hands on the boy's shoulders. If only it was the army marching below instead of the SA, he said to himself, remembering the glittering parades of the old Imperial army. Although Karl supported Hitler, he would not accept that there should be any other force for the protection of the State other than the army.

As a true Prussian, it was the army that stirred Karl's imagination, and had played such a vital role in the formation of his country. In 1415 the eastern part of the medieval German state of Brandenburg beyond the Elbe was leased to Count Frederick of Hohenzollern. This remote frontier province of Prussia gradually spread across northern Germany. It had no natural frontiers, and its only means of survival was by the military prowess of its army. The army became the most important institution in the state. Mirabeau was once quoted as saying *Prussia is not a state with an army, but an army with a state.* The people were taught obedience, sacrifice and duty. It was these combinations in the Prussian way of life that made the country the dominant state in Germany, and enabled Bismarck to successfully carry out his plan of unification.

Karl believed the SA had become too powerful and was now a threat even to the army itself, and he considered that now Herr Hitler had come to power he would have to do something to restrain these Brownshirts.

By the Treaty of Versailles the Regular German Army had been restricted to one hundred thousand men but the SA, being a political organisation and not part of the armed forces, had grown over the years to twenty times that number and now boasted two million men. They had originally been formed to protect Nazi meetings, and to terrorize and break up the meetings of those who opposed Hitler. But now that Hitler had come to power, some of the leaders hoped to see the SA supplant the regular army. But Hitler had other ideas. The SA had been useful to him in his rise to power - they had won for him the streets of Germany - but now that he was Chancellor it was the army he needed, not a band of brownshirted street brawlers. It was a problem he was to deal with in his own good time.

"If only Robert was here to see all this. Just listen to those bands," Karl Heinz called back to his parents as he leant out into the fresh night air.

"Perhaps we could have the window closed now, the room is becoming quite chilly," said Natascha. She had huddled close to the blazing fire while her menfolk had been standing at the open window. The excitement of the day had not provoked any feelings of elation within her, in fact quite the contrary, for she did not share the enthusiasm of her husband and son for the events taking place in her adopted land. German politics had never held her interest, but the sheer power of these marching formations filled her with apprehension.

"But Mother they're still coming. I can see the torches right up the street," Karl Heinz called back once again, still leaning out as far as he could. He felt his father's grip tighten on his shoulders.

"Shut the window, Karl Heinz," Karl ordered.

Karl Heinz was about to object again but thought better of it. He had learnt early in his life that failure to obey quickly would be met by swift and painful punishment, and even now at the age of fourteen, when he considered himself almost grown up, the cane would still be brought from the cupboard when he failed to comply with his father's rigid code of discipline. For all that, he loved his father dearly and accepted without question whatever punishment was meted out to him. This, his father had taught him, was the duty of a good German boy.

"Yes, Father." Karl Heinz shut the window and then moved quickly to the fire to warm himself.

Natascha looked up at her son from her chair. She had never objected to the strict upbringing her husband had insisted upon for Karl Heinz, even though the punishments the boy had received were more frequent and harsh than she would have wished. She knew that such was the deep love between father and son that these things were able to take place between them without any loss of affection or resentment on the part of the boy. Had it been otherwise her son would not have grown in body and mind to his present strong and healthy state. She thought how smart he looked standing there in his black short trousers and brown shirt. Round his neck was a black triangular scarf, the two ends of which hung down the front of his shirt like a tie, being fastened at the neck by a small leather band. On his left arm the distinctive red armband of the Hitler Youth, with the white band running round the centre and the black swastika standing out boldly on a white square background. Uniform suited him, she decided. He was such a good looking boy.

Natascha had tried hard to suppress her worries since Karl Heinz had become a member of the movement, for the last twelve months had seen a rise in street violence between the Nazis and the Communists. It had even reached a state when, on one occasion, the Communists had used firearms and opened fire on a SA march. A number of Hitler Youth members had been killed in street brawls over the last few years, but it was one particular incident which had taken place just over a year ago that Natascha couldn't erase from her mind. It had occurred on a Sunday morning in the Wedding district of Berlin - known as 'Red Wedding' because it was predominantly Communist. A small group of Hitler Youth boys had gone into the district to put up Nazi posters in the streets, when they were attacked by a troop of Communists. The Hitler Youth boys scattered, but one, called Herbert Norkus, was cornered and killed. When his body was recovered it was found that he had five stab wounds in the back and two in the chest. His face had been mutilated and his upper lip was completely missing. He was 12 years old, Natascha had prayed for Karl Heinz not to become involved in this sort of activity, and so far her prayers had been answered. Her hope was that now Herr Hitler had become Chancellor the street battles between the Nazis and Communists would cease. It was a hope that was to be realised in a very short time.

"You look very smart, my dear," she said, looking admiringly at her son.

"Yes, we are very proud of you, Karl Heinz," said Karl.

"Thank you," the boy replied modestly.

Karl Heinz was wearing his best uniform with his cross strap and dagger, because he had been on parade earlier in the evening as part of the celebrations. Parades and marches gave vent to his energy. He always enjoyed them - and the food he was given afterwards. To the poorer, unemployed boys in the troop, who paid no membership fees, this free food was a welcome gift. It was also great fun when he travelled free with his troop to other parts of Germany for these activities, especially when he was allowed a few days away from school to take part.

"And have you thanked your father for letting you stay up late?" Natascha asked.

"Thank you very much, Father."

Karl nodded with satisfaction. "And now it's time for bed, my son."

Karl Heinz kissed his parents and left the room, but a moment later he had returned. "There's somebody knocking on the front door, Father," he said.

"Whoever can that be at this time of night?" Karl frowned. "I think Marie has gone to bed, Karl Heinz, so just go down and see who it is."

"Yes, Father."

Karl rented a spacious four storey house in the city centre, the living rooms and kitchen being on the first floor and the bedrooms on the upper floors. It was a most suitable arrangement for it meant that the ground floor could be entirely given over to his surgery and dispensing room and the other rooms required for the efficient running of his medical practice.

As Karl Heinz made his way down the wide, carpeted staircase to the ground floor, the banging on the front door became more urgent, and he heard raised voices and scuffling in the large porch outside. He knew from looking out of the window above, that the pavement was still crowded with people watching the torchlight parade, but why there should be people in the private porch way he could not understand. He switched on the hall and porch way lights, and then opened the door. He started back with astonishment, because as he opened the door what he thought were two bundles of clothing fell at his feet. He quickly realised that these bundles were a man and a boy who must have been huddled together on the ground against the door, and had fallen across the threshold into the hallway as the door was opened. The man had obviously been trying to shield the boy from the kicks which were still being aimed at them by a number of youths who thronged the porch way.

The moment the door had opened and the assailants had seen the uniformed figure standing there, they had drawn back. Even though he was still a boy, the wearing of the uniform and Nazi armband had, on that particular night, made Karl Heinz as one not to be challenged, especially by those who were not in any Party organisation.

"Heil Hitler!" one of the youths shouted, raising his arm in salute.

"Heil Hitler!" Karl Heinz answered, stepping forward so that the man and boy on the ground were behind him.

The faired haired youth, who was obviously the leader of the group, spoke again. "We're dealing with these dirty Jews." He made to push by, but Karl Heinz stood in front of him.

"This is private property, you have no right here. I will deal with them," Karl Heinz replied, shutting the door firmly. His reply was firm and clear, for in the few months he had served with the Hitler Youth he had been taught to drill a squad and give orders sharply. The seeds of authority had already been sown within him, and he had been noticed as material for leadership.

Now that they were safe the man and boy struggled to their feet. "Herr Weltlinger!" Karl Heinz exclaimed as he recognised the man. "And Joseph. What have they done to you?"

"What's going on, Karl Heiriz?" Karl called out from the top of the stairs.

"It's Herr Weltlinger and Joseph, Father. They've been attacked."

Both the man and the boy were in a state of shock, and their faces covered with blood. Aaron Weltlinger was an elderly man who owned much property in the district, including the house in which the Heinemann family lived. He and his family had been some of Karl's first patients when the medical practice had been set up in the neighbourhood. Old Aaron had set a fair rent for the premises, and a mutual trust had grown up between the two men. In the difficult years when, on occasions, Karl's fees had not been paid, and he had been unable to pay the rent on time, old Aaron had not pressed the matter, knowing that Karl was an honourable man who would pay directly he had the money.

Karl quickly came down the stairs and assisted the old man into the surgery, where he was given a seat and the blood was washed from his face. Karl Heinz copied his father and did the same for the boy. He knew the Jewish boy by sight, for they both attended the same school, but they had little contact with each other, Joseph being younger.

It came to light as the two sat there having their cuts dressed, that Aaron and his grandson had been returning late from a synagogue meeting. They had been delayed in the throng and had stopped to watch the parade when they were set upon.

"Your injuries are only superficial, Herr Weltlinger," said Karl.

"They would have been a lot worse if it hadn't been for the prompt action of your son, Doctor," the old man replied.

"You must report this attack to the police," Karl urged.

"I think not, Doctor. I fear we Jews are not popular with the authorities at the moment. But I am sure that when Herr Hitler has established himself as Chancellor he will protect us, and things will return to normal." Old Aaron, rose unsteadily to hi's feet and walked towards the door. "Come, Joseph, we must go" he added.

"Will it be safe, Grandfather?" the boy asked.

"It is only a short distance to go," his grandfather replied. And then turning to Karl he said, "Perhaps we may be allowed to go out through the back door, Doctor."

When the visitors had gone it was a thoughtful boy who went to his bedroom that night.

The following afternoon when Karl Heinz returned from school he did not seek out his mother as was his normal practice before going to his room to do his homework. Natascha heard him go straight to the bathroom, and then heard him filling the basin with water.

Karl Heinz was two minutes late for dinner that evening, and when he arrived in the dining room he found his parents already seated. "You're late!" snapped Karl.

"I'm sorry, Father," Karl Heinz stood at attention by his chair hoping his father would let him sit down and not send him back to his room without having eaten.

Karl's face was stern. "You know I cannot abide unpunctuality," he said. "If I am slack and two minutes late a patient could die. Just remember that your actions affect others."

"Yes, Father."

"You may sit down, but if it happens again you'll be punished."

"What has happened to your face, Karl Heinz?" Natascha inquired. She had noticed that there was bruising and an abrasion on the boy's left cheek.

"It's nothing, Mother."

"And just look at your hands. You've knocked the skin off your knuckles. What have you been doing?" Natascha persisted.

"I'm all right, Mother. Don't fuss."

"Stand up!" Karl commanded impatiently, glaring at his son. He'd had a tiring day and was in no mood to allow Karl Heinz to prevaricate.

Karl Heinz sprung out of his chair and stood to attention.

"When your mother asks you a question, you will answer it properly. Now, how have you come by these injuries? Have you been fighting?"

"Yes, Father."

"Perhaps he could be allowed to sit down, Karl," said Natascha gently.

Karl nodded at his son, and the boy sat down again.

Karl .Heinz then explained that a number of boys had set upon Joseph Weltlinger in the playground, and he had gone to the younger boy's aid. Some of the boys were Karl Heinz's own friends and they stopped when he told them to leave the boy alone. "But that Max Bauer called me a dirty Jew lover and a traitor, so I punched him on the nose and we had a dreadful fight," Karl Heinz related.

"Did you win?" asked Karl.

"I'm not sure. I think so, but we didn't finish. He got a bloody nose and a black eye."

"Go on, let's hear the rest," smiled Natascha.

"It would have been all right, but everyone wanted to watch and they made such a row that Doctor Krödel must have heard, because the next thing we knew he had grabbed our ears and was marching us to his study."

"Did he thrash you?" asked Karl.

"Yes, Father. After the beating he asked what it was all about," Karl Heinz replied.

"I should have thought he would have asked that before beating you," said Natascha, looking a little puzzled.

"Nonsense!" Karl retorted. "They had broken the school rules so they were punished. The reason had nothing to do with it."

"But Karl Heinz was protecting an innocent boy. Why should he be beaten for that?" Natascha rejoined.

Karl thought his wife a little obtuse at times. "He was not beaten for that. He was beaten for fighting. Now please let the boy finish his story."

Karl Heinz then went on to relate how Max Bauer had accused him of being a traitor in front of the headmaster. "I told him he'd better be careful because you're a friend of Gauleiter Ley."

"And the doctor, what did he say?" asked Natascha.

"He slapped Bauer round the head and told him to shut up."

"I believe Doctor Krödel is a National Socialist himself," said Karl.

"He asked me if I went to church," Karl Heinz remarked. "He didn't seem to mind when I said I did. He said something about always remaining true to one's convictions."

There was silence at the table for a time until Karl Heinz said, "Herr von Schirach has said he doesn't want anyone in the movement who doesn't believe in God."

"Well, that's something, I suppose," Natascha commented.

"Why aren't Jews Christians?" Karl Heinz asked.

"The first Christians *were* Jews." Karl replied, and then added. "But I don't think there are many Jewish Christians nowadays."

Karl Heinz looked puzzled. "Is that why they're different? I mean, because they're not Christians, they are different, aren't they?"

Both Karl and Natascha felt that the question was best left unanswered. It would be so easy for the boy to innocently misquote them.

"Perhaps I shouldn't have stood up for Joseph."

"What makes you think that, dear?" asked Natascha.

"Because he's a Jew. My *Bannführer* says all Jews are swine and the cause of all Germany's troubles. He says Herr Hitler hates them, and every pure Aryan German boy should do the same."

"And what do you think?" Karl asked.

Karl Heinz thought for a moment and then said, "I'm not quite sure. Herr Hitler can't be wrong, can he? They're making our German race impure, you know, and I've seen pictures of the terrible things they do."

"Then why did you help poor Joseph?" It frightened Natascha that such thoughts had been planted in her son's young mind.

"I don't really know, Mother. Sometimes I get in such a muddle. When I listen to the lectures it all seems to make sense, but it's different when it's someone you know. I'm sure Joseph isn't wicked. I just couldn't stand by and see him hurt."

But over the next few months many good Germans had to stand by and see others hurt or face the consequences which disagreement with the new government would swiftly bring.

*

To hold the honourable office of Chancellor of Germany was one thing, but to have absolute power was something quite different. And it was absolute power that Hitler was determined to have. From the moment he became Chancellor he worked towards that end.

When the Reichstag building was burnt down on 27th February, Hitler lost no time in blaming the Communists, and the following day he persuaded President Hindenburg to sign a decree suspending all civil liberties as *a Defensive measure against Communists' acts*. He used this new power to further his cause in the forthcoming elections.

Karl believed these measures were necessary and once again voted for the National Socialists on 5th March in the last democratic elections he was to know. But for all the intimidation and suppression, Hitler did not get a clear majority in the Reichstag which was necessary if he was to change the constitution and govern in his own way. However, when the newly elected Reichstag assembled in the Kroll Opera House on 23rd March they had before them the Enabling Act, which would give the Chancellor and his Cabinet full powers for four years in order to destroy the communist menace. In effect it would give Hitler the power he wanted, and except for the Social Democrats, all Parties voted in favour. The Reichstag had voted itself out of power.

"Do you think it wise to give the government so much power?" Natascha asked. She and Karl had lingered at the breakfast table that Saturday morning discussing the latest political events that had been taking place in Berlin during the week.

"If we wish the Chancellor to deal with the communists he must have the means to do it. We don't want a revolution," Karl replied.

"Of course we don't. But surely it's not necessary to give the government the power to change the constitution just to deal with the communists?" Natascha persisted. Although German politics did not generally interest her, recent events had caught her attention and had brought a feeling of concern for the future, not so much for herself and Karl but for Karl Heinz.

"It is our duty on occasions like this to give up certain freedoms for the good of the state. We are law abiding and loyal Germans so what have we to fear. It's only the communists and criminals who will be crushed." Karl could see that they were not going to agree, but put it down to Natascha being Dutch, and her lack of understanding of German political thinking. And then there was the English influence in her life which did not help matters. "You mustn't worry, darling. Everything will be for the best."

"I hope you're right," Natascha smiled.

"I was talking to Robert Ley last week,'" Karl went on. "He said that the future looks bright, and that the Party will look after its supporters. He asked me if I should like to own this house."

"Whatever made him say that? It's not our house, and I'm sure Herr Weltlinger has no intention of selling."

"That's exactly what I said. He just smiled and said that as the house was owned by a Jew it wouldn't be difficult to get it made over to me."

"What a strange thing to say," Natascha pondered. "What did you say to him?"

"I didn't know what to say. I didn't really understand what he was talking about, but he said time would tell."

At that moment Karl Heinz entered the room. He was in uniform, because that afternoon the local branch of the Hitler Youth was off into the country for sports and training. "I've just had an idea," he said. "That is if you will allow it," he added.

"Well, what is it?" Karl inquired.

Karl Heinz hesitated not knowing quite how to put it. "You see, I told my *Bannführer* that my cousin is the son of an English general and he said he would like to meet him. He said the Führer respects the English. So I was wondering if Robert could come to stay with us in the summer holidays?"

"What you mean is that you want Robert to stay with us," Natascha laughed. "There's no need to put the responsibility on to your poor *Bannführer.*"

Karl Heinz grinned sheepishly. "Yes, Mother."

Karl Heinz had a small room set aside for him to use.

"Well, Karl, shall we allow it?" Natascha asked, pretending to be serious. She saw the look of hopeful anticipation on her son's face, and was enjoying teasing him.

Karl also tried to look serious and stroked his chin as if giving the matter deep thought. "Do you think our son has been good enough to deserve a guest, my dear?" he asked.

Karl Heinz was looking from one to the other as his parents pretended to make up their minds, his face a picture of uncertainty, and his eyes pleading with them to say yes. "Please, I promise to be very good. And you do like Robert, don't you?" he said.

"Yes, I think he's a fine boy," said Karl. "He can't help being English, but at least it's the next best thing to being a German." Karl looked at his son and smiled, and then said, "Yes, Robert may come."

Karl Heinz's face lit up with joy. "Oh, thank you, Father! Thank you, Mother!" he exclaimed. "I shall go and write to him straight away. He was in such a hurry to leave the room that he almost knocked over the maid who was just entering to clear the breakfast table. "Sorry, Marie," he cried as he caught hold of the bewildered girl and whirled her round in a joyful dance before rushing from the room.

Karl Heinz had a small room set aside for him to use as a study, and it was to this room he went to prepare his letter. Clearing a space, he placed the writing pad on the table, and then, opening a bottle of ink, he carefully put it down in the centre of the table so as not to knock it over. He didn't wish for any accidents, and he was determined to be on his best behaviour from now on, otherwise Father might change his mind about Robert coming to stay. Having fitted a brand new nib to his pen, he sat down and began to write.

Robert's letters to Karl Heinz were always written in German, and Karl Heinz always wrote back in English, except for the opening greeting which he wrote in German.

> *You know where,*
> *25th March 1933,*
> *Mein Lieber Robert,*
>
> *I have got such good news; I can hardly wait to tell you. Father says that you can come and stay with me in the summer holidays. Please write back quickly and say you will. It will be such great fun.*

*

"Yippee! Karl Heinz has asked me to stay with him in the summer holidays," Robert cried. He had come down to breakfast and found the letter waiting for him on the table. He had been in such a hurry to read it that he ripped it open even before serving himself with his porridge, and read the first few lines while leaning against the sideboard. "Can I go, Father?"

"I always knew there was something wrong with Karl Heinz," grinned Joanna.

Robert glared at his sister. "What are you talking about?" he snapped.

"Well, he must be barmy to want you to stay with him," Joanna laughed.

"Oh, shut up!" Robert retorted, but he was too happy to keep a straight face and couldn't prevent himself from grinning. He stuffed the letter into his pocket while he carried his plate to the table and sat down.

"And have you got enough money to pay the fare?" asked John.

"No, Father," Robert grinned sheepishly at John.

"So who's going to pay?"

"I thought perhaps. . ." Robert hesitated.

"Watch out Pops, he's after your money again," Joanna interrupted.

"You can talk! You're always on the scrounge. It's not fair. You're always slobbering him with kisses and getting what you want," Robert retorted. He then began to mimic his sister. "Daddy dear, I've just seen the most gorgeous dress. It hardly, costs a thing, dearest Daddy. I know you'll get it for me. Oh, do say you will."

"Well I must say there is a certain amount of truth in what you say, m'lad," John chuckled.

When Joanna had controlled her laughter, she said, "Why don't you make him work his passage down the Rhine on a barge?"

"What a splendid idea," said John. "What do you think of that, Robert?"

"Oh, yes! That would be super. Does that mean I can go?"

"I think I'd better let him go, don't you, Beth? If only to prevent him sitting on my knee and slobbering me with kisses," said John.

"In that case, perhaps you'd better. I'm sure Hugo could arrange a suitable barge," Elizabeth replied.

"I wish it could be the one we bombed," Robert blurted out, and then put his hand over his mouth when he realised what he'd said.

"Bombed? What do you mean, bombed?" John looked puzzled.

"Oh, nothing, Father," Robert replied.

"Don't ask questions, Daddy. There are lots of things that you mustn't know about the last summer hols, aren't there, Robert?" said Joanna meaningfully.

Robert didn't answer. He quickly pulled out the letter and started to read the rest of it:

> *All my friends want to meet you and my Bannführer says you can come with me when I go to Hitler Youth meetings and take part just as if you were a member. I've got a spare uniform you can wear. We are the same size so it will fit you just right. You won't be able to wear the armband though, because you are not a member. But that doesn't matter. I know you will enjoy it.*
>
> *I had a really good fight, or should I say bad fight – anyway, it was a fight. It was a few weeks ago now. This boy Max called me a traitor so I punched his nose. Then he hit me in the face and we bashed each other for about 5 minutes before our Headmaster stopped us. We got the stick – ouch!! Anyway, Max has joined the Hitler Youth now, and he said he was sorry for calling me names so we are friends again.*
>
> *I still remember how to make water bombs. I taught some of my friends in my troop to make them and after parade one evening we had a good battle and got very wet. I thought my Scharführer, that's my local branch leader, was going to be angry, but he wasn't. He said he thought it showed good spirit. Then he taught us how to lob them like grenades.*

> *I have to go now, Robert. Do say you will*
> *come. We will have lots of fun. Specially wrestling*
> *in the bedroom!!! And you know what that means.*
>
> *With love from*
> *Karl Heinz.*
> *P.S. We won't have Lisa to pester us either.*

"Look at him sniggering away with his nose in that letter. Come on let's have a decco," said Joanna.

"Not likely!"

"There! I knew it! I bet those two have got some dark secret," Joanna teased.

Robert coloured up, remembering the naked wrestling-bouts with his cousin and knowing them to have been just an excuse to pursue their awakening boyish desires. Why did that wretched girl always have to say things like that, he asked himself? The trouble was it happened to be true. Robert put the letter back into his pocket. "Oh, no we haven't!" he lied. He then quickly changed the subject. "Mother, will you write to Uncle Hugo today about the barge?"

"There's plenty of time, dear. You don't break up until the thirty first of July, so you won't be going until August," Elizabeth replied. "I'll write soon."

"And you'd better make sure you work hard, next term or you won't be going at all," John interposed.

"I promise," Robert replied. Then his stomach turned over at the thought of the school report his father would be receiving in a few days. Oh, crumbs!, he thought, what would he say?

"I've heard that before," said John. . . "And you'd better start saving some money, as well. I shall raise your pocket money to one and sixpence, and you must save a shilling a week. By the time you go you should have saved about seventeen shillings."

Robert thought this was a reasonable financial deal. "Thank you, Father. . . As it's Friday today, could I have my first one and sixpence now?"

John felt in his pocket and brought out the coins. "You can put your cap on and come up and receive it like a soldier," he said.

"Yes, sir," Robert replied, leaving the table to fetch his cap. Being Friday it was OTC parade at school in the afternoon, and Robert was dressed in his khaki army uniform. The jacket with a high collar and black buttons was fastened right up to the neck. On each shoulder strap was a black metal insignia giving the name of the school. There were small black metal hooks at each side of the waist where the webbing belt rested. This belt had to be freshly covered in green blanco before each parade and the brass buckle and other brass pieces had to be highly polished. Black boots had to be worn, and puttees were wound round the legs from the ankles to just under the knees with the trousers neatly turned over and overlapping the top of the puttees by about two inches. The khaki cap had on it the Royal Sussex Regiment badge in bronze.

Robert was always very particular in the way he wound on his puttees, for he knew his father's critical eye for uniform would not allow him to be anything but smart. When he returned to the breakfast room, Robert was wearing his cap but not his clean belt. This had been carefully placed, in a bag ready for afternoon parade. He dare not let it get dirty or he would be pulled up when inspected. He marched in and came to a halt in front of his father, and, standing to attention gave a very smart salute. "Cadet Rutherford ready for inspections sir!" he said with a grin on his face.

"Well, Cadet Rutherford, you look exceptionally smart today, and I think you're worth one and sixpence." John pressed the coins into the eager young hand, and with his own hand gently closed his son's fingers over them. For a moment he did not let go. The bright eyes looking at him from under the khaki cap reminded him of another boy into whose hand he had pressed a coin so many years ago. *All Sir Garnet, Robert!*

"All Sir Garnet, Father!" Robert knew all about, the expression which his father used on occasions. It always meant he was in Father's

good books. He gave another smart salute and said, "I must go now, or I'll be late for school."

The Easter holidays, which commenced the following week, did not start well for Robert. Firstly, he had to wait a week before he could present his father with his school report - John being away for the first week of the holiday - and secondly, when the report was eventually read, Robert's prediction that it would not be favourably received was no understatement. As he stood there wringing his hands behind his back, and waiting for the storm to break, while his father read the dreaded document, he ventured a remark. "I suppose *All is Not Sir Garnet* today, Father."

John looked up and saw the pained expression on his son's face. He tried not to smile, but couldn't help admiring the boy's humour. "No it damn well isn't, you cheeky young devil," he replied. "I thought you'd started to improve last year, but since then you've got worse. I'd a jolly good mind to give you a damn good flogging."

Robert gripped his bottom hard at the thought of it. "I really promise I'll do better next term, Father."

"Now understand this, Robert. If you get a report like this again you'll be caned. And you won't be allowed to go to Cologne. I don't expect miracles, but just try your best," John lectured.

"Yes, Father, I promise. May I go now?"

"Yes, perhaps you'd better, before I change my mind," John sighed.

Robert left the room much relieved that he had managed to escape without punishment. Nevertheless, he felt decidedly guilty because he knew he had been very slack during the past term and had not kept his promise to work harder. It also weighed on his conscience that he had, yet again, upset his father who, he had to admit, was being exceptionally patient with him.

Robert kept his promise during the summer term, and even surprised himself with the extra effort he put into his work. He considered it the best term he'd ever had at the school. Even old Cavey had found no reason to haul him out in front of the class and slap his head, and he'd managed to avoid the wrath of that Welsh demon in the chemistry labs.

His great joy for this particular term was that he had got his place in the cricket first eleven and was now an established member of the team.

Another thing that had surprised him and also pleased his father was that he quite enjoyed his Friday afternoons with the OTC. He enjoyed the physical activity, and then there was the other consideration that he was out in the open air and not stuck in a classroom as were those boys who were not in the corps. He had soon picked up the drill movements and, although he found the rifle rather heavy at first, he could now carry out the arms drill without the after effect of aching muscles. He had taken naturally to shooting and was developing into a good shot.

He found it all great sport, and at that stage it had never crossed his young mind that the basic purpose of all this training was, for whatever reason, to kill people. It was the reality of this fact that he would have to face as he matured towards manhood, but for the present he basked in the sunny security of his youth, blissfully ignorant of the clouds gathering on the horizon.

By the end of the term all the necessary arrangements for Robert's German holiday had been made. He would take the usual route to Rotterdam where he would remain for two days with Uncle Hugo and family. A German barge would take him the rest of the way to Cologne. He would only take a small case for his underwear and a few other items, because Karl Heinz had suggested and Robert had willingly agreed that he should dress as a German boy in some of Karl Heinz's clothes. Then we will look like brothers, Karl Heinz had written.

John had been better pleased with Robert's school report and was relieved that he had not had to enforce his threat of refusing to allow the holiday to take place. He was also pleased for the excuse to give Robert some money as a present for his improvement.

"We'll come and see you off at Harwich, dear," said Elizabeth. She wanted Robert to have his holiday because she knew how much it meant to him, but she had still not come to terms with the fact that her young son was to travel on his own for the first time, and her protective instinct towards him was causing her to feel a little apprehensive. How she would miss him, she thought.

"I'd prefer it if you didn't, Mother. I'd like to try to do it all on my own," Robert replied. He felt a little unkind when he noticed the disappointment on his mother's face. He sat down beside her and put his arm round her. "Please don't be sad, Mother. I don't mean to be unkind. I just want to do it myself. I am fourteen and a half now." Robert paused and took his arm away. He sat on the edge of the settee with his chin resting in his hands. "I'm sorry, I'm not putting this very well, am I?"

"I think you've made your point, Robert," said John. "The boy's right, Beth, he's not a baby anymore. He should learn to stand on his own feet. He's a strong, strapping lad, and he's got a tongue in his head to ask if he's not sure of anything."

"Yes, I'm being very silly."

"Don't worry, Mother, I'll be all right, and I'll be back before you know it."

When, the great day eventually arrived, it was not only Elizabeth who was affected by the parting. Robert had been in a state of excitement all the morning, but in the afternoon when the car was brought to the front door and the moment came to say goodbye, he felt a lump in his throat at the thought of leaving his family for the first time. Each in turn hugged and kissed him, and then he quickly got into the car beside the chauffeur. He took out his handkerchief and pretended to blow his nose, furtively dabbing the wet from his eyes and hoping no one would notice. As the car went down the drive he leant out of the window and waved until out of sight, and then sat back in his seat feeling a little sad. Why did they all seem to love him so much when he was such a naughty boy, he wondered? Father had made the travel arrangements. Mother had written to Uncle Hugo, and even Joanna had given him a half-a-crown to buy some food on the journey.

The Southern Belle was standing at the platform as Robert went through the ticket barrier. This was now an electric train, the steam locomotive having been withdrawn from this particular service on the 1st January that year. It was an all Pullman train which John frequently used, and he had felt it would be an interesting experience for Robert to travel on it.

While waiting for the train to start Robert passed the time reading a comic he had just bought at the book stall. A number of other passengers entered the carriage, but there were still a number of tables free. Two rather elegant, elderly ladies came in and stood in the gangway by Robert's table. Robert looked up and noticed the taller of the two had white hair, and the other grey hair.

"Shall we sit in our usual place?" said one.

"Oh yes. I'm sure this young gentleman will not mind," the other replied, smiling down at Robert.

Robert stood up as the two took their seats opposite him. "I'm sorry if I have taken your seat," he apologized.

"But you haven't, my dear. We always sit with our backs to the engine," the white haired woman beamed.

At last the whistle blew and Robert felt the train move and quickly picked up speed. The great adventure had really begun. "I'm on my way, Karl Heinz," he silently whispered to himself. He blinked his eyes as the train moved out from the dingy station into the bright sunlight of the hot August afternoon, and then sat back in his seat, happy just to watch the scenery flash by. It was a non-stop train, and having passed through the first station a little way up the line, only seconds later the sun was blotted out and the lights came on as he was whisked into the short Patcham tunnel and then out again for a minute or two before entering the long Clayton tunnel.

He thought of his friend Ian, because this tunnel passed almost under his garden. It was funny to think that Ian might be standing on top of him.

This tunnel seemed to go on for ever and he wondered how long it was taking to get through. It must be well over a minute. He smiled to himself as he imagined old Cavey setting him one of those beastly problems he was always dreaming up just to torture poor boys. He wouldn't be smiling if it was actually happening, but it was fun to think about it when he was safe from his tormentor's clutches. Stand up, Rutherford, and answer this question. If an engine driver spent 6 minutes each, day inside a tunnel, and worked for 6 days a week for 40 years, how much of his life would he spend in a tunnel? If old Cavey had asked him that in class he would have been stumped, but now it was actually happening the problem didn't seem so difficult, because an engine driver working on this line would spend that time each day in a tunnel - probably more. Robert tried to work it out. He had a pencil stub in his pocket and wrote down the figures on his comic. He wasn't sure whether he was right, but he made the answer 48 days. Fancy spending forty eight days in a tunnel. What a bore, he decided,

He glanced up and noticed the two ladies looking at him with interest. "You seem to very engrossed, young man," said the grey haired one. Robert just smiled. He felt a little self-conscious travelling on his own, and missed having the family to do the talking for him. He had never been a chatter-box like Joanna, but rather reticent in the presence of strangers, and he remembered his father telling him that he must speak up for himself and not be shy, because he has sensible thoughts in his head so he should not be afraid to use them. But the two ladies gradually engaged him in conversation and drew him out. When they ordered tea from the steward they included him, and he was soon tucking into scones and cream cakes.

CHAPTER 8

Karl Heinz had spent the morning by the river, returning home at mid-day for something to eat. He was so impatient for Robert's arrival, he could settle to nothing. "Stop gulping your food, Karl Heinz, and try to relax. It won't make Robert arrive any sooner by stuffing your mouth like that," said Natascha.

"I'm sorry but I do wish he'd hurry up. I can't wait to see him."

"And don't speak with your mouth full."

But nothing Natascha said could restrain her son's impatience, and directly he had eaten he made his way back to the river. It was a ten minute walk to the great Hohensollern Bridge, which spans the Rhine a short distance from the Cathedral, and once there, Karl Heinz took up a position where he could get a view of the barges coming up river.

Robert stood at the bow of the barge watching the Hohenzollern Bridge get closer and closer, and then he caught sight of the figure of Karl Heinz standing near the archway which leads under the bridge at the side of the river. They both waved frantically to each other, and continued to do so until the barge passed underneath the massive girders and slid quietly alongside the landing stage on the far side. Robert's journey was over, and he had made it by himself.

Karl Heinz had run to the landing stage, and, the moment he was able, he leapt aboard to greet his cousin. The weeks of waiting were over and he almost danced for joy as they threw their arms round each other's shoulders, once again locked together as brothers.

The barge remained alongside just long enough for Robert to introduce his cousin and say his farewells, and then with Karl Heinz carrying the small case the boys stepped ashore and stood waving as the vessel continued on its way up river.

Although Robert had lived in Cologne for a few months when John had been stationed there as part of the British army of occupation, he had been too young to have anymore than faint memories of the town. He fancied he remembered the towers and the castle like archway at the end of the great Hohenzollern Bridge, and perhaps the Cathedral had made some impression on him, but he could not bring to mind the quarters where he had lived. However, he did have a vague recollection of being taken for walks by the river, and he had carried in his mind a picture of the new bridge, but this was probably because it hung on great cables like the one at Clifton, which his father had pointed out to him on a number of occasions.

The boys walked with their arms linked. As an only child Karl Heinz had always longed for a brother, and his cousin filled that gap in his life. He wanted the whole world to know that this was his brother. "I can hardly believe you're here, Robert. This must be the best day of my life."

"It's really good to be here," Robert replied. He gazed up at the tall buildings, a number of which had long red banners with the black swastika on a white circular background draped from the upper floors. "You look very smart in your uniform, Karl Heinz," he remarked. "Do you wear it all the time?"

"Not all the time. But it's a good time to wear it at the moment, because it shows I'm loyal to our Führer... Anyone in the Hitler Youth is important now, because we are the new Germany. That's what the Führer says, anyway."

"Have you been properly sworn in yet?"

"Oh yes, last October, when I was fourteen." The boys stopped for a moment to gaze up at the great spires of the Cathedral. "What's that small star on your epaulette?" Robert continued, still interested in his cousin's uniform.

"I'm a Kameradschaftsführer. That means I'm in charge of a squad of about fifteen boys." Karl Heinz then pointed to the number eleven above his rank star and said, "This means my unit belongs to the Cologne-Aachen *Gebiete*"

"You're very young to have been promoted."

"They needed more leaders because so many new boys have joined since the Führer became Chancellor. We don't have grown-ups leading us, they hold only the very high ranks. The idea is that youth should lead youth. Even our Bannführer is only twenty five and he has about three thousand boys in his group."

"I bet you're a jolly good leader," Robert remarked, pleased to think his cousin was so important.

From the square, in front of the Cathedral the boys walked into the street where Karl Heinz lived. Before entering the house Karl Heinz said, "We must be quiet until we get up the stairs, because Father has a surgery going on at the moment." They opened the front door and crept into the silent hall, the only sound being the loud *tick tock* of a grandfather clock. But once up the stairs and entering the drawing room Karl Heinz called out, "Robert's here, Mother!" Whenever he came into the presence of Aunty Natascha, Robert's thoughts were invariably the same. It was Mother standing there - and yet it wasn't. He had never ceased to marvel at the likeness between the two sisters. It must be the reason why he and Karl Heinz were so alike.

Natascha put her arms round Robert and kissed him. "Well, my handsome Prince, how you've grown. You boys will soon be looking down on me."

"It's awfully kind of you to have me, Aunty," Robert said.

"We've all been looking forward to it, my dear. And Karl Heinz has been like a caged lion all day, prowling up and down not knowing what to do next."

"Your first job this evening, Robert, is to play the piano," said Karl Heinz. "Music always sooths Father's temper down and I'm hoping it will make him forget he was annoyed with me at breakfast this morning."

"He'll have forgotten all about it by now," said Natascha.

"I bet he hasn't. It wasn't fair, anyway. I know I knocked the coffee over, but that's not bad manners. It was an accident," Karl Heinz protested.

"Of course it was, dear. Your father is a little worried at the moment and I think it's making him irritable," Natascha replied. She knew that Herr Weltlinger had been visiting Karl on certain occasions during the past few weeks. His visits had always been well after dark when Karl Heinz had gone to bed, and Karl had seemed worried when he had returned upstairs after seeing the old Jew. But he had said nothing.

"And, Robert, please don't play any Mendelssohn," Karl Heinz instructed.

"Why ever not?"

"Because he was a Jew."

"What's that got to do with it? Uncle Karl likes Mendelssohn. He told me so last summer."

"It's different now," said Karl Heinz. He was a little unsure how to explain. "Look, Robert, we just mustn't listen to Jewish stuff anymore. "Promise you won't play any."

"How do I know who's Jewish and who isn't?" Robert complained looking puzzled.

"Just promise, Robert."

"Okay, I promise." Robert replied uncertainly. He looked at Natascha, who raised her eyebrows and said, "Don't worry, Robert, I'm as baffled as you are."

When Karl came upstairs after surgery Robert found him quite affable. "I am pleased you've come, Robert. Now, perhaps Karl Heinz will calm down," said Karl, shaking his nephew's hand. And then, turning to Karl Heinz he said, "And I haven't forgotten that I wish to speak to you."

"No, Father," Karl Heinz replied, glancing at his mother as if to say I told you so.

All the rooms in house were large, and the long dining room table matched the size of the room. Robert considered it far too long for a small family. His uncle and aunty sitting at each end seemed to him to be miles away. He sat opposite Karl Heinz, and he wondered whether Uncle Karl had measured the position of his chair with a ruler to make sure it was exactly halfway along the side. It would have been cosier if they had all eaten at one end, he thought.

Karl Heinz was instructed to say grace before the meal which was something Robert was never called upon to do at home unless the vicar was present." John believed that if anyone wished to thank God for food they should do so quietly in their own mind.

Robert felt the meal was rather formal, but then Uncle Karl was rather a formal person. He really didn't know his uncle very well, and had never been completely at ease in his presence. He believed he was very strict with Karl Heinz, but then Father was strict as well, Robert thought. At least you know where you stand with Fathers like that, and both of them were very fair men. Perhaps he would come to like Uncle Karl if he got to know him better.

"Perhaps you would play for us after dinner, Robert?" said Karl.

"Yes, Uncle, of course," Robert had a feeling of satisfaction that Uncle Karl should wish him to play, for Uncle was not one to try to be popular with boys. He was a straightforward man like Father, and would not have asked unless he really wished him to play. At least that was one point in his favour, he decided.

Karl Heinz winked at Robert across the table.

His nephew was a pleasant enough boy, Karl considered. Rather mischievous like Karl Heinz, but at least that showed spirit, and provided it was controlled with discipline, there was no harm in it. He was a strange mixture of a boy. Tall and strong; good at games and athletics and yet sensitive and certainly a talented musician. Karl had always pictured musicians as rather frail and studious types, but Robert was anything but that. He looked at the two boys and wondered whether there might be any truth in these racial theories that certain members of the Party were expounding. If ever there were two pure Aryan boys, these fitted the picture, he thought.

After dinner Robert sat at the piano admiring the quality of the instrument while he waited for the others to make themselves comfortable. "It's a lovely piano, Aunty," he said.

"It's not played as much as it should be," Natascha replied. "Karl Heinz can play quite nicely, but he's very naughty when it comes to practising."

"Do you wish me to play anything in particular, Uncle?"

"I always enjoy Chopin, Robert."

Robert played for some time, lost in the delicate poetry of the music. He loved Chopin himself and played many of the pieces from memory. Others he sight read from the large selection of sheet music which was available.

Karl Heinz sat on the settee with his head resting on the arm of the chair, happy now in the presence of this cousin whom he loved so much. He could see his father had relaxed; and it was almost certain he would escape any further reprimand for the breakfast incident.

"You really are incredible, Robert, the way you remember all that music," Natascha said when the recital had finished. "I thought the violin was your instrument, but you are equally as good on the piano."

"Yes, Robert, that was most enjoyable". I feel very privileged to have such a professional player in my home. I hope we shall have many such evenings while you are here," said Karl.

Robert was pleased to have gained such praise from his uncle. "Thank you, Uncle," he replied.

"'We'll go to bed now," said Karl Heinz.

"It's very unusual for you to volunteer to go to bed so early," Natascha smiled.

But Karl Heinz just smiled, kissed his parents good night, and left the room with Robert. He had other plans before going to sleep, and Robert knew what they were.

When the boys had gone, Karl and Natascha sat quietly talking for sometime. "I'm expecting Herr Weltlinger later this evening so it is as well that the boys have gone to bed." Karl said.

"You have never explained why he keeps calling so late," Natascha remarked.

I'm sorry, my dear, but I didn't want to worry you. He comes late because I wish no one to know about it, not even Karl Heinz. It's not that I don't trust my son, but an unguarded slip of his tongue at the wrong time could cause me. . ." Karl hesitated as he searched for the right words - "Great embarrassment with my Party friends. And I cannot risk being known as a Jew lover."

"I don't understand. You have never kept your good relationship with Herr Weltlinger a secret before." said Natascha,

"Times have changed, Natascha, as you well know. I have you and Karl Heinz to consider, and I have no intention of ruining my medical practice just because I happen to disagree with certain policies of the new government. You may remember I told you some time ago it had been suggested that we should own this house."

"Yes, I remember."

"Well, we do own it now." Karl then explained that a few weeks ago one of his patients, who is a high ranking officer in the SA, had informed him that it had been suggested to Herr Weltlinger that, in order to keep some of his numerous properties, he should consider giving away two of his houses to the present tenants, Karl being one of them, and the SA officer the other. This action, Herr Weltlinger was told, would show his loyalty to the new regime and ensure that his family came to no harm."

Karl continued, "My patient thought he was doing me a favour, and he knows, of course, I'm a personal friend of Gauleiter Ley. No doubt he hopes his action will bring him advantage within the Party. It has certainly brought him a free house."

In return, for the gift which had come to him by the good offices of the SA, Karl would be expected to make a relatively small donation to SA funds. Consequently, Herr Weltlinger had made over the property to Karl, who had in turn made a donation to SA funds.

"So the house is now ours," Karl concluded.

"But this is quite wrong, Karl. You should have objected." Natascha protested.

"My dear, you don't understand. At the present time one does not object to anything the SA suggests."

"But why is Herr Weltlinger still visiting you?" Natascha inquired.

"You must promise me, Natascha, never to tell anyone what I am about to say. Not even Karl Heinz."

"Of course, my darling, if that is your wish."

"It is," Karl replied. "Each time Herr Weltlinger has visited me, I have given him a sum of money in cash. I have not got the money to pay him what the house is worth, but I have tried to give him something to make up for his loss. He is going to emigrate, and it will be more than enough to pay the fares to America for him and his family."

"That's very generous of you, Karl."

"I don't feel particularly generous, my dear, but I consider it the honourable thing to do,' but remember I wish no one to know about this."

"I thought he was quite wealthy," said Natascha. "He is, but most of his wealth is in property, and he will have to leave it behind. He's having to pay a great deal to get his family out, and it has been difficult for him to find the ready cash."

"Can he not sell his other property?" Natascha asked.

"Perhaps, but that takes time and he wishes to get out of the country now. Some people are reluctant to deal with Jews at the moment."

"Surely the SA cannot confiscate property like this?"

"They haven't confiscated it. They've just made certain suggestions, and you know what that means. I don't like it anymore than you do, Natascha, but there's nothing we can do about it."

"There must be something. Can't the Church do something? Surely they don't condone this persecution?" It was something that had been on Natascha's conscience for some time, but somehow, she thought, it was not a Christian issue in Karl's mind.

"If our government wish Germany to be rid of the Jews, then who are we to oppose it. As for our Lutheran Church, Martin Luther himself had wanted the same thing, and he had wanted their synagogues and schools set on fire and their houses destroyed." Karl was not alone in his thinking, for Luther's anti-Semitism and his passionate belief in absolute obedience to the political power was deeply inbred into the minds of many German Protestants, including their Pastors.

When Karl heard the door bell he got up and went downstairs. A short time later he returned looking quite cheerful. "Well that's an end of it," he said, seeing Natascha looking at him, obviously waiting for the latest news. "The Weltlingers leave for America next week. They've got their papers, and they've sold as much as they can. The rest they will just leave behind."

"Poor people." said Natascha sadly.

"It's not our worry," Karl replied.

"I'm sorry, Karl, but I think it is. Where is it all going to lead?"

When the boys came down for breakfast the following morning Karl had already left to take his morning surgery. Normally, Karl Heinz was expected to take his breakfast with his father and mother, but Karl had allowed that while Robert was staying with them the boys could come down later and take breakfast on their own.

"Isn't this terrific, just the two of us!" exclaimed Karl Heinz as they sat eating.

"I should say!" Robert replied enthusiastically.

Natascha entered the room and both boys stood up, each receiving a kiss. "Robert, my dear, you look very dashing in that uniform," she remarked, seeing her nephew dressed, as a Hitler Youth boy. "You really do look like twins now. . . And how are you going to amuse yourselves today?"

"Robert's going to meet my friends, and I'll show him round the town."

When Karl Heinz had first joined the Hitler Youth Natascha had not allowed him to wander the streets dressed in uniform for fear he became involved in a brawl with communist youths. But now it was different and there were no longer any street battles. For those in Party uniform the streets were safe. The communists had been suppressed, and Nazis power was supreme. Even communists were now joining the SA - Berlin's SA was referred to as *Beefsteak Nazis,* brown outside and red inside. The Hitler-Youth was also rapidly expanding as other German Youth Associations were either discouraged or instructed that their members were now part of the Hitler Youth. Even former members of the Communist Youth Association were being accepted into the movement. The fine, strong, bright eyed young men who were later to sweep into Poland, France and Russia and conquer Europe for their Fuhrer were in the making.

"Be back in time for lunch, boys. I must make sure Robert doesn't starve or Aunty Elizabeth would never forgive me," she laughed.

One of the things Robert noticed as they set out along the street was the number of people who acknowledged Karl Heinz, obviously pleased to see him. It seemed as if they were being stopped every few yards so that he could be introduced to someone.

"You seem to know everyone," Robert said admiringly.

"Most people round here have known me since I was quite small, because Father's their doctor. He's a very good doctor, you know, Robert, and everyone likes him."

The street in which Karl Heinz lived was quite narrow for most of its length. At one end it joined the large square in front of the Cathedral, and at the other end it widened into a small tree lined square. It was to this tree lined square that Karl Heinz took his cousin, for this was the meeting place for the local boys.

Karl Heinz found some of his friends there and proudly introduced Robert. Seeing Robert dressed as a Hitler Youth the boys were surprised to learn that he was the English cousin they had heard so much about. "He's a temporary member, and has special permission to wear our uniform," Karl Heinz explained.

At first Robert found that the boys appeared somewhat reserved towards him, but, being Karl Heinz's cousin, this attitude soon thawed and he became accepted into their company. One boy, who was bigger and stronger than the others, pushed Robert in the chest. "Can you fight, English boy?" he asked belligerently.

"What for?" Robert asked. He didn't mind wrestling for fun, but otherwise he had to have a good reason to fight.

"To show you're not weak," the big boy replied, giving Robert another push.

"That's stupid," Robert retorted.

"Are you calling me stupid?" The other boy was beginning to show temper.

"Shut up, Max!" Karl Heinz interrupted. "Robert can handle you any day, so watch out." Karl Heinz was unsmiling and looked steadily at the other boy.

The big boy thrust his hands into his pockets and sat down under one of the trees. "All right, no need to get like that," he grumbled, chastened.

They all sat down under the trees to talk, glad to be in the shade out of the hot sun. It was obvious to Robert that his cousin was a popular boy with his friends, and if anyone was the leader, it was Karl Heinz. One of the boys Robert particularly liked was called Paul. He was small for his age and wore a Hitler Youth uniform, which appeared to Robert to be rather scruffy. "The two sat talking quietly together.

"I've never met an English boy before," Paul said. "I wouldn't have known you were English, if Karl Heinz hadn't said so. You're just like one of us."

Robert was pleased to be accepted by his cousin's friends. He said, "I see you're in the Hitler Youth, as well."

"Yes." Paul looked about him furtively, then added in a whisper, "But don't tell anyone. I don't like it very much."

"Why not?" Robert asked quietly, following the other's lowered tone.

"It gets a bit rough sometimes. The Führer thinks all boys should box, but I don't like boxing. And I don't like the courage tests either. I'm not very good at that sort of thing." Paul was pleased to have someone to confide in and went on talking to Robert quite freely. "There are some good things, though. There's no class distinction. When I first joined, some of the grammar school boys wouldn't talk to me because I come from a poor home. But that was soon stopped and they were punished."

"What happened to them?" Robert asked.

"They were sent out into poor homes to do all the chores. For two months they had to spend all their spare time doing this. They were really nice to me afterwards. I think they saw what it's like to be poor."

"If you don't like it, why do you stay in it?"

"Most of my friends are in it and I don't want to be left out. Besides, my family's poor so I don't have to pay a membership subscription, and we all get free food when we attend parades. They've even given me food to take home. And they found me a job too."

"Come on, Robert, let's go. See you tomorrow evening at the meeting, Paul," Karl Heinz called.

"Will I see you again, Robert?" Paul asked his new friend.

"Robert will be at the meeting as well," said Karl Heinz.

The two cousins continued on their way. In one of the streets a small open back lorry crammed with SA men drove by. It drew up some way further on and Robert saw some of the men get off and go into a shop. He thought no more of it and stopped for a few minutes to look in a shop window. When he and Karl Heinz eventually approached the place where the lorry had stopped, Robert saw that a few people had gathered on the pavement, including two members of the Hitler Youth, both of whom were a little older but wore the same rank insignia as Karl Heinz. One SA trooper was standing by an old bearded man who was painting a sign on the shop window.

Robert's curiosity got the better of him. "What's he's painting, Karl Heinz?" he asked.

"The Star of David," Karl Heinz replied. "Come on, let's cross over," he added hastily, trying to get Robert away from the scene.

But Robert was trying to see what was going on. He saw that two other troopers were standing over two youths who were down on their knees scrubbing the pavement. The older youth had started to object to his treatment, but the man standing over him merely beat him across the back with his rubber truncheon until he began scrubbing again. The younger boy of about fifteen was obviously too scared to object and was working hard at his task. From time to time he would receive a severe kick in the buttocks from one of the Hitler Youth boys.

Karl Heinz was acquainted with the two boys in uniform and hoped they hadn't seen him, but before he could get Robert to the other side of the street one of his friends called to him. "Hallo, Karl Heinz, come and join the fun." The youth ran up and took Karl Heinz by the arm and led him to the front of the shop, followed by Robert. Robert couldn't take his eyes from the scene before him. He had never seen the likes of it before. The older youth was still being beaten into submission and was scrubbing furiously, at the same time weeping with anger and humiliation. An SA trooper slammed his rubber truncheon across the youth's buttocks the moment he slowed in his work, bringing another howl of pain. The same was now happening to the younger boy. The old man, who had finished his painting was being forced to watch.

"Come on, Karl Heinz, kick a dirty Jewish arse." Karl Heinz was pushed forward. Robert saw him put his foot on the younger boy's backside and give a sharp push so that the victim went forward flat on his face.

"You can do better than that," said one of the troopers.

As the boy, who was now crying bitterly, tried to kneel up Karl Heinz kicked him down again.

"That's a better one, Karl Heinz," said his friend.

Eventually, the storm troopers tired of their work, and, getting back on the lorry, drove away. The few people who had been watching also melted away. Karl Heinz's two friends remained and continued to taunt the two Jewish boys. The younger of the two victims was still down on his hands and knees with his head bowed and almost touching the pavement. He was convulsed with sobs as the other weeping youth, who appeared to be his brother, and the old man tried to lift him on to his feet.

"Shouldn't we do something to help?" Robert asked.

Karl Heinz took his cousin by the arm and pulled him. "Just come away!" he exclaimed.

The two boys walked away, neither making any effort to speak, Karl Heinz wishing that Robert had not seen the incident. Somehow, in spite of all that he had been taught in the past few months about Jews, he felt distinctly uneasy in his conscience for what he had just done. And yet, when he had kicked the boy, he had felt a strange sense of elation. In any case, he thought, it would have been difficult to refuse, for he had no wish to be thought of as anything but a loyal German boy, and he certainly had no intention of being called a Jew lover by his friends. On the other hand, he knew that Hitler Youths should not became involved with the SA on their operations against Jews, for although the Hitler Youth had at one time been under the SA, it was now a separate organisation, and its leader, Baldur von Schirach, did not approve of this sort of behaviour by his youths.

Karl Heinz took Robert into a coffee house and ordered two ice coffees with plenty of cream on the top, and there they sat for some time contentedly sipping their drinks. Karl Heinz was the first to break the silence, "Robert, please don't tell Mother that I kicked that boy. She wouldn't understand."

"Why should I? I'm not a sneak," Robert replied. He thought his cousin looked a little sheepish. "Why was that soldier with a gun watching?" he asked.

"He was a policeman, not a soldier."

"Then why didn't he stop it? Surely it's against the law to beat people like that?"

"The police don't interfere with the SA, and they can't arrest a Hitler Youth in uniform."

"Did you like kicking that boy?"

Karl Heinz dropped his eyes as if he was studying his coffee. "I'm not sure," he murmured.

"Why did you do it?"

"I had to. They were dirty Jewish swine," Karl Heinz replied, still not able to look Robert in the eyes. "Besides, the Fuhrer says we must put the common interest before self," he added, quoting words he had been made to learn by heart from *Mein Kampf.*

"I just don't understand why you hate Jews so much. Some of my friends at school are Jews, and they're decent enough."

"You haven't seen pictures of what they do to German women. The Führer says they are not Germans, and they've corrupted our nation with their poison," Karl Heinz replied with a little more confidence.

"What poison?" Robert asked, looking puzzled.

"The wicked things they put in their newspapers, and books."

"What wicked things?"

"Oh, I don't know, Robert. I don't read newspapers. In any case, they're racially inferior."

"And what does that mean?"

Karl Heinz hesitated. He had been taught so many things in the last few months, but now he was called upon to explain what he had accepted without question, he was finding difficulty. "It means they're not of a pure race like we are.

"Why is our race pure and theirs is not?" Robert persisted.

"How should I know?" Karl Heinz retorted, wishing Robert would shut up about the subject. "For heaven's sake, let's change the subject," he added impatiently. "How's Lisa?"

Robert gave a detailed description of his few days stay in Rotterdam. Heedless to say the part that most interested Karl Heinz was the bedroom incident on the first night. "The cheeky cat!" he sniggered. "I wish it had been me. I'd have soon dealt with her."

"I'd like to have seen you," Robert laughed as they both left the café.

As each day passed it seemed to Robert more enjoyable than the last. Although he was introduced to an endless number of people as Karl Heinz's cousin, he was treated as if he was a twin brother, much to the delight of both boys. Many of the things they did each day were not particularly exciting or especially memorable, but it was enough just to be in each other's company.

The local branch of the Hitler Youth to which Karl Heinz belonged met each Friday evening in a hall, which was loaned free of charge by a local businessman, who supported the Party. There were about fifty boys in the *Schar* (troop) under a *Scharführer*, a boy of sixteen. The *Schar* was made up of three *Kameradschaften*, with about fifteen boys in each under a *Kameradschaftsführer*, of which Karl Heinz was one.

On the evening that Robert was first taken to a meeting he felt apprehensive as to how he would be received. But he need not have worried, for, once again, with Karl Heinz present, he was soon accepted by the other boys. He was assigned to Karl Heinz's *Kameradschaft*.

After the fees had been collected the boys formed up in lines, because their *Bannführer* was due to inspect them that evening. On arrival the young man walked down the lines, and when he got to Robert, Karl Heinz introduced his cousin. Robert was standing to attention the way he had been taught in the OTC with his hands tightly closed and the thumb towards the front.

Bannfuhrer Grund was a tall, fair haired, athletic-looking man. He extended his hand and said, "We have all been looking forward to meeting you. You are most welcome here."

Robert shook hands smartly, remembering to click his heels, and then stood to attention again.

The *Bannführer* looked Robert up and down and nodded his approval. "Very smart," he said, "But you must stand to attention in the German way. We always have our hands open with fingers straight and the palms flat against our thighs," he explained. Robert immediately opened his hands in the German fashion. "Also, when we march, we keep our hands open, and bending the elbows we swing the arms up and across in front of us. I believe you English march swinging your arms straight ahead from the shoulder."

"Yes, sir," Robert replied."

Before the evening's activities commenced, Robert, much to his embarrassment, which he tried to conceal, was taken up on to a platform at one end of the hall by the *Bannführer,* who then began to speak.

He said, "For the next few weeks we have the honour to have with us Robert Rutherford from England. There is no class division in the Hitler Youth, but he is the son of an English general, who holds the highest award his country can bestow for bravery, and for that we honour both father and son. I would remind you that our beloved Führer greatly admires the English, and it is therefore our duty to make our guest welcome. Heil Hitler!"

"Heil Hitler!" the assembled youths roared back.

There was something new and exciting in the atmosphere which seemed to bridge all class barriers; rich and poor, aristocrat and worker mixed together as comrades. For whatever reason a boy initially joined the movement, once having done so, even if he did not like some of the activities, it would be difficult not to be infected with the enthusiasm and sense of fellowship which pervaded the movement.

Robert had caught the feeling and was immensely happy to have been welcomed into this dynamic movement. He was soon engaged in the activities which had been arranged, for the evening. Firstly, they had to learn off by heart the words of a marching song. This was considered important because when they went on their marches through the city they were expected to sing to show that young national socialists were happy to march for their Führer.

A political text from Mein Kampf was supposed to be discussed, but as no one had any useful comments to make this proved to be boring and quickly ended. An adventure story about a German hero of the past was then read out by one of the older boys. This was far more interesting and captured the imagination of the boys. However, there was little time for reading and thought, because the restlessness of youth demanded action, and it was marching and sporting competitions and other such activities that filled most of the time.

The evening finished up with a field game in a nearby park which Robert found much to his liking.

Boys were expected to give all of Saturday to Hitler Youth activities, and sometimes Sunday as well. So the following day the two cousins returned to the meeting hall. For the first twenty minutes an SA officer lectured on *Lebensraum* (Living Space). From what Robert could make out it seemed that it was Herr Hitler's idea that Germany had the right to expand eastwards into the Slavic lands of Poland and Russia. Evidently the Slavs were only second class people so it didn't matter whether they liked it or not. It was a bit rough on the Slavs, he thought, but he didn't think he ought to say so because it was a lecture, not a discussion, and in any case no one questioned anything Herr Hitler said. But he had to admit that what was said interested him, especially when the subject changed to the Treaty of Versailles. It was strange to hear a different view from what he had heard at home at the dinner table when important guests would discuss things with Father. He must tell Father about it when he got home.

After the lecture all the boys had to strap packs on their backs and march out into the country. They sang their way through the city, feeling important and proud of themselves as people looked on in admiration at their happy faces. Robert had learnt the words of the Hitler Youth Anthem - *Das Fahnenlied*, written by the young Youth Leader of Germany, von Schirach - so was able to join in the singing:

"Wlr marschieren für Hitler
Durch Nacht und durch

Mit der Fahne für Freiheit und Brot. . .
Unsere Fahne ist mehr für uns alsder Tod."
(We march for Hitler through night and suffering
With the banner of freedom and bread. . .
Our banner means more to us than death.) ^(see P625)

Once out into the country they marched for miles along hot, dusty roads before being allowed to rest. The heat was sweltering and Robert was thankful that he was not wearing his OTC uniform with its thick khaki serge and puttees. At least he was wearing only shoes and socks turned down to the ankles, shorts and shirt. But the pack was weighing heavily on his shoulders. They had to keep in step and swing their arms, and from time to time the *Scharführer* would make them sing. Some of the boys were finding it difficult to keep going in the heat, but nobody fell, out for fear of being classed as a weakling. In any case the *Scharführer,* an older boy of sixteen, was a real martinet who exercised iron control over his charges. Eventually, after some miles, they crossed some fields and arrived on the bank of a small river where they were halted. Although they were all exhausted and yearning to throw themselves into the cool water, they were made to stand at attention for ten minutes, facing the river, while they were lectured on endurance.

"There is no room for weakness in the new Germany. The strong will survive," the *Scharführer* barked. "The Führer wants you to be as hard as flint. We are not playing games. . ." The rest of his words were lost on Robert, who could think only of the sparkling water gently flowing in front of him. He was pouring sweat and his whole body was aching with fatigue. Oh, God? How much longer is he going on, he asked himself? But when the talk finished the *Scharführer* instead of letting them rest, gave the order to march on. There was no whisper of dissent at the continuance of the march, for this again would have shown weakness.

After another mile the order came to halt. The boys were allowed to remove their packs, and these had to be placed on the ground in neat rows. Every boy, whether they could swim or not; was then ordered, to strip naked and jump in the river. Those who could not swim were the responsibility of those who could. A boy was expected to help his less skilful comrade for the common good.

The indescribable relief that Robert felt as the water caressed his naked body filled him with joy and gave him the feeling that the hard march he had endured had all been worthwhile. His new friend, Paul, who could not swim, was floundering about near the bank. Like everyone else the boy was relieved to be in the water, but he was fearful of letting go the bank.

"Try swimming to me, Paul," Robert called from a few yards away.

"I can't."

But Robert was not to be put off, and, with Karl Heinz on one side and himself on the other, they managed to encourage their friend to make his first uncertain strokes.

The swim over, they all lay on the bank eating the food they had brought, and drying themselves in the sun. "I bet Lisa would love to be here," laughed Karl Heinz.

"Thank goodness she's not. I've had enough of her seeing me like this," Robert replied.

"Everyone get dressed!" came the order, and when this was done and the packs were strapped on their backs once more, the long march home began.

Under the blazing afternoon sun it wasn't long before Robert felt as if that glorious swim had been but a dream. One of the boys was overcome by the heat and his pack was taken off and carried by another. In order to continue the march the casualty had to be supported by two others. Then Paul collapsed, and the same had to be done for him. Robert took his pack and, with Karl Heinz, supported him for the rest of the way back.

It was two weary boys who returned home that evening. They struggled up the stairs to the drawing-room and stood supporting each other in the doorway.

"Good heavens! What have we got here?" Natascha exclaimed, looking at the two suntanned figures before her, their shirts and shorts saturated with sweat.

That evening after the sheer luxury of a bath, a change of clothes and a good meal, the two boys were content to lounge in the drawing-room with Karl and Natascha relating the events of the day. It had been a hard and exhausting day, but they felt fitter and stronger than ever, and they had endured to the end without complaint, and even taken on an extra burden by assisting their friend.

There was no wrestling in the bedroom that night. They hardly had time to strip themselves and climb into bed before they were asleep.

The days that followed passed quickly, and before they knew where they were the week-end had come round again. This time their *Schar* met at the SA barracks for a Saturday parade. Robert had obviously proved himself acceptable in the troop, for he was called before the *Bannführer* and invited to accompany them to the Party Rally at Nuremberg at the beginning of September. "That's wonderful!" Karl Heinz exclaimed when he heard the news. "And just think, you'll see the Führer."

"I'll have to write home and ask if I can stay on a little longer," Robert said. "That is if Uncle Karl will allow me to."

"Of course he will," Karl Heinz replied confidently.

The day was filled with unending activity, all of which was geared to continuous competitive struggle. Although individual success was commended, it was made clear that this should never be at the expense of the group. Training commenced with drill on the barrack square, followed by athletics and boxing. Then there was close combat-fighting, which Robert found quite rough, but being tall for his age and strong managed to cope. He could understand why Paul didn't like it. Another thing he learnt, which he had not understood when Paul had mentioned it, was what was meant by a courage test.

During the afternoon each boy was made to run along the top of a six foot high brick wall, and then jump off the end, landing properly so as not to injure himself. An athletic looking SA officer, who was evidently a gymnastic teacher, stood nearby shouting instructions on the correct way to land, and the boys were made to carry out this exercise time after time until they got it right. After this they were marched away and lined up in front of one of the barrack blocks. Robert, saw that a rope extended to the ground from an open first floor window, and wondered what was to happen next. He was soon to find out.

"Each one of you will climb the rope to the window," ordered an instructor. "You will then jump to the ground, landing properly as you have been taught."

Robert gulped. Bloody hell! He said to himself. Admittedly there was soft earth to land on, but it's a bloody long way down, he thought. He was supposed to be on holiday enjoying himself, and yet here he was racking his poor body with long marches in the heat, exhausting himself in athletics, and doing all sorts of things which he never dreamed he could do. And now this. He must be mad. He glanced out of the corner of his eye at Karl Heinz and wondered whether he was feeling nervous as well. But then Karl Heinz seemed to revel in this sort of thing and had probably done it before.

The instructor spoke again. "This is not only a test of your physical toughness, but of your courage. But no one has to make the jump. It's up to you."

And a fat lot of comfort that is, Robert groaned. At that moment he would have given anything to have been one of the boys who, for one reason or another, decided not to jump. But how could he get out of it without showing himself to be the coward he was? Being the English boy, everyone would be watching to see if he would do it. And being the son of a general, which on occasions had advantages, meant that others often expected so much more from him. There's no way out, Rutherford, you'll just have to do it, and if you break your bloody neck it's your own bloody fault for getting yourself into this, he moaned to himself.

Robert was fifth in line to climb and jump, with Karl Heinz immediately in front of him. The first two boys were successful in their jumps, although one was shouted at for not landing correctly. The third boy made the climb but found he could not bring himself to jump, so climbed, down again. Karl Heinz climbed eagerly and jumped confidently, making a good landing which brought a word of praise from the instructor. Just as Robert, was about to make his climb, the Bannführer came up and stood watching with another officer.

Just my luck, Robert thought. He probably wants to see the English boy make a fool of himself. He was quite used to climbing ropes, for it was the way he got into his tree house, which his father had made for him in the garden at home. But this was a little different because he would be scaling the side of a building; which meant he had to walk up the wall leaning well back. This was something else he had just been taught. Up he went not daring to stop or look down. If he hesitated he knew he would have to climb down again like the other boy. So directly he had made the climb he turned and jumped. As he struck the soft earth a feeling of elation came over him. He had done it, and had been successful. He picked himself up and noticed the Bannführer nod his approval. He felt so pleased with himself that he wished he could do it all over again.

As with most boys of his age, Robert had little knowledge of politics and certainly gave no thought to the deeper reasons for the training that thousands of German boys were receiving in the Hitler Youth. All he knew was that the harder the task he was set, the more satisfaction he got when he had successfully completed it. And this in turn gave him confidence and a sense of achievement. Other boys to whom he spoke confessed that they too felt much the same. They all found themselves striving towards same obscure nationalistic ideal, which encouraged a strong feeling of fellowship towards one another.

Because of the many physical activities in the Hitler Youth there was little time for any systematic ideological indoctrination, but the sheer dynamic idealism of the movement which inspired unquestioning loyalty, obedience and unselfish sacrifice, combined with a deep love of their country ensured that these young minds developed in the way their Führer desired. The same sense of dedication that Karl Heinz had for this Führer of his began to affect Robert. The fitter and stronger he became, the happier he became. He was bursting with life, and, as with the other boys in the movement, his healthy young mind was eager to receive whatever new ideas might be sown by those that led them. With Robert, being only temporarily in this environment, what was sown was not given a chance to germinate.

But for Karl Heinz and the German boys of his generation it was a different story.

The community spirit and service to the state was encouraged in the Hitler Youth, and boys were expected to give some of their spare time to community service. All were expected to take part in the street collections for the Winter Relief Fund, and many chose to help old people. Most were encouraged to spend some of their time working on the land, assisting to bring in the harvest. It was this last activity that Karl Heinz and Robert decided upon to fulfil their duty, and they spent four days working hard in the fields loading hay carts for a farmer.

One week-end the boys attended a Hitler Youth camp. This had been set up to accommodate about three hundred boys and was situated some five miles out of the city. During the day, activities in the nature of military manoeuvres took place, but it was the warm evenings that Robert enjoyed most of all, when they all sat round the camp fires with their arms about one another, singing the folk tunes of old Germany. Together they swayed to the music bound by the joyful spirit of youth and comradeship. But in the days to come it was the end of the day he remembered best, when the camp fires were dying, and three hundred young voices broke out into the moving tune *Gute Nacht Kameraden*.

Robert obtained permission from his parents to stay the extra days in order to attend the Party Rally in Nuremberg.

There was great excitement on the morning the boys were to leave, and after a good breakfast they set out with their rucksacks on their backs for the main railway station. This was near the Cathedral and only a short walk from the house, and it was here that the local branch was to assemble.

Robert found the journey good fun, with plenty of singing, and harmless larking about. But there was no lack of discipline, nor was the comfort of other passengers interfered with, for this would have brought discredit on the movement. When Hitler had first come to power there had been certain acts by members of the Hitler Youth which had caused concern to the authorities, and these had to be stopped. Some youths, thinking they no longer had to obey their teachers, had disrupted their schools. But this attitude was soon suppressed and the Hitler Youth was admonished to respect the authority of school and parents. It was also made clear that a healthy family life for the German people was the policy of the new national Socialist government.

The train was crowded with Hitler Youths and others travelling to the *Parteitag*, and on arrival in Nuremberg it appeared to Robert that the town was overflowing with people, many of whom were sleeping in tents in the surrounding area. Robert's *Schar* had their tents placed near the ground where the Hitler Youth was to assemble to be inspected by the Führer, so they would not have far to march. The Hitler Youth were involved in some of the events, the climax being when thousands of them would stage an exhibition of formation exercises in the vast Zeppelinwiese stadium. Robert would remain a spectator to this as he had not been trained to carry out the complex movements.

The *Parteitag* covered four days and consisted of SA rallies, speeches, meetings, parades and inspect ions. In later years the *Parteitag* became established as a staged political show with new buildings and a permanent arena to contain the thousands involved, with foreign diplomats invited to attend. But this stage had not yet been reached in the first year of the new Germany.

The weather was fine and warm - Führer weather as it was called - and Robert found it, pleasant sleeping under canvas. He was awake early on the first day, and having got up and washed, sat on the grass outside the tent eating his breakfast with Karl Heinz and some of the other boys of his *Schar.* Their part in the rally was not until the following day, so once they had done their camp duties and attended the morning parade the rest of the day was their own, or so Robert thought. But after the parade the Scharführer rushed into the tent and ordered him and Karl Heinz and the others with whom they shared the tent to put on their best uniforms. When this was done the six of them had to clamber on to a small open back lorry. "I wonder where we're going?" Karl Heinz remarked as the lorry began to move. But they soon, realised that they were being taken into the centre of the town. Robert noticed that many of the buildings were decked with flags, most being the now familiar party banners which hung down from the upper floors. But there were also other flags to add to the colourful scene, and Karl Heinz pointed out the old Imperial flag, now not often seen. The sound of bands indicated that a parade was taking place, but the lorry avoided the streets where this was happening and arrived in a large square. Large stands, on which there were row upon row of seats, had been erected on three sides of the square and these were already packed with people, many of whom were wearing the brown uniform of the SA.

The lorry stopped on the road which ran along the end of the square where there was no stand, and the boys were ordered off. Then the Scharführer said, "In a short time the Führer will arrive here and you are to act as a guard of honour. When you are put in your position you will not move from there until ordered."

The Führer's car was to stop at an exact point. The boys were placed three on each side of this point, facing inwards, with enough space for the Führer and his entourage to walk between them into the square.

The centre of the square began to fill with SA troopers carrying the large banners of the district in which they served. Half an hour past before the square was packed to capacity and was a mass of Party flags. Then there was more waiting and Robert felt his legs aching. If only he could sit down just for a minute, he thought.

A car drove into the square and for a moment Robert thought it was the Führer arriving, but it wasn't. It stopped near the boys just long enough for a number of black uniformed men to get out. "Who are they?" Robert whispered out of the corner of his mouth without turning his head.

The boy next to him whispered back, "SS."

People had begun to gather on tune pavement behind the boys in order to greet their Führer. Robert could feel them lightly pressing in on him, but they made no attempt to move in front and block the entrance.

It was Hitler's policy to arrive late for these events in order to let the tension build up. And that is exactly what was happening, for Robert could feel the atmosphere of anticipation and excitement.

After two more false alarms wild cheering was heard coming from the streets some blocks away, and then a convoy of large, gleaming, black Mercedes-Benz open tourer cars, glided into the square. The front car, which carried the personal standard of Adolph Hitler on the front mudguard, stopped exactly between the two lines of boys. The crowds in the vicinity went wild with delight. As was usual for him when saluting the crowds lining the streets, the great man was standing in the front of the car next to the driver. Robert, who was nearest to the car on his side of the two lines of boys, saw an SS man rush to open the door, and Adolph Hitler stepped out. For a moment the man who held Germany in the palm of his hand hesitated as if he was lost and was waiting for someone to show him what to do. Robert thought he looked bewildered with all the clamour going on about him, and for some reason, which he couldn't explain, he felt sorry for him. He had imagined that the Führer would be a real show off and terribly conceited, but he wasn't. And he doesn't look at all fierce, he thought. In fact, he looks, well, just ordinary.

If Robert had stretched out his hand he could have touched him. He noticed the small dark moustache and the hair falling forward over the left side of the forehead. The Führer wore no coat and no hat, but was dressed in similar fashion to an SA trooper, in jack boots, brown breeches, brown shirt and tie. There was the Nazi Party armband on his left arm, but he wore no badges of rank. Of all the men who accompanied him he was dressed in the simplest fashion. However, what he prized most highly, he wore on his shirt just below the left pocket lapel; the Iron Cross 1st. class, which he had won for bravery while serving in the Imperial Army in the Great War. (Even his enemies and detractors could not deny the authenticity of this.) Below the Iron Cross he wore the Wound Badge.

The other cars had drawn up behind Hitler's car, and a number of high ranking party officials began to collect about their leader. Then a group of what were obviously high ranking SA officers came from the other direction to greet their Führer. The leader of this group was a stocky man with a large round face and double chin. Set above his tight lips was a triangular moustache, but it was the deep scar across his left cheek that caught Robert's eye. Of all the officials he appeared to be on very familiar terms with his Führer, but even this was not to save Ernst Rohm's life the following year.

Once the greetings had been made, Hitler began to lead them forward towards the centre of the square. The crowds were shouting their adulation and the noise was deafening. Robert was standing rigidly to attention, waiting to relax when the Führer had moved away. Surprisingly, the Führer didn't move away, but to Robert's consternation the Reich Chancellor of Germany stood in front of him. Robert felt himself tremble but tried to stop it showing by tensing himself. He knew little about this man, but what he did know was that Adolph Hitler was all powerful in Germany even if he did look ordinary. Perhaps he was to be arrested and shot as a spy, or put in one of those beastly concentration camps he'd heard about. He would never see his home again. Should he fall on his knees and beg for mercy? Oh God! He was being spoken to!

"Young man, you are not wearing the Party armband." The voice was quiet and not unpleasant.

"I..I beg your pardon, Herr Reich Chancellor," Robert stammered. "I'm only a visitor here. I'm English and,..." Robert was cut short.

"English! An English boy in my youth organisation?" The great man grasped Robert's right hand and held it affectionately between both of his own hands. "What is your name?"

"Robert Rutherford, Herr Reich Chancellor." Robert could feel himself trembling.

"Are you afraid, Robert?" The face before him had softened into a smile,

"Yes, Herr Reich Chancellor."

Robert's honesty brought a laugh from his questioner, and a number of the important men present joined their Führer in his amusement. "I like your honesty. But there's no need to be afraid. You are amongst friends. I admire the English."

At that moment Robert felt he would do anything for this man. He isn't a bit stuck up, he decided. Yet there was something about him which held Robert under a spell. Perhaps it was the Chancellor's eyes that fascinated him, or his charming manner. But of one thing he was sure, and that was, out of all the thousands present at that moment, this man's attention was concentrated only on him, Robert Rutherford, and on no one else. Robert sensed that this was no act, nor was he playing to the crowd - he had no need to - but a genuine concern for a nervous young visitor to his country.

Adolph Hitler unpinned a small badge, in the shape of the German eagle over a swastika, from his own tie and fastened it on Robert's black scarf. "Now you are a member of my Hitler Youth. It is against the rules as you are not a German boy, but I make an exception in your case," he said. He patted Robert gently on the cheek and was gone, disappearing among his officials, all of whom turned and quickly followed.

Robert felt as if he was walking on air, such was the effect this man had had on him. His legs had been aching but he would stand for hours if need be just to see the great man again. He was now surrounded by people all of whom wanted to shake his hand and congratulate him for having been so honoured by the Führer. A young woman came up and touched the badge he had been given. Eventually the Scharführer came and took his six boys away for a rest, because it would be some time before the Führer left the square.

The boys were taken to some spare seats in the stands where they got a good view of the Führer inspecting the SA standards before mounting the rostrum to make a speech. Robert could not remember much of what the speech was about, the Führer seemed to be praising the army which struck Robert as strange as it was an SA gathering. It went on for some time and then, directly it was over, the boys had to take up their positions again near the waiting car.

As the Führer returned to his car the spontaneous enthusiasm of the crowd was greater than ever. He walked with his right arm bent at the elbow and hand raised in salute, stopping to shake the hands of a few people. And then he was in his car and away.

The boys were allowed to remain in the town for the rest of the day.

Back at the camp that evening Robert was again the centre of attention; with everyone wishing to congratulate him and examine the badge he had been given.

The next morning when the group formed up on parade ready to march off to the assembly ground for the Hitler Youth rally, a black car drew up and an SS Hauptsturmführer got out holding a very large brown envelope in his hand. Robert saw the black uniformed officer go and speak to the Bannführer, who was standing in front of the assembled group, and then he heard his name called. For a moment he didn't know what to do and just stood still. Then Karl Heinz nudged him and whispered, "He's calling you out. Go on."

Robert marched smartly out and stood to attention in front of the two officers. It was the SS officer who spoke. "Are you the English, boy, Robert Rutherford?"

"Yes sir."

"The Führer has commanded me to present you with this," said the man, handing Robert the envelope.

Once again Robert didn't know what to do.

The Bannführer was speechless, being completely overawed by the fact that the Führer himself had seen fit to honour the English boy.

"You are to open it immediately," said the SS officer.

Robert could feel there was something solid inside. It was obviously not just paper. He began to fumble in an effort to tear it open without damaging the envelope, because it bore the official German emblem and he thought it would be nice to keep.

"Here, use this," said the officer, handing Robert his dagger.

Robert carefully slit it open and handed back the knife. He put in his hand and drew out a Hitler Youth dagger with the words *Blood and Honour* inscribed on it. He held, it lovingly in his hand not knowing what to say. At last he said, "Is this really mine?"

"Read what it says on the blade," smiled the SS officer.

Robert drew the dagger out of its sheath and read out the inscription on the blade. "To my young English friend, Adolph Hitler."

"What an honour!" exclaimed the Bannführer, taking the dagger to read the inscription himself.

Robert then drew out from the envelope a brand new Hitler Youth armband. The SS officer took it from him and carefully put it on Robert's left arm, and then clipped the dagger on to his belt. When he was able to take his eyes from his new dagger and armband, Robert drew out the other contents of the envelope. There was a signed photograph of Adolph Hitler; a photograph of Hitler holding Robert's hand on the previous day which he had not realised at the time was being taken, and a short note on official paper reading:

Robert Rutherford - I hope you will have happy memories of Germany,

Adolph Hitler.Sept. 1933.

Emotions within him had been stirred which bewildered his young mind. A feeling of joy lifted him to such a height he could quite easily have given his life for this man under whose spell he had fallen. He understood now the wild adoration of the crowd he had witnessed the day before. He stood gripping the envelope not knowing what to do.

"Heil Hitler!" The SS officer flung out his arm in the Nazis salute.

Robert instantly sprung to attention and reacted in the same fashion as if to give the salute was perfectly natural to him. "Heil Hitler!" he replied, and then returned to his place in the ranks.

During the rally that followed, Robert saw the Führer only in the distance as he spoke from a rostrum to the assembled boys. But it didn't matter, for he had actually met him and held his hand, and that experience could not be taken from him, and he had his dagger and the other things to remind him of that fleeting moment in his life. But in spite of this, even though he looked the same, spoke the same and wore the same uniform, he felt set apart from the thousands of youths standing in their ranks about him, because nothing could change the fact that he was English.

For the two days that remained of the *Parteitag* Robert felt he was often the centre of attention within his group. He was the boy to whom the Führer had spoken.

When Robert and Karl Heinz arrived home in Cologne it was Karl Heinz who rushed up the stairs with the news of Robert's honour. Robert followed him into the drawing room and quietly kissed his aunty and shook his uncle's hand, and then sat listening to his cousin relating the story.

"Calm down, Karl Heinz," Natascha laughed. "You have been talking non-stop for five minutes, and you haven't even greeted me or your father with a kiss."

"I'm sorry, Mother, but it's so exciting. The Führer passed so close to me I could have touched him. I'm sure he smiled at me." Karl Heinz stopped talking and kissed his parents, but then immediately continued, "But he actually held Robert's hands, and just look at what he gave him."

"I feel awful that it was me and not you he spoke to," said Robert. "After all he is your Führer, and I'm only a visitor."

"You mustn't feel like that, Robert. I'm so proud of you. And you're no longer just a visitor, but a real member of the Hitler Youth. The Führer said so. Karl Heinz didn't know how to contain his excitement.

But whatever Robert was, his time had almost run out, and his holiday was coming to an end. Three days later he stood, on Cologne station with the little family he had come to love so much, trying to suppress the sadness of parting.

"We shall miss you so very much, Robert," said Natascha as she kissed him goodbye.

"Yes, we will," said Karl.

To Robert's surprise Karl hugged him as well as shaking his hand. He had come to realise that there was another side to his uncle, and that he was not just the man with the strap.

The two boys held each other in a long embrace. It might have been a childish act when they had cut their arms and mixed their blood, but it was real enough to them that the same blood ran in their veins. In their minds they were brothers and nothing could alter that.

It was always the same when they parted, the feeling of being torn in half, and the days of heart-ache when getting used to the idea that the other was no longer there. As the waving figure leaning out of the carriage window disappeared from sight, Karl put his arm round his son's shoulders and led him home.

CHAPTER 9

Nothing stays the same for long, John thought. He was staring out of the window watching trees and hedgerows flash past as the Southern Belle swiftly made its way through the Sussex countryside on that bright September evening. It occurred to him that life was like the passing scenery, for nothing could prevent it from rushing by. In four months he would be fifty six. Not a great age, of course, but he could no longer consider himself a young man. And the children were growing up so fast. It was difficult to believe that Joanna was well over eighteen, and it only seemed yesterday that he was holding her in his arms for the first time. She must have been about five months, and he had come home on his first leave of the war. What was that song he had softly sung in her little ear? He hummed the tune quietly to himself and then remembered the words.

And when I tell them, and I'm certainly going to tell them
That you're the girl whose boy one day I'll be
They'll never believe me, they'll never believe me
That from this great big world you've chosen me. (see P625)

From the very first he had swamped her with love. He was sure it hadn't spoilt her. Just think, she had already completed a year at Oxford. She was a clever girl. To study Law was no doubt most commendable, but what would she do with it? Perhaps she could be a solicitor's clerk, and yet she talks of being a barrister. Well, she's certainly got the gift of the gab, and women were into everything nowadays. Women judges one day, he supposed. Who was that young man he met years ago who was going to study law, he tried to think? But the thought slipped away.

The rhythmic sound of the wheels on the lines changed to a roar as the train pounded through Hassocks station. It went through so fast he couldn't even read the station name. Now the South Downs were looming up high in front of him - always a welcome sight, indicating he would soon be home. He had been away for the week and was looking forward to a relaxing weekend.

As the carriage lights came on for Clayton tunnel, John smiled to himself as he remembered Robert's letter from Germany, which had arrived two weeks ago asking permission to stay on for a few extra days. He had wired back to say it was all right. It was a nice letter and gave a good description of his journey, and his activities in Cologne. And what was it the boy had said? Something about train drivers spending forty eight days of their lives in a tunnel. He could be an amusing boy, intelligent too, and he should do very well if only he would put his mind to his work. A dreamer, that's what he is. But what was he going to do with his life? He can't live on dreams, and surely he wouldn't wish to take up music. He'll have to go into the army, it was the only answer. Besides, he'll probably make a damn good soldier. Why the hell do they have to grow up so quickly? He would miss the boy when he left home. He'd already missed him over the past few weeks, so how he'll feel when the lad had gone for good didn't bear thinking about.

John saw the familiar Brighton sign on the side of the signal box as the train moved slowly into the station. On leaving the carriage he walked quickly along the busy platform, happy with the thought that Robert would be home tomorrow.

The following morning John, anticipating Robert's arrival, was unable to settle to anything. "John dear, do come and walk in the garden with me. You'll wear that carpet out prowling up and down," Elizabeth smiled. She took him by the hand and led him out through the French doors on to the lawn.

"But what if Robert telephones?"

"It's too early yet. He will ring when he gets to Victoria, and he won't be there until lunch time," Elizabeth replied. "You really are an old fuss pot, John. I'm sure you're the calmest man in England, except when it comes to your children. And then you fuss about like an old hen."

He grinned at her perception and then, on impulse, he stopped and enclosed her in his great arms. "And you, my darling, are the most wonderful woman in the whole wide world." He put his finger under her chin gently tilting her head back, and, leaning down, gently kissed her. He noticed the attractive flush on her cheeks which had been there when he had first kissed her sitting in the carriage on the *Maasdijk* all those years ago.

"John, the servants!"

"Can a man not kiss his wife?" he smiled, kissing her again.

"How happy we've been together," she said.

"And always will be," he replied. "With you I almost feel young again. You who gave me back my youth." He took her hand and they walked on. "I've never forgotten the moment I first set eyes on you. You were sitting at the piano and the sun was lighting your hair, and from that moment my life was never the same again."

She smiled up at him and squeezed his hand, rendering words unnecessary.

At the sound of the gong they returned to the house for luncheon.

"Maitland, will you kindly put the telephone beside me," John instructed as he sat down at the table.

"Certainly, sir," the butler replied. "Might I ask, sir, if we expect Master Robert to call very soon?"

"Any moment I hope, Maitland."

The dining room door was flung open and Joanna burst in. "Hallo all! Any news of that brother of mine yet?"

"Joanna, when are you going to enter a room like a young lady and not blow in like a whirlwind?" Elizabeth asked.

"Sorry, Mummy, but everything is such a dash. I hope Robert isn't too long, because I simply must get to the tennis club this afternoon. There's this gorgeous boy down there."

"Not another one?" said John. "What's this one's name?"

"I've no idea, Daddy, but he's very dashing."

"By the way, young lady, I have told His Majesty that you will be coming out next, year. He asked the other day when this was to be."

"Oh, Daddy, that's wonderful! Let's have a ball here."

At that moment the telephone rang. John snatched the earpiece from the hook. "Hallo! Hallo! Is that you, Robert?"

Joanna rushed to her father's side and put her ear as close to the receiver as she could. "It is, Mummy. He's at Victoria."

"All right, son, we'll be there. Goodbye. Goodbye now." John replaced the earpiece. "Well, we've got time for a good lunch before we go to the station."

"Platform four," said John, taking up a position a few yards outside the ticket barrier where he could get a good view of the train coming in.

"Here it comes!" said Joanna a short time later as the London train nosed its way into the station. "It seems years since we've seen him. I wonder whether he's changed much?"

"I should hardly think so, dear. He's only been away five weeks," Elizabeth replied.

The train squeaked to a stop, doors were flung open and a mass of passengers alighted and hurried towards the barrier.

"There he is!" cried Joanna, waving frantically. "Doesn't he look gorgeous? I'm sure he's taller than ever. I can hardly believe it's my baby brother."

John looked with pride at the boy coming down the crowded platform. That's *my* son, he felt like shouting.

Elizabeth sensed a new confidence in her boy.

As Robert stepped down on to the platform it was his father he spotted first, standing head and shoulders above all. This massive, quiet man, whom he loved so much. This wonderful father who filled him with awe, and yet in whose presence he felt completely secure. And there was Mother with Father's arm round her. They always stood close to each other, he thought. He could never imagine them apart. To him they were one person. He could see Joanna waving, and lifted his hand to let them know he had seen them.

Once through the ticket barrier he ran forward, quickly put down his case, and, in his excitement, tried to embrace them all at the same time.

"You look absolutely marvellous," said Joanna, throwing her arms round him and kissing him. "I'm sure you've grown taller and more handsome than ever."

Robert was quite taken aback by the affection of his sister's greeting.

"Come along, Joanna, let me kiss my son," Elizabeth smiled. She took him in her arms and kissed him. He would never be as big or have the exceptional strength of his father, but she knew that one day he would develop into a tall, strong man. "It's so good to have you home, my darling," she said.

"It's good to be home, Mother." He had been sorry to leave Karl Heinz, and it was sad that the holiday had come to an end, but it suddenly occurred to him how happy he was to be back in familiar surroundings amongst his own family. He also felt a sense of achievement that he done what he had set out to do.

John took Robert by the shoulders, holding him at arms length and casting his eye over his son. "I've never seen you look so fit and brown. Germany must have agreed with you." He pulled Robert close and embraced him.

"It did, Father. It was wonderful." Robert, pointed to the small badge on the lapel of his jacket and said proudly, "And look, Father, this was given to me by Herr Hitler himself."

"Oh, come on, Robert, not one of your stories already," Joanna laughed.

"I swear it!" Robert exclaimed. "He took it off his own tie and gave it to me. And he shook my hand and touched me on the cheek, and what's more I can prove it."

"Come on, let's go home," said John. "You can tell us all about it on the way, Robert."

Robert did exactly that. He didn't stop talking the whole way home, and even when they arrived at the house there was more to tell.

"We'll hear the rest at teatime," said John as his son hurried from the car to fling his arms round Agnes and greet the other servants.

Robert then ran up to his bedroom and flung himself on the bed, and there he lay, with his hands clasped behind his head, content just to be surrounded by his own treasures. His very own room, and his very own bed. His pink donkey was still lying on the spare bed beside him where he had left it on the day he had gone away. He reached over and, picking it up, held it in his arms. It had been given to him when he was a baby by Uncle Reggie. Mother had told him that it had arrived through the post with just a label round its neck, which was typical of Uncle Reggie; he had always been such a joker.

Robert had taken the pink donkey to bed with him at night for as long as he could remember, and still did, unless he had a friend to stay. He knew he was now too old to do such a thing and tried to keep it a secret. Agnes knew, of course. But then she knew almost all his secrets; he even had a nasty suspicion that she knew about the naughty things he did to himself, but she never said anything.

As he lay there hugging the pink donkey, he felt a strange sense of relief, which he couldn't account for. He was once more in his own country, his own town, his own home; and for all the interesting places he had seen and the wonderful people he had been with, it was here he belonged. Gone were the uniforms; the marches; the banners; the rallies; the cheering crowds. Gone were the forceful lectures on the eastern question, the Slavs and the Jews, which had begun to open his mind to new and bewildering thoughts. He remembered the smiling face of Herr Hitler and the excitement of being spoken to by the great man. But now it was all just a memory.

The picture of the two Jewish boys returned to his mind. How the SA troopers had beaten them, and how they had yelled. It was difficult to make sense of it, because it all seemed without reason, except, that they were Jews. He had been beaten himself by Father and others, but there was something different about the way the Jewish boys had got it. There had always been a reason for his own punishments and he had never felt degraded by them, only sore. Perhaps that was the difference; the Jewish boys appeared to have done no wrong and yet they were being degraded in front of other people. On the other hand perhaps they did deserve to be beaten; he remembered thinking so after one of the lectures when it had been explained to him what terrible things the Jews did to good German women. Karl Heinz seemed to think so although even he wasn't too sure.

How he missed Karl Heinz.

Robert got up from the bed and went to the window. He looked across the lawn, now a little parched after the long, hot summer, to the trees beyond which were rustling in the gentle afternoon breeze. And there was the rope hanging down from his tree house. "Poor Karl Heinz," he said to the pink donkey. "He has only houses to look at from his window, and I have all this. Thank God I live here. And thank God I'm an English boy."

He opened his case and took out all the little presents he had brought back for the family and the servants, and for Uncle Reggie and Aunty Daisy.

Later, having distributed the presents, he sat down in the drawing-room with John and Elizabeth and related the rest of his story.

*

This year Robert's birthday fell on a Saturday. He decided, much to his parents' suppressed amusement, that, as he was now almost a man he no longer wished for a boys party. "May I have a proper dinner party like you have with your friends, Mother? Just a family affair with Uncle Reggie and Aunty Daisy, and I could ask Ian and then he could stay the night."

"If that's what you want, dear," Elizabeth had promised.

As Robert's birthday was always on Armistice Day he had to attend school in uniform. It had become a tradition of the school on Armistice Day that the boys would work for the first two periods and then assemble in the hall after break for a Remembrance Service, ending with a two minute silence and a bugler playing The Last Post. After the Service the boys were given the rest of the day off.

"It's a swindle, Ian. I mean being a Saturday we don't gain a thing, it's a half day anyway," said Robert, as he and his friend walked to school that morning.

"You're right. They ought to give us another afternoon off to make up for it."

The boys felt proud walking through the streets in uniform, and today even more so with their red poppies standing out brightly in their button holes. "They were too young to have any deep understanding of the sadness and despair of those who had lost their loved ones in the war, but the atmosphere which surrounded them on Armistice Day did enable them in their own small way to honour the dead in their young hearts.

When the whole school had assembled in the hall that morning the usual silence fell on the boys as the headmaster mounted the platform. He was followed by a few of the school governors including John, as chairman, who was in uniform. He would normally have been at the Cenotaph with the King, but this year he had been released from this duty so that he could attend the school.

"Hymn five eight four, O valiant hearts," the headmaster announced.

John opened his hymn book but made no effort to find the right page, for when they started to sing, the four hundred voices brought a lump to his throat, and he realised he would not be able to join in. Instead he studied the rows of young faces standing before him, and asked himself what madness had come upon mankind that had allowed such as these to be cut down in their thousands only a few short years ago. Every year as the clock crept up to the eleventh hour on this day he remembered that other young face, and the life that had flickered out like a candle as he had held the boy in his arms. The experience had finally exhausted his spirit for a time. And yet at that moment a new candle had been lit, and the flame of life had burnt on in the birth of his own beloved son. It had been as if God was proving to him that, for all the folly of the war years, life was never extinguished, and he was not to despair. The sight of Robert's face amongst the mass of boys below him, so full of life, seemed to endorse this message. In a few minutes the boy would be exactly fifteen years old, but what did the future hold for this bright young life, in fact what did it hold for all these boys?

At breakfast that morning he had told Robert that at eleven o'clock he would make a sign with his hand to acknowledge the moment of Robert's birth. It was to be a secret sign between the two of them. This had pleased Robert immensely, and as the time approached he kept his eyes fixed on his father, waiting for the sign.

The hymn ended, the prayers said, and the moment came. Robert saw the sign and furtively raised his own hand in acknowledgement. In the crowded hall an invisible bond stretched out between father and son to the exclusion of all others. The OTC bugler, who stood outside in the small covered yard between the hall and the Gymnasium, sounded the Last Post. The two minutes silence was kept. The bugle sounded again and then it was over for another year, except for those like John who had done the fighting, and those whose loved ones had never returned for them, it was never over.

After the Service Ian accompanied Robert home to spend the day and stay the night with him. Changing out of their uniforms, the boys stood looking out from the bedroom window. Through a gap in the trees they could see one of the new houses, which were being built on the other side of the garden wall. The estate bordering the north side of the Rutherford garden had sold most of the land for new building, and houses were beginning to spring up where once only gardens had been. But this new building work had not spoilt the privacy of Robert's home or garden, because it was the gardens of the new houses which would abut the Rutherford property, and there was the high wall and a large border of shrubs and trees to act as a barrier.

Robert had not actually been forbidden to enter the building sites on the other side of the garden wall, but Elizabeth had suggested that he keep away. However, sometimes his curiosity got the better of him, and when the workmen were not there and no one else was looking he would scale the garden wall and drop down the other side to spend time clambering through the unfinished houses.

The day had been showery but during the afternoon it had brightened up and Robert decided that an expedition over the garden wall should be undertaken. It was easy to get on top of the garden wall opposite the new house that they had seen from the bedroom window, because a tree branch overhung it at this point and Robert had fixed his rope ladder to the branch, so it was just a matter of climbing the ladder. Having reached the top of the wall, they sat there for a moment and were just about to drop down the other side when a girl about their own age appeared from the unfinished house.

"Damn!" whispered Robert, "Who the hell's she?"

"Hallo! What are you doing?" the girl asked brightly.

Doing handstands on the lawn. What does it look like, Robert was about to say, but thought better of it? He shouldn't be rude, he decided, especially on his birthday when everyone was being so nice to him. "Just looking," he replied innocently. "We like sitting on walls, don't we Ian?"

"Oh, yes! We always sit on walls. It's our hobby, you know," said Ian, trying not to laugh.

"Would, you like, to come and see my new house?" the girl asked.

"Your new house?" Robert sounded surprised.

"Yes, I'm coming to live here when it's finished. And my family, of course."

"No thanks." Robert felt a little put out by this intrusion into what he considered his territory.

"Why not?" the girl persisted.

Robert quickly tried to think of an excuse. "We daren't. They would think we were trying to escape, and we'd be whipped and locked up in a dark cell as punishment." Robert spoke with such gravity that Ian had to stop himself giggling.

"Whatever do you mean, trying to escape?" the girl asked, obviously concerned for the two boys.

"Didn't you know this is a reform school? That's why there's a high wall," Robert went on. "We're only allowed out on Saturdays." He quickly added, "But not over the wall."

"You poor boys! What happens for the rest of the time?"

"Please don't ask. It's too terrible. Look, my friend's crying at the thought of it."

Ian was helpless with laughter. He had taken out his handkerchief and was holding it over his face.

"You must be very wicked to deserve such punishment," the girl persisted.

"Oh, yes, we are! My friend pushed, his grandmother down the stairs and she broke her neck."

"Why ever did he do that?"

"Er. . . " Robert hesitated as he tried hard to think of a reason. "She wouldn't give him any pocket money," he added quickly.

"And what about you? What did you do?"

Robert was having to rack his brains to continue his yarn. "I poured hot water on my baby brother, because he wouldn't stop crying."

"What beasts you are!" the girl exclaimed.

"Oh, we are!". Robert replied, his tone full of remorse. "Sometimes we wake up in the night screaming for mercy because we've been so wicked."

"I don't think I ought to be talking to you."

"No, you shouldn't," Robert replied.

"Wendy, it's time to go darling!" A man appeared at the side of the house accompanied by a woman and a small boy.

It certainly is, thought Robert. "Come on, Ian, quick, let's go!"

"Ah, I see you have two young friends. I thought I heard you talking." The man sounded very pleasant, but the boys didn't wait to see, and were already clambering down the rope ladder.

"Come away, Daddy, you mustn't talk to them, they are reform school boys," Robert heard the girl say. The boys remained at the foot of the wall trying to hear what else was said.

"What are you talking about, Wendy?" said the woman.

"That's a reform school, and those boys are terribly wicked. One poured hot water on his baby brother."

The boys were holding their hands over their mouths to stifle their laughter.

"What nonsense," laughed the man. "I believe the house belongs to a general.

"Then they must have been lying, Daddy."

"Teasing, my dear, more like."

The voices on the other side of the wall faded, and the boys ran back to the house in fits of laughter. They rushed in through the side door nearly knocking Agnes off her feet in their hurry. Robert caught her round the waist and whirled her along the corridor into the hall, loudly humming *The Blue Danube* waltz as he went. "Put me down, Robert!" she cried.

"But darling, you're so beautiful," he said, smothering her objections by kissing her so that she couldn't speak, and holding her so tightly she couldn't force him away.

"Robert!" Elizabeth came from the drawing room, smiling. "Will you leave poor Agnes alone."

"It's my birthday and I'll do what I like with the women in this house," Robert laughed as he released Agnes.

"You're next, Elizabeth." Robert took his mother in his arms and kissed her passionately.

"What the devil's going on out here?" Hearing the commotion, John emerged from his study.

"I am sorry, sir, but I'm passionately in love with your wife," said Robert dramatically, putting on a French accent. "You must surrender your wife or your life."

"And, if I refuse?" John smiled.

"Then I'll run like blazes," Robert laughed, releasing his mother and running up the stairs. "Come on, Ian," he called, and both boys disappeared along the passage to Robert's room.

"Well, I never did," Agnes exclaimed. What are we going to do with that boy, Sir John? He's getting so strong."

They all laughed.

Robert had asked if he might receive his birthday presents just before dinner that evening. It would be more exciting to have them at the end of the day rather than at breakfast time. Of course, he had received the usual ribbing from Joanna who had said "And what makes you think you're getting any?" But his wishes were to be complied with.

That evening, before dressing for dinner, Robert was drying himself after his bath, when Agnes entered the bedroom. "I thought you might like to know your cousin Lisa has arrived," she said.

"Oh, good. I was hoping she'd make it."

"And she's brought a friend with her."

"Bloody hell! The rotten cow," Robert exclaimed. Agnes slapped him hard across his bottom. "Ouch!"

"You're to stop using language like that," she ordered.

"Sorry... But she is." He remembered his last meeting with Lisa in the summer, and her threat to bring her friend to meet him. Of course, it may not be the same friend, he thought, but he bet it was, knowing Lisa, and she was sure to have told her everything. How bloody embarrassing. Why were girls such a nuisance?

"Now hurry up," Agnes said. "You're the host this evening, and you must be there to welcome your guests."

'When the boys were dressed Agnes cast a critical eye over the starched white shirts and the neatly tied black bow ties. "You look very smart," she said.

Having passed her inspection they went down to the drawing-room.

Robert said, "By the way, thanks for coming, Ian. It's made the day much more fun."

"I always like coming here. It's great .fun."

When his parents entered the room, Robert went forward and bowed. He took his mother's hand and kissed it. "Lady Rutherford, you are more beautiful than ever," he said, grinning at her. "Thank you for coming to my birthday dinner." .

"Thank you, young sir," Elizabeth replied, thinking how grown up he looked in his dinner suit.

"And if you look behind the curtains over there," said John indicating the bay window, "You may find something to interest you."

Robert drew back the curtain, and there was a brand new, shiny black bicycle with its chrome handlebars and wheel rims glinting in the light of the room. He stood there speechless, just looking in wonder. He knelt down beside it and lovingly ran his hands over the smooth enamel surface of the mudguards. He noted the three speed gear on the cross bar, the lamp on the front; and the red rear light. He had always dreamed of a cycle like this, and joy welled up inside him. He looked round and saw that his parents were watching him, and quickly moving across to them he flung his arms round Elizabeth and kissed her. Forgetting for a moment that he was supposed to be grown up, he blurted out, "Oh, thanks, Mummy! Thanks, Dad, Father, I mean. I'm in such a whirl; I don't really know what to say." He let go of Elizabeth and quickly kissed John on the cheek. "It's the most marvellous bike in the world. Come and have a look, Ian." But Ian was already admiring the machine. "I'll be able to ride out to your place on it."

"There's one condition," said John. "Never ask me to ride it. I've sworn never to ride one of the wretched things again."

"I can't understand why you hate them so much, my darling. After all, if it wasn't for your cycle tour we would never have met," Elizabeth reminded him.

The four of them gathered round the gleaming cycle, both John and Elizabeth feeling a glow of satisfaction as they watched the sheer joy on their son's face.

At that moment Lisa and her friend entered the room. "Robert," Elizabeth whispered, indicating that he should go and welcome them. He went across the room with a shy smile on his face, feeling himself go hot under the collar. He held out his hand to Lisa and said, "Thanks for coming Lisa."

"I wouldn't have missed it for anything," she said. "Oh, this is Tessa." Lisa looked intently at her cousin and saw him colour up. "I've told you about her," she added meaningfully with a faint smile and a wicked look in her eyes. "And this is my cousin Robert, Tessa."

God! It's her, Robert thought to himself. He swallowed hard and held out his hand. "I'm very pleased to meet you," he gulped. Even though they were only a few months older than himself, he thought both girls looked terribly grown up in their long dresses, and they seemed so calm and composed, which was more than he could say for himself.

"I've heard so much about you," said Tessa, looking Robert up and down. "In fact, Lisa has described you in such detail; I feel I already know you intimately."

Robert ran his hand across his forehead. I bet she has, he thought. But his thoughts mellowed towards his cousin when, she presented him with a large parcel which the butler had just brought into the room for her. "This is for you, Robert. It's from all of us at home."

"Whatever is it?" said Robert.

"Why not open it and see," Lisa suggested.

Everyone crowded round as Robert cut the string and tore off the brown paper wrapping to reveal a large cardboard box on which were the words *Genuine Waterproof Camping Tent*. "Thanks, Lisa, it's smashing! I've always wanted a tent. However did you know?"

"You'll be able to sleep in the garden on a hot summer night as you've always wanted to," said Lisa.

"Wouldn't it be fun for all of us to sleep in it," said Tessa.

Not on your life, thought Robert. Fancy sleeping in the same tent with girls. "It's only for two," Robert retorted.

"All the better," Tessa whispered to him.

"What a lovely present," said Elizabeth.

"You're a very lucky boy."

"Yes, I know."

"Happy birthday Old Bean!" Joanna rushed in wearing a mackintosh, and beret, and pushing a parcel into his hands, flung her arms round Robert's neck and kissed him so vigorously that he sat back on the arm of the settee to steady himself. "Sweet fifteen and never been kissed! Anyway, brother dear, I made it. I would have done it for no one but you." Robert's face was a picture of resignation as he sat on the arm of the chair with his sister's arms round his neck, waiting for the moment when she would at last allow him to open his present. But she hadn't finished. "And I simply had to rip myself away from college, there's so much going on. I shall miss two parties tonight, but no matter, I simply had to see you on your birthday. And I've met the most divine man. If it hadn't been for him I would have still been clattering along on that beastly train. He drove me all the way from Oxford. Wasn't that sweet of him?"

"It was," said Robert, glad to have been able to get a word in. "Now can I open my parcel?"

"Well, of course you can. While you're doing that I'll just dash upstairs and fling on some old rags. See you at dinner!" Joanna called, hurrying from the room.

"Phew. You can see why I'm the quiet one," said Robert. He opened his parcel and found it contained a large, real leather saddlebag for his new cycle. He was about to fix it on the saddle when the butler entered and announced, "Mr. and Mrs. Sanders and er. . .wheelbarrow."

"Wheelbarrow!" exclaimed John.

"Wheelbarrow, sir," Maitland repeated with even more dignity. But before the butler could explain Daisy entered the room followed by Reggie pushing a wheelbarrow which contained something large covered with a blanket.

"All the fun of the fair, you chaps! Where's my godson?"

Robert went forward to greet the newcomers.

"In the name of heaven, Reggie, what are you up to this time?" asked John.

"A little something for the boy, don't you know. Don't worry about your carpets, Beth old girl. Had the compost hosed off the barrow, ha ha."

Reggie stood on one side of the barrow and organised Robert to stand on the other side, each holding a corner of the blanket. "When I give the word, old boy, we whip it off. Hey Presto! And off it comes."

The removal of the blanket uncovered a solid oak cabinet, Robert looked baffled as he helped, his uncle lift it on to the floor, but his face soon lit up when Reggie lifted the top to reveal the turntable of a gramophone. "Happy birthday old son. Hope you like it," said Reggie.

"Is it really mine?"

"Well, of course it is, dear," said Daisy.

Reggie removed a small handle from a clip alongside the turn-table and inserted it in a hole in the side of the cabinet. "You wind it up here," he said. He pulled open two small doors in the front of the cabinet and said, "This is where you store your records. We've put a few in for you as a start," he added.

"I don't know what to say," said Robert. But before he could say anymore or examine his present more closely the butler entered and said, "Master Robert, Ladies and Gentlemen, dinner is served."

Elizabeth whispered in his ear, "You are the host tonight Robert. Choose a lady and lead us into dinner."

Without having to think the choice was already in his mind. If the room had contained a thousand people his choice would have been the same. "May I escort you into dinner, Cousin?" he requested.

Lisa looked at him, but said nothing. She showed no surprise, just accepting his arm as if it was her right and that no one else should be at his side. Robert felt the touch of her hand and once again, as in the park at Rotterdam, it affected him in a way he was unable to account for. Since their Rotterdam meeting he had often thought of her, and sometimes in bed at night he would drift into sleep picturing himself as her hero, the finest swordsman in England defending her to the death from her enemies, or her devoted slave offering himself for sacrifice in her place.

All took their seats at the table. That is, all except Joanna, who, now hurried in, quickly kissing her parents and then Reggie and Daisy. "Sorry I'm late, but life is so hectic." she said, taking her seat. "I really must tell you all about Matt. His name is Matthew, really, but I call him Matt."

"So we have a name this time, do we," John remarked dryly.

"Of course we do, Daddy dear. It's the real thing this time, I know it."

"And what makes you so certain?" John inquired.

"It's the way he looks at me, "Joanna sighed.

"Oh God! Isn't it sickening," said Robert.

"Robert dear, don't be blasphemous," Elizabeth scolded.

"Sorry, Mother, but she's so soppy. All this love talk."

"You wait 'till you're in love," Joanna retorted.

"You won't catch me falling in love. It's stupid, all that soppy kissing and cuddling, and darling this and darling that." Robert would, have continued if there had been no guests present, but as he had just put a large piece of buttered roll in his mouth, he considered he ought to show good manners by not talking with his mouth full.

"So, you consider your parents soppy, do you my lad?" Elizabeth smiled.

"Oh no, Mother," he mumbled, and then clearing his mouth he added, "Parents are different."

"Well, I'm glad to hear that, dear. But what about soppy lovers who become parents?"

Robert could think of no suitable reply.

"Anyway, I don't care what you think, Robert. You're too young to understand. Matt and I are desperately in love," Joanna rejoined.

"He must be soft in the head," Robert retorted.

"Might I ask how long you've known this fellow?" John gave his daughter a quizzical look.

"I met him last night at a college party."

"Last night!" John exclaimed. "Isn't that rather a short time for becoming so desperately in love, as you put it?"

"It was love at first sight, Daddy."

Robert decided to rejoin the attack on the lovers and said, putting on an affected accent, "I suppose he's awfully, awfully strong and handsome, with gorgeous dark hair."

"As a matter of fact he's not handsome at all, but he's very intelligent and his eyes are so penetrating. It's as if he sees right through you."

"He obviously hasn't seen through you so he can't be that intelligent," Robert sniggered.

"I shall ignore that remark as it's your birthday," Joanna replied haughtily. "She continued with a dignified air. "I shall continue my description to those who appreciate it. Matt is rather thin and pale, but he has dark hair with some sweet little wisps of grey over the ears."

"For God's sake, how old is this man?" said John.

"John dear, don't be blasphemous," Robert mimicked without thinking, causing everyone to laugh. He looked at his father out of the corner of his eye and was thankful to see a smile on his face.

"Oh, he's in his thirties," Joanna replied confidently. "He's an up and coming barrister, you know."

John decided not to pursue the matter, because, as with all Joanna's other boy friends, this Matt would be forgotten in a few days. "And as for you, my lad," he said, looking at Robert, "I'll give you John dear, you cheeky young monkey!"

"The lad bowled you middle stump that time, old boy, ha ha," Reggie laughed.

The chatter at the table increased as the meal progressed and everyone relaxed. Robert wished Tessa, who was sitting on the opposite side of the table at the far end, would stop looking at him. She had such a confident manner and her sweet smile made him feel uncomfortable. He knew what she was thinking, and he could have killed Lisa for bringing her.

Robert glanced at Lisa, who was sitting on his left, and thought how much better looking she was than Tessa. In fact, he couldn't think of a better looking girl than Lisa. Anyway, what did it matter what she looked like; she was a blasted nuisance like all girls. And yet, it was nice to be with her. Lisa turned her head and gave him one of her enigmatic smiles. "Wasn't it kind of Tessa to come tonight," she said.

"I suppose you told her everything," Robert whispered out of the corner of his mouth.

"Of course. I described you in detail, and she's crazy with jealousy. So my little scheme worked."

"Just you wait till get you alone, Lisa van der Leyden."

"I shall look forward to that." Lisa furtively stretched out her hand under the table, gripping it in his ticklish spot just above the knee. Robert's leg shot up and his knee struck the underside of the table making a loud bang. He just managed to stifle a howl. John looked at him but said nothing. Lisa looked completely innocent and continued eating. Daisy giggled, remembering her own young days.

Just before the sweet was served, the butler and one of the maids brought in two silver ice buckets each containing a bottle of champagne and placed them on the sideboard.

John looked on in surprise and said, "I gave no order for champagne tonight, Maitland."

"No, I did, old boy!" said Reggie, getting up from the table and going to the sideboard. "I'll do the honours, Maitland," he added. "It's my godson's birthday and he's going to have a swig of the very best bubbly."

"But Reggie, old friend, I don't allow him to drink alcohol," John replied.

"Oh, please let me have a taste, Father, just this once," Robert pleaded. Without thinking he said. "I had some beer in Germany." And then realising what he had said and knowing he had been strictly forbidden to drink alcohol he quickly explained. "I couldn't help it, sir. Some of us in the Hitler Youth had been working a farm all day and the farmer gave us each a pot of beer. I just couldn't refuse or they would have thought the English were stupid."

"You know what I said I would do to you if I ever caught you drinking," said John.

Robert was relieved to see that there was a flicker of a smile on his father's face. "But Father, you haven't caught me yet," he replied, grinning sheepishly, willing his father to relent.

"Ha ha, he's bowled you out again, old boy," roared Reggie, who had not taken the slightest notice of John's protestations, but had just drawn the first cork and was beginning to fill the glasses.

John smiled. "Well, just this once, "he said. "You spoil this boy of mine, Reggie, you really do."

"Of course I do, old boy, that's what godfathers are for.

"Thanks, Father! You're a brick!" Robert exclaimed.

As the servants served the sweet, Reggie acted as wine waiter and placed a glass of champagne in front of each person as if he was handling a priceless piece of delicate antique china. "Now, Robert my lad, don't gulp it. Take the glass lovingly in your hand remembering it contains the most precious nectar in the world, the drink of the gods. Caress it, savour the moment, let it . . . " Reggie would have continued but Daisy interrupted.

"For heavens sake, Reggie, stop your chatter and let the boy 'ave a swig."

"Sorry, old girl. Get carried away, don't you know."

Robert took a sip, but wasn't quite sure whether he liked it or not. It was certainly better than that German beer. Perhaps he did like it, he decided. He noticed his uncle, who had taken his place again at the table, watching him, waiting for his comment. "It's jolly nice, Uncle. Thanks very much."

"Yes, Reggie, this is the best. Your kindness is much appreciated," said John. "You really shouldn't spoil us like this."

"Think nothing of it, old boy," Reggie beamed, rising from his chair. "And now, with your permission, John, I'm going to say a few words about someone very dear to my heart."

John nodded and smiled, and Reggie continued. "At this time fifteen years ago I was sitting at another table in another country. For four years, like millions of others, I had lived with nothing but death and destruction. But on that particular day two things happened. Firstly, the killing stopped, and secondly, a new life entered the world, and I have had great pleasure in watching that child grow into a strong and healthy boy. Sometimes he is mischievous, as I know to my cost. Sometimes, I am told, he can be downright naughty. Reggie paused and winked at Robert, who was grinning up at him. "I don't wish to embarrass him, but I see his true nature as one who is kind and loving. He is not aggressive, nor is he a bully. He is a boy who feels the beauty of life and demonstrates it to others in many ways, especially with music. He is polite and obedient to his elders, he is considerate to all, and it is always good to be in his company."

"Who is this mythical character, Uncle?" Joanna interrupted. "I'd love to meet him."

Reggie gave one of his hearty laughs but was not put off his stroke. "Having no son of my own," he continued, "He has been of special joy to me, and I must give thanks to you, John, and you, Elizabeth, for allowing me a share in your son. So let's, all stand and drink the very best wine as a toast to the very best of boys – Robert."

Robert sat with his head bowed as everyone stood and raised their glasses towards him. His hands were under the table tightly gripping his legs. He felt himself go hot and knew his face had coloured up. It was then he heard his father say those words which he had always known would be said to him one day. And this was that day. When he had asked for a dinner party it had not occurred to him that this would happen.

"Robert, you must stand up and reply."

"Yes, speech!" cried Joanna.

For as long as he could remember he had dreaded the moment when he would have to stand up and make a perfect fool of himself in front of other people. If only it didn't have to be now. After all, it was his birthday and he had been enjoying himself. His mind raced, trying to think how to get out of it. It seemed an age that he sat there, still with bowed head, knowing that all eyes were on him. He heard Joanna again. "Come on, Robert, speech!" It was then he felt the touch of a hand gently resting on his hand. He glanced to his left and saw Lisa smiling at him. It was as if she was saying, come on Robert, there's nothing to worry about, I'm here. She slipped her hand into his and held it tight as he rose from his chair. He had wanted to be her hero, well now was his chance, he thought. Surely he could do anything if she were beside him.

Having stood up, Robert's mind went blank. Oh God! What was he going to say? "Father, Mother, Ladies and Gentlemen," he commenced uncertainly, but the hand he was still holding gave him a gentle squeeze. "For one moment I thought Uncle Reggie was talking about me, but then, as he went on I knew it must be some other boy. I'm sure my parents would not agree with the polite and obedient bit, and as for being kind and considerate I can't help feeling a bit of a failure. But thanks anyway, Uncle, for the kind words, and, er..." Robert hesitated and once again felt his hand pressed. "Oh, yes, and thank you for the smashing presents and for making this a very happy evening for me. . .er . . . and thanks, Mother and Father, for being such wonderful parents and putting up with me for fifteen years. I hope the worst is over, but I can't guarantee it." Robert grinned and everyone laughed. "That's about all, I think . . . I know, let's drink to my parents." Robert picked up his glass and everyone followed and raised their glasses to John and Elizabeth. When he sat down he felt Lisa withdraw her hand, but he wished she hadn't. He turned and looked at her. "Let me hold it again," he whispered.

"Not now," she said. But then, seeing his disappointment, she added, "One day, maybe."

"Oh, my sainted aunt!" Robert exclaimed. It was the Saturday following his birthday, and John and Elizabeth had picked him up in the car after morning school. As they arrived home, George's Daimler was seen to be standing outside the front door. "Look what the blinking tide's washed up!"

"Robert, where do you pick up all these dreadful expressions?" asked Elizabeth.

"Aunty Daisy" he replied, but his mind was elsewhere, working out how he was to avoid his relatives. "I'm going upstairs."

"Oh, no you're not! You'll come and pay your respects," Elizabeth said firmly.

"I just hope that blasted Jason isn't here," Robert muttered.

The butler was at the door as the family entered. "I have placed Sir George in the morning room, sir. He is accompanied by Lady Rutherford and Mr Percy."

"Thank you, Maitland."

John found it disturbing to see the deterioration in his brother's condition. It had been seventeen months since he had first noticed the tremor of George's right hand. When he had seen him six months ago the infirmity had spread and George was finding difficulty in walking. But now the condition had advanced even further. He was no longer the slightly overweight pompous man he had once been, but a shadow of his former self. He lacked animation, because his muscles had lost their strength, and his hand, shook continuously.

"This is a pleasant surprise," said John. Then going to his brother, who had made no attempt to rise, he said, "George, you've lost weight."

"Excuse me for not rising, but the truth is I'm a bloody wreck," George replied, extending a shaky hand.

Henrietta glared at her husband. "At least you can control your language, George, even if you have difficulty in controlling that disastrous body of yours," she rebuked cuttingly. But her husband seemed not to hear.

Percy, whose long frame had been sprawled on a settee, lethargically heaved himself on to his feet and shook hands with his uncle. It had always surprised John that Percy had a firm handshake, for it didn't seem to match, what John considered, his otherwise languid character. John nodded to his nephew, but neither spoke and Percy moved across and kissed his aunt. "Aunty, dear, you become more beautiful than ever. And as for you, handsome cousin," he went on flippantly, looking at Robert, who had remained in the background hoping to escape the attentions of his relatives. "You'll be breaking a few hearts before you're much older."

Percy offered cigarettes to his father and uncle, and, having lit them, returned to his lounging position on the settee. He produced a cigarette holder, which must have been at least six inches in length, and with exaggerated care placed a cigarette in the end, then, lighting it, began to puff away himself.

Elizabeth sat down next to Henrietta and said, "You look well, Henrietta dear."

"No thanks to that husband of mine," snapped Henrietta. "Since this odious thing has come upon him and he's been forced into early retirement, the whole weight of responsibility for running our family affairs has fallen on me."

"What the Mater means is, that now Pater's got the shakes, she has to wait at least three minutes longer for him to sign a cheque for her," Percy drawled. He was lounging cross legged on the settee with his elbow resting on the arm, and had removed the cigarette holder from his mouth just long enough to make his remark.

Robert sniggered, but, seeing his aunt glaring at him, pulled a straight face. He glanced at Percy and received a wink through the haze of smoke which enveloped his cousin.

When luncheon was announced they all prepared to move into the dining room. Considering George's condition, Elizabeth was concerned as to how much assistance he would need to get to the dining-room, and also how he would cope with a meal. But immediately it became apparent that George wished to rise, Percy was at his father's side assisting him to his feet. The cigarette had been stubbed in the ask tray, the long holder disappeared into a pocket, and for a moment the nonchalant, disinterested attitude vanished. Percy was in command, handling his father with an ease and consideration which surprised his relatives. "Steady now, Pater old thing, this isn't the hundred yards sprint," he said, putting his arm round George to prevent him stumbling.

When he had seated his father at the table, Percy, without hesitation, or reference to the servants, arranged the place set in front of him so that George could eat and drink with his left hand. Elisabeth watched her nephew with admiration as he took the large napkin, and after spreading it out, tucked it into George's collar. When the meal was served Percy was once again at his father's side, this time to cut up the food into small pieces so that George could manage to eat with one hand only. Whenever George was in difficulty Percy was there dealing with the matter without apology or excuse to the onlookers, but with his own particular brand of comment.

"And how is Jason, Henrietta?" Elisabeth inquired. "He must have been on his training ship for over a year now."

"Training ship!" Henrietta stormed. "Prison ship, more like, from what the poor dear boy has told me. There's some beastly man who is called a boat swine or some such equally barbarous name."

"Bo'sun, Mater," Percy corrected.

"Don't interrupt! As I was saying, this wicked man continually flogs poor Jason with the end of a rope."

"Rope's end, Mater," said Percy, interrupting once more.

"Whatever it's known as is of little consequence," Henrietta retorted, becoming irritated with her son. "What is of consequence is that poor Jason is being beaten by it."

"Serves him right. Should have been done years ago," Percy drawled.

Robert, who was listening with interest, agreed.

Henrietta continued in an indignant tone. "Because of this disgraceful treatment I have decided to withdraw Jason from the merchant navy."

"Just because the blighter's got a sore bum, Aunty," Percy drawled, glancing at Elizabeth."Good reason to keep him in, I would have thought."

Robert found the conversation much to his liking and sniggered at Percy's remarks.

"Don't be so vulgar, Percy!" commanded his mother.

The meal over, Percy assisted George to John's study where he left the two brothers to enjoy a glass of brandy on their own.

"Not supposed to touch the stuff according to the damn quack," said George, breathing in the fumes of the golden liquid. "But who cares, better enjoy myself while I can."

"I'm sorry to see you like this, George. Can nothing be done?" John asked.

"Nothing, I'm on the way out, John, and that's a fact. Percy's turned up trumps though. Don't know what I'd do without him."

"So I've noticed," John replied,

"Do you know he even shaves me everyday? He's so gentle too. Won't let anyone else touch me. And when he's not waiting on me he sits in his room writing plays. It's a funny sort of life for a young man, but he never complains. Although he's my son I've never known what to make of him. Always putting on an act. God knows what's going to become of him! If only he could find a good woman to marry."

"He's a strange chap, I must say. Not my type, of course. Hasn't he got any interests?

"I'm told he's quite an expert on pictures, for what use that is. And, of course, he's forever at some theatre or other. Oh yes, and he flies."

"Flies!" John exclaimed. "Flies what? Kites?"

A flicker of a smile passed, over George's face. He was not sure whether John was being facetious. "An aeroplane of course. Belongs to some flying club or other. God knows what for. Says it's relaxing."

"I should have thought he was relaxed enough without needing any assistance," John remarked. "Besides, in my opinion aeroplanes are more likely to have the opposite effect. Damn dangerous things. Can't imagine Percy wanting to fly an aeroplane. He appears far too indolent."

"Well he does, and they say he's rather good at it."

"Where does he get the money?"

"Some wealthy chap he knows in the art world seems to indulge his whims."

"That sounds an unhealthy relationship," John concluded.

George made no further comment but changed the subject. "By the way, can you do something for young Jason? He's decided on the army, after all."

"Has he now! Is he suitable, do you think?"

"I've no idea, John. But it would be a comfort to me to know he's settled before I go. This is actually what we've come to see you about."

"Steady on, old chap, you're not finished yet," John comforted. "Don't worry I'll see what I can do for the boy."

The brothers were silent for a time, and then George closed his eyes, and John thought he had dropped off to sleep. Still with his eyes closed, he said sadly, "I know you've never really liked Henrietta, and I admit she's a difficult woman. The boys are not everyone's cup of tea either. But it would be a comfort to know that when I'm gone you will keep an eye on them."

"I doubt if they'll want much to do with me," John replied. "But I'll be here if they want me. Blood is thicker than water, I suppose," he added without enthusiasm.

"Henrietta's worried about Jason. He's having a rough time on that training ship. Can't understand why."

"My dear George, everyone has a rough time on a training ship. That's what training ships are for. He's been to public school so he should be used to discipline. He's a strong boy, and from what I can see, a rough time won't have done him any harm. He won't find the army a picnic, you know."

Robert had escaped to his room after lunch to do some homework which he should have completed the previous evening. After half an hour he became restless and getting up from his desk wandered aimlessly to the window, where he stood with his nose pressed flat on the glass. He could see the large tree overhanging the garden of the new house where he and Ian had sat on the wall and made that girl believe they were reform school boys. Girls are so stupid, he thought. Fancy believing all that rubbish. Turning away from the window he looked with satisfaction at his new gramophone. It really, is a smashing present, he said to himself as he opened the lid. Uncle and aunty were so kind to him. Having wound it up he placed a record on the turntable and pushed the little release lever which allowed it to spin. Then he carefully swung the arm over the record and lowered the head, making sure that he didn't scratch the record with the steel needle.

Using a chair the wrong way round he sat astride it with his arms along the top of the back, and his chin resting on his arms.

The record he had put on was one which Reggie had given him, the great love duet from the opera *Madam Butterfly*. He had heard it for the first time a few days before, and it had so moved him that he had asked his mother about the opera. He sat enraptured as the music soared to the heights of passionate love, his romantic young soul lost in his imaginings of the tragic story; and tears rolling down his cheeks. The music finished and the needle began to scrape at the end of the record as the turntable continued to spin. But for a moment, he was lost in thought, asking himself how it was possible to love a girl with such passion and then desert her for another? If he ever fell in love - which he wouldn't, he quickly reminded himself - but if he did, he would always be faithful.

Returning to reality, he lifted the arm off the record, and was about to put it on again, when there was a knock on the door. He quickly took out his handkerchief and dried his eyes before going to open the door. To his surprise Percy was lounging against the opposite wall of the passage. "Ah, hallo old thing. Heard the music, don't you know. Never could resist music. Mind if I come in?"

Robert did mind but was too polite to say so. "If you like." He knew he sounded offhand, but he hadn't bargained for being disturbed by Percy.

"Don't sound so frightfully enthusiastic," Percy chuckled as he nonchalantly strolled past Robert into the bedroom. "So this is the den where you escape to when your ghastly relatives arrive. I bet some naughty things go on in here," he grinned, looking Robert straight in the eyes. Robert blushed and turned away, going to the gramophone where he busied himself taking off the record. How did Percy know what he was like, he asked himself? Perhaps Jason had told him, he thought. "Don't worry, your secrets are safe with me," Percy grinned.

"I don't know what you mean," Robert stammered, feeling distinctly guilty, and thinking to himself that it was all Jason's fault that he had got into bad habits.

Percy stood for a moment slowly turning full circle as if he was examining every aspect of the room. Although his bodily movements were lackadaisical, his eyes were never still and Robert gained the impression that his cousin had missed no detail.

Robert put the record away and closed down the top of the gramophone.

"I thought you might play me something," said Percy.

"I've finished now," Robert replied abruptly.

"Never mind," smiled Percy, not appearing to be put out by his cousin's clumsy refusal. He continued his stroll round the room, stopping opposite a small picture on the wall. Taking out an eye glass he studied it carefully. "Worth a fortune," he commented, then moved on to carefully examine Robert's collection of books. He picked out a book and flicked through the pages, then, without looking up, drawled, "Been blubbing?"

"No I haven't!" Robert retorted defiantly.

Percy gave Robert a quizzical look, and then said in a kindly tone of voice. "Why be ashamed of it?"

"I'm not," Robert snapped, wishing his cousin would go away. He had resumed his position on the chair and again, sat with his chin resting on his arms watching Percy study the book and waiting for him to leave.

"So you were blubbing," Percy grinned.

"What if I was? It's my business!"

Percy ignored the rebuke. "I often have a quiet blub myself," he said.

"You!" Robert could hardly believe that this cousin of his, who had such a cynical and flippant attitude towards life, was a cry baby like himself. "I don't believe it."

"Why not? It's a perfectly natural function of the body, and besides, there's nothing like good blub to free the emotions. When I'm stirred by the beauty of music, or the sadness of great and moving words, I drop a few tears." Percy looked pensively at the wall, and then glanced at Robert. "In any case, all life is a tragedy and it's a hard heart that doesn't weep for the sufferings of poor old humanity. Take the poor old Pater for instance, that's enough to make you weep." Percy sat down at Robert's desk and cast his eye over the exercise book lying open there.

"Don't you care if people know?"

"Not a fig. They think I'm peculiar anyway."

"Doesn't that worry you?" Robert persisted.

"Why should it? It's all rather amusing."

"I didn't know you liked music, Percy," said Robert in a more reasonable tone.

"Of course you didn't, old darling. In fact, like most other people, you know nothing about me at all. I'm just that odious fop of a cousin, who puts in an appearance every now and again and drives everyone to distraction with his idiotic remarks."

Robert was trying hard not to soften his attitude towards Percy but couldn't prevent a flicker of a smile at his cousin's description of himself. It matched Robert's own description.

Percy gave the impression that his interest was in the book he held in his hand, but his quick eye hadn't missed the changing expression on his young cousin's face. Still turning the pages he continued, "You be careful, my beauty, not to stick a label on a box before you know what's inside. All life's one big act, and some are better at acting than others. But when you clean off the wretched grease paint you find most people are the same underneath." Out of the corner of his eye Percy could see the blank look on Robert's face. "Take you, for instance. People see a strong, good looking, mischievous boy, without a care in the world, living through the best days of his life. But what's the truth that lies beneath this fair exterior, my sweet?"

"I do wish you wouldn't call me that," Robert objected.

Percy continued ignoring his cousin's protest. "The truth is that you have as many worries, relative to your age of course, as any other poor soul. You don't like horses and you obviously don't want to join the army, so I suppose; you worry your little head that others will think you a coward. Though how anyone in their right mind can like those dreadful creatures, I can never imagine. And as for being a soldier, even the thought of it is too tedious for words."

When Percy paused, Robert interrupted. "You won't tell anyone, will you Percy?"

"Tell 'em what?"

"Well, you know, about the tears."

"Of course not, darling. But why on earth you should want to hide it beats me. I suppose you think you're a cry baby and other people will laugh at you."

Robert nodded, wondering how Percy seemed to know so much about his feelings. "Sometimes I think I'm quite grown up. But other times I feel such a baby. It's so stupid." He asked himself why he was telling Percy all this.

"It's not stupid at all," Percy replied. "It's all to do with growing up, when you're half a man and half a boy and your feelings get mixed between the two stages. But don't ever suppress your tender heart and sense of beauty with the mistaken idea that these feelings are childish, because they're not, and you'll carry them, and your tears, to your life's end. You'll never be rid of them. You may suppress them, but if you do, then you'll be but half a man. And just remember that all people are far more sensitive than it appears on the surface." He was silent for a moment and then pondered. "Unfortunately, tender hearts so often get broken."

By now Robert sat taking in every word Percy uttered. It was the first time anyone had ever spoken to him about his own inner worries, and with such depth of feeling. Percy had answered questions which, as yet, Robert had not been able to formulate in his mind. He had known that he wanted an answer to these problems, and now he'd got one without even having to ask.

"How do you know so much, Percy?"

"It's quite simple, old thing. Just look inwards to your own heart, and there you'll find a miniature of the whole world."

Percy went on to relate in a most amusing way how he was called a cry baby at school. That is until the day he'd had enough of it and punched his tormentor on the nose and made it bleed. This boy happened to be the toughest boy in the form, but instead of turning on him in anger the two had become firm friends. "And from that day forth," Percy went on, "I was allowed to blub in peace if the mood took me, and anyone who called me names got a jolly good buffeting from old Polly Perkins. Actually his name was Paul, but I always called him Polly. He seemed to accept it from me, but when others tried it Polly used to twist their arms until they howled. Polly was an absolute dear. Which brings me to my point, idiotic though it might be, if you feel like blubbing, then blub, and be damned to everyone."

Robert found it hard not to laugh at the way Percy related his little story. "You really don't care what people think of you, do you Percy." he said.

"I'd be a nervous wreck if I did, sweetie. I act my part, other people act theirs. As I said, life is one long act, and you can't change your part halfway through the play.

Percy picked up Robert's exercise book, and leaning back in the chair, stretched out his legs and placed his feet on Robert's desk. "Is this ghastly piece of work yours?" he said, holding the book at arms length between two fingers as if it was giving off a repugnant smell.

"Is it that bad?" Robert asked, looking a little crestfallen. His homework had been to write a character study of Lady Bracknell from *The Importance of Being-Earnest.*

"It's absolute bilge, dear thing."

"But the play is so boring," Robert objected.

"Rubbish, you young Philistine! It's one of the wittiest plays ever written, but I suppose you and all the other duffers in your class just sit there half asleep wondering what it's all about when you're forced to read it. Instead you should be laughing your heads off. It needs to be acted, properly, then you might understand it." Percy then began to recite line after line of the play, changing his voice to suit the different characters, and as he did so the play began to have some meaning to Robert. Percy flung the text book at his cousin. "Here! Page thirty nine. You be Jack. I'll be Lady Bracknell," he said.

Robert was unable to stop himself laughing at Percy's antics, but managed to read his own part successfully.

"You're a jolly good actor, Percy," he remarked when they had finished.

"My word, there's praise indeed for poor old Percy. I wish my agent had your confidence."

With his better understanding of the play, and with some helpful suggestions from Percy, Robert sat down to re-write his homework, having the feeling that he might get a reasonable mark for a change. He heard the bedroom door open, and glancing up saw it close as Percy quietly disappeared. He felt a little ashamed at his behaviour towards his cousin, because, when he came to think of it, he had never done him any harm. Getting up from his chair, he went to the door with the intention of saying he was sorry and offering to put on another record, but Percy had disappeared.

After tea that afternoon Robert stood with his parents in the drive as their relatives prepared to depart.

"Goodbye, young Robert," said George, thrusting a ten shilling note into his nephew's hand as Percy assisted him into the car. "Have it on account while you've got the chance."

"Thanks. Uncle, that's jolly generous of you!"

Having settled his father, Percy got in beside the chauffeur and the Daimler slowly moved away.

CHAPTER 10

There was an air of excitement about the house on that May Saturday morning. Maitland and Perks were moving furniture and rolling back carpets in the drawing-room while the maids were dusting and sweeping and generally tidying up after the men had done their work.

Joanna was sleeping late and had so far not put in an appearance much to the relief of Elizabeth who felt she and the housekeeper could organise the household far better without the interference of her vivacious daughter.

Robert had gone to school, and John was not due to return from London until the afternoon. He had made a special point of staying at his club the previous night in order to keep out of the way *while his house was being turned upside down,* as he put it.

Although Joanna had become nineteen in April it had not been convenient to hold the ball on her birthday, "In any case," she had said, "May is so much more romantic than April." But the deciding factor in her mind was that the date chosen was convenient, for Matt to put in his first appearance and meet her family.

Much to the surprise of her family the name of Matt had not faded from Joanna's conversation. On the contrary, it was the one subject that remained constant. John had decided it was time that he met this Matt, and the ball offered a suitable opportunity, so there was a double sense of expectancy pervading the household that day.

The work completed and the house made ready, Elizabeth sat down for coffee in the breakfast room with the housekeeper. "How is Millicent settling down, Mrs Bennet?" she inquired. Millicent was sixteen and had recently been taken on as a maid.

The housekeeper hesitated for a moment, making up her mind how best to answer the question. "I think her work is satisfactory but she has a tendency to gossip and takes a little longer over her duties than she should."

Elizabeth nodded and said, "I'm sure that can be put right under your supervision, Mrs Bennet."

"However, there are one or two things I feel I ought to mention, your ladyship. She is rather forward and has a little too much to say for herself for one of her station in the household. She is also good looking and knows it." The housekeeper hesitated again and then added, "I just hope she doesn't attract the attention of Master Robert."

Elizabeth passed no comment on Mrs Bennet's last observation but thought it a matter to be closely watched even though Robert had as yet, shown little interest in the opposite sex. On the other hand, she remembered, when Lisa had last visited, there had been a subtle change in his attitude towards her, so perhaps there was a dawning taking place.

Joanna entered the room and helped herself to coffee. "Good morning, Mummy. Good morning, Mrs Bennet. What dark household secrets are you discussing?" she said. But Joanna didn't wait for an answer. Her mind was too full of the coming event and Matt's visit.

The housekeeper got up and left the room leaving Joanna to talk to her mother.

Joanna asked, "Do you think that Daddy really minds that Matt is so much older than me? After all, Daddy's ten years older than you so I don't see how he can object."

"Object to what?" Elizabeth enquired.

"Marriage, of course."

Elizabeth had recently begun to realise that there was more to her daughter's affair than just another short infatuation. "Surely your Matt isn't contemplating marriage. You *are* rather young?" she said, eyeing her daughter carefully. "Are you keeping something back, my girl?"

Joanna looked sheepish. "Actually, Matt has asked me to marry him."

"Has he now!" Elizabeth exclaimed. "And what about your father's permission?"

"He's going to speak to Daddy tonight."

"It all seems very premature to me."

"Not if he's the right one. Look at your marriage."

"I was twenty six, not, nineteen," retorted Elizabeth.

"I do hope Daddy isn't going to be stuffy about it. After all it is nineteen thirty four."

"I think we'll wait and see your Matt before making any judgements."

When Robert arrived home from school he noticed the new maid busily dusting the hallstand. He couldn't remember her name, but it was strange how often she was dusting the same piece of furniture when he came through the front door. "Good afternoon, Master Robert," she said as Robert hung up his cap.

"Hallo."

Millicent looked him up and down with a slight smile on her face. He decided it was rather a saucy look, but he didn't mind too much because she certainly wasn't unpleasant to look at.

"Are you looking forward to the ball tonight?" she asked. Millicent came from a small town in the west part of the county and spoke with a slight country accent.

"I suppose so."

"Can you dance?"

"A bit," Robert replied, backing away towards the dining-room. He was starving and had no intention of prolonging this conversation when there was food waiting for him.

"I could teach you," she offered.

"It's all right, thanks, I'll manage."

Agnes passed through the hall and Millicent's conversation was cut short, enabling Robert to make his escape.

"Ah, my favourite brother," said Joanna as Robert joined her and Elizabeth at the table for luncheon. "And how did you get on this morning?"

"Okay thanks. I got a good mark for my essay on the Hitler Youth. Old Pascoe said it was quite interesting. He made me read it out to the class. They didn't seem to know there was such a thing,"

"I hope you didn't mention the Jews," Elizabeth remarked.

"Why should I? What have they got to do with it? Anyway, they're not allowed in it. I think some have tried to join, though, but they won't let them."

"I just wondered. I'm glad you didn't, because it could be hurtful to the Jewish boys in your class."

"But they're my friends. Why should I want to hurt them?" Robert replied indignantly.

"I'm glad to hear you say that. I would hate to think you had been involved in that sort of thing."

"You needn't worry, Mother, I wasn't. It's the SA who bash up the Jews. I don't know why, but they do. The Hitler Youth are not supposed to get involved, although sometimes they do," he replied, remembering what he had seen in Cologne. He had told no one of the incident and wished he could forget it himself. "Uncle Karl says it is anti-semi . . ." Robert hesitated, trying to remember the word.

"Anti-semitism, dear," Elizabeth prompted.

"Yes, that's it. Well, he says it's nothing new in Germany. It's been there for centuries."

"That doesn't make it right," Elizabeth replied.

"I suppose not," said Robert. "By the way, what's that new maid's name?"

"Oh, you mean Millicent."

"Have you got a pash on her?" Joanna grinned.

"Oh, shut up, of course not!" Robert retorted, colouring up. "She's quite nice looking though," he added.

"That's a change, coming from you," Joanna laughed. "Who's the boy who says all girls are soppy? You must be growing up at last."

Robert thought it was time to wriggle out of this conversation. "What time is lover boy arriving?" he countered.

"Now Robert, you be polite when he arrives," Elizabeth instructed.

"Yes, no stupid remarks or showing off," rejoined Joanna.

"I shall be a perfect gentleman." Robert put on an affected accent. "How do you do, Mr Lover. It's so good of you to come. It's really frightfully jolly of you to marry my sister and take her off my hands. I've been waiting so long for some idiot, sorry I mean gentleman, to take her away for good. And the best of luck."

"Shut up, you pig!" exclaimed Joanna. "I'll kill you if you don't behave yourself."

When John arrived home he found Elizabeth and Joanna taking tea in the drawing roam, and he had no sooner settled down to be served with a cup when the butler announced that Mr Matthew Irving had arrived. Joanna flew from the room, a moment later returning on the arm of a sharp featured, slim man, of medium height, whose age John estimated at being about thirty five. He had the confident air of a man who knew where he was going. John rose to greet his guest as Joanna made the introductions.

Matthew Irving came forward and gently took Elizabeth's offered hand. "As a young man I heard of your legendary beauty, Lady Rutherford, but I have had to wait over fifteen years to witness it for myself."

Elizabeth smiled at the newcomer, but was puzzled as to how he could have known of her so many years before. Perhaps she could understand Joanna's liking for this man.

He was certainly not handsome, but there was a strong character behind those alert, intelligent eyes. "If this is how you flatter the female members of a jury, Mr Irving, it is no wonder you are a successful barrister."

Turning to John, Matthew Irving said, "I have had the honour of meeting you some years ago, sir."

John looked carefully at his guest, but could not recollect the face. "Then you have the better of me, sir," he said.

"It was Armistice Day nineteen eighteen at a celebration, dinner in a chateau near Mauberge," the younger man started to explain, but was cut short.

"I remember you," John interrupted. "You were the young officer who gave the speech. The one who was too intelligent to remain in the regular army, as my friend remarked."

John continued to reminisce until he was stopped by Joanna, who suggested that their guest might be allowed to sit down and take tea. But it was obvious to Joanna that her father liked Matt, and her hopes rose that the recent proposal of marriage might be favourably received.

Robert had been amusing himself that afternoon climbing the tree which had overhung the wall bordering the new house where the faired haired girl now lived. He had been incensed when his father had ordered the branch to be cut back so that it didn't Inconvenience the new neighbours, grumbling that it wasn't right to cut trees about just because they overhung somebody's garden. But at least he could still use what was left of the branch to get on to the garden wall. In some ways he resented the new houses that were springing up in what had once been gardens, but on the other hand, since the arrival of the new family, he had found himself taking an increasing interest in what was going on over the wall. He seemed to be drawn to climb this particular tree in the hope that he might catch a glimpse of the girl. He hadn't spoken to her since the day he had teased her with his story, but today he was in luck because she was sitting in the garden reading a book.

The new family had moved in a few weeks before, and John had discovered that the man was the new manager of a local bank.

Robert had made his climb making sure that he drew attention to himself, but at the same time pretending that he hadn't noticed the girl. He sat on a branch in full view of her garden hoping she would say something. She was quite nice looking, he thought, and her legs were just about right. He didn't like girls to have fat legs or thin legs, they had to be medium legs, he decided.

The girl glanced up from her book as if she had just noticed him, but in fact she had been watching him from the moment he came into view above the garden wall. "Oh, hallo. You're not trying to escape, are you?" she asked seriously.

"Hallo," Robert replied, wondering whether she still believed his reform school story or if she was teasing him in return. He wasn't quite sure. "I wish I could, but I daren't."

"I suppose they starve you," she said.

"Oh yes, terribly."

"You don't look starved." The girl thought for a moment and then said, "I know, I'll fetch you some food and drink." She got up and went towards her house.

"Please don't bother," Robert called after her, but she took no notice and disappeared inside.

A few minutes later she returned carrying a glass of water and a large chunk of bread. "Come on down," she called.

"I'll sit on the wall," he said. "I daren't come any further." It was the girl's parents he didn't wish to meet just in case they knew about his fibs. They were sure to think he was an idiot. The girl stood on a garden chair and handed him up the food and drink, and there she remained to ensure that he ate every last scrap of the bread and drank every drop of the water. Although Robert was invariably hungry, at that moment dry bread and water did not appeal to him at all. But he forced it down.

"Where's your friend today?" she asked.

Robert's mouth was so full of bread that he was at first unable to answer. "Er, well. I think he's locked in his cell." Before he could continue a voice came from behind him

"There you are, Robert! You're wanted in the drawing-room immediately." It was Agnes.

"I must go," he said, quickly handing back the glass. He lowered himself from the wall, and as he followed Agnes through the shrubbery, he said in a loud voice, "Please Mara, I wasn't trying to escape. Please don't punish me."

"What are you talking about, Robert?" said Agnes. But Robert just grinned and ran past her back to the house, taking no notice as she called after him to wash his hands and smarten himself before going to the drawing-room.

"Who wants me?" he said as he trotted into where his parents were sitting.

"Robert, what a mess you look, and just look at those dirty hands," Elisabeth scolded.

"Sorry, Mother, but you said come immediately." Robert stood grinning in the centre of the room. He noticed the stranger and now guessed why he had been called in.

"This is Robert, Mr Irving. Please excuse his disgraceful appearance."

Robert went forward and saw the man rise from his chair. So this was the famous Matt. Perhaps now that everyone had met him Joanna would talk about something else for a change. Still he didn't look a bad sort of chap, a bit old maybe, but not at all as he had imagined. "How do you do, sir," he said, rubbing his hand down his trousers before offering it. "Sorry I'm a bit of a mess."

"Think nothing of it, Robert," Matt replied, taking the grubby hand without hesitation. "It would be a strange boy who wasn't in a mess sometimes." Matt grinned at the boy before him. What an attractive and interesting face, he considered. "I've heard a great deal about you."

"Oh, no!" Robert exclaimed, feeling his face flush. "What's she been telling you, sir?"

"Don't worry, it's all complementary, Robert," laughed Matt. "And please call me Matt."

"I say, that's jolly decent of you," Robert replied, feeling that his sister's friend was going to be all right after all.

"And now, Robert, when you've washed your hands you may have some tea," said Elizabeth.

"I'm not hungry, thank you."

"Why ever not?"

"He must be sickening for something," declared Joanna. "He's usually such a pig when it comes to food."

"I've just been force fed with a great big chunk of bread by that girl over the wall."

"My, my, how romantic. The girls are really starting to fall for you," laughed Joanna. "What with Lisa and her friend, Millicent, the maid, and now the girl over the wall, I ask myself who will be throwing herself at my handsome brother next?"

"Oh, shut up!" Robert grinned shyly.

"You can see what we have to put up with in this house when these two get

together, Mr Irving," Elizabeth smiled.

"I find it most refreshing, Lady Rutherford. It's the sign of a happy home."

"I do believe you're right, Mr Irving."

Matthew Irving had made a good first impression on the family he hoped to enter. Although it was Joanna he was determined to marry, to be accepted by her family was also important to him. He had few close relatives of his own, and, having lost both parents early in life, had been brought up by a maiden aunt, and it was his earnest wish to be favourably received by his future wife's family.

Before the ball commenced, Matthew found John alone in his study.

"Come in, Irving," John said in answer to the knock and the appearance of his guest's head round the door. "I've just escaped for a few minutes for a quiet smoke." John offered Matt a chair and a cigar.

"I'm glad of this opportunity to speak to you, sir," Matt said. "I will come straight to the point," he continued. "I am thirty-five years old. In addition to a large private income, I have a very successful practice in law, facts which tend to indicate that I know my own mind, and on that point, sir, I can assure you I do." He spoke with the confidence of an advocate sure of the justice of his case, stating the facts clearly himself so that his adversary had no chance of taking the initiative.

The point of the conversation was beginning to dawn on John, but he remained silent while Matt continued.

"I wish to marry Joanna. But before you raise the valid objection that, although I may know my own mind, she is too young to know hers, I can give an assurance that the marriage will not take place for three years. This will give her time to pass her examinations and to be certain that I am the man she wants. I realise there is an age gap, but it cannot be helped, and in any case, love overcomes such things. I am a very busy man, but I can promise that my wife and the children I hope to have will take first place in my life. Nothing will come before them."

When Matt had finished John sat for a moment blowing smoke into the air. He said, "Your legal training does you credit, Irving. I certainly cannot fault the way you have so expertly put your case. It is all very sudden, and loving fathers are notoriously reluctant to part with their daughters. I am no exception to this rule. Joanna, of course, is far too young to marry, but from what I've heard over the past few months she certainly appears to love you. So, as you very sensibly agree to wait for three years, I will give my consent on that condition." John rose from his chair and offered his hand which Matt eagerly grasped.

"There is one thing I ought to tell you," John continued. "I have already made enquiries about you in certain quarters, so I am not completely unaware of your background. Such is the father's protective instinct," John smiled and then added, "But I had not connected you with the young officer I met all those years ago. Now that I have, it is to your advantage."

As it was Joanna's ball Robert anticipated that no one of his own age would be invited. It was going to be a boring evening for him. However, he had been told that he must put in an appearance for Joanna's sake, but he need not stay to the end. He saw the musicians arrive in the hall and had then gone to his room for a bath. That finished, he dressed, in his dinner suit and then sat on the edge of the bed and read for half an hour before making the effort to go downstairs. He was feeling hungry now, and hoped he might be able to scrounge something to eat from the buffet which had been laid out in the dining-room. At the top of the staircase he wished he could lean over the banisters and slide down as he used to when he was younger, but restrained himself as a sacrifice to the cause of growing up. Sometimes this business of growing up could be a blasted nuisance, he thought, but when he heard the voices of his parents outside the drawing-room door, he was glad he hadn't given way to his impulse.

As he reached the bottom of the stairs and looked towards; the drawing-room an exclamation of surprise escaped his lips. "Oh, no!" he whispered to himself, for there was the girl with the long fair hair and her parents talking to his parents. He quickly turned to creep upstairs again. But it was too late. His mother had seen him.

"Robert." Elizabeth called.

He reluctantly went towards them, making sure not to look directly at the girl, and wondering what she was thinking. How hellishly embarrassing, he thought. What could he say to them? He really must stop making up stupid stories. He heard his mother introduce him, and shook hands with the three new arrivals. Their name was evidently Marsden. Elizabeth had been introduced to them by the vicar at a recent church function, and had invited them to the ball as a gesture to new neighbours, and to assist them to get to know other residents in the area.

"So this is the boy on the wall," said Mr Marsden, smiling at Robert. "That's what you're known as in our family. We've all been looking forward to meeting you, Robert, although I believe you have already met Wendy."

Robert smiled but didn't know what to say. He saw the girl grinning at him. "Which is your cell?" she asked innocently. "You know, the one they lock you in when you're very wicked."

John and Elizabeth looked at Wendy and then at Robert, both wondering what the girl was talking about. "Cell?" Elizabeth queried.

"Oh, you tell your mother. Robert. You're much better at telling stories than I am," Wendy urged.

"It's nothing, Mother, honestly." Robert tried to evade the question, but Elizabeth knew her son and her interest was aroused.

"Robert," Elizabeth rejoined in a tone of false severity and a flicker of a smile on her face. "What have you been up to now?"

"I only told Wendy this was a reform school," Robert admitted, going red in the face.

"Well I'm blessed!" exclaimed John. "You must excuse my son. I'm afraid his sense of humour is liable to get the better of him. But with the antics he gets up to, perhaps this should be a reform school."

They all laughed at Robert, and he, shyly grinning back at them, thought it was time to retreat. He made his excuses with the idea of getting away to the dining-room.

"Take Wendy with you. Robert dear, and get her a drink," Elizabeth suggested.

Robert hesitated, but, being unable to think of a good reason why he shouldn't, reluctantly took his guest to the dining-room, where, in silence, they both helped themselves to food and drink. Robert then went and sat down at a small table in the corner of the room, thinking that the girl might return to her parents. But she came and sat opposite him.

"If I'd known that reform schools served such good food I wouldn't have bothered to feed you this afternoon," said Wendy.

Robert gave her one of his winning smiles. "I'm sorry for teasing you," he said.

She looked at him seriously and said, "And there was I believing you were suffering all sorts of terrible punishments, and all the time you were living in luxury."

"I said I'm sorry," he replied, looking crestfallen.

Wendy burst out laughing. "Don't look so worried," she said, "It was quite fun really. We all had a good laugh about, it when I told my parents. I think I believed you at first. Almost, anyway."

"I bet your parents think I'm an absolute idiot."

"Of course they don't. It was only a joke, after all."

Robert felt reassured, and began to find Wendy pleasant company,

"What a lovely house," she said, looking up at the high ceiling. "You must be terribly rich."

"I suppose we are. I've never really thought about it, and father never mentions it. He certainly doesn't let me have everything I ask for. I have to manage on one and six a week, which I suppose isn't too bad."

"Your father looks very kind."

"Not when he's angry," Robert replied.

"Can you dance?" Wendy inquired.

"A bit. Would you like to try?" Robert felt a little nervous at the thought of holding a girl in his arms. In his view, dancing and girls had come under the same heading – soppy. That is until recently when it was noticeable that his attitude had begun to change, and he had asked Elizabeth to teach him the steps of the popular dances. He had practised with Joanna when, she had been home from college one week-end, but he'd never danced with anyone else.

"Oh, yes, I'd love to!" Wendy replied enthusiastically.

The house had now filled with guests and there was little room on the dance floor when they arrived in the drawing-room. "Let's wait for a slow waltz," Robert suggested, thinking he would be less likely to make a fool of himself with the simple step and the slow speed.

The floor cleared after the quickstep, and after a short interval, the band started again with the slow waltz.

"Come on," said. Wendy, taking his hand. She felt his hand shaking and gripped it harder.

Let's wait a minute," Robert suggested. "We don't want to be first on the floor."

"Are you nervous?" she smiled.

"No, of course not!" he lied. "I hope I don't tread on your toes, though."

"Don't worry, I won't mind."

After two other couples had taken to the floor, Robert plucked up courage and followed suit. It was pleasant taking her hand, but when he put his arm round her and lightly touched her waist the sensation made him catch his breath. He had held his mother and sister when practising his dancing steps, but it had not been, like this. He had thought it stupid when he had seen older boys putting their arms round girls, but perhaps it wasn't so stupid after all, he decided.

He made the first few steps holding Wendy away from him so that he could, look down at his feet and avoid treading on her.

"No, Robert, not like that," she said, stopping for a moment. She pulled him close so that their bodies were touching, and held him firmly round the waist. "Like this. Relax. Don't be so tense." she added.

Robert couldn't have answered if he had tried, and allowed her to do with him as she wished. The closeness of her body had taken his breath away, and he could feel his heart beating faster with excitement.

"That's better," she said, as they started, to dance again.

When the dance was over Robert considered he had done quite well, having managed to avoid standing on his partner's feet. But it was the thrill of being able to hold a girl close that made him return to the dance floor as often as he could during the evening.

Unfortunately for Robert, he was, from time to time, dragged away by his parents from this new found pleasure to be introduced to some of the guests who had expressed a wish to meet him. One of these was the present commanding officer of John's old battalion, a rather crusty man, Robert thought, with a fierce looking moustache.

"This is my son, Robert," said John.

Robert shook hands and then stood to attention waiting to be spoken to.

"Well, you're a fine, strapping young man, Robert. How old are you, boy?" asked the colonel.

"Fifteen, sir."

"It won't be long now before we have you at Sandhurst, eh what! Looking forward to it?"

"I'm not sure, sir."

"What's this? Not sure!"

Robert felt himself go hot under the collar. He wondered what his father was thinking and hoped he wouldn't be angry with his evasive answers. "I don't think I'm clever enough for Sandhurst, sir."

"Nonsense! You're your father's son, and that's good enough for the army. One day I hope to see you in command of the battalion. Just you make sure of it, young man."

"Yes, sir." Robert's reply was unconvincing, and he saw his father look hard at him. The introduction over he quickly made his way back to Wendy.

When he arrived back at her side he found her talking to one of Joanna's college friends. "Oh, you must be Robert," said the young man.

Oh, must I, thought Robert. He didn't like the other's condescending manner, or his flattened greasy hair. Where *does* Joanna dig these people up from, he wondered? "Yes," he replied.

"I'm Mark Bailey, one of your sister's friends."

Robert made no reply, hoping the young man would go away, because he wanted to return to the dance floor so that he could put his arm round Wendy again. But Mark didn't go away and seemed determined to engage the two youngsters in conversation, or more correctly, to lecture them on subjects on which he considered himself an expert.

Politics seemed to be uppermost in his mind, and he explained that, as the capitalists were ruining the country, he had joined the communist party to further the cause of the revolution.

"What revolution?" Robert inquired.

"The workers revolution, of course. Like they had in Russia."

"Who wants a rotten revolution like that. All that killing. I hate killing!" Robert retorted.

"Don't we all? But sometimes it can't be helped when you are trying to bring freedom to the people."

"They didn't have to kill the Czar and all his family," Robert snapped, glaring at Mark.

Wendy thought Robert, sounded quite angry, and looked at him admiringly.

"That was necessary for the good of the cause and it couldn't be helped," Mark replied evenly.

"It wasn't necessary and it damn well could be helped!" Robert snapped back. He remembered his father discussing this very subject quite recently at the dinner table. "Fancy killing women and children," he went on. "Those reds were just a lot of rotten murderers, and you should be ashamed of yourself for standing up for them. You and your stupid revolutions!" It was not often that Robert lost his temper, but people like Mark annoyed him with all their silly talk about causes. It was the way this sort of person was prepared to overlook the murder of innocent people because it happened to suit their politics that made him unable to restrain himself from answering back. Robert knew little about the subject, but he had listened intently to what his father had said, and had formed definite opinions as to the rights and wrongs of the matter. Some of the guests standing nearby turned their heads to see who it was raising his voice in such indignation.

"You cheeky young puppy! What do you know about it?" stammered the much subdued Mark indignantly.

Robert ignored the last remark, and taking Wendy by the hand firmly pulled her away to their small secluded table tucked away in the corner of the dining-room. He sat her down, and, fetching two drinks from the bar, sat down opposite her.

"You're very forceful when you're angry," Wendy grinned. She had enjoyed seeing Robert put the young man in his place, and had also been impressed by the firm way he had taken her by the hand and pulled her away,

"I shouldn't have lost my temper, but I hate killing, and stupid politics for that matter. That Mark is such a show off." He then added mournfully. "But I suppose I'll have to apologize."

"Why should you! You were right."

"Maybe. But he's a guest, and it's a strict family rule that one must not be rude to guests. When Father finds out I'll be for it,"

"But it wasn't your fault."

"You tell that to my father."

"I will," Wendy replied with determination. "Anyway, what will he do about it?"

"Cane me, I expect."

"Cane you? Is this another one of your stories, Robert? Fathers don't do that sort of thing nowadays, do they?"

"Mine does. And I know some of my friends get it at home."

Wendy looked at him sympathetically. "You poor boy," she said. "Are you often caned?"

"Oh, no. Father's really very fair."

"Does it hurt terribly?"

Robert nodded.

At that moment Joanna arrived and sat herself down on Robert's knee with her arms round his neck. "Hallo you two! Enjoying yourselves? I bet you are from what I've seen," she laughed. "I say, Rob old thing, you certainly put Mark in his place. What a wheeze! It's about time someone shut him up about his silly old politics. He's quite nice really, just, a bit of a bore, that's all."

"But what if father finds out?" Robert asked.

"Don't worry, I've seen to it," Joanna laughed.

"Thanks sis, you're a real sport."

"Think nothing of it, old bean. Must rush, we're just about to announce our engagement."

"Engagement!" Robert exclaimed. But his sister had already disappeared out of the room.

"Isn't she terrific!" said Wendy."

"She's certainly useful at times," Robert admitted.

Robert went to fetch two more drinks, and when he returned to the table he pulled his chair round so the he was sitting beside Wendy. As they sat drinking he noticed her hand resting on the table, so, as he put down his glass, he made sure that his hand touched hers. She made no attempt to take it away, and very gradually he let his fingers entwine with hers.

"Your eyes are a lovely blue," he stammered. The excitement of touching her hand made him wish to say nice things to her. If only he could impress her by saying something really poetic. But he felt tongue-tied.

"Do you like me?" she asked modestly, lowering her eyes.

"I think you're very pretty."

"I bet you've had lots of girls," she grinned.

"I haven't had much to do with girls," Robert admitted.

"Haven't you ever kissed a girl?"

Robert coloured up and shook his head. He was finding the conversation really daring, and wondered what Wendy would say next.

"Would you like to kiss me?" she asked.

Robert's heart was pounding, and he found he could hardly speak with excitement. "Oh, yes!" he panted.

"So there you are! We've been looking everywhere for you." It was Wendy's mother who spoke and she was accompanied by Elizabeth.

Robert snatched his hand away from Wendy's and stood up feeling hot with embarrassment.

"It's one o'clock and time we were going," said Mrs Marsden.

"Oh, please Mummy, not yet. We were having such a good time," Wendy pleaded.

"So it would appear," her mother replied.

But Mrs Marsden would not relent, and much to Robert's irritation Wendy had to leave.

Damn and blast! Robert thought to himself as the front door closed on his new friend. Why did they have to go so early?" he pouted to Elizabeth,

"And who's the boy who didn't want to come to the ball and wasn't going to stay up late?" asked Elizabeth.

"Yes," said Joanna, who was also present, having just said, good-bye to her guests. "And who's the boy who thinks girls are soppy? I saw you holding hands."

"Oh, shut up!" Robert replied. "I'm going to bed," he added making his way up the stairs.

"Did you kiss her?" Joanna called after him.

"Certainly not!" he called back, feeling a sense of frustration at having been reminded of what he might have done if he'd been left with Wendy just a little longer.

"Damn! Damn! Damn!" he swore as he sat on the edge of the bed removing his shoes and socks. "Why the hell did she have to go?" But the moment had passed and he began to feel quite exhausted. Having stripped, he crawled into bed, and, imagining the kiss he might have had, fell asleep.

*

During the weeks that followed the ball Robert saw little of Wendy. They would smile at each other in church on Sunday morning, and meet briefly after the service in the presence of their parents. But Robert made no effort to further their friendship, because, for some reason, he now felt ashamed of the feelings that had come over him when they had been together that night. Besides this reason, there had been little time to spare. Being the summer term, cricket was occupying much of his spare time, and when he wasn't engaged with this he was being made to stay at home and study.

As with the three previous years 1934 was turning out to be another hot summer. By the middle of July the drought in the United States had already lasted 100 days and the heat wave had caused 50 deaths. But the good weather suited Robert's sporting activities, and even made the enforced studying more pleasant, because he was able to take his books to the summer house at the far end of the lawn and sit quietly reading in the evening sun. But even the sun couldn't alter his dislike for some of the subjects he was having to study, and his mind would often wander to more pleasant thoughts such as the coming visit of Karl Heinz and Lisa in the summer holidays.

At Easter the whole family had gathered at Grave with Jan and Flora, so by way of a change it had been decided that in the summer holiday they would gather in England.

From the moment the three cousins were together again it was as if they had never been apart. They needed nothing but one another's company to keep them happy, and the long summer days were spent swimming and lounging on the beach, or roaming on the downs. Sometimes they would meet with some of Robert's friends for cricket or some other game.

One particular Saturday had become sultry and the heat was oppressive. The youngsters had gone to the beach. Jan and Flora had remained in the drawing-room trying to keep cool, and John was working in his study. The rest of the family sat in the garden under the shade of a tree with Hugo on the ground propped up against the trunk, while the three women sat round in deck chairs.

"It wouldn't surprise me if there was a storm later on, it's so still," Kate remarked.

Maitland came across the lawn carrying a picnic hamper followed by Millicent carrying a rug. The rug was laid out on the grass and Maitland started to open the hamper.

"Thank you, Maitland, we can do the rest," said Elizabeth.

"Thank you, m'lady. I'll inform Sir John that luncheon is served, and I'll bring out the iced drink."

"Haven't seen, that maid before," Hugo remarked when the servants had gone.

"We've only had her for about four months," Elizabeth replied.

"Good looking girl."

"Trust you to notice that," said Kate.

John came out of his study through the French doors and crossed the lawn. "I'm damned if it's not hotter than India!" he exclaimed, wiping his forehead with his handkerchief. "It's all right for you lazy lot, but it's a hard life for us chaps who have to work for a living," he grinned. "I've been slaving away at that blasted report all morning and it's still not finished."

"You poor darling," Elizabeth sympathised. "Come and have some lunch." She had got up from her chair to serve the others with their food, and then sat down on the rug. "Let's sit back to back, John, just as we did on that glorious summer Sunday all those years ago in our first little house. Do you remember?"

"How could I ever forget? I can see it as if it was yesterday." John sat down and leant back on his wife. "It was the day the old world began to fall apart," he remembered.

"How times have changed," said Hugo.

"What does Karl think about the latest events in Germany?" John asked Natascha.

"He had no love for Rohm or any of the SA leaders. He thought they were getting too powerful, but he was shocked that they were gunned down like that. What worries me is that the purge was used to get rid of innocent people as well," Natascha replied.

"They were no doubt inconvenient to the government," John commented.

"And now that Hindenburg is dead, who is there to restrain Hitler," said Hugo.

"The army could if they had a mind to, but even they'll find it difficult now, having sworn allegiance to the man," said John. "Now he's put down the SA and is not only Chancellor but also Supreme Commander of the Armed Forces, I don't think it will be long before we see Mr Hitler's true colours."

Natascha said, "Karl still supports him. He believes he will do great things for Germany."

"We shall see," said John.

"Have things changed much?" Elizabeth asked Natascha.

"No, I don't think so. Our way of life is much the same." Natascha sounded uncertain and, hesitated in her answer as If she couldn't express herself as precisely as she would have liked. "Some things have improved. There's no more political street fighting, and crime has dropped dramatically. I must admit, though, I worry about the Hitler Youth Movement. It's beginning to control the lives of far too many of our young people. They've already taken over a number of other youth organisations. In my opinion, some of the young leaders have been given too much power and it's making them arrogant."

"I hope Karl Heinz isn't becoming arrogant," said Elizabeth."

"Thankfully, no. He's still an obedient boy. I think most German children are, it's only the few who aren't. In any case, Karl is still very strict with him." Natascha sighed, and then said, "I sometimes wonder what the future holds. I don't think I've mentioned it, but we've just been instructed that Karl Heinz is to attend one of the new National Political Institutes of Education. He's to start in September." Natascha went on to explain that the *Nationalpolitische Erziehungsanstalt* were new schools set up by the Party under the supervision of the SS for the education of the elite. They were to use a grammar school curriculum and restore the education formerly given at the old Prussian military academies. In addition, special training in national socialist principles was to be included. "In some ways," Natascha continued, "they are similar to the English public school with the prefect system and fagging."

"Have you no say in the matter?" Elizabeth inquired.

"None whatsoever. We cannot refuse to let him go. Evidently Karl Heinz has been noted as a promising boy, no doubt because of his rapid advance in the Hitler Youth. He is now a *Scharführer* which means he's in charge of a local branch of about fifty boys," Natascha replied.

John had finished his lunch and was getting to his feet to return to his work. "And what does Karl Heinz think about it?" he asked.

"He's thrilled and can't wait to go."

John made no comment. "I shall see you all later," he said, walking back across the lawn.

"Isn't Karl Heinz rather young to be in charge of fifty boys?" Hugo asked.

"I think he is," Natascha replied. "But the policy of the Hitler Youth is that youth should lead youth."

There was not a breath of wind that afternoon, and the curtains in John's study were hanging absolutely motionless even though the French doors were wide open. John did not return to his desk but sat in his favourite armchair which he had pushed behind the study door in the coolest part of the room. He sat there reading his report, but must have dosed off for a short time because he awoke to the sound of quiet voices in the passage outside the door, which was slightly ajar.

"I tell you I saw them, naked as the day they was born." It was Millicent's voice. She and Agnes must be preparing to take their afternoon off, he thought. They obviously didn't know he was there.

"And how did you come to see them?" Agnes was heard to ask.

"From my window I can see right down into Robert's room."

"Master Robert, to you!" Agnes exclaimed, indignant at the other's familiarity,

Millicent took no notice of the interruption and continued with her story. "And there they was with the light on and the curtains not drawn."

"You shouldn't have been peeping."

"I wasn't peeping. I was just drawing my curtains, and there they was having a right old time."

John heard Millicent giggle.

"It's no laughing matter, my girl. You ought to be ashamed of yourself," Agnes scolded.

"It wasn't my fault, I couldn't help it."

Agnes tried to sound disinterested, but she was determined to have the full facts. "What were they doing?" she asked.

"You know what boys do. Blimey, Agnes! Don't you know anything?"

"I know you're a young hussy, and that's the truth," Agnes replied indignantly.

But Millicent wasn't, to be put down so easily. "If you really want to know," she said, and then went on to describe in detail everything she had seen Robert and Karl Heinz do to each other. "And now you know," she added defiantly, and began to giggle again.

"That's quite enough!" came the reply as the voices faded.

For a moment John sat motionless, hardly believing his ears. Then he got up and started to pace the room. Could it be true that a son of his could do such things? The thought kept going round and round in his mind. Surely it's not possible? On the other hand why should the girl lie? Perhaps it is true and he is a blasted pansy in which case he would thrash it out of him.

He must have paced the room for half an hour trying to assess the matter calmly. He couldn't settle to his work anymore so he eventually returned to the garden and flung himself into a deck chair.

"You do look hot, schat. Let me pour you a drink," said Elizabeth.

He didn't answer, and Elizabeth saw the scowl on his face. She said nothing, but poured his drink and placed it on the table beside him, understanding him well enough to know that the reason for his irritation would be divulged in his own time.

John sat in silence sipping his drink. The others saw he was brooding on something. His mind went over the whole matter again and again. Is it possible the boys were doing this sort of thing? It had happened in the dorm at school, not that he'd ever taken part, so why should his son be unnatural? But the boy did have a soft streak in him, what with his music and dislike of horses. Yet he doesn't look effeminate, and he doesn't act like it. And then there's Karl Heinz. He's a tough young nut. Nothing sissy about him either. Perhaps it's not true and the girl was joking or lying? No, she wouldn't make up a story like that. How the devil was he going to broach the subject with Natascha? It was a damn nuisance that Karl wasn't here, it would have been easier to discuss with a man. Perhaps he should forget the matter? No damn it! The boy must be confronted, and he couldn't deal with Robert without involving Karl Heinz, so he must speak to Natascha.

"What's the matter, John, you look as black as thunder," said Natascha cheerfully.

John did not reply immediately, his mind fighting to find the most suitable and diplomatic words. Eventually he said, "I have something .to say, but I'm not sure how to start. To tell the truth I don't know how to say it in front of you ladies."

"Would you like us to leave you alone with Hugo?" Natascha asked, trying to be helpful.

"No, no!" John exclaimed emphatically. "It concerns you."

"Oh dear! What have I done?" she said, putting both hands on her heart feigning surprise.

John was in no mood for her humour. "Do try to be serious just for a moment, Natascha."

"I'm sorry, John, please go on."

"It's about the boys," he began.

"What about them?"

"If you'd kindly be patient, I'll explain." He paused and the others looked at him in anticipation. He was beginning to wish he had not brought up the subject, but, having done so, was now determined to go on with it. "It's come to my notice," he began again, but this time he was interrupted by Elizabeth.

"John dear, don't sound so pompous."

"I'm trying to find the right words," he replied impatiently. "Kindly let me finish." He paused again and then said, "The boys have been doing things to each other."

"What sort of things, dear?" Elizabeth asked innocently.

"They were in their bedroom without any clothes on, and were doing things that they should not have been doing."

"He means, masturbating." Natascha cut in nonchalantly, giving John a provocative look.

Kate looked shocked. Hugo, on the other hand, was never surprised at anything his sister came out with. Elizabeth sat composed, seemingly unaffected by the forbidden tunnel. She glanced at Natascha but said nothing.

"Good heavens, Natascha!" John exploded. "Do you have to be so damned indelicate! I was trying to spare your feelings." He felt quite put out, and his face flushed with embarrassment.

Natascha looked at her brother-in-law with a twinkle in her eye and said, "My dear John, for goodness sake stop looking so serious. You're talking to the van der Leydens. We're not prudes, you know. And let me remind you," she went on in a more serious vein, "that I am a doctor and know a great deal more about this sort of thing than you do. Fancy you, an army man and a man of the world, making such a fuss." She had a great affection and respect for John, but wanted, to make it perfectly clear to him that she was a woman of experience and wished to discuss all matters on equal terms. Natascha had seen life. She had served in the German army field hospitals during the war, and, since then she had assisted Karl build up his practice. Her knowledge and understanding was extensive. "And kindly stop treating us like innocent school children," she scolded.

John mopped his brow with his handkerchief. "I'm sorry, Natascha, that wasn't my intention at all," he said. "But this sort of thing worries me. Who knows what it might lead to, and supposing they develop feminine tendencies."

"Oh, John, what nonsense! Surely you know your own son. I certainly know mine, and, I can tell you there's nothing wrong with either of them. You're worrying unnecessarily." Natascha was now speaking not only seriously, but with a force of argument which quite surprised John. "I do know about this sort of thing, I've had a lot to do with the young."

Elizabeth had remained silent, thinking it best to let the other two deal with the matter. Hugo and Kate had discreetly taken a walk round the garden.

"Are you saying that nothing should be done about it?" John asked.

"Our boys are not perfect, John, I realise that. But as you say in this country boys will he boys, and that's just what they are being. I think it best to ignore the matter, because it'll come to an end quite naturally. Most boys go through this stage, but they'll soon get over it when they begin to notice the girls."

"Well, I respect your point of view," John replied. "But I'm not prepared to let the matter rest. It's my intention to question Robert, and if what I've heard is true I shall cane him." He felt he must demonstrate to the boy that what he'd done was wrong, and that it must be stopped before it went further. "It could develop into other abuses," he added.

"Does he have to be beaten?" Elizabeth asked quietly. "Perhaps another punishment would be more suitable."

"I've made my decision, Beth."

"I think you'll be making matters worse," Natascha declared. "There's nothing wrong with our boys. Their eyes are already on the girls. But I won't argue the matter if that's your decision. If Robert is to be punished then Karl Heinz must be punished as well. I shall leave it in your hands,"

Elizabeth said, "Are they not too old to be caned, dear? They are fifteen."

"Certainly not! They're still boys and will receive a boy's punishment." John replied rather more sharply than he intended. He could not abide weakness when dealing with boys and believed that swift punishment should follow a misdemeanour. He got up from his chair and started to walk back to his study. "Send them to me directly they return," he called back.

When he had gone the two sisters looked, at each other, and Elizabeth said, "You must forgive John. I'm afraid he's developed a phobia over the years that Robert could become unnatural. It seemed to stem from the time when Robert refused to ride. The boy dislikes horses, and John just cannot understand it, although what that's got to do with being unnatural I can't imagine. And then there's Robert's music. John doesn't believe it's a suitable pastime for a man, or at least not for his son. Thank heavens for cricket! At least that redeems Robert in John's eyes."

The conversation gradually died away and both women lay back in their chairs and gazed up lethargically at the cloudless sky. It was too hot even for reading, thought Elizabeth as she let her book fall to the ground. The buzz of insects in the shrubbery and the faint sound of traffic on the London Road at the end of the drive was all that disturbed the stillness of the afternoon. Hugo and Kate had returned from their stroll in the grounds and lay listlessly on the rug with their eyes closed.

The sound of the front door slamming followed by laughter and happy voices came from the house. "They're back," Hugo smiled. "Peace over." A moment later the three youngsters burst out on to the lawn from the back door. The boys kicked off their sandals and each grabbed one of Lisa's hands and ran as fast as they could across the lawn dragging her with them. Up the slope at the end on to the upper lawn they went, and then down again with Lisa laughing and screaming for them to stop. When they arrived in front of their parents Lisa dropped to the ground out of breath, and the boys stood leaning against each other with their arms round each other's shoulders.

"That'll teach you to put ice cream down my bathing costume," panted Karl Heinz.

"You shouldn't have ducked me in the first place," laughed his cousin.

Elizabeth looked at the boys standing in front of her. Each wore only a pair of khaki shorts. They were old shorts specially kept for beach wear. She considered they were beginning to grow out of them, but at least they weren't those dreadful long shorts that some English boys were forced to wear. What a picture of health and energy they look, she thought. Their strong, well proportioned bodies, the fair smooth skin browned by the sun, and their fair hair falling forward over their foreheads. Their hair was not quite so fair as it had been when they were younger. They were tall for their age, but they had always grown in proportion to their height and neither had gone through the lanky stage. How alike they were. John must be wrong. They cannot be what he fears. But still, they will have to be punished. What a pity to ruin this happy scene. She had always hated it when Robert was caned, and could not bring herself to break the bad news to them.

Natascha had no such qualms. "You boys are in trouble," she said. "Uncle John wants to see you in his study."

"What have we done?" asked Karl Heinz.

"It's possible you've been very naughty boys, and if so your interview is going to be painful," Natascha replied.

"Oh, no!" Robert exclaimed. He nervously put his hands on his buttocks and looked at his cousin. He tried to rack his brain to think what they had done, but even though he couldn't think of anything a cold sweat came over his brow and he knew he was looking guilty.

The conversation had made Lisa sit up, but far from being downcast she appeared to be enjoying her cousins' discomfort. "Perhaps you'd better put on some thicker pants," she suggested, teasing them. "On the other hand don't bother, because Uncle will sure to whack your bare bottoms."

"Shut up, you!" Robert snapped, knowing what she said was true and trying to cover his fear.

"Stop it, you two!" ordered Natascha, waving the boys away to their unwanted appointment.

They crossed the lawn, unspeaking, with their heads bowed. They did not enter the study by the open French doors, but went into the house and knocked on the door. John called them in and looked at them sternly.

God! He's in one of those moods, thought Robert, remembering previous times when his father had beaten him. He saw the cane hanging menacingly over the back of a chair and his stomach turned over."

John was also feeling uncomfortable and was still unsure how to handle the matter, but he was used to hiding his feelings.

The boys stood before John. Karl Heinz standing at attention looking directly at his uncle. Robert standing straight but with his arms behind his back twisting his fingers in his nervousness.

When John spoke Robert felt his inside jump. "Robert, is it true that you two boys carried out certain disgraceful acts with each other last night?" John spoke sternly, looking piercingly at his son.

"I don't know what you mean, sir." Robert tried to sound innocent, but he didn't feel innocent.

"You know very well what I mean. Now, were you doing things together that you shouldn't have been doing without any clothes on?"

"No, sir," Robert lied. He looked at the floor, wishing it would open up and swallow him. He didn't know why he had lied. It just seemed to slip out, and he felt sick in his stomach.

John wondered for a moment whether what he had overheard was not true, but he knew in his heart that his son was lying. "Look at me, boy. I'll ask you once more. Did you commit any shameful act last night?"

"No, sir," Robert stammered, looking down at the floor again. He noticed the curtain at the French doors move slightly and glancing up saw Lisa peeping through.

He heard his father speaking again, this time to Karl.

"Karl Heinz, I now ask you. If you can confirm what Robert has said that will be the end of the matter. Did you and Robert do the things I have mentioned?"

Karl Heinz bit his lip, his mind in turmoil. He loved his cousin, and it would, hurt him deeply to betray him as a liar. But he was a German boy and a Scharführer in the Hitler Youth and he had been taught it was dishonourable and weak to lie. To lie would be to betray the Fatherland and he could not do it. His uncle was looking hard at him and he heard him say, "I'm waiting for an answer, Karl Heinz. Is it true or not?"

"Yes, Uncle," the boy replied.

"Oh God, no!" Robert whispered. He wished he could run from the room, but felt rooted to the floor. He could never face Father again. What would become of him? If only he hadn't lied.

"So Robert has lied to me, Karl Heinz?"

"I think he was only trying to protect me, Uncle."

"I'm sorry to say that I do not share your charitable opinion of him," said John, glaring at Robert in disgust. "Why did you lie to me, Robert?"

"I don't know, sir."

"Of course you know and I'll have an answer if you please." John felt his anger rising. He had meant to keep calm and not let his emotions cloud his better judgement, but was finding that Robert was frustrating his good intentions. "Look at me, boy, when you speak." Robert looked up and John saw a tear run down his son's cheek. "Please, I'm sorry, sir. I . . I" The boy's voice faded into silence.

"It appears to me that you are a liar and a coward, Robert. There seems to be no other explanation for your conduct."

His father's words had stung Robert like a whip lash. He had always know in his heart that this was his true nature, but to hear it said was as if the condemnation had been branded on his heart.

After a moment's silence, John said, "I have nothing further to say except that these goings on between you will stop. There is only one suitable punishment for you and that's a damn good beating."

The boys looked at each other but remained silent. From outside the french doors Lisa saw the boys remove their shorts. She loved them both, and of one thing she was certain, that sometime in the future she would take one of them for herself, and she knew in her heart which one it was to be. Her heart beat faster when she saw Karl Heinz bend over a chair. She knew she shouldn't be watching, and yet couldn't drag herself away. She found her feelings impossible to understand. Perhaps she wanted proof of their manliness, or just wished to be able to comfort them afterwards. Whatever it was she had to see it happen.

Robert couldn't take his eyes from his suffering cousin, and with each swish and crack of the cane he winced in anticipation of his own punishment to come. He counted six strokes and braced himself to take Karl. Heinz's place over the chair, but to his horror the beating continued with Karl Heinz gasping with the pain. Even Karl Heinz couldn't prevent himself from crying out as the tenth, eleventh and twelfth strokes cut into him. When it was over Karl Heinz stood up biting his lip, his face contorted in agony and tears running down his cheeks. He gripped his buttocks as he stiffly walked to the armchair to retrieve his shorts.

Robert went forward and bent over the chair. Out of the corner of his eye he saw Lisa still watching, but then even she was blotted from his mind as the first stroke cut into him and took his breath away. With tears flooding from his eyes he tried desperately not to cry out, but after six strokes the pain was so excruciating he could no longer control his feelings, and he began to sob without restraint. Each stroke felt as if a red hot poker had been laid across his buttocks. He cried out and squirmed in agony, wondering how much more he could take. When he thought it had finished he heard his father say, "And now six more for lying."

How he got through the final cuts he never knew. When it was over, he stood for a moment in agony grasping his backside as if trying to tear out the pain. Then, unable to bear it any longer and not waiting for Karl Heinz or stopping to put on his shorts, he fled from the room. Outside the study he almost ran into Millicent, who had just returned from her afternoon out and hearing the sounds of punishment had been listening at the door. But he didn't care. Neither did he care who else witnessed his shame as he ran up the stairs to his bedroom, feeling his buttocks were on fire. He slammed the bedroom door behind him and flung himself on to his bed to sob his heart out.

Karl Heinz had stood waiting to be dismissed.

"Go to your room, Karl Heinz, and stay there for the rest of the day," said John in a slightly less severe tone.

"Yes, Uncle," Karl Heinz whispered painfully.

John's anger had subsided, and he now felt that perhaps he had been a little hard on the boys. But then he always felt like this after caning Robert. But why did the boy have to lie to him, he asked himself? As a straightforward man he couldn't abide liars, and he was finding it difficult to understand his son. Perhaps he would speak to Elizabeth about the boy. She seemed to understand him.

The sharp witted Millicent had returned to the kitchen where she found Mrs Hicks preparing dinner. Agnes was also there.

"You're late, my girl," said Mrs Hicks crossly. She was not quite sure what to make of this girl. She worked well, but as Agnes had said, she's too clever by half.

"No I'm not, Mrs Hicks. I was in before six."

"Then where've you been?" put in Agnes as if she had at last caught the girl out with a master stroke of interrogation.

Millicent ignored the question, and with a smug look on her face, said, "There'll be two less for dinner tonight, Mrs Hicks."

"How do you know?" asked the cook.

"The master has just given them two boys a right whopping and sent them to bed."

"Have you been listening at keyholes again?" Agnes asked sharply.

"No I haven't!" said the girl indignantly. "I could hear it all without that, and then Master Robert comes running out without a stitch on. I ask you, what an innocent girl has to put up with in this house. I bet it was all about what I was telling you, Agnes."

"And what was that, might I ask?" Mrs Hicks inquired.

"It's as well you don't know, Mrs Hicks, a lady like yourself," Agnes replied. Then turning to Millicent she wagged, her finger and said, "You'll get the sack if you're not careful, my girl. You and your gossip. And there's nothing innocent about you."

There was a knock and Lisa poked her head round the kitchen door. "Excuse me, Mrs Hicks, but my aunty says to tell you that there will be two less for dinner tonight."

"Thank you, miss."

A look of satisfaction came over Millicent's face, but as Lisa was present, she said nothing further.

Lisa went up to the cook and quietly told her that the boys had been sent to their room without dinner. "Do you think you could give me something to take up to them, Mrs Hicks?" she asked.

"Of course, dear. You come back after dinner and I'll have something ready for you."

"Thanks, Mrs Hicks, you're a real sport."

When Lisa had gone Millicent said, "There, I told you so!" But, much to her disappointment, the other two women did not pursue the conversation.

Karl Heinz, who had now managed to control his tears, had returned to the bedroom and painfully removed his shorts. He lay on his bed beside Robert and put his arm round his weeping cousin's shoulders. Robert's tears were now due as much to frustration at what he considered his cowardice than to the pain, which was still bad enough. He wished he was dead. Why did he have to cry so much when Karl Heinz managed to control himself?

After a few minutes, Robert, his voice still shaking as he tried to get the words out, asked sulkily, "Why did you have to tell him?"

"I had to. It's dishonourable to lie. You know that." Karl Heinz spoke softly but with conviction.

Robert couldn't object to his cousin's answer, because he knew it was true.

"You know the Hitler Youth are taught not to lie, not to cheat and not to steal. If we're weak we can't serve the Fatherland, and that's a dishonour."

"I lied," Robert said miserably, the tears still flowing down his cheeks. "Why am I so weak? And why am I such a coward?"

"You're not really, Rob. You just made a mistake, that's all. It could happen to anyone," Karl Heinz comforted.

"It didn't happen to you. And why do I cry more than you?"

"You're sensitive, you're not a coward. Besides, you got a bigger thrashing than I did," Karl Heinz replied.

"I hate Father. He's a bloody swine, flogging us like that!" Robert blurted out. He buried his face in the pillow, trying to put the pain out of his mind.

"You shouldn't say things like that. It's not like you, Rob," Karl Heinz scolded.

Robert lifted his face from the pillow, feeling ashamed that he should be rebuked by his cousin. He said, "We are brothers, aren't we?"

"Of course we are and always will be."

"Nothing can change that, can it?"

"What could possibly change it?"

"I don't know. Maybe it won't be the same when we grow up. Grown-ups seem different somehow."

"Of course it'll be the same. You worry too much, Rob. Nothing will ever come between us." Karl Heinz took his arm from Robert's shoulder and held it out. He pointed to the small scar on the forearm. "You haven't forgotten that?"

Robert shook his head.

"Well, nothing has changed, and nothing will."

Robert examined his own scar, and catching his cousin's confidences his black mood and fears for the future began to fade.

For some time the boys lay still and quiet in the heat of the evening. The red, hot burning sensation on their backsides having turned into a fiery glow and a constant throbbing as the blood pulsated along their weals. The bedroom windows were open but there was not a breath of wind. They heard the distant voices of their parents coming from the far end of the lawn, and the chink of cups and saucers as the butler served after dinner coffee. Robert was feeling hungry to say nothing of feeling thirsty, and he would have given anything for a cool drink. He ran his hand lightly over his bottom and let his fingers go up and down across the weals. He knew from past experience that it was going to be painful to sit down for some days. He wondered how many days, because he had never been beaten so severely before.

"What do you think of Lisa, Robert?" Karl Heinz broke the silence.

"I think she's a rotten sod, and I'd like to get my hands on her. Fancy peeping like that. It's a pity she doesn't get thrashed, and then perhaps she wouldn't be so keen to watch others."

"I didn't mean like that."

"What did you mean then?"

"Do you ever think of her as more than just a cousin?"

"As a sort of girl friend, you mean?"

"Yes, that's it."

Robert thought for a moment. He had to admit to himself that there were occasions now when he felt she was more than just a playmate, and lately he had gained a certain pleasure from just looking at her. "I don't know, really." he replied. "Do you then?"

"Yes. Sometimes I feel I want to do things to her," said Karl Heinz.

"What sort of things?"

"You know. Like we do to each other." Karl Heinz smiled and bashfully buried his face in the pillow.

"How can you do that to a girl? They're different.

Karl Heinz felt he was not making himself understood. "I know that. I don't mean exactly the same, but wouldn't you like to see her without any clothes on?"

"Of course I would," Robert replied. He began to feel uncomfortable lying on his front. Lately he had imagined this sort of thing when lying in bed at night and found that it had excited him.

Nothing more was said, but the talk of Lisa had stirred their feelings and they were unable to resist what John had forbidden happening again. Both boys were so engrossed with each other that they failed to notice Lisa enter the room holding a tray on which was the supper she had obtained for them. When they did notice her, for a moment neither boy knew what to do. Then they quickly flung themselves on to their stomachs, covering their shame.

"Get out!" Robert cried angrily.

"Oh, all right," said Lisa, nonchalantly turning and walking towards the door. "If you don't want any supper I'll just take it away again. Of course, I'll have to tell Uncle John what you were doing," she said as she reached the door."

They both called after her, pleading for her to come back, so she returned and sat at the foot of Karl Heinz's bed with the tray on her knees.

"You shouldn't creep in on us like that," Robert grumbled.

"I didn't creep in. I can't help it if you're such dirty beasts that you didn't hear me knock," she retorted, knowing very well she didn't knock."

"We're not dirty," snapped Karl Heinz.

"Then what are you so ashamed of?"

Neither boy could think of an answer to this so there was silence until Robert pleaded for her to look the other way while they put their shorts on.

"No," she said. "You'll stay as you are as a punishment."

"But we've been punished," said Karl Heinz.

"Obviously not enough."

"It's not fair, we never see you like this," Robert whined.

"No you don't, and you're not going to either. Now if you want your supper you had better turn over and take it," she instructed.

Karl Heinz was the first to move. He knew that Lisa had them at her mercy, and that it was useless to try and get the better of her. So he boldly turned over. He felt more ashamed at being in the power of a girl than by being caught in the act. But at least the girl was Lisa, and that wasn't so bad.

Robert saw his cousin hungrily tucking in to the food, but it was the ginger beer that finally overcame his embarrassment and forced him to turn over and join the feast. But he had to fire a last desperate shot at Lisa in an effort, to make her feel guilty. "You shouldn't have watched the caning," he said.

But if Lisa felt any remorse she didn't show it. "Didn't you squeal and squirm," she said to Robert with relish.

"I do believe you enjoyed it. You're a bloody sadist!" he snapped back.

"What's a sadist?"

"I don't know, but whatever it is you're one."

In a short time there was nothing left on the tray. The boys lay back on their beds satisfied and in a better frame of mind. They had to admit to themselves that they were glad Lisa was with them even though she was obviously enjoying herself at their expense.

After they had eaten she made them lie face down. They were beyond argument and meekly obeyed. She then brought in a bowl of warm water from the bathroom and gently bathed their wounds, and after drying them she tenderly applied some soothing cream to their weals.

Robert had never felt such rapture as her smooth fingers moved over him. Her touch was so exquisitely light. He had never been touched like this before. But it was not, only her touch that had stirred new feelings within him, but the very fact that she should want to nurse him and relieve his pain. The adventures with Karl Heinz satisfied the desires of his young body, but this was somehow different. His whole being was involved, and although he was still too young and immature to realise it the early dawn of love would soon be bringing new light into his life. Where the cane had failed to change his desires, the gentle hands of a girl might succeed.

In the cool of the evening the rest of the family sat out on the lawn in front of the summer house. The high spirits and chatter of the young ones was absent, much to the disappointment of Jan and Flora, who had ventured out of the house now that the heat of the day had subsided. The conversation was spasmodic and John sat moodily sipping his drink but saying little.

"You're not still brooding over those wretched boys?" Elizabeth asked him.

"I suppose I am."

"You certainly didn't spare the rod from what I heard."

"Robert lied to me."

"He was probably afraid, schat."

"Surely you're not condoning it, Beth?"

"Certainly not. He was very wrong, but you can be rather terrifying sometimes." She smiled at him lovingly.

"What utter rubbish! You know damn well the whole pack of you twist me round your little fingers. Especially you women."

"I must admit that we women do get the better of you on occasions, but it's different for Robert, he hasn't got our feminine wiles. He's afraid of you sometimes."

The conversation had done nothing to comfort John's feelings, in fact it had added to his problems. Why on earth should the boy fear him so much as to lie? He didn't want that. "Karl Heinz didn't lie; neither did he cry as much. I sometimes fear Robert's going to turn out...Well, you know what I mean."

Natascha looked at John and said, "We all worry for our children, John dear. Perhaps Karl Heinz doesn't cry enough. Sometimes I imagine that one day tears will be all he has left, and then it'll be too late to cry."

"There's no need to worry about either of them," said Hugo. "They're both fine boys, and you should think yourselves lucky you've got them. I wish I had sons like them."

"Well said, Hugo," Flora concluded, as they all got up to move into the house.

Robert took a long time to get to sleep that night, what with the heat and his throbbing backside. When morning came he lay wondering whether he had slept at all. He managed to drag himself out of bed, but as he walked to the window every step felt as if his weals were being torn open. Agnes came in and ran his bath, suggesting it might ease his discomfort. It did up to a point, but he was unable to sit on the hard enamel surface so had to kneel or lie down during the operation.

He asked Agnes if she would sneak same food up to the bed-room so that they didn't have to go down for breakfast.

"I suppose you're too ashamed to be seen at breakfast," she replied.

Robert didn't reply but gave her one of his pleading looks, which she couldn't resist, and breakfast duly arrived on a tray.

Karl Heinz, who had been sleeping soundly, eventually awoke and forced himself out of bed. Both boys, knowing they had to attend church that morning, put on their grey suits and eventually ventured downstairs. They waited in the drawing-room for the rest of the family to assemble for the walk to church, but neither wished to sit down so they both lent across the grand piano. Hugo came in, and much to their surprise, spoke to them as if nothing had happened. They had been expecting everyone to ignore them, such was their disgrace.

Robert thought it was good to have Uncle Hugo around, because he was so understanding. He had never known him to be angry or miserable, just a pleasant, steady type of person.

As the rest of the family put in their appearance one by one no mention was made of the boys disgrace. Natascha was amused by their posture over the piano. The butler came in and announced that Miss Wendy Marsden had called asking for Master Robert.

"I can't see her," said Robert, feeling embarrassed.

"Robert! Don't be so rude and unkind;" Elizabeth scolded. "Please show her in, Maitland."

Seeing that Robert made no attempt to go forward and greet his guest, Elizabeth did it for him. "Come in, my dear," she said, putting her arm round the girl's shoulders and introducing her to the family.

Wendy had called to ask if she might accompany the family to church that morning as her mother was not well. "Of course, dear, we are pleased to have you," said Elizabeth.

Oh no we're not, thought Robert. He knew he was being unkind and couldn't understand why. He had enjoyed her company at the ball, but afterwards feeling ashamed for letting his emotions rise and for wanting to kiss her, he had avoided meeting her again. He still wanted to kiss her, and he wanted to kiss Lisa, as well. Why was life so complicated, he wondered? He furtively glanced at both girls. Lately, the mere thought of them had an unsettling effect on him, and new desires had begun to disturb his mind and body. Both girls were so good looking in their different ways. One so open and fair with bright smiling eyes, the other dark with her mysterious thoughts hidden behind that beautiful face.

John entered the room but ignored the boys. Elizabeth brought Wendy across to Robert and then everyone made to leave the house, the youngsters bringing up the rear.

Wendy asked Robert why she hadn't seen him lately, but finding his reasons unconvincing didn't pursue the subject. Robert tried not to sound offhand but felt he hadn't succeeded, for the girl looked unhappy at his attitude. He really mustn't be so rotten to her, he chided himself.

On the way to church she noticed that he was walking stiffly as if in pain, and that he kept putting his hands on his bottom.

"Are you all right, Robert?" she asked with concern.

"Of course I am," he snapped.

"It's all right, Wendy," Lisa chuckled, "He was flogged yesterday, and he's got a sore bottom."

"Do you have to tell everybody?" Robert retorted angrily.

But Wendy didn't take Lisa's light hearted view of Robert's discomfort and was obviously upset by the fact that he was in pain, but her concern only seemed to irritate him all the more so she relapsed into silence.

The hard church seats ensured that the service was torture for the boys, and a lot of the time they spent fidgeting much to the annoyance of John, who, from time to time, glared at them in an effort to make them keep still. If Father doesn't like him fidgeting he bloody well shouldn't have made him came to church, Robert thought defiantly.

After the service Robert and Karl Heinz escaped from the church as quickly as possible, and Lisa had to run and catch them up along the road. Wendy hadn't been so quick off the mark and had remained behind with the rest of the family while they chatted to friends and the vicar at the church door.

"Wait for me you two!" called Lisa. "What's the hurry?"

Robert replied, "I want to get home. I must get this suit off, it's so blinking hot."

As they passed the end of one of the roads leading off the main road, Karl Heinz exclaimed, "Hey, look up there! Isn't, that your friend Albert? Looks like he's being bashed up."

Robert followed his gaze and saw a boy he knew from the farm cottages lying on the grass verge about a hundred yards away with, a much bigger boy sitting on him. The boy held Albert down by the wrists and was kneeling on the muscles of his arms, causing him to cry out in pain. Three other boys stood watching, enjoying the fun.

Without hesitation Karl Heinz pulled Robert by the arm and started towards the boys. "Come on!" he cried.

But Robert didn't share his cousin's enthusiasm. "They're bigger than we are," he objected. "And there's four of them."

"Can't be helped," Karl Heinz replied," not slackening his pace,

Albert was in tears when Karl Heinz and Robert reached him. "Get off, you bloody bully!" growled Karl Heinz, but the boy just looked at him with contempt and made no attempt to comply.

"Who's going to make me?" he sneered.

But Karl Heinz had not come for a verbal battle and just, threw himself on the boy. The two of them went sprawling on the grass, and so violent was the attack that two of the other boys went to their friend's assistance. Seeing this, Robert made a half hearted attempt to stand in their way, but his school cap was snatched from his head and went flying into the road. He was pushed in the face for his trouble; making him fall backwards and sit down heavily on the grass. He let out a cry of agony as his raw buttocks touched the ground. The hard push had caught Robert on the end of his nose and made it bleed, and if there was one thing certain to make him lose his temper it was to be struck on the nose. In a flash he was on his feet again his fists flailing at his assailant's face with such ferocity that the unfortunate boy's nose also began to bleed. Robert felt himself gripped round the waist from the rear as the third boy attempted to control him. But Robert was struggling so violently that all three of them fell to the ground on top of Karl Heinz and the other boy.

Lisa stood watching the twisting mass of bodies and the flailing arms and legs as the fight continued on the grass. There were four bicycles lying on the grass nearby belonging to the boys, so she did no more than start letting down one of the tyres. The fourth boy, who had not yet joined the scrum, came rushing over to stop her.

"You put one hand on me and I'll jump on the spokes," she threatened, forcing the boy to back off. But it wasn't just Lisa's threat that made him pick up his bike and prepare to ride away. He called urgently to his friends, but they were too involved in the fight to hear, so he disappeared down the hill on his own, riding on a half flat tyre in his panic. Lisa had also seen the policeman approaching.

Mr White was a tall, brawny man, who had been the local policeman for a number of years. He knew how to deal with boys as Robert had found out early in life. His majestic figure stood looking down at the heaving mass before him, waiting to be noticed. One by one the boys saw the uniform and the fighting gradually ceased.

It didn't take the policeman long to assess the situation, and having taken the names and addresses of the three bigger boys and made the usual dire threats about what was to happen to them - threats he had no intention of carrying out - he sent them on their way. He then turned his attention to Robert and Karl Heinz, who stood before him with grass stained suits, and bruised faces. Robert's nose had stopped bleeding but the blood had covered his white shirt and school tie, and had spotted the front of his jacket.

"I'll not 'ave fighting in my streets, young Robert," said the policeman.

"No, Mr White," Robert replied.

"It wasn't their fault, Mr White," piped up Albert.

"Speak when your spoken to, Albert Thompson," commanded the policeman. "When I want your advice I'll ask for it."

Albert said no more.

When Mr White enquired what Robert's father would say on hearing his son had been fighting in the street, Robert felt weak at the knees. "I dread to think, Mr White," he answered.

Lisa retrieved Robert's cap, and then they all returned to the main road just in time to meet the rest of the family returning home. Elizabeth was horrified when she saw the state of the two boys and the presence of the policeman. "Whatever's happened? Just look at the state of you," she said to the boys. "Has there been an accident, Mr White?"

The boys were sent on home while their parents spoke to the policeman.

When the boys got home they changed from their suits and went to the bathroom to bathe their wounds. Lisa came in with her ointment and gently tended Robert's face. "I think we lost that fight," Robert remarked.

"It doesn't matter, we stopped them bullying your friend," Karl Heinz replied. "Only cowards won't fight. We had to do something."

"I suppose you're right," Robert, replied, not feeling completely convinced. "But it's made my bum ache worse."

"You fought like a tiger, Robert," said Karl Heinz."

Robert was pleased with the compliment, but he didn't feel much like a tiger, in fact he felt a bit of a fraud. He knew he'd been reluctant to take on the bigger boys, but was glad this reluctance hadn't been noticed. Anyway he'd done it, "But what he'd have done if Karl Heinz hadn't been there to lead the way into battle he just didn't know, and he tried not to think about it.

"You were both terrific," said Lisa.

Her remark made Robert swell with pride. It was worth being bashed about just to hear her say it. It was even worth the extra punishment he was anticipating for fighting in the street. At any moment he was expecting his father to send for him, but nothing happened, and nothing was mentioned at luncheon. However, later in the afternoon his mother called him aside into the drawing-room while the rest of the family were in the garden.

Elizabeth mentioned nothing about the fight which surprised him. "You were not very kind to poor Wendy this morning," she rebuked. "I was rather ashamed of you."

Robert bowed his head. He hated being told off by his mother, because she had the knack of making him feel ashamed of himself without even raising her voice. In addition to which she was invariably right in what she said... "I'm sorry, Mother" he replied, feeling contrite,

"It's not me you should be apologizing to. You must go and say you're sorry to her."

Robert nodded.

"I thought you liked her?"

"I do."

"Then you have a strange way of showing it," Elizabeth replied. She made to leave the room, but stopped when he pleaded, "Please don't go for a moment."

She turned and faced him, and as always his appealing look melted her heart."

"Are you terribly angry with me?" he asked.

"You can't expect me to be particularly pleased with you considering your disgraceful behaviour."

"But I have been punished, Mother, so please don't pretend you hate me for too long," he smiled sheepishly.

Elizabeth had to fight back a smile. Her son was obviously more astute about her serious looks than she had bargained for, and one of her difficulties had always been to resist, his charm and sense of humour after he had been naughty.

He then asked, "Isn't Father going to speak to me again?"

"Of course he is, but you've been very naughty and you'll have to give him time. You are not the only one with feelings, young man. Just remember that parents have feelings as well as you. And the fact that you lied has been, very hurtful to him. It would help if you went and said you were sorry."

"I can't!"

"It takes a real man to be able to say sorry when he is in the wrong." She looked hard at him, forcing him to bow his head as her words cut into him. Elizabeth left him to think about what she had said.

Robert returned to the garden to find his cousins, but Karl Heinz and Lisa were nowhere to be seen, and he had to search the garden for them. When he did find them it was behind the shrubbery near the wall bordering Reggie's garden. To Robert's surprise Karl Heinz had his arms round Lisa's waist and was kissing her on the lips. He didn't feel jealous, because there could be no such thought in his heart for Karl Heinz, but he did wish that it was him doing the kissing. Robert stood watching until his cousins had finished their embrace. Seeing him, they showed no sign of embarrassment or resentment that he should be there, but happily joined him and wandered back to the lawn where the three of them lay lazily under the hot afternoon sun.

"I reckon those boys bashing Albert were Jews," Karl Heinz remarked thoughtfully.

"Whatever makes you think that?" Robert asked.

"Well, it's just the sort of filthy trick Jews get up to."

"They're not Jews. They come up from the village. I've seen them before," Robert replied.

"I suppose you wouldn't have rescued Albert if he'd been a Jew?" Lisa cut in.

"Of course I wouldn't," Karl Heinz replied.

"Why not?" asked Robert.

"Because he's stupid," Lisa grinned.

Karl Heinz ignored her, and then said, "Jews don't count. They're just vermin. It's a waste of time helping them; they'll only stab you in the back. They made us lose the war."

"That's not true!" Robert pushed himself up and rested on his elbow, looking at his cousin. "Now who's saying things he shouldn't say. You don't really believe all that, do you?"

Karl Heinz painfully turned over on to his back and stared up at the sky. "Of course I do."

"You told me you once helped a Jewish boy," Robert persisted.

"Maybe, but I know better now," Karl Heinz concluded. "He isn't a Jew, is he?" he added quickly, frowning at Robert.

"Who?"

"Albert, of course."

"Not that I know of."

Karl Heinz looked relieved and showed no further interest in the subject. He lay shading his eyes from the sun and searching the clear blue sky. The sound of an aeroplane had attracted his attention. He could hear it somewhere but as yet it hadn't come into view. "There it is!"

The others looked to where Karl Heinz was pointing. The plane was very low and had come into view over the trees on top of the hill, which rose steeply from the railway cutting on the other side of the main road. It chugged lazily across the blue, sunlit sky, the sound of its light engine pleasantly breaking the stillness of the quiet afternoon and adding the smallest particle to the storehouse of their memories to be brought to mind at some future time as a reminder of a fleeting moment on a glorious summer's day when they were young.

"It's a bi-plane," said Karl Heinz.

"It's a Tiger Moth," said Robert, being precise and pleased that he knew the name of the machine. "I bet it comes from Shoreham Aerodrome." He had been taken to an open day at the airport by Reggie, and had taken a great interest in what he had seen. He was even able to boast that he'd had a flight in the new DH89 Dragon Rapid.

Karl Heinz was most impressed with Robert's knowledge. "You lucky thing," he remarked. "I've never even seen an aerodrome."

"Actually, it's only a big field with huts and things, but it's jolly exciting having a flight."

Robert related that his Uncle Reggie had told him that he had witnessed the first flight from Shoreham in 1910, when a man called Harold Piffard had taken off in a Humming Bird, which was a plane similar to that used by the Wright brothers. "When I was there I saw some of our air force planes," he added.

Karl Heinz said, "We're not supposed to have an air force, and it's not fair. But you wait and see. I bet the Fuhrer will do something about it."

"What do you want an air force for?" Robert asked.

"All countries need an air force," Karl Heinz replied.

"No they don't. Not unless they're going to war."

"You've got one. Why shouldn't we have one?"

"We've got an empire to defend."

"And we've got to defend the Fatherland."

Lisa had had enough of the argument. "For goodness sake you two shut up about your silly air-forces."

*

When John left for London for the week on the Monday morning, neither he nor Robert had been able to bring themselves to talk to each other. Robert had watched his father leave with feelings of frustration in as much that he hadn't found the courage to apologize. However, the week apart from each other had given them both time to think and regret the rift which had opened between them. So it was with pleasure that John saw his son sitting on the steps outside the front door when he arrived home in the car on the Friday evening.

Robert opened the car door for his father and took his brief case. Neither spoke, but both greeted the other with a flicker of a shy smile, and then together they walked into the house. John made straight for his study and flopped down in his arm chair. Robert followed him in and put the brief case on the desk, and then poured his father a drink, which he placed on the table beside him.

"Thank you, Robert," said John, pleased to have broken the silence between them.

Elizabeth came in and greeted John, but, thinking it might be a good idea if father and son were left alone together, left the room almost immediately.

Robert sat down on the arm of John's chair with his back partly towards his father. He clasped his hands between his legs and hung his head. There was a long silence, and then he said, "Father."

"Yes, Robert?"

There was another pause as Robert struggled to get the words out. "I. . I'm. . I'm terribly sorry," he stammered. "That is for last week-end." Robert glanced over his shoulder at John's face and was relieved to see that there was no black scowl. "I'm sorry I lied to you."

"Why did you?" John asked. He saw Robert looking at him, and their eyes met. How he loved this boy. If only he was capable of showing his feelings as others seemed to do, but it was so difficult. Perhaps it was the war? Or was it that he never had been capable of letting the boy know his heart? He must try, he sighed.

"I was ashamed...and afraid." Robert whispered.

"Are you often afraid of me?"

"Sometimes, Father."

John put his arm round the boy's waist and let his hand rest on his leg. "Thank you for being honest with me and for apologizing. I want you to promise that you will never lie to me again, because where there are lies there can be no trust."

"I promise, Father." Robert got up from the arm of the chair. He felt as if a great load had been lifted from him, and his cheerful spirit returned. He bent and quickly kissed his father's cheek and then went to leave the room.

"Thank you for coming," John said as Robert reached the door.

Then as an afterthought he said, "I regret that I may have been rather too severe with you."

"Don't worry, Father. I'm all right now," Robert replied, and then, grinning, he added, "Almost, anyway."

As the holiday continued it regained the happy state that had existed before the painful week-end, although it was two weeks before the boys could sit down with comfort, and even then the marks on their backsides had not disappeared.

Lisa had remained on after Karl Heinz had left for home, for she was to return to school direct from Brighton. Now that he had her to himself Robert was determined to find an opportunity to follow Karl Heinz's lead and kiss her. One afternoon he tried to encourage her to walk with him to the shrubbery, but she seemed reluctant to leave the drawing-room, and just stood moodily at the open french windows. Robert, standing beside her, felt he could stand the temptation no longer. He leant across and quickly kissed her on the cheek, but to his astonishment she gave him a hard slap across the face, bringing the tears to his eyes. "How dare you!" she snapped. "Who do you think you are?" But, seeing the sorrowful look on his face and knowing that her slap had been hard, she immediately regretted her action.

"I'm sorry," he apologized, holding his hand on his cheek. "I didn't mean to upset you. After all, you let Karl Heinz do it. I suppose you like him the best?"

"That's my business. Besides you're only a couple of silly schoolboys, so why should I like one of you better than the other?" Lisa tossed her head, and then added imperiously, "When you're grown men, and if I decide to choose one of you, it will be the strongest one."

"But I love you now!"

"Don't be silly, Robert, you're only a boy, and you know nothing about love. Besides, I thought you loved Karl Heinz.

Robert went red in the face. "That's different," he retorted. "Why are you so beastly to me?" He stood with his head bowed, believing that he had no chance against Karl Heinz for the first place in Lisa's affections.

Lisa knew she was trying her best to hurt him. She couldn't understand why, and was angry with herself for being so cruel. Then in a gentler tone of voice she said, "Anyway, I don't feel like that sort of thing today."

"Why not? You felt like it the other day," Robert replied, looking puzzled.

"Because girls are different and we don't always feel like being mauled about. You wouldn't understand."

Robert didn't understand, in fact, he thought, the more he got to know about girls the less he understood.

Lisa walked towards the door of the room.

"Don't go!" he called after her. "I've got something for you."

She stopped abruptly and turned to face him, her dark eyes puzzled. Robert took something from his pocket and shyly held it out to her. "It's only a small one, but it is real silver," he said, looking at her apprehensively, wondering whether she would like it.

"A silver rose," she said, holding it in the palm of her hand and caressing it with a finger. "It's lovely, Robert but why? It's not my birthday."

Robert hesitated, not knowing quite what to say. "I just want you to have it, that's all."

"But you shouldn't waste your money on me. I'm not worth it. It must have cost an awful lot."

"It's got a pin on the back so you can wear it," Robert said hopefully. "Will you wear it?"

Lisa closed her hand round the rose and held it close to her. "One day, perhaps," she replied softly.

"But when?"

She went towards the door and then turned again. "You'll find out," she smiled. Before disappearing she added, "By the way, I'm sorry I slapped you."

Robert went to his room and flung himself on the bed. He would never understand girls, especially that one, he thought. They are such a pain in the neck. You never know how they are going to be from one moment to the next. If Karl Heinz can kiss her why shouldn't he? He knew she liked Karl Heinz best, which was understandable, because everyone likes him best. But surely she could let him have a kiss as well?

His thoughts had been churning round his head for about, ten minutes when he heard his bedroom door open. Millicent entered. I've come to tidy up," she said. Robert didn't argue even though Agnes had already tidied up as usual earlier in the day, which seemed to account for the fact that Millicent had little to do except talk to him.

Millicent led the conversation to boy-girl relationships and try as he would, Robert couldn't get her to change the subject. He learnt that she had been watching when he had received his recent slap, and she began to offer him unasked for advice on the best way of achieving his desire. She told him that if he wished to kiss a girl he should choose the right time.

"How do I know when the right time is?" he asked sulkily. If you like something, one time is as good as another."

"Girls don't always feel like it," Millicent replied.

"Why don't they."

"Blimey! Don't you know anything about girls?"

"I know they're a blinking nuisance," Robert replied, getting up from the bed.

"You should lead up to it, not just peck a girl on the cheek," Millicent explained. "Like this," she said, slipping her arm round his waist and holding him close to her.

Robert thought he ought to push her away, and yet he didn't. He felt her hands stroking the back of his neck and gently pushing his head forward, and then, before he knew what was happening, their lips touched. At first he stood shyly with, his arms to his side, but as the pleasure took hold of him he became bolder and let his hands slide on to her back.

She felt his strength as he held her close, and in the end she had to gently prise him away. "I think that's enough for one day," she said. "You learn fast, Master Robert."

Robert sat down on the bed. He had enjoyed the experience. "Can we do it again?" he asked.

"I expect so, but not today," she said, making her way to the door. She had every intention of doing it again, and more besides.

Robert was unable to try out his new found pleasure on Lisa, for she returned to school before he could pluck up courage for a second try. However, he conveniently remembered that it was time he apologized to Wendy for his recent offhand behaviour.

He had never called at the Marsden house before, only having made contact over the garden wall. One afternoon after school before the summer faded he stood outside the front door waiting for an answer to his ring. It was Mrs Marsden who opened the door. "Why, Robert! What a pleasant surprise," she said, beaming at him, and inviting him in.

Robert thought she seemed pleased to see him, although he couldn't think why. He was immediately invited to stay for tea, and having accepted, began to feel at home.

After tea Robert suggested to Wendy that they go for a walk on the downs, and to his surprise she enthusiastically agreed.

"I'm sorry I was rotten that Sunday," he said, as they ambled across the golf course towards the Roman camp.

"You were upset, weren't you?" she smiled.

Robert nodded. "But it was no reason to take it out on you," he said. "You're always so kind to me, Wendy, and yet I don't deserve it, you know."

"It's easy to be kind to someone you like."

When they arrived at the ramparts of the ancient camp, Robert took Wendy by the hand and pulled her up the grassy bank. Once on the top neither made any attempt to unclasp their hands as they walked round the circular mound to find a suitable place to sit down.

Lying below them to the south, where the downs sweep down to the sea, the town had spread along the coast like a grey scab over the green countryside. But beyond, the silver Channel glinted in the evening sunlight.

"I've never been up here before," she said, as they stood gazing at the view.

Robert released her hand and let his arm slide round her waist, wondering as he did so whether he had chosen the right time for his boldness, as Millicent had advised. Evidently he had, he decided, because he received no slap round the face on this occasion. It was exciting to have his hand gently holding her waist, and feel her body nestling into his. What a pity that Lisa hadn't let him do the same with her.

Robert knew every fold in the downs, and was glad to show his knowledge by pointing out all the landmarks to this girl, who was looking up at him with such admiration.

Along the great hills to the west the famous Chanctonbury Ring stood out boldly in the clear evening air. This clump of trees, he explained, had been planted by a boy in 1760. Then, if she looked carefully, she would see the Isle of Wight sitting faintly on the far western horizon, almost imperceptible behind its shroud of haze. "You can only see it on the very clearest of days," he said.

They sat down on the grassy bank, and Wendy lay back looking up at him sitting close beside her. He gazed into the distance,

"Wendy, do you remember at the ball what you said I could do?" he asked hesitantly.

She remembered very well, and her heart missed a beat at the thought of it. "What was that?"

He lent over her with his face close to hers, looking down into her eyes. "You remember," he said breathlessly as their lips touched. At first he was restrained, but when he found that he was not rebuffed he kissed her again and again, wishing he could go on doing it for ever. At first he was somewhat clumsy in his efforts, but then, remembering what Millicent had taught him, he became gentler and more relaxed.

Wendy could hardly breathe as his mouth smothered hers. "Don't eat me, Robert," she managed to whisper. Feeling his excitement rising as he pressed hard against her, she calmed him by gently stroking his cheek until their lips parted.

For a moment he couldn't speak. Then he said, "I'm sorry, Wendy."

"Don't be sorry." She smiled into his appealing eyes. "I didn't mind a bit. You're very good at it."

"Am I?"

"You know I like you terribly, don't you?"

Robert felt new confidence welling up inside him. "Do you!" he exclaimed, looking surprised. Wendy was such a happy person, he thought. Why didn't Lisa say things like that? And why didn't Lisa let him kiss her as Wendy had done?

"Of course I do! But you mustn't go too far," she smiled.

He wasn't quite sure what she meant, but it didn't matter, because he had found a new joy in living, and life was young and all was right with the world. Happiness in his heart, he took her by the hand and pulled her to her feet. "Come on," he said, "Race you home!"

PART 3

CHAPTER 11

During the past two years Victoria Station had come to represent different moods in Robert's mind depending on which way he was travelling. When bound for home it was a place of happy anticipation with thoughts of his coming leave uppermost in his mind. But on the return journey to Berkshire he was invariably depressed at the thought of yet another term, at the Royal Military College, and the drab building and draughty platforms only tended, to lower his spirits still further. However, on this chilly October afternoon matters were in reverse, and he would have been only too pleased to be travelling in the opposite direction from home.

Time and again he turned, over in his mind how he would broach the subject to his father. He would normally have gone into the refreshment bar while he waited for the fast train to Brighton, but the anticipation of a blazing row had taken away his appetite, and he sat unhappily on a bench in view of the train departure information board. He pulled his mackintosh more closely round him and turned up the collar in an effort to keep warm, and then hunched himself over his newspaper, reading the headlines:

MR. CHAMBERLAIN DECLARES
'IT IS PEACE IN OUR TIME'

5000 British Troops
Will Be Sent To
Sudetenland

PRAGUE'S DAY OF SORROW

It brought to his mind an early morning in March two years before. He had been staying in Cologne with Karl Heinz, and had been awoken by the sound of horses in the street below. Getting out of bed and looking out of the window, he had seen the street filled, with German cavalry units making their way towards the Hohenzollern Bridge. The German army had crossed into the Rhineland, and Hitler's march towards war had begun. So he's got his way again, he thought. It was only to be expected. How could Chamberlain hope to cope with a man like Hitler? The German leader would twist him round his little finger with that charm of his. Robert remembered the eyes of the man who had held him spell bound all those years ago. No wonder he gets what he wants. Father thinks there will be war in spite of Chamberlain's efforts.

The thought of his father made his stomach turn over, bringing to his mind the incident that had finally led to him being sent to Sandhurst. It had been in the summer before his seventeenth birthday. He had reached the difficult stage in his youth when he had come to believe that he had been blessed with more knowledge and wisdom than his parents, and for that matter most other people as well.

Robert smiled to himself as he remembered Agnes saying, "You're a proper know-all nowadays, Robert, and that's for sure."

To add to his conceit and against all the forecasts, he had managed to scrape a pass in the school certificate examination.

His parents had suffered this stage in his life with patience, hoping that mercifully it would be of short duration. It was.

In the summer of 1935 Robert had started with a new music teacher, his previous one having given up the post, because, as she had honestly admitted, there was little more she could teach him, and he needed someone of a far higher standard to develops his talent. A somewhat elderly German, but none the less a first class performer and teacher had been recommended to Elizabeth, and this man had agreed to take the post.

Robert had liked and respected his previous teacher and had never given her any trouble. She had been strict with him, but the new man was different. A great player in his time, and an excellent teacher, but being completely absorbed in his love of music, had no thought of placing his student under any discipline. That was his pupil's problem. He would teach, giving the benefit of all his knowledge and experience, but it had been up to Robert how he reacted to this. He was a kindly man and his patience with his young pupil seemed inexhaustible. But Robert had sensed a lack of firmness in the way he was being handled, and remembered how he had begun to take advantage. He had come to resent criticism, and in his frustration, when he found that he couldn't at first master what he was being taught, would sometimes lose his temper.

One afternoon he had been particularly difficult, so much so that he had been made to play one phrase over and over again. He had become so incensed by his inability to get it right that eventually, in sheer frustration, he had flung his instrument to the ground, knocking the bridge out of position.

Robert remembered how he had sat on the settee, holding his head in his hands. "What's the use? I can't do it! I wish I was dead!" he had cried.

The old teacher had said nothing. He had quietly packed his things and left the room. Robert had run after him to apologise, but had found him in the hallway talking to John.

"Leaving already, Mr Goldstein?"

"I think it best, Sir John. I feel I'm not the right one to teach Robert."

"Why ever not? Has the boy no talent?"

"Oh, yes, he has talent, there's no doubt about that. But perhaps I'm not the right one to draw it out of him. I find his playing an enigma. Something is there. It may be the spark of greatness, but whether it will ever burst into flame, who knows? Only time will tell."

When the teacher had left, Robert recalled, he had been ordered into his father's study. He could see Father now, sitting at his desk, looking him straight in the eyes. He had been invited to sit down, and then Father had wasted no time, saying, "It's the army for you, my lad. You'll go to Sandhurst in the autumn next year."

When the words had sunk in he had replied, "But, Father, I don't want the army. I want to do music."

"You'll do as you're told! After what that teacher fellow told me you'll waste no more time on this music nonsense. I'll not have a son of mine throwing tantrums like that. What the devil do you think you're playing at!"

"I'm sorry. I didn't mean it. I promise it won't happen again." Robert had felt himself near to tears. "Please don't stop my music, Father. Please!"

"Haven't you any other aspirations?"

"No."

"Then you're a fool, boy. Look at you, you're intelligent, tall, strong, good looking, with all the advantages life can offer, yet all you want to do is waste your life away."

"It's my life."

"Yes, and it's my duty to see that you don't waste it playing that damned fiddle."

"Supposing they don't accept me?"

"They'll accept you because you're my son."

"That's just it! I'm no blasted good, but they'll take me just because I'm your son." Robert had retorted angrily. He remembered his words as if he had just uttered them. He had never before spoken to his father with such defiance in his voice, and he waited apprehensively for the wrath to break over him. But his father had just sat looking at him.

John had realised his mistake, and had tried to put matters right, but whatever he said he couldn't shift the thought he had confirmed in his son's mind, that his entry into the army would be only on his father's merit.

"Others do what they want, why can't I? I'm not a child anymore."

"Then stop acting like one."

"You know I'll be no good as a soldier. You've always thought me a sissy, and a coward, and a cry baby, and no good at anything. I'll hate the bloody army. I'll hate it! Hate it! Hate it! But you don't care. I can't be like you, I just can't," Robert had sobbed. It had all came spilling out. He had covered his face with his hands as tears of frustration overflowed down his cheeks.

John had sat watching his son with astonishment. He had never realised the boy had such thoughts in his head. Surely he didn't really believe he thought those things about him?

Robert remembered feeling his father gently remove his hands from his face. He had opened his eyes to see this great man squatting down in front of his chair looking up at him with a kindly expression on his face. He had heard him say softly, "Now listen, Robert. I think none of those things, and I believe you are growing into a very fine young man. For my sake, if not for your own, do as I ask. You'll see, it'll be for the best."

He remembered nodding his agreement, and Father saying, "Good man."

Robert glanced up at the station clock. Hell! How the time was dragging, he thought.

Before going to Sandhurst, Robert had remained at school for a further year, leaving during the summer of 1936. That was a summer he'd always remember, when he and Karl Heinz had spent a wonderful holiday together touring Germany by train and on foot. Their joy in each other's company had not diminished as the youthful years had slipped away, and they matured happily together towards manhood. It had seemed as if nothing could ever spoil the sunshine of their young lives as they hiked through the German countryside or sat drinking coffee in a coffee house in one of the great cities. And then the time had come to keep his promise to his father. He had passed the entrance examination to Sandhurst, but then had the nerve racking experience of having to attend the interview.

On the lonely chair in front of the Interview board he had sat almost unable to speak from nervousness. The officers on the board had at first found him shy and withdrawn. One captain had in fact lost patience with him and wished to fail him, but a colonel, who was chairman, of the board, persevered with the questions, and having drawn him out, found the young man not only intelligent but interesting, especially with regard to his knowledge of Germany.

Robert had gradually found his confidence, which was partially due to his irritation with this particular captain, giving him the desire to hit back.

"Can you ride?" had been one of the captain's abrupt questions.

"No, sir."

"Why not?"

"I hate horses, sir."

"Hate horses!" the officer had exploded. "Then what damn good, are you going to be as a soldier?" He was plainly exacerbated with this young idiot.

"I don't think I'm going to be much damn good at all, sir."

"Are you trying to be impertinent?"

"No, sir."

The colonel had suppressed a smile at the young man's reply.

Robert, had taken a dislike to the captain, and secretly hoped he might fail the board. "Horses weren't much good in the last war, sir. And they won't be much good in the next against tanks and aeroplanes, so what's the point in a soldier being able to ride, sir?"

"When we want your opinion on military matters, we'll ask for it. Meanwhile, we'll ask the questions," the captain had snapped back.

"I note from your record that you were in the OTC at school and that you were a good shot," the colonel remarked evenly. "Do you like shooting?"

"Yes sir," Robert had replied, and then added, "At targets."

"Explain yourself"

"Well, sir. I wouldn't like it if it meant shooting people or animals."

The unpleasant Captain butted in again, this time addressing the chairman. "Sir, if this candidate is going to be squeamish about whom he shoots, is there any point in continuing this interview? How can we possibly accept him into the army with such an attitude as this."

"May I ask a question, sir?" Robert had requested.

"You may," the chairman replied.

"I see by your ribbons, sir, that you fought in the war. Did you want to shoot other human beings?"

"You ask a pertinent question, young man. Point taken."

Another officer spoke to Robert. "I understand you went to a grammar school."

"Yes, sir."

"Most of our candidates are from public schools. Do you think this is to your disadvantage?"

"No, sir."

"Why not?"

"My school is as good as any public school."

"Why were you not sent to your father's college?"

"My parents wished to bring me up themselves. They didn't want anyone else to do it."

"Do you think this was a good idea?"

"I think home is the most wonderful place in the world."

"Answer the question. Was it a good idea?"

"Yes, sir."

"Why?"

The questions were being fired at him so fast that Robert had hesitated for a moment. All eyes had been fixed on him. Father had told him to look them straight in the eyes, boldly but not insolently.

"It was a good idea, sir, because I had the benefit of being brought up by two very special people, and whatever happens nobody can ever take those happy years away from me. They taught me more than, any housemaster could have done."

The officer nodded his head as if satisfied, but the unpleasant Captain had another question. "So you've been tied to your mother's apron strings," he remarked. "I take it that with this, so called, happy upbringing, there was a sad lack of discipline, which, to me, seems to stand out a mile?"

"No, sir."

"What do you mean, no, sir?"

"I mean there was no lack of discipline, sir. I was brought up firmly, sir, as anyone would understand if they had served under my father."

The colonel had nodded and smiled. "I think I can vouch for that," he had remarked.

Robert had wondered how long the ordeal was to last. But eventually it had come to an end and he had been released.

Before the official result of the interview was received John had known that Robert had been accepted. He was no longer a serving officer, having retired from the army that year; John now held a high and influential post in the King's service at Buckingham Palace. The new king who had long admired and respected John, had particularly asked him to serve on his staff, and there was little that went on in high places about which he didn't know?

When the previous King had abdicated, John had continued to serve his brother with equal loyalty.

"I'm proud of you, Robert," John had said on hearing the news.

"Thank you, Father."

"I'm told you gave the interview board a run for their money," John had chuckled.

"I only spoke the truth, Father. Anyway, a lot of the questions seemed stupid to me," Robert remembered replying.

Robert was beginning to feel cold sitting in the draughty station. It won't be long now, he thought. The damn train should be in soon. He shut his eyes and remembered how depressed he'd felt when travelling to Sandhurst for the first time. How he'd hated leaving home. To him it had marked the end of his boyhood. In spite of the occasional severe beating during his young life, his early years had been idyllic. No boy could have been happier, and because of this the wrench from home had been the greater. It had taken him some time to settle down at the college, but when he had, life had not been as bad as he had imagined.

He had made new friends and found that he could cope with most of the training programme. He still found Maths a problem, but he was good at map reading, and found that he was also quite good at sketching, a subject at which all cadets were expected to become proficient.

However, there was one cadet for whom he had taken an immediate dislike. Courtney Babington-Smith - Babs to his friends, which did not include Robert, was considered by Robert to be a supercilious snob. From the moment the two had met the dislike had been mutual, but whereas Robert had been content to let matters rest, Babington-Smith had never lost an opportunity to provoke him.

"You'd have never been accepted in the army if it wasn't for that father of yours," Babington-Smith had said haughtily. He had a habit of tilting his head back so that he looked down his large hooked nose at the one to whom he was speaking.

"I can't help it if my father happened to be a general," Robert had replied evenly. "It's not my fault that yours was only a major," he had added mischievously, knowing the best way to irritate his antagonist. Robert, had grinned as Babs had stalked off. He had found himself wondering whether it was necessary for Babs to hold his head back in order to counter balance the weight of the nose.

During discussions on current events Robert was usually quiet, but on one occasion when the subject had been Germany he had put his view rather forcefully.

"Trust you to stick up for the bloody Huns," Babs had remarked.

Robert had replied, "Well, it's ridiculous to say that all Germans are bad just because you happen to disagree with what their government is doing. I've got German relatives and they're good people."

"I might have known it! You should be kicked out of the army as a traitor."

"That will do, both of you," the instructor had interrupted.

But the matter had not ended there. After the class had finished the two had continued to argue until Robert had been challenged to a fight in the gym with the boxing gloves on.

That evening the gym had been crowded with cadets, all eager to watch the fun. A clear space had been left in the centre to act as the ring, and when Robert accompanied by his seconds, had nervously pushed his way through the crowd, he had found Babs confidently waiting for him. "So you've come then. I must say I'm surprised, knowing what cowards you Hun lovers can be." The face behind the large hooked, nose leered at Robert.

Robert had ignored the insult. He'd had no wish to speak in case his voice betrayed his nervousness.

Babs was a keen rugby player, strong and well built, and had all the confidence of the extrovert. Unlike his opponent, he was obviously enjoying being the centre of attention.

"For God's sake keep your distance, Rob, and only go in when there's an opportunity. Then hit him hard," one of Robert's friends had advised.

Robert didn't like boxing and remembered not enjoying the experience. Fortunately he had remembered much of what he'd been taught of the art in the Hitler Youth and it was this that had saved his face from a battering.

In the first round Babs had hit out wildly, but although he held twice landed punches on Robert's body, it was obvious that he had no idea how to box. Robert heeded the advice of his friend and tried to keep his distance, giving the impression to his opponent that he was afraid to fight, which in Robert's mind was not far from the truth. Babs confidence increased, and when the round finished he had been surprised that he had not already flattened Robert.

When the second round commenced, Babs had come rushing out of his corner with his arms flailing, but finding that Robert had successfully dodged his blows he had momentarily hesitated, wondering how best to deal with his elusive opponent. It was at that moment that Robert had quickly stepped forward, and with all his strength had slammed his fist upwards squarely on to his opponent's protruding jaw. To everyone's surprise, Courtney Babington-Smith had stood for a few seconds swaying on his feet with a stupid expression on his face – at least more stupid than usual. Robert grinned to himself as he brought the incident to mind. Babs arms had dropped to his side, and then slowly he had fallen forward like a felled tree, his face striking the floor with a sickening thud.

Robert had been as successful at covering his surprise at his victory as he had earlier covered his nervousness. Babs had broken his nose when he had struck the floor. When he had recovered consciousness, he had refused to shake Robert's hand, in fact he never spoke to Robert again, always making a point of avoiding him.

The one part of the training Robert dreaded had been the riding lessons. Most of the other cadets were already good riders, and those who were not appeared keen to learn. Not so Robert. It was only with the greatest determination that he overcame his fear and forced himself up on to the animal's back. But however hard he had tried it was obvious to all that he would never become a good rider. He didn't like the horse, and had sensed that the animal had known it. The feeling appeared to be mutual. On occasions he knew he had made a fool of himself, and had often wondered why some of the more arrogant cadets had not laughed at him. It had never occurred to him that his performance in the boxing ring had ensured his immunity from too much ridicule.

His greatest surprise since passing into the Royal Military College had been that he had managed to pass out. He'd even felt proud of himself on the passing out parade, especially as his parents were watching. The sun had been shining, the band playing, the immaculate lines of the newly commissioned subalterns and his own success had intoxicated him. But the moment had been short lived, and when the excitement of the day was over, and he'd had to report to the regimental depot at Winchester, the old feelings returned, and he had found that he still lacked enthusiasm for the army.

Robert had arrived at the depot and reported to the adjutant, who had taken him to the colonel. "Mr Rutherford reporting for duty, sir," the adjutant had announced. Robert had entered the office, and standing rigidly to attention had given a smart salute. He hadn't seen this rather fierce looking man since Joanna's ball. "So you've come to us at last, young man," said the colonel. He nodded with approval at the smart turn out of his new officer.

Robert had been allowed to sit down. The colonel lifted a sheet of paper from his desk. It was Robert's report from the Military College, and the two had sat in silence while the colonel read it to himself.

> *This officer has done all that has been required of him,* and *has done well in some subjects. But he has not shown the enthusiasm normally expected from cadets with his military background. Consequently, he has not allowed his talents to be* developed *as*

might have been the case if he had adopted a more positive attitude. He has been inclined to 'Hide his light under a bushel'.

He has first class leadership qualities, but the difficulty has been in trying to persuade him that this is so. In this we have failed, and these qualities have remained dormant. His courage in overcoming difficulties he experienced in certain aspects in the training programme has been noted.

It is agreed by all instructors that this officer has been difficult to assess, but the decision to grant him a commission has been in all cases considered the correct one.

A young man of promise, providing he is willing to give of his best to the army.

"A damn strange report!" the colonel had grunted at last. "If the truth is known, they don't seem to know what to make of you."

Robert had remained silent.

"What's all this about not showing enthusiasm? Eh, what?" The colonel had glared at Robert, waiting for an answer.

"I tried to cover it, sir, but I obviously didn't succeed."

"Damn it, man! Are you telling me you lack enthusiasm?" The colonel had realised he wasn't going to get an answer so continued. "Look here. I don't want anyone in my battalion who's not absolutely one hundred per cent."

"I understand, sir," Robert had replied. Then taking an envelope from his pocket, he had stood up and handed it to the colonel. "That's why I request that you accept this, sir."

"What is it?"

"My resignation, sir."

Robert remembered the colonel exploding when the word resignation had been mentioned, but then all thoughts of the past quickly disappeared as he felt himself poked in the chest by an umbrella. Looking up, he saw a tall, slim figure in a black pin-striped suit. From under a bowler hat a long nose pointed down at him, and the face to which it belonged wore an amused expression. For a moment Robert looked blank, and then, standing up, he exclaimed, "Percy! I didn't recognise you."

"I say, old thing. I do believe you're pleased, to see old Percy."

"Well, of course I am," Robert replied warmly. His attitude towards Percy, whom he once detested, had changed over the years of his youth, and he had come to realise that his cousin genuinely desired his friendship. A certain mutual admiration had grown up between them. "You look quite the city gent, Percy. I never thought to see you all togged up like this."

"I told you once before, darling cousin, all life's an act. And this is Percy's mourning come Baronet costume," he grinned.

"What are you talking about?"

"I'll explain, dear thing, but first things first." Percy put his hand on Robert's shoulder and then said, "How would you like to spend the night with old Percy. Plenty of room in the old shack, you know. You can tell me all your troubles."

"How do you know I've got troubles?" Robert felt his stomach turn over at the thought of having to face his father with the news of his resignation.

"When I saw you deep in thoughts I said to myself, Percy, old thing, that boy has a problem. So, how about it?"

Robert looked doubtful.

"You'll be quite safe," Percy remarked with a twinkle in. his eye.

Robert blushed. "Okay, Percy, I'd like to. Thanks," he smiled shyly.

"I do so love it when you blush. It's absolutely heavenly," Percy drawled. "Come on, let's get a taxi."

On the way to St. John's Wood, where Percy had his hovel, as he put it, the two cousins discussed family affairs. They had last met when Robert had attended his Uncle George's funeral, now over a year ago. Since that time, Percy related, Henrietta had remained on in the family home even though, all her sons were living away. "And I live in London now," said Percy. "I can't stand too much of the old mater. She's such an old grouser."

Percy went on to relate that he had just returned from a visit to his mother at Wimbledon. A few days previous she had telephoned him at Kenley – Percy did not explain what he was doing there – to say that she had received a message from the War Office that young George had been killed on active service in Shanghai. "The old thing was in such a state that I had to rush over and calm her down," he continued. "What actually happened, I have since found out, was that young George was sozzled at the time, and accidently blew his brains out – if that was possible," he quickly added. "He evidently picked up a loaded revolver in mistake for a cork screw, and the beastly thing went off. Mind you, I haven't told the old mater this. She still thinks he was some sort of hero, which I suppose he was in a way, having put up with the army all these years."

Robert tried not to laugh, but the way his cousin related the story made it almost impossible not to. "Percy, you really are dreadful. You make it all sound like a comedy act."

Percy grinned, "I'm sure young George would have seen the funny side of it. After all, what a wonderful way to go. Sloshed out of his mind, and then, Pop – exit young George stage left. Didn't feel a thing." He paused for a moment while he made great play of fixing a cigarette into his long holder. The taxi filled with smoke as he lit up, and Robert started to cough, so before the conversation could continue the window was opened to clear the air.

"Sorry about that," said Percy, flapping his hand up and down in front of Robert's face.

"You don't seem very sorry about young George, Percy," Robert remarked.

"Well, my dear, it's no good crying over spilt milk or in young George's case, spilt whisky. He's gone and that's that. We were quite close as boys. He was good to me at school, I remember. But then we all have to grow up, and. . ." The sentence trailed off and Percy became thoughtful for a moment. Then his normal affectation returned, "Now that young George has popped off, so to speak," he continued, "You realise what it means?"

Robert didn't.

"It means, dear thing, that old Percy is a Baronet. So I want a little respect from you, young cousin," he chuckled.

"Good Heavens!"

"Is that all you've got to say? I'll make a jolly-good Baronet."

"Yes, Sir Percy," laughed Robert.

"The Hon Cynth thinks it's an absolute scream. Says even daddy dear won't mind the old knot being tied now."

Robert looked bewildered, finding it difficult to keep up with his cousin's train of thought.

Percy apologized, and realising that Robert knew almost nothing of his life, went on to relate even more news. Robert learnt that the Honourable Cynthia Cartwright-Craddock was Percy's fiancée. Evidently her father had at first not taken to the idea of Percy as a son-in-law, considering him a most peculiar fellow, and his theatrical connections an unsuitable recommendation for entry into the family of a Viscount. But Cynthia's father was beginning to relent, Percy explained; especially now he was a Baronet.

"First bumped into the Hon Cynth in the National Gallery. It was love at first bump," Percy chuckled. "She's a wizard with the old paint brushes. Daddy's absolutely loaded. Have to keep in with the dear old buffer in the hope a little loot might trickle my way some day. Not that I really need it anymore."

"Percy, you really are a wag. You've quite cheered me up," Robert laughed.

"Well, what are friends for? I always wanted to be your friend, Robert. It wasn't easy at first, you know."

Robert grinned, "Sorry, Percy. I know I was damned awkward some times as a boy. You once came to my room, I remember. I wasn't very polite, was I? But I was sorry when you'd gone."

Having paid off the taxi, Percy led Robert into an exclusive block of flats, where they took the lift to the penthouse apartment.

"I say, what a wonderful place, Percy!" Robert exclaimed. From a small entrance hall, Percy led his cousin through a door into a spacious living-room, most of which was a fully carpeted lounge area scattered with deeply cushioned armchairs and large, luxurious settees. On one side of the room there was an equally spacious bay window area. Here the floor level was raised and set aside as a dining area so that those sitting at the beautifully polished mahogany table might gaze out over the park through the large picture window. Through an archway on the other side of the room a passage led to the bathroom and bedrooms. The kitchen opened directly on to the dining area. The tasteful decoration and the luxury of the furnishings left Robert in no doubt that here was affluence.

Seeing his cousin's astonished look, Percy said, "I suppose you're wondering how old Percy comes to live in such luxury? It's plays, old thing, which bring in the loot. I scribble 'em out, and the West End theatres do the rest. Then there's the book. Absolute trash of course, but it's made me a fortune. Lucky the old mater doesn't know or she'd be tapping me for a few bob," he laughed. "She never comes to London now. Thinks I live in some Bohemian dive in Soho." Percy enjoyed his pseudonym.

It occurred to Robert that he was the only one in the family who knew of his cousin's success.

Percy explained that it was his man's day off, and that he and Cynthia had intended to meet some friends for a meal in the West End. "But old Cynth can rustle up something here instead," he declared.

Meanwhile Robert was given a bedroom, and told he could take a bath before dinner if he wished.

Percy remained in the bedroom and watched Robert closely while he stripped. Seeing his cousin's interest Robert asked, "Is there something wrong with me?"

"Absolutely not!" Percy exclaimed. "I was just admiring your perfect body. Adonis could not have had such perfection. Such smooth, lightly browned skin. And such perfect proportion. And not a hair on your chest." Percy enthused.

"Oh, do shut up, Percy. I'm not a girl."

"There's nothing girlish about you, old thing. In fact, quite the opposite. But the male form can also be beautiful, and I simply love beautiful things. Get quite carried away, you know. It's the artistic temperament, I suppose." Percy then took his young cousin to the bathroom where he sat and talked while the bath was taken.

"You must be six feet tall now, Robert?"

"Yes. Not as tall as Father, though."

"If only the Hon Cynth could see you like this. She would simply adore painting you. But of course you'd be too embarrassed."

"I certainly would," Robert replied, looking worried. "By the way, she's not liable to come in here, is she?"

Percy laughed and calmed his cousin's fears. The front door was heard to slam, and the sound of someone entering the living room made Percy get to his feet and go to the bathroom door. "Is that you, darling?" he called.

"Cynthia here, dearest." Robert heard the voice call back. There were footsteps along the passage.

"No entry, sweet one," said Percy, standing at the half open door, barring the way. "I have cousin Robert in here taking a bath, and he's simply paralysed with fear that you might see him in the buff."

"Is that the absolutely divine boy you are always raving about, darling?"

Percy confirmed that it was, and Robert saw a hand come round the door and wave at him, and the low mellow tone of Cynthia's voice called out a greeting.

"There's just one snaggy pooh, sweetest," said Percy. "You'll have to cook the dinner tonight. And while cousin Robert finishes washing his adorable body, I shall ring Bunty and tell him it's all off this evening."

Robert breathed a sigh of relief at being left alone to finish his bath. What a strange fellow Percy is, he considered. Full of surprises, but his heart's in the right place. He wondered what Cynthia would look like? She sounded nice.

When he eventually arrived, clean and fresh, in the lounge, he could hear Cynthia singing in the kitchen. Percy was obviously in his room. He wandered slowly round the room, looking at the paintings on the walls and the many books lining the shelves of a large bookcase. On a low table by one of the armchairs he noticed an expensive looking silver picture frame. Picking it up, he saw it contained a photograph of a group of Royal Air Force officers standing in front of a Gladiator fighter aircraft.

"Why, hallo there, dear boy." Cynthia had emerged from the kitchen and was advancing towards him.

Robert quickly replaced the photograph on the table, and turned to gain his first impression of Percy's future wife. Tall, she had a bright, rather thin face. Definitely an outgoing personality, and certainly arty, he noted. But not unattractive, although her nose, like Percy's, was perhaps a shade too long. Somewhat like a model of the type he'd seen in Joanna's fashion magazines. Percy is thirty two. Cynthia must be about the same, he decided. Robert was about to offer his hand, but the Honourable Cynthia enthusiastically enclosed him in her arms and kissed his lips.

"So you are Robert! What a gorgeous boy! Absolutely divine," she said in. her sultry voice, stepping back and looking Robert up and down. "Percy never stops raving about you, darling. I simply seethe with jealousy." She gave him a knowing look and then added, "But I do see what he means. . . I really must pop you on canvas." Cynthia, came forward again and lightly stroked his cheek. "What beautiful features and such eyes. Yes, the eyes are the key, so full of life - and yet." She paused, and standing back to get a proper perspective, stroked, her chin, and then added, "The eyes of a dreamer. But there, I embarrass you."

"Not at all," Robert lied, smiling. "I was often called a dreamer at school."

"I see you were looking at my Percy's photo. Doesn't he look marvellous in uniform? Daddy dear didn't believe me when I told him." Cynthia lowered her voice to her confidential level and giggled, "Daddy thinks Percy's a bit of a pansy." She went off into peels of laughter, "Just imagine it, Percy a pansy!" she hooted, holding her sides.

Robert stood, looking blank.

Cynthia saw the lost expression on his face and it began to dawn on her that he had not seen Percy in the photograph. She stopped laughing and picked up the silver frame, and, pointing to one of the figures leaning against the aircraft, asked, "Don't you recognise him?"

Robert looked closely. "Good God! But he's in RAF uniform."

"Of course, dear thing, he's in the auxiliary air force? He's been flying for years. In fact he's been standing-by at Kenley with his squadron for the past few days because of this beastly Czech crisis. That man Hitler is really too naughty for words. I do so wish he'd stop walking into places, it's so disrupting to the social calendar. We've already missed one absolutely divine party because of this standing-by business. I did suggest that he stood-by at the party, but my Percy is so conscientious, he said it would be too difficult to scramble from there. To tell the truth, Robert darling, I didn't know what on earth he was talking about. Anyway, we didn't go." At last Cynthia paused to draw breath.

"I had no idea," Robert just managed to reply before his hostess continued.

"That's typical of Percy. He keeps reality in the background, because so often he finds it unpleasant. He likes to live in a world of make-believe with his books and plays. I suppose that's why he's been so successful." Cynthia hurried back to the kitchen still talking as she went.

It was at the dinner table that Robert was able to tell of his resignation from the army. He told of how he had thought the colonel was going to burst when the letter of resignation was handed to him. But for Robert there was no going back on his decision no matter what the colonel thought. "I thought he might have been pleased, because he'd just been rating me for lack of enthusiasm at Sandhurst," he said. But the colonel wasn't pleased and had tried hard to make Robert change his mind. But whatever argument he put forward, he could not shake Robert's resolve. He had even got up from his chair, and going to Robert, had put his arm round his shoulder, asking him to think again.

"And now you're going home to break the news to your father," said Percy.

Robert nodded. "Have I done right, Percy?" he asked.

"Only you know that, my sweet. If you have doubts, then you may have made a mistake. But if you feel yourself to be really happy and filled with a sense of relief to have left the army, then you've probably made the right decision. At least you've made your own decision."

"I'm sure there's going to be a fearful row when I get home," said Robert.

Percy rubbed his cheek. "Perhaps," he said thoughtfully. Uncle John will certainly be broken hearted." Percy looked directly at Robert and then said, "You be careful how you break the news to him, and just remember what I once said to you about people being sensitive below the surface."

Percy then went on to remind his young cousin that if there was a war, Robert would find himself back in the army whether he liked it or not.

"Supposing I'm a conscientious objector, could I get out of it then?" Robert asked.

"Are you?" asked Cynthia.

"I might be. I'm not sure. I'm thinking of joining the Peace Pledge Union." Robert had read somewhere that the Reverend Dick Sheppard, Canon of St. Paul's, had formed this union in May 1936 with a view to abolish war. Its members were called upon to renounce war. A membership application form had arrived, but as yet he had not returned it. There were still too many contradictions in his mind. He was quite prepared to say that he renounced war, that was easy, but at the same time he was well aware that he was not prepared to make the necessary sacrifices to back up these principles.

Percy gave Robert a long, steady look and then said seriously, "Now you listen to me, Robert. You're not one of these conchie fellows, and don't you ever tell anyone you are, because if you do you'll be storing up trouble for yourself." Percy's lecture was a long one as he explained his thoughts that to be a conscientious objector was not just a matter of not wanting to kill other human beings. "Most people object to killing others," he went on, "but most people also believe that there are times when to kill is the lesser of two evils, and that sometimes it becomes necessary. And the majority of people believe it right to defend themselves. A genuine conscientious objector would not accept this reasoning. Their minds are absolutely closed to any variation of the command *Thou shalt not kill.* And unless you're prepared to give up everything including your life for this principle, then you're not one of these people. And another thing young cousin," Percy continued, "this Peace Pledge Union of yours will come to nothing, you mark my words. Lloyd George once said '*You must renounce war in the hearts of men*', but it's all fancy political talk. Men's hearts are not so easily altered."

Robert had no answer to this. When it was put to him in this way he realised he was not prepared to give up his life for the principle of not killing, because to give up his life would defeat the object of his objection to fighting, which, if he was truthful with himself, was to save his own life. So looked at in this way he was a coward, he decided. He was afraid to fight in case he got hurt, and was just using this as a way out. Was this the real reason why he had resigned his commission, or was it his genuine desire for a musical career? Or perhaps something else? He wished he knew. "I wish I could be like Gandhi," he said. "Father thinks he's a damned trouble maker, but just think if we were all like him it would be a paradise here on earth." Robert's face lit up with youthful enthusiasm.

"Well you're not Gandhi!" Percy retorted. "And you're forgetting that man was kicked out of paradise. This is a sinful old world, Robert, and there's nothing you can do about it."

For a time Robert sat deep in thought, but remained silent. He felt the conversation was getting out of his depth. Then his thoughts were interrupted by more advice from his cousin.

"And don't forget what I said, dear child," Percy drawled. "Be a good boy and be gentle with your father when you break the news."

"I don't think he's going to be very gentle with me. He'd put the stick across me if I'd been a bit younger," Robert replied.

"What are you, nearly twenty now? Your days of being whipped are over, which is probably a pity considering your stupid ideas about being a conchie," Percy grinned. "Row or not, there'll certainly be a sad man trying to understand his wilful son. So do as I say and try and soften the blow."

"I thought you didn't like Father," said Robert.

"Percy is a real softie underneath," interjected Cynthia.

"Uncle John and I have never seen eye to eye, but that doesn't mean I want to see him hurt."

"I'll try to do as you say, Percy."

"And another thing, for heavens sake don't mention this nonsense about being a conscientious objector."

Robert agreed.

"I must say having your dear daddy as an uncle has done me a bit of good. It was a real wag watching the change of attitude in the old future pater-in-law when I spilt the beans that your daddy was my uncle. I really went up in the old man's estimation. Nothing like family connections," Percy laughed. He then added seriously, "But just you remember what I said, my sweet."

"Yes, Sir Percy."

Robert then questioned Percy about his flying activities. For some time Percy had believed there was going to be war. He also believed that to stand the best chance of surviving a man needed to be an expert in his field of fighting. He had joined one of the City of London squadrons of the auxiliary air force, so that if he had to fight at least he wouldn't be a novice at the game.

The auxiliary air force squadrons that had been raised usually took the name of towns or cities. The City of London had two squadrons, numbers 600 and 601. The pilots of these squadrons were part time volunteers.

"And besides," Percy went on. "Flying is by far the most comfortable way to die. At least you're sitting down, not splashing about in mud or getting squashed by some beastly tank. It's so much more civilised than having some dreadful sergeant fellow shouting obscenities at one, or having to push one of those ghastly bayonet things into some heavenly German youth, with whom one would much prefer to be drinking coffee on the Unter den Linden, or wherever Germans drink coffee. I don't think I could put up with that. It would be too frightful for words."

"But do you really think there'll be a war?" Robert asked, hoping for reassurance that it would not happen.

"Of course there'll be a war. Do you really believe that your friend Adolph is going to be satisfied just because he's got Austria and the Sudetenland? Of course he's not. The trouble is, it's going to be such a long tedious business. Those Germans are such professionals when it comes to fighting. If only it was the French, it would be so much easier to knock them about instead. But there, we really should choose our enemies more carefully," Percy concluded.

The three had sat talking into the early hours of the morning, and after retiring to bed Robert awoke to find it was almost noon. His clothes, which he had flung off before getting into bed, had disappeared, and a new set had been neatly laid out for him. A young man, only a few years older than himself entered the room and introduced himself as Stevens, Sir Percy's manservant. Robert sat up and Stevens placed a tray on the bed, and said, "Just a snack, sir, to keep you going until luncheon."

When Robert eventually arrived in the lounge he found Percy sitting at his desk, typing, and Cynthia prancing round the room with a pencil in her mouth. She had just arrived back after spending the night in her father's London home. Evidently daddy strongly objected to her sleeping in one of Percy's spare bedrooms. As Percy had explained to Robert, "Daddy insists there's no monkey business before the nuptial knot's tied. Doesn't want any little bastards cluttering up the family tree."

On seeing Robert Cynthia removed the pencil from her mouth, and the greeting he received, Robert thought, would have been more suitable for one whom she had not seen for ten years.

"Darling boy!" she gushed, flinging her arms round him, and kissing him with even more ardour than she had the previous evening. "If only you'd sit for me, you heavenly thing. I'd be in an absolute frenzy of inspiration."

Percy had stopped typing. "She'll inveigle you into it in the end, dear boy, so you might as well let her have her way now," he chuckled.

Robert laughed. "I'm afraid I'm no artist's model. Anyway I must go soon. Another time perhaps Cynthia."

"Is that a promise?"

"Yes, okay," Robert replied quickly and without conviction, to pass the matter off.

"You know you're welcome to stay on as long as you like, dear boy," said Percy.

But Robert felt he must get home. He couldn't delay facing his father any longer, so after lunch he caught an afternoon train for Brighton. The journey gave him more time to consider the advice Percy had given him regarding way he should break the news to John. What Percy had said had also cleared his mind of any ideas that he might be a genuine conscientious objector. But what would he do if war did come? To that question he had no answer, so it was pushed to one side in the hope that it may never arise.

He arrived home just before teatime. Being a Sunday the house was quiet as he opened the front door and set down his cases in the hall. The sound of the grandfather clock was all there was to be heard. He flung his mack on a chair and crept towards the drawing-room. His mother was sitting reading in front of the fire, and for a moment he stood silently in the doorway just looking at her. "Hallo, Mother," he said quietly.

Elizabeth looked up. "Robert!" she said, with surprise written all over her face. "I thought you were in Winchester. Whatever are you doing here?" She noticed he had the same look on his face as when he used to return from school after having been in trouble. Elizabeth got up and went towards him with outstretched arms. "What's wrong?" she asked, embracing him.

Robert kissed her but made no attempt to answer her question. He took her by the hand and led her back to the fireside. Still holding hands they sat together on the settee. "Mother, I've resigned my commission." There was a long pause while he waited for a comment.

"I see," Elizabeth replied without emotion. "Perhaps you'd better tell me everything."

Agnes came in with the tea trolley, and couldn't contain her joy at seeing her boy again. Robert embraced and kissed her, and when she had gone he related his news and tried his best to explain himself to Elizabeth. "I'm sorry, Mother. I know I'm a rotten son," he concluded.

"Robert, don't talk such nonsense. You're a wonderful son, and don't you ever forget it. But I can't think what your father will say."

At that moment John came briskly into the room, rubbing his hands in anticipation of a hot cup of tea. "Tea ready, Beth?" he asked. "Good Lord! What are you doing here, Robert? Not leave already?"

Robert got up and John shook his hand. "Not exactly, Father."

John was oblivious of the worried look on his son's face, and happily sat down. "Well this is pleasant having the newest subaltern in the regiment with us, isn't it, Beth?"

"Perhaps you ought to reserve judgement on that, Father."

"Robert has something to tell you, schat," Elizabeth said as soothingly as she possibly could.

John looked from one to the other. "What's this, a conspiracy?" he smiled. "Well, come along, boy, out with it."

Robert sat with his hands clasped between his knees and his head bowed. Another of his traits, Elizabeth remembered. He had always sat in that way in his younger days when about to confess some new piece of mischief. There was a long pause while Robert considered how best to start. Percy had told him to be gentle, but he could not think how to soften the blow. He would just have to come straight out with it, he decided. He breathed deeply and then quietly said, "I've resigned my commission."

"You've what!" John spluttered, sitting up straight. He felt himself fighting for breath and for a moment was unable to say more. He gripped the arms of the chair hard in an effort to control his anger.

Elizabeth noticed the little twitch under her husband's right eye. She also saw the same on her son's face.

"I've resigned, Father," Robert repeated.

John made a move to stand up, but as fast as the tension had built up within him it quickly subsided, and he slumped back into his chair as one exhausted. "I see," he eventually remarked. Thoughts rushed through his mind. He'd had disappointments before, but nothing to compare with this. Such a fine boy, and such a waste. He would have made a good officer. Perhaps it was his own fault for insisting the boy went to Sandhurst in the first place. He remembered his own youth when he had been sent into the army against his will, but at least he had done his duty by Father and not resigned.

"I'm terribly sorry, Father."

"Are you!" John replied curtly. "I find you very difficult to understand, Robert. If you'd been a failure," John reasoned, wondering to himself whether there was any point in continuing the conversation. "But you weren't a failure. You'd have made a good officer."

"I did try for your sake, sir, but I'm no soldier, at least in my heart I'm not. I don't want to be a fighter. I just want peace."

"Don't we all!" John glared at his son, feeling himself becoming agitated again. "We all want peace, but sometimes peace has to be fought for, as one day you may find out," he snapped. "And just remember it's the fighting services that enable us to live our lives in this peace you talk about."

Robert asked himself why everyone appeared so much wiser than he. All his reasoning seems to be useless when others put an entirely different view. First Percy, now Father. If only he could be honest and tell the world that he couldn't be a soldier because he was a bloody funk, instead of making up excuses, he thought.

"And what the devil do you think you're going to do now?" John asked.

"I don't know," he replied,

"You don't know," John repeated disdainfully. "Well, it's time you did. Don't expect me to keep you. You get yourself a job."

"Perhaps I could go to music college? Robert tentatively suggested.

"And perhaps you can't!" John snapped back. "I thought I'd made myself perfectly clear on that score when that music teacher fellow walked out after that tantrum of yours."

"But I was only sixteen, Father. It'll be different now."

"Different or not, the answer's no," John retorted, and then, getting out of his chair and making towards the door, added, "Better still, I'll get you a job. No time like the present."

"What job?" Robert asked doubtfully.

"Something in the city. Merchant banking perhaps," John replied.

"But I don't want that sort of job," Robert objected.

"How do you know till you've tried it? I'll have no more nonsense, Robert. You'll do as you're told!"

When John had gone Elizabeth said, "You'd better do it, Robert, for a time at least. He's terribly upset, you know."

"I wish I was a boy again. Then it was a quick caning. Now I'm going to be imprisoned in a blasted bank for the rest of my life."

"Come now, Robert, it won't be that bad. You may even like it. Just let things take their course, dear. I'm sure everything will turn out for the best."

Robert leant over and let his head rest on his mother's shoulder. "Why does life have to be so frustrating, Mother? Perhaps I should have stayed in the army." He felt his mother running her hand through his hair and stroking his head, trying to sooth away his troubles. "You know what I really want don't you?"

"Yes, I know," Elizabeth sighed.

"Sometimes I feel I can't live with music, but deep down I know I can't live without it. . . What *am* I going to do, Mother?"

When John had left, the drawing-room, he had taken the secret way into Reggie's house.

"All the fun of the fair, old boy!" exclaimed Reggie, waving a toasting fork in the air as John walked into the drawing-room. He and Daisy had their chairs drawn close up to the fire and were sitting with their feet in the grate. "We're not trying to roast ourselves, old boy, just toasting the old crumpets. Daisy insists we toast 'em ourselves. None of the old grilling for her, don't you know."

"What was good enough for my old mum, is good enough for me," said Daisy. "Something wrong John dear? It ain't like you to be 'ere for Sunday tea."

John sat down and came straight to the point. "'Robert's resigned his commission," he said.

"Good for him," laughed Reggie. "Got a bit up top like his Uncle Reggie." Reggie tapped his head with a finger. "Ha, ha. Have a crumpet, old boy. That'll keep the old pecker up." Reggie gingerly took the hot crumpet off the fork and handed it quickly to Daisy, who put it on a plate and buttered it.

"You won't get any sympathy from Reggie, John dear. Not where that boy's concerned. Robert can do no wrong in 'is eyes," said Daisy, handing him the plate.

But John shook his head. He hadn't come here to eat, he had more serious matters on his mind. "It's all right saying that, Reggie, but what's going to become of him? That's what worries me."

"For heavens sake, old son! The army isn't the only occupation open to a young man of Robert's calibre."

"Reggie's right, dear," Daisy interrupted. You're the most sensible and unruffled man I know, John, except when it comes to dealing with Robert. You worry about 'im, far too much. He'll be all right, dear, you'll see. He's got his head screwed on, and at least 'e's not running off to fight in Spain like some other silly young twerps."

John said, "Now look here, Reggie, I want a favour."

"Anything you like, old boy."

"I thought you might get the boy fixed up with something in the city."

"Leave it to me. I'll have a scout round tomorrow. Sure to be something suitable."

The door of the room opened quietly. Daisy glanced up and blurted out, "Blimey! Look what the tides washed up now. We'll soon 'ave the 'ole family 'ere."

Robert stood in the doorway not expecting to see his father already sitting in the room. "I'm sorry, I didn't mean to intrude," he said. But he too received his usual warm greeting, and was made to sit down next to John.

"So you want a job in the city, Robert," said Daisy.

"What he wants has nothing to do with it," John interjected. "This is my idea."

Robert remained silent.

"Not a very good basis for a successful career," Reggie remarked.

"Maybe not," John replied. "But at least it'll be a start. Who knows, he may come to like it." He stood up. "Well, I must go."

"But you've only just come, dear," said Daisy.

But John felt restless, and he knew that the shock and disappointment of the afternoon would make him bad company for the rest of the day, so, leaving the others to chat amongst themselves, he returned to his own fireside and disconsolately flung himself into his chair. He said to Elizabeth, "Reggie'll fix him up with something."

But seeing the look of uncertainty on her face, he added, "The job, for Robert. I've asked Reggie to find him something."

"I hope you know what you're doing, dear," Elizabeth remarked.

"What makes you say that?"

"Well, we don't want the boy bored to death, do we."

John was about to answer when the telephone rang. He picked up the receiver and the incredulous expression which came over his face when the caller spoke gave Elizabeth a fit of the giggles.

"I say, who is that?" John barked. "No, this is not your heavenly boy. Are you sure you have the right number?" There was a long pause while John listened to some sort of explanation. Then he said, "Yes, I'll tell him you called. Goodbye, er. . . " There was a loud click as the caller rang off.

Elizabeth gave way to her laughter. "Your face John! Whoever was it?"

"God knows! Thought I was Robert. Heavenly boy indeed! Some woman calling herself the Hon somebody or other."

"Is that what she called you, her heavenly boy?" Elizabeth was now helpless with laughter.

John scowled at his wife. "That boy of yours has got some damn strange friends!" he exclaimed. "I hope he's not picking up with the wrong sort."

When Robert returned John said to him, "I trust your uncle has given you some good advice. You seem to be able to take it from him."

"At least he understands, which is more than you do."

"Robert, that's unkind!" said Elizabeth. "Apologise to your father."

"No, don't apologise if that's what you think," John interjected. "But it may surprise you to know that I understand more than you think, young man. Perhaps the army is well rid of you if you're unwilling to fight. They have a name for that sort which I have restrained myself from using."

"I'm sure Robert didn't mean it, dear," Elizabeth said.

"I'm sorry, Father."

There was an awkward silence for a time, and then John said, "By the way, some person rang for you. The Hon someone; a woman's voice."

"The Hon. Cynth!" Robert exclaimed.

"Who the devil's she!"

"It's cousin Percy's fiancée, the Honourable Cynthia Cartwright-Craddock."

"Percy's fiancée! I don't believe it."

"It's true, Father. They're going to be married."

"Married! But I thought Percy was a. . . Well, never mind what I thought. How do you know all this?"

Robert explained how he had spent the previous night at Percy's flat.

"How look here, Robert. I don't want you getting involved with these people. They're a most peculiar set, if you ask me. Not the sort for a son of mine to mix with. They could lead you into all sorts of unsavoury things."

"What sort of things?" Robert snapped, back indignantly.

"You know very well what I mean. I thought I had beaten that sort of thing out of you and Carl Heinz, but sometimes I'm not so sure."

"God! Why did you have to bring that up?" Robert coloured up. "We were only boys. You always think the worst of me."

"Then give me reason to do otherwise," John retorted.

"Besides, Percy's all right when you get to know him."

"Well, you've changed your tune a bit. But don't say I haven't warned you," John concluded.

Robert couldn't wait to find out what Cynthia wanted, so he left the room for a few minutes to ring her. When he returned it was obvious to his parents that he was happy about something. It turned out that Cynthia had found him an engagement with an hotel quartet. Evidently one of the violin players had fallen sick and a temporary replacement was needed. "It's just for ten days, darling, and the pay is under forty bob," Cynthia had said. "And you simply must come and stay with Percy while you're in town."

Robert did not mention the music engagement, saying only that he had been invited to stay with Percy for ten days. John felt unable to forbid it so gave his consent providing Robert was available for any job interviews that might come up. But he was not pleased about the matter. "You just remember what I've said while you're with these people."

"I'll be all right, Father."

Robert left the next day for London. The arrangement to stay with Percy was most convenient, because the hotel was within walking distance of the apartment.

He was almost late for his first morning session at the hotel, and when he arrived out of breath it was to find the other members of the quartet sitting waiting for him. The pianist was a middle aged, bald headed man, who, Robert thought resembled a pig. Both the other violinist and the cellist were grey haired, elderly ladies. They looked at one another as Robert introduced himself and stood before them waiting for one of them to say something. There was a long pause, during which his new colleagues eyed him with expressionless faces.

"He's rather young," said the violinist to the other lady.

"You're rather young," the cellist repeated to Robert.

"Yes, Mam, I suppose I am," said Robert respectfully, although what his age had got to do with it he didn't know.

"We didn't expect anyone quite so young," the violinist remarked.

"No. We didn't expect anyone quite so young," the cellist repeated.

Robert wondered whether all their conversation was in duplicate, and he was finding it difficult to keep a straight face.

"We can't do anything about that now," interrupted the pianist impatiently. "We'll just have to try him, and if he's no good he'll have to go."

"If you're no good you'll just have to go," repeated the cellist.

"But he is polite," said the violinist, giving Robert a weak smile.

"You are polite," came the inevitable statement from the cellist.

The pig face decided it was time for action, and pointed to a vacant seat, in front of which was a music stand. After Robert had taken his place, the man came and handed him some music, and began to explain in a somewhat aggressive north country accent what was required of him. "If it's too difficult you'd better say so now," he concluded.

"I think I'll manage, thank you," Robert replied.

"He thinks he'll manage, Hilda." This time it was the cellist who spoke first.

"I sure he'll manage, Myrtle, he's so refined, and such a nice looking boy."

"You're a nice looking boy."

"Thank you. You're very kind," Robert replied.

Both ladies nodded and smiled at him, but the man had had enough, of their dithering and made ready to play.

The coffee lounge had begun to fill with people, and it reminded Robert of the time he had played on board ship coming home from India. How nervous he had been then, but he was too amused with his colleagues to be nervous on this occasion, and in any case the music looked so easy. When the time came to play, they all started more or less together - Hilda having to quickly get herself in time - but they hadn't played more than a few bars when the two ladies stopped and let Robert continue alone, accompanied only by the piano. They stared at him and then looked at each other. They had rarely heard such exquisite intonation from one so young, and the technique of the boy had taken them completely by surprise.

When the piece had finished there was polite applause, and then the pianist remarked abruptly to Robert, "You'll do." Then turning to the ladies he inquired, "Are you two on strike? If you don't buck up this young upstart will do you out of a job."

The ladies nodded and smiled at Robert, praising him in turn for the way he had played. From that time on they made a great fuss of him, but having had no dealings with young people, treated him more like a thirteen year old than a youth, of nineteen. Robert didn't mind and resigned himself to their quaint ways, feeling quite touched by the kind attention they paid him. Whenever the occasion allowed after a performance they would buy him an ice cream, insisting that, as all boys liked ice cream, their boy was not to be done out of such a treat.

But the time passed quickly, and soon the engagement came to an end. He said his goodbyes to the pianist and to two tearful ladies, and left, the hotel for the last time slightly better off than he had been.

Robert's next engagement in the world of the arts was not so much to his liking. That evening at dinner Cynthia informed him that she was going to start painting his portrait directly the meal was over.

"Full length, absolutely starkers, sweetie," Percy chuckled.

"Oh, no! I can't!" Robert objected.

But Cynthia was not to be put off. "You promised, darling, and I just can't wait to get you on canvas."

"I didn't mean it, it was just a slip of the tongue," Robert hedged.

But when the meal was over, Cynthia dragged her unwilling subject to the centre of the lounge and began to remove his clothes. Robert was not to be spared his embarrassment. He knew in his mind that he should not allow it to happen, but he felt helpless to stop it. Is this what Father was talking about, he asked himself? Perhaps he was allowing himself to sink into corrupt ways. The thought of his father made him feel ashamed.

Percy flung himself full length on a settee and lounged back enjoying the spectacle as Cynthia coaxed the last piece of clothing from her unwilling model. Having done so she launched into an effusion of praise for the subject before her, and then walked, round and round Robert, who was standing uncomfortably in the centre of the room, sizing him up from every angle.

"Do stop drooling over the beautiful boy and get on with it Cynth," drawled Percy.

"Patience, dear heart, I must get the perspective right," Cynthia replied, getting hold of Robert and arranging his stance to her satisfaction.

"What have I let myself in for?" Robert groaned.

"Don't worry it'll be quite painless," Percy laughed.

"Maybe, but it's jolly embarrassing," Robert objected.

While Cynthia was still settling Robert's position the door leading from the entrance hall opened and Stevens entered to announce a visitor. But before he could do so the visitor, who was wearing a green coloured velvet jacket, green trousers and a green shirt, and was holding a handkerchief to his forehead, burst into the room with all the dramatic affectation of a Victorian melodrama. Stevens, lifting his eyes in despair, gave up his task and withdrew, leaving the newcomer to sweep into the centre of the room on his own.

He was a middle aged man with a long narrow face and a large Roman nose. The hair on one side of his head had been allowed to grow long so that it could be brushed across to the other side thus covering the area on top which was beginning to show signs of baldness. A long black cloak had been allowed to slip from his shoulders on to the floor as he advanced.

"Darlings!" he wailed, mopping his brow. "Disaster! Bunty is ruined! My heart has been simply torn from my breast."

"Do stop making such a commotion, Bunty,'" said Percy, remaining completely unmoved by his friend's dramatic entrance.

"It's the end, darlings, it's all over," Bunty continued, not at all put off by the lack of interest from his audience. "I've lost the lovely Peter," he declared. His tone changed from one of despair to irritation. "It's that odious Monty Marchbank. The wretch has carried the dear boy off to the south of France."

"Bunty, we've no wish to hear about your sordid love affairs," said. Percy.

But Bunty's dramatic entrance had come to a sudden halt. His eyes had come to rest on Robert.

It had been Robert's inclination to run for cover into the bedroom when the door had opened, but Cynthia had made him stand still, and, not taking the slightest notice of the interruption, had continued to push her subject from one position to another until she got the effect she wanted.

"I say!" exclaimed Bunty, taking an eye-glass out of his top pocket. "Who's this heavenly child?" .

Robert watched the newcomer slowly run his eyeglass down the full length of his body, pausing for a moment at a part of special interest. It came to his mind that the Christian slaves must have felt much as he did as the stranger eyed him.

"Lor! What a divine creation. Such beautifully smooth skin. Just a shade of powder needed to cover the poor thing's blushes." Bunty seemed to have forgotten the lovely Peter and was now giving his full attention to Robert.

Percy, still stretched out languidly on the couch, said, "Bunty, let me introduce my cousin, Robert. And don't get any ideas, he's not one of your sort, so hands off."

"Alas, alas, poor Bunty." Bunty sighed, and sank clown into an arm chair, still keeping his eyes on Robert.

"And this is Bunty Fortesque, Robert. He's an absolute reprobate where young men are concerned, but otherwise a dear friend, and certainly a useful old thing to know if you wish to enter the music world.

Cynthia wouldn't let Robert move so a nod had to suffice for the introductions.

"I do wish you wouldn't wear those dreadful green things, Bunty darling, I can hardly bear to look at you," Cynthia scolded.

"But darling, I'm in mourning for the loss of the divine Peter. I always wear green when I'm in mourning; it reminds me of a graveyard. The teeny bit of orange," Bunty continued, fingering his bow tie, "is to cheer poor Bunty up."

Cynthia swept across the room and picked up the fallen black cloak. Taking it to Bunty, with a great sweeping motion she dramatically spread it over him, leaving only his head uncovered. "Sorry, darling, but I'm trying to paint this dear boy and the green is affecting my inspiration. It's not a day for green."

Robert was quite bewildered by the proceedings, but he noted that Bunty didn't seem at all put out by being almost completely submerged in his cloak. In fact, due to Robert's presence, Bunty's spirits had revived considerably.

When Robert was eventually allowed to dress - much to Bunty's disappointment - and to sit down and talk to the visitor, he found Bunty a very knowledgeable and interesting person. According to Percy, what he didn't know about music and London's musical fraternity wasn't worth knowing. His main occupation in life being that of a music critic. At Percy's suggestion Bunty agreed to hear Robert play.

"Well, what do you think?" Percy asked when Robert had finished. "An honest answer now, Bunty, because you won't get any favours from this boy whatever you say."

"A bit rusty at the moment, dear boy,' but with the right teacher he could go a long way. Needs to be heard by the right people. As the old saying goes, it's not what you know, it's who you know. And you know Bunty. Enough said. I'll arrange a recital. It'll take a few weeks to get the right people together, so be patient."

"It's awfully kind of you, Bunty, but. . . " Robert hesitated. He knew this was a chance not to be missed, but it would have to wait. His first priority was to avoid having to take up banking, and he had decided that he would go to Rotterdam without telling his father, and ask his Uncle Hugo for a job. He would try to keep up his music at the same time, then, hopefully, he thought, Father might relent and let him run his own life. And then there was Lisa. Lately she had been constantly in his thoughts, and he yearned to be near her. He hadn't seen her since Joanna's wedding, which was over a year ago, because, since then, she had been away at finishing school in Switzerland. Sometimes the thought of her nearly drove him to distraction, and he had to relieve his feelings in the only way he knew. "I'm going to Rotterdam," he added.

"Rotterdam! Dear child, there's no music in Rotterdam!"

Percy, who had been taken into Robert's confidence, interrupted. "He's not going there for music. He going to visit a dark eyed maiden and until he's had his way with her music will have to take second place."

Robert saw Percy grinning at him and knew his cousin was right. But he'd never yet had his way with Lisa, and probably never would. He'd never even properly kissed her, and it was obvious she didn't love him. But he couldn't help himself; he just had to see her again.

"The randy beast!" exclaimed Bunty. He sat thoughtfully stroking his chin with his eye glass and then said to Robert, "When you return to earth from your romantic adventure, contact Bunty and I'll see what can be done for you."

Robert spent the next few days being lavishly entertained by Percy in the West End. He was introduced to the world of theatre, music and art. But his spare moments were taken up with him standing naked in the middle of the room while Cynthia enthusiastically went to work with her brushes. When the picture was finished and he was allowed to look at it, he knew it was a first class job. "It's too good. Everyone will recognise me," he objected.

"Well of course they will, darling. There's nothing to be ashamed of," Cynthia replied.

"I'm not so sure about that. You could have made it a little less revealing and left something to the imagination."

"That would have spoilt it. It's meant to portray the life and vigour of youth," Cynthia enthused.

"It certainly does that," Robert replied. "A bit too much in my opinion. I hate to think what Father would say, and Mother would be shocked." At the thought of his parents a feeling of shame came over him. He should have refused, he decided. But it was too late now. "Promise you won't show it," he pleaded.

"Don't worry, darling, I'll hang it in the bedroom," Cynthia promised.

*

True to his promise Reggie found a position in a city merchant bank. Robert was to start his new career in the second week of January which gave him a few weeks at home before it was necessary to escape to Rotterdam. He hated deceiving his parents, but could see no other solution to his problem.

Wendy was Robert's constant companion during the last weeks of the year. She was studying at the local technical college and was still living at home. The two had become very fond of each other, neither having forgotten the first time their hands had touched at Joanna's ball, or their first kiss on that summer evening on the downs when they were still only fifteen. There had been many kisses since, but their close relationship had never gone too far, although on some occasions Robert had become over passionate and had wished to go further. But Wendy had not allowed this to happen, and when he had become frantic with desire had gently calmed his pent up feelings.

It was an easy, happy and uncomplicated relationship as far as Robert was concerned. He found her cheerful spirit brought out the best in him. Always willing to listen to his problems, she wouldn't allow him to dwell on them too long and sink in to a mood of depression. He knew she was good for him, and enjoyed the way she had of encouraging him to talk about his favourite subjects.

From the moment Wendy had seen the good looking, untidy boy sitting on the garden wall no other boy had been able to gain the special place in her life as had Robert. To her he was the perfect boy, not only in looks but in other respects. She found him kind and considerate, full of fun, and yet with a deeply sensitive nature giving to his character a certain seriousness which fascinated her. Just to be in his presence was the joy of her life, and when he kissed her and she felt the nearness of his body it was as much as she could do to prevent him having his way. But she was determined not to allow it until she had won his heart as well as his desire, and young as she was, she realised that this moment might never come.

On New Year's Eve the Marsdens had been invited to a small party at the Rutherford home. It was just a small family affair with a few local friends included. It was the homely gathering that Robert enjoyed. The great log-fires all lit and burning brightly in every room, and the lights on the Christmas tree adding to the warm, cosy atmosphere.

As the Marsdens arrived Robert came trotting down the stairs and swept Wendy away from her parents.

Wendy's mother had begun to wonder whether there was more in her daughter's relationship with Robert than just a passing fancy. "I hear Robert's going abroad," Mrs Marsden remarked to Elizabeth.

"Abroad?" Elizabeth looked puzzled.

"Yes, I thought I heard him mention Rotterdam to Wendy."

"That's the first I've heard about it," Elizabeth replied. "He's going to London to start a new job."

"Perhaps that was it," Mrs Marsden decided. "I hope so. We should miss him. We've just got used to having him in and out of the house again."

Elizabeth let the matter drop. She had no intention of interfering with her son's plans. If he wished to go to Rotterdam without telling her, then so be it. But she rightly suspected that Robert's secrecy had stemmed from the fear that his father would refused him permission to go. Of course, the boy was very naughty not to say something, especially now that a position in a bank had been arranged for him, but it was something he was going to have to handle himself, she decided.

Robert poured Wendy a drink, and then whisked her off into the seclusion of the small music room, where they sat together on a settee in front of the blazing fire. He wasted no time in slipping his arm round her waist.

Wendy looked at him quizzically. "You're in a hurry tonight, Robert," she grinned. She felt his lips lightly on her cheek, and turning to face him their lips touched and pressed together. From the very first she had enjoyed the ardent way in which he kissed her. There was nothing sloppy about the way Robert kissed, and one of the things that fascinated Wendy about him was the mixture of shyness and passion in his nature.

Breathing heavily, he drew away and panted, "God! I've been waiting all day for that."

"You are on fire tonight, you naughty boy," Wendy declared.

Robert smiled sheepishly, and for some time they sat happily together in silence. "Wendy?" Robert eventually said. He hesitated as he tried to pluck up courage to ask the question which had been on his mind for some time. He saw her looking at him in anticipation, and he had to look away before he could speak. He took his arm from her waist and sat forward with his elbows on his knees and his hands covering his face, and said quietly, "Can't we. . .well, you know, go too far?" He hesitated; glancing at her from behind his hands. "I want you, Wendy. Please," he pleaded.

There was a moment's silence, and then he felt her hand on his shoulder, gently turning him to face her. She took his hands from his face and held them together in hers. "If you ever fell in love with me, Robert. . ."

"But I. . ." he began to say, but she put her finger on his lips and stopped him.

"No, Robert. Don't say it, because you know it wouldn't be true. It's not me you love."

He turned his head away, unable to look her in the face, because he knew she was right. "I'm sorry, Wendy. Oh, God, I'm sorry! But I can't help it."

"I understand." She gently put her hand on his face and turned it towards her. "You're the sweetest boy I've ever met, and I know you're fond of me, but until you love me. I'll not be completely yours. And to me love means marriage." Holding his face in her hands she pulled him to her and kissed him. "I'll always be here, waiting. Even forever," she whispered.

When he was released from her tender grasp, Robert saw there were tears in her eyes. "Please don't cry, Wendy," he pleaded. "What a selfish brute I am." He picked up his drink and sat back in the chair moodily staring at the glass. "I don't know why you put up with me. You're too kind, and I don't deserve it."

She wished to say how much she loved him, but the words died on her lips. "Cheer up, Robert. We've had lots of fun together, and we're still friends. Anyway, who knows what might happen." Wendy took him by the hand and stood up. "Come on, let's put a record on and dance," she said brightly.

Robert's mood soon changed, and the evening passed happily. Just before midnight John, switched on the wireless to hear Big Ben striking the hour. As it did so the toast was drunk and the New Year greetings exchanged. Robert kissed his mother and father, Joanna, Daisy and Agnes, and then quickly returned to take Wendy's hand and kiss her.

"Nineteen thirty nine," John declared. "A happy New Year to you all. And I wish you young ones a bright future," he said raising his glass.

"All the best, you two, for nineteen thirty nine," was Reggie's greeting as Robert, with Wendy hanging on to his arm, shook his hand.

"What I wouldn't give to be young again, dear," said Daisy as she kissed Wendy. Daisy winked at Robert. "What a lovely girl. You can choose 'em all right, you naughty boy," she added, giving him one of her knowing looks.

*

Robert left home on the Friday before he was due to start his new job in London ostensibly to take up lodgings in the city. But he had arranged no lodgings, and his intention was to travel straight to Rotterdam. John was in London so only Elizabeth was present when the time came for Robert's departure.

Robert hugged and kissed his mother and then got into the waiting car.

"Take care of yourself, Robert," Elizabeth said.

"Don't look so sad, Mother," he replied. He was going to add that he would be back next week-end but thought better of it. He didn't wish to deceive his mother more than necessary. Instead he leant out through the window and took her hand gently squeezing it.

As the car drew away Robert heard Elizabeth say, "Give my love to Hugo and Kate." He turned in surprise and saw a wisp of a smile on his mother's face as she stood there waving. How ever did she know, he wondered? Perhaps he should go back and apologize, but he made no attempt to tell Perks to stop or go back.

His conscience was still pricking him as he passed through the ticket barrier at Brighton Station. Then he felt a tug on his arm, and turning, saw Wendy looking up at him

"Wendy!" he exclaimed. "What are you doing here?"

"I just had to see you off. I hope you don't mind," she smiled.

"Mind! Of course I don't mind." He put his arm round her and they walked down the platform until he found a suitable compartment. Having put his case on his seat, he jumped back down on to the platform and enfolded her in his arms. They stayed, talking quietly, until it was time for him to go, and then he got back into the carriage and leant out of the open window. "Thanks for coming, Wendy. It's really nice," he said.

"I couldn't let you go without saying goodbye." She looked up at him sadly as the train, began to move. "Remember what I said about waiting for you," she called.

"I'll remember."

"I love you, Robert;" she called after him, but the screech of a train whistle drowned her words, and she knew he hadn't heard.

He stayed at the window, waving until she was out of sight.

The journey was uneventful, and he arrived in Rotterdam the following morning. He had written to Hugo and Kate - not explaining the reason for his visit – and found them waiting for him at the station. He was disappointed not to see Lisa waiting with her parents, but was soon informed that she was away skiing in Switzerland and would be returning in a few days.

Hugo had always enjoyed having his nephew to stay in his home, but when he heard that Robert wished to stay for some months, perhaps even on a semi-permanent basis, his pleasure was obvious. However, both he and Kate were curious to know why their nephew had suddenly taken it into his head to visit them.

"Are you on leave, Robert?" Kate inquired.

"Well, not exactly, Aunty." Robert hesitated, and then said, "Actually, I've resigned."

"What, given up the army altogether?" Hugo looked at his nephew in surprise.

Robert nodded.

"Oh, dear," said Kate. "What ever did your father say?"

"He wasn't very pleased."

"I bet he wasn't," Hugo grinned.

Kate looked hard at Robert. "I presume he knows you're here?" she asked.

Robert glanced sheepishly at his aunt. "Well, a-actually, no," he stammered.

"I think you'd better explain, young man," Kate suggested.

So Robert told the whole story and ended by asking Hugo if it was possible for him to be found a job.

"Of course I'll find you a job," Hugo replied. "But you really should have discussed the matter with your father first, you know."

"I know, Uncle. I'll write and explain. I just want to show him I can stand on my own feet."

"I don't think he's ever doubted that, Robert," Kate interjected.

Kate instructed Robert to write to his parents immediately, and Hugo, although he did not mention it to Robert, decided that he would write to John with a promise to give Robert a thorough training in commerce, and to assure him that his son was trying his best to gain his approval.

Hugo's offices were within walking distance of his home, in fact, they were only half a mile away in the Willemskade in a house situated beside the river and once occupied by another old merchant family. Robert had been there before and knew some of the staff, so when he accompanied Hugo on his first morning at work it was not a completely new experience for him.

Hugo's delight at having his nephew working for him was obvious to all, and it was only with difficulty that the chief clerk managed to prise Robert away from him in order to start teaching the young man the rudiments of the business. "Mr Robert must learn the job from the bottom," the chief clerk said to Hugo. "You can't keep him to yourself all day."

Hugo smiled. "Of course you're right as always, Mr Peterson. I wish Mr Robert to be my personal assistant, but I suppose he'd better learn the job first."

Robert tried his hardest to concentrate, and to his surprise found that he was actually enjoying himself and easily taking in what he was being taught. Some of the mathematical problems, which he had found so difficult at school when old Cavey had tried to drum them into his unwilling brain, now seemed, to make sense. However, there were occasions when his mind wandered, and sometimes the anticipation of seeing Lisa again interrupted his train of thought, but Mr Peterson was a good teacher and soon brought him back to earth.

"When Miss Lisa returns she will assist me with your tuition," said Mr Peterson.

For a moment Robert looked blank. "Surely she doesn't work here," he said.

"She certainly does, and a very astute young business lady she is."

It was a few days later when Robert and Hugo arrived home from the office that they heard Lisa's voice coming from the drawing-room. Just the sound of her voice made Robert's heart jump for joy, and he had difficulty in restraining himself from running into the room to greet her. As he entered the room Robert saw her standing with her back to the fire, facing him. That she was now a mature young woman somewhat surprised him, and the poise she had gained since he had last seen her greatly impressed him. She was more beautiful than ever, he thought. But the sight that met his eyes did not please him, for standing beside her was a man with his arm round her waist. The man was shorter than Robert, but had a confident air about him. Robert considered him old, at least thirty five.

When she saw Robert, Lisa could not hide her delight. She freed herself from her admirer and came forward to greet him. Robert got the impression that underneath her new found sophistication she was still the same Tom-boy he had known in the past.

"Robert!" she exclaimed, kissing him on the cheek. "It must be the longest we've ever been apart. Over a year, I think. You haven't changed a bit."

For a moment their eyes met. What were they saying to him? Perhaps nothing, and yet could they be challenging him, he wondered? It pleased him that she had noticed, the time gap during which they had not seen each other. He felt himself being taken by the hand and dragged towards the stranger. "Come and meet Mr Charlton," Lisa said. "He's from the United States."

"Please! Call me Brent," said the stranger loudly.

Robert shook his hand, but could not get rid of the feeling that he was being patronised.

The American had met Lisa during her skiing holiday, and had decided to spend a few weeks in Rotterdam to further the friendship - a friendship Robert considered had gone far enough.

In the days that followed it amused Lisa, to watch her two admirers vie with each other for her attention. Brent appeared put out when the two cousins talked of times past of which he knew nothing. But at the same time Robert felt cut out when Brent took Lisa out to shows and expensive restaurants. He could understand Lisa falling in love with Karl Heinz, but it was beyond him how she could let this man maul her about. The mere thought of it had begun to make him angry.

One evening when Lisa had been taken out Robert could not settle to anything. Kate watched him fidgeting in his chair, and then get up and pace the room. "Do you think Lisa really likes that man, Aunty?" he asked.

"I know one thing for sure, Robert, you don't."

"I'm sorry, has it been that obvious? Being a guest here I tried to hide it," Robert apologized.

"My dear boy, you're not a guest in this house, you're part of the family, and don't you ever forget it."

"Thanks, Aunty. I suppose it's none of my business, but it does irritate me when he's always taking Lisa out."

"Then why don't you do something about it and take her out yourself?"

"I can't afford it. I wish I could. All these expensive restaurants and his car. "You wouldn't think I come from a rich family. I've got the wages I earned last week and a few quid in the bank. Do you know, even at Sandhurst my allowance was half the size the others got. Father said I was there to work, not spend money."

"Your father is a very sensible man," Kate remarked. She stretched out her hand to Robert and said, "Come and sit down here." Keeping hold of his hand she continued, "Has it ever occurred to you that Lisa may not require you to spend money on her?"

Robert shook his head.

"I think I know my own daughter," Kate went on.

"I wish I did," Robert put in.

Kate smiled at him. "You've always liked her, haven't you."

Robert nodded, "I wish she liked me a bit more."

"What makes you think she doesn't?"

"Well, she was sweet on Karl Heinz, and now there's this Brent fellow."

Kate smiled. "Never be put off by the wiles of women, Robert."

Robert gave his aunt a quizzical look, but she said no more on the subject.

Robert's irritation with Brent got the better of him on the following Sunday afternoon. Brent had called and was waiting to take Lisa for a drive. Having dressed for the outing and put on her coat she came down the stairs and made towards the drawing-room. But Robert was waiting for her in the hall. He took her firmly by the hand and pulled her towards the front door.

"I'm glad to see you've got your coat on," he said. "What we need is a nice walk." Robert opened the front door, and before Lisa could object she was outside, down the steps, across the road and in the park."

"I'm going out with Brent!" she objected, trying to release her hand.

"No you're not, you're going for a walk with me," Robert grinned, still holding her hand firmly.

"Let me go, Robert, or I shall never speak to you again."

Robert laughed and tightened his grip. "Is that a promise?" he goaded.

Lisa thumped his chest with her free hand. "Let me go! you. . . you rotten beast."

"Temper, temper," he grinned, catching hold of her other hand. "What's all the fuss about? I'm doing you a favour."

"What makes you think I want to go out with you? Who do you think you are, anyway? At least he's a mature gentleman with good manners, not a stupid boy."

"He's no gentleman. He's a smarmy Yank. It's sickening to see the way he drools over you. And he's old enough to be your father," Robert added for good measure.

"I'll go out with whom I like! It's nothing to do with you, Robert Rutherford."

"Oh, yes it is! Lisa van der Leyden."

"You can't tell me what to do."

"Yes I can!"

"You're jealous!"

"What if I am?"

Robert managed to drag her, protesting, as far as the lake and, having got fed up with pulling his captive, they stopped by the water's edge. Lisa pulled hard, trying once again to release her hands from his grip.

"Let me go, you beast!" she demanded again.

"You're just a spoilt brat!" Robert retorted in frustration. "Someone should have put you over their knee long ago. Go back to your fancy man! See if I care!"

Lisa gave one almighty tug to free her hands at the same time as Robert let go. Having nothing to hold her, she staggered backwards into the lake and, losing her balance, sat down in the water.

Robert stared in disbelief as Lisa sat there with the water swirling round her waist and astonishment written all over her face. After controlling himself for a moment, Robert burst into laughter. "I never thought I'd see the day when Lisa van der Leyden got a wet bum," he roared.

"Oh, shut up, you idiot! I'll never. . ."

"I know, you'll never speak to me again." He collapsed on the bank helpless with laughter.

Some passers-by glanced at the young couple with amusement.

"Don't just sit there you bloody fool! Give me your hand and get me out of here."

"Naughty, naughty. That's not the way for a young lady to speak," Robert taunted, just managing to get the words out before his next burst of laughter.

"Oh, shut up!" Lisa extended her hand.

Still laughing, Robert got to his knees and held out his hand which Lisa grasped firmly. But before he was ready, Lisa pulled with all her strength and Robert, being unprepared, fell full length into the water. Lisa quickly threw herself on top of him to make sure he became *completely* submerged.

When Robert got his breath back after coming to the surface, he sat beside Lisa with water dripping down his face. "You bloody minx!" he exclaimed, pushing her backwards so that she too was completely saturated.

For a moment they sat glaring at each other trying to keep straight faces. But they were unable to control themselves for long, and burst into peels of laughter. They wrestled together for a few moments until the icy water began to make them shiver. Then, struggling to the bank, they ran back towards the house.

Bursting in through the front door, oblivious to the presence in the hall of Kate and Brent, Robert caught Lisa round the waist and the two of them started to wrestle with each other. "I'll teach you, you minx!" Robert laughed.

The astonished Brent just stared.

"What have you two been up to?" Kate demanded with a look of resignation on her face. "You're absolutely soaked!"

"I've just saved your daughter's life, Aunty," Robert replied, trying to hold Lisa still.

"You lying beast! He pushed me in, Mother. Don't believe a word he says."

"Stop it, both of you! You naughty children," Kate ordered. "You'll catch your death of cold. You're both to go and have a bath immediately." Kate stood pointing up the stairs with a look of mock severity on her face.

Robert gave her an engaging smile. "Both together, Aunty?" he asked innocently.

"Robert!" Kate tried to look stern. "You naughty boy!"

Lisa sniggered and ran up the stairs. "Bags the best bathroom." At the top of the stairs she stopped and called back, "Sorry, Brent, see you later".

When Robert and Lisa had disappeared Kate turned to Brent and said, "I'm so sorry that your arrangements have been upset, Brent. But you see how it is with these young people. Their lives have been bound together for so long that it is very difficult for others to enter their world." Kate spoke in a kindly way, but her words were full of significance.

Brent waited patiently until Lisa returned downstairs. When she entered the drawing-room he got up and closed the door, hoping they would be undisturbed.

Lisa sat down, but Brent stood looking down at her with his arm resting along the mantelpiece.

"How would like to come to the States?" he asked.

"Very much," Lisa replied.

"That's settled then."

"What's settled. Brent?"

"I gotta go back shortly. You come too. It's a great idea, honey."

"Steady on, Brent. I can't go back with you."

"For heavens sake, why not? You'll love it over there. I got a great place, swimming pool, everything you want."

"Well, for one thing it wouldn't be quite right. And, besides, my parents wouldn't allow it."

"I'm sorry, honey, I've put this all wrong. You're the most beautiful girl I've ever met and I love you. You must know I wanna marry you."

"But you hardly know me."

"I knew you were for me right from the start. I know I'm no chicken, but a great girl like you doesn't want a baby faced boy like that cousin of yours."

"How do you know what I want, Brent?"

"Look; Lisa, I got a feel about it. You'll see everything'll be fine."

"Brent, I'm very fond of you. You've been so kind to me, but I'm not ready to marry anyone."

"Okay, okay, honey, if that's how you feel. But you won't put Brent Charlton off that easily. You'll come around."

A few days later Brent left for home much to Robert's delight. Now he had Lisa to himself, and her presence at home and at the office held him in a permanent state of happiness. He made no advances to her, although sometimes he had to take firm control of himself prevent this from happening. For a time the mere presence of her was enough. And for her part, Robert had noticed, Lisa seemed content to be in his company. On the other hand, when she received letters from Brent, she always made great play of flaunting them in front of him.

The winter began to move towards spring, and one morning in March, Robert came down to breakfast to find an envelope lying in his place at the table. "It's from Karl Heinz!" he exclaimed, ripping it open and pulling out the one sheet of paper inside.

"Come on, what does he say?" Lisa asked. "And none of your secrets," she sniggered.

Robert glanced at her and went red in the face.

It was only a short letter, obviously written in a hurry. "He's got his commission, and he's now a *Leutnant*. He says he's thrilled because he's got into a panzer regiment, which was just what he wanted. He's okay and enjoying life. Oh yes, and he sends his love to you all."

"Where is he at the moment?" Kate inquired.

Robert looked at the letter again and said, "It was written, ten days ago. It's from a place called Gmünd near the Czech border."

A few minutes later Hugo entered the room looking worried. "Have you heard the news?" he asked. "German troops are pouring across the Czech frontier."

CHAPTER 12

Jan's interest in his birthdays had long since faded, but this year he was eighty, and he found himself looking forward to the event, because his three children and five grandchildren had all promised to be present on the day. But his pleasure was tinged with sadness, because as each year passed it became less likely that the family would gather in his presence again. It was not only that his own health was failing, but circumstances were beginning to affect the lives of the young people. Isabel had married a man whose business interests compelled him to spend much of his life in the Far East. At the end of the summer the couple were due to take ship for the Dutch East Indies. And then there was Karl Heinz, now an officer in the German army. It was fortunate that he had been able to get leave for the celebration on this occasion, but a soldier's life was uncertain, and it was unlikely that this would happen again.

But by far the greatest consideration in Jan's thoughts regarding this matter was the European political situation. He prayed there would be no war, and yet could see no way of escape from it. The thought of his grandsons becoming enemies saddened him, but events seemed to be moving irrevocably towards this very thing.

Hitler had taken Czechoslovakia and now renewed his demands on Poland which were immediately rejected. Britain and France had declared, that they would guarantee the independence of Poland against any aggressors, so the line up for war had taken place.

Summer came, and the arrival of the family, especially the young people, brought the old house at Grave to life once more. John had accompanied Elizabeth and Joanna, but Matt missed the opportunity to visit the house, because he was involved in a highly complicated fraud case at this time. Karl and Natascha had come up from Cologne, and Hugo had driven Kate, Lisa and Robert down from Rotterdam. Isabel and her husband had also arrived.

On the day that Karl Heinz was due to arrive, Robert and Lisa drove to Nijmegen station to meet him. Spotting his cousins waiting for him Karl Heinz ran towards them and embraced Robert as he always had done. Then, flinging his arms round Lisa, he eagerly kissed her. The mutual enjoyment of the kiss did not escape Robert's notice.

Returning to the house, the three cousins ran up the garden path arm in arm and burst noisily through the front door. Their holiday had begun. They were together again.

Robert and Karl Heinz still slept in the same room as they had done from the time they were babies. That night when both had stripped, Karl Heinz jumped into bed, but seeing Robert kneel to say his prayers, immediately climbed out again and knelt beside his cousin. He felt ashamed of himself for having forgotten that they had always done this together before getting into bed for as long as he could remember. His days away at school, then in the labour corps and the army, had removed the habit from his life; but to be doing so again gave him a comfortable feeling that nothing had changed, and life was still the same for the two of them as it had been when they were boys.

When both had climbed into bed, they lay awake talking into the early hours of the morning, reminiscing about the happy days gone by, and expressing their dreams for the future, promising themselves that in the years to come they would not be out of each others presence for longer than necessary.

The years of spartan discipline and indoctrination in national socialist principles had gradually closed Karl Heinz's mind to some of the normal and broadening principles of education. His own intelligence and loving family life had countered the worst excesses of Nazi ideology, but much of the sinister teaching had found a place in his thoughts. The young of Nazi Germany had grown up with strong and healthy bodies, but the minds of many had been filled with a deadly poison which in the end would bring disaster to their generation.

Robert admired his cousin's confidence and the love he had for his country, but he found the blind faith that Karl Heinz had for his Führer somewhat ridiculous. But what Robert didn't understand was that the confident attitude Karl Heinz adopted was the result of an inner turmoil whereby his true nature struggled desperately not to be submerged, by the unhealthy regime which surrounded him.

But if Karl Heine had changed in any way, he had not changed in his affection towards Robert. They might disagree on certain subjects, but their brotherly love remained as strong as ever.

"Are you still a Christian, Karl Heinz?" Robert asked.

"Of course I am! Why do you ask?"

"I thought Herr Hitler was against the Church."

At the mention of his Führer's name Karl Heinz became defensive and a hardness crept into the tone of his voice. "He doesn't want any interference from the Church, but the churches are still there and nobody has been stopped from attending them. I still go to church and so do many other party members."

"How can you accept Jesus if you hate the Jews? After all, he was a Jew himself, and he said that we mustn't hate one another."

Karl Heinz thought for a moment and then replied, "Martin Luther was a great Christian, but he hated the Jews. Anyway, Jesus was different; it was all different then. The Jews had their own country and they hadn't spread out and polluted other nations."

Karl Heinz caught hold of Robert's wrist, and forcing him on to his stomach, twisted his arm up his back. "Stop interrogating me, Robert, or out of bed you go." Laughing, he held his cousin over the edge of the bed so Robert's head was nearly touching the floor.

"All right, I promise," Robert laughed. But directly he was released, he said, "But what about all the Pastors who have been arrested?"

"What can they expect if they speak against the Führer."

"Well it doesn't sound right to me," said Robert.

"Of course it's right," snapped Karl Heinz indignantly. "The Führer's creating a new Germany, and these treacherous swine are trying to stop him."

"They're only speaking out against what's wrong."

"You don't know anything about it, and if you don't shut up I'll . . ."

"There!" Robert exclaimed triumphantly. "Threatening force again."

For a moment there was tension between them. Then Karl Heinz saw his cousin grinning at him, and they both began to laugh.

After lying silent for a time, Robert changed the subject and asked, "Do you love Lisa?"

"Yes, I think so. Why?"

"It's just the way you kissed her. I've never really kissed her at all."

"Do you want to then?" Karl Heinz asked.

"I should say!"

"Then why don't you? You must take what you want from life, Robert, or you'll never get anything."

"I don't think she wants me to. I tried once and she slapped my face. I'm not going to force myself on her."

"Why not? People need a little force sometimes. If you want to kiss her then do it, and if she doesn't like it it's just too bad."

Robert grinned at his cousin's forthright policy. "You're copying your Führer again. He seems to get what he wants by force."

"If one is in the right, what's wrong with using force? The Führer's right to take back what belongs to Germany."

Robert didn't want another political discussion so he changed the subject back to Lisa. "Do you want to marry her?"

"One day, but not yet. There are too many things I've got to do first," replied Karl Heinz without hesitation.

"I'd marry her tomorrow if she'd have me,"

"I'll wrestle you for her," laughed Karl Heinz.

"Not likely!" Robert grinned. "I wouldn't stand a chance."

"The trouble with you, Robert, is you're too modest," Karl Heinz thought for a moment. "Tell you what then, we'll let her choose between us. And may the best man win."

"What makes you think she wants either of us?"

"Who knows what she wants? But I expect we'll find out one day. There's just one thing, Robert. We must never fall out over her."

"I agree."

On the day of Jan's birthday a dinner party had been arranged, and it was a happy family that took their places round the great table. With the outside world shut out, it seemed as if nothing could disturb the peace and stability of their lives on that carefree summer evening. The party went on far into the night with dancing and games for all who wished to take part.

On two occasions during the evening Robert saw Karl Heinz and Lisa locked in an embrace. After the second occasion Robert sat down on a settee, moodily wishing he could do the same thing. What a fool he was to think he could stand up to competition such as Karl Heinz. He had always known in his heart that Lisa loved his cousin, and that he himself was second best in her affections. He tried not to sink into a mood of depression and spoil the party. After all, he thought, he was only guessing and he may still stand a chance. But then he remembered Lisa once saying that she wanted the stronger of the two, and his mind once again lapsed into a turmoil of doubt.

"You look very serious sitting here all on your own, boy," John remarked as he sat down beside his son. "Aren't you enjoying yourself?"

It had been an embarrassing moment for Robert on meeting his parents for the first time since he had escaped to Rotterdam, but, although his father had rebuked him for being deceitful and ungrateful, the matter had eventually been dropped. John had to admit to himself that the boy had shown some initiative in finding himself a job, and from what Hugo had said he was making excellent progress. At least there had been no more talk of a musical career.

"I'm all right, Father. Just thinking, that's all."

"I'm pleased to hear you're doing so well, Robert, but don't you think it's time you came home? There could be war you know."

"Not yet, Father."

"Do you realise that the government has announced conscription, and the first batch of your age group have already been called up."

"I don't want to be conscripted."

"Is that why you're not coming home?"

"Perhaps." Robert sat forward on the chair with his hands clasped tightly between his legs and his head bowed.

John took an official looking brown envelope from his pocket. "This came for you," he said.

Robert tore it open and read the contents. "It says I'm to register for military service."

"Then you'd better come home and do so."

"Well, I'm not going to. I'm quite happy here."

"Robert, I really find you difficult to understand. Don't you realise there's going to be a war? We're going to need all our young men."

"What as, cannon fodder?"

John looked hard at his son. "Don't make stupid remarks," he said sharply. "You don't seem to realise what we'll be up against. They're an evil lot these Nazis."

"Karl Heinz isn't evil."

"Robert, sometimes you can be exceptionally obtuse. It is not what Karl Heinz *is* as an individual, it's the wicked few who are hiding behind the likes of him. The soldiers of the German Army for the most part are decent men, but they have sworn, allegiance to this gangster Hitler, and if they're prepared to defend him they'll have to take the consequences."

"He didn't see in like a gangster to me."

"My dear boy, you were fourteen at the time, and were with him for a few minutes. You can't judge a man on that." John got up and looked down on his son. "They say the devil has a smiling face," he remarked as he moved away. He felt that Robert would soon make up his own mind to come home. Perhaps it would be best not to push the boy too much.

For the next few days the three cousins tried to relive times past by doing all the things they had done as children. But, as always, their pleasure was not just in the things they did; it was that they did them together. They swam in the river, or just lazed on the bank and watched the barges go by. Sometimes they walked, but usually they cycled through the countryside. Once they even clambered along the underside of the bridge just to see if they could still do it.

One of their cycle rides took them to Ravenstein, and that meant a visit to Elsa Meijer at the ferry house. Luckily Dignus was out on the ferry when they arrived, but Elsa was there to give them their usual welcome. The place was the same as ever, untidy and none too clean with the inevitable cats curled up on the chairs. The young people were more particular about what they ate and drank than they had been when they were children so they diplomatically refused any refreshment. In any case, Elsa's sweet home made brew did not appeal anymore. But they sat patiently and listened while she told them all her news. She informed them that Dignus was now a leading member of the local branch of the national socialist party, considering himself an important man in the district. To Elsa it was a huge joke. "But it keeps him happy," she concluded.

They had already mounted their cycles ready to leave when Dignus arrived. They had seen him coming but had not been able to get away from Elsa before he came up to them. Dignus was only interested in Karl Heinz, and greeted him in the way he had always done since learning he had joined the Hitler Youth. "Heil Hitler!" he snapped, giving the salute.

"Heil Hitler!" Karl Heinz replied. He had been taken by surprise the first time Dignus had greeted him in this manner, but since then he had always proudly returned the greeting. However, he was never happy about the attitude of his cousins towards what he considered a serious matter. They seemed to think it funny, and this frivolous attitude made him angry.

"Heil Hitler," Lisa shouted at Dignus, keeping a serious look on her face and thrusting her arm vertically into the air.

Robert thought her salute resembled a traffic policeman's stop signal, and didn't know what to do to stop himself laughing. He started to snigger and turned away, putting his hand over his face.

"Heil Hitler!" Dignus answered. He then came and stood in front of Robert. "You English are stupid!" he spat out with venom. "'But soon you'll be laughing on the other side of your degenerate faces."

A shiver went down Robert's spine, and his amusement vanished when Dignus glared into his eyes. But it was Dignus who dropped his gaze and turned away, angrily walking into the house.

The cousins quickly pedalled away, and nothing was said until they were well clear of the ferry house. "I'm sure that Dignus Is mad," Lisa declared.

"You shouldn't make fun of him like that," Karl Heinz admonished.

"He didn't know I was teasing so what does it matter? Or are you annoyed because you think I've insulted your Herr Hitler?" Lisa chuckled.

"It wasn't very polite, that's all," Karl Heinz replied. "I don't insult your Royal Family so you shouldn't make fun of the Führer," he added seriously.

"Sorry," Lisa said penitently. Her large dark eyes glancing, humorously, at Karl Heinz.

"It's not funny," he said angrily.

"I've said I'm sorry. Don't be so arrogant." Lisa then turned to Robert, who was riding on the other side of her. "Old Dignus certainly told you where to get off. Fancy laughing at the poor man like that," she said with a twinkle in her eye.

"I was laughing at you, you idiot!" Robert grinned at her, and then said seriously, "That Dignus gives me the creeps. It was strange though. When he came close and glared at me, I could have sworn he was . . . well, afraid."

Lisa laughed and began to pedal ahead, "That's not surprising," she called back, "Your face is enough to frighten anyone."

"You cheeky cat!" he shouted after her, increasing speed to catch her up,

Madly they raced home along the Maasdijk, swerving and bumping to get in front of one another. "First to the mounting block is the winner," shouted Karl Heinz as he pulled ahead of the others. They swept down the slope leaving the Maasdijk and pedalled furiously along the straight to Velp, and once through the village they careered into the rough track, bouncing violently over the uneven surface in their frantic efforts to be first. Hugo and Kate driving sedately up the track were overtaken in the mad rush. Karl Heinz leapt from his machine on to the mounting block, the cycle continuing on until it keeled over through lack of momentum. "I've won!" he proclaimed.

Robert struck the grass bank and fell off, being overtaken by Lisa at the last moment. "Blast it!" he swore, running to Karl Heinz, pulling him down from the winning post and rolling him on the grass. As they wrestled Lisa flung herself on top of them adding to the tangle of bodies.

Hugo drew up alongside the struggling mass. "You mad young devils," he chuckled, enjoying the fun and wishing he was young enough to join in.

Robert tried to struggle to his feet but Lisa jumped on his back, so with her still holding on he piggybacked her along the garden path being chased by Karl Heinz. They burst in through the front door and collapsed on the floor in the hall, where the three of them lay flat on their backs exhausted. It was in this position that Jan found them. "I thought there'd been an explosion," he remarked dryly. "I might have known it was only you three making your usual sedate entry."

"We've just raced all the way from Ravenstein, Grootvader," said Lisa.

"I won!" Karl Heinz declared. "Germans always win!"

"There you go again!" Lisa retorted, digging her cousin in the ribs. "Show off!"

Jan looked down with satisfaction at the happy faces of his grandchildren, who had given him such deep joy over the years. What wonderful young people they are, he thought. "Do you intend to lie there for the rest of the day cluttering up my hall?" he inquired.

"I think we might, Grootvader, it's jolly restful," said Robert.

Jan dropped an envelope on to Karl Heinz's chest. "That arrived for you, Karl Heinz."

"Thanks, Grootvader." Karl Heinz tore open the envelope while still lying on his back. "I don't like the look of this," he said. The others looked at him as he read the letter, noticing the frown appear on his face. "Damn! I've been recalled. I've got to go to Gleiwitz."

"Where's that?" asked Lisa.

"Polish frontier, I think. My regiment must have moved."

"Just as we were having such fun," Lisa pouted.

"What if there's a war?" Robert remarked.

"Who with, you and the French?" Karl Heinz joked. "You'd never fight," he added contemptuously.

A party was quickly organised for Karl Heinz that evening, and it was the early hours of the following morning when the young ones dragged themselves to bed. The rest of the household had retired earlier, but the three cousins had remained talking together, reluctant to be apart during time left to them before Karl Heinz departed.

After breakfast that morning, Hugo made ready to drive his nephew to the station. The family gathered at the front gate, and, having bid them farewell, Karl Heinz got into the car.

Robert caught hold of Lisa's hand and pulled her towards the car. "Come on, let's go as far as the bridge with him."

They both leapt into the back of the car and sat one on each side of Karl Heinz. It was only a few minutes before the car was on the bridge, and the extra time together was soon over.

"Stop here, Uncle," said Robert.

Lisa kissed Karl Heinz and got out of the car. Then Karl Heinz turned to Robert and they firmly gripped each other's hands with an intensity forged by the bond that had always existed between them. Parting had always been difficult, and for a moment they sat motionless just looking at each other. Karl Heinz tried to smile, but Robert sensed an air of uncertainty about his cousin as one who was about to be led dawn an unknown path away from all that he held dear. Then Robert was out of the car, watching it recede into the distance with Karl Heinz still waving from the window.

As he stood there sadly gazing at the now empty road, Robert felt Lisa standing close to him. He put his arm round her, expecting to be rebuffed, but instead he found that she slipped her arm round him. For a moment it didn't registered with him what she had done." Then he felt her hand gently gripping his waist, and a feeling of satisfaction spread over him. They stood looking down at the great river flowing beneath them.

Robert said, "Do you realise it's ten years since this bridge was completed. We've grown up with it, haven't we?" He grasped one of the great girders, admiring its strength. "It's always been a frontier to me."

"A frontier?" Lisa looked up at him her dark eyes wide with interest.

"Yes. You see, that's the magic land," Robert pointed to the south side of the river where the town and the old house were situated, "Where life is always happy," He paused and then pointed to the other end of the bridge, "And on that side is the real world. The world of goodbyes where the magic doesn't work."

Lisa slowly turned him to face her and took his hands in hers. "And what about here in the centre?" she asked.

"This is the place where time stands still, and if we stood here for a thousand years we would, never grow old. And I could dream my dreams forever."

"What are your dreams, Robert?"

He turned his head away and looked at the river, and then said, "To hold you and never let go."

"Then perhaps we'd better walk towards your fairyland, because the real world sometimes pulls people apart." She made to walk on, but he held her firmly and slowly drew her towards him. Gently he tilted her chin and almost imperceptively their faces moved towards each other until finally their lips touched and blended together.

They lost all sense of time as again and again they kissed, revelling in the sensation and yearning to go on and on. It mattered not that they stood in view of the passing traffic, for in their timeless world they were oblivious to all except each other.

On his return from the station Hugo saw them locked in their embrace, so he tactfully drove by.

"I've wanted to do that for so long," Robert said as they walked back hand in hand across the bridge. "You didn't slap my face this time."

"Perhaps I should have done," she replied, giving him a wicked smile. "You should be ashamed of yourself taking advantage of a poor innocent girl."

Robert smiled and then said, "You know I love you, don't you?"

"I know," she replied. She spoke softly and in a way that seemed to indicate to him that she had always known. But she said no more.

*

The holiday at Grave over, Robert did not return to England with his parents, but went back to Rotterdam to continue his life working for Hugo. Even though the situation in Europe was deteriorating, he showed no sign of wishing to leave Rotterdam. Many times after returning from Grave he told himself that he ought to go home, but his yearning for Lisa had become so great that he knew it would be impossible to tear himself away from her. He was so in love with her, but she never spoke of her feelings for him even though they were now often in each others arms. But she no longer refused him the delight of her kisses.

As September dawned, Robert's dreams of peace were shattered when the news came through that the German army had moved across the Polish frontier. The fire was lit and the world began to burn. All illusions about Adolph Hitler were soon to vanish in the flames.

"What will happen now, Daddy? Will Britain and France go to war?" Lisa asked. She sat at the breakfast table trying to cover her concern.

"It's a certainty. They'll send an ultimatum and when it's not complied with, which it won't be, they'll declare war," Hugo replied. He turned to his nephew and said, "And you, Robert, will you return home?"

"Do you mind if I stay on a bit longer, Uncle?"

"Of course not. Stay as long as you like." Lisa found the talk of war depressing and changed the subject to something far more pleasant. "What time are we leaving for the ball tonight?"

The Merchants' Ball was one of the big events in the year for the family, and caused much excitement in the household. Kate and Lisa had talked of nothing else for weeks. Robert was also looking forward to it, especially now that Lisa had chosen him as her escort. At first she had made it known that she was considering other young men, but this was just to tease her cousin. Unknown to him, Robert had been her choice from the beginning.

The maid entered with a silver cardboard box tied with crimson ribbon, and handed it to Kate. "What's this? It's not my birthday," Kate said, taking the box.

"What an exciting looking box," said Lisa going to her mother's side. "Do hurry up and open it, I can't wait to know what's in it," she urged,

Kate carefully cut the crimson silk binding.

"I bet it's from some secret admirer," said Robert.

"Be quiet you naughty boy," Kate smiled, lifting the lid.

"Red roses!" Lisa exclaimed. "Aren't they beautiful! Quick, Mummy, see what's on the card."

Kate took hold of the card and read out.

"With grateful thanks for giving me a second home. From your loving nephew, Robert.

"Robert! You dear boy." Kate left her chair and going to Robert, cradled his head in her hands and kissed his forehead. "You've quite touched my heart. I don't know how to thank you."

"You already have. Aunty, with all you've done for me."

Kate lovingly held one of the roses to her cheek, caressing its fragrant beauty. She looked at Robert and said, "'Where I come from, if a boy gives a girl a rose and she wears it, it means she loves him. I wonder if I might be permitted to wear one without making Hugo jealous."

"And what if it's a silver rose, Aunty, does that mean the same thing?" Robert asked.

Kate looked at him quizzically. "Even more so I would have thought," she smiled.

"And this is for you Uncle, for the same reason." Robert leant over and handed Hugo a small box.

Hugo opened the box and took out a pair of silver cuff-links inscribed with his initials. For a moment he was quiet, seemingly finding it difficult to find the right words. "You must forgive me, Robert, I really am at a loss for words. You've no idea what this means to me," he said, turning the silver objects over and over in his hands. "Thank you so very much, my boy."

That evening Hugo and Robert stood talking in the hall at the foot of the stairs. It was time to leave for the ball, but Kate and Lisa had not yet put in an appearance. Kate was the first to appear. Her elegant black gown, set off by a single diamond necklace and a red rose made her an attractive sight to behold. "You look lovely, my dear," said Hugo.

At that moment Lisa began to descend the stairs.

"I never could compete with this girl," said Kate, looking up at her daughter with pride and then smiling at Robert. But Robert hardly heard, his eyes were riveted on Lisa. He had always known she was good looking, but it was as if he was seeing her for the first time in all her dark, radiant beauty. Her midnight blue gown was plain and simple jewellery was unnecessary to enhance her beauty, and she wore none - but as she came towards him, Robert saw that she was wearing the little silver rose he had given her five years before.

Robert's mind flashed back over the years, remembering how she had entered more and more into his thoughts and desires. Words she had said which gave him hope that she loved him came to mind, only to be dashed down by others which tended to prove she didn't. And now she was wearing his rose. Was she wearing it because of what Kate had said, or was it just coincidence? Perhaps it was for Karl Heinz?

Neither of them spoke on the way to the ball, and when they arrived Lisa seemed to be the centre of attraction for so many people, especially young men, that Robert found himself being pushed, into the background. Eventually he became irritated and forcing his way past those who had gathered about her, took her firmly by the arm and led her on to the dance floor. "I was wondering when you were going to do that," she grinned.

Robert did not reply, but when the dance finished, still holding her firmly by the hand, he took her out on to a balcony. At least he was determined to have her to himself for some of the time. They leant over the balustrade, looking down at the gardens below and across the lake beyond, and then he turned to face her and touched the silver rose. "Have you ever worn it before?" he asked.

"Never." Her answer was short and to the point.

He couldn't make up his mind whether or not he was disappointed. "Then why are you wearing it now?"

"You're full of questions tonight, Robert," she said. A provocative grin spread across her face. "Perhaps what Mummy said was true."

"But I gave you the rose, not Karl Heinz."

Lisa casually turned her face away and looked towards the lake, but out of the corner of her eye she could see the expression on his face. "So you did," she said. "How silly of me not to remember."

"You do love Karl Heinz then." His words were neither a statement nor a question, but just an acceptance of what he had always known to be true.

"Yes, I love him deeply, "Lisa replied softly. She could see the crestfallen look on his face." I'm sorry, Robert, but I can't have both, of you."

He turned away and bowed his head. "No, of course not," he sighed. "Karl Heinz always was the one. I think I've known for a long time . . ." The words faded on his lips. Lisa had turned and was smiling at him.

"Oh, Robert, what a foolish boy you are! Don't you see that it's you I love? It's always been you. There's never been anyone else." She saw the puzzled look in his eyes, and gently touched his cheek with her fingers.

For a moment he couldn't .speak, then he stammered, "But. . . but I don't understand. I just can't believe it."

"No, you never could believe in yourself, Robert. If you ever did, then the world would have to look out."

He took her in his arms and held her close. "Oh, my darling Lisa, all my dreams have come true. I shall hold you forever and never let you go," he whispered, letting his lips move down her cheek on to her lips. "I can hardly speak, I love you so much," he added breathlessly. "Lisa, my sweet one, will you marry me? Please, please say you will."

"Of course I will, my darling, with all my heart. It's all I've ever wanted."

When he eventually led her back into the ballroom they found a secluded table where they sat and talked. "I still can't believe it's true. Tell me again you love me."

They sat close to each other and Lisa slipped her arm under his jacket and held him round the waist. "I love you, my darling Robert, I always have. I think I knew it from the day we sat on the river bank, and you and Karl Heinz cut your arms with that knife."

"I was in a blue funk," Robert grinned.

"Yes, I know you were, but you overcame it, and that took courage. That's what I call being strong. In physical strength you are the same as Karl Heinz, but inside you are the stronger. It was easy enough for Karl Heinz, because he had no fear. It was hard far you, but you did it. And then you risked a strapping to go down the cellar, and that took courage."

"I wished I hadn't when Uncle Karl laid that damned strap across me. God, how it hurt!"

"Yes I know, I was listening. And it was all for me. I'm so in love with you, Robert."

"Why did you keep it from me for, so long?"

"I wanted you to be free of me until the right time," she answered.

They talked for a long time about the happy days gone by when the sun always seemed to be shining, and even the painful moments could now be seen as sweet memory. But being young it was their plans for the future which excited their thoughts more than the past.

"Let's go and tell Daddy and Mummy," Lisa urged.

"I'd better ask permission first rather than tell them," Robert said.

"Good idea. But Daddy would never refuse you anything." Lisa grinned and then added proudly, "And in any case I'm twenty one."

"Well, I'm not."

"But you soon will be."

They returned to the table where Hugo and Kate were sitting. "What have you two been up to all this time?" Kate asked. She looked at them with a suspicious smile on her face. Their preoccupation with each other over the past few weeks had not escaped her notice.

Robert looked shy and wondered how he was going to broach the subject with Hugo. Lisa encouraged Kate to leave the table on a pretext of meeting one of her friends, leaving Robert alone with her father.

Hugo chatted away happily as he always did when he had his nephew to himself, and it was a few minutes before Robert was able to overcome his nervousness and bring the conversation to the subject of marriage.

"Something on your mind, Robert?"

"Yes, Uncle," Robert stammered. "There's something I want to ask you."

"Fire away, lad!"

"Well, Uncle, it's about Lisa and me." Robert felt his face go red. " I . . . That is we are very much in love." He hesitated and then quickly added, "Can I have your permission to marry her, Uncle? I promise I'll look after her and protect her, and I'll work hard to give her a good life. I've always loved her, you know."

Hugo looked at the embarrassed youth and said, "You're a bit young, Robert, and I wasn't banking on losing Lisa quite so soon." He saw the look of disappointment on his nephew's face.

"I'll be twenty one in November, Uncle," Robert replied brightly, as if he had found a trump card.

"Put like that what can I say? I think I can trust her to you, Robert. You're almost a son as it is, and in any case I'm sure you must realise that I have a deep affection for you."

"Does that mean it's all right, Uncle?" Robert asked uncertainly.

"Yes, Robert, that means it's all right."

Robert got up and took Hugo's hand. "You're so kind to me, Uncle, I don't know how to thank you."

"It will be sufficient if you keep those promises you've just made."

When mother and daughter returned to the table they could see the answer which Robert had been given written on his face. "It's all right," he said happily.

"Well, what did you expect?" Kate laughed.

The rest of the ball was like a dream for Robert as he danced Lisa into the early hours of that unforgettable Sunday morning.

The family rose late that morning to be greeted with the news that Britain had at last made a stand in support of Poland and declared war on Germany. Later in the day France also declared war, anticipating the expiry of her ultimatum, not due until the following day.

But as the weeks went on the war made little impression on Robert. It was true that Poland was being destroyed, but it all seemed so far away and in any case there was nothing he could do about it.

The SS Athenia was sunk by a U-Boat with the loss of 112 lives; the first units of the British Expeditionary Force crossed into France; French patrols crossed the German frontier. But the armies on the western front faced each other without fighting, waiting in vain for diplomatic moves to be made.

Robert was not alone in his thoughts on the war, and for him and the majority of people in Western Europe life went on much as usual. Nothing appeared to be happening, giving the illusion that there was no war. Polish resistance ceased, but still the western front remained quiet. It was true that British ships were being sunk; a German submarine had even penetrated the naval Base at Scapa Flow and sunk the Battleship *Royal Oak* with the loss of 786 lives, but there was still no movement on the western front.

The wedding had been arranged for Saturday 18th. May, and Robert wrote home of his joy and the happy turn his life had taken. Both John and Elizabeth could sense a new optimism in his letters, but there was no mention of him returning to England. Deep within him Robert knew that there would come a day when he would have to face this problem, but to return home before he was married was out of the question. In the first flush of his young love, to be out of Lisa's presence for a few hours was a torment to him, but to leave her behind while he went home would have been more than he could bear. Why should he leave to fight in this damn war, he asked himself? Surely there must be other ways of settling the matter.

Both John and Elizabeth were very fond of Lisa and approved Robert's choice of a wife. However, it was John's opinion that his son was too young for marriage and that he should wait for two years. But Robert couldn't wait, and John put no obstacle in his way, so the wedding plans went ahead.

In his happiness the war was pushed into the background of Robert's mind, only to interrupt his thoughts of love when incidents of special interest were reported. At the end of November Russia invaded Finland, and then in December the German pocket battleship, *Admiral Graf Spee,* was scuttled in Montevideo harbour. At Christmas the armies on the western front celebrated within the concrete of the Maginot and Siegfied Lines, and still all remained quiet and the *phoney war* went on.

It was Robert's first Christmas away from his family. After a large Christmas lunch he had taken Lisa into the park to walk it down. On returning to the house, they found Hugo and Kate in the drawing-room listening to the wireless.

"Hush, children! It's your King speaking, Robert," said Kate, as he and Lisa quietly sat down to listen.

They all listened to the slow, hesitant voice bringing the speech to an end by saying, "In the meantime I feel that we may all find a message of encouragement in the lines which, in my closing words, I would like to say to you;

And I said to the man who stood at the *gate of the year:*
'Give me a *light that I may tread safely into the unknown.'*

And he replied:

'Go out into the darkness and put your hand into the hand of God.
That shall be to you better than light and safer than a known way.'
May that Almighty Hand guide and uphold us all. " (see P625)

The King's voice ceased, and then Robert said, *"So I went forth and finding the hand of God, trod gladly into the night. And he led me towards the hills and the breaking of day in the lone East."*

Lisa squeezed his hand and looked up into his eyes with pride.

"That was lovely, Robert," said Kate.

"I found it in a little second hand book of verse when I was a boy," Robert replied. "There are three more verses, but I can't remember them."

"I think your King is a good man. He sounds so kind," Kate remarked.

It was a happy Christmas-tide for Robert and the family. Hugo arranged seats at the theatre and meals at the best restaurants. There were dances, parties at the houses of friends, and a party at Hugo's home. And then there was the New Year's Eve ball; when Robert and Lisa hugged each other tightly as midnight struck, their lips tasting the delight of each other rather than the champagne they had been given to toast in 1940.

As the weeks advanced into the New Year, it seemed to Robert that his love for Lisa increased with each day. He also found it increasingly difficult to restrain himself from possessing her completely as his love making became more passionate. But Lisa kept a firm control on him. "You must wait till our wedding night," she said on one occasion, when he became frantic with desire.

But however much they ignored the war, the distant menace was always there in the background of their lives. In March the war between Russia and Finland ended. But in April the Germans invaded Denmark and Norway, and the flames seemed to be creeping nearer.

"Surely they won't invade Holland," said Kate at the table one day when the subject had arisen.

"'Of course they won't," Hugo replied optimistically, trying to allay his wife's fears. "They left us alone in the last war, and there's no reason why they should act any differently now. And in any case, they've professed nothing but friendship for us."

"Father has written to say that we should all go to England," said Robert.

"So John thinks we are in danger," said Kate.

Robert knew his father believed that the Germans would never attack France along their heavily fortified mutual frontier. This meant that the attack would come through the Low Countries. In the last war the right wing of the German army had wheeled through

Belgium, but John considered that this time they would extend even further to the right and this would mean moving through Holland.

"He feels we should be on the safe side, Aunty."

"It's out of the question for me," said Hugo. "But perhaps the rest of you should go."

"I shall not go without you, Hugo," Kate replied. And don't forget we have the wedding next week. It's only nine days away."

But professions of friendship, weddings and the love of young people had no place in Hitler's plans. Orders had already been issued by the German High Command to the German forces that the offensive in the west was to commence the following day.

Robert slept badly that night. He felt hot and restless, and had the windows wide open. He woke early and lay watching the light stream in through a small gap in the curtains. Turning over, he glanced at the clock. It was just after five thirty. As he lay there, his mind picked up the sound of an aeroplane, and then, it gradually dawned on him that it was not just one aircraft he could hear. He dragged himself out of bed and, drawing back the curtains leant out of the window. He was right, there was more than one, in fact there appeared to be a whole fleet of them slowly moving across the east side of the city. He saw something fall out of the first plane and a parachute open, then another and another. His first thought was that the crew were bailing out, but then the sky became filled with parachutes, and the terrible truth struck him. They were Germans. He stood as if mesmerised, watching the parachutes slowly descend and pass out of sight behind the roofs of the nearest houses. The aircraft disappeared, the sound of their engines fading into the distance. Then, quickly pulling on his underpants, he rushed from his room down to the telephone in the hall.

He had to tell somebody what he'd seen, and the police were the only people he could think of. But the line was engaged. It was probable that others were doing the same thing, he thought. Then he managed to get through to the operator and was informed that the matter was being dealt with. Replacing the receiver, he sat at the bottom of the stairs holding his head in his hands, the dreadful reality of the situation taking shape in his mind.

Hugo, having heard someone running down the stairs, appeared in his dressing gown on the landing above. "Robert, what are you doing there half naked?"

"We're being invaded, Uncle! German parachutists. . . hundreds of them!"

Hugo hurried down the stairs. "Are you absolutely sure?" he asked.

"I saw them, Uncle. The telephone operator confirmed it. I tried to phone the police, but the line is jammed."

Hugo picked up the receiver, and Robert saw him quickly dial a number. Hugo had friends in high places in the military and seemed to know exactly who to call. As he was talking, Kate came down the stairs, and then two of the servants appeared. Everyone waited in silence for Hugo to finish his conversation. Eventually he put the phone down and looked at the anxious faces about him.

"The German army crossed our borders this morning," he said gravely. They've gone into Belgium as well. They've dropped parachute troops on the bridges at Dordrecht, Moerdijk and here in Rotterdam. They're in the southern outskirts of the city. Our army is fighting back as well as they can, and we've opened the dykes."

There was a moment's silence, and then Kate asked, "What's to be done, Hugo?"

"We must try and keep calm, and carry on as usual," Hugo replied. He gave the servants the option of leaving if they were worried about their families in other parts of the country. But they did not wish to go. "In that case" he continued, addressing the housekeeper, "We will have an early breakfast."

When the servants had gone about their duties Hugo said to Robert, "I'll arrange for you and Lisa to be taken to England as soon as possible."

"But what about the wedding, Uncle?" Robert protested.

"There'll be no wedding, Robert. Your safety comes first. Now go and put some clothes on, and pack your things ready to go at a moments notice."

Kate woke Lisa and gave her the news, but her daughter's reaction was one of silence. And when she appeared, for breakfast, Lisa said little. She knew now there would be no wedding. When, she walked to the office that morning, hanging on Robert's arm, there was an uncanny atmosphere pervading the streets. Few people had ventured out, but the docks were still working and ships were putting to sea. The sporadic sound of gunfire could be heard in the southern suburbs.

"If we were ever parted, you would still love me, wouldn't you?" she asked.

"You know I would," Robert replied. "Why do you ask?"

"I just wanted to hear you say it, that's all."

They said little more to each other, but their eyes told of their feelings that all their plans were falling apart.

The news at the end of the day was serious, for although the Dutch army was fighting bravely with its obsolete weapons, they were no match for the Germans.

Robert went to his bedroom early that night, but when he had stripped he found himself restless and made no attempt to switch out the light or get into bed. Now that there could be no wedding he knew that his burning desire to possess Lisa would have to be suppressed until they could marry in England. The mere thought of her had started to arouse his passion as he sat naked on the edge of the bed, and although he tried to fight the surge of feeling, he knew that, as always, his lust would become uncontrollable, and there would have to be relief by his own hand.

Silently and without any warning the bedroom door opened and Lisa stood in the room. Robert looked at her in surprise, but this time, as he rose from the bed, he made no attempt to hide his naked body as he had done in the past. He stood before her, his proud manhood erect with his passion plain for her to see. He felt no shame, only a desire to take her in his arms and fill her body with his own. They both knew that the moment had come and they could wait no longer, for if they did they might have to wait forever.

Lisa had enjoyed seeing him naked before. But this time she revelled in what she saw, knowing it all belonged to her and her alone. Although now fully mature, Robert's body had retained its youthful beauty. His smooth light brown skin was hairless, except in the usual place, and his face had not lost that boyish look – he still hardly shaved. Her desire for him had become impossible to resist any longer. Slowly she unfastened her dressing gown – she wore nothing else – and let it fall to the floor, revealing at last the full flower of her dark beauty that Robert had yearned to see and to hold for so long.

Robert gasped at the sight before him. His chest felt tight, and he could hardly breathe with excitement. He could feel his whole body throbbing as his passion pounded through his veins. He stretched his hand and gently pulled her towards him until their bodies touched and their arms enclosed each other.

The excitement was too much for him, and life burst from him at the touch of her body. She held him tightly as he lost control, feeling him jerk against her, groaning with relief, and then led him to the bed where she gently caressed back his desire. In the frantic passion that followed, when they were locked together in the ultimate joy of their love, they found an ecstasy beyond their wildest dreams. At last they were one, each body and soul possessed of the other, their union complete.

They lay, their youthful bodies moulded together, their pure love protecting them from any thought of shame in what they were doing. Lisa whispered in Robert's ear, "I don't feel wicked, do you?"

"No," Robert faltered, still breathless with excitement. "Only deliriously happy." He kissed her lightly on the end of the nose. "Let's marry ourselves now," he suggested. "God will understand." His passion temporarily spent, Robert took himself from her, and going to a drawer in a small table standing near the bed he took out the wedding ring. Returning, he knelt on the bed, sitting back on his heels. Lisa, seeing him do so, got up and knelt beside him, holding his hand.

Robert began to speak quietly. "Lord, we don't believe we've done wrong. We just couldn't wait any longer. I want to marry Lisa now, and I promise to love and protect her always until death us do part."

"And I promise, Lord, always to love and obey Robert until death us do part," Lisa said.

He placed the ring on her finger, and then, holding her hand, said the words he had heard so often when, he was a choir boy.

"With this ring I thee wed, with my body I thee worship, and with all my worldly goods I thee endow: In the name of the Father, and of the Son, and of the Holy Ghost. Amen."

"Amen," Lisa repeated. She kissed him and said, "And now we are man and wife in front of God, and however far we might be apart, nothing can ever change that."

Once more they lay together whispering their love, their young bodies possessed of each other in a rapture of unbelievable joy. The night went on, and again and again as the passion returned, so again and again it burst forth in the frenzy of their love. Together they reached the heights of ecstasy, until at last, exhausted, they drifted into sleep in each other's arms.

They awoke late the following morning, but it did not matter, because breakfast was always a little later on Saturdays. In any case, there was nothing for them to do except wait for the moment when they were to depart for England. At breakfast Hugo informed them that he had not yet be able to organise their departure for England. The situation was serious and the country was in a state of confusion. In Belgium many towns had been bombed, and in England Winston Churchill had been asked to form a government.

"You two youngsters are not to go far from the house." Hugo ordered. "You may go in the park, but no further."

"Yes, Uncle," said Robert.

Lisa got up to leave the table, and as she did so Kate noticed that her daughter was wearing the wedding ring. "Lisa, the ring. You're wearing it already?"

Robert went to Lisa's side and took her by the hand. "I gave it to her last night, Aunty," he said. He could feel himself becoming hot with embarrassment, but he felt no shame in what he had done, and was determined to confess his happiness. "Last night we were married," he confessed.

Hugo and Kate looked at him in bewilderment and then at each other. "What do you mean, married?" Kate asked.

Robert continued to stammer out his explanation. "Please don't be angry with me with me but . . ." he came to a stop, not knowing how to continue.

Kate saw the shy look on his face as he stood fidgeting before her. "Go on, Robert," she instructed.

"Well, Aunty, as our wedding has been cancelled, we married ourselves."

"What are you talking about?"

"We made our promises before God, and asked his blessing. Last night we . . . we . . ."

"We slept together, Mummy," Lisa interrupted firmly.

There was silence in the room for a moment, and then Robert blurted out, "We're not ashamed!"

"Then you should be!" Kate declared.

"But, Aunty, we couldn't help ourselves. Try to understand."

"Understand!" Kate exclaimed. She was about to say more but fell silent on seeing Hugo shake his head at her.

"Sit down, both of you," Hugo said firmly.

"Are we very wicked; Daddy?" Lisa asked.

"You certainly are. You know very well you shouldn't have done it. And as for you, Robert, you deserve a good whipping." Hugo tried to sound stern, but felt he wasn't making a very good job of it.

Robert bowed his head and said, "Yes, Uncle. It would be worth a whipping." He glanced up at Hugo. "You know we desperately love each other, and we would have waited, but what's the use of waiting for a wedding which isn't going to take place."

"You are both very naughty!" said Kate crossly. "You should have waited until you got to England, and then got married properly. I really don't know what you young people can be thinking of nowadays."

Robert replied, "But we've done nothing morally wrong, and we don't feel any shame, Aunty. After all, when people go to a church they marry themselves. The priest only tells them what to say, and acts as a witness."

"There's more to it than that, Robert," Kate scolded. She was shocked and looked to Hugo for a lead.

Hugo looked sadly at the two youngsters, trying hard to understand their impatience. "In normal circumstances you most certainly would have been wrong," he said. "But circumstances are not normal, and we can't undo what is done, so as far as I'm concerned you are man and wife, and you have my blessing." Hugo smiled at the two worried young faces before him.

Lisa went to her father, and, flinging her arms round his neck, kissed him. "Oh, thank you, Daddy!" she exclaimed. "And what do you say, Mummy?" she added.

"I cannot pretend that I'm not very angry with both of you. I don't know what things are coming to. How could you do such a thing? But your father is right; we cannot undo what is done. Now you're to promise me that directly you get to England you'll have a proper wedding."

"We promise," said Robert.

Robert and Lisa had no difficulty in obeying Hugo's instructions to keep within the vicinity of the house, for except for a short walk in the park, they spent the greater part of the day locked in a bedroom. Burning with desire and unable to wait for the night, they spent hour after hour entwined naked in each other's arms, their young bodies quivering with delight as their passion was spent time and time again.

Sunday came and went in the same way for Robert and Lisa. They were so lost in the ecstasy of their love that the news of the war made little impression on them.

The 7th French army, which had entered the Netherlands, was now falling back from Breda. The Dutch army was still fighting, but time was running out, and the war made no allowance for young love.

On Monday Hugo heard the news that the Dutch army was beginning to collapse, and that Queen Wilhelmina and her government had left for England. He had at last arranged for a fishing boat to take Robert and Lisa to England. "You will be at the quay at the bottom of the road, at ten o'clock tomorrow evening," he said at dinner that evening to the two youngsters. "It's only a small boat, but the two men who run her are reliable and will see you safely to

England." Realising he had not got their full attention; he spoke to them again, only this time more sharply. "You two had better come down to earth, because if anything goes wrong and you don't get out tomorrow evening it may be too late to get out at all. Is that clear?"

"Yes, Uncle." Robert replied.

Hugo could see that they were tired, and knew the reason for it. But, although he had forbidden them to make love again before they were married, he made no attempt to enforce his order. "And you'd better get some sleep tonight." He ordered, looking knowingly at Robert and trying not to sound too severe. But he was worried and was firm in what he said. "You must have your wits about you tomorrow," he added.

But who could face tomorrow if it was known what tomorrow would bring? The Dutch army was withdrawing to what was known as the *Dutch Fortress,* an area which included Amsterdam, Rotterdam and Uttrecht. German parachute troops were still holding the outskirts of the south side of Rotterdam, but the Dutch army held lines on the north side of the river to the sea.

"At least your boat will be able to get safely to the sea this evening," said Hugo just before leaving for the office on that fateful Tuesday morning. Robert and Lisa accompanied him into the street, something they had never done before, and watched him all the way to the corner where he turned and waved before disappearing.

When they returned to the house Robert caught her round the waist. "Let's go to the bedroom again. I still need it badly," he grinned.

"You're insatiable, Robert, you naughty boy," Lisa laughed.

"What can you expect now that I've got you after all these years? I could, go on doing it forever."

"Come on then, just once more. Then we'll go for a walk in the park," she replied.

But when the bedroom door was closed and locked, and they were once more seized by their sensuous rapture, the world outside did not exist, and it was lunch time before they appeared downstairs again. After lunch they took the walk in the park which they had intended to take earlier. But they were too tired to walk far, and after a short distance they returned to sit on a seat not far from the house.

They sat with their arms round each other. Robert gave Lisa a wicked look and whispered, "What about the bedroom again?"

"Robert, control yourself!" Lisa ordered. "There'll be no more until we get to England."

"But we've got time for one more session."

But Lisa wasn't listening to him. She was straining her ears trying to make out a faint droning sound. "Hush, Robert, I think I can hear aeroplanes somewhere."

"You're right," he said. He searched the sky but could see no sign. "It sounds like quite a lot of them."

"Maybe it's more parachute troops coming," Lisa suggested. "I think we'd better get home." She got up and pulled Robert to his feet. "Look, there they are!" Lisa cried, pointing, as a large formation of aircraft came into view over the city. "They're coming this way."

Robert felt Lisa grip his arm tightly. He knew that the war had come to them at last. "They're German!" he exclaimed, staring hard up into the sky. He enclosed Lisa in his arms and held her close to him, but then stood transfixed as he watched wave after wave of aircraft come into view, and make their leisurely way across the city. Even when the first wave was right overhead Robert could not take his eyes from them. His mind went back to when he had seen the parachute troops leave their aircraft a few days before, but the objects falling from the planes this time appeared much smaller. For a moment he couldn't believe his eyes. It was springtime, and he was standing with his loved one in the park which held such happy memories for him. Yet suddenly the dreadful reality dawned on him.

"Down!" he cried, flinging Lisa on to the grass, and trying to cover her with his own body. "They're bombing us!"

From where he lay Robert heard a dull thud, and watched as the earth erupted a short distance away, sending debris high into the air. And then again and again as the stick of bombs moved steadily across the park. Horrified, he saw the explosions move closer and closer to their home, until there was a sickening cracks and it appeared that all the lights had been switched of in the house as a blinding flash lit up the windows. For a second it seemed as if time stood still, but then with a crash every window in the house blew out. He watched, fascinated, as the front door burst open and was hurled across the road as if it was no more than a piece of cardboard. At the same time the four pillars supporting the balcony over the front entrance snapped like matchsticks, and the balcony collapsed into pile of rubble. A sheet of flame shot up on the right hand side of the house, and smoke began to pour from a ground floor window.

"Don't move!" Robert shouted to Lisa as he leapt up and ran towards the house. He scrambled over the rubble of the fallen balcony, and, without thought for his own safety, rushed into the burning building. "Aunty!" he screamed. The heat was already building up as the flames slowly spread up one side of the hall. He took off his coat and put it over his head. It was impossible to get near the room that was burning, and if he didn't find Kate soon he would be forced to leave without her. Debris was falling from the ceiling, and he stumbled over something on the floor. To his horror he saw it was the body of one of the maids lying there in a sickening mess with her head blown clean off. There was no time for sorrow; if he didn't get out quickly the whole place would collapse on him. He could see the ceiling beginning to give way in places. Madly he scrambled into the dining-room on the opposite side of the hall to the flames, but found no one there. He ran back into the hall, and then stumbled up the stairs to check the first floor. But the smoke was beginning to affect him, and he couldn't see properly. On the landing he tripped and fell, but, as he went to crawl away back down the stairs his hand touched someone lying there beside him. "Aunty!" he gasped with relief. But Kate had been struck on the head and was unconscious. For a second he collapsed across her exhausted. A section of ceiling plaster fell on top of him, filling the air with dust, but driving him back into action. Using all his strength he dragged Kate down the stairs. But he had still to get across the hall to the front entrance, and the heat was becoming almost unbearable. He staggered across the hall, once more tripping over fallen debris and falling flat on the floor. "God, give me strength!" he cried out, picking himself up and again taking hold of Kate's limp body. A sheet of flame shot across the landing where Kate had been lying, as the fire took hold of the upper stories. The hall ceiling collapsed over the stairs and, although Robert did not know it, it was about to come down over the place where he was standing. With one final effort he dragged his casualty to the front door as the rest of the ceiling collapsed behind him.

He never knew how he got Kate into the street, but as he did so he heard a loud crash as the roof caved in. With the inrush of air there was a mighty roar and the whole house burst into flames. Lisa and other people quickly came to assist him as he collapsed exhausted in the street. Cut, bruised and with slight burns on his arms, Robert lay listening to the now raging fire in the house, and the explosion of more bombs as Rotterdam was destroyed. Then he remembered Hugo. "Stay with her Lisa. I'll be back in a minute," he said, forcing himself to his feet. His effort to save Kate had drained the strength from him and he shook with fatigue. But he had to do something to find Hugo.

Running to the end of the road, Robert turned into the Westerkade, and then made his way as fast as he could alongside the river to the Willemskade, where Hugo had his office. But it was unbelievable chaos and destruction that met his eyes. The whole block had been hit, and what hadn't been blown down was burning furiously. Rubble covered the street and smoke filled the air. Across the river he could see that the docks had been hit and were burning. The murderous attack still continued as new waves of aircraft unloaded their deadly cargo over the defenceless city. The sky had now become darkened as the smoke gathered like a cloud over the burning ruins. From time to time smoke swirled around Robert so that he was unable to see more than a few yards in front of him, only to clear again as the rush of wind caused by the raging fires took it high into the sky. Stumbling on, Robert heard more explosions behind him as another stick of bombs made their deadly way down the street. He flung himself flat, feeling the rush of air pass over him, as one bomb fell behind him and another in front of him. But he was careless of his own life in his efforts to reach the office. The whole front of Hugo's office building had been blown out, and the rubble was spread across the street. What was left standing was in flames. He fell on his knees amongst the rubble trying to clear it in a desperate and futile attempt to find Hugo. "Uncle!" he screamed. "Uncle Hugo!"

In his frantic search he found one body, but it was not Hugo. And then, moving some bricks, he saw a hand and the glint of something being grasped in it. Pushing open the fingers he recognised the silver cuff-links which had given Hugo such pleasure. In a frenzy he flung away more bricks, but then collapsed on his face in horror, finding that there was no body attached to the arm. What energy he had left deserted him, and he lay exhausted, convulsed with sobs and the tears pouring down his blackened cheeks. His mind raced, trying to make sense out of what was happening. He had been so happy in his little world of love. But now this world had been shattered.

It had taken fifty Heinkels just fifteen minutes to destroy the city centre of Rotterdam and drag yet more innocent people into the hell of war.

Robert tried to tell himself that it was all a bad dream, but the explosions, the roaring fires, the smoke, and the chaos burnt the reality into his brain. And the dead bodies, hideously twisted by fire or torn in pieces by the explosions, sickened his tender soul – he had never seen death before. Had he been sent into this hell as a punishment for what he had done to Lisa, he asked himself? No. Surely God was not like that.

A policeman came and assisted him to his feet, telling him to go and take cover. There was nothing more he could do here. Hugo was dead. He made his way unsteadily back to the park where Lisa was kneeling beside Kate.

Kate had regained consciousness and was being attended by a doctor. She took Robert by the hand when he knelt beside her. "Thank you, Robert dear. You are so brave," she smiled.

"Have you found Daddy?" Lisa asked. She could see where the tear marks had left streaks down his blackened cheeks, and saw the look on his face.

Robert stood up and drew Lisa aside. Opening his hand, he revealed the silver cuff-links. He tried to speak, but his voice was breaking with emotion. In any case, words were unnecessary, for she knew what he was trying to say. He took her in his arms and they wept.

As the city burnt so the flames of war burnt away their dreams. Their world was collapsing about them.

Kate was taken to a hospital, and Robert was also treated for minor burns and cuts. Lisa then took him to the home of some friends, who lived on the outskirts of the city. The welcome the youngsters received was overwhelming in its kindness. Robert was able to bath and was given a room where he could rest before going to the docks to meet the fishing boat. As he had lost all his possessions he was also given a change of clothes, which were suitable for his sea journey, and included a polo-neck pullover and a warm seaman's jacket.

After his bath Robert returned to the room, but the afternoon had become hot so he lay naked on the bed, intending to relax for a few minutes before dressing and going downstairs to find Lisa. As he lay there he could feel the tears rolling down his cheeks as the terrible events of the day began, to sink into his mind. He found it difficult to believe that Hugo was dead, Kate injured, and the house and all their possessions completely destroyed. And yet this was the reality. The hell he had been through was no dream. Only the thought of Lisa as his wife brought him the consolation that he searched for.

An explosion seemed to shatter the silence in the room, and the ceiling began to fall in on him. He cried out in terror, and screwed his body up into a ball in an effort to protect himself. He felt something slicing at his arm. "Not that!" he screamed.

"Robert darling, wake up." Lisa stood by the bed gently shaking his arm. She saw him open his eyes and stare at her, the perspiration standing out on his forehead. For a moment he looked bewildered. "You've been dreaming," she smiled, taking his towel and tenderly wiping his brow.

"How long have I been here?"

"It's half past eight now. I've been in before but you were sound asleep. I've brought you something to eat." Lisa drew up to the bed a small table with a tray of food on it, and then sat on the bed while Robert ate. "How are your burns now?" she asked.

"Oh, they're okay thanks. They weren't much anyway."

"You were so brave, Robert. If it wasn't for you Mummy would be dead."

The memory of running into the burning house and what might have happened to him made him shudder. "Would to God I could have saved poor Uncle! Why did they have to do this to us? Why couldn't they leave us alone, we've done nothing to them? Surely it must be a terrible mistake? They couldn't have meant to do it."

Outwardly, Lisa appeared to have taken the death of her father calmly, but inwardly her heart had been torn in shreds, and a deep hatred of those responsible had taken possession of her. She said coldly, "The filthy swine meant it all right, and their invasion is no mistake. But I swear to God that one day we'll have our revenge."

Robert finished his food and got up to dress. "What time are we leaving for the docks?" he asked.

"In fifteen minutes. I'll come and see you off, Robert, but I can't go with you."

For a moment he didn't comprehend her last remark, and then it dawned on him what she had said. Half dressed, he turned to face her, his voice unsteady. "What do you mean, you can't come with me? You must come! It's all arranged."

"You must understand, Robert. You know I can't leave Mummy now. I must stay and rebuild the business. So many people will be relying on me."

"Then I'm not going! You're my wife and I'll stay with you."

"Don't be silly, it's impossible for you to stay. The Germans will be here soon, and you'll be sent to prison or worse. You've got to go!"

Robert sat down on the edge of the bed, holding his head in his hands. "Oh, God!" he sighed. "What's happened to us? We had so many dreams."

"There's no more time to dream, my darling. We've got to be strong and do our duty, then one day it'll all come right again."

"Damn our duty! Damn everything! I can't live without you!" He flung himself round on to the bed and buried his face in the eiderdown. Lisa sat down beside him and ran her fingers through his hair.

"You'll manage, Robert, I know you will. We still have our love. They can't take that away."

Robert raised himself up, and, taking her in his arms, held her close. "Why couldn't it have gone on forever? Without you, there'll be nothing left for me."

There was a knock on the door, and a voice informed them that it was time to go. Robert finished dressing and Lisa helped him on with his coat, and seeing his eyes full of tears lightly dabbed them with her handkerchief. "Now you're ready," she said, trying to sound cheerful.

"You'll never wipe the tears from my heart," he said. "Promise you'll come to me as soon as you can."

"I promise," she smiled. Then her smile faded and she said, "Don't worry, I'll survive. Those German swine won't get away with this."

They went, unspeaking, downstairs, and were taken to the waiting car. As they were driven back towards the river they could see the glow in the sky above the blazing city centre. A pall of smoke hung like low cloud over what a few hours before had been, a peaceful, thriving community. It would be five years before the cloud of oppression would lift from the life of this small nation.

The nearer the centre they got, the worse the chaos and destruction became. It was getting towards ten o'clock, and still they had some way to go before reaching the river.

"We must hurry, the boat won't wait," Lisa urged.

Just before reaching the north end of the park, they were forced to stop at an army check point. There was a barrier across the road, and the soldiers there seemed edgy. They stood staring hard at the car with their rifles at the ready as an officer came over to speak. "Who are you, and where are you going?" he asked the driver curtly.

It was now ten o'clock and Lisa was getting impatient. She got out of the car and gave the man a pleasant look. She pointed across the park and said, "My home is over thnere, Lieutenant."

"Nobody is allowed through," he replied sharply. "The Germans are on the other side of the river. You must turn round and go back."

"Please, Lieutenant, couldn't you let us through. We'll only be a few minutes. My father was killed today, and I want to kneel and say a prayer at the place he died." If only he'd hurry up, she said to herself. She glanced at her watch. It was now five past ten.

The young officer looked at the beautiful face and the large dark eyes which seemed to be pleading with him to relent. He looked into the car and saw Robert hunched in the rear seat. "Who's he?" he asked.

"That's my brother. He's terribly upset," Lisa replied.

"All right, you can go through, but be careful. The Germans could even be on this side of the river by now. I'll give you fifteen minutes."

A few minutes later they arrived at the end of the Westerlaan where there were some steps leading down to the river, and it was here that the boat was to make its pickup. The car stopped at the top of the steps, and Robert and Lisa got out. The place was deserted and there was no boat.

"We're late," said Lisa anxiously.

"Perhaps they've already gone, or won't come at all," Robert sounded as if he didn't care one way or the other.

The dock area was still burning, and from time to time the river was lit up as new flames shot up into the night sky only to die down again and return the water to darkness. Robert looked sadly at the smouldering shell of the old house, which stood only a few yards up the street. Then his heart bled once more with thoughts of Hugo as he glanced towards the destroyed Willemskade,

But Lisa's thoughts were on the boat. If it didn't arrive she would have to arrange some other way of getting Robert to England, and that would be a problem. But she would do it even if it meant losing her life in the attempt. She felt herself enclosed in his arms, and a surge of confidence lifted her spirit. He always had that effect on her. It flashed through her mind how passionately he had loved her as they had lain together during the last few days. The indescribable joy she had experienced when seeing him gripped in an uncontrollable frenzy of desire at the sight of her body.

They stood locked in each other's arms for some minutes, forgetting the boat. Then the chugging of an engine could be faintly heard coming down river, and they knew that their time was running out. There was so much to say, and yet words were inadequate. Only their eyes spoke. They kissed again and again, desperately trying to hold on to the moment.

Robert tried to speak, but Lisa, looking up at him, lightly touched his lips with her finger. "There's no need for words, my darling. Our hearts are saying all that needs to be said." A tear ran from the corner of her eye as she spoke.

The boat was at the foot of the steps. A gruff voice called up, "Come on, hurry up!"

Robert felt Lisa's arm gripping him tightly as they went down the steps together. In a daze, he was forced to let her go as he stepped aboard the boat. She handed him the small packet of belongings he had been given, and he put them down on the deck. With tears running down their cheeks, they stretched out their hands to hold each other for just a moment longer. They could, hear the engine gently ticking over below the deck, and knew that at any moment the note would change, and the boat would begin to move away.

They stood waiting, their hands clasped together in one last token of their love. "Don't ever forget me, Lisa."

"You know I won't, my darling. You'll always be in my heart as long as I live."

The engine began to thump, and almost imperceptively the boat began to draw away from the quay. They could feel their hands being torn apart. Inch by inch they slipped away from each other until only their fingers were touching. And then there was only the feel of the night air on their tender young skin as the boat moved away into the darkness.

"I love you, Robert!" Lisa called after him.

"Lisa! Lisa!" he cried out, his voice choked with despair. But her form was now gradually fading into the shadows of the harbour wall. He saw a movement up the steps to the road above, and then she was gone. He slowly sank down on to the bench at the stern of the boat, gripping his stomach as if trying to rip out the pain within. He sat bent double, quietly weeping, his heart broken, not caring whether he lived or died.

It was a smart fishing boat just over fifty feet in length with a wheelhouse amidships. A hatchway led to the small engine room at the stern, and steps within the wheelhouse led down to the fore cabin. An old, hardened seaman called Koos Kruyff owned the boat, working it with his son Piet.

"You'd better come to the cabin, you'll get cold just sitting there, boy." Koos had left Robert alone for a time, but seeing the youth hadn't moved thought it time he said something. Robert still didn't move or look up, so the old man took him by the arm, and gently pulling him to his feet, led him unresisting to the cabin. "We should be safe all the time our army controls the right bank," he remarked. "It's only thirty kilometres to the sea, and we should be clear by two o'clock."

Robert did not reply, sitting silently on a bunk while Koos made him a hot drink. He sat with head bowed, making no attempt to hide his tears. From time to time he quivered and caught his breath as he fought to control his emotions. In a few hours his happy life had been torn apart. From the heights of ecstasy he had been dragged down into a nightmare of death and destruction. Completely beyond his experience, his youthful mind was having difficulty in adjusting to such sudden change of fortune.

From the moment of his birth he had always been wrapped in the security of a loving family and the stability of a happy home, which was in stark contrast to what he had experienced in the last few hours. But his upbringing, although not anticipating such horrors, had given his character a hidden strength to cope with such distress.

Having finished his drink, Robert lay back on the bunk and was soon asleep. He awoke once during the night to find the cabin almost in darkness, the oil lamp swinging from a beam having been turned right down. A blanket had been placed over him as he slept so he was comfortably warm. He could feel by the motion of the boat that they must be out at sea. He caught sight of Koos's sea boots disappearing up the ladder, and realised that it was probably the sound of the old fisherman moving about that had awoken him. A few minutes later

Piet came below and heaved himself onto another bunk. He grinned at Robert and said, "It'll be getting light soon."

Robert nodded and closed his eyes again. The next time he awoke it was to find Piet standing over him with a hot drink.

"Here, drink this," Piet handed him the mug and then returned to the old stove where he was preparing breakfast. Having served Robert, and finished his own breakfast, Piet went to relieve his father at the wheel.

Koos came below and set about eating his breakfast, but he hadn't been there for more than a few minutes when there was a shout from Piet. "There's a boat coming at us at high speed, Father!"

Robert followed Koos up into the wheelhouse. At least he might as well take an interest in what was happening, he thought. In any case he was getting bored just sitting below. Koos trained his binoculars on the grey shape in the distance. Robert could see by the high bow wave that it was travelling fast.

"Curse it!" Koos exclaimed. "It's German!"

"What are we to do, Father? Do you think they'll guess where we're going?" Piet asked.

"I hope not. We'll pretend we're just about to drop our nets. But knowing these German swine they're as likely to start shooting without asking questions. We'll soon know."

"I've an idea, if you'll let me try," said Robert quietly. He felt he owed it to these men to try and help, and in the face of danger his natural sense of self preservation had raised itself above his despair and mood of depression.

"What can you do, boy?" snapped Koos.

"I can speak German for a start."

The two fishermen looked at each other as if they were resigned to try anything. "Do what you like, boy," Koos shrugged.

"I want to get alongside them and go aboard," Robert said as he made to leave the wheelhouse.

"Are you mad? They won't let you on board," Koos declared.

"They might. Don't say anything unless they speak to you, and then just say you're taking me to England," Robert instructed.

"You *are* mad," said Koos.

"Please do as I ask," Robert begged.

Koos shrugged, then nodded agreement.

Robert stood on the deck waving the E boat to come alongside. It drew in close and slowed to the speed, of the fishing boat, so that both vessels were running parallel to each other about twenty yards apart. A German machine gunner had his weapon trained on Robert.

Robert took a deep breath in an effort to stop himself shaking. He had done some acting at school and had always enjoyed it, but this time he would have to act for his life. He cupped his hands round his mouth and shouted across with authority in his perfect German. "I wish to come aboard." He signalled Piet, who was at the wheel to move in close and stop. When, this had been done, and the Germans had taken a line from Koos, a Lieutenant, who was obviously the captain of the E boat, waved Robert aboard.

There was only a gentle swell running so Robert had little difficulty in clambering up on to the German boat. He noticed a number of German sailors had appeared armed with rifles. Some kept a close watch on the fishing boat while one pointed his weapon at Robert.

Robert realised that his boyish looks may be against him, but that was a chance he would have to take "Heil Hitler!" he barked, clicking his heels and raising his arm in salute. He saw the German Lieutenant hesitate in surprise, but the young man recovered himself and returned the greeting, but with a naval salute rather than the *deutsche Grass*.

Before the German officer could say anything Robert took the initiative and, with a touch of arrogance in his tone, snapped out, "I'm *Hauptsturmführer* Heinemann of the *Sicherheitsdienst.*"

The German looked uncertain but Robert did not give him time to dwell on his suspicions. "A word with you, *Oberleutnant,* then there'll be no mistakes."

Once again the officer was about to speak but Robert cut him short. "I'm bound for England on a special mission. It's essential I'm not delayed." Robert spoke aggressively, but felt anything but aggressive. Under his clothes fear had made him clammy with sweat.

"Your papers please, Herr Hauptsturmführer." If the German lieutenant had any doubts about this baby faced and rather arrogant SD officer they were covered by the extra courtesy he extended towards him. He was aware that some of the young fanatics in the SD may have youthful features, but beneath their often charming exterior they were killers, and he considered it sensible to be cautious.

"Come, come, *Oberleutnant,* do you really expect me to be carrying papers on a secret mission to England." It struck Robert that his two years at Sandhurst had at least given him some confidence and helped him to think quickly in awkward circumstances. He prayed that they wouldn't search him, for amongst what had survived of his personal papers was a letter which he had intended to send to Karl Heinz but had forgotten to do so because of the bombing. It would be difficult to explain away.

The German lieutenant felt a little foolish and did not pursue the matter of the papers. "Who are they?" he asked, pointing to the two Dutchmen.

"Dutch fishermen working for us. They are members of the NSB."

The German had no idea what NSB stood for, so not wishing to show his ignorance he let the matter drop. "What is this mission of yours?" he asked.

"That's not your business. But I can tell you that I have a rendezvous with a Spanish freighter making its way to London."

"And how do I know that you're telling the truth, Herr Hauptsturmführer?"

"You don't, *Oberleutnant.* But when I was in the Hitler Youth I was trained as a leader to assess a situation and use my initiative. It must have been the same with you."

With mention of the Hitler Youth, Robert had purposely put into the German's mind another subject by which to test his authenticity.

"Where was your unit?" The lieutenant's tone was now less formal, and he asked the question conversationally.

"Cologne. My home town," Robert replied nonchalantly. He gave Karl Heinz's address to back up his story.

"What was your *Gebiet* number?"

"Eleven," Robert replied with a note of impatience in his voice. He noticed that a rifle was still being pointed at him, and it was apparent that he had not completely convinced the German even though it was most unlikely that anyone who had not been involved with the Hitler Youth would know a Gebiet number.

The young lieutenant still hesitated. "I must contact headquarters. Perhaps they have some information about this matter," he decided. ''Kindly wait there, Herr Hauptsturmführer.'' He turned to go to the wireless room.

"They will know nothing, *Oberleutnant*. But hurry up. If this delay causes me to miss my rendezvous, it will be headquarters contacting you. *Gruppenführer* Heydrich will wish to hear why a special mission organised by him personally has been, obstructed." Robert had heard Karl Heinz mention Reinhard Heydrich, head of the SD, as a man to be feared, and by the expression he saw on the German officer's face realised he had found a trump card.

"*Gruppenführer* Heydrich! Why didn't you say so? Of course you must go on immediately."

With the mention of Heydrich's name it appeared to Robert that the German couldn't get rid of him quickly enough. He was assisted over the side back on to the fishing boat. The lines were cast off, and the E boat slowly moved away.

When back in the wheelhouse Robert said to Piet, "For God's sake let's get away from here!" He went below into the cabin and sat on the bunk holding his arms tightly across his chest. He could feel his heart beating fast with the nervous tension of the past few minutes, and he took deep breaths to try and calm himself.

Koos came down to him. "You look quite pale, boy," he said.

"M . . . my legs are shaking, I can hardly stand," Robert stammered. "Thank God that German didn't notice."

Koos took a small bottle of whisky from his pocket and handed it to Robert. "Here, drink," he ordered.

Robert took more than he meant to. He had never tasted whisky before, and felt that his throat was being burnt away. "Water!" he gasped, jumping up and holding his throat.

Retrieving his bottle, Koos just laughed. "That's got you on your feet," said the old fisherman.

When the burning sensation had worn off, Robert collapsed on the bunk. "I'll never touch that stuff again," he promised.

Koos said, "I don't know what you said to those Germans, but whatever it was certainly did the trick. I like you, boy. You've got guts. And I don't say that to many people."

As the day went on the weather remained fair and they made good progress. Robert was even allowed, to take the wheel for a time. "Watch the compass," said Koos, showing him how to keep the boat's head in the right direction. He had to steer halfway between *west by south* and *west south west*, which would take them into the Thames Estuary. "Keep it on that, or we'll end up down the English Channel," Koos instructed.

The bow swung from side to side until Robert got used to handling the wheel. But he soon got the feel of it and kept a reasonably straight course. The recent event with the E boat, and then learning to steer properly kept his mind occupied, and temporarily lifted him out of his depression. But after a time his thoughts reverted back to Lisa and the feeling of hopelessness returned.

Hour after hour passed with the constant throb of the engine drumming in his ears. He tried to be of use in any way he could throughout the day, but Koos and Piet had their routine and needed little help, and other than his turn at the wheel and clearing up after they had eaten, there was little for him to do.

After the evening meal Robert sat in the cabin with a bucket of hot water at his feet cleaning the mugs and plates as best he could. He worked mechanically, thinking of other things, and yet even now the full impact of what he had recently experienced had not properly sunk into his mind. A sudden roar and sharp cracking sounds burst in upon his thoughts and startled him to such an extent that he dropped the plate he was washing back into the bucket. He heard glass smashing and a heavy thump, in the wheelhouse above, and then it felt as if the boat was turning. The roar was obviously a low flying aircraft, and it came to him that it was a machine gun he'd heard. He quickly went to the steps leading up to the wheel house.

"What's happened?" he called up. But there was no answer from above. Robert rushed up the steps, and the ghastly sight that met his gaze made his stomach turn over. The floor of the wheelhouse was covered with glass and blood, and there was Koos, lying grotesquely against the door with his head almost severed from his body. It went through Robert's mind that what he had heard was one long burst of machine gun fire as the plane went over. The bullets must have come straight through the windscreen and struck Koos in the throat. "Piet!" he shouted. But again there was no answer.

The engine was still chugging away, but with no one at the wheel the boat was turning in a circle. Robert pulled back the throttle so that the engine was just ticking over. Perhaps Piet was in the engine room and hadn't heard. "Piet!" he yelled. He pulled Koos's body away from the door and went to the open hatchway over the engine. Looking down he saw Piet hunched over the engine with a screwdriver in his hand. "Piet!" he called. But Piet didn't move. And then he noticed blood on the Dutchman's back and holes in his shirt. "God! Not you as well!" he cried. Robert eased himself down into the engine room and tried to turn Piet to face him, but as he did so the man slowly slid off his stool on to the floor.

For a moment Robert just knelt beside the body in the cramped space, but there was nothing he could do, so he pulled, himself back up on to the deck and sat with his feet dangling through the hatchway. He buried his face in his hands, feeling weak with shock at the death of the two fishermen, and his own narrow escape.

It went through his mind how ironic it was that in trying to avoid the war he had found it with a vengeance. Mistakenly, he believed he had tried to run away from it, but in condemning himself, he had failed to take into account his burning love for Lisa. The reality of death had entered his life, but for the moment he felt numb. It was as if his young mind had put up a barrier of protection against the horrors he was experiencing. He wondered whether he was becoming hard, because the sight of the two dead Dutchmen had brought only a sickening revulsion, no deep sorrow or despair as had Hugo's death. Perhaps he hadn't known them long enough for his deeper feelings to be affected, or perhaps his relationship with them was purely selfish, and they were only a means of ensuring he reached safety.

"Now what am I going to do?" he whispered to himself. He remembered again the words of old Cavey, 'Don't just sit there, Rutherford, the problem won't solve itself. Do something, boy, even if it's wrong'. If only he was back sitting in that safe and secure classroom. So often he had sat and dreamed of adventures and far away places, but at this moment he would have given anything just to be back with his old school friends. He could have even, put up with old Cavey slapping his head to make him pay attention. But perhaps old Cavey wouldn't remember him, and there would be another boy sitting at his desk now. How sad the passing of time can be, he thought. He would never be a boy again, and all the fun had gone from his life. If only . . . But what's the use of thinking of the past? He was alone with two dead men on a small boat, and he didn't know where the hell he was.

Robert stood up. The wind ruffled his hair, and the evening chill, made him shiver. For a moment the feeling of desperate loneliness gripped him as he looked out over the empty water. The engine was still idling and the boat drifting. He went into the wheelhouse and pulled Koos's body out on to the deck, then returning, he pushed the throttle forwards and as the boat picked up speed he turned the wheel until he was back on the course Koos had told him to steer. He would just keep going, and with any luck he might reach the Thames. He looked at his watch. It was 6.30 p.m. The boat had reached the sea at about 2 a.m. that morning, so he'd been at sea for sixteen and a half hours. At roughly five knots, it would mean he'd already covered over eighty miles. He picked up an old chart, which was clipped to a board and leaning against the side of the wheelhouse at his feet, he decided that after another ten hours he might sight the coast of Kent. God knows how he would keep awake that long. It all seemed a bit hit and miss, he thought, but if he kept going west he was bound to reach England. Thank God he'd paid attention to some things at school.

He let his thoughts race round in his head. Anything to stop the boredom, as hour after hour he stood holding the boat on course. It must have been a German bomber going home that had loosed off its machine gun at the boat. What a senseless thing to do to a harmless fishing boat. It's a wonder they didn't come back and try another burst. Perhaps they were short of fuel. It was strange to think he might have once met the men flying it. Surely the Germans he knew wouldn't do a thing like that, but perhaps war changes people. How strange to think he had seen more of the war than all the people at home.

He tried not to think of Lisa, because the very thought of her gave him physical pain in the pit of his stomach, as well as mental anguish as he pined to have her in his arms. But it was no good, his mind kept returning to her, and over and over again he tortured himself by imagining her naked body and the things they had done together.

Darkness fell, and Robert found he was becoming drowsy even though the cool night air was blowing on to his face. As the windscreen had been smashed the upper part of him had no protection. On one occasion he jerked back into consciousness after finding he had fallen asleep standing there. Fortunately the boat had remained on course, although the wheel had begun to feel sluggish and it somehow felt more difficult to steer. Perhaps it was because he was tired.

He decided to tie the wheel in position so that he could go below and make a hot drink. The idea seemed to work, for the boat kept reasonably steady.

Having made his drink, he sat on the edge of the bunk daggling his legs over the side. He pulled a blanket round his shoulders and gradually a little warmth began to seep into him. He rested his shoulders back against the side of the cabin, enjoying the warmth and comfort for just a few minutes longer. Closing his eyes, he imagined himself in his own bed at home. He smiled at the thought of his pink donkey, and wondered whether it was still lying on his pillow where he had left it before leaving for Rotterdam. How lucky he had been to have such a room. Millicent wouldn't be poking around in there anymore. She had been sent packing after Agnes had caught them together on his bed. He hadn't liked Millicent all that much, but she had taught him a thing or two, he remembered. It was lucky that

Father hadn't found out, he thought, and that the relationship had been stopped before it had gone too far. Agnes had been furious, and, after sending Millicent back to the kitchen, she had, for the first time ever, used the cane on him. The humiliation had been worse than the pain, he remembered, because at the age of seventeen he had considered himself past such punishment. As if that wasn't enough, and to add to his punishment, he had then been forced to have a cold bath to cool him down, as Agnes had said.

He shuddered at the thought of that cold bath. That was punishment enough without being beaten with that damn cane. He could almost feel again the cold water on his feet as he had stepped into the bath, Agnes watching with a stern look on her face, and menacingly holding the cane in her hand. Before lying down, he had slowly knelt until the water had covered his legs. His vivid thoughts of the past made the sensation seem almost real. Why were his feet so cold? He jerked upright, opening his eyes. "Blast!" He must have fallen asleep again. "Oh, my God! It is real!" he exclaimed, seeing that his feet and the lower part of his legs were daggling in water. For a moment his mind couldn't make out what was happening. The cabin was awash, the water almost up to the edge of the bunk. The engine had stopped, and all he could hear was the gentle lapping of the water against the cabin sides. "God, I'm sinking!" he cried as his mind cleared and the reality of the situation forced itself upon him.

With the water above his knees Robert quickly paddled across to the steps and went up on deck. It was still dark, but by the light of the lantern in the wheelhouse he could see that the boat was settling down into the water. It was going down very slowly, but evenly. "Those bloody Germans must have shot holes in the bottom," he murmured. Quickly returning to the cabin he grabbed a blanket and wrapped in it as much food as he could find. Then, grabbing a can of water and taking the oil lamp from the beam he returned on deck. He held his watch close to the lamp. It was ten past three. He went to the dinghy, which was lying on the deck at the bows, praying that it too hadn't been holed by the machine gun bullets. Mercifully, but not for Koos and Piet, the bullets had passed over the top of it and struck the wheelhouse and engine room instead. Placing the food and water in the small boat, he returned to the wheelhouse to see if there was anything else he needed to take. He couldn't detach the compass, but he took the chart, for what use it would be, and he also found a box of flares and some matches.

The boat was now settling down fast, with water having started to come in through the scuppers onto the foredeck. Robert made sure the dinghy was free to float off, and then got in it and sat waiting for the old fishing boat and its dead crew to sink beneath him.

In ten minutes it finally disappeared, and Robert sat shivering in his drifting dinghy. He had to get warm in some way, so he set the oars in the rowlocks and began to row. He could see the faint light of dawn on the eastern horizon so he rowed in the opposite direction. At least he would be going towards the English coast, although he had little idea how far it was likely to be. But there must be ships in the vicinity, he decided. He hoped that the day would be clear so that he could take his direction by the sun.

As dawn broke and the sun began to struggle above the horizon he was surprised to see a number of ships in the distance. They were too far away to be able to see him, but if he could light a flare it was possible he could attract their attention. He opened the box and, taking out a flare, tried to read the faded instructions without much success. He would just have to guess what to do. The damn thing looked a bit too old to be safe, he thought. But he would have to risk it. He put an old bailing tin on the stern seat and then stuck the flare in it. His hands were so cold he had difficulty in handling the match box, but when he did manage to get out a match and strike it, it was too damp to light. Match after match refused to light. "Bloody hell!" he swore, losing his temper and flinging the box into the sea. Cold and depressed he started to row again.

Throughout the whole day the only ships he saw were too far off to attract their attention. Fortunately the sea remained calm and Robert congratulated himself for having had the presence of mind to bring food and water from the fishing boat. He spent the day alternately rowing and resting, but as darkness closed in once more there was still no sign of land. He tried to keep up his rowing into the night, but weariness overtook him, and sometime during the small hours he awoke to find himself lying in the bottom of the boat and no oars in the rowlocks. Drowsily, he realised that they must have slipped away as he slept and that he was now drifting, but he was too tired to care and closed his eyes again.

It was the squawking of seagulls that eventually woke him. He squinted up into the lightening sky watching them circle and dive overhead. He lay for a few minutes trying to collect his thoughts, and then it began to dawn on him that something was different, but his tired mind was finding it difficult to decide what it was. Then it struck him that there was no motion and that the boat was being held fast. He stiffly raised himself and peered over the gunwale, and saw the early morning mist floating eerily over the saltings. The boat was high and dry on the mud of a small inlet. He felt tears of relief welling up into his eyes. It can only be England, he thought.

CHAPTER 13

Robert arrived home late that evening and as he walked past the lodge into the drive that strange feeling of security came over him as it always had done when, as a boy, he had returned from a trying day at school. He glanced down at his filthy clothes and the mud caked hard on his shoes, and wondered how he would he received by his parents. Perhaps they wouldn't even recognise him, he thought.

After leaving his boat, he had struggled across the saltings, and then, with wet mud dripping from his trousers and covering his shoes, had trudged along a road to the nearest town, which turned out to be Southend. Luckily he'd had just enough English money to pay his train fare to London. He had walked across town and called at Percy's flat to borrow some money for his fare to Brighton. Cynthia had answered the door carrying her new baby, and had given him her usual overwhelming welcome. He had been reluctant to enter the penthouse owing to the state he was in, but Cynthia had insisted so he had relented but immediately wished he hadn't, because there was Henrietta sitting in the lounge.

"It's Robert, Mother dear," Cynthia had said as she had led him into the room. "He needs some money for the train."

"I would have thought it was a bath he needed," Henrietta had snapped, eyeing Robert closely. "You look disgusting, boy."

"I'm sorry, Aunty, but . . ."

"And you smell," Henrietta interrupted, placing her handkerchief to her nose. "And as for that disgraceful portrait hanging in the bedroom," Henrietta had continued, "You ought to be ashamed of yourself!"

"Yes, Aunty," Robert had replied, and then quickly changed the subject by asking after Percy.

Evidently, Percy had just returned from France and was now stationed with his fighter squadron at Biggin Hill.

"What a lovely baby, Cynthia. I heard I had a new cousin," he had continued. "How old is it?"

"Not it, darling, him." She had grinned at Robert, then cooed at the child, "Isn't he naughty. This is little Adrian, and he's seven months next Tuesday."

Robert had done his best to show interest in the child, but he was exhausted, and his one desire had been to get home and sleep, so as soon as he could he had taken his leave.

The Brighton train had been crowded and he had stood in the corridor trying to be inconspicuous, feeling all the time like a fugitive. At Brighton station he had been stopped by the police, who wanted to see his identity card, and to know why he was entering a restricted area. If it hadn't been for Mr White, the policeman who had known him since he was a boy, he would probably have been arrested. But now, at last, he was home, standing at the front door. He rang the bell and waited. It was Agnes who opened it. "Yes?" she said.

Robert stood looking at her and watched her face change as she realised who it was. "Robert!" she cried taking him in her arms and kissing him, unable to contain her excitement that her boy had returned.

Hearing the commotion in the hall, and the sound of Robert's voice, Elizabeth came out of the drawing-room, and for a moment stood looking at her son. "Robert," she said quietly. "Oh, Robert, my dear boy, you're safe. We've all be so worried." She came quickly forward and threw her arms round him, kissing him gently. Then, holding him away from her, she looked him up and down. "What a state you're in. What has happened to you?"

"I'm all right, Mother. It's only mud." He tried not to sound unresponsive to her concern for him, but he was too tired for further conversation. "I must go to bed," he said, "we'll talk later."

"But you've only just arrived, dear. Won't you come and sit down, just for a minute or two," Elizabeth suggested. "You must have so much to tell me. . .Surely you want something to eat?"

"Not now, Mother. I just want to sleep," he replied, slowly backing away up the stairs.

"You can't go to bed like that," Agnes called after him, "You must have a bath."

But Robert was too tired to listen, and had disappeared along the passage.

Going to his room a short time later with a tray of food and drink for him, the two women found Robert lying fully clothed on the spare bed. He had only managed to remove his shoes before falling asleep. Agnes prepared his own bed, and then, while he slept, they stripped him and with some difficulty moved him into it and tucked him up properly, leaving him to sleep.

When John arrived the following morning to spend the week-end at home, Robert was still sleeping soundly. It was not until the afternoon, when John and Elizabeth were chatting in the drawing-room, that their son eventually joined them.

"So the wanderer has returned at last," said John as Robert, wearing only a dressing gown, entered the room. "And not before time," he added.

"You don't seem very pleased to see me, Father."

"I would have been better pleased if you'd come home some time ago."

"But why? I was perfectly happy . . . at least I was until. . ."

"And why aren't you properly dressed?" John interrupted. He had been looking forward to seeing Robert again, but now the moment had came he found himself censuring the boy.

"I'm going back to bed," Robert replied. "I only popped down to say hallo." He sat down, beside his mother on the settee.

"Why, are you ill?"

"No, Father. Just tired."

"What nonsense! A young chap like you tired. Get yourself a bath, and spruce up a bit, and you'll be as right as rain."

"He's had a long journey, dear." Elizabeth interjected.

"Maybe. But it's fortunate for us that our young men in France don't scuttle off to bed every time they feel tired," John retorted. "How did you manage to get out?"

"On a fishing boat. Father."

"Well, we're glad you're safely home. Now it's time you got into uniform. You can't run away from it any longer. We've already had the police up here asking why you haven't registered."

Robert sat with bowed head only giving half his attention to what his father was saying. He had started to think of Lisa again, and couldn't get it out of his mind, that this was to have been the wedding day. "Don't worry, Father, I'll go," he replied absently.

"Good. We'll get you your commission back," said John, sounding better pleased.

"No!" Robert exclaimed. "I don't want any favours just because I'm your son. And, I'm certainly not being pushed into your regiment."

"And why not, might I ask?"

"Because, for one thing, I've no intention of going anywhere near Jason."

"I'll have you know that Jason has done damn well in the regiment. Just got his captaincy. At least he's got the guts to be serving his country in France. I don't know what you've got against him."

"It's as well you don't," Robert said quietly more to himself than to his father.

"Then what are you going to do?" John asked.

"I'll join the ranks."

"Don't talk nonsense! You're a trained officer. You're more entitled to a commission than most of those being granted them now."

"Look, Father, I don't want to go at all, but I've got no option. But I'll do it my way."

John shrugged. "All right, if that's what you want."

"We were so sorry about the wedding, dear," said Elizabeth.

"Yes, that was unfortunate," John agreed. "I must admit though that I have certain reservations about the match."

"Why?" Robert asked belligerently.

"Because you're very young and I think you should have mixed more with other girls before making your choice. After all, you've never really taken much interest in the opposite sex, have you? Except, perhaps, the Marsden girl."

"It's Lisa I want, not other girls. It's always been her."

"That's just my point. You've have no standard to judge by. What does Hugo think?"

"He's dead," Robert replied sharply, and then realised what he had said.

"Dead?" Elizabeth gasped.

Robert quickly moved close to his mother and took her hand. "I'm sorry, Mother, it just slipped out. I was going to tell you, but not like that. I really am sorry." He felt himself break out in a cold sweat as the memory of that terrible day returned to his mind. He saw the tears on his mother's cheeks, and put his arm round her.

"Couldn't you have been a little more tactful," said John, scowling at his son.

"I've said I'm sorry," Robert replied. He turned, to Elizabeth and added, "I didn't mean to be hurtful, Mother."

Elizabeth squeezed Robert's hand and said, "It's all right, dear, don't upset yourself. I'll be alright in a minute."

Gradually, Robert choked out something of what had happened during his last few days in Rotterdam.

"So much for your friend Hitler," John remarked when Robert had finished.

"It must have been a mistake," Robert replied. "He couldn't have ordered that. It was pointless, smashing up a defenceless city."

"You've got a lot to learn, about war, Robert. And about Hitler and his gang."

"Hugo so loved that house," Elizabeth remarked. "Has it all gone?" she asked

"Almost," Robert replied. "It was completely gutted, and the roof fell in."

"Then how did Kate get out if she was unconscious?" John wanted to know.

"She was pulled out just in time," Robert replied.

"And where were you when all this was going on?" John asked.

"In the park with Lisa." Robert got up from the settee and went to leave the roam. "Will you excuse me," he said, "I don't want to talk about it."

They watched him go, and when the door had closed behind him Elizabeth said, "Don't be too hard on him, John dear, he's only young, and we don't know what he might have been through."

"Hard on him!" John exclaimed. "It's time he realised there's a war on. We're fighting for our very existence in France, and he's still reluctant to join up. And I do wish he'd stop making excuses for the Germans."

They sat for a few minutes in silence, and then the door opened and John's eyes lit up as a small child tottered unsteadily towards him followed by Joanna.

Robert returned to his room and flung himself on the bed. He felt angry with himself for not breaking the bad news in the gentle way he had planned. But the speed of events over the past few days had been bewildering, and now he was home and safe and had had time to think he found himself depressed and weary. He yearned only for Lisa. They had been so happy together, but now he could see only a bleak future without her, and he didn't care what happened to him.

There was a knock on the door and Joanna's head appeared. Robert got up as she entered, and they hugged and kissed each other, and then both sat on the bed.

"I'm so glad you're safely home, Rob. We've missed you so much."

"Thanks, sis. The old man doesn't seem so pleased to see me."

"Of course he is! You know what he's like. He keeps it all underneath."

"I haven't been home two minutes and he wants to pack me off into the army. . . Anyway, how's, Patrick?"

"He's fine. He's downstairs entertaining his grandparents. He's walking well now. . . You know, Rob, Matt could probably do something for you, when you join up. He's a major in some sort of intelligence job. It's all hush hush, but you might be useful with your languages."

"I'll think about it," Robert replied, but the last thing he could put his mind to at the moment was his future in the army.

*

After a few days at home, Robert registered for military service, and was then called for a medical examination. Some weeks later he received his call-up papers and reported to Catterick for his initial training.

He had put his name down for the intelligence corps, but after his initial training he found himself posted to an infantry battalion. But he didn't care one way or the other. As far as Robert was concerned, as it was impossible for him to lead the life he wanted it was of little concern what was put in its place.

He spent many months training with his battalion in different parts of the country, but although the life in many ways was hard and sometimes boring, he did not dislike it. Time had partially healed the pain of Rotterdam, and he could now cope with the memory, without sinking into a mood of depression. But his yearning for Lisa had not diminished, and he still could not bring himself to seek the company of other women as many of his friends did even though they were married.

To the men in his platoon it was obvious that Robert's upbringing had been very different from their own, and that here was a young gentleman who appeared more suited to the officer's mess than the barrack hut. But they also realised that he was no snob, and, for his part, Robert made a point of never mentioning his family or his father's position. They made fun of his refined accent, and the fact that he drank little alcohol when he went with them to a pub, but for all that he was popular, and, although often quiet and withdrawn, they enjoyed his company.

It was also apparent to Robert's, commanding officer that here was a young man who was officer material, and it was suggested on a number of occasions that he make application for a commission. At first Robert was reluctant to apply, because he was happy with his new friends and felt no particular desire to be an officer, but eventually, thinking he should show Father that he could do something off his own bat, he decided to submit an application.

Returning from a week-end leave before attending the War Office Selection Board, Robert had just passed through the ticket barrier at Victoria station when he heard his name called. Turning, he saw an officer standing there smiling at him. Robert saluted and then noticed the ribbon of the military cross on the smart tunic that faced him.

"Don't be so damned formal, young Robert!"

"Jason!" Robert exclaimed. "I didn't recognise you behind that moustache." It had been some years since he had seen his cousin, and it was difficult to realise that this debonair young officer was the same boy who had bullied him whenever the opportunity had presented itself during their youth.

"Nice to see again, Robert," said Jason, shaking his cousin's hand. "I'm just on my way down to your place in Brighton. Wondered whether I'd see you there."

"No, I'm on my way back," Robert replied without enthusiasm, unable to completely disguise his relief at having missed the impending visit.

"Pity. I'm taking my fiancée down to meet uncle and aunty." Jason saw the questioning look on his cousin's face. "Surprised?" he grinned.

"Yes," Robert admitted. He could not imagine anyone wanting to marry Jason. "I had no idea you were engaged," he added to cover the true sense of his rather abrupt admission. He saw his cousin's eyes light up as they were approached by an attractive looking girl.

"Here she is!" Jason exclaimed, catching up the newcomer in his arms and kissing her. "Alice, let me introduce you to my cousin Robert."

"Robert, how nice to meet you! Jason has often mentioned you."

Robert took her hand and was reminded of Lisa. It was probably the dark hair, he thought. She hadn't Lisa's beauty, but she was a charming girl and he felt she had a warmth about her. Whatever did she see in Jason, he wondered?

"Robert only tolerates me," Jason grinned. "He's never really forgiven me for bossing him about when we were boys."

Robert coloured up, knowing the truth of his cousin's remark, but considering it an understatement of what actually had taken place when they were young.

"I'm looking forward to meeting your parents. Robert," Alice said.

"Yes," Jason agreed, keeping his arm firmly round her waist. "Uncle John has been a real brick since the old man died. Can't seem to do enough for me. Takes a great interest in everything I do, and wants to meet Alice."

"It pleases him to think there's one member of the family in the regiment," Robert remarked. "I'm afraid I haven't come up to his expectations."

"Don't say that, Robert. I'm sure he thinks the world of you," Jason replied. Then, looking at his watch, he said. "Must go, or we'll miss the train."

Robert watched them go through the ticket barrier arm in arm, and thought how lucky they were to have each other. In some ways the Jason he had just met seemed like a stranger to him, and yet it was difficult to rid himself of the dislike he had for his cousin, even though Jason's corrupting influence had had little lasting effect on him. But as he walked away his mind turned from Jason to the more pressing thoughts of the forthcoming selection board.

*

The selection procedure, which he passed easily, and the training courses which followed took some time, so it was not until early in 1942 that Robert received his commission. Having previously spent two years at Sandhurst, he had not found the training course difficult. Some aspects of officer training had altered, the war having taught new lessons, and the assault courses were far more realistic. But he coped well and passed out top of his intake.

Having gained their commissions, Robert and his fellow officers were all impatient to know their postings. Directly the list was posted up a crowd collected round the notice board, those at the front eagerly searching for their names, and those at the back jostling to move forward. Eventually Robert reached the front, but to his surprise his name was not on the list.

"They've forgotten me," Robert complained to those standing around him.

"Probably marked you down for a secret mission, old boy, to cut Hitler's throat," a voice piped up.

Robert didn't feel amused. He went to the adjutant's office to find out what was to happen to him. "Oh, yes, Rutherford. I was asked not to put your posting on the list," the adjutant remarked. "You're to report immediately to a Major Irving at this address in Baker Street London." He handed Robert a slip of paper.

"But, sir, I don't understand."

"Nor do I, Rutherford, just get on with it," the adjutant replied impatiently, bringing the interview to a close.

Two days later Robert made his way to the address in Baker Street. The previous day he had arrived at John's London house in Eaton Square where he had dumped his kit and stayed overnight. His father had not been able to throw any light on Matt's mysterious summons. John knew Matt was involved with some branch of military intelligence, but what he actually did was never mentioned between, them.

Inside the building Robert found himself none the wiser to what it was being used for. It appeared to be some sort of staff headquarters. He was taken to a room and told to wait while his escort disappeared into another office. A few moments later the door opened and he was greeted by Matt. Robert came to attention and made an exaggerated salute, at the same time giving Matt a cheeky smile. "And you can cut all that out, you cheeky young devil," Matt grinned. Then after a pause he said, "I expect you're wondering why I've made you come here."

Robert was, but remained silent, just giving a nod.

Matt went on. "I can't give you much information, but you would be useful to us here. You speak Dutch, German and French, and you're absolutely loyal to this country. We are looking for people who have quiet, unobtrusive courage."

"That rules me out," Robert interjected.

"Don't be stupid, Robert! I believe you have this quality. Now what do you think?"

"How do I know what to think? You haven't told me what the job is."

"At this stage I can only tell you that we need your knowledge of Dutch," Matt replied, and then added as an afterthought, "Oh, yes, and it could be dangerous."

"Dangerous!" Robert exclaimed. "Are you trying to get rid of me? I was hoping you'd find me something cushy, not bloody dangerous. A fine brother-in-law you've turned out to be."

Matt grinned at his young relative. "There is a war on, young Robert, and sooner or later you are going to have to do something that has an element of danger in it."

"Not if I can help it."

Matt chuckled. "You really are the limit. You've always belittled your own courage and abilities. Anyway, I don't think you mean half you say. I want you to go for an interview, and after that you can decide whether or not to continue. That is if you are passed as suitable for the training."

"It seems I have no choice."

"Oh yes you have, but you'll do it anyway," Matt smiled.

Robert was sent to a requisitioned hotel which was near the War Office. He was shown into a small room which was completely bare except for two chairs. A naked light bulb hung from the ceiling, he noticed. He waited for a few minutes then the door opened and a middle aged man entered and started to speak to him in Dutch. He was invited to sit down but the man gave no name and made no attempt to introduce himself.

"How do you come to speak fluent Dutch?"

"My mother is Dutch and I was born in Holland," Robert replied.

"What parts of Holland are you familiar with?"

"Brabant, especially around Grave. That's where I was born. I know the rest of Holland quite well. Oh, yes, and I also know Rotterdam well, or I did before the bombing."

The man looked hard at Robert. There had been a catch in the voice at the mention of Rotterdam. "Do you know many people in Holland?"

"Yes. Quite a few."

"What do you think of the Nazis?"

Robert stopped, to think for a moment. He found it a difficult question. "I think they've got to be beaten."

"Why?"

"Well, their policies are unacceptable."

"That sounds a very mild opinion considering what they've done to Europe. Don't you hate them?"

"Perhaps. I don't know really."

"Would you kill a German if you had to?"

"I suppose so. I certainly wouldn't kill one unless I had to."

"If we accept you, it will be a secret war that you will be dealing with. We don't want brisk, decisive types, you understand. We want reflective people who are not impulsive. Prudent people with courage. Do you think you fit that description?"

"I don't know, sir. I'm certainly not brisk or decisive. They tell me I'm a bit of a dreamer."

"I want you to go away and have a think. Come and see me again in three days, same time. Consider yourself on leave until then."

"Yes, sir." Robert got up and went to the door, but before he left the room the man spoke again.

"By the way, don't mention this interview to anyone."

Returning to the street again, Robert wandered, towards Trafalgar Square not knowing what to do with himself. He mingled with the throng, most of whom, like himself, were in uniform. Many wore unfamiliar foreign uniforms of the countries overrun by the Germans. Then it occurred to him that when he was last home on leave, Mrs Marsden had told him that Wendy had been posted to the Admiralty. He would go and see if she was available, and take her out to lunch.

"First Officer Marsden, you say?" said the commissionaire at the reception desk in reply to Robert's enquiry. "I think you might have just missed her, sir."

Robert made to leave, feeling disappointed, but the man called after him.

"One moment, sir, she's coming now."

Robert turned to see Wendy approaching accompanied by a naval officer. "Robert!" she exclaimed with surprise. "How lovely to see you! It's been so long," They stood looking at each other, neither knowing quite how to greet the other. Then Wendy said, "Let me introduce Lieutenant Commander Horton."

Robert's hand was gripped firmly and shaken enthusiastically. "How d'you do," the officer said breezily. Robert thought he was one of those brisk, decisive types who his interviewing officer had just mentioned.

Robert said, "I'm in London for a few days, and I was wondering if I could take you to lunch somewhere." He didn't notice Wendy's look of disappointment.

"I'm so sorry, Robert, but I've already got a lunch appointment with Commander Horton."

"Yes, sorry, but we must go." Horton made little attempt to cover his impatience at the delay and took Wendy's arm to lead her away. "Nice to have met you," he muttered unconvincingly.

As Wendy was pulled away she called back over her shoulder, "I'll get in touch, Robert."

Don't bother, he thought as he returned to the street. He walked down The Mall feeling lonely and depressed. If only he had a friend to talk to, but since leaving school he had lost touch with most of his friends, because, like him they were in the forces and spread all over the country. It had irritated him that Wendy had gone off with that naval officer; although in his heart he knew that he had no right to expect her to be at his beck and call just because he happened to be at a loose end. After all, he wasn't in love with her. But for all that, he couldn't bear the thought of her being in love with someone else. Damn her, why couldn't she have come with him.

He returned to Eaton Square, and on entering the house went upstairs to the drawing-room where he flung himself on to a settee. Kicking off his shoes, he put his feet up, lay back against the arm with his hands clasped behind his head, and relaxed. He started to think about the interview, and wondered whether or not he should volunteer for this job - whatever it might be. He guessed that he was being asked to become some sort of agent. Surely they wouldn't expect him to go back to Holland? That could be bloody dangerous. But supposing they did? He could see Lisa again; then it would be worth the risk. At the thought of Lisa he closed his eyes and let his imagination run wild, torturing himself with erotic thoughts of their love. He could almost feel her soft skin caressing his body as he remembered the first time they had stood naked in each other's arms.

It was some time later he awoke. The room was in darkness, lit only by the blazing log fire with its leaping flames making the shadows dance along the walls. He slowly swung his legs off the settee and sat staring into the fire, holding his head, his elbows resting on his knees.

"So you're awake at last."

Robert started, and sat up. In the glow of the fire he made out the figure of Wendy sitting in an armchair at the side of the fireplace. "God! You gave me a start," he groaned.

"I'm sorry," she apologized. "I didn't want to disturb you. You were sleeping like an innocent."

"I don't feel very innocent. In fact I feel awful. I shouldn't have dropped off like that. What's the time?"

"Six o'clock."

"How long have you been here?" he asked.

"Some time."

Robert shook his head, in an effort to clear the sleep from his brain.

Agnes entered the room with a tea tray. "I've put the blackout up. Would you like the light on?" she asked.

"Yes, thanks, Agnes."

The tea tray was placed near Wendy, who took charge of the pouring without being asked. "Do you always talk in your sleep?" she grinned.

"How should I know?" Robert retorted, feeling uncomfortable. "What did I say?" he asked apprehensively, hoping nothing embarrassing had come out.

"Ah, that would be telling. Come on, what were you dreaming?"

"Never you mind. What did I say?"

"Never you mind," Wendy grinned.

"Touché. I can never get the better of you damn women." Robert almost smiled, but remembered that he was supposed to be angry with her. "What are you doing here, anyway? I thought you'd be with that blinking seasalt."

"He's not a blinking seasalt. Howard's a very nice man."

"Oh, it's Howard now, is it!"

"And why not. I do believe you're jealous, Robert."

"Jealous!" Robert exclaimed indignantly. "Of course I'm not jealous."

"I must say, you really know how to give a girl confidence." Wendy pouted at him and grinned.

She had such a lovely face, he thought. "I didn't mean. . ." Robert hesitated. "Oh God. I don't know what the hell I do mean. I suppose I am jealous. I've got no right to be, but I am. In any case, you shouldn't need confidence with your looks."

Wendy laughed. "Well, thank you, kind, sir," she said. "That's the nicest thing that's been said to me for a long time."

"I'd have thought your precious Howard would have told you that."

"Well he didn't. And he's not my precious Howard. At least, not yet," Wendy provoked.

Robert could not decide whether she was teasing him. "Anyway, what are you doing here?" he asked.

"I came to say how disappointed I was that I couldn't lunch with you today. thought you looked a little put out."

Robert felt his heart jump for joy when she spoke.

"I wasn't at all put out," he lied. "It's nothing to do with me who you lunch with."

"Oh, in that case you won't mind if I lunch with Howard again tomorrow." Wendy turned to place her cup and saucer on the tea trolley, but, glancing at Robert out of the corner of her eye, noticed his look of disappointment.

"But. . ." his voice tailed away when he saw her smiling at him. "You know damn well I mind."

They both laughed.

For a time neither spoke. They sat gazing into the fire content to enjoy each other's presence and the feeling of security their friendship gave them.

The door opened and Elizabeth entered the room. "My dears!" she said, crossing the room and embracing first Wendy, then Robert, both of whom had stood up to receive her. "How nice to see you, Wendy. I hear you are working In London. You should have called before."

"I didn't like to, Lady Rutherford. I know how busy you are with your Red Cross work."

Elizabeth replied, "I must say it takes up a lot of time. I've been at headquarters all day, but one must do something. Anyway, my dear, Sir John and I are never too busy to see you." She then directed her attention to Robert. "Robert how untidy you look, you naughty boy. And why haven't you got your shoes on? What a way to entertain a young lady."

"Mother, I was asleep when this young lady crept in on me, so I couldn't help it." Robert turned to Wendy and added with a grin, "She still treats me like a schoolboy."

"And a very naughty one you were sometimes," Elizabeth laughed.

"For God's sake don't let's go into that, Mother!" Robert exclaimed.

Elizabeth then set about organising the rest of the evening. She had already dined, so arranged for the two young people to have their supper on their own in front of the fire. "You just stay where you are and I'll have it brought to you." she told them. "Wendy, you must, stay the night. We can't have you wandering out into the blackout tonight."

"I can get a taxi," Wendy suggested half-heartedly.

But Elizabeth wouldn't entertain the idea. "We'll get you a taxi in the morning," she decided.

When Elizabeth had left the room, the young people sat down together on the settee. "Do you ever get the feeling that Mother is just a little bit of a match maker?" Robert asked.

Wendy looked at him and then asked seriously, "Us, you mean?"

Robert turned his face away. "I want you, Wendy. You know that, don't you?"

"But you don't love me,"

Robert rested his elbows on his knees and clasped his face in his hands. "I don't even know if that's true anymore," he said quietly. "After all, what is love? To physically want someone? To share your life with them? To enjoy their company? To do things together?"

"That's true enough; but it goes deeper than that, Robert. For me anyway. I could never take second place in the affections of a man who wished to marry me. It must be all or nothing. In marriage there can be no half measures, if you understand what I mean."

"Yes I do understand. But, what if someone loves two people?"

"You're talking about love. I'm talking about being in love, and that's different. You can't be in love with two people, because one will always take second place."

"Is that why you've never allowed me to make love to you?"

"All I want is to marry and have children, but that won't happen until I've found a man who puts me before everything and everyone. I know exactly what I want, and perhaps even who I want, but I'm not prepared to compromise." She stretched out and gently prised his hand away from his face and took it in both of hers. "Don't you agree that this is the right way?"

"I suppose so," he sighed.

"You don't sound sure."

"Would it make any difference if I was?"

"Of course it would. You've got to make up your mind what you want then stick to it."

There was a pause in the conversation, and then Wendy said, "I'm so pleased you got your commission. Where are you being posted?"

"I don't know. I have a decision to make, and I haven't made it yet. Unfortunately, I'm not allowed, to talk about it."

It was a decision that Robert had still not made when he returned to continue the interview three days later.

He sat in the same bare room with the Interviewing officer, but this time the man was more explicit about what the job would entail. He explained that the job was not just that of an interpreter, but one where a successful candidate would actually go into Holland to work in some subversive activity.

"I had guessed it was something like that, sir," Robert replied.

"There's no need for me to spell out the danger."

Robert was not asked for his decision, but once again told to go away and think about it which was just as well because he still hadn't made up his mind.

It was only at the third interview that he was asked whether he wished to take the job. He didn't really want the job and considered that he would make a very poor agent, but for some reason the officer had decided that he was the right material.

"Yes, I'll do it," Robert said on the spur of the moment, thinking more of seeing Lisa again than serving the purposes of this organisation, whatever it was.

*

Robert was sent to Hampshire for the initial part of his training. Arriving at his destination, he found it to be a country house on a large estate. After paying off the taxi, he stood gazing at the building, considering it to be a most pleasant place. Going in through the front door he found, the entrance hall even more inviting. The house had a warm atmosphere and was appointed like a country hotel.

"Good afternoon, sir." A sergeant standing behind the reception desk greeted the new arrival with a smile.

Robert dumped his kit on the floor. "Good afternoon, sergeant. I'm Second Lieutenant Rutherford. I hope you're expecting me."

"We are, sir. I'm Sergeant Drake, sir. I act as chief steward and barman. I'm here to look after you, sir, so if there's anything you require, just ask."

"Thank you, Sergeant."

Robert was taken upstairs and shown to an attractive room overlooking the front of the house. "This is your room, sir," said the sergeant. "Please be downstairs in the lounge at sixteen hundred hours, because the commandant wishes to welcome the new intake."

He had an hour before he was required downstairs. He lay down on the bed feeling pleased that he had a bedroom to himself, and thinking that if this was what being an agent was all about he was glad that he'd volunteered. But he allowed himself to relax a little too much, and awoke to find he had two minutes to get downstairs to the meeting. He entered the lounge at the same time as the commandant, who happened to be a stickler for punctuality. He eyed Robert closely.

Sitting down quickly at the back of the room, Robert saw that there were about twenty other trainees; men and women of varying ages, gathered in the lounge. Two of the women, who were perhaps a little older than Robert, had noticed him slip into the room, and wondered who the handsome young officer was.

The commandant began to speak exactly on time. He explained that the course would consist of physical training, with many cross-country runs and other exercises. The students would learn to use certain pistols and sub-machine guns, and would study elementary map reading. Once again Robert relaxed, knowing that he had trained in all these things before. It should be an easy three weeks, he thought.

"And now ladies and gentlemen," the commandant went on, "I would like you to stand up in turn and introduce yourselves, giving your name and what you did in civilian life."

Other than the few regular officers, there were among the trainees, clerks from banking and insurance, a stockbroker, a lawyer, three teachers, two typists, and an interpreter. Being at the back of the room, Robert was last to stand and give his details.

His natural bent for devilment got the better of him. "Robert Rutherford, conscientious objector," he said. He didn't know whether to grin or keep a straight face when some of those in front turned to look at him. But he couldn't resist trying to irritate the commandant, whom, he considered a little stuffy.

"I see you have a sense of humour, Mr Rutherford. "You may need it if the Gestapo ever get hold of you." The commandant looked sternly at Robert.

Robert couldn't make up his mind whether or not they believed him. In any case, he didn't care what they thought of him. He noticed that the commandant's look had softened, and thought he almost caught a twinkle in his eye. Perhaps he wasn't so stuffy.

The commandant was not sure how to take this young man. "I think Mr Rutherford is amusing himself at our expense, ladies and gentlemen," he concluded.

When the commandant had spoken of the training programme, he had not mentioned that during the course all the trainees would be constantly watched by the instructors both while training and during leisure hours.

During the evenings it was especially noted how much a person drank at the bar, and how that person, reacted to drink. A man or woman affected adversely by alcohol would be of little use as an agent.

It was expected that all students would spend some time during the evening in the lounge mixing with one another. Robert usually found himself a quiet corner and sat reading. Sometimes, if he was noticed, others would come and join him for a chat. One evening the two girls who had thought him handsome when he entered the room for the first time came and sat near him.

"I'm Nancy and this is Jane," said the more talkative of the two.

"How do you do. I'm Robert." He shut his book and smiled at them.

"We hope you don't mind us talking to you," said Nancy.

"Of course not, why should I?"

"Well, you seem rather quiet."

"I'm sorry. I don't mean to be unsociable. But I don't drink much and I'm quite happy just to sit and read."

"You see! I told you we'd disturb him," said Jane.

"No, it's all right! Really it is!"

"I see you're reading a book on music," said Nancy. "It looks terribly technical. Can you play the piano?"

"A little, but only when I'm on my own," Robert smiled. He had begun to enjoy the company of these two girls. Neither looked like his idea of an agent, although what an agent should look like he wasn't too sure. At least he didn't have to exert himself to make conversation, because Nancy kept that flowing quite well without any help from him.

"You're a bit of a wag, telling the commandant you were a conscientious objector," said Jane.

"It's true," Robert protested, grinning at them. "Don't tell anyone, but I still am."

"We don't believe you," Jane laughed. "How can a soldier be a conchie? You're having us on."

"Robert," Nancy looked at him quizzically. "You don't mind me calling you Robert, do you?"

"Of course not."

"Oh, good. Robert, do you think you could help us with our map reading, and give us a few tips about shooting? I'm sure you must know all about these things being a soldier."

"We don't know anything," said Jane. "Nancy was a teacher and I was a typist. We answered the advertisement because we both speak French."

Robert's days of keeping himself to himself were over. Wherever he was, the two girls were to be found also. They gave him the impression that they were so grateful he had become their friend, and listened intently to any advice he gave on the course subjects. At the end of the course, when all three had passed - and some didn't - the girls put their success down to his instruction.

For the next part of the training those who were successful in the Initial course were sent to Scotland. By this time the trainees had all become familiar with one another, but the two girls still treated Robert as a special friend and seemed to hang on his every word.

The training school was established in a large house, which was situated in the wild country of Arisaig. For much of the time during the course the sky was overcast and a great deal of rain fell, but Robert was fascinated by the bleak, deserted countryside. The girls were less enamoured of the place especially when out on an exercise and the skies opened on them.

Much of the course was taken up in small arms training. The trainees were expected to handle many weapons, even to the extent of being able to strip and reassemble each type in the dark. Then there was unarmed combat, an extreme version being taught by expert instructors.

As the training continued, those unable to cope were sent away as unsuitable for the task. The others, including Robert and the girls, moved for further training to another country house. It was here that they learnt at last exactly what they were being trained for. They were to go into enemy occupied territory and cause chaos. This was the brief of the organisation to which they belonged.

Here also they learnt the finer points of working as an agent in occupied territory, and what would happen to them if they were caught. It was this last point which caused Robert, and no doubt others as well, a great deal of heart searching as to whether he wished to continue in this line of work. If he were caught by the Gestapo, he was sure that he would never be able to bear the pain that they would inflict upon him if he failed to answer their questions. But for all his doubts and fears he continued with the training.

Robert then attended a course on parachute jumping, after which he was sent to a wireless school near Oxford, where he learnt to become an operator. It was a few more weeks to delay his participation in the active service side of the job; he thought, and he did find, the work interesting. But even this came to an end, and he awaited his next posting with apprehension, knowing that the time had come when, he may be sent on active service.

However, to his surprise, he was posted to headquarters in Baker Street as a junior staff assistant. It was merely a temporary position until the time came for him to be sent into Holland. This sort of war suited him very well, he decided. Living at Eaton Square, having lunch with Wendy on occasions, and generally enjoying himself in London. "Long may it last, Robert, m'boy," he muttered to himself on his first day in his new office.

CHAPTER 14

The first half of 1942 had been a disastrous time for the Allies. Singapore had fallen, the mighty British battleships *Prince of Wales* and *Repulse* had been sunk, and the Japanese were pushing the frontiers of their Pacific empire ever outwards. In the Atlantic German U-boats were sinking more ships than the British and Americans were able to build. In the early summer the German army had struck towards the Don and would soon be threatening Russian oil fields in the Caucasus. In North Africa Rommel had taken Tobruk and driven a defeated British army back into Egypt.

Yet, in spite of all the set backs, and the worsening situation, the Americans and Russians were pressing Churchill for a second front in Europe. Even responsible British newspapers had asked: *Where's that second front?* But Churchill was not a man to lack the offensive spirit, and needed no encouragement from his allies to get to grips with the enemy. So prevalent was this trait in his character, that shortly after Dunkirk he was demanding that preparations be made for raiding the coastline now occupied by the Germans. One result of this was the formation of the Commandos. There were, of course, occasions when he had to be restrained by his Chiefs of Staff from putting into operation some of his wilder ideas, but with a man of his fighting spirit this was only to be expected.

However, for all his offensive spirit, Churchill knew that it was impossible for the British and Americans to make a full scale invasion of France at this stage of the war.

On the other hand, some offensive action was needed against mainland Europe, not only to appease the Allies but as a morale booster for the British public, and the newly formed Combined

Operations Organisation were given, the task of selecting a suitable target for a large scale raid. The choice made was Dieppe.

"All this talk about a second front strikes me as nonsense," John commented. "We're just not ready for it." He was supporting his newspaper with one hand and stirring his coffee with the other. "The first thing we must do is get Rommel out of North Africa, and we're only just managing to hold him at this place . . . what's it called?" he mumbled, scanning the article. "Ah yes, El Alameln. If we fall back any further Gerry'll be in Alexandria."

It had been quiet at the breakfast table until John had broken the silence.

Elizabeth glanced at her two men folk with pride, happy that Robert was able to live at Eaton Square during his present posting in London. As it was convenient for their work, John and Elizabeth had moved into their London address for the duration of the war, only returning to Brighton on occasional week-ends. "Do you think the Germans will get to the Suez Canal, schat?" she asked.

"Not without a hell of a battle and Rommel may not have the resources to cope with that. He must have a supply problem, because his lines of communication are hundreds of miles long, and his supply ships are being sunk in the Med."

"Do you think Churchill was right to kick out Auchinleck as GOC at this crucial time, Father?" Robert asked.

"Oh, yes, I think so. Alex should make a go of it, and this chap Montgomery seems to have the right idea. Plenty of confidence, anyway."

After a pause Robert said, "The newspapers have been saying that the Canadians have been training for something big. Surely they're not thinking of a second front yet?"

"I should have thought a second front was out of the question at the moment," John replied. "I believe that the Chiefs of Staff would be most unhappy to mount a full scale invasion of France without first gaining some experience of what this could entail. There'll have to be a practice run sometime or other. A large scale raid, perhaps."

"They say the Canadians can't wait to have a crack at Gerry."

"So I've heard. They're fine men, but enthusiasm is not enough. They lack fighting experience, and to mount a seaborne attack against defended positions without experience could be a disaster," John concluded, looking at his watch. "Well, Robert, it's been nice having a chat, but I must go," he said.

"Before you do, Father, may I have a private word with you?" Robert asked.

Elizabeth got up from the table. "I'll leave you two men together," she smiled, pleased that Robert should wish to confide in his father. She knew it also pleased John.

"I'm sorry. Mother, but the matter is secret."

Robert had never spoken of his work to anyone except John, whose military rank and high position in the Royal Household allowed confidences not given to others. When asked about his job, Robert had been instructed to reply that he worked, at the Ministry of Economic Warfare. John knew this was just a cover and that his son was engaged with a new subversive organisation which had agents working all over the world.

"I have a problem, Father."

John nodded.

"As you know, I'm working for these special operations people. I'm in the Dutch section and it's one of my jobs to check through the messages that come from our agents in Holland before passing them on to the officer in charge of the section."

John listened intently. His relationship with Robert had gone through a difficult period, but now this had improved. At least the boy was taking an interest in something at last, he thought.

Robert continued, "Every wireless message received from an agent should contain a safety check known only to the agent and to us at headquarters. This ensures that all is well with him."

Robert went on to explain that the safety check was based on the misspelling of a word. If the sixteenth letter in the message, or a multiple of sixteen, was incorrect then it was known that all was well with the agent. But, if these spelling mistakes were omitted then this meant danger.

"In the few weeks I have been doing this job, Father, I have received messages from agents which do not contain this safety check. It has happened more than once. The copy of the message comes in from our cipher branch clearly marked security check omitted."

"Go on," said John.

"Each time I've pointed this out to my superior, but he does nothing. I've even put it in writing that something's wrong. Yesterday, which was the last occasion it happened, I was almost rude and insisted, as much as a junior officer can insist, that something was done. And do you know what I was told?" The exasperation he was feeling showed in Robert's voice, "I was told to instruct all agents to use security checks. It's absolute madness, Father. We have security checks and then ignore them. If the Germans have arrested our agents and are using them, we're playing right into their hands. I think that this is exactly what's happening, and I don't know what to do about it."

"Have you spoken to Matt about it?" John asked.

"No. You see he's In charge of a different section. I didn't think I should involve him."

"Quite right." John considered for a moment and then said, "Make out an application for an interview with the officer in overall command. You will have to submit it through the officer in charge of your section and let him know why you're doing it. If he refuses to submit your application then we'll consider the next step later."

"Thank you, Father. I've a feeling he will refuse."

Later, when Robert arrived in his office, it appeared almost as if his application had been anticipated. He had just sat down at his desk when the telephone rang and he was summoned to his chief's office.

As Robert entered the office the major looked up at him and smiled, thinking to himself, bloody nuisance, it's time he was hooked out of his cushy job. "Ah, Rutherford," he said, pleasantly, "Do sit down."

Robert sat down wondering what was coming next.

"On a number of occasions lately you've come to me insisting that something should be done about these absent security checks from our chaps in Holland."

"Yes, sir. I'm sure something's wrong out there."

"Yes, you've already made that quite clear. Now you can do something about it." The major thought he recognised a look of surprise on Robert's face, but he was mistaken. Had he known, it was more a look of suspicion, for Robert had got over his initial surprise at being summoned to the office and was now becoming wary about what was to follow. "I've decided that you will go over and make contact with our group in Holland and find out what's going on. It's time you had a crack at the job we've trained you for." The major beamed, expecting the young officer to glow with pleasure at the thought of being entrusted with such an important task. But once more he was mistaken.

"I'm not going over there, sir! I don't mind a calculated risk, but this is madness. Gerry'll be waiting for me." Robert spoke with a confidence that surprised even himself.

"What nonsense! You've worked yourself up into phobia about these security checks."

"Maybe, sir but I'm still not going."

"Are you refusing this instruction?" The smile had vanished from the major's face and he was beginning to become irritated.

"Yes, sir, I am. It's my right."

Robert knew that he was within his rights to refuse. Any would be agent could refuse to be sent into enemy territory. This was his right, and no accusation of cowardice could be made against him.

The major managed to hide his frustration, but consoled himself with the thought that at least now he could get this young nuisance out of the section. "I'm well aware of your rights, Rutherford. But I must admit to a little disappointment with you. You were recommended to us by Major Irving as a first class chap, but I think you've let him down. However, since you have exercised your right I must inform you that the section has no further use for your services. I shall submit your name for a posting immediately."

Do what you bloody well like, Robert thought to himself. He left the office with a sense of relief that he had stood up for himself. He hadn't realised the gradual sub-conscious build-up of tension within himself at the thought that one day he would have to face the experience of being dropped into Holland. Now this was not to be, and he knew he was happy about it. His only regret was that the opportunity to contact Lisa was lost. His one concern was where he would be sent next, but he hadn't long to wait to find out.

It was a few days later when his posting came through. He was sent to Combined Operations Headquarters where, on arrival, he was interviewed by a staff colonel and informed that, until a permanent posting had been found, for him, he would be attached to a Commando unit to act as an observer throughout a certain operation which was due to take place in the next few days.

"You must understand young man, that you are with this unit just for this one operation," said the colonel. "The job should be done by a far more experienced officer than yourself, but unfortunately the major who had been nominated has just been killed on a training exercise, and you just happen to be available."

Robert wondered what exactly he was suppose to be observing, but the very fact that it was a Commando unit involved led him to the conclusion that it was going to be the real thing.

"I must remind you that you are not expected to become involved in any of the action you might witness," the colonel went on. "It's your job to observe what happens. When you return, you will report fully on what you've seen. You will also be closely questioned on every aspect of the operation, so make sure you keep your eyes open. The information we gain from you and the other observers will be noted and used in future operations."

It didn't strike Robert as a particularly difficult assignment, although he had to admit it all seemed a little vague. For security reasons, he was told, no details of the operation could be given to him until later. His orders were to report to Seaford, a small seaside town on the Sussex coast about 10 miles east of Brighton. Robert knew the place, having passed through it on a number of occasions when, as a boy, he had been taken on outings by his parents to Eastbourne.

His most vivid memory of the place was how the sea at high tide sent spray right across the promenade. He remembered once after a gale much of the beach had ended up on the seafront road.

He travelled down to Seaford on the Sunday, taking a train to Brighton and then changing for the short trip along a line familiar to him through Lewes and Newhaven. He had no difficulty in finding the unit he was to be attached to, and arrived at the officers quarters, a large house at the east end of the town near the seafront, at teatime.

That evening when Robert entered the officers' mess he had the usual feeling of apprehension that a new boy feels when arriving at his school for the first time. For a moment he stood at the door glancing round for a quiet place where he might sit on his own. The room was full of officers, some standing chatting with drinks in their hands, some sitting quietly smoking away from the crush round the bar.

"You must be Rutherford." The voice was brisk but welcoming, and Robert found his hand firmly gripped, and shaken by a tall, well built officer in his early thirties. "Major Forbes. I'm second in command here. You're most welcome."

Robert felt relieved that someone had spoken to him. "Thank you, Major," he replied gratefully.

A drink was thrust into his hand and he was introduced to a number of other officers and left in the company of one group that had gathered near the bar. He hadn't been standing there long, when he heard the sound of a voice behind him which seemed familiar and belligerent. "Rutherford! What the hell are you doing here?" Robert turned and came face to face with Courtney Babington-Smith.

"Why Babs, how nice to see a familiar face!" Robert exclaimed, offering his hand.

"Captain Babington-Smith to you," Courtney rasped, ignoring Robert's hand. "You may remember I'm only Babs to my friends."

Robert was a little taken aback by the other's attitude towards him. After all, they had only been eighteen when they quarrelled and fought each other at Sandhurst, and Robert bore no grudge. After the fight he had tried to made friends with Babs, but the other had always remained cool towards him.

"We can do without your sort here," Babs sneered at Robert as he pushed his way into the circle of officers. He then asked caustically, "What regiment are you from?"

"I've been attached to the Ministry of Economic Warfare," Robert replied evenly.

Babs continued in a loud voice, "I might have known it, a bloody funk hole. Still, I suppose they have to keep bloody German lovers away from the front." He turned to the others in the group. "You didn't know he's a German lover, did you? Got no right to have a commission. The swine should be in an internment camp."

Robert felt himself flush with embarrassment, but he also felt his anger rising. It was with great difficulty that he remained silent.

"Steady on, Babs old boy. That's no way to speak of a fellow," an elderly Captain in the group protested. Harry Bourne had been a regular officer and had come out of retirement when the war had broken out. He now acted as an administrative officer at the unit's headquarters.

But Babs was not to be stopped. "You don't know him, Harry, like I do," Babs retorted.

Robert didn't know what to say. Some others in the group looked uncomfortable and moved away. "That will do, Babs," Harry Bourne declared. "You are being discourteous to a fellow officer in the mess, and I'll not allow it to continue." He spoke with the firmness of experience and glared straight at Babs, who moved away, piqued, to another group.

Robert felt his arm gripped and he was pulled away by Harry into a corner where the two of them sat down. He noticed Major Forbes talking to Babs, and it struck him that Babs was not pleased with what was being said to him.

"Sorry about that. I'm afraid Babs gets rather childish at times, especially after a few drinks," Harry said. "You've obviously come across him before."

Robert nodded and said, "I'm afraid there's some truth in what he says. About the Germans, I mean."

Harry smiled at his new friend, thinking how young he looked. Almost too young to be out of school, he decided. "There's no need to explain, it's your business and nothing to do with anyone here."

But whatever comfort Robert drew from Harry's kind words, he couldn't help feeling that his reputation had already been blackened in the mess, and Babs was unlikely to stop spreading his poison. It was all so damned embarrassing, he thought.

However, on the following day Robert had little time to think about Babs, for although he was only attached to the unit as an observer, he was kept busy by Harry helping with the preparations for the forthcoming operation, whatever it might be. That evening he sneaked away on his own to a Brighton cinema which was showing *Beyond the Blue Horizon*. He had no wish to meet Babs again in the mess.

No-one seemed to know what was happening, but rumours were flying round that there was to be a big raid on the French coast. There were Canadian Regiments in the area and for some time now it had been put about that they had been promised action of some sort. A raid by the Canadians had been called off a few weeks earlier, and it was believed the target on that occasion was to have been Dieppe. Now orders had been received that the operation was to take place after all, but for security reasons, only a few senior officers knew the destination. Some guessed it was Dieppe again, but others thought it unlikely that the same place would be chosen a second time.

Two units of British Commandos were to support the Canadians and it was one of these to which Robert had been attached.

On the Tuesday morning the order came in that the show was on, and Robert was told to be ready to leave early that evening. He was to attach himself to Lieutenant Price, a very young officer in charge of one of the platoons.

All over south eastern England that day men were being transported to the embarkation ports at Southampton, Portsmouth, Gosport, Shoreham and Newhaven. On arrival at Newhaven the town was so congested with troops that the commandos had to wait for some time before they were able to embark. Most of the commandos sailing from Newhaven were to make the whole crossing in their small landing craft. These small wooden boats were fast, manoeuvrable, and could operate right inshore. They carried about 25 soldiers, but the plywood construction afforded little protection for their occupants against enemy fire.

As his boat cleared the harbour arm the slightest of breezes brushed across Robert's face. It was a fine summer evening, and he was thankful the sea was smooth. Outside the harbour he could see that his boat had formed up with over twenty other landing craft all of which were being led by a steam gunboat. An armed motor launch and a flak landing craft gave protection at the rear. The little convoy was sailing on the eastern side of the main force, which was at this time leaving from the other harbours down the channel.

He stood at the stern for a time, watching the cliffs recede into the distance. As the boat drew away and more of the coastline came into view, the great white cliff faces of the *Seven Sisters* came into view, standing out boldly in the clear evening light. How well he remembered another such evening long ago when he had seen these same white cliffs from the deck of a paddle steamer. He must have been twelve at the time, and his parents had taken him for a day trip to Eastbourne on one of the old Campbell's boats. How wonderful it had been on that hot summer's day with Father, Mother and Joanna. It was strange how in childhood memories the sun was always shining. How happy he had been then, and how secure he had felt. But now he was leaving this beloved country and he may never return. Oh God, bring me back safely, he silently prayed. If he could have just one more chance, he thought, he would try to do better with his life. If only he'd told his parents how much he loved them before he'd left. But he'd been in such a rush that all the things he should have said only came to mind after he had left. Perhaps he would never see them again, these dear people who had patiently loved him all these years. And then there was Lisa. To hold her in his arms just once more was his dearest wish.

Robert turned his back on the now distant shore and asked himself what fate awaited him over the darkening horizon. They had been designated to land on the extreme left of the raiding force at a place called Berneval in support of the main Canadian landings at

Dieppe. Berneval was a small village about 5 miles east of Dieppe, and it was here that there was a heavily defended German coastal battery which the commandos had been ordered to put out of action. He promised himself that being just an observer, he would keep out of harm's way, but even this was little comfort, knowing that an exploding shell would make no allowance for his passive role, and if one hit this small craft there would be little chance of survival for anyone in it. Restless though he felt, he sat down beside Lieutenant Price.

The young officer seemed eager to talk to Robert, which surprised him because Price appeared to be one of Bab's cronies. "When do you think we'll be passing through the minefield?" asked Price.

The Germans had laid minefields along the French coast to protect their coastal convoys from attack by the Royal Navy. Minesweepers had gone ahead of the raiding force to clear a way through.

"Not yet awhile," Robert replied, hoping that the minesweepers had done their job properly. It was going to be bad enough when they got on shore without any danger at sea, he thought, but the danger at sea was not to come from minefields.

A radar station on the Kent coast had picked up a German convoy, consisting of 5 coastal motor vessels, escorted by an armed minesweeper and 2 submarine chasers of the German navy, moving down channel from Boulogne. Eventually the signal faded but it was picked up again about midnight by Portsmouth radar, and it was noted that these unidentified ships and the Dieppe raiding force were drawing closer together as the night went on. A signal was sent to alert the leading destroyer acting as escort to the raiding force, but the signal was not received. Consequently the two destroyers sent to protect the left of the raiding force were not informed. The German convoy with their escorts, and the commandos who had sailed from Newhaven were on collision course.

The moon had set at one o'clock and there was little that could be seen on the darkened boat except for the occasional glow of a cigarette as a soldier lit up to calm his nerves. Robert lay on the floor with a blanket over him, staring up into the night sky, his hands clasped behind his head. He tried to sleep but with little success, and the hours seemed interminable. Occasionally the boat passed through a patch of sea mist, and the stars were blotted out for a short time, but generally the night remained clear. The sea had remained smooth. It must be getting on for four o'clock, he decided. He could see the form of Lieutenant Price with a blanket round his shoulders sitting on the seat above him. Price was leaning back against the side of the boat, and, like Robert, trying to catch some sleep.

When the star shell exploded high above the boat, Robert was still lying staring at the sky. For a moment his tired mind was unable to take in what was happening. Time seemed to stand still as the slowly descending flare burnt away the darkness of the night. What had previously been the dark forms of men huddled in the boat were now revealed in the eerie light as ghostly apparitions.

"Christ! Keep down!" The Sub-Lieutenant at the wheel screamed, as the German submarine chasers were illuminated by the light of their own star shell.

The warning had no sooner been shouted when the silence of the night was shattered as the British and German escort vessels opened up on each other. Robert lay as if paralysed, watching the green star shell burn itself out, its light now replaced by tracer shells ripping their way through the darkness. He had no intention of doing otherwise than keeping down.

Suddenly there was a sharp crack, and he was covered in smouldering wood splinters as tracers tore their way through the thin side of the boat. It was not only wood splinters which showered over Robert. Lieutenant Price, who had been resting back against the side of the boat above Robert, had no time to throw himself to the floor. Robert saw the young man's chest burst open, pouring smoke, as the tracer shells hit him. There wasn't even time for him to cry out. He fell forward and collapsed on top of Robert.

The night had turned into an inferno, so fierce had the engagement become. When Robert finally extricated himself from under the body of Price, he was just in time to see the Sub-Lieutenant sent crashing to the deck hit by machine gun bullets. The boat began to turn off course. Robert scrambled to the steering position and took the wheel. From this vantage point he could see the chaos of the battle. He could also see that he had no protection at all standing at the wheel, and was completely exposed to the gunfire. A gigantic flash lit the night sky as one of the German submarine chasers blew up. In the light of the explosion he could see that the other commando landing craft had scattered, and that the Royal Navy gun boat, which had led the raiding force was in a bad way pouring steam and with all its guns out of action.

"Christ! We've got to get out of here!" Robert shouted at himself against the noise of the guns. He pushed the throttle forward and felt the boat surge ahead. He didn't care where he was going, just steering for a dark patch away from the firing. At one moment a German boat seemed to be turning towards him firing as it came. He turned the wheel violently to avoid the tracers, but as he did so the German boat ceased firing and turned away, and the night was silent once more.

The Germans had believed that their convoy was under one of the usual attacks by Royal Navy motor torpedo boats which happened frequently in this part of the channel. They had not realised that they had run into part of the Dieppe raiding force. Directly the German ships had passed safely towards Dieppe, the escorting submarine chasers broke off the engagement. The battle had been exceptionally fierce, but short.

Robert gripped the wheel tightly to stop his hands shaking. A commando sergeant had crawled to the side of the wounded Sub-Lieutenant and bandaged his arm and shoulder. The wounds were superficial, the bullets having passed right through. After being tended, the officer took over the wheel again. "I think I can land you almost in the right place," he grinned.

The only right place to land in Robert's mind was home, but he didn't say so. Far over to the right he could see a flashing light which was obviously on the harbour arm at Dieppe. The Germans, not realising a raid was coming, had left the light on to guide their convoy in.

The sergeant stood by Robert as the boat reduced speed for its run in to the beach. "You'll take over now, sir, as Mr Price is dead?" he asked respectfully.

Robert felt his stomach turn over when he realised the sergeant was addressing him. He knew that the respectful question was more of a statement. It was a question with only one possible answer. Robert was now the only officer in the boat, except for the naval Sub-Lieutenant and his job was to get the troops to the right beach and nothing more. God, why did that idiot have to get himself killed, Robert groaned to himself? He glanced at the sergeant and felt like blurting out that he was only here as an observer and it was up to the sergeant to take command. "Yes, of course, Sergeant," Robert drawled, successfully covering his reluctance. "Make sure the men are ready to go. We'll be there shortly."

"Sir!" the sergeant replied, pleased that this officer appeared to be competent.

Robert went to the bows of the boat and stood beside the sergeant facing the men. It was beginning to get light, and he could just about make out their strained faces. "When we land follow me to the top of the beach. Don't go ahead of me, and don't bunch up," Robert ordered. He cursed himself for being such a bad soldier. If only he knew what the hell he was doing. These poor wretches were relying on him. He nearly lost his balance as the boat ground on to the beach. At any moment he expected machine guns to open up from the cliff tops, but nothing happened and all remained quiet except for the drumming of the boat's engine and the sea lapping the pebbles.

Robert didn't know whether he was on the right beach or the wrong beach, and he didn't much care. But he had to do something. "Come on lads." he called, jumping from the landing craft. It's better than Brighton beach on a bank holiday, I can tell you." He ran to the top of the beach and flung himself down on the pebbles facing the entrance to a narrow gully, signalling the men to spread out and lie down in a line either side of him. The sergeant lay beside him.

In the increasing daylight, Robert could see that the gully went back some distance, and was obviously an easy way to the top of the cliffs on either side. Too damned easy, he thought. There was barbed wire at the far end, but other than that it appeared undefended. He saw the sergeant looking at him and knew that he would have to make a quick decision.

"Shall we move forward, sir?" the sergeant asked.

"No," Robert replied. He was feeling calm now that the action had started. "We must find another way up. It's too bloody innocent here, and Gerry's no fool. Do you know what I think, Sergeant, I think it's mined."

"I think you're right, sir," the sergeant replied, looking at Robert with respect. He liked an officer who didn't go blundering into trouble without thought for the safety of his men.

Until this moment Robert's landing craft had been the only one to arrive at this beach. He believed they'd landed too far to the right. But hearing the sound of an engine, and the grinding of pebbles, he turned to see another boat striking the beach. Another platoon ran up the beach, and taking a lead from Robert's men lay down in a line to await instructions.

Captain Courtney Babington-Smith came rushing up. He had not noticed Robert lying there, but he had seen the sergeant. "Are you in charge of this lot, Sergeant?" he bellowed, glaring down at the line of men.

Robert looked round. "No, I am," he said.

"I might have known it!" Babs growled. "Where the hell's Price?"

"Dead."

"Get on your bloody feet when you speak to me, Rutherford."

Robert got up. If only he could tell Babs what a bloody stupid show-off he thought he was, but it wouldn't be right in front of the men. What a perfect target the two of them made for a sniper, standing here like this, he thought.

"What the hell are you waiting for? Get your men up that bloody gully," snarled Babs.

"I think it's mined. We were just about to try somewhere else."

"What the hell do you know about it? You're just a bloody desk wallah. I always knew there was a yellow streak in you." Babs strode through the line of troops still lying flat on the beach. Ignoring Robert he looked down, at the sergeant. "Come on! Get moving!" he shouted, trotting towards the entrance to the gully.

The sergeant disliked, this blustering captain. It was no way to speak to a junior officer in front of the men, he thought, and his attitude showed the captain was no gentleman. In any case the young officer had done his best. He hesitated and looked up at Robert. His hesitation to advance with the captain saved him.

Babs entered the gully but got no further than twenty five yards when there was a sharp crack and the beach erupted under him. He screamed as the lower half of his right leg was torn off and flung into the air with a shower of pebbles, then, gripping his stomach, he collapsed to the ground.

"Stay where you are!" Robert shouted to the line of men, who had just started to move forward. "Keep down." The stupid bastard, he thought. Now what am I going to do?

The sergeant began to strip off some of his equipment. "I'll go and bring him in, sir," he said.

"No you won't, sergeant. I'll have to do it," Robert replied. Christ! What had he said? He felt his knees almost buckle beneath him. Oh, what a bloody fool he was. Why didn't he keep his mouth shut and let the sergeant do it. But Father had told him that it was an officer's responsibility to take the lead, and he must not hide behind his sergeant. If only he had Father's guts.

Robert felt himself shake and his body turn to jelly as he took the first step into the gully. He had taken the sergeant's knife to try and flick away some of the pebbles in an effort to reveal the mines before taking each step forward. On the other hand, he imagined himself touching the detonator with the knife and the mine blowing up in his face as he bent forward. Step after step he went forward, almost choking with fear each time he placed a foot on the ground. If the beach had been sandy he could have placed his feet in Babs' footprints as he went forward, but being large pebbles he could not tell where Babs had trodden. At one point his hand was shaking so much he dropped the knife, the clatter making his heart miss a beat. He had gone ten yards when, pushing back some pebbles, a deadly metal casing was revealed. He bent and cleared the stones from round it so that he could see it on the way back if he ever got that far.

Halfway he had to stop and gain control of himself. His vivid imagination had got the better of him, and he could see a picture of himself lying on the beach screaming, and squirming in agony with his legs and arms blown off. Perhaps the dreams he had as a boy were about to come true. Then the horrific thought came to him that what was between his legs could be torn off in an explosion, and, he would never be able to make love again. It was a thought that had never occurred to him before, and it sickened him with fear.

Babs was now only a few yards away. Robert felt his underwear saturated with sweat, and drops of moisture running down his face. How long had he taken? Each step seemed like hours. Supposing his hands were blown off, or his fingers; he would never be able to play the violin again. Lisa's face came into his mind. She was praising him for being brave when he had cut himself with that knife by the river on that sunlit day so long ago. Life was good then. What had happened to the world? Perhaps this is what hell is like - everlasting fear.

Robert almost stumbled over the squirming figure of Babs. He tried to pull the wounded man over his back so that he could lift him clear of the ground, but Babs started to scream and fought off his rescuer.

"For God's sake, shut up you stupid bastard!" Robert cried, relieving his pent up fear and frustration.

He tried again, but Babs still pulled away, so he hit him as hard as he could, and for the second time in his life he knocked Babs unconscious.

This time he managed to get the wounded man across his back, but fear had drained his strength and the unconscious man was a dead weight. Robert found that he couldn't stand up.

By this time more landing craft had come in to the beach, and Major Forbes had arrived. The major rushed up the beach to the sergeant and got a full explanation about the minefield. Together they watched as Robert tried again to stand with the wounded Babs on his back. "Shall I give him a hand, sir?" the sergeant asked.

"No, stay where you are, Sergeant. He'll do it in a minute, and I don't want anymore unnecessary casualties."

With a supreme effort Robert at last managed to stand. Then he began the hazardous way back. This time there could be no careful study of the ground where he was to tread. If he bent too far forward with Babs on his back he would lose his balance and fall. He tried to see where his footsteps were so that he could use them again, but this was impossible, and he knew that each step could be his last.

Babs regained consciousness and began to struggle and scream again. "Shut up, for Christ's sake, Babs! You'll have us both down in a minute." Robert tried to get a firmer grip on his burden, but in his panic took his eyes from the ground and failed to notice his foot was on the side of a large pebble. As all the weight came down on the foot, the pebble moved and the ankle twisted. He let out a cry of pain and nearly collapsed to the ground, but just managed to save himself by transferring all the weight to the other foot. For a moment he couldn't move, and it was just as well he didn't, because, looking down, he saw the glint of metal. His foot was only inches away from a detonator head.

Five more paces and he would probably be safe, but now he was fixed. He could put no weight on his injured ankle, consequently all the weight was on the other leg. "Hold on, sir, we're coming," said the sergeant as he and two other men slowly made their way forward carefully removing the top layer of pebbles. In the short distance three mines were uncovered. When they got to Robert and relieved him of his burden he almost collapsed in the sergeant's arms.

"Well done, Rutherford," said Major Forbes, then turning to the sergeant he added, "Get Mr Rutherford and Captain Babington-Smith back to one of the boats, and then follow me along the beach."

"But, sir, I'm supposed to go with you!" Robert protested.

"Can you climb cliffs with an ankle like that?"

"No, sir!"

"Then don't be such a bloody fool, man!" The major watched as Robert was helped away down the beach. "You've done your bit, lad," he called after him.

The sergeant assisted Robert back on to a landing craft and made him comfortable. As he made to leave the boat he turned and looked at the modest young officer who had been the first ashore.

The youngster had not only competently led the platoon for those first critical few minutes, but, without doubt, had saved their lives. He had guts as well. "Thanks for everything, sir," he said, and then ran quickly up the beach to join his men.

Robert wondered what the sergeant was talking about. It never occurred to him that he had saved his men from the minefield. The boat backed away from the beach and then turned out to sea to find one of the escorting destroyers so that the two injured officers could be transferred aboard, for medical attention. It seemed to Robert that hours had passed since the moment he had stepped on to the beach, and yet here he was back on board, being taken out again after only about twenty minutes.

As Robert was taken on board the destroyer he could hear the sound of gun fire. Some of the destroyers were bombarding Dieppe as the Canadians went in. A roar startled him as Hurricane fighters swept low overhead to attack buildings on the seafront of the town. But that was the last he heard of the battle. He was taken below and given a hot drink, and then he lay down on a bunk, feeling mentally and physically exhausted.

A fat lot of good he'd been as an observer, he thought as he lay there comfortably on the bunk. What would they say when he got back and found that he couldn't tell them anything about the operation, he asked himself? He'd been a fool to go up that gully. If he'd moved away down the beach in the first place instead of waiting, that idiot Babs might never have got himself blown up. Time and again he turned over in his mind what he should have done, cursing himself for his incompetence. The only thing he'd done successfully was to twist his blasted ankle. "And what did you do at Dieppe, Robert?" he whispered, mimicking his father. "Oh, I bravely twisted my ankle, Father," he grinned.

He began to chuckle quietly, asking himself whether they gave medals for twisting ankles. He imagined himself being invited to Buckingham Palace to give an account of his experiences to the King and the Prime Minister. The Prime Minister would tell the King that *Never in the field of human conflict was so much owed by so many to one man, who had not only twisted his ankle, but had done it on the wrong beach, and not even under fire. Could there be a braver act, Your Majesty?*

His humour soon subsided, and he broke out in a sweat, living again the moment when he had stepped on to the beach expecting to be cut to pieces by machine guns. Why hadn't the Germans been waiting? Especially after that sea battle with the German sub chasers; it had been like firework night at home, and with all that row going on it was difficult to understand why the Germans hadn't been alerted. The thoughts swirled round and round in his mind until sleep gradually overtook him. But as he slept it was a different story for the Canadians - they were being mown down on the beaches at Dieppe.

"Time to wake up, sir."

Robert opened his eyes to see a medical orderly looking down at him. He sat up and slowly swung his legs over the side of the bunk. "Have I been asleep all that time?" he queried, looking at his watch. "Where are we?"

"Portsmouth, sir. We're going to get you ashore now."

Try as he would Robert found that he could put no weight on his ankle and had to be assisted ashore. He was about to be put into an ambulance when the staff colonel he had seen at Combined Operations Headquarters confronted him. "You're one of my observers," said the colonel, eyeing Robert carefully.

"Yes, sir."

"What the hell are you doing here? You're unit's suppose to be at Newhaven," the colonel bellowed.

"I twisted my ankle on the beach, sir."

"Then you're a bloody fool, sir! You were sent to observe, not twist your confounded ankle."

"Yes, sir. I'm sorry."

"It's no damn use being sorry, man! It was information we wanted, not apologies. I suppose you got nothing."

"We were attacked at sea, sir, and I think we landed on the wrong beach."

"You think. Don't you know?" The colonel was becoming exacerbated.

Robert thought that if he'd been sure in the first place which was the right beach, which he wasn't because he'd never been told, he'd have known whether or not the one he landed on was the wrong beach. But he felt his argument was not convincing so he just commented. "It was all a bit of a muddle, sir."

"That's a blasted understatement if ever I've heard one!" the colonel snorted, walking away and vowing never again to entrust a young idiot like that with a responsible job.

Robert, much relieved to see the colonel disappear, smiled sheepishly at the orderly who was still supporting him.

"Seems like he's got it in for you, sir," the orderly smiled as he helped Robert into the ambulance.

Robert was taken to the naval hospital where it was found that he had no bones broken. The ankle was properly bandaged, and after being issued with a pair of crutches he was sent home on sick leave.

He arrived at Eaton Square that evening. Agnes came to the front door. "Robert!" she cried, "What a state you're in. What have you done? Are you wounded?"

"It's all right, Agnes, calm down. Don't fuss, I've only twisted my ankle," he explained.

But Agnes was not to be put off. For years she had fussed him, and nothing was to stop her now. Robert knew it was no good fighting the inevitable where Agnes was concerned. He was in her care now so he might just as well sit back and enjoy it.

That week-end he received an unexpected visit from Joanna and Matt. Robert was sitting in the drawing-room with Elizabeth when they arrived.

"Jo! Matt!" he cried with pleasure. "God, it's wonderful to see you!" He glanced at Elizabeth who was just about to scold him. "I know, Mother. Don't be blasphemous, Robert," he grinned. "But, it's so good that we're all together again."

A few minutes later John also arrived home for the week-end and the family was complete.

"So you went to Dieppe, Robert," John remarked, when they had all taken their seats for luncheon.

"How did you know, Father?" Robert asked.

"Dieppe!" Elizabeth cried; looking shocked. She had read the official account in the newspapers, but she had also heard the rumours which were beginning to circulate, that the raid had been a disaster. "Robert, why didn't you tell me? Is that where you were wounded?" she questioned.

"I wasn't wounded, Mother. I just twisted my ankle, that's all."

"I bet you were jolly brave, Rob," Joanna interrupted enthusiastically.

"Brave! Me! That's a joke, sis," Robert scoffed.

"I heard you did rather well," said Matt.

"I was only there a few minutes."

"'What were you doing there in the first place?" John asked, looking sceptically at his son.

"I was attached to a commando unit as an observer."

"Then why were you there for such a short time?" John persisted.

Robert thought he had made this clear. He felt that his father was not satisfied that his reason for leaving the beach was genuine. "Because I twisted my ankle," he replied impatiently.

"Then you didn't carry out your assignment."

"No, Father, I didn't." Robert replied in a more tolerant tone of voice, realising that, as he hadn't told his father the full story, he had no right to expect him to understand.

"All sounds damn careless to me."

"You're safe now, dear. That's all that counts," Elizabeth interrupted.

Robert remembered his prayer on the boat. He had asked to be brought back safely to his family, and his prayer had been answered - this time. But what the future held, he wished he knew.

Chapter 15

It might have been true when Earl Mount batten of Burma said that the battle of Normandy was won on the beaches of Dieppe. It was certainly true that the disaster at Dieppe taught the Allies many lessons, the most important of these being that there was no easy way back into Europe. When the time came to land the Allied armies on the continent and break Hitler's west wall, the operation had to be so vast that little was left to chance. They had learnt that it had to be done differently from the Dieppe raid.

But for the entire complex organisation it must have occurred to some of the fighting soldiers, who landed on the Normandy beaches that June day in 1944, that success was by no means a foregone conclusion. It was certainly a thought that went through Robert's mind as he had once again approached the shores of France. He could distinctly remember asking himself as he had run up the beach on that memorable day whether the Dieppe fiasco was to be repeated. It was something that was to remain in his mind during the weeks that followed, when he led his company through the bitter and vicious fighting round the small town of Caen.

But Normandy was now far behind. He had entered Brussels with his battalion a few days previous to a jubilant welcome from the population, and then moved forward again to a position almost at the Dutch frontier.

"What do think Monty will do next, Dave?" Robert asked. He was lounging on the soft grass with his back against a tree, enjoying the warmth of the September afternoon.

"Bash straight into Holland, I shouldn't wonder, if Ike'll let him," Dave replied. Captain Dave Brooks and Robert had been firm friends ever since Robert had arrived at battalion headquarters almost exactly two years before. Together, they had worked hard during the months of waiting for D-Day to make their company an efficient fighting unit, and in this they had been successful. They had fought together in Normandy, and during the past weeks had swept through France and Belgium as part of the 2nd British Army. Now they waited for the next move forward.

The battalion was established in a wood, their vehicles camouflaged under the trees just behind the most advanced units. The two friends were sitting out in a large clearing to get the benefit of the sun. A few of their men were amusing themselves kicking a ball about on the opposite side of the clearing.

"Why shouldn't Ike let him, if it's the right thing to do?"

"Well, I think Ike's got problems. We know Monty's the best, but I've heard some of the yank generals don't like him. Ike has to keep the peace, between them, and Monty doesn't always get his own way."

Robert dangled a piece of grass in his mouth and looked up into the sun, his eyes half closed and an expression of contentment, on his face. "God, it's peaceful here! If only we could sit out the rest of the war like this."

Dave grinned. "Some hopes of that," he said.

"Gentlemen!" The regimental sergeant major stood before the two friends and saluted as only sergeant majors can.

"Whatever it is, Mr Watkins, tell Captain Brooks," Robert grinned, looking up at the imposing figure. "I'm too busy, and besides it's nearly teatime."

"Begging your pardon, sir, it's you that's wanted. The colonel wishes to see you immediately."

Dave began to laugh. "I say, you are in demand, young Robert."

Robert stood up, put his helmet on straight, and dusted himself down. "I wonder what he wants."

"Perhaps he's inviting you for tea," Dave chuckled.

"That'll be the day," Robert retorted. "Back in a minute," he called as he walked away following the sergeant major.

Battalion headquarters had been set up about 300 yards down the road which ran through the wood. As Robert approached, he saw the colonel standing beside a staff car talking to the adjutant. He went straight up and saluted. "You sent for me, sir."

"Robert, I don't know what all this is about, but you're to go to London and report immediately to a Colonel Irving. I'm told you know the address in Baker Street."

"When have I got to go, sir?"

"Now. My orders are that this is top priority."

"Then I'd better hand over to Captain Brooks and collect my things."

"Leave all that to me," the colonel ordered. "Your things will be sent on to you. Just get in the car and go."

Robert obeyed, but wished somebody would tell him what was going on.

"And, Robert," the colonel added before the car moved away, "Thank you for all you've done. It's been a pleasure having you in the battalion."

Robert was rushed to an advanced landing strip about 10 miles back from the line, where, to his surprise, a Lysander was waiting for him with its engine running. Without delay he climbed into the aircraft, and before he had time to collect his thoughts, he was in the air on his way to England. He tried to make sense out of what was happening. Why had Matt sent for him? Why was he being treated like top brass? Surely they didn't want him back in that special operations lot or whatever they called themselves? If they did, they'd be unlucky. He wasn't going through all that agent stuff again.

The efficiency of the arrangements for his journey to London continued when he landed at Tempsford in Bedfordshire. Once again a car was waiting, and he was driven direct to Baker Street. Still carrying his steel helmet Robert was taken up to Matt's office.

Matt rose from his desk and came forward. He shook Robert warmly by the hand. "Robert, it's good to see you! Do sit down."

Robert dropped into a chair. "Come on, Matt, what's this all about?"

But Matt was not to be rushed. "Can I offer you a drink, Robert?"

"No, but I could do with a damn good meal. I'm starving. I missed tea because of you."

"Of course. How thoughtless of me. I'll get something sent up."

Robert sat impatiently waiting for an explanation as Matt picked up the telephone and ordered some food for his hungry young brother-in-law.

Matt sat back in his chair and began to chat unhurriedly, even though he sensed Robert's impatience. "Joanna once told me that you know the countryside around Grave better than anyone. Evidently you were always playing about near the bridge and cycling around."

"That's true I suppose," Robert admitted, giving Matt a suspicious look. "But you haven't rushed me all the way from Belgium just to talk about my boyish pranks."

Matt grinned, and then spread out a map on his desk. "This is a map of the area. It's not a very good one because it lacks details but it'll have to do. I want you to write in the details. Put down anything you know about the area within about a mile of the bridge.

"Is that all?" Robert asked, still eyeing Matt suspiciously.

"No, it's not all, but it'll do for the moment."

Robert set to work. It didn't take him long, and when he had finished. Matt examined his work and nodded his approval. Then, after a few extra questions regarding fences, ditches and the course of the dyke, Matt rolled up the map and left the room.

He returned a few minutes later without the map but accompanied by an ATS girl who was carrying Robert's meal. He placed Robert in his own chair so that his guest could eat more comfortably at the desk. He went to a cabinet, and, after pouring himself a drink, sat down in an easy chair.

"Joanna told me you once got a good hiding for going down the cellar at your grandfather's house." Matt spoke casually, holding his glass up to the light and pretending to examine the golden liquid.

"What made you bring that up?" Robert asked inattentively, his meal taking priority over any conversation.

"She also said that you claimed to have found a tunnel under the house which led to the bridge."

"Fancy her remembering all that."

"Did you?"

"Did I what?"

"Find a tunnel."

Robert nodded, taking another mouthful of food. "I believe I did." he mumbled. Clearing his mouth he added with a grin. "I only told them to try and get out of a strapping. No one believed me."

"I believe you."

"Well, that is a comfort I must say," Robert laughed. "A fat lot of good it is now!"

"Could you find it again?"

"What?"

"The tunnel, of course."

"Of course I could. It's only up the chimney in the cellar."

"Where did it lead?"

"To a gully almost under the end of the bridge."

"So someone entering the tunnel from the cellar could get to the underneath of the bridge unseen."

Robert was beginning to take note of what was being said and this was no idle conversation. Matt was serious. "What are you driving at, Matt?"

"Could they get there unseen?"

"Yes, they could. I did."

"Now listen carefully, Robert. There's something big coming off. I can't give you the details, but it is absolutely vital that the bridge at Grave remains intact. The Germans will already have it wired for demolition, and that must not happen."

"Surely it's not likely to at the moment, we haven't even crossed into Holland yet," Robert commented.

"Situations can change overnight."

"Why are you telling me all this?"

"Because you are going to Holland to save that bridge."

"Me!" Robert cried. "I'm not volunteering for that. I should never have got involved with your lot in the first place, and I've no intention of doing so now."

"You're not being asked to volunteer, Robert. This is an order, and it's come from the top. Monty wants that bridge saved, and you'll do as you're told."

"Bloody hell!"

"You'll go to the old house at Grave and ask for Liro."

"Who the devil's that?"

"We don't know. What we do know is that it's the code name for the local Resistance leader who will be waiting for you."

"How do you know all this?"

"We're in wireless contact."

But Robert was not to be put off, and continued to object. "If the Resistance have the house, then tell them where the tunnel is by wireless. Why send me all the way over there?"

Matt replied patiently, "You probably don't know, but you were proved right about the situation in Holland. It was eventually discovered that our whole organisation in Holland was in German hands, and that the messages we were receiving supposedly from our agents were in reality coming from the Germans."

"Well, I warned you," Robert smiled smugly.

"You did and you were right," Matt grinned. "I hope it's some comfort to you."

"It's not really. But I did think it was bloody stupid to go on feeding information to operators who were leaving out their security checks."

"However, to get back to your point, because of this previous disaster with our Dutch agents we have been instructed that no information of any sort will be passed to the Resistance about this operation."

"What is the operation?"

"You only have to know your part in it, and that's to get to the bridge unseen and cut the wires to the demolition charges. It's essential that this is done by thirteen hundred hours on Sunday."

"What happens at that time?"

"You'll know when it happens."

"How am I going to get there?"

"One six one squadron are laying on a Halifax especially for you. You'll take off from Tempsford tomorrow evening."

."You're not expecting me to parachute in, are you?"

"Of course. There's no time for you to go any other way. Besides, we gave you some training when you were with us."

"That wasn't the real thing. It was only from a tower," Robert protested.

Well it taught you how to land. The other bit is only jumping out of the plane and floating down."

"It's all right for you to sound so bloody confident," Robert grumbled.

"Don't worry, I've arranged a quick crash course for you," Matt paused and grinned. "Sorry," he continued, "That was an unfortunate word. I meant refresher course."

Robert raised his eyes in mock despair. "You seem to have thought of everything. By the way, just one small point," he went on sarcastically, "Is the bridge guarded?"

"Yes. That's why the tunnel is so essential. We're told that there is a twenty millimetre flak gun on a tower near the south end of the bridge. There are second grade troops in the area, probably anti-aircraft gun crews and labour corps."

A bed had been prepared for Robert in a room above Matt's office. He had hoped to be allowed home for the night, but Matt forbade it. He was to have no contact with any outsider before leaving for Holland.

As Robert made to leave the office for his bedroom Matt said, "There's just one snag, Robert."

"Only one?" Robert scoffed. "I wish I had your confidence. What is this one snag?"

"It's a moonless period so we can't drop you at night. It would make your landing too dangerous in the darkness. You'll have to be dropped at dusk. This will give you time to get to the house before it's completely dark. The problem is that somebody might see you coming down. It's a risk we'll have to take."

"We'll have to take!" Robert exclaimed. "I like that. I'm the one taking the bloody risk. It's all right for you."

Matt grinned and continued with what he was about to say. "Your aircraft will not follow the usual bomber route across Holland. Now that we've taken practically all of Belgium, it means that it can cross the south Dutch border and be over enemy occupied territory for only a short while. It'll go in low and try to get beneath the German radar screen, just getting enough height for your jump. We hope to get the plane in and out again before the Germans react." Matt could see that his young brother-in-law was not impressed by the plan.

"And how are you going to get me out again after I've done this marvellous deed?"

"Don't worry, Robert; it's all arranged. I'll have you back here for some leave by Monday evening if all goes well," he concluded.

Somehow, Robert did not feel so optimistic.

The following day was hectic for Robert. After breakfast he was rushed to a parachute training depot, where he gained sufficient skill in the art of falling properly to be fairly certain, of making a landing without breaking his legs, or so he hoped. By the afternoon he had been returned to Baker Street and was ordered to sleep for a few hours. When he awoke he was issued with civilian clothes and false papers, and a little Dutch money just in case of emergency. It was not expected that he would need the papers or the money, because it would be dark just after he landed and it was unlikely that he would meet anyone before reaching the house.

That evening he was driven to the airfield where a Halifax was waiting for him. He'd had little time to stop and think during the day, but now, as he climbed up the ladder into the aircraft and sat down on the canvas seat with his back against the fuselage, his mind tried to catch up with what was happening to him.

Everything was happening so fast. Yesterday afternoon he had been with his company in Belgium, resigned to finishing his war service in the infantry. But now here he was about to be dropped into Holland on a secret mission, having no idea what it was all about.

He could, feel the butterflies in his stomach, and cursed himself for being so nervous. Why the hell did he always get this sickly feeling? If only the war would end. When it did end the first thing he would do would, be to find Lisa. Then, maybe he'd take up music seriously.

His thoughts were interrupted as the noise of the four great engines increased to a deafening roar. The whole fuselage was vibrating and he felt himself bounced and shaken in his seat as the aircraft picked up speed for take-off. Eventually the wheels left the ground and he was able to sit more comfortably. He wished he could read to pass the time, but he couldn't settle to anything. For something to do he poured himself some hot cocoa from a flask he had been given. He didn't really feel like it, but he was chilly and it helped to warm him.

He wondered whom he would see at the old house. Would Grootvader and Grandma still be there? Perhaps there would be news of Lisa and Aunty Kate. On the other hand, there may only be strangers in the old place now.

After what seemed an age, an RAF sergeant sat down beside him. "Are you ready to go, sir?" he asked.

"Is it time?"

"Five minutes, sir."

He stood up feeling cold and stiff. He tried to exercise some warmth back into his limbs, but then his time ran out. The sergeant checked that his parachute cord was hooked over a wire ready for the jump. He checked it himself as well. A small hatch was opened in the floor of the fuselage and Robert felt the cold air rush into the aircraft. It had been a clear evening, but dusk was settling over the land, so from his present height what he could see below was not clearly defined. It was a great void beneath him into which he must jump, and he felt his heart thumping within him in anticipation. "Sit here, sir. When the green light shows, just push yourself out," drawled the sergeant.

Robert sat on the floor with his feet dangling out through the hatch and his arms across his chest holding himself tightly. He could feel himself shaking. He couldn't do it, he panicked. He wouldn't do it! Why the hell should he? If he refused and went back home they couldn't do anything about it - it would be too late. His eyes were watering with the cold air and he never did see the green light. All he felt was a push in the back and he was falling, falling, falling into the greyness. Then suddenly he was jerked upright and the noise and the rushing wind had vanished as if by magic. He lost all sense of motion, feeling he was suspended in time and space. His fear had given way to a sensation of peace as he floated silently towards the ground. But his contentment was short lived as reality returned to stare him in the face.

As he drifted lower and lower, the land below began to take shape in the failing light. It became plain to him that they had dropped him in the wrong place, because the town he could see wasn't Grave, but Ravenstein, and that was much too far west. He should have landed in the fields about half a mile from the house so that he could get there before darkness set in. Also, if he was seen as he came down he would stand a chance of disappearing into the house before any-one could get to him. Now it had all gone wrong, and he would have miles to walk before he got to his destination. Why the hell don't they get things right, he moaned?

He could make out the Maas on his left, and seemed to be drift-ing towards it. He wasn't sure which would be worse, to fall in the river with a chance of drowning, or into the centre of the town with the certainty of getting caught.

But now the ground was rushing up at him. Would he just make the south bank? He struck the soft grass, successfully rolling over as he'd been taught, and the parachute slowly collapsed beside him. He had no difficulty in releasing himself from the straps, and was relieved to find that his legs and ankles were intact with nothing broken. His landing had been successful It had all been so easy.

He had made a safe landing at the right time, but he had the problem of being in the wrong place. Just a few yards away in the gathering dusk was the Edith Bridge which carried the railway across the Maas at Ravenstein. Perhaps the RAF navigator had mistaken it for the bridge at Grave, he thought. Whatever the man had done it was no use dwelling on it, because it didn't help his difficulty.

He bundled up his parachute and tried to conceal it as best he could, but having nothing with which to dig a hole his efforts were not completely successful. He sat for a moment considering what he should do. It was five miles or so to the house, and to walk would take so long especially when it became pitch black with no light to guide him. He must get there before the darkness really set in. Besides, the sooner he got there, the sooner he could get some sleep, which he was going to need if he was to be up before dawn. He'd be lucky if he got there before dawn, he despaired.

Then an idea struck him. He looked around before moving. Everything was quiet and the place deserted. If anyone had seem him drop, then they appeared to have done nothing about it. But in this he was mistaken. He got up and began to walk, passing under the railway bridge and alongside the edge of the small town. So that his footsteps would not be heard in the silence of the evening he remained, on the large expanse of grass, which ran parallel to the town between the river and the Maasdijk. Passing the Maaspoort, Robert saw the old ferry house loom into view. Remaining on the grass, he drew level with the house. It was in darkness and no sound came from it. He crossed the Maasdijk and made for the old wooden shed which had been built against the side wall of the house. He knew that Dignus Meijer had always kept his cycle in the shed. He would use that to get him to Grave. It's about time that Dignus did something to help the war effort, he grinned to himself, wondering whether that strange man was still so keen on the Germans after over four years of occupation.

Opening the shed door, he went inside. The shed had no windows, so it was difficult to see in the gloom. A crash made him jump. He had accidentally dislodged a tin full of nails, which had fallen to the floor. "Blast it!" he whispered as he groped about. But try as he would, he could find no cycle. He held open the door to let in what light there was but still without success. "Damn!" He would have to walk after all. He stepped back outside. It was still quiet. Nobody could have heard the noise he had made. But as he made to walk away he started with fright. He felt something poke him in the back. A voice he well remembered snarled, "One false move and I'll shoot."

Robert was not allowed to turn round and face his captor, but was pushed roughly towards the ferry house. The cycle for which he had been searching was leaning against the wall of the house beside the front door. Once inside, Dignus Meijer switched on a dim light and then forced his prisoner across the room until he was standing hard up against the old dresser.

Robert remembered everything in the room to be just as it was when he was a boy. Even the box of kitchen utensils still stood on the dresser.

"Now slowly turn round, and don't try any tricks," said Dignus, holding his pistol against Robert's head.

Robert did as he was told and when he had turned felt the pistol jammed under his chin.

"Dignus," he said, wondering whether the use of the other's name might help him. But seeing the green uniform realised his mistake. Dignus was obviously still a member of the Dutch Nazi Organisation.

At the sound of his name Dignus' eyes narrowed and he looked hard at his prisoner. "I remember you!" he growled slowly, as recognition dawned on him. "You're that English brat who was always laughing at me. Well, you won't be laughing much longer."

Robert could see the hatred in his captor's eyes. "I was only a kid, Dignus. I meant no harm," he said trying to keep an even tone in his voice."

"You filthy English are trying to ruin the Führer's new order in Europe. You're all Bolsheviks and Jews."

Dignus had not changed, and frequently assisted the German authorities against the Resistance movement. It was while returning from one such unsuccessful operation that evening, that he had heard an aircraft overhead, and spotted the dark shape of a parachute floating down somewhere near his home. He had made his way up through the town, believing that the parachutist would have landed somewhere near the Maasdijk. He emerged from under the Maaspoort just in time to see Robert disappearing into the gloom towards the ferry house. Seeing the intruder enter his shed, he had quietly crept up on him.

Robert did not like the expression on Dignus' face, and realised he would have to do something soon or he would be shot by this fanatic. "The war's lost, Dignus. The Germans are retreating everywhere. In a few weeks they'll be out of Holland and then everyone'll turn against you. Help us now and you'll be well rewarded."

"Help you?" There was a trace of hysteria in the voice. "You communist swine! You must all be shot!"

Robert felt himself pushed back hard against the dresser, the pistol now being held to his mouth. To steady himself his right hand went back on to the box of utensils. Under his palm he could feel the bone handle of the carving knife, which had always made him shudder when he was a boy. His hand closed round it, the fear of death now ordering his every action.

Dignus seemed crazed with the power he had over his prisoner. He had seen the SS execute people and had envied them their power, but now it was his turn to kill one of the enemy and please his superiors. Once he had been only a humble ferryman, but now he had status and was a man to be reckoned with. He put his free hand up and clapped it over Robert's face, pushing his head back and at the same time trying to force the gun into his victim's mouth. It was a method of execution which appealed to him.

The blade plunged deep into Dignus just below the ribs, the point travelling upwards towards the heart. Dignus jerked, air expelling from his mouth, before letting out a deep groan. His hand fell from Robert's face and the gun clattered to the floor. He took a pace backwards; the knife still buried in his side, and stood for a moment with a bewildered expression on his face, one arm stretched out in front of him groping the air. His lips moved, trying to form some last word, but no sound came, and he collapsed to the floor.

"Oh, my God!" Robert stood for a moment unable to take his eyes from the dead man, horrified at what he had done. He supported himself against the dresser, feeling as if he was going to vomit. He had seen death in the heat of battle, but that had been impersonal. This was different. He had killed someone whom he had known since he was a boy. He may not have liked Dignus, but to have killed him sickened his soul. How much deeper had he to sink into the wickedness of this war before it ended, he silently cried out to himself? He must get out of the room. He went quickly to the door, and once outside, took Dignus' cycle and rode away towards Grave.

In the past it had always been a great joy for Robert to ride along the Maasdijk, but now with thoughts of the dead man in his mind, and the possibility of being stopped by a German patrol it was a nightmare. He knew the road well, and rode as quickly as he could, the night air cool on his face, his one intent being to get to the old house before it became pitch black. After a mile he stopped to get his breath. With the cycle between his legs, he leant forward across the handlebars, panting, and turning over in his mind what he had done. It struck him that Elsa would probably find the body in the morning. He should have dragged it into the river to save her the shock. But it was too late now; he must go on. Poor Elsa. Cycling on, he went down the slope where the road left the dyke, and then came the straight before Velp, where he could hear the tyres splashing through puddles left by rain which had fallen earlier in the day. Silently passing the few houses and the convent he soon came to the rough track and was forced to slow down. Pedalling slowly up the track he made the right angled turn at the end and was quickly in front of the old house. All was quiet, and the house in darkness.

Dismounting, he walked to the garden gate, pausing for a moment to stare at the dark form in front of him. What would he find there? Would Grootvader and Grandma still be there? Who was this Liro he had to contact? Oh, God, if only he could be back in the happy days before the war.

He went up the garden path and rang the front doorbell. Almost immediately the flap behind the old grill on the door opened - he could not remember it ever having been used before - and two eyes stared out at him. "Who is it?" said an unfamiliar voice.

"Piet has sent me. I've come to see Liro."

The flap closed and the door opened. "Come in."

Robert stepped into the hall and the door was closed behind him. Somehow he resented being asked into this house, his own birthplace, by a stranger. He noticed the man was in his early thirties and wore dark trousers and a black polo neck pullover. He carried a pistol in his hand.

"You're late!"

"Am I?" Robert replied abrasively. He hadn't come all this way to listen to the unnecessary remarks of some damned stranger. In any case, the only reason for keeping to the actual time of arrival was so that he could get to the old house before it became dark. He was led into the dining-room where he stood for a moment gazing round and remembering days gone by. Everywhere he looked conjured up a fresh memory. He had expected to see the mysterious Liro, but the room was empty. "Where's this Liro person?" he questioned. He was feeling tired and his irritation showed.

"Here!"

For a moment he stood rooted to the floor as if afraid to turn and face the voice which addressed him from behind. Turning slowly, fearful in case it was all a dream, he saw her standing in the doorway. For years he had imagined this moment. His desperate hope that she would be here at the house had driven him on to carry out this mission, even though, in his heart, he had known it was just a daydream. And yet, it really was her. "Lisa!"

"My God! Robert!" she cried. "My darling Robert."

She came towards him, her dark beauty unimpaired by the years of separation, and they flung themselves into each other's arms.

"I can't believe it," he whispered. "Is it really you? It's been so long."

In their joy all else was forgotten and words became unnecessary. All that mattered was that they were in each other's arms, and they must never be torn apart again.

"Are you two going to be all night?" The impatient voice of the other man interrupted their joy.

Lisa gently held Robert away her looking up into his eyes. "He's right, my darling. We must hear what instructions you've brought from London. We'll have plenty of time for ourselves later," she smiled shyly. "By the way, Robert; this is Klaas Kruyff. He is second-in-command of our Resistance group. He's a demolition expert and was in the Dutch army before the surrender."

Robert nodded at the man.

"This is my husband Robert, Klaas,"

"*So* you're the one," said Klaas, looking Robert up and down.

"Have London told you nothing?" Robert enquired.

"Nothing, except that we were to expect someone who would bring urgent instructions," Lisa replied.

Robert was given food and a hot drink, and they all three sat together at the dining-room table while he ate. He explained his instructions that the bridge must be saved.

Klaas looked at him in sullen surprise. "Our job has been sabotage and destruction, now you come here and tell us we're to save this bridge. What's going on? Why have we got to save it?"

"I don't know, but those are the instructions," Robert retorted. He had not taken to this man.

"The bridge is well guarded, and it'll be difficult to get at. We'll have to wait for the right time, which might be days," Klaas remarked,

Robert looked at his watch. "It's just after eleven so we can all get some sleep before we go. The job must be done in the daylight, so we'll leave about half an hour before dawn and be under the bridge just as it's getting light," he said. "All the charges must be defused by thirteen hundred hours tomorrow,"

"You must be mad! It's impossible!"

"I'm the leader of this group, Klaas. I'll decide what's impossible," Lisa sharply interrupted.

Klaas knew better than to argue. Lisa van der Leyden was a lovely young woman. She could also be charming. He had known her for many years, but had noticed that since she had returned to Grave from Rotterdam during the early part of the war there was toughness about her which he hadn't previously noticed. She had developed into a natural leader, and was ruthless in the fight against the German occupation.

"Have you a plan, Robert?" she asked.

"Yes. That's why they've sent me. There's a tunnel leading from the cellar to the bridge. With any luck we can get under the bridge without being seen."

"A tunnel! In the cellar?" Lisa looked puzzled. "How do you know?"

"You remember the time when we were kids and you dared me to go down the cellar."

"How can I ever forget it," she smiled.

"And Grootvader came down when I was in there?"

"I remember."

"Well, I stood on the old stove to hide from him. Then I saw these metal things sticking out of the chimney breast. They were actually footplates, so I climbed up a little way." Robert went on to explain how he had found the tunnel, and how, walking through it, had come out at the other end near the bridge. "My clothes got ripped to pieces on brambles, and then I got soaked on the way home in that thunder storm," he concluded.

"So that's how you managed to hide from Grootvader and why you were in such a mess."

"You wouldn't believe me about the tunnel."

"That's not surprising," Lisa grinned. "You were always full of stories." Lisa paused for a moment, pondering what Robert had said. "My own house, and I never knew," she added thoughtfully.

"Your house?" Robert queried.

"Our house, now, my darling," she replied. "You see, Grootvader died in forty one, and Grandma in forty two, and then everything was left to me."

Robert felt a sadness come over him as he remembered the two wonderful people he had loved so much. "Both dead?"

"Yes. Neither of them really got over the shock of Father being killed." Lisa's face hardened. "Neither have I," she added with bitterness. "And life has never been the same since the Germans came."

"And, what about Aunty? Is she all right?"

"She's never got over Father's death, but she's very brave. She's upstairs asleep. You'll see her in the morning."

Robert took her hand and squeezed it. He got up from his chair and gently pulled her to her feet. "We must get some sleep and then get this wretched job over with. But when we get back. . ." he broke off and looked into her eyes. "I want you so badly," he said breathlessly.

"I can't wait" she replied, stretching up and kissing his cheek. "And I've got a surprise for you when we get back."

The three of them went to the drawing-room and each collapsed into a comfortable chair to rest." By the way," Robert asked, "Why this name Liro?"

"The first two letters of my name, and the first two of yours," she replied.

"Well I'm damned!" Robert chuckled.

Robert and Lisa awoke to the sound of an alarm clock to find that Klaas had already left the room.

In the excitement of finding Lisa again Robert had forgotten about Dignus, but his first thoughts on waking were of the dead ferryman. He held his head in his hands, trying to rid himself of the scene at the ferry house.

"Are you all right, Robert?" Lisa asked.

"Yes," he replied. "But I had a bad experience on the way here. They dropped me too far to the west, and I thought I would borrow Dignus Meijer's cycle. But he caught me and threatened me with a gun. I'm sure he was going to kill me."

"I wonder why he didn't?" Lisa interrupted. "He's been the cause of many deaths in this area since his German friends arrived."

"He didn't because I killed him first."

Lisa had got out of her chair and was making towards the door. "Good for you," she said without emotion.

"I killed him, Lisa! Don't you understand?"

Lisa turned and faced him. "Yes, I understand," she replied. "You killed him, and good riddance. What do expect me to do, pretend I'm sorry? There's been too many of his sort in my country, and the sooner they're wiped out the better."

"But. . ." Robert tried to interrupt, but was cut short.

"No Robert, you listen! You've never had to live under these Nazi swine, and you've no idea what happens when people like Dignus gain a little power. Well, the tide is running the other way now, and the likes of him are about to get what they deserve. If you hadn't killed him, someone else would. So forget it."

Robert followed Lisa through the door. There was obviously no more to be said, on the matter. He comforted himself with the thought that perhaps Lisa was right.

Klaas was waiting for them in the hall. He gave them each a pair of wire cutters and a torch. On Robert's suggestion they also took with them a pair of garden rose cutters to deal with the brambles, and a spade in case they had to dig themselves out at the other end of the tunnel. They also took a hammer in case more bricks had to be chipped away from the chimney breast to make entry to the tunnel easier.

They changed their shoes for plimsolls to ensure silence and to give them a good grip as they clambered about underneath the bridge.

"Let's go then," said Robert, leading the way down the passage. He paused before opening the cellar door, staring at the leather strap which was still hanging on the wall. A strange emotion ran through him and he shut his eyes. "I feel just as if it was that day all those years ago. Would to God it was," he sighed. He put his arm on the door jam and rested his head on it, searching his mind in an effort to bring back a picture of those lost years.

"Come on, Robert, we can never go back," Lisa put her hand on his shoulder.

"No, of course not," he said, recovering himself and opening the door.

But each step down into the cellar was another step back into the past for Robert. It was strange, but the old stone steps didn't seem so steep and difficult as they had done before, and even the deepest step halfway down was not as deep as he had remembered it to be.

At the bottom he switched on the light and noticed that there was something different in the cellar. At first he couldn't think what it was. Then it came to him that the archway, leading to that part of the cellar used to store the wine, had been bricked up.

"I had it bricked up," Lisa explained, "just in case those German pigs ever came down here. Not that they ever have. In fact, they've never come near the house. We have meetings here, and light the stove sometimes to give us a little warmth. The temperature change would not do the wine any good. When the war's over I'll have it dismantled. Then we'll really celebrate."

"I thought it felt warm down here." Robert glanced across the cellar and saw that a small new stove now stood in the large fire place alongside the old iron stove. Being well over to one side it would not interfere with their climb up the chimney.

Going to the fire place, Robert clambered on to the old stove and climbed upwards on the footplates. With the hammer and some stout nails he soon removed enough bricks to enlarge the tunnel entrance sufficiently so as to make access easy. He found it warm in the heat given off by the small stove below, but fortunately it had a long metal smoke stack so that the smoke was not released into the chimney until it was well above him.

Having enlarged the hole in the chimney wall, Robert clambered into the tunnel, and the other two climbed up the foot plates and followed him in. They wasted no time, immediately setting off into the darkness with Robert leading the way. As with the stone staircase and the cellar itself, the tunnel appeared smaller than his childhood memory had imagined. But it certainly hadn't deteriorated much since that time, he decided. He squeezed past the shoring pole in the centre still firmly holding up the roof, and then remembered to keep left where the tunnel branched. The tunnel not only seemed smaller, but the distance appeared shorter. His torch beam glinted on a metal object, and he knew that they were nearing the end. It was the old torch, now completely covered in rust, which he had thrown down in temper when its light had failed him those 12 years before. He bent down and picked it up. "Do you remember that torch, Lisa?" he grinned."

"Good heavens!"

The spade had to be used before the exit was large enough for them to squeeze through, and many brambles had to be cut away. It was still dark, and the night was now overcast, when they eventually made their way along the gully, but it would soon be getting light. German voices could be heard coming from the flak tower, but this was near the end of the bridge, and out of view from the bottom of the gully. The end of the gully became shallow where it sloped up to meet the path which ran on top of the dyke, and from this point it was only a few yards to the underneath of the bridge. But these few yards of path could be seen from the top of the bridge.

Robert peered over the top of the gully, but he could see nothing in the pitch black. So, one at a time, they broke cover and moved silently along the track to where they knew the first concrete support stood. Once there, under the bridge, they were out of the sight of the Germans above.

They sat on the grass bank waiting for the dawn. They had not long to wait, and soon the light began to spread across the eastern sky. Directly there was sufficient light for their purpose they quietly clambered up on to the girders and started to move stealthily under the roadway above.

Robert led the way, surprising his companions by the speed with which he was able to negotiate the girders. He had done it many times before and knew exactly what he was doing. He also knew how to remain concealed from the view of three spans of the bridge were built. For, although they could not be seen by those on the bridge, it was from the fields and from the river itself, when they got that far, that they could be spotted if they did not take care. The fields were usually deserted, but the river was another matter with the barge traffic passing underneath. Their careful checks under the first three spans revealed no demolition charges, but underneath the end of the fourth span Robert found a large explosive charge cemented on to the concrete support with the detonation wires running towards the north end of the bridge. It was exactly how he had expected it to be. The Germans would blow only the spans of the bridge which were actually over the river, and this would obviously be done from the north bank. If his calculations were right he would find more charges under the centre of the next span and also on the next concrete support.

After cutting the wires, they moved on, now over the river itself. More charges were found under the fifth span. They were not difficult to find, because the Germans had no need to conceal them, but the work took time.

It was the same under the sixth span, but here, as they busied themselves rendering the charges safe, a barge was approaching them going up river towards Grave. It got within 50 yards before Robert noticed it. Lisa was supposed to be keeping watch while the two men did the wire cutting, but her attention, had been diverted by Klaas requiring her to hold an awkward wire while he cut it.

"Look out! There's a barge coming!" Robert whispered frantically.

In the scramble to conceal themselves Lisa turned sharply and her elbow knocked the wire cutters out of Klaas' hand. They fell with a clatter, striking the edge of a girder an arms length below, and were about to topple into the water. Lisa, nearly losing her balance, shot her arm downwards and caught one side of the handle between her first and middle fingers. The barge was almost under the bridge, and she could feel the cutters gradually slipping away. "I can't hold them," she wailed softly. Desperately, she tried to get a better grip, but then they were gone, falling with a dull thud on to the moving deck below.

"Damn!" Robert whispered.

As the barged moved away a man came out of the wheelhouse and stood on the deck looking up at the bridge.

"I think he saw me," said Lisa. "Oh, what an idiot I am!"

"It's my fault," Klaas admitted.

"It doesn't matter whose fault it is. We must get on," Robert urged. He looked upstream and saw that the barge was putting into Grave. "If that man reports seeing us here, we've had it. Let's hope he keeps his mouth shut."

They examined the last three spans as quickly as possible, cutting every wire they could find. It was still early, and although they heard the odd vehicle passing overhead and the voices of the German guards at the end of the bridge, generally the surrounding area remained deserted and they had little difficulty in completing their task.

However, it took them a long time to return to their starting point at the other end of the bridge, because by the time they were ready to re-cross the water, the river traffic had increased and they had to wait some for a long enough interval between barges. They did not want to run the risk of being spotted again.

It was apparent that their presence had not been reported, because no police or extra German troops appeared on the scene. Once across the river they had no difficulty in returning unseen to their starting point under the first span. But it was here that they had to face a problem. It was one thing to cover the few yards from the gully to the bridge in darkness, it was quite another to return over the same distance in the daylight with the German guards on the bridge just above.

"What are we going to do, Robert?" Lisa asked, Klaas interrupted, "Why don't we stay here till it's dark? I don't fancy getting caught just for the sake of getting back to the house a few hours sooner."

"And I don't fancy staying cramped up here," Lisa retorted.

"We must go back now," Robert declared. "If we're caught under here they'll know what we've been up to. And I have a feeling it'll be somewhat unhealthy around here at about one o'clock.

"What makes you say that?" asked Klaas.

"Well, that's the deadline for completing the job," Robert replied. He sat thinking for a moment, and then said, "Now listen you two, get yourselves ready to walk briskly to the gully. Don't run, but put your arms round each other, and if the worst comes to the worst and you hear a guard challenge you from the bridge, don't take any notice. Just stop and embrace each other. If he persists, then go to him and pretend you've been making love on the grass under the bridge."

"And what are you going to do?" Lisa asked.

"I'll climb round the side of the bridge and carefully look over the top. I'll give you the signal to go when the guards aren't looking. I just hope that nobody will see you from that damn flak tower. Whatever you do, when you reach the gully, get into the tunnel out of sight. Don't wait for me. Have you got that?"

"Yes, sir," Lisa grinned.

"What are you grinning at?"

"I was just thinking how like Uncle John you've become, issuing all your military instructions."

"That's enough from you, my girl," Robert quietly chuckled. "There'll be a few more instructions for you when I get you home."

"Oh, yes please! I can hardly wait," she said coyly.

"For God's sake, let's get on with it!" exclaimed Klaas.

Lisa and Klaas dropped down on to the grass bank and then stood waiting on the dyke path, but still under the bridge. Robert clambered to the side of the superstructure and then forced himself upwards, slowly allowing his head to appear above the side girder. He could see the flak tower and the gunner leaning over the side talking to a guard below. A second guard was walking in Robert's direction so he had to duck down. He considered that these soldiers looked rather slovenly, so perhaps the information that Matt had given him was true, and the troops in this area were second class.

The second guard came to a point level to where Robert was hiding. He turned and moved towards the side of the bridge and then stood looking out towards the town. As he hung on to the side of the bridge, hardly daring to breathe, Robert could feel the closeness of the man.

Robert's attention was then attracted by the sound of a large vehicle approaching the bridge, and then he heard a shout. The guard, above him quickly moved away, and Robert resumed the position where he could see what was going on. It appeared that another guard had arrived, probably a corporal, he thought, and was upbraiding the others for slackness. There was immediate activity, and the approaching lorry was stopped. One guard stood in front of the lorry with his back to Robert, while the other, accompanied, by the corporal, went to the driver and began to check his papers. As luck would have it, the lorry had also claimed the attention of the man in the flak tower and he was looking away from the dyke path.

Robert quickly ducked down and signalled the others to go. Lisa and Klaas covered the few yards, as they had been told, and disappeared into the gully. Robert made his way to the end support and lowered himself down on to the grass bank. He quickly crossed the path,

And then ran down the side of the dyke into the field. He came out from under the bridge and could have been seen by anyone standing on the bridge above him, but not by the guards in their present position some yards down the roadway. Climbing the bank again exactly opposite the gully, where he would only have the width of the path to cross, he peered over the top. At that moment the lorry moved off, and for a few seconds all the guards were on the opposite side of it and out of view. The man in the flak tower was looking in the opposite direction as if he'd seen something approaching from down the road. Without any hesitation Robert flung himself across the path into the gully. He lay panting on the grass, his heart thumping in trepidation that he'd been seen.

He would make no move towards the tunnel until he was satisfied that the soldiers were not coming for him, because if the tunnel was discovered the consequences for the others, including Kate and any servants in the house, would be disastrous. His heart jumped when he heard another shout from the bridge and the sound of heavy boots running and stamping. Oh God! They were coming tor him, he cried to himself. He lay on the grass gripping his stomach in an effort to control his fear. What was he going to do? He could almost feel the barrel of a rifle being poked into his back as he lay there waiting for them.

He decided that he could do no more than just lie and wait. But nothing happened, and then all was quiet for a moment, except for a distant rumble down the road. Tanks! He'd know that distinctive clanking anywhere, he thought. He heard a shouted order and the sound of a car and motor cycles moving across the bridge. He breathed a sigh of relief that he was not the cause of the disturbance on the bridge. But the shock had made him feel quite weak and he lay for a moment longer to compose himself. Although he couldn't see any of the activity going on so near him, he could guess what was happening. It must be a Panzer regiment making its way back from the front. The car he could hear was probably a staff car, and the guard corporal had obviously lined up his men and saluted as it past. The motor cycles would be the escort, and would have sidecars with mounted machine guns.

Robert didn't wait to hear anymore. He stumbled through the brambles to the tunnel entrance and then eased himself through. Once inside, he sat down on the pile of earth which had been removed to enlarge the entrance, and held his head in his hands. "We did it," he panted.

Lisa sat down beside him and pulling his head towards her, kissed him. "We did it, thanks to you," she said.

It was strange how this bridge - his bridge – had become part of his life, and how fate had called upon him to save it from destruction. At least he'd done something worthwhile in his life, he considered, even if he had been reluctant to take on the task.

As they sat resting, they could hear the rumble as the tanks moved on to the bridge, the vibration causing little rivulets of earth to run down the tunnel walls. But they were safely out of sight, and after replacing some of the cut brambles and other undergrowth over the tunnel entrance in an effort to conceal it, they made their way back to the cellar.

*

"That's Grave over there, sir, and Nijmegen is about ten kilometres up the road," Untersturmführer Ullrich reported with enthusiasm. He was barely seventeen and had joined the 9th. SS Panzer Division Hohenstaufen just in time for the vicious fighting at Caen in Normandy a. few weeks before. But for all his youth he, like so many other ex-Hitler Youth boys, had proved himself a fighter to be reckoned with as many an Allied soldier had come to realise. What he had lacked in experience he had made up in courage, idealism and a passionate desire to save his Fatherland. Now he lacked neither experience, nor had his fighting spirit been broken by the long retreat through France and Belgium.

The boy's regiment - or what was left of it - had stopped for a brief rest after crossing the Maas. The few tanks and half-tracks were parked at the side of the road waiting for the order to move on towards Arnham where they were to rejoin their division, which was resting in the area after being badly mauled in Normandy. But unknown to them there was to be little rest for the 9th Panzer Division during the next few days.

The young officer glanced with pride at the tall man standing next to him wearing the Waffen-SS pattern black Panzer uniform. To the boy, the Obersturmbannführer was the hero of whom he had always dreamed. He looked longingly at the decorations on the black uniform; the gilt close combat clasp on the left breast, and below that on the chest the Iron Cross 1st class, the tank assault badge, the wound badge, and the ribbon of the Iron Cross 2nd class affixed to the open collar of the jacket. But the award that the boy coveted most was the Knight's Cross worn at the collar of his commanding officer's black shirt. The Führer himself had presented it to the Obersturmbannführer.

The Obersturmbannführer had no need of the information the young officer had just given him, but said nothing to dampen the boy's enthusiasm. He looked at the bridge and then stood gazing across the great river, fixing his eye on the roof of a house which could just be seen nestling in some trees behind the dyke on the far side. There was nothing the eager boy could tell him about this area. The sight of it all conjured up in his mind a picture of his long forgotten youth, and for a brief moment he was struck with a yearning for those whose love for him had made for such happiness in days gone by. But what was love, he asked himself? He had almost forgotten what it was to love and be loved - the fighting on the Russian front had seen to that. He had loved his parents, but they had been taken from him. He had loved his regiment when serving in the army, but had become so highly decorated that the Führer had insisted he transfer to the SS, because Doctor Goebbels required young heroes with film star good looks for his propaganda campaigns. Now it was all different. The great days of victory had long passed, to be replaced by death and defeat. He had loved his old comrades, but they had vanished in the vastness of Russia, and the men he commanded now were no more than boys.

Although he had been reluctant to transfer to the SS, the Obersturmbannführer had come to respect the fighting qualities of these regiments. At first he had been posted to the 1st SS Panzer

Division Leibstandarte Adolf Hitler, in which his own soldierly qualities had soon brought promotion. At the end of 1942 he was given command of a regiment in the newly raised Hohenstaufen Division.

Removing the cigarette from his mouth, he flung it to the ground. He had never smoked as a youngster, but now he needed the comfort a cigarette could bring. "Do you see that house over there, Max?" he said, pointing across the river.

"The one through the trees, sir?"

"Yes." The Obersturmbannführer lit up another cigarette while his young companion waited for him to complete what he was going to say. "I'm going over there to have a look at it."

"But, sir. Is that wise? The Resistance are becoming active now that we are moving back."

The older man put his hand on the other's shoulder. "Don't worry, Max, I'll be alright."

"At least let me get Hirsch to arrange an escort."

"If you must," the Panzer leader sighed, a faint smile flickering across his face. He had become resigned to the boy fussing over his safety. When Ullrich had left him, he strolled across to the leading tank and gave instructions to his second-in-command that the regiment was to move on and that he would join them within the hour. Then before setting out on his private venture, he stood at the side of the road and waited until every vehicle had moved away.

Having received his instructions to arrange an escort for his commanding officer, Sturmscharführer Hirsch set off in his armoured scout car to examine the old house which had been pointed out to him across the river. He decided to go on ahead to check the house before the Obersturmbannführer arrived. He couldn't understand why his commanding officer had suddenly taken it into his head to visit this particular house, but since he had, Hirsch was determined to ensure his safety.

The scout car sped back across the bridge following behind a motor cycle and sidecar with mounted machine gun. Once over the river the two vehicles turned right along the road which led to Velp and Ravenstein. It was not difficult to find the location of the old house, and soon they were bouncing up the rough track. Stopping alongside the garden gate, Hirsch, his driver and one of the motor cycle crew, with their sub-machine guns ready in their hands, quickly moved towards the front door, leaving one SS man to guard the vehicles.

In reply to the heavy thumping a young maid nervously unfastened the lock and half opened the front door of the old house. Hirsch roughly pushed the door wide open and strode into the hall followed by his men. He gave instructions to one of the soldiers to search the ground floor rooms, and the other he sent upstairs, while he himself remained, in the hall with the frightened maid. A few minutes later the soldiers returned, reporting that the house was empty except for a woman and a small boy. Kate and the child accompanied one of the soldiers down the stairs.

"Good morning." Kate addressed Hirsch calmly trying hard to hide her apprehension. "Is there some way I can help you, er. . .?" she hesitated, wondering how to address the man, not being familiar with the rank insignia of the SS. Unlike Lisa, her German was not good, but she could make herself understood.

"Sturmscharführer Hirsch," he said, introducing himself. "Who else lives here?"

"Only my daughter," she replied.

"Soldier, Grandma." The boy pointed up at the tall, thick set man in front of him.

"Yes, dear, soldier."

Hirsch squatted down and held out his hand to the boy. "A fine boy," he said, his voice taking on a less aggressive tone.

At first the child put his thumb in his mouth and tried to bury his head in Kate's skirt, but with a little coasting his curiosity got the better of him and he went forward and began fingering the *Old Fighter's Chevron* on the soldier's right arm. It was a badge of which the SS man was particularly proud, denoting that he had been affiliated to the Nazi Party before January 1933.

Hirsch stood up and patted the boy's head. "Where is your daughter?" he demanded abruptly.

"I'm not quite sure," Kate replied. She sounded uncertain and was about to go on, but the words died on her lips.

Without warning the house suddenly resounded with the ear-splitting report of a German sub-machine gun.

The maid screamed and rushed into Kate's arms, hugging her with fright. The child started to cry and buried his face in Kate's skirt.

Hirsch turned to see one of his men with his smoking gun pointing down the passage which led to the cellar door.

Robert, Lisa and Klaas had successfully made their way back to the cellar. They hadn't carried guns while actually under the bridge, but Klaas had taken a revolver and a sten gun to the end of the tunnel just in case they were needed. On arriving back in the cellar he had the sten gun in his hand, and it was he who led the way back up the stairs to the ground floor of the house.

From the very first days of the occupation no German had ever set foot near the house, let alone in it, and consequently Klaas had become slack in the precautions he took when emerging from the cellar door into the passage. He had opened the door and stepped out with the sten gun in his hand straight into the view of one of the SS men who was standing in the hall and facing down the passage. The SS man, seeing a gun pointing at him was not slow to react.

The bullets struck Klaas full in the chest and he was knocked back down the passage, dead before he touched the floor. Before Robert and Lisa realised what was happening, the SS soldier was at the open cellar door and had his weapon pointing at them.

Kate could feel herself shaking with shock at the deafening noise of the gun, but she was too occupied with comforting the child and the maid to worry about herself.

Hirsch was not slow to take action. He had the other soldier take Kate and her sobbing charges upstairs and lock them in a room. Then, striding down the passage, he examined the two prisoners, who were now standing facing the wall with their hands raised.

Robert turned and looked into the cold eyes of his captor. For a fleeting moment he thought he detected an expression of surprise on Hirsch's face. He felt it was as if the man had recognised him, but couldn't remember where he had seen him before. Hirsch hesitated, but almost immediately recovered himself.

The soldier guarding the vehicles had come running in on hearing the shots. Hirsch called to him, "Go and fetch my whip," he ordered. Since fighting in Russia he had never gone anywhere without his whip, keeping it to hand in the scout car. His expertise in extracting information from those unwilling to give it had begun on the streets of Berlin, where, as a member of the SA, he had brawled for the Party and seized communists and others, taking them to cellars for torture. He had come to the notice of Himmler, who had taken him into the SS in 1934, just in time for him to take part in the liquidation of some of his ex-comrades in the SA during the Röhm purge. On the Russian front he had rarely failed to get the information he wanted from prisoners, and when he did, those who managed to resist the persuasion never lived to enjoy their triumph. Now he was convinced that he had stumbled by chance on to a Resistance cell, and any information he could extract from these two young people would be of value to the Gestapo.

Having telephoned Gestapo headquarters at Nijmegen, Hirsch, his whip in his hand and accompanied by two of his men, forced Robert and Lisa back down into the cellar. The two prisoners were both made to strip themselves naked so that their bodies and their clothes could be searched thoroughly for weapons or other incriminating evidence. As Robert removed his shirt he remembered the medallion was round his neck. He knew he should have left it at home, and cursed himself for his stupidity. He furtively removed it and tried to conceal it in his hand, but Hirsch spotted him. The SS man nonchalantly crossed to where Robert was standing and stood in front of him. He said nothing, just holding out his hand, and Robert reluctantly handed over the medallion which, after being closely examined, was thrown down on top of his discarded clothing.

Robert felt himself trembling with fear and anger. Fear of what was to happen to them, but anger for the way they were treating Lisa. It was obvious that the SS were enjoying the sight of her beauty, and the soldier who was searching her was carrying his thoroughness to the extreme. Robert could stand it no longer. "You filthy swine!" he shouted, making a dash towards the man. Hirsch, ever alert for any violent retaliation from those he oppressed, was quick to react and kicked out at Robert with his heavy boots, catching him in the groin and sending him crashing to the floor.

Hirsch looked down at his naked victim writhing in agony at his feet. "Any more displays of gallantry from you, and I'll put a bullet in the girl's brain," he threatened coldly. He stood tapping the handle of his whip in the palm of his hand. "Do you understand?" he shouted.

"Yes," Robert gasped, as he dragged himself to his feet.

"In that case we can proceed," Hirsch smiled. He began to slowly pace up and down in front of the two young people. "The matter is quite simple," he continued, his manner now very precise. I wish to know who you are. I wish to know what you were doing in this cellar with an armed man. And I wish to know the names of the rest of your group. I must have names." He smiled at them. "If you tell me now, it will save you much pain. If you don't . . .Well, I can assure you that you will be begging to tell me later." He stroked the handle of his whip. He would start with the man, he thought, and save the girl for later.

Lisa realised that whatever story she made up was unlikely to be believed. The SS man was no fool. But she had to play for time. He might not even believe the truth, about the bridge. What was certain, Lisa sensed, was that the man had every intention of using his whip on Robert. If it became necessary she would give some information; she might even sacrifice herself, but whatever happened she would not give the names of others in the Resistance. What she couldn't understand was why he had not started on her. She had held herself frigid and aloof when they had mauled her, and had steeled herself for what was to follow, but it appeared that it was Robert who was going to suffer if they didn't talk. Perhaps they were saving her for later. "What are you talking about, a group?" she snapped, unable to disguise her hatred of these foreigners. She spoke in German in an effort to impress Hirsch, but nothing seemed to impress the man.

Hirsch smiled. "I'm quite happy to have a little game and pretend you know nothing, but don't waste my time for too long.

"I am Lisa van der Leyden and this is my cousin William de Lange." She spoke boldly as if she was ordering the German to believe her. She knew that she must be careful, but her hatred of Nazis and the SS in particular was too deep for her to show anything but contempt for these men. Thank God she had looked at Robert's false papers before they set out for the bridge, she said to herself. But in her heart she knew it would make little difference however convincing her story might be. It might help, though, in her effort to play for time, she thought.

"Who was the man we've just shot, and why did he have a gun?" Hirsch persisted.

"He was a stranger. He'd forced his way into the house demanding money."

Hirsch laughed. "You'll have to do better than that." He turned to Robert. "And what have you to say?" he asked.

Robert remembered it was a question his headmaster had always asked before caning him. It had made no difference what he had said as a boy, and it would probably make no difference now. But he had to try to delay the inevitable. "It's the truth," he claimed. "We are just ordinary people. We've always cooperated with you Germans." He said anything that came into his head just to waste time. He told Hirsch how he had met the Führer at one of the early Party Rallies when he was a boy, and was about to tell him that he had German relatives when Hirsch cut him short.

"You're wasting my time," Hirsch snapped. He motioned to one of his men, and Robert was forced at gun point to spread-eagle himself face down across the large table. Cord had been found and his wrists and ankles were bound, the cord being pulled tightly and secured so that he was unable to move and the cord bit hard into his flesh. He could see Lisa looking at him. Their eyes met, expressing their love as well as any words could have done. She attempted, to go to him, but one of the soldiers roughly pushed her back.

Why had everything suddenly gone wrong, Robert demanded of himself? He felt he could scream with frustration, but there was time enough for screaming when the whipping started. What would Lisa think of him when he did start to scream, he agonised? If only that fool Klaas had taken more care he would have been lying with

Lisa in his arms by now, but once again his dreams had been shattered by the turn of events.

"We're citizens of the Third Reich, surely the Führer doesn't want his people to be treated like this," Robert blurted out.

"Citizens are you. Traitors more like. I'm sure the Führer won't be too upset by one young Dutchman having his back laid open with a whip," Hirsch smiled. He made a point of always sounding pleasant to those he was about to torture. It seemed to add to his enjoyment.

So this is what Hitler's New Order had brought to Europe. Robert could see in his mind the sunny day long ago when the great man had taken his hand and then patted him on the cheek. The compelling eyes and charming smile had caught the imagination of the impressionable boy which he had been in those halcyon days of the new movement. But now it had come to this, and he himself was to suffer at the hands of men who gave their allegiance to his one time hero. Was it possible that the charming Führer could have sunk to this? Then he remembered Rotterdam and a remark his father once made that *the devil has a smiling face.*

Hirsch walked slowly towards the table, uncurling the whip as he came and enjoying the look of terror in the eyes of his victim. Robert felt the end of the whip laid lightly across his bare back as Hirsch measured the distance for the first lash. Many times he had woken in the night when he was training to be an agent, believing the Germans had got him. Now the nightmare had become reality. He knew what was to happen and couldn't save himself. If he had been alone he would have told everything. He would have told them he was a British Officer and that he had cut the wires under the bridge. But if he confessed anything at all they would shoot Lisa for assisting him. He racked his brains in an effort to think of other ways of playing for time. Perhaps rescue would come at one o'clock. Matt had said something was going to happen. If only he could hold out that long. He was not sure that he could hold out at all, for when the flogging began he might go to pieces and tell everything he knew. When they had taken his watch from him he had noticed the time was showing eleven-forty so there was over an hour for him to endure if Matt was right about the timing of the operation.

*

Shortly before noon on that September Sunday morning, airfields all over southern England were alive with the roar of engines as the great air fleet of troop carriers and gliders began to taxi to their take off positions. At the given signal throttles were pushed forward and the first aircraft moved down the runways gradually taking up the slack in the neatly looped tow ropes of the gliders behind, and then picking up speed for the slow climb into the sky. The destination was Holland, Operation Market Garden had begun.

It was Montgomery's bold plan to drive a spear right through the centre of Holland, outflank the Siegfried Line, cross the Rhine at Arnhem, and envelop the great industrial centre of the Ruhr from the north, thus shortening the war by months.

To carry out this operation an airborne carpet was to be laid by dropping 3 Airborne Divisions along the Eindhoven-Nijmegen-Arnhem road. It was the task of these Divisions to capture the bridges over the Maas, the Waal and the Neder Rijn (Lower Rhine), and a number of smaller waterways. XXX Corps of the 2nd British Army led by the Guards Armoured Division was to smash a hole in the German front line at the Belgium border, and then race north along this road to relieve the paratroops holding the bridges. The prize was the bridge at Arnhem. But if the bridges below Arnhem were not taken and held, and the relieving armour could make no headway, then the prize would be lost, and the operation would not fulfil its objective.

Rick Radowski of the 504 Parachute Regiment wore the Stars and Stripes emblem on the right sleeve of his combat jacket. On his left arm there was a square red badge, in the centre of which there was a blue circle with the white letters AA – the badge of the United States 82nd Airborne Division, whose task it was to take the vital bridges at Grave.

"Come on, Radowski, move it!" the sergeant yelled, giving the young paratrooper a hefty push towards the open door of the waiting Dakota transport plane.

Since joining the battalion just three weeks before, the tall young private had been the bane of his sergeant's life. It was not that the sergeant disliked his new charge or that Radowski meant to be difficult, it was more that the young man found it difficult to come to terms with army routine. He was a dreamer, and his mind was usually far away when he should have been concentrating on what the sergeant was saying. He was invariably last on parade, in fact he was usually last in most of the activities that the army required of him. Sometimes the sergeant wondered how he had managed to get into a parachute regiment, but then Radowski would surprise him, and for a time, carry out his duties with reasonable efficiency.

The rest of his unit were already seated when Rick stumbled into the plane followed by the sergeant. The door was fastened, and as Rick staggered to his seat the aircraft began to move.

"Hey, Radowski, it's sure nice of you to join us. Sure you can spare the time?"

The young man took little notice of the catcalls and whistles made at him as he made his way to his seat. At one point he lost his balance and almost sat on the lap of one of the older men who roughly pushed him away. "Get lost you son of a bitch!"

"I'm sorry, I couldn't help it," Rick apologized.

"I'm sorry, I couldn't help it," the man mimicked. "Keep off me, fancy boy!"

"Put a sock in it, Moran! Leave the kid alone," the sergeant ordered.

Rick eventually reached his seat at the end of the row and sat down. He was soon forgotten by the others, everyone now being engrossed, with their own thoughts about the coming battle.

When the sergeant wasn't looking, Rick furtively took the Dogs Tags from round his neck and slipped them into his jacket pocket. He hated anything hanging round his neck, and in any case if he was killed it was of little importance whether or not he was identified. He was alone in the world and there was no next of kin to inform.

The noise of the engines increased to a roar as the aircraft began to pick up speed for take off.

"Watch out, Adolf, here we come!" someone was heard to call out.

*

The black car pulled up behind Hirsch's armoured scout car outside the old house. Normally, the Obersturmbannführer would use a scout car himself when travelling in convoy with his battalion. But the battalion had lost so many vehicles in the retreat from Normandy that he had commandeered a French police car for his own use. He sat gazing at the house. He had no intention of going in; it was just that he wanted to see it again.

The SS soldier, who had been left outside to guard the vehicles, approached the car and smartly raised his arm in salute.

"Where's Sturmscharführer Hirsch?" asked the officer.

"Inside the house sir. They've just shot a Resistance man, and the Sturmscharführer is questioning another man and a woman in the cellar."

The officer made no move to leave the vehicle. He didn't particularly wish to witness what he knew would be going on in the cellar. He was a fighting soldier and even now, although he acknowledged the necessity for extracting information by any means, he did not like this form of violence. He remembered how, in the early days of the war, it would have shocked his sense of honour to have even considered using such practices. But the Russian front had changed all that. After the barbarities committed on his own men by the Partisans in the rear of the front line, he had gradually come to realise that the only way of finding out their hiding places was to allow Hirsch his way with any prisoners they came by. Whether or not Hirsch enjoyed the game was of little importance; it was results that mattered and Hirsch invariably obtained the information he required.

Robert had given up trying to bite back the pain, and now with each lash he flung back his head and cried out in agony.

When the lashing stopped, Hirsch looked with satisfaction at his handiwork. The back and the buttocks of the strong young body which lay before him were now covered in bleeding weals. But for all his efforts he had gained no information. "Turn him over!" he ordered.

Robert let out another cry as the cords were temporarily loosened and he was roughly turned over. He tried to arch himself in an effort to keep his torn flesh from touching the table, but Hirsch forced him down, pushing hard on his stomach. He groaned in agony as he was again tied down. "No more," he begged.

"Then talk," Hirsch ordered.

But Robert remained silent. Hirsch smiled and gently laid the whip across his chest in preparation for another flogging.

Lisa flung herself towards Hirsch and tried to tear at his face. "Swine!" she cried, "Stop it! Stop it!" But Hirsch just struck her to the floor, and one of the other soldiers grabbed her and, holding her firmly, forced her back against the wall.

While the Obersturmbannführer sat in his car lost in thought, another car pulled up. Two men got out, both wearing long raincoats, the younger of the two obviously in charge.

Gestapo, the Obersturmbannführer decided as the blond young man approached him. It seemed that Hirsch had wasted no time in contacting them. He'd had no contact with the Gestapo over the years, at least not until the bomb plot on the Führer's life in July. Not that he'd been involved in this act of treachery - he was a loyal SS officer and above suspicion - but he had noticed their presence since that time as their net dragged through the officer corps of the Wehrmacht. He knew these men were dangerous, but then so was he.

The Obersturmbannführer slowly got out of his car and leant back against it nonchalantly taking a cigarette from his mouth.

"Hauptsturführer Kube, Gestapo." The young man clicked his heels and introduced himself, his cold blue eyes assessing the SS officer lounging in front of him. He had read about this hero of the Reich, and recognised him by the photographs which had appeared in the newspapers each time the Führer had decorated him. "I believe, Herr Obersturmbannführer, that your men have arrested some of the

Resistance in this house," he said with the arrogant courtesy of one who was used to receiving a nervous deference from the majority of those he addressed in the course of his duty.

But if Kube expected to find any such fear in the man he addressed, he was disappointed. The SS officer had stood face to face with death on too many occasions to be apprehensive of a young man who had never even seen the enemy. He nodded his acknowledgement of the Gestapo officer and replied with little interest, "So I believe."

"Perhaps the Obersturmbannführer would care to accompany me while I interrogate these traitors," said Kube.

The SS officer nodded and strolled towards the front door followed by Kube and his companion. He would have to enter the house after all, he thought. In any case, it was time he got Hirsch out and left the matter in the hands of the Gestapo. He didn't wish to be delayed any longer. It crossed his mind that it might be one of those occasions when Hirsch had become carried away by his lust for cruelty. Sometimes the man went too far.

Entering the hall, he stood for a moment glancing round and thinking that perhaps he shouldn't have come here after all. He hesitated at the cellar door, glancing at the old strap hanging there, and then made his way down the stone steps followed closely by the two Gestapo men.

When the Obersturmbannführer appeared in the cellar, Hirsch and his men immediately sprang to attention. But their officer did not notice. He had been about to order them back to their vehicles; when his eyes fell first on the naked body of Lisa, and then on the victim lying in agony on the table. For the first time for as long as he could remember his power of decision failed him, and his inner composure relapsed into a state of confusion. For years he had steeled himself against sentiment and weakness, and his self discipline had been successful. Constantly at the front, it had kept him remote from the suffering around him. But now it was as if the steel shell which encased his feelings had been breached. Life had been simple. He believed in his Führer and his country, he knew the enemy and had fought them with every means at his disposal. But here was his own cousin lying writhing in agony before him. Where now did his loyalty lie? He stood rooted to the spot, staring at the scene before him.

As she recognised him, the look on Lisa's face changed from one of contempt to astonishment. She had been about to pour out her hatred against the black uniformed newcomer. Instead, after a moments hesitation, she ran forward, "Karl Heinz!" she cried, flinging herself at him. "For God's sake stop them!" But her cousin had recovered himself and stood unmoved while a soldier dragged her away. "What's the matter with you?" she shouted, "Why don't you do something? Don't you recognise us?"

Robert slowly raised his head at the sound of his cousin's name. He stared hard at the black uniformed figure, for a moment unable to believe his own eyes. "Karl Heinz," he gasped with relief, thinking his ordeal to be at an end.

But as their eyes met Karl Heinz turned away.

"Karl Heinz it's me!" Robert cried.

But Karl Heinz remained silent. This was no time for sentiment, he told himself. It was people like this who were ruining the Führer's vision of a pure German race and a united Europe. If only the English hadn't started the war. But then Father had always said they were a strange people and couldn't be trusted. Why hadn't they supported the Führer against the Bolsheviks? But they hadn't, and now they were the enemy.

The Gestapo officer looked, at Karl Heinz in surprise. "You know these traitors?" he asked.

Karl Heinz nodded. "We cannot choose our relations," he replied coldly.

"Relations!" Kube exclaimed, asking himself if the Obersturmbannführer might also be a traitor?

"Don't look at me like that, Kube," Karl Heinz snarled. "The Reichführer himself knows my family connections. It's not your business."

"Of course, I meant no offence," Kube replied with respect, recalling that this officer was a personal friend of Reichführer Himmler.

Karl Heinz glanced down at Robert. "What are you doing here?" he asked.

"You know I can't tell you that. I'm a British officer. My rank is captain and my number. . ."

"Damn your number!" Karl Heinz retorted sharply before Robert could finish. "What are you doing here?" he demanded again.

"Is that all you can say after all this time? What's happened to you? I thought we were brothers."

Although Robert's words pierced his heart, Karl Heinz was determined to keep all thoughts of the past far from his mind. "Either you tell us what we want to know or you'll suffer," he said coldly, angry with his cousin for encouraging emotions best forgotten.

Kube was becoming impatient. "I'm sure the Obersturmbannführer will not object if we continue with the interrogation," he interjected.

Karl Heinz shrugged. "If you must," he assented.

"Karl Heinz! No!" Robert cried.

Lisa stood in astonished silence unable to understand her cousin's attitude. How could he allow the torture to continue, she asked herself?

Kirsch lashed his whip across Robert's chest, bringing another cry of pain, but then Kube stopped him. "Enough of that, you're wasting time," he ordered, sounding irritated. He looked dispassionately at the naked man on the table. He was not interested in torture for the sake of it, but only as a means of gaining information, and if a victim would not talk then greater pain had to be applied.

Kube went across to the stove and thrust a long flat iron bar, which was used as a poker into the fire. He nodded to Hirsch. "Use that," he instructed. Hirsch grinned and stood waiting for the iron to heat up.

Robert forced his head up from the table in an effort to see why the whipping had stopped. He saw Hirsch, with a thick piece of rag in his hand, coming towards him holding the red hot iron. At that moment his eyes grew wide with terror as it dawned on him what was to happen. He squirmed in his terror, frantically jerking at the cords holding his arms and legs in a futile effort to free himself, but he was too firmly secured, to move anything but his head. "No! No! Not that," he screamed. "Karl Heinz, stop them! Please!" he pleaded.

Kube nodded at Hirsch, who was now standing beside the table holding the red hot iron over his squirming victim, enjoying the look of terror in the young eyes and the frenzied entreaties for mercy.

Horrified, and with sweat pouring from him, Robert saw the glowing instrument of torture slowly lowered towards him. Fighting for breath and almost choking in his fear, he shrieked as the searing pain burnt its way into his flesh. Lisa flung herself at Hirsch in another desperate effort to stop the torture, but this time she was caught round the waist by Karl Heinz, who lifted her, kicking and struggling, off her feet and held her firmly under his arm.

When the iron had cooled, Hirsch replaced it in the fire to reheat.

"It's time you two started to talk," said Kube.

"Go to hell!" Lisa screamed back at him, Karl Heinz flung Lisa over his shoulder and carried her still struggling up the cellar steps.

"No more!" Robert pleaded when Hirsch stood over him once more, ready to repeat the torture. "Stop! I'll tell you everything" he cried, his words changing scream as Hirsch, applied the iron again.

"A British officer are you," said Hirsch nonchalantly, smiling at his writhing victim. "A spy, more like."

Reaching the top of the steps, Karl Heinz and Lisa heard the screaming start again. Karl Heinz knew he had the power to stop the torture, but he fought off any such thoughts. He went quickly through the cellar door and slammed it behind him in an effort to deaden the sound of Robert's distress. He carried Lisa up the stairs and into one of the bedrooms, where he lowered her on to the bed and stood looking down at her.

"Now what, you bastard?" she spat out, her eyes blazing with anger.

"What do you think!"

"No never. Not that!" she shouted at him defiantly. "I hate you!"

Karl Heinz unfastened his pistol belt and hung it on the chair beside the bed, and then began to remove his jacket. "I've always wanted you, and you've wanted me, so don't deny it."

You conceited swine! Don't fool yourself. It's bastards like you who killed Father!" she screamed at him, tears of anger rolling down her cheeks.

"You bloody people think you're the only ones to have suffered in this war!" Karl Heinz hit back at her angrily. "It was your precious allies who killed Father and Mother."

Lisa's expression changed. "Not them as well? Not Auntie Natascha?"

"Yes, them as well," Karl Heinz replied bitterly. "In a Cologne hospital, by your bombs. So don't you be so bloody self righteous!"

Even in the bedroom they could here the shrieks coming from the cellar. "For God's sake go down and stop them," Lisa shouted at him. "You can do what you like with me then."

"No. He'll suffer till he talks." He tried to placate his conscience with the thought that Robert was the enemy - the enemy who had killed Father and Mother - but he saw the reproach in her eyes. "For heavens sake, Lisa, it's not my doing, you brought it on yourselves!" he exclaimed. "I didn't want this to happen. If I'd known it was you in here I. . ." He stopped abruptly. He didn't have to make excuses, he told himself, but then added defensively, "I'll do my duty."

"Your duty," she spat back contemptuously. "Since when has it been anyone's duty to whip and burn and torture? You bastards have done that all over Europe, and for what? Do you ever stop to think? You contaminate and ruin everything. But it's all right if it's your duty, isn't it." Lisa's blazing anger, coldly suppressed over the years of the German occupation, boiled over.

"That's not true!" he shouted back. "I've fought honourably for my country," he tried to explain, "but she cut him short.

"Honourably!" she cried. "What do you know of honour? You Nazi scum have spread nothing but misery and destruction. You... you and that bloody Führer of yours, and all the rest of his filthy gang."

"Shut up!" he shouted back furious at her insults of all he held sacred.

"And if I don't? Are you going to have me whipped and branded? That's your answer for everything, isn't it?"

He turned from her and began to remove the rest of his clothes.

Lisa saw her chance. She slowly moved to the edge of the bed and quietly unfastened the pistol holster, taking out the gun. She knelt on the bed and pointed it at him. "You're not having me, Karl Heinz," she said, speaking very deliberately.

He made no attempt to turn and face her until he had undressed, but when he did and saw the gun in her hand his face clouded. "Put that thing down and don't be stupid," he ordered.

"Stay back," she said unconvincingly, her determination wavering"

"Put it down! Or you'll get something you hadn't bargained for," he threatened.

Lisa was now unsure of herself. Now that the black uniform had been removed she saw him no longer as the highly decorated panzer leader. No longer was he one of those who had killed her father and ravaged her country. It was just Karl Heinz standing there, the boy who had always been there in the memory of her young days, when all had been laughter and sunshine.

"I'm warning you, Karl Heinz!"

In a sudden movement he stretched out and grabbed the gun, flinging it on to a chair. For a moment Lisa was taken aback, but then her anger flared and she threw herself at him clawing at his face.

"You bloody cat!" he shouted, catching her by the wrists. Then in one movement he sat on the bed and pulled her across his knee, beating her in a frenzy of anger and relief until his hand was stinging with the effort.

He pushed her down on the bed, and flinging himself on top of her, took her firmly in his arms. "You needed that," he said breathlessly.

The tension between them vanished, and Lisa, still smarting from the violence of his slaps and feeling the strength of his desire, realised her resistance had gone. They had both been starved of their natural desires for too long and were hungry for love, and the touch of their bodies now made it impossible to prevent the inevitable from happening.

Shrieks could be faintly heard coming from the cellar. "Please, Karl Heinz," she whispered, trying to salve her conscience, "Do something about Robert."

But it was too late, she had surrendered to him. She could resist her desire no longer, and Robert's agony was forgotten in the ecstasy of their passion.

Hirsch returned to the stove to re-heat the iron, and Robert lay groaning on the table, his whole body trembling and covered in sweat. He had sunk into an abyss of unimaginable pain, his whole body burning as if engulfed in flames. He cried to Hirsch and offered himself for any degradation if only he would stop the torture. As the iron was applied again he shrieked with pain and screamed for mercy, and denounced Lisa as the local resistance leader uncaring in his agony what they did with her. He told them everything he knew, but they thought he had still more to tell, and the torture continued. They wanted the reason why the detonation wires under the bridge had been cut, but he could not give it. He was beyond shame at what he believed to be his cowardice, and would have certainly told them had he known the answer. He had managed to resist the pain of the whip, but they had broken him with the red hot iron, and other exquisite tortures that Kube inflicted on him whilst waiting for the iron to reheat.

Once again Robert saw Hirsch returning with the iron, which was now almost white hot. Again lie squirmed in terror and begged not to be branded again. He cried like a child, and through his tears saw Kube looking at him unmoved by his distress. He tried to cringe away from his tormentor, but they had now driven nails through the palms of his hands and he was held so firmly that any move-ment brought more agony. Hirsch caught him by the hair, forcing his head up to ensure that he could see what was happening, as the iron was lowered on to him. Robert shrieked and shrieked until he could shriek no more. Eventually Hirsch let go his hair and he lay back whimpering and groaning in his agony.

It was at this point that Karl Heinz and Lisa returned to the cellar. Lisa ran to the table meaning to take Robert in her arms, but recoiled in horror at the sight before her. The cords holding Robert's wrists had broken, but large nails had now been driven through the palms of his hands securing him to the table. She wanted to scream her hatred at his tormentors, but her own sense of shame and guilt for having forgotten him while in the arms of Karl Heinz forced her into silence. She put her hand on his brow in an effort to comfort him, but, although he looked at her his eyes were unseeing and her presence made no impression on his mind.

Kube said to Karl Heinz, "We'll get no more from him, but the girl can tell us a great deal."

Karl Heinz caught Lisa by the arm and held her in front of him. "Tell them what they want to know," he entreated her.

I've nothing to say!" Lisa sneered at Kube.

"Release him, and put the girl on the table," Kube ordered.

Robert screamed again as the nails were pulled out and he was roughly dragged from the table on to the floor. His mind had begun to wander and he could no longer fix his thoughts on anything but the unending agony. Shock had taken hold of him and he couldn't stand without assistance. He lay there on his side groaning, bending his knees up towards his chin and making himself into a ball as he had often done at home in bed when he was a boy. But all movement brought more pain, and again he cried out in agony as his knees came up and the weals on the back of his thighs opened up again. He clasped his hands together and pushed his knuckles into his mouth like a child seeking comfort.

Karl Heinz had an impulse to rush to the aid of his suffering cousin, but still he would not give way to weakness in front of his men.

Lisa was tied face down on the table. She looked reproachfully at Karl Heinz. "And you said you loved me," she said, her voice breaking with emotion.

He stood motionless, lost in thought and unable to cope with the contradictions that were pulling him apart. With unquestionable loyalty he had dedicated his life to the Fatherland and the Führer, planning his career carefully and with foresight. By his strength of will he had dispelled his earlier confusion, but he had failed to allow for his heart. His faith in his Führer had enabled him to sacrifice

Robert in the name of duty, but now a stronger power had captured his affections. Suddenly the crack of the whip jerked him back to reality, and, for the first time in his life, he realised he was in love. For a moment he hesitated and then there was a second crack and a gasp from Lisa. "Stop!" he shouted.

Hirsch instantly obeyed.

Kube turned in surprise. "Herr Obersturmbannführer, is something wrong?" he asked calmly.

"Enough of this! Release her!" Karl Heinz ordered sharply, and by the tone of his voice Hirsch knew that his commanding officer had decided on a course of action from which nothing would shift him.

But Kube had no such knowledge of the Obersturmbannführer and found it difficult to understand that another officer – even one of higher rank than himself – would dare to go against the wishes of the Gestapo. "It would be unwise to obstruct a Gestapo officer carrying out his duty, Herr Obersturmbannführer." His words were polite but full of menace. He nodded at Hirsch to continue the whipping, but Hirsch made no move to do so. He would take orders from none but his commanding officer.

The other Gestapo man snatched the whip from Hirsch, but Karl Heinz moved himself between the man and the table. "Release her," he ordered.

"I suggest you stand out of the way, Herr Obersturmbannführer," Kube snarled from behind, still maintaining his excessive politeness.

Karl Heinz turned to see the Gestapo officer pointing a pistol at him.

"It would be unfortunate if I had to use this on such a distinguished officer," Kube sneered. But at that moment a sub-machine gun was pushed into his side and his pistol was removed from his hand. He glanced round the cellar and saw that Hirsch and his men had raised their weapons and were pointing them at him and his man.

"Hirsch, escort these two gentlemen to their car," Karl Heinz instructed.

Hirsch motioned to Kube with his gun that he was to leave, and the two Gestapo men reluctantly walked towards the stone steps. Before leaving the cellar, Kube turned and spat out, "You've not heard the last of this, Herr Obersturmbannführer. You've protected traitors."

"Get your facts right, Kube," Karl Heinz replied icily. "I'll decide what happens to my prisoners."

Kube was about to reply, but Karl Heinz cut him short. "I could have you shot for pointing a gun at me," he snapped. "The Reichführer doesn't like his friends threatened."

At the sound of Himmler's name Kube said no more and quickly mounted the steps followed by Hirsch and the other SS soldiers.

When his men had disappeared, Karl Heinz released Lisa and helped her from the table, telling her to dress.

Robert was still writhing in agony on the floor, gasping for breath as his body convulsed with sobbing.

Lisa, in pain herself, remained silent as she dressed. Her anguish for Robert and her lack of understanding at Karl Heinz's erratic attitude towards her had cast her emotions into turmoil. She knelt down to comfort Robert, but quickly realised he did not recognise her. "God in heaven!" she exclaimed, looking at the numerous brand marks and his bleeding back and pierced hands. "We must get a doctor."

"You can treat him upstairs, but then he'll have to come with me. He's a prisoner of war."

"For God's sake Karl Heinz! Don't you understand he's not fit to travel."

"It's you who doesn't understand. When they come back they'll shoot him. Kube'll be back, make no mistake. And you'd better get away from here too."

At that moment footsteps were heard; hastily descending the cellar steps, and Hirsch came hurrying to Karl Heinz. "What is it, Hirsch?" he asked."

"We must get out, sir, quickly!" he urged.

"Why, what's the matter?" asked Karl Heinz.

Enemy aircraft, sir. They're dropping paratroops to the southwest. The sky's black with them."

"So they do want the bridge." Karl Heinz pondered. How far away are they landing?"

"About a kilometre."

"They're coming for you, Hirsch," Lisa interjected with venom in her voice.

"Right! We must go," Karl Heinz declared. "Give me a hand to get the prisoner upstairs, Hirsch."

"No! Keep your filthy hands off him!" Lisa cried, glaring at Hirsch. "I'll do it."

"All right, Hirsch, go upstairs and keep a lookout," said Karl Heinz.

Lisa picked up Robert's trousers and tried to pull them over his feet, but he cringed away from her.

"Come on, there's no time for that," said Karl Heinz impatiently. He noticed the medallion lying on Robert's clothing and quickly picked it up and put it in his pocket.

Gently, but firmly Lisa and Karl Heinz lifted Robert, groaning in agony, to his feet. He was too weak to stand on his own so they supported him one on each side, and slowly made their way up the steps.

In the sky above the American air fleet was gradually unloading its human cargo. Hundreds of steel helmeted paratroopers were moving in orderly queues towards the open doors of their transport aircraft, and in quick succession were throwing themselves out over the flat countryside of Holland below.

"For God's sake, Radowski, move it!" the sergeant shouted. His men had started to jump and the line was moving quickly along the fuselage and disappearing out of the open door. That is, all except the last man. Radowski was still sitting in his seat fiddling with his parachute straps.

"It's tangled, Serg," Rick called out.

The sergeant hurriedly pushed his way to the rear of the fast disappearing line of men. Out of a hundred and fifty million American citizens they had to send him Radowski, he commiserated with himself. But the sergeant was efficient. Like lightning he sorted out the young soldier's problem, clipped up his strap, and was pushing him towards the door. "Let me know if it don't work, kid," the sergeant shouted against the noise of the engines and the rushing air, giving the young man a heavy push in the back.

Rick went through the open door, followed immediately by the sergeant. When his own chute had opened, and he was able to see what was going on, around him, the sergeant noticed with a certain amount of relief that Rick was floating down safely just a short distance in front of him. But the few seconds delay in jumping meant that the two men would land some distance away from their company and closer to the bridge.

As he drifted down the sergeant could see that he was going to land not too far distant from an old house nestling in some trees just south of the dyke. He could clearly make out the black cross on the side of a German armoured scout car, which was standing in front of the house. There was also a black car and a motor cycle with sidecar. A German soldier ran down the garden path to join another soldier standing near the vehicles. The two of them tried to elevate a machine gun on the sidecar towards him, but before they could open fire he and Rick had dropped out of view behind the trees.

Landing safely, both the sergeant and Rick were out of their harnesses in a few seconds and had run for cover into the wood. "What now, Serg?" said Rick.

"Just stick with me, kid. Did you see what I saw?" the sergeant asked.

"You mean those Germans?"

"You got it, son. We're going to bust 'em up. I don't want our boys running into trouble when they come up. The Krauts might have set up a strong point in that house."

The two Americans circled the house, keeping well out of sight of the German soldiers. They entered the garden at the rear of the house, and concealed themselves in the shrubbery for a few moments to ensure they had not been seen. The house appeared quiet. The sergeant pointed out a rear door to Rick. "If it's open, we go in. If it's locked, we use that open window over there," he indicated. "Now listen, kid. Blast anything that moves in German uniform, but be careful because there may be civilians in there. If we get to the front of the house without any trouble we can knock off those Krauts outside with no problem. If we have to start shooting in the house get to the front door quick, because those boys outside are going to come running, and we can knock 'em off as they come up the path. Got it?"

"Got it, Serg."

"Let's go!"

They rushed across the lawn to the door. Then, crouching down, sub-machine guns ready, the sergeant quietly tried the door handle. The door was not locked and was silently pushed open. Slowly they made their way through the kitchen, and quietly opening an inner door moved out into a passage. The sergeant could hear voices. He turned to his young companion and put his finger to his lips. "Germans," he mouthed. Ahead the passage turned at right angles. Pausing, the sergeant peered round the corner. Now he could see that it went straight ahead into what appeared to be a room, or maybe an entrance hall, and it was here from where the voices were coming.

At the end of the passage the two American soldiers poised themselves ready for action.

"Now!" The sergeant and Rick flung themselves into the hall. In a split second the sergeant reacted to what he saw. The German soldier standing by the front door didn't even have time to turn his head before the bullets struck him. Hirsch, who caught the sergeant's second burst of fire, staggered backwards holding his stomach before collapsing on the floor. It was all so quick that even Rick was bewildered for a moment. He saw a girl and a German in a black panzer uniform supporting a naked man between them. He fired a burst wide to the right in an effort not to hit the girl and the man she was supporting, one of his bullets finding its mark in the panzer officer. Karl Heinz slowly slid to the floor holding his chest.

Immediately after firing, the sergeant bashed a fresh magazine into his gun and ran to the window. As he had predicted, the SS men outside with the vehicles, having heard the shots, were now running up the garden path. He ran to the front door and, flinging it open, sent a hail of bullets crashing into the approaching men. None of them stood a chance, and it was all over in seconds.

Meantime, Robert, not fully aware of what was going on around him, felt himself lose the support on one side and instinctively grabbed the banister post at the foot of the stairs to steady himself. The sergeant, having made sure there were no more Germans outside, came across and looked at Robert. "Who is this guy?" he asked Lisa, seeing the state of Robert's body.

"He's a British officer. They've been torturing him," Lisa replied.

"Holy Mother of God!" he exclaimed, shocked at the sight which met his eyes. "The bastards!"

Robert had begun to shake as the shock took hold of him again. Rick took off his combat jacket. He gently eased Robert's arms into it and lifted it on to his shoulders, turning him and taking Karl Heinz's place at his side in support.

Rick said kindly, "Don't worry; we'll get a doc to take a look at you. You'll be fine."

After, seeing the state Robert was in, the sergeant turned on Karl Heinz, who was kneeling on the floor holding his chest. "You Nazi son of a bitch!" he yelled. He kicked Karl Heinz in the chest and sent him sprawling back on the floor. It was his last act.

Hirsch was not yet dead. He lay on the floor slowly bleeding to death, his sub-machine gun still clutched in his hand. But no one had noticed him move. In a last act of defiance, using all his remaining strength, he lifted the gun and pulled the trigger, at the same time blindly sweeping it round in an arc. The sergeant was sent sprawling forward on to his face with a line of bullet holes across his back. Lisa saw it coming and screamed a warning. But it was too late. Rick, who was still supporting Robert, was not quick enough to open fire, and was hit in the chest and staggered backwards before collapsing. The last of the magazine struck Robert. Lisa felt him wrenched from her grasp as he crashed backwards to the floor, striking his head against the banister post as he fell. He lay motionless, his head lolling to one side. Then, giving a deep sigh, he lay still.

Had the magazine of Hirsch's gun not run out of ammunition, Lisa would also have been shot. "Robert!" she screamed, kneeling at his side. The unbuttoned combat jacket had fallen open, revealing a chest covered with blood and the tell tale puncture marks where the bullets had entered. "Robert! Robert!" she cried, falling across the still body. "Don't leave me!"

Losing control, and in a frenzy of despair and hatred, Lisa snatched up Rick's weapon and emptied the magazine into the now dead body of Hirsch. "You filthy bastard," she cried hysterically. Then, flinging down the gun, she sank to her knees with her hands covering her face, and wept as she had never wept before.

It was minutes before she managed to control herself. She wiped her eyes and fought to regain her composure. She had always been determined and strong, and now she would need that strength to fight her grief and to bring up Robert's son on her own. The child was to have been a surprise for him when they returned from the bridge, but now he would never see the boy. It was not the first time her heart had been torn in shreds, but now the hurt could not be healed. With a supreme effort she forced herself to push these thoughts from her mind, knowing that it was the living who needed her now, not the dead. There would be time enough for tears in the long years ahead. She must go to Mother and little Robert.

She got to her feet, and turning, saw that Karl Heinz had dragged himself to where Robert was lying, and was holding the motionless head of his cousin in his hands, his tears falling on to the ashen brow. She watched as he took the medallion from his pocket, and saw him gently place it round Robert's neck.

Lisa knelt beside him. "It's too late for tears, Karl Heinz." There was a harshness in her voice which she couldn't hide. "You should have wept long ago."

They were together again in a place they had all loved, the three of them, but the sound of their happy young voices was only an echo of the past.

Lisa suddenly jumped up and rushed to the window. There had been the sound of firing coming from the direction of the bridge and the town, but now she had heard the sound of shouted orders outside. "American soldiers!" she cried. "They're at the front gate." She wanted to rush out and welcome them, but instead she hurried back to Karl Heinz. "Quickly!" she urged. "Leave Robert. We can do no more for him. You must hide. They'll kill you in that uniform."

Karl Heinz glanced up at her. "Isn't that what you want?" he asked unhappily.

"It should be, but it isn't," she retorted.

He clung to Robert for a moment longer, kissing him on the cheek, and then allowed Lisa to assist him to his feet and help him along the passage and through the cellar door. On reaching the bottom of the steps, Lisa could feel that her cousin was losing his strength and that she could no longer support his weight. Gradually, she lowered him to the floor and sat him resting back against the wall. Kneeling beside him, she opened his jacket and found his shirt soaked in blood. "I must get bandages," she said urgently.

"No, don't leave me!" he begged.

"I must."

"No! Don't go, Lisa," he pleaded, grasping her wrist. "It's too late. I'm finished."

"Don't talk nonsense! You'll be all right," She saw a trickle of blood issue from the side his mouth and run down his chin.

He smiled at her. "Who would have guessed it would all end like this?" he said, his voice becoming weaker. "We were so happy once. We were happy, weren't we?"

She nodded, the tears welling up into her eyes.

"Kiss me," he whispered.

She leant forward and took him in her arms, gently brushing his lips with hers. "I love you," she heard him say faintly. For a moment he struggled to say more, but she only caught one whispered word, "Sorry. . .," before he fell silent. He closed his eyes and sighed, and she felt him go limp.

How long she wept over him holding him in her arms Lisa never knew, for the next thing of which she was conscious was a hand on her shoulder gently shaking her, and an American soldier looking down, at her with a puzzled grin on his face. "Hey, miss, you gerna sleep all day? You gotta wake up now!"

For a moment she found it difficult to focus her exhausted mind on what had happened, and then, finding herself lying across the body of Karl Heinz, it all began to come back to her. She reached out and took hold of the young soldier's offered arm and was slowly assisted to her feet. "Was I asleep?" she asked unnecessarily.

"You sure were. Flat out on this guy," the American replied, indicating Karl Heinz with his gun.

"What time is it?"

"Sixteen thirty."

"Three hours!" she whispered to herself, hardly believing she could have been lying there for so long. She looked down at Karl Heinz, and the events of the day rushed back into her mind. She stood for a moment, fighting back the tears, sorrow gnawing at her heart.

"You okay, miss?"

Lisa nodded.

"Say, this guy didn't hurt you, did he?" he asked, noticing the SS uniform.

"No. He didn't hurt me," she replied softly.

Lisa was escorted by the soldier from the cellar back to the hall, to find the house alive with American troops. But to her surprise there was no sign of the dead Germans or the two American soldiers who had been lying on the floor when she had taken Karl Heinz to hide. And there was no sign of Robert's body.

"Look what I found, Captain!" The soldier handed Lisa over to an officer.

The American officer looked at Lisa and smiled, asking a question that the soldier had taken for granted. "Do you speak English?"

"Yes."

"Can I ask who you are, miss?"

Lisa introduced herself and then added, "I'm the owner of this house."

"Captain Sherwood, Miss van der Leyden. Sorry about all this," he apologized. "We need to have a temporary headquarters near the bridge."

"It's all right, Captain Sherwood. Stay as long as you like. Thank God you've come."

"Sorry it took so long."

"By the way, have you got the bridge?"

"Sure. And do you know something; the Krauts didn't even try to blow it."

"How strange. I wonder why?" she said quietly. "Oh, Captain Sherwood," she added. "Can you tell me what happened to the bodies that were lying here?"

"Bodies? I don't remember any bodies."

Seeing the puzzled look on the captain's face, Lisa tried to explain. When she had finished the captain said, "Someone said the medics have taken a couple of our boys who were still alive."

"But there were others, some Germans and a man who'd been tortured."

"Sorry, miss, I don't know about that. I wasn't first here. When I arrived there were no bodies." The captain could see the look of disappointment on Lisa's face, but he knew there was little he could do for her. "Look, give it time," he went on. "When the fighting stops things'll settle down, then you'll be able to find out where they've taken him."

Lisa realised that there was nothing she could do at the moment to ensure Robert had a proper burial. Her duty was now to the living. She made her way up the stairs. "Mother!" she called. "Where are you?"

"We're in here, dear," Kate called from one of the bedrooms.

Lisa entered the room to find Kate and the maid sitting on the bed with little Robert between them. "Isn't it wonderful, dear! The Americans here, I mean," Kate said. "They've been so kind. . . We thought we'd stay up here out of the way. . . I've been so worried about you. Whatever's been going on down there?"

"It's best you don't know, Mother."

"But we heard shooting downstairs. That was hours ago. There's been more shooting outside so we stayed away from the window."

"It's all over now, Mother. We're free at last."

"What's free, Mummy?"

Lisa caught the boy up in her arms and hugged him. "It's something very precious, Robert. Something you don't appreciate until you've lost it." She saw the puzzled look on his face and knew he was too young to understand, but it didn't matter. Perhaps his generation would never need to understand. She looked into his large brown eyes and tried to smile, but a single tear rolled down her cheek.

*

On that September Sunday afternoon, Grave became the first town in Holland to be liberated. "The famous American 82nd Airborne Division not only liberated the town, but achieved their objective in capturing intact the vital bridge over the Maas. Before dark that day they had also captured a bridge over the Maas-Waal canal, thus opening the way to Nijmegen.

Eight bridges, including the bridge at Nijmegen, were seized along the corridor from the Belgium frontier, but the strategic objective of the whole operation was frustrated, because the final bridge - the bridge over the Neder Rijn at Arnhem - although bravely held for many days by a battalion of the British 1st Airborne Division, could not be reached by XXX Corps, and consequently the break-out over the Rhine was not achieved. The greater part of Holland remained in German hands for another seven tragic months.

But for Lisa the indescribable relief that the Germans had gone, and the joy of liberation was overshadowed by the loss of Robert and Karl Heinz. For the sake of her son she was determined not to let her life be affected by her anguish. The grief in her heart was her own affair, and she would keep her tears for the moments when she was alone.

In the following days she tried to trace where Robert had been taken. She discovered where the dead Germans had been buried after the Americans had removed their bodies from the house, but Robert was not among them, nor for that matter were the two American soldiers. Then she found the dressing station where the wounded in the fighting on that first day had been taken. "The man I'm looking for was British. He had been badly tortured," Lisa told the American doctor.

"Sorry, miss, I've had no British here," the doctor replied. "Perhaps they took him down to Eindhoven. Any identification on him?"

Lisa shook her head. "All I can tell you is that he was wearing an American army jacket," she said.

"Tell me who isn't, miss," the doctor smiled.

An orderly, who was standing nearby listening to the conversation, interrupted. "I saw some guys put on a truck. And there's only one road out of here, lady, and that's to Eindhoven."

But during the next few days it was impossible for Lisa to use the road to Eindhoven, because it was the one road along which the Allied troops were advancing, and it was choked with military traffic.

Frustrated in her efforts, Lisa sat in the garden one afternoon trying to make up her mind what she should do. Although still in the area, the Americans were no longer using the house, so it was with some surprise that she saw an American jeep draw up outside the garden gate. She watched an officer get out and enter the garden. He came towards her beaming, obviously expecting to be recognised.

"Surprise! Surprise! Remember me?" he called, holding out both hands as if expecting Lisa to run into his arms. Then, seeing Lisa's blank look, he took off his helmet. "Come on, Lisa, you remember me. Brent Charlton."

"Brent!"

"Yes, mam, Major Brent Charlton, at your service."

Lisa was unsure whether she was pleased to see her visitor or not. His boisterous, self-assured attitude did not match her mood. But then it struck her that he may be able to help trace Robert, so she went forward smiling and took his hand.

"Say, don't I get a kiss after all this time?"

"Of course," she said, pecking him on the cheek.

Taking him into the house, Lisa remembered that he was an easy man to entertain, and from that point of view he hadn't changed. She only had to sit and listen while her visitor talked incessantly - mainly about himself. In the first few minutes Lisa learnt that his insurance business back home had become even more successful since their last meeting. It had been left in the hands of his partner while he was away in the army.

"And why didn't you write?" Brent continued.

Lisa tried to think of an excuse. "The war, of course," she replied.

"I mailed you letters before we came in," he persisted. "Now what do you say about that?" he chuckled, amused with himself that he'd caught her out.

Lisa shrugged. "I can't remember. Too much has happened, Brent. It hasn't been easy."

"Well, we can start all over again. Brent Charlton doesn't intend to let you go this time."

It was only with difficulty that Lisa managed to turn the conversation to the favour she wanted. But when she did Brent was full of enthusiasm to help her in any way he could. He was almost child-like in his pleasure at having found something he could do for her, and promised he would make immediate enquiries about Robert. Lisa explained that the two of them had once met, but Brent hardly remembered this cousin Robert, and, in any case, his only interest in tracing him was to gain Lisa's affections.

In the next few days Brent kept his promise, but all he could find out was that an ambulance had run over a mine near Eindhoven, and had been found burnt out. The occupants had been so badly burnt that they were beyond normal recognition.

Lisa decided that to enquire further about Robert would be useless. In any case, a grave was not essential to keep his memory alive, for he would live in her heart for the rest of her life.

CHAPTER 16

At first, through his drowsiness, Robert could not make out what it was he was staring at, but then, as his eyes began to focus, he realised it was a bunch of holly and a small sprig of mistletoe. A sense of peace pervaded his whole being, but his arms and legs felt heavy, and it was an effort to turn his head. He could see that he was lying in bed in a small room that had a clinical appearance about it, and then he noticed that his arms and hands were completely covered in bandages.

For some time he tried to concentrate on something, anything, that would help him understand the questions that were very slowly forming in his mind. He saw the holly move slightly as the white door beneath where it hung swung open. The door was directly in front of his bed so he was able to watch the young nurse enter the room. At first she did not notice that his eyes were following her, but when she did, she looked at him in surprise and quickly left the room to return a few minutes later with a doctor in a white coat.

"So you're awake at last," the doctor said.

But although Robert struggled to reply, he was unable to force out even one word.

It was some days later that he managed to speak his first word. That morning he awoke to find a nurse looking down at him. "Happy Christmas, Rick," she smiled.

"Christmas?" he whispered hoarsely. "It can't be. . . Where am I? What's happened to me?"

"All in good time, Rick. You just rest now."

"Why do you keep calling me Rick?"

The nurse picked up some army identity discs which were lying on top of the small cupboard beside the bed. "Rick R. Radowski," she read out. "That's you, honey. They were found in your pocket."

"But where am I?" he persisted.

"My, you are full of questions today. You must be getting better. You're in the Walter Reed army hospital."

"Never heard of it!"

"Washington," the nurse declared.

"Washington!" he exclaimed faintly. "But that's America."

"Well, what d'you know!" she teased. "Why so surprised? The good old U.S. of A. Where else should a wounded G.I. be?"

"A GI? But I'm. . ." His words faded as his mind struggled for an explanation, but he could not even recall his own name.

The nurse noticed her patient's puzzled look. "You got badly shot up in Holland. Remember?" she asked. But it was obvious that he did not remember. "Now don't you worry, honey," she comforted. "It'll all come back to you. Just give yourself time."

"How long have I been here?" Robert asked.

"Since October, I guess," she replied, and then went on to explain that a Dutch farmer had found him near a burnt out ambulance, wearing nothing but an American combat jacket, and it was thought that he must have been blown clear as the vehicle had gone over a mine. "You've been unconscious for weeks. It's a miracle you survived," she concluded.

The New Year came and went, and Robert's memory gradually returned. The peace he had felt on awakening from his coma vanished, and, as the days passed, he began to relive the torture he had suffered in that cellar. He made no effort to reveal his true identity, preferring, at least for the present, to remain among people who did not know him and had no idea that he had betrayed the one he loved. The thought of his betrayal of Lisa constantly gnawed at him, and became magnified in his mind out of all proportion as he remembered seeing her carried away to be shot.

Weeks turned into months, but still Robert remained silent about himself. The doctors were pleased with the way his body had healed and the fact that he was walking again, but they were concerned that the shock of the explosion was still affecting him. It had been noticed that sometimes, for no apparent reason, he would start to shake and the sweat would stand out on his forehead, and in the night he would frequently cry out in his sleep. What they did not know, and could not get from him, was the remorse he was suffering for what he believed was his cowardice.

Each day Robert expected to be confronted with the fact that he was not Rick Radowski, but as the American soldier's record showed he had no next of kin there was no one for the authorities to inform who could have identified him. The records even covered Robert's English accent, because Radowski's mother was English and he had lived in England for some years.

Robert realised that by failing to say who he was his conduct was completely irrational, and that he would be causing grief to his family, but until he felt stronger in mind and body the thought facing his father filled him with apprehension. To be wounded was one thing, he told himself, but to be sent home and seen weeping and shaking with fear was something to be delayed as long as possible.

On one of those early autumn days, when, the midday sun still gives the illusion of summer, Robert was sitting by the open window when the doctor entered the room and quietly drew up a chair beside him. "Well, Rick," he began, "We've done all we can for you. You've healed up well, and you're walking normally again. I guess it's time you were discharged."

Robert nodded, asking himself what was he to do now?

The doctor continued, "I'd still like to know how you came by those weals on your back. Who whipped you, Rick? And you know as well as I do that the marks on your hands were not caused by bullets. They look like nail marks to me. And what about those burn marks? Just what did happen out there?"

"I can't remember," Robert lied.

"Look, Rick, you'd feel better if you talked about it." The doctor looked hopefully for an answer from his patient, but getting no response he said, "Let me get one of our psychiatric boys to see you."

"Why, do you think I'm mad or something?" Robert retorted.

"Of course not! But there's something on your mind and you need a bit of help. Then you'll be fine."

Robert shrugged. He had intended to confess that he was not the American soldier, but once again he said nothing.

The next day Robert saw the doctor approaching him accompanied by another officer. "This is Major Collins, Rick. He wants a few words with you," the doctor said, leaving the major to sit down beside Robert.

"You're wasting your time, sir," Robert said. "I don't want to talk about it." He saw the quizzical look on the major's face and then asked, "You are the psychiatrist aren't you?"

"Me a psychiatrist! Not me, son," the major smiled. "Now listen, I'm told you have a gold medallion."

Robert looked suspiciously at the officer, but admitted he had.

"Can I see it?" the major asked, holding out his hand.

Robert took the medallion from round his neck and handed it over.

The major examined it carefully and then said, "I'm a friend of Colonel Matt Irving." He held up a letter in front of Robert. "I've had this from him. Need I say more, Robert?"

"I suppose not," Robert replied, feeling a strange sense of relief that the decision to admit who he was had been forced upon him. "I'm sorry, I meant to tell them. I just never got around to it."

The major smiled. "Think nothing of it, son. You've had one hell of a time. There's no saying what shock can do to a guy."

"What now?" Robert asked.

"It's time to get you home."

*

Major Collins was as good as his word, and in a short time had arranged a flight for Robert on a United States air force bomber which was making a routine trip to England. As Robert alighted from the B17, he saw Matt waiting for him on the tarmac. He was surprised when Matt came quickly forward and hugged him, for he had not thought Matt to be a particularly demonstrative person.

"You've no idea how good it is to have you back, Robert," Matt said softly.

Later, as Matt drove the two of them through the countryside towards Sussex, he adopted a firmer tone with his young brother-in-law. "Why the hell didn't you write, or tell someone you were alive," he remonstrated. "Don't you realise what you've done, letting us think you were dead."

"I'm sorry."

"And so you bloody well should be! I've had a hell of a conscience about sending you into Holland, and as for Mother and Father, they've had to live with their grief for months, thinking you were dead. And I was the one who had to tell them."

Robert looked sheepish. "How did you find me?"

"Well, we got a message from Holland saying you were dead. I had a lot of enquiries made but there was no trace of you. It was your friend Wendy who remembered the gold medallion. She kept on to me, saying she was sure you were still alive. A woman's intuition, I suppose," Matt grinned. "I was sceptical about you being alive I must admit, but she talked me into checking again. And then someone at the General Hospital, Cherbourg remembered an American soldier with a medallion. It struck me that it could be a case of mistaken identity, and that it was just possible you could have been shipped to the States. Mind you, I still thought you dead. It was your body I was trying to trace. It was a long shot, but I got Collins to check the casualty records over there. He also checked the Military Hospitals for anyone with a gold medallion. You know the rest."

At the mention of Wendy Robert had ceased to listen to what Matt was saying. It surprised him that the sound of her name should give him such pleasure. So often he had treated her badly, he thought, and he blamed himself for making use of her friendship when Lisa was not available. Was that the reason now for his renewed interest, he asked himself?

Since John and Elizabeth had moved back to Brighton, Wendy had become an intimate friend of the family, Elizabeth finding the presence of a young person who had known Robert so well a great comfort. Wendy was also a frequent visitor to Matt and Joanna's home at Ditchling, a small village nestling beneath the downs near Brighton, where she was a firm favourite of the two children.

For sometime there was silence in the car, and then Matt asked, "What did happen out there, Rob?"

"For God's sake, Matt, don't you start! Ever since I woke up in that hospital they kept on and on about it."

"I just want your version to finish off my official report. After all, I'm still your CO, and it was my responsibility sending you out."

"Anyway, I can't remember," Robert replied.

"Don't talk nonsense! Of course you remember!"

"Look, it's all over now. We saved the bloody bridge! That's what they wanted, wasn't it? So let's just forget it."

"All right, Rob, don't get so aerated. You did a damn fine job. I've put you up for an MC."

"Oh, no!" Robert exclaimed. He turned his head away and looked out of the side window. "I don't think I could stomach that," he added. Not after what happened, he thought to himself.

"What are you talking about? I thought you'd be pleased."

"Well I'm not. I may be many things, but I'll not be a bloody hypocrite."

"I don't know what the hell you're talking about!"

"Then let's just drop it," Robert concluded.

Matt said no more. But he was determined that sooner or later he would uncover the truth.

Robert had come to realise that with Lisa dead there was no one to tell of his cowardice, unless of course Karl Heinz had survived the war. But he had often wondered about the welcome he would receive when he arrived home, considering his strange attitude in not immediately revealing his identity to the Americans, and not having his parents informed that he was alive. But he need not have worried, because the welcome he received clearly demonstrated that the one concern of his family was to have him safely home. Elizabeth shed tears of joy, and John found it difficult, as he had those many years before when informed of Robert's birth, to keep his emotions under control as he embraced his son. Joanna had no such inhibitions, nor had the two children, who were soon demanding the full attention of their uncle.

Robert would have preferred to have stayed in his room that evening, but Agnes insisted that he went down for dinner. "You can't disappoint the family on your first evening home," she scolded.

He sat at the table lost in his own thoughts saying nothing unless he was spoken to, and all the time conscious of the marks the nails had left on his hands.

"You must have so much to tell us, dear," said Elizabeth.

"No, Mother, not really," Robert replied inattentively.

John said, "What actually happened to you?"

"I evidently got blown up. They said I was in an ambulance that went over a mine. I can't remember."

"Why not?" John asked.

"I was unconscious. I'm only telling you what I was told."

"But why were you unconscious in the first place?" John persisted. "Something must have happened for you to have been in an ambulance."

"Look, Father, do you mind if we change the subject?" Robert said sharply, and then seeing the look of frustration on John's face, he added, "Well, you would never talk about the war."

John sighed. "I'm sorry, I didn't mean to pry," he said. "I was just interested to hear your story. But no matter."

There was a strained silence at the table for a few moments, and Elizabeth could feel John's disappointment.

"Well, you saved the bridge," Joanna declared brightly, breaking the silence, "Didn't he Matt?"

"Yes, I was complementing him earlier on the fine piece of work he did," Matt replied.

"What about this award you mentioned, Matt?" John inquired.

"I don't want an award," Robert snapped.

"Balderdash!" John exclaimed."Damn it! You did a good job. It should be acknowledged."

"I just want to forget the bloody war!" Robert could feel the perspiration standing out on his forehead, and mopped his brow with his napkin, hoping that no one would notice that his hand was shaking. "I'm sorry," he apologized, "But do we have to keep talking about the war."

"Why is it that you never tell us anything?" John demanded irritably,

"Now, now, John dear, Robert's back, and that's all that matters," Elizabeth interjected. "Are you fully recovered, dear?" she asked Robert.

"Yes thank you, Mother, I'm fit enough now."

"Anyway, Robert, it's a great relief to have you home," John smiled. "I expect you're looking forward to taking up your music again. We thought you might like a new violin for your birthday, didn't we Beth?"

"That's kind of you, Father, but I shan't be playing anymore."

"Why ever not, dear?" Elizabeth asked.

"Yes, Rob, why not?" Joanna interjected. "Is it your hands?"

So they had noticed, Robert thought, quickly snatching his hands out of sight below the table. He ignored Joanna's question, but remarked cynically, "I'd have thought you'd have been pleased, Father."

"Now, Robert, that's unkind," Elizabeth scolded.

"I'm sorry. But you never liked my music, did you, Father?"

"That's not fair. I never said that. I admit that I did not wish you to become a professional musician," John replied, thinking to himself that perhaps he had made a mistake with the boy. He had not realised how much he would miss the days when he used to hear Robert playing. "I just thought it would be, nice for you to play again."

"Well, it's too late, Father, I can't, and even if I could I'm not sure I'd want to."

"Why ever not?" John asked.

But Robert ignored the question, and then John asked, "What are you going to do with your life?"

"I couldn't care less what I do, as long as I get out of the army," Robert sighed.

"Well, that's a fine attitude!" John retorted.

"Maybe it is, Father, but it's the way I feel . . . Perhaps I'll go and see Percy. He could find me something to do."

John was about to object to this idea of Robert's, but was interrupted by Joanna. "What is wrong with your hands, Rob?" she asked again with concern.

Robert rose from the table. I'm sorry, you'll have to excuse me, I'm tired," he said, quickly leaving the room.

For a short time there was silence at the table, then John said, "What the devil's the matter with the boy? Don't seem to be able to talk to him."

"He does seem very withdrawn," said Elizabeth.

"He's a bit tense, I must say," Joanna added.

"I think you're going to have to be very patient for a time, Mother," said Matt. "I have the feeling he's been through more than we know."

"What do you mean?" asked Joanna.

"I'm not quite sure. But those marks on his hands; he didn't get them by being blown up."

John looked quizzically at his son-in-law. "What are you driving at?" he asked.

But Matt would not comment further, especially in front of Elizabeth. "Let's just say that perhaps we should keep off the subject of his hands when Robert is present."

The next morning Robert woke to the sound of Agnes drawing the curtains. He pulled the covers over his head in an effort to keep the bright light from his eyes, and made no attempt to get out of bed. He hoped that he had not screamed out in the night as he had often done in the hospital. The reoccurring nightmares had became fewer as the months had past, and he would now awake normally on most occasions without the vision of a red hot iron being slowly brought towards him, or the sickening thud of the hammer as the nails were driven through his hands.

"Come on, lazy, your bath is ready," said Agnes.

Robert slowly dragged himself from under the bedclothes and sat on the edge of the bed, holding his head in his hands. He glanced round the room, but not even the familiar objects that he had known for so long gave him any pleasure. Why was it that nothing seemed to interest him anymore, he asked himself? He got up and went to the window, and longingly looked down at the garden, hearing across the years the youthful laughter that had once been in those hot summers long ago, but seeing only the golden leaves being gently brushed lifeless from the branches of the trees at the far side of the lawn by a light autumn breeze. He found no satisfaction from the scene as he once would have done, and turned from the window to see Agnes looking at him.

"Pyjamas now, is it," Agnes remarked, remembering how he had never used them from about the age of fourteen to be like Karl Heinz. "Getting shy in our old age are we?" she laughed.

But Robert made no reply. He went to the bathroom and, to Agnes' surprise, put the bolt on the door; something he had never done before. He had no intention of allowing Agnes to see the marks of shame on his body, knowing that if he did there would be more questions.

Robert left the house directly after breakfast and spent much of the day aimlessly wandering the streets of Brighton. His return, home from America, had happened so quickly that he needed time to think. In hospital he had pushed, thoughts of the future out of his mind, but now, faced with the reality of life again, he could no longer hide from the decisions that had to be made.

That evening, he was in the drawing-room with Elizabeth, when Wendy was announced. Elizabeth got up to welcome the visitor, while Robert stood silently watching. To his surprise, he felt his spirits lift, and shyly smiled at the newcomer. "I'll leave you two young people alone," Elizabeth said, making to leave the room.

"There's no need to go, Mother," Robert said without conviction. But Elizabeth just smiled and disappeared from the room.

Wendy felt her heart leap at the sight of him. He still looked as young as ever, she thought, but there was a subtle difference in his countenance, although what it was she could not decide.

"It's kind of you to call, Wendy," he said formally, making no move to go towards her.

"I'm glad to see you're safely home," she replied in the same manner.

They stood for a moment just looking at each other, then Wendy could not contain herself any longer and moved quickly forward, flinging her arms round him. "Oh Robert, Robert!" she wept, "I thought you were dead. Thank God you've come back!"

He looked down at her in surprise, taken aback by her outburst of affection. He saw the tears in her eyes, and felt her tender concern kindling warmth back into his heart. Gradually his arms enfolded her and they stood in silence, content just to hold each other. He led her to the settee and they sat holding hands in front the fire.

Conversation had always been easy between them, and Robert had always known that she was good for him. He felt her stroking his hands and knew that sooner or later the question would come about the scars. They discussed many things, but when she asked about his hands, he felt himself begin to shake and knew that the sweat was standing out on his brow. Again he felt the whip cutting into his back, and the searing agony as the branding iron was held against his naked body. Again he heard his shrieks and pleas as the nails were driven through his hands, but what was now worse was the memory of his shame at having degraded himself to his torturers, and his betrayal of Lisa. If only he could tell her what he had done, he cried to himself. If he could just tell somebody.

"What ever is the matter?" she asked, seeing his distress. She gently pulled him towards her, kissing him, and then, holding his head to her breast, stroked the back of his neck. "What's happened to you?"

"They nailed me to a table!" he blurted out.

At first she could hardly believe what he was trying to tell her, but as the story gradually unfolded of how he had been broken by unbearable suffering and degradation, she burst into tears and hugged him tightly.

When he had finished she raised his head and held it against hers, their tears mingling on their cheeks. "Oh, Robert, Robert, I can't bear to think of it," she whispered, knowing that any words would be inadequate.

"You're the only one that knows," he said, getting control of himself and sitting back in the chair, but still holding her hand. "I had to tell someone."

They sat in silence for a short time, and then Robert said, "If only it hadn't been Karl Heinz. Why didn't he stop them?"

"War changes people," she said.

"But we were so close . . . Closer than brothers."

"You must stop torturing yourself, Robert. It's all over and done with, and as for Karl Heinz, he paid the price."

"What do you mean?" Robert asked.

"Well, him being dead."

"How do you know he's dead?"

"It was in Lisa's letter."

"Letter? What letter? What do you mean?" he demanded. "Lisa's dead!" he exclaimed. "They shot her. I didn't tell you, because..."

"No, Robert!" she interrupted, "You're mistaken. There was this letter from her months ago. Your mother let me read it. It never mentioned what they did to you, just that something had happened, and you and Karl Heinz were dead."

Abruptly, he released her hand and sat forward on the settee. "And all the time I thought she was dead," he murmured. He stood up and went to the fireplace, and putting both hands on the mantelpiece gazed into the fire. "I don't understand. Why didn't someone tell me?"

Wendy noticed his agitation and could feel his sudden change of mood. "I don't expect they realised. You not knowing, I mean. Come and sit down," she said.

He returned to the far end of the settee and flung himself down. "I must go to Holland!" he declared.

But you've only just got home. Don't leave us again so soon," she pleaded, knowing very well that he was slipping away from her, and that Lisa had come between them again.

"I must!"

"Robert, I'm asking you not to go," she said firmly. This time she was determined not to lose him so easily.

"But she thinks I'm dead!"

"Of course she does. We all did. Now why don't you write first?"

"Why are you trying to stop me?" he snapped.

"I'm afraid you might get hurt again. A lot can happen in a year. Things could be very different now."

Robert was about to ask what she meant, but at that moment Elizabeth came back into the room. "Do you mind if I join you?" she said, "I'm having coffee brought in for us all."

"Mother, why didn't you tell me that Lisa's alive?" Robert demanded.

"I'm sorry, dear, but the thought never entered my head," Elizabeth replied gently. "I'm sure none of us realised you thought her dead."

"Well, I did! I'm going to Holland tomorrow."

"Oh, Robert," Elisabeth began to protest, but then seeing John enter the room she turned to him and said, "Robert says he's going to Holland tomorrow."

John said, "But you've only just got home. I'd have thought you'd had enough of that place. Why all the hurry anyway?"

"I've got to see Lisa."

"Oh, I see, that's it," John grunted disapprovingly. "Haven't you got over that yet? Time you found yourself a nice English girl."

"Just like you did, Father," Robert replied sarcastically.

Elizabeth smiled at her son's remark, but at the same time she realised that it would be useless to try any further to dissuade him from returning to Holland. Two days later Robert arrived at Njjmegen station and immediately took a taxi to Grave. It was only after leaving the taxi, as he walked along the rough track towards the old house, that doubts began to enter his mind. During the greater part of the journey he had been impatient to arrive at his destination, but now he had he began to ask himself whether, after his betrayal of her, she would want him again. He knew that he still loved her, so surely her love for him would be strong enough to forgive his cowardliness, he told himself. Maybe she wouldn't be here at all, he thought as he went through the garden gate. He would soon know.

He pressed the door bell and stood waiting. It was all so peaceful, he thought, and everywhere he looked brought back a fresh memory, the scenes from his happy boyhood blotting out the horror of his last visit. A young maid opened the door, and he remembered the last time he had rung the bell and a stranger had stood before him. Forgetting that it was he who was the stranger, he stepped into the hall uninvited, and stood gazing at the scene he remembered so well.

The maid, at first taken aback that a stranger should enter the house uninvited, recovered herself and demanded, "What do you want?"

Robert looked at her and smiled, realising what he had done. "Oh, I'm sorry," he said. "May I see Lisa van der Leyden."

"Who is it, Anna?" a voice called from the drawing-room.

"I don't know, madam."

"Well do hurry up, girl! We're leaving soon and there's a lot to do," came the impatient reply.

The sound of the voice made Robert's heart jump for joy.

"It's someone asking for you, madam," the maid replied, now flustered that she had failed to announce the stranger in the proper manner.

"Why didn't you say so?" said Lisa, hurrying into the hall and coming face to face with the visitor. "I'm so sorry. . ." she began. But the words faded on her lips, and the colour drained from her face. She stopped in her tracks, her heart palpitating, and her strength draining away with the shock of seeing him standing there. She took a step back to support herself against the door jamb. "My God!" she gasped, trying to get her breath.

The maid looked concerned, seeing her mistress' agitation. "Are you all right, madam?" she asked.

But Lisa ignored the question, for her whole attention was focused on this ghost from the past. "Robert. . .but you were dead. . . I don't believe it."

"Lisa," he said softly, unable to take his eyes from her. Quickly he went forward and took her in his arms, whispering her name again and again. Hardly realising what was happening, and both trying to grasp the reality of the other's presence, they held each other more in mutual support than in a passionate embrace. Then Lisa gently released herself and held him away.

"Is it really you?" she asked softly, trying to compose herself, and not knowing what else to say. "For heaven's sake! Where have you been? I thought you were dead."

He tried to stammer out an explanation, but it was too soon for explanations and he lapsed into silence again. The joy of finding her alive had pushed all else for his mind, including the fear of having to face her with the shame of his cowardice. Only their love mattered now. He made to take her in his arms again, but she drew back, holding out her hand to stop him.

"No, Robert, "she pleaded, the tears running down her cheeks, "we mustn't." Then, at a loss to what she should do, Lisa ordered the maid to fetch some coffee. She took Robert into the drawing-room and they sat down opposite each other.

There was another awkward silence, and then Robert suddenly exclaimed, "For God's sake, Lisa, what's the matter with us? We should be dancing for joy. We've found each other again."

She smiled at his new found optimism and said, "Things have changed, my dearest."

"Why won't you let me hold you?" he asked. "Don't you love me any more?"

"Of course I do! But there are things you don't know. I daren't let you hold me."

"Why not, for God's sake?"

"Because you know what would happen, and it mustn't."

The maid entered the room with the coffee followed by a small boy. "Mummy, when are we going?" the child asked excitedly.

"Soon dear. Now say good afternoon to this gentleman, and then run along with Anna." She glanced at Robert and noticed his astonishment.

"You! His mother?" Robert faltered, glaring at Lisa with thoughts of infidelity creeping into his mind. He turned away to receive the small hand that was held out to him. "What's your name?" he asked the boy.

"Robert, sir," the boy replied.

Robert would have liked to engage the boy in further conversation, but the maid took the child by the hand and led him from the room.

"And the father?" Robert asked with a touch of bitterness in his voice.

"You, of course! Who else, with looks like that?"

"Me!" he cried, flabbergasted.

"Is it so surprising after what we did that weekend?" Lisa grinned. "Didn't you see how like you he is?"

Robert looked away shyly, remembering the first flush of their young love, his heart swelling with pride at the thought of having a son. He felt, guilty at having doubted her, and a pang of sorrow pierced his heart at the thought of the years he had missed of his son's life.

"Why didn't you tell him?" he asked. "Call him back, I want to see him again."

"No, Robert, you must give me time to explain things to him. We're leaving for America in half an hour, and this is not the time."

"America!" he cried. "What the devil are you going there for?"

"I'm selling this house. Mother died suddenly, and things are not the same here anymore."

"Oh, no. I'm so sorry, Lisa," he said sadly. "Poor Aunt Kate. She was always so good to me. And poor you." He was silent for a moment and then said, "But you can't go now I've come back. We can start again, just the three of us."

"I'm sorry, Robert, we can't," she replied, looking uncomfortable. "I don't want anything to unsettle little Robert before we go. I've just got him used to the idea, and he's just beginning to accept Brent," she added.

"Brent? Who's Brent?" he asked.

"Brent Charlton. You met him in Rotterdam years ago, you may remember."

Robert looked disinterested. "Vaguely. What's he got to do with it?"

"Robert, there's something I must tell you. You see, I was certain you were dead," she stammered. "You do believe that, don't you? Everything fell apart for me, and Brent's been very kind."

"What are you trying to say?"

She turned her face away and hesitated, reluctant to hurt him. "Brent and I. . . we're married," she confessed.

For a moment he was unable to speak, trying to convince himself that it wasn't true. But the joy of finding her again shattered, and his hopes for the future began to tumble away. He got up from his chair and seized her firmly by the wrists, pulling her to her feet. "But you're *my* wife!" he cried, almost shouting the words at her.

"Not according to law, Robert."

"Damn the law! Doesn't our love mean anything to you any more?"

"Of course it does. But what was I to do? I'd lost you, and Karl Heinz, and I'm left with two sons, and Brent kindly. . . " Lisa was cut short by another outburst from Robert.

"Two sons? Do you mean to say that this Brent . . .?"

"No," she interrupted. "It's not his. Brent's been perfectly honourable and very kind. We were married only six weeks ago."

"Then whose is it?" he demanded."

Seeing his anger, Lisa hesitated, not knowing how to begin. She released herself from his grip and moved across the room, turning from him to gaze out of the window. "You remember that last morning here," she began uncertainly.

"Do you expect me to forget it?" he retorted. He followed her across the room and stood behind her.

"Karl Heinz took me from the cellar."

At the mention of his cousin's name, Robert felt himself gripped by a hopeless longing for the boy he had known and for the happy times they had spent together, but he knew he must force these memories from his mind. Then it began to dawn on him what Lisa was trying to say. "You and Karl Heinz?" he questioned, speaking very deliberately.

Lisa nodded.

"But how could you?" Then it all came back to him and he remembered how, through his tears, he had seen Karl Heinz carry her up the stairs. "You left me on that table while you . . !" he taunted in anger, words failing him. "You let him have you to save your own skin."

"That's not true!" she protested, turning to face him.

"Then he was the one you loved!" he exclaimed. "And I thought it was me."

"No!" she cried. "It didn't happen like that. I couldn't stop it. God knows! I tried . . . " She flung her arms around him. "You must believe me, Robert. It's you I love."

He saw the tears rolling down her cheeks, and realised for the first time that it was not only he who had succumbed to weakness, but that Lisa and Karl Heinz had also been unable to stand firm against temptation. As quickly as his anger had flared it subsided, and he felt a sudden weariness come over him. "I'm sorry," he said gently. "It seems we all betrayed one another? What happened to us?"

"I suppose we grew up and lost our innocence."

He took her in his arms and kissed her.

There was a knock on the door and the maid entered, carrying a baby and holding little Robert by the hand. "The car's here, madam," she announced.

"I'm just coming, Anna. Get the boys in the car," Lisa instructed.

"But you can't go!" he exclaimed. "There's too much to be said. Give him up!" he added impulsively as a last desperate attempt to keep her.

"I can't. It wouldn't be right, you know that. It's better this way, Robert." She took him by the hand and led him to the open front door. "Let's make it quick," she said.

They flung their arms round each other and for a moment their lips touched. "I'll always love you," she whispered.

Robert felt her release herself, and then she was gone, walking quickly down the garden path. For as long as he could remember it had always been her that he had loved. With her he had reached the heights of ecstasy, and known the depths of despair, but in his heart he knew that it was a passion that had become too intense to live with.

He stood watching until the car was out of sight.

"Can I get you some refreshment, sir?" the maid asked.

"No thank you," Robert replied. "I'll just stroll along the dyke to the bridge, then I'll go."

Robert walked through the garden and climbed the bank on to the dyke. And there was the bridge ahead of him. It was a sight that had once thrilled him, but now there was a feeling of emptiness within him and all seemed different. He realised it was the loved ones he had known that had made his happiness and not the bridge or the house or the river. He knew now that it had been a mistake to return, because to see again the places he had known with the eyes of a boy or a youth was impossible. Youth had died in the cellar on that fateful Sunday morning.

In a few minutes he reached the bridge and made his way to the span over the centre of the great river. He stood close to the side, feeling the strength of the girders as he gripped them firmly in his hands. Looking down, the sparkling river seemed to be enticing him, its reflections sending pictures of the past dancing before his eyes. Once beneath the cool waters all the pain and longing would cease, he told himself. Life was of little value without love, so why hold on to it? It would all be so easy. He tightened his grip on the girder. There would be few who would miss him, he decided. After all, he had been dead to them before so what difference would it make, and his own son did not know him.

Lost in his thoughts, he gradually became aware of a hand lightly touching his elbow. "Robert." There was a note of uncertainty in the soft voice.

Startled, he quickly let go the girder and turned. The shy, smiling features; the soft tender eyes, and the long fair hair, had had no place in his thoughts since leaving home, making his surprise even more evident. "Wendy!" he gasped in astonishment. "What are you doing here?"

"I followed you," she smiled.

They stood looking at each other, both wondering what to say, yet knowing that words were unnecessary. He looked down into her loving eyes. She had never demanded anything from him, not even his love. Yet she had always been there had he only realised it. He knew then that he could never find happiness in the past, but if he looked to the future that might be another story. He glanced for the last time at the old house nestling in the trees, knowing he would never pass this way again.

"Come home, Robert," she said quietly, her eyes pleading with him. She took him gently by the hand, and they slowly walked away, his mood of despair vanishing in the sunlight as does the blackness at the end of a dark tunnel.

QUOTES

In 1910, Frederic E Weatherby, an Englishman, who had never set foot in Ireland, wrote the words of 'Danny Boy'. Initially, the words were set to a tune other than the Londonderry Air. Then in 1913, he changed the lyrics, to fit the rhyme and meter of Londonderry Air.   P185

The Hitler Youth Anthem 'Das Fahnenlied' written by Baldur von Schirach   P297

The song 'They Didn't Believe Me' by Jerome Kern, was first sung in Paul Reubens operetta, 'The Girl from Utah' (1914). The song became very popular in England after being put in the Gaiety production of 'Tonight's the Night' (1915) Words by M.E.Rourke.   P313

A quotation of Minnie Haskins read by King George VI in his Christmas Broadcast 1939.   P469